This special signed edition is limited to **1000** numbered copies.

This is copy ___651___.

Elizabeth Hand

THE BEST OF
ELIZABETH HAND

THE BEST OF ELIZABETH HAND

Edited by Bill Sheehan

SUBTERRANEAN PRESS 2021

The Best of Elizabeth Hand
Copyright © 2021 by Elizabeth Hand.
All rights reserved.

Dust jacket illustration
Copyright © Album/ Alamy Stock Photo.
All rights reserved.

Interior design
Copyright © 2021 by Desert Isle Design, LLC.
All rights reserved.

See pages 559-560 for individual story copyrights.

First Edition

ISBN
978-1-64524-005-1

Subterranean Press
PO Box 190106
Burton, MI 48519

subterraneanpress.com

Manufactured in the United States of America

For John Clute,
Who stirred the Cauldron of Story
With all my love

TABLE OF CONTENTS

LAST SUMMER AT MARS HILL 9

PAVANE FOR A PRINCE OF THE AIR 63

THE BACCHAE. 95

CLEOPATRA BRIMSTONE 113

GHOST LIGHT 171

THE HAVE-NOTS 175

THE MAIDEN FLIGHT OF
McCAULEY'S *BELLEROPHON* 193

EAT THE WYRM 249

FIRE. 255

THE LOST DOMAIN—THREE STORY VARIATIONS
      ECHO. 265
      THE SAFFRON GATHERERS 275
      KRONIA 293

NEAR ZENNOR 299

THE OWL COUNT. 359

THE LEAST TRUMPS 383

ILLYRIA. 443

STORY NOTES 549

Last Summer at Mars Hill

EVEN BEFORE they left home, Moony knew her mother wouldn't return from Mars Hill that year. Jason had called her from his father's house in San Francisco—

"I had a dream about you last night," he'd said, his voice cracking the way it did when he was excited. "We were at Mars Hill, and my father was there, and my mother, too—I knew it was a dream, like can you imagine my *mother* at Mars Hill?—and you had on this sort of long black dress and you were sitting alone by the pier. And you said, 'This is it, Jason. We'll never see this again.' I felt like crying, I tried to hug you but my father pulled me back. And then I woke up."

She didn't say anything. Finally Jason prodded her. "Weird, huh, Moony? I mean, don't you think it's weird?"

She shrugged and rolled her eyes, then sighed loudly so that he'd be able to tell she was upset. "Thanks, Jason. Like that's supposed to cheer me up?"

A long silence, then Jason's breathless voice again. "Shit, Moony, I'm sorry I didn't—"

She laughed, a little nervously, and said, "Forget it. So when you flying out to Maine?"

Nobody but Jason called her Moony, not at home at least, not in Kamensic Village. There she was Maggie Rheining, which was the name that appeared under her junior picture in the high school yearbook.

But the name that had been neatly typed on the birth certificate in San Francisco sixteen years ago, the name Jason and everyone at Mars Hill knew her by, was Shadowmoon Starlight Rising. Maggie would have shaved her head before she'd admit her real name to anyone at school. At Mars Hill it wasn't so weird: there was Adele Grose, known professionally as Madame Olaf; Shasta Daisy O'Hare and Rvis Capricorn; Martin Dionysos, who was Jason's father; and Ariel Rising, née Amanda Mae Rheining, who was Moony's mother. For most of the year Moony and Ariel lived in Kamensic Village, the affluent New York exurb where her mother ran Earthly Delights Catering and Moony attended high school, and everything was pretty much normal. It was only in June that they headed north to Maine, to the tiny spiritualist community where they had summered for as long as Moony could remember. And even though she could have stayed in Kamensic with Ariel's friends the Loomises, at the last minute (and due in large part to Jason's urging, and threats if she abandoned him there) she decided to go with her mother to Mars Hill. Later, whenever she thought how close she'd come to not going, it made her feel sick: as though she'd missed a flight and later found out the plane had crashed.

Because much as she loved it, Moony had always been a little ashamed of Mars Hill. It was such a dinky place, plopped in the middle of nowhere on the rocky Maine coast—tiny shingle-style Carpenter Gothic cottages, all tumbled into disrepair, their elaborate trim rotting and strung with spiderwebs; poppies and lupines and tiger lilies sprawling bravely atop clumps of chickweed and dandelions of truly monstrous size; even the sign by the pier so faded you almost couldn't read the earnest lettering:

MARS HILL
SPIRITUALIST COMMUNITY
FOUNDED 1883

"Why doesn't your father take somebody's violet aura and repaint the damn sign with it?" she'd exploded once to Jason.

Jason looked surprised. "I kind of like it like that," he said, shaking the hair from his face and tossing a sea urchin at the silvered board. "It looks like it was put up by our Founding Mothers." But for years Moony almost couldn't stand to even look at the sign, it embarrassed her so much.

It was Jason who helped her get over that. They'd met when they were both twelve. It was the summer that Ariel started the workshop in Creative Psychokinesis, the first summer that Jason and his father had stayed at Mars Hill.

"Hey," Jason had said, too loudly, when they found themselves left alone while the adults swapped wine coolers and introductions at the summer's first barbecue. They were the only kids in sight. There were no other families and few conventionally married couples at Mars Hill. The community had been the cause of more than one custody battle that had ended with wistful children sent to spend the summer with a more respectable parent in Boston or Manhattan or Bar Harbor. "That lady there with my father—"

He stuck his thumb out to indicate Ariel, her long black hair frizzed and bound with leather thongs, an old multicolored skirt flapping around her legs. She was talking to a slender man with close-cropped blond hair and goatee, wearing a sky-blue caftan and shabby Birkenstock sandals. "That your mom?"

"Yeah." Moony shrugged and glanced at the man in the caftan. He and Ariel both turned to look at their children. The man grinned and raised his wine glass. Ariel did a little pirouette and blew a kiss at Moony.

"Looks like she did too much of the brown acid at Woodstock," Jason announced, and flopped onto the grass. Moony glared down at him.

"She wasn't at Woodstock, asshole," she said, and had started to walk away when the boy called after her.

"Hey—it's a joke! My name's Jason—" He pointed at the man with Ariel. "That's my father. Martin Dionysos. But like that's not his real name, okay? His real name is Schuster but he changed it, but I'm Jason Schuster. He's a painter. We don't know anyone here. I mean, does it ever get above forty degrees?"

He scrambled to his feet and looked at her beseechingly. Smaller even than Moony herself, so slender he should have looked younger than her, except that his sharp face beneath floppy white-blond hair was always twisted into some ironic pronouncement, his blue eyes always flickering somewhere between derision and pleading.

"No," Moony said slowly. The part about Jason not changing his name got to her. She stared pointedly at his thin arms prickled with gooseflesh, the fashionable surfer-logo T-shirt that hung nearly to his knees. "You're gonna freeze your skinny ass off here in Maine, Jason Schuster." And she grinned.

He was from San Francisco. His father was a well-known artist and a member of the Raging Faery Queens, a gay pagan group that lived in the Bay Area and staged elaborately beautiful solstice gatherings and AIDS benefits. At Mars Hill, Martin Dionysos gave workshops on strengthening your aura and on clear nights led the community's men in chanting at the moon as it rose above Penobscot Bay. Jason was so diffident about his father and his father's work that Moony was surprised, the single time she visited him on the West Coast, to find her friend's room plastered with flyers advertising Faery gatherings and newspaper photos of Martin and Jason at various ACT-UP events. In the fall Jason would be staying in Maine, while she returned to high school. Ultimately it was the thought that she might not see him again that made Moony decide to spend this last summer at Mars Hill.

"That's what you're wearing to First Night?"

Moony started at her mother's voice, turned to see Ariel in the middle of the summer cottage's tiny living room. Wine rocked back and forth in her mother's glass, gold shot with tiny sunbursts from the crystals hung from every window. "What about your new dress?"

Moony shrugged. She couldn't tell her mother about Jason's dream, about the black dress he'd seen her wearing. Ariel set great store by dreams, especially these last few months. What she'd make of one in which Moony appeared in a black dress and Ariel didn't appear at all, Moony didn't want to know.

"Too hot," Moony said. She paused in front of the window and adjusted one of three silver crosses dangling from her right ear. "Plus I don't want to upstage you."

Ariel smiled. "Smart kid," she said, and took another sip of her wine.

Ariel wore what she wore to every First Night: an ankle-length patchwork skirt so worn and frayed it could only be taken out once a year, on this ceremonial occasion. Squares of velvet and threadbare satin were emblazoned with suns and moons and astrological symbols, each one with a date neatly embroidered in crimson thread.

Sedona, Aug 15 1972. Mystery Hill, NH, 5/80. The Winter Garden 1969. Jajouka, Tangiers, Marrakech 1968.

Along the bottom, where many of the original squares had disintegrated into fine webs of denim and chambray, she had begun piecing a new section: squares that each held a pair of dates, a name, an embroidered flower. These were for friends who had died. Some of them were people lost two decades earlier, to the War, or drugs or misadventure; names that Moony knew only from stories told year after year at Mars Hill or in the kitchen at home.

But most of the names were those of people Moony herself had known. Friends of Ariel's who had gathered during the divorce, and again, later, when Moony's father died, and during the myriad affairs and breakups that followed. Men and women who had started out as Ariel's customers and ended as family. Uncle Bob and Uncle Raymond and Uncle Nigel. Laurie Salas. Tommy McElroy and Sean Jacobson. Chas Bowen and Martina Glass. And, on the very bottom edge of the skirt, a square still peacock-bright with its blood-colored rose, crimson letters spelling out John's name and a date the previous spring.

As a child Moony had loved that skirt. She loved to watch her mother sashay into the tiny gazebo at Mars Hill on First Night and see all the others laugh and run to her, their fingers plucking at the patchwork folds as though to read something there, tomorrow's weather perhaps, or the names of suitors yet unmet.

But now Moony hated the skirt. It was morbid, even Jason agreed with that.

"They've already got a fucking quilt," he said, bitterly "We don't need your mom wearing a goddamn *skirt*."

Moony nodded, miserable, and tried not to think of what they were most afraid of: Martin's name there beside John's, and a little rosebud done in flower-knots. Martin's name, or Ariel's.

There was a key to the skirt, Moony thought as she watched her mother sip her wine; a way to decode all the arcane symbols Ariel had stitched there over the last few months. It lay in a heavy manila envelope somewhere in Ariel's room, an envelope that Ariel had started carrying with her in February, and which grew heavier and heavier as the weeks passed. Moony knew there was something horrible in that envelope, something to do with the countless appointments Ariel had had since February, with the whispered phone calls and macrobiotic diets and the resurgence of her mother's belief in *devas* and earth spirits and plain old-fashioned ghosts.

But Moony said nothing of this, only smiled and fidgeted with her earrings. "Go ahead," she told Ariel, who had settled at the edge of a wicker hassock and peered up at her daughter through her wineglass. "I just got to get some stuff."

Ariel waited in silence, then drained her glass and set it on the floor. "Okay. Jason and Martin are here. I saw them on the hill—"

"Yeah. I know, I talked to them, they went to Camden for lunch, they can't wait to see you." Moony paced to the door to her room, trying not to look impatient. Already her heart was pounding.

"Okay" Ariel said again. She sounded breathless and a little drunk. She had ringed her aquamarine eyes with kohl, to hide how tired she was. Over the last few months she'd grown so thin that her cheekbones had emerged again, after years of hiding in her round peasant's face. Her voice was hoarse as she asked, "So you'll be there soon?"

Moony nodded. She curled a long tendril of hair, dark as her mother's but finer, and brushed her cheek with it. "I'm just gonna pull my hair back. Jason'll give me shit if I don't."

Ariel laughed. Jason thought that they were all a bunch of hip-pies. "Okay" She crossed the room unsteadily, touching the backs of chairs, a windowsill, the edge of a buoy hanging from the wall. When the screen door banged shut behind her Moony sighed with relief.

For a few minutes she waited, to make sure her mother hadn't forgotten something, like maybe a joint or another glass of wine. She could see out the window to where people were starting downhill toward the gazebo. If you didn't look too closely, they might have been any group of summer people gathering for a party in the long northern afternoon.

But after a minute or two their oddities started to show. You saw them for what they really were: men and women just getting used to a peculiar middle age. They all had hair a little too long or too short, a little too gray or garishly colored. The women, like Ariel, wrapped in clothes like banners from a triumphant campaign now forgotten. Velvet tunics threaded with silver, miniskirts crossing pale bare blue-veined thighs, Pucci blouses back in vogue again. The men more subdued, in chinos some of them, or old jeans that were a little too bright and neatly pressed. She could see Martin beneath the lilacs by the gazebo, in baggy psychedelic shorts and T-shirt, his gray-blond hair longer than it had been and pulled back into a wispy ponytail. Beside him Jason leaned against a tree, self-consciously casual, smoking a cigarette as he watched the First Night promenade. At sight of Ariel he raised one hand in a lazy wave.

And now the last two stragglers reached the bottom of the hill. Mrs. Grose carrying her familiar, an arthritic wheezing pug named Milton: Ancient Mrs. Grose, who smelled of Sen-sen and whiskey, and prided herself on being one of the spiritualists exposed as a fraud by Houdini. And Gary Bonetti, who (the story went) five years ago had seen a vision of his own death in the City, a knife wielded by a crack-crazed kid in Washington Heights. Since then, he had stayed on at Mars Hill with Mrs. Grose, the community's only other year-round resident.

Moony ducked back from the window as her mother turned to stare up at the cottage. She waited until Ariel looked away again, as Martin and Jason beckoned her toward the gazebo.

"Okay" Moony whispered. She took a step across the room and stopped. An overwhelming smell of cigarette smoke suddenly filled the air, though there was no smoke to be seen. She coughed, waving her hand in front of her face.

"Damn it, Jason," she hissed beneath her breath. The smell was gone as abruptly as it had appeared. "I'll be *right there*—"

She slipped through the narrow hallway with its old silver-touched mirrors and faded Maxfield Parrish prints, and went into Ariel's room. It still had its beginning-of-summer smell, mothballs and the salt sweetness of rugosa roses blooming at the beach's edge. The old chenille bedspread was rumpled where Ariel had lain upon it, exhausted by the flight from LaGuardia to Boston, from Boston via puddlejumper to the tiny airport at Green Turtle Reach. Moony pressed her hand upon the spread and closed her eyes. She tried to focus as Jason had taught her, tried to dredge up the image of her mother stretched upon the bed. And suddenly there it was, a faint sharp stab of pain in her left breast, like a stitch in her side from running. She opened her eyes quickly, fighting the dizziness and panicky feeling. Then she went to the bureau.

At home she had never been able to find the envelope. It was always hidden away, just as the mail was always carefully sorted, the messages on the answering machine erased before she could get to them. But now it was as if Ariel had finally given up on hiding. The envelope was in the middle drawer, a worn cotton camisole draped halfheartedly across it. Moony took it carefully from the drawer and went to the bed, sat and slowly fanned the papers out.

They were hospital bills. Hospital bills and Blue Cross forms, cash register receipts for vitamins from the Waverly Drugstore with Ariel's crabbed script across the top. The bills were for tests only, tests and consultations. Nothing for treatments; no receipts for medication other than vitamins. At the bottom of the envelope, rolled into a blue cylinder and tightened with a rubber band, she found the test results. Stray words floated in the air in front of her as Moony drew in a long shuddering breath.

Mammography results. Sectional biopsy. Fourth stage malignancy. Metastasized.

Cancer. Her mother had breast cancer.

"Shit," she said. Her hands after she replaced the papers were shaking. From outside echoed summer music, and she could hear voices—her mother's, Diana's, Gary Bonetti's deep bass—shouting above the tinny sound of a cassette player—

*"Wouldn't it be nice if we could wake up
In the kind of world where we belong?"*

"You bitch," Moony whispered. She stood at the front window and stared down the hill at the gazebo, her hands clamped beneath her armpits to keep them still. Her face was streaked with tears. "When were you going to tell me, when were you going to fucking tell me?"

At the foot of Mars Hill, alone by a patch of daylilies stood Jason, staring back up at the cottage. A cigarette burned between his fingers, its scent miraculously filling the little room. Even from here Moony could tell that somehow and of course, he already knew.

Everyone had a hangover the next morning, not excluding Moony and Jason. In spite of that the two met in the community chapel. Jason brought a thermos of coffee, bright red and yellow dinosaurs stenciled on its sides, and blew ashes from the bench so she could sit down.

"You shouldn't smoke in here." Moony coughed and slumped beside him. Jason shrugged and stubbed out his cigarette, fished in his pocket and held out his open palm.

"Here. Ibuprofen and valerian capsules. And there's bourbon in the coffee."

Moony snorted but took the pills, shooting back a mouthful of tepid coffee and grimacing.

"Hair of the iguana," Jason said. "So really, Moony, you didn't know?"

"How the hell would I know?" Moony said wearily. "I mean, I knew it was *something*—"

She glanced sideways at her friend. His slender legs were crossed at the ankles and he was barefoot. Already dozens of mosquito bites pied his arms and legs. He was staring at the little altar in the center of the room. He looked paler than usual, more tired, but that was probably just the hangover.

From outside, the chapel looked like all the other buildings at Mars Hill, faded gray shingles and white trim. Inside there was one large open room, with benches arranged in a circle around the walls, facing in to the plain altar. The altar was heaped with wilting day lilies and lilacs, an empty bottle of chardonnay and a crumpled pack of Kents—Jason's brand—and a black velvet hair ribbon that Moony recognized as her mother's. Beneath the ribbon was an old snapshot, curled at the edges. Moony knew the pose from years back. It showed her and Jason and Ariel and Martin, standing at the edge of the pier with their faces raised skyward, smiling and waving at Diana behind her camera. Moony made a face when she saw it and took another swallow of coffee.

"I thought maybe she had AIDS," Moony said at last. "I knew she went to the Walker Clinic once, I heard her on the phone to Diana about it."

Jason nodded, his mouth set in a tight smile. "So you should be happy she doesn't. Hip hip hooray." Two years before Jason's father had tested HIV-positive. Martin's lover, John, had died that spring.

Moony turned so that he couldn't see her face. "She has breast cancer. It's metastasized. She won't see a doctor. This morning she let me feel it..."

Like a gnarled tree branch shoved beneath her mother's flesh, huge and hard and lumpy. Ariel thought she'd cry or faint or some-thing but all Moony could do was wonder how she had never felt it before. Had she never noticed, or had it just been that long since she'd hugged her mother?

She started crying, and Jason drew closer to her.

"Hey," he whispered, his thin arm edging around her shoulders. "It's okay, Moony, don't cry it's all right—"

How can you say that? she felt like screaming, sobs constricting her throat so she couldn't speak. When she did talk the words came out in anguished grunts.

"They're dying—how can they—*Jason*—"

"Shh—" he murmured. "Don't cry, Moony, don't cry…"

Beside her, Jason sighed and fought the urge for another cigarette. He wished he'd thought about this earlier, come up with something to say that would make Moony feel better. Something like, *Hey! Get used to it! Everybody dies!* He tried to smile, but he felt only sorrow and a headache prodding at the corners of his eyes. Moony's head felt heavy on his shoulder. He shifted on the bench, stroking her hair and whispering until she grew quiet. Then they sat in silence.

He stared across the room, to the altar and the wall beyond, where a stained glass window would have been in another kind of chapel. Here, a single great picture window looked out onto the bay. In the distance he could see the Starry Islands glittering in the sunlight, and beyond them the emerald bulk of Blue Hill and Cadillac Mountain rising above the indigo water.

And, if he squinted, he could see Them. The Others, like tears or blots of light floating across his retina. The Golden Ones. The Greeters.

The Light Children.

"Hey!" he whispered. Moony sniffed and burrowed closer into his shoulder, but he wasn't talking to her. He was welcoming Them.

They were the real reason people had settled here, over a century ago. They were the reason Jason and Moony and their parents and all the others came here now; although not everyone could see Them. Moony never had, nor Ariel's friend Diana; although Diana believed in Them, and Moony did not. You never spoke of Them, and if you did, it was always parenthetically and with a capital T—"Rvis and I were looking at the moon last night (They were there) and we thought we saw a whale." Or, "Martin came over at midnight (he saw Them on the way) and we played Scrabble…"

A few years earlier a movement was afoot, to change the way of referring to Them. In a single slender volume that was a history of the Mars Hill spiritualist community, They were referred to as the Light Children, but no one ever really called Them that. Everyone just called them Them. It seemed the most polite thing to do, really, since no one knew what They called Themselves.

"And we'd hate to offend Them," as Ariel said.

That was always a fear at Mars Hill. That, despite the gentle nature of the community's adherents, They inadvertently would be offended one day (a too-noisy volleyball game on the rocky beach; a beer-fueled Solstice celebration irrupting into the dawn), and leave.

But They never did. Year after year the Light Children remained. They were a magical commonplace, like the loons that nested on a nearby pond and made the night an offertory with their cries, or the rainbows that inexplicably appeared over the Bay almost daily, even when there was no rain in sight. It was the same with Them. Jason would be walking down to call his father in from sailing, or knocking at Moony's window to awaken her for a three A.M. stroll, and suddenly there They'd be. A trick of the light, like a sundog or the aurora borealis: golden patches swimming through the cool air. They appeared as suddenly as a cormorant's head slicing up through the water, lingering sometimes for ten minutes or so. Then They would be gone.

Jason saw Them a lot. The chapel was one of the places They seemed to like, and so he hung out there whenever he could. Sometimes he could sense Them moments before They appeared. A shivering in the air would make the tips of his fingers go numb, and once there had been a wonderful smell, like warm buttered bread. But usually there was no warning. If he closed his eyes while looking at Them, Their image still appeared on the cloudy scrim of his inner eye, like gilded tears. But that was all. No voices, no scent of rose petals, no rapping at the door. You felt better after seeing Them, the way you felt better after seeing a rainbow or an eagle above the Bay. But there was nothing really magical about Them, except the fact that They existed at all. They never spoke, or did anything special, at least nothing you could sense. They were just *there*; but Their presence meant everything at Mars Hill.

They were there now: flickering above the altar, sending blots of gold dancing across the limp flowers and faded photograph. He wanted to point Them out to Moony, but he'd tried before and she'd gotten mad at him.

"You think I'm some kind of idiot like my mother?" she'd stormed, sweeping that day's offering of irises from the altar onto the floor. "Give me a break, Jason!"

Okay, I gave you a break, he thought now. *Now I'll give you another. Look, Moony, there They are!* he thought, then said, "Moony. Look—"

He pointed, shrugging his shoulder so she'd have to move. But already They were gone.

"What?" Moony murmured. He shook his head, sighing.

"That picture," he said, and fumbled at his pocket for his cigarettes. "That stupid old picture that Diana took. Can you believe it's still here?"

Moony lifted her head and rubbed her eyes, red and swollen. "Oh, I can believe anything," she said bitterly, and filled her mug with more coffee.

• ◆ •

IN MARTIN DIONYSOS'S kitchen, Ariel drank a cup of nettle tea and watched avidly as her friend ate a bowl of mung bean sprouts and nutritional yeast. *Just like in* Annie Hall, she thought. *Amazing.*

"So now she knows and you're surprised she's pissed at you." Martin raised another forkful of sprouts to his mouth, angling delicately to keep any from falling to the floor. He raised one blond eyebrow as he chewed, looking like some hardscrabble New Englander's idea of Satan, California surfer boy gone to seed. Long gray-blond hair that was thinner than it had been a year ago, skin that wasn't so much tanned as an even pale bronze, with that little goatee and those piercing blue eyes, the same color as the Bay stretching outside the window behind him. Oh, yes: and a gold hoop earring and a heart tattoo that enclosed the name *JOHN* and a T-shirt with the pink triangle and SILENCE=DEATH printed in stern block letters. Satan on vacation.

"I'm not *surprised*," Ariel said, a little crossly. "I'm just, mmm, disappointed. That she got so upset."

Martin's other eyebrow arched. "*Disappointed?* As in, 'Moony, darling, I have breast cancer (which I have kept a secret from you for seven months) and I am very *disappointed* that you are not self-actualized enough to deal with this without falling to pieces'?"

"She didn't fall to pieces." Ariel's crossness went over the line into full-blown annoyance. She frowned and jabbed a spoon into her tea. "I wish she'd fall to pieces, she's always so—" She waved the hand holding the spoon, sending green droplets raining onto Martin's knee. "—so *something*."

"Self-assured?"

"I guess. Self-assured and smug, you know? Why is it teenagers are always so fucking smug?"

"Because they share a great secret," Martin said mildly, and took another bite of sprouts.

"Oh, yeah? What's that?"

"Their parents are, all assholes."

Ariel snorted with laughter, leaned forward to get her teacup out of the danger zone and onto the table. "Oh, Martin," she said. Suddenly her eyes were filled with tears. "Damn it all to *hell*..."

Martin put his bowl on the table and stepped over to take her in his arms. He didn't say anything, and for a moment Ariel flashed back to the previous spring, the same tableau only in reverse, with her holding Martin while he sobbed uncontrollably in the kitchen of his San Francisco townhouse. It was two days after John's funeral, and she was on her way to the airport. She knew then about the breast cancer but she hadn't told Martin yet; didn't want to dim any of the dark luster of his grief.

Now it was her grief, but in a strange way she knew it was his, too. There was this awful thing that they held in common, a great unbroken chain of grief that wound from one coast to the other. She hadn't wanted to share it with Moony, hadn't wanted her to feel its weight and breadth. But it was too late, now. Moony knew and besides, what did it matter? She was dying, Martin was dying and there wasn't a fucking thing anyone could do about it.

"Hey," he said at last. His hand stroked her mass of dark hair, got itself tangled near her shoulder, snagging one of the long silver-and-quartz-crystal earrings she had put on that morning, for luck. "Ouch."

Ariel snorted again, laughing in spite of, or maybe because of, it all. Martin extricated his hand, held up two fingers with a long curling strand of hair caught between them: a question mark, a wise serpent waiting to strike. She had seen him after the cremation take the lock of John's hair that he had saved and hold it so, until suddenly it burst into flames, and then watched as the fizz of ash flared out in a dark penumbra around Martin's fingers. No such thing happened now, no Faery Pagan pyrotechnics. She wasn't dead yet, there was no sharp cold wind of grief to fan Martin's peculiar gift. He let the twirl of hair fall away and looked at her and said, "You know, I talked to Adele."

Adele was Mrs. Grose, she of the pug dog and suspiciously advanced years. Ariel retrieved her cup and her equanimity, sipping at the nettle tea as Martin went on, "She said she thought we had a good chance. You especially. She said for you it might happen. They might come." He finished and leaned back in his chair, spearing the last forkful of sprouts.

Ariel said, "Oh, yes?" Hardly daring to think of it; no don't think of it at all.

Martin shrugged, twisted to look over his shoulder at the endless sweep of Penobscot Bay. His eyes were bright, so bright she wondered if he were fighting tears or perhaps something else, something only Martin would allow himself to feel here and now. Joy, perhaps. Hope.

"Maybe," he said. At his words her heart beat a little faster in her breast, buried beneath the mass that was doing its best to crowd it out. "That's all. Maybe. It might. Happen."

And his hand snaked across the table to hers and held it, clutched it like it was a link in that chain that ran between them, until her fingers went cold and numb.

• ◆ •

ON WEDNESDAY EVENINGS the people at Mars Hill gave readings for the public. Tarot, palms, auras, dreams—five dollars a pop, nothing guaranteed. The chapel was cleaned, the altar swept of offerings and covered with a frayed red-and-white checked table cloth from Diana's kitchen and a few candles in empty Chianti bottles.

"It's not very atmospheric," Gary Bonetti said, as someone always did. Mrs. Grose nodded from her bench and fiddled with her rosary beads.

"Au contraire," protested Martin. "It's very atmospheric, if you're in the mood for spaghetti carbonara at Luigi's."

"May I recommend the primavera?" said Jason. In honor of the occasion he had put on white duck pants and white shirt and red bow tie. He waved at Moony, who stood at the door taking five dollar bills from nervous, giggly tourists and the more solemn-faced locals, who made this pilgrimage every summer. Some regulars came week after week, year after year. Sad Brenda, hoping for the Tarot card that would bring news from her drowned child. Mr. Spruce, a ruddy-faced lobsterman who always tipped Mrs. Grose ten dollars. The Hamptonites Jason had dubbed Mr. and Mrs. Pissant, who were anxious about their auras. Tonight the lobsterman was there, with an ancient woman who could only be his mother, and the Pissants, and two teenage couples, long blonde hair and sunburned, reeking of marijuana and summer money.

The teenagers went to Martin, lured perhaps by his tie-dyed caftan, neatly pressed and swirling down to his Birkenstock-clad feet.

"Boat trash," hissed Jason, arching a nearly invisible white-blond eyebrow as they passed. "I saw them in Camden, getting off a yacht the size of the fire station. God, they make me sick."

Moony tightened her smile. Catch *her* admitting to envy of people like that. She swiveled on her chair, looking outside to see if there were any newcomers making their way to the chapel through the cool summer night. "I think this is gonna be it," she said. She glanced wistfully at the few crumpled bills nesting in an old oatmeal tin. "Maybe we should, like, advertise or something. It's been so slow this summer."

Jason only grunted, adjusting his bow tie and glaring at the rich kids, now deep in conference with his father. The Pissants had fallen to Diana, who with her chignon of blonde hair and gold-buttoned little black dress could have been one of their neighbors. That left the lobsterman and his aged mother.

They stood in the middle of the big room, looking not exactly uneasy or lost, but as though they were waiting for someone to usher them to their proper seats. And as though she read their minds (but wasn't that her job?), Mrs. Grose swept up suddenly from her corner of the chapel, a warm South Wind composed of yards of very old rayon fabric, Jean Nate After Bath, and arms large and round and powdered as wheaten loaves.

"Mr. *Spruce*," she cried, extravagantly trilling her *rrr*'s and opening those arms like a stage gypsy. "You have come—"

"Why, yes," the lobsterman answered, embarrassed but also grateful. "I, uh—I brought my mother, Mrs. Grose. She says she remembers you."

"I do," said Mrs. Spruce. Moony twisted to watch, curious. She had always wondered about Mrs. Grose. She claimed to be a true clairvoyant. She *had* predicted things—nothing very useful, though. What the weather would be like the weekend of Moony's Junior Prom (rainy), but not whether she would be asked to go, or by whom. The day Jason would receive a letter from Harvard (Tuesday, the fifth of April), but not whether he'd be accepted there (he was not). It aggravated Moony, like so much at Mars Hill. What was the use of being a psychic if you could never come up with anything really useful?

But then there was the story about Harry Houdini. Mrs. Grose loved to tell it, how when she was still living in Chicago this short guy came one day and she gave him a message from his mother and he tried to make her out to be a fraud. It was a stupid story, except for one thing.

If it really had happened, it would make Mrs. Grose about ninety or a hundred years old. And she didn't look a day over sixty.

Now Mrs. Grose was cooing over a woman who really *did* look to be about ninety. Mrs. Spruce peered up at her through rheumy eyes, shaking her head and saying in a whispery voice, "I can't believe it's you. I was just a girl, but you don't look any different at all…"

"Oh, flattery, flattery!" Mrs. Grose laughed and rubbed her nose with a Kleenex. "What can we tell you tonight, Mrs. Spruce?"

Moony turned away. It was too weird. She watched Martin entertaining the four golden children, then felt Jason coming up behind her: the way some people claim they can tell a cat is in the room, by some subtle disturbance of air and dust. A cat is there. Jason is there.

"They're *all* going to Harvard. I can't *believe* it," he said, mere disgust curdled into utter loathing. "And that one, the blond on the end—"

"They're all blond, Jason," said Moony. "*You're* blond."

"I am an *albino*," Jason said with dignity. "Check him out, the Nazi Youth with the Pearl Jam T-shirt. He's a legacy, absolutely. SAT scores of 1060, tops. I k*now*." He closed his eyes and wiggled his fingers and made a *whoo-whoo* noise, beckoning spirits to come closer. Moony laughed and covered her mouth. From where he sat Martin raised an eyebrow, requesting silence. Moony and Jason turned and walked outside.

"How old do you think she is?" Moony asked, after they had gone a safe distance from the chapel.

"Who?"

"Mrs. Grose."

"Adele?" Jason frowned into the twilit distance, thinking of the murky shores and shoals of old age. "Jeez, I dunno. Sixty? Fifty?"

Moony shook her head. "She's got to be older than that. I mean, that story about Houdini, you know?"

"Huh! Houdini. The closest she ever got to Houdini is seeing some Siegfried and Roy show out in Las Vegas."

"I don't think she's ever left here. At least not since I can remember."

Jason nodded absently, then squatted in the untidy drive, squinting as he stared out into the darkness occluding the Bay. Fireflies formed mobile constellations within the birch trees. As a kid he had always loved fireflies, until he had seen Them. Now he thought of the Light Children as a sort of evolutionary step, some-where between lightning bugs and angels.

Though you hardly' ever see Them at night, he thought. *Now why is that?* He rocked back on his heels, looking like some slender pale gargoyle toppled from a modernist cathedral, the cuffs of his white oxford-cloth shirt rolled up to show large bony wrists and surprisingly strong square hands, his bow tie unraveled and hanging rakishly around his neck. Of a sudden he recalled being in this same spot two years ago, grinding out a cigarette as Martin and John approached. The smoke bothered John, sent him into paroxysms of coughing so prolonged and intense that more than once they had set Jason's heart pounding, certain at This Was It, John was going to die right here, right now, and it would be all Jason's fault for smoking. Only of course it didn't happen that way.

"The longest death since Little Nell's," John used to say, laughing hoarsely. That was when he could still laugh, still talk. At the end it had been others softly talking, Martin and Jason and their friends gathered around John's bed at home, taking turns, spelling each other. After a while Jason couldn't stand to be with them. It was too much like John was already dead. The body in the bed so wasted, bones cleaving to skin so thin and mottled it was like damp newsprint.

By the end, Jason refused to accompany Martin to the therapist they were supposed to see. He refused to go with him to the meetings where men and women talked about dying, about watching loved ones go so horribly slowly. Jason just couldn't take it. Grief he had always thought of as an emotion, a mood, something that possessed you but that you eventually escaped. Now he knew it was different. Grief was a country, a place you entered hesitantly, or were thrown into without warning. But once you were there, amidst the roiling formless blackness and stench of despair, you could not leave. Even if you wanted to: you could only walk and walk and walk, traveling on through the black reaches with the sound of screaming in your ears, and hope that someday you might glimpse far off another country another place where you might someday rest.

Jason had followed John a long ways into that black land. And now his own father would be going there. Maybe not for good, not yet, but Jason knew. An HIV-positive diagnosis might mean that Death was a long ways off; but Jason knew his father had already started walking.

"...you think they don't leave?"

Jason started. "Huh?" He looked up into Moony's wide gray eyes. "I'm sorry, what?"

"Why do you think they don't leave? Mrs. Grose and Gary You know, the ones who stay here all year." Moony's voice was exasperated. He wondered how many times she'd asked him the same thing.

"I dunno. I mean, they *have* to leave sometimes. How do they get groceries and stuff?" He sighed and scrambled to his feet. "There's only two of them, maybe they pay someone to bring stuff in. I know Gary goes to the Beach-Store sometimes. It's not like they're under house arrest. Why?"

Moony shrugged. In the twilight she looked spooky, more like a witch than her mother or Diana or any of those other wannabes. Long dark hair and those enormous pale gray eyes, face like the face of the cat who'd been turned into a woman in a fairy tale his father had read him once. Jason grinned, thinking of Moony jumping on a mouse. No way. But hey, even if she did, it would take more than *that* to turn him off.

"You thinking of staying here?" he asked slyly. He slipped an arm around her shoulders. "'Cause, like, I could keep you company or something. I hear Maine gets cold in the winter."

"No." Moony shrugged off his arm and started walking toward the water: no longer exasperated, more like she was distracted. "My mother is."

"Your *mother?*"

He followed her until she stopped at the edge of a gravel beach. The evening sky was clear. On the opposite shore, a few lights glimmered in Dark Harbor, reflections of the first stars overhead. From somewhere up along the coast, Bayside or Nagaseek or one of the other summer colonies, the sounds of laughter and skirling music echoed very faintly over the water, like a song heard on some distant station very late at night. But it wasn't late, not yet even nine o'clock. In summers past, that had been early for Moony and Jason, who would often stay up with the adults talking and poring over cards and runes until the night grew cold and spent.

But tonight for some reason the night already felt old. Jason shivered and kicked at the pebbly beach. The last pale light of sunset cast an antique glow upon stones and touched the edge of the water with gold. As he watched, the light withdrew, a gauzy veil drawn back teasingly until the shore shimmered with afterglow, like blue glass.

"I heard her talking with Diana," Moony said. Her voice was unsettlingly loud and clear in the still air. "She was saying she might stay on, after I go off to school. I mean, she was talking like she wasn't going back at all, I mean not back to Kamensic. Like she might just stay here and never leave again." Her voice cracked on the words *never leave again* and she shuddered, hugging herself.

"Hey," said Jason. He walked over and put his arms around her, her dark hair a perfumed net that drew him in until he felt dizzy and had to draw back, gasping a little, the smell of her nearly over-whelming that of rugosa roses and the sea. "Hey, it's okay, Moony, really it's okay."

Moony's voice sounded explosive, as though she had been holding her breath. "I just can't believe she's giving *up* like this. I mean, no doctors, nothing. She's just going to stay here and die."

"She might not die," said Jason, his own voice a little desperate. "I mean, look at Adele. A century and counting. The best is yet to come."

Moony laughed brokenly. She leaned forward so that her hair once again spilled over him, her wet cheek resting on his shoulder. "Oh, Jason. If it weren't for you I'd go crazy, you know that? I'd just go fucking nuts."

Nuts, thought Jason. His arms tightened around her, the cool air and faraway music nearly drowning him as he stroked her head and breathed her in. *Crazy, oh, yes.* And they stood there until the moon showed over Dark Harbor, and all that far-off music turned to silvery light above the Bay.

◆ ◆ ◆

TWO DAYS LATER Ariel and Moony went to see the doctor in Bangor. Moony drove, an hour's trip inland, up along the old road that ran beside the Penobscot River, through failed stonebound farms and past trailer encampments like sad rusted toys, until finally they reached the sprawl around the city, the kingdom of car lots and franchises and shopping plazas.

The hospital was an old brick building with a shiny new white wing grafted on. Ariel and Moony walked through a gleaming steel-and-glass door set in the expanse of glittering concrete. But they ended up in a tired office on the far end of the old wing, where the squeak of rubber wheels on worn linoleum played counterpoint to a loudly echoing, ominous *drip-drip* that never ceased the whole time they were there.

"Ms. Rising. Please, come in."

Ariel squeezed her daughter's hand, then followed the doctor into her office. It was a small bright room, a hearty wreath of living ivy trained around its single grimy window in defiance of the lack of sunlight and, perhaps, the black weight of despair that Ariel felt everywhere, chairs, desk, floor, walls.

"I received your records from New York," the doctor said. She was a slight fine-boned young woman with sleek straight hair and a silk dress more expensive than what you usually saw in Maine. The little metal name-tag on her breast might have been an odd bit of heirloom jewelry. "You realize that even as of three weeks ago, the cancer had spread to the point where our treatment options are now quite limited."

Ariel nodded, her arms crossed protectively across her chest. She felt strange, light-headed. She hadn't been able to eat much the last day or two, that morning had swallowed a mouthful of coffee and a stale muffin to satisfy Moony but that was all. "I know," she said heavily. "I don't know why I'm here."

"Frankly, I don't know either," the doctor replied. "If you had opted for some kind of intervention oh, even two months ago; but now…"

Ariel tilted her head, surprised at how sharp the other woman's tone was. The doctor went on, "It's a great burden to put on your daughter—" She looked in the direction of the office door, then glanced down at the charts in her hand. "Other children?"

Ariel shook her head. "No."

The doctor paused, gently slapping the sheaf of charts and records against her open palm. Finally she said, "Well. Let's examine you, then."

An hour later Ariel slipped back into the waiting room. Moony looked up from a magazine. Her gray eyes were bleary and her tired expression hastily congealed into the mask of affronted resentment with which she faced Ariel these days.

"So?" she asked as they retraced their steps back through cinder-block corridors to the hospital exit. "What'd she say?"

Ariel stared straight ahead, through the glass doors to where the summer afternoon waited to pounce on them. Exhaustion had seeped into her like heat; like the drugs the doctor had offered and Ariel had refused, the contents of crystal vials that could buy a few more weeks, maybe even months if she was lucky, enough time to make a graceful farewell to the world. But Ariel didn't want weeks or months, and she sure as hell didn't want graceful goodbyes. She wanted years, decades. A cantankerous or dreamy old age, aggravating the shit out of her grandchildren with her talk about her own sunflower youth. Failing that, she wanted screaming and gnashing of teeth, her friends tearing their hair out over her death, and Moony…

And Moony. Ariel stopped in front of a window, one hand out to press against the smooth cool glass. Grief and horror hit her like a stone, struck her between the eyes so that she gasped and drew her hands to her face.

"Mom!" Moony cried, shocked. "Mom, what is it, are you all right?—"

Ariel nodded, tears burning down her cheeks. "I'm fine," she said, and gave a twisted smile. "Really, I'm—"

"What did she *say?*" demanded Moony. "The doctor, what did she tell you, *what is it?*"

Ariel wiped her eyes, a black line of mascara smeared across her finger. "Nothing. Really, Moony, nothing's changed. It's just—it's just hard. Being this sick. It's hard, that's all."

She could see in her daughter's face confusion, despair, but also relief. Ariel hadn't said *death*, she hadn't said *dying*, she hadn't since that first day said *cancer*. She'd left those words with the doctor, along with the scrips for morphine and Fiorinal, all that could be offered to her now. "Come on," she said, and walked through the sliding doors. "I'm supposed to have lunch with Mrs. Grose and Diana, and it's already late."

Moony stared at her in disbelief: was her mother being stoic or just crazy? But Ariel didn't say anything else, and after a moment her daughter followed her to the car.

◆ ◆ ◆

IN MARS HILL'S little chapel Jason sat and smoked. On the altar in front of him were several weeks' accumulated offerings from the denizens of Mars Hill. An old-fashioned envelope with a glassine window, through which he could glimpse the face of a twenty-dollar bill—that was from Mrs. Grose, who always gave the money she'd earned from readings (and then retrieved it at the end of the summer). A small square of brilliantly woven cloth from Diana, whose looms punctuated the soft morning with their steady racketing. A set of blueprints from Rvis Capricorn. Shasta Daisy's battered *Ephemera*. The copy of Paul Bowles' autobiography that Jason's father had been reading on the flight out from the West Coast. In other words, the usual flotsam of love and whimsy that washed up here every summer. From where Jason sat, he could see his own benefaction, a heap of small white roses, already limp but still giving out their heady sweet scent, and a handful of blackberries he'd picked from the thicket down by the pier. Not much of an offering, but you never knew.

From beneath his roses peeked the single gift that puzzled him, a lacy silk camisole patterned with pale pink-and-yellow blossoms. An odd choice of offering, Jason thought. Because for all the unattached adults sipping chardonnay and Bellinis of a summer evening, the atmosphere at Mars Hill was more like that of summer camp. A chaste sort of giddiness ruled here, compounded of equal parts of joy and longing, that always made Jason think of the garlanded jackass and wistful fairies in *A Midsummer Night's Dream*. His father and Ariel and all the rest stumbling around in the dark, hoping for a glimpse of Them, and settling for fireflies and the lights from Dark Harbor. Mars Hill held surprisingly little in the way of unapologetic lust—except for himself and Moony, of course. And Jason knew that camisole didn't belong to Moony.

At the thought of Moony he sighed and tapped his ashes onto the dusty floor. It was a beautiful morning, gin-clear and with a stiff warm breeze from the west. Perfect sailing weather. He should be out with his father on the *Wendameen*. Instead he'd stayed behind, to write and think. Earlier he'd tried to get through to Moony somewhere in Bangor, but Jason couldn't send his thoughts any farther than from one end of Mars Hill to the other. For some reason, smoking cigarettes seemed to help. He had killed half a pack already this morning, but gotten nothing more than a headache and a raw throat. Now he had given up. It never seemed to work with anyone except Moony, anyhow, and then only if she was nearby.

He had wanted to give her some comfort. He wanted her to know how much he loved her, how she meant more to him than anyone or anything in the world, except perhaps his father. Was it allowed, to feel this much for a person when your father was HIV-positive? Jason frowned and stubbed out his cigarette in a lobster-shaped ashtray, already overflowing with the morning's telepathic aids. He picked up his notebook and Rapidograph pen and, still frowning, stared at the letter he'd begun last night.

Dearest Moony,

(he crossed out est, it sounded too fussy)

I just want you to know that I understand how you feel. When John died it was the most horrible thing in the world, even worse than the divorce because I was just a kid then. I just want you to know how much I love you, you mean more than anyone or anything in the world, and

And what? Did he really know how she felt? His mother wasn't dying, his mother was in the Napa Valley running her vineyard, and while it was true enough that John's death had been the most horrible thing he'd ever lived through, could that be the same as having your mother die? He thought maybe it could. And then of course there was the whole thing with his father. Was that worse? His father wasn't sick, of course, at least he didn't have any symptoms yet; but was it worse for someone you loved to have the AIDS virus, to watch and wait for months or years, rather than have it happen quickly like with Ariel? Last night he'd sat in the living room while his father and Gary Bonetti were on the porch talking about her.

"I give her only a couple of weeks," Martin had said, with that dry strained calm voice he'd developed over the last few years of watching his friends die. "The thing is, if she'd gone for treatment right away she could be fine now. She could be fine." The last word came out in an uncharacteristic burst of vehemence, and Jason grew cold to hear it. Because of course even with treatment his father probably wouldn't be all right, not now, not ever. He'd never be fine again. Ariel had thrown all that away.

"She should talk to Adele," Gary said softly. Jason heard the clink of ice as he poured himself another daiquiri. "When I had those visions five years ago, that's when I saw Adele. You should, too, Martin. You really should."

"I don't know as Adele can help me," Martin said, somewhat coolly. "She's just a guest here, like you or any of the rest of us. And *you* know that you can't make Them..."

His voice trailed off. Jason sat bolt upright on the sofa, suddenly feeling his father there, like a cold finger stabbing at his brain.

"Jason?" Martin called, his voice tinged with annoyance. "If you want to listen, come in *here*, please."

Jason had sworn under his breath and stormed out through the back door. It was impossible, sometimes, living with his father. Better to have a psychic wannabe like Ariel for a parent, and not have to worry about being spied on all the time.

Now, from outside the chapel came frenzied barking. Jason started, his thoughts broken. He glanced through the open door to see Gary and his black labrador retriever heading down to the water. Gary was grinning, arms raised as he waved at someone out of sight. And suddenly Jason had an image of his father in the *Wendameen*, the fast little sloop skirting the shore as Martin stood at the mast waving back, his long hair tangled by the wind. The vision left Jason nearly breathless. He laughed, shaking his head, and at once decided to follow Gary to the landing and meet his father there. He picked up his pen and notebook and turned to go. Then stopped, his neck prickling. Very slowly he turned, until he stood facing the altar once more.

They were there. A shimmering haze above the fading roses, like Zeus's golden rain falling upon imprisoned Danaë. Jason's breath caught in his throat as he watched Them—They were so beautiful, so *strange*. Flickering in the chapel's dusty air, like so many scintillant coins. He could sense rather than hear a faint chiming as They darted quick as hummingbirds from his roses to Mrs. Grose's envelope, alighting for a moment upon Diana's weaving and Rvis's prize tomatoes before settling upon two things: his father's book and the unknown camisole.

And then with a sharp chill Jason knew whose it was. Ariel's, of course—who else would own something so unabashedly romantic but also slightly tacky? Maybe it was meant to be a bad joke, or perhaps it was a real offering, heartfelt, heartbreaking. He stared at Them, a glittering carpet tossed over those two pathetic objects, and had to shield his eyes with his hand. It was too bright, They seemed to be growing more and more brilliant as he watched. Like a swarm of butterflies he had once seen, mourning cloaks resting in a snow-covered field one warm March afternoon, their wings slowly fanning the air as though They had been stunned by the thought of spring. But what could ever surprise *Them*, the Light Children, the summer's secret?

Then as he watched They began to fade. The glowing golden edge of the swarm grew dim and disappeared. One by one all the other gilded coins blinked into nothing, until the altar stood as it had minutes before, a dusty collection of things, odd and somewhat ridiculous. Jason's head pounded and he felt faint; then realized he'd been holding his breath. He let it out, shuddering, put his pen and notebook on the floor and walked to the altar.

Everything was as it had been, roses, cloth, paper, tomatoes; excepting only his father's offering, and Ariel's. Hesitantly he reached to touch the book Martin had left, then recoiled.

The cover of the book had been damaged. When he leaned over to stare at it more closely, he saw that myriad tiny holes had been burned in the paper, in what at first seemed to be a random pattern. But when he picked it up—gingerly, as though it might yet release an electrical jolt or some other hidden energy—he saw that the tiny perforations formed an image, blurred but unmistakable. The shadow of a hand, four fingers splayed across the cover as though gripping it.

Jason went cold. He couldn't have explained how, but he knew that it was a likeness of his father's hand that he saw there, eerie and chilling as those monstrous shadows left by victims of the bombings at Hiroshima and Nagasaki. With a frightened gasp he tossed the book back onto the altar. For a moment he stood beside the wooden table, half-poised to flee; but finally reached over and tentatively pushed aside his roses to fully reveal the camisole.

It was just like the book. Thousands of tiny burn-holes made a ruined lace of the pastel silk, most of them clustered around one side of the bodice. He picked it up, catching a faint fragrance, lavender and marijuana, and held it out by its pink satin straps. He raised it, turning toward the light streaming through the chapel's picture window, and saw that the pinholes formed a pattern, elegant as the tracery of veins and capillaries on a leaf. A shadowy bull's-eye—breast, aureole, nipple drawn on the silken cloth.

With a small cry Jason dropped the camisole. Without looking back he ran from the chapel. Such was his hurry that he forgot his pen and notebook and the half-written letter to Moony, piled carefully on the dusty floor. And so he did not see the shining constellation that momentarily appeared above the pages, a curious cloud that hovered there like a child's dream of weather before flowering into a golden rain.

• ◆ •

MOONY SAT HUNCHED on the front stoop, waiting for her mother to leave. Ariel had been in her room for almost half an hour, her luncheon date with Diana and Mrs. Grose notwithstanding. When finally she emerged, Moony could hear the soft uneven tread of her flip-flops, padding from bedroom to bedroom to kitchen. There was the sigh of the refrigerator opening and closing, the muted pop of a cork being pulled from a bottle, the long grateful gurgle of wine being poured into a glass. Then Ariel herself in the doorway behind her. Without looking Moony could tell that she'd put on The Skirt. She could smell it, the musty scents of patchouli and cannabis resin and the honeysuckle smell of the expensive detergent Ariel used to wash it by hand, as though it were some precious winding sheet.

"I'm going to Adele's for lunch."

Moony nodded silently.

"I'll be back in a few hours."

More silence.

"You know where to find me if anyone comes by," Ariel nudged her daughter gently with her toe. "Okay?"

Moony sighed. "Yeah, okay"

She watched her mother walk out the door, sun bouncing off her hair in glossy waves. When Ariel was out of sight she hurried down the hall.

In her mother's room, piles of clothes and papers covered the worn Double Wedding Ring quilt, as though tossed helter-skelter from her bureau.

"Jeez, what a mess," said Moony. She slowly crossed to the bed. It was covered with scarves and tangled skeins of pantyhose; drifts of old catering receipts, bills, canceled checks. A few paperbacks with yellowed pages that had been summer reading in years past. A back issue of *Gourmet* magazine and the *Maine Progressive*. A Broadway ticket stub from *Prelude to a Kiss*. Grimacing, Moony prodded the edge of last year's calendar from the Beach Store & Pizza to Go.

What had her mother been looking for?

Then, as if by magic, Moony saw it. Its marbled cover suddenly glimpsed beneath a dusty strata of tarot cards and Advil coupons, like some rare bit of fossil, lemur vertebrae or primate jaw hidden within papery shale. She drew it out carefully, tilting it so the light slid across the title.

MARS HILL: ITS HISTORY AND LORE
BY
ABIGAIL MERITHEW COX
A LOVER OF ITS MYSTERIES

With careful fingers Moony rifled the pages. Dried rose petals fell out, releasing the sad smell of summers past, and then a longer plume of liatris dropped to the floor, fresh enough to have left a faint purplish stain upon the page. Moony drew the book up curiously, marking the page where the liatris had fallen, and read,

LAST SUMMER AT MARS HILL

Perhaps strangest of all the Mysteries of our Colony at Mars Hill is the presence of those Enchanted Visitors who make their appearance now and then, to the eternal Delight of those of us fortunate enough to receive the benison of their presence. I say Delight, though many of us who have conjured with them say that the Experience resembles Rapture more than mere Delight, and even that Surpassing Ecstasy of which the Ancients wrote and which is at the heart of all our Mysteries; though we are not alone in enjoying the favor of our Visitors. It is said by my Aunt, Sister Rosemary Merithew, that the Pasamaquoddie Indians who lived here long before the civilizing influence of the White Man, also entertained these Ethereal Creatures, which are in appearance like to those fairy lights called Foxfire or Will O'The Wisp, and which may indeed be the inspiration for such spectral rumors. The Pasamaquoddie named them Akiniki, which in their language means The Greeters; and this I think is a most appropriate title for our Joyous Guests, who bring only Good News from the Other Side, and who feast upon our mortality as a man sups upon rare meats...

Moony stared at the page in honor and disgust. *Feasting* upon mortality? She recalled her mother and Jason talking about the things they called the Light Children, Jason's disappointment that They had never appeared to Moony. As though there was something wrong with her, as though she wasn't worthy of seeing Them. But she had never felt that way. She had always suspected that Jason and her mother and the rest were mistaken about the Light Children. When she was younger, she had even accused her mother of lying about seeing Them. But the other people at Mars Hill spoke of Them, and Jason, at least, would never lie to Moony. So she had decided there must be something slightly delusional about the whole thing. Like a mass hypnosis, or maybe some kind of mass drug flashback, which seemed more likely considering the histories of some of her mother's friends.

Still, that left Mrs. Grose, who never even took an aspirin. Who, as far as Moony knew, had never been sick in her life, and who certainly seemed immune to most of the commonplace ailments of what must be, despite appearances, an advanced age. Mrs. Grose claimed to speak with the Light Children, to have a sort of understanding of Them that Ariel and the others lacked. And Moony had always held Mrs. Grose in awe. Maybe because her own grandparents were all dead, maybe just because of that story about Houdini—it was too fucking weird, no one could have made it up.

And so maybe no one had made up the Light Children, either. Moony tapped the book's cover, frowning. Why couldn't she see Them? Was it because she didn't believe? The thought annoyed her. As though she were a kid who'd found out about Santa Claus, and was being punished for learning the truth. She stared at the book's cover, the gold lettering flecked with dust, the peppering of black and green where salt air and mildew had eaten away at the cloth. The edge of one page crumbled as she opened it once more.

> Many of my brothers and sisters can attest to the virtues of Our Visitors, particularly Their care for the dying and afflicted...

"Fucking *bullshit*," yelled Moony. She threw the book across the room, hard, so that it slammed into the wall beside her mother's bureau. With a soft crack the spine broke. She watched stonily as yellow pages and dried blossoms fluttered from between the split covers, a soft explosion of antique dreams. She left the room without picking up the mess, the door slamming shut behind her.

◆ ◆ ◆

"I WAS CONSUMPTIVE," Mrs. Grose was saying, nodding as she looked in turn from Ariel to Diana to the pug sprawled panting on the worn chintz sofa beside them. "Tuberculosis, you know. Coming here saved me."

"You mean like, taking the waters?" asked Ariel. She shook back her hair and took another sip of her gin-and-tonic. "Like they used to do at Saratoga Springs and places like that?"

"Not like that *at all*," replied Mrs. Grose firmly. She raised one white eyebrow and frowned. "I mean, Mars Hill saved me."

Saved you for what? thought Ariel, choking back another mouthful of gin. She shuddered. She knew she shouldn't drink, these days she could feel it seeping into her, like that horrible barium they injected into you to do tests. But she couldn't stop. And what was the point, anyway?

"But you think it might help her, if she stayed here?" Diana broke in, oblivious of Mrs. Grose's imperious gaze. "And Martin, do you think it could help him, too?"

"I don't think *anything*," said Mrs. Grose, and she reached over to envelope the wheezing pug with one large fat white hand. "It is absolutely not up to me at all. I am simply *telling* you the *facts*."

"Of course," Ariel said, but she could tell from Diana's expression that her words had come out slurred. "Of *course*," she repeated with dignity, sitting up and smoothing the folds of her patchwork skirt.

"As long as you understand," Mrs. Grose said in a gentler tone. "We are guests here, and guests do not ask favors of their hosts."

The other two women nodded. Ariel carefully put her glass on the coffee table and stood, wiping her sweating hands on her skirt. "I better go now," she said. Her head pounded and she felt nauseated, for all that she'd barely nibbled at the ham sandwiches and macaroni salad Mrs. Grose had set out for lunch. "Home. I think I'd better go home."

"I'll go with you," said Diana. She stood and cast a quick look at their hostess. "I wanted to borrow that book..."

Mrs. Grose saw them to the door, holding open the screen and swatting threateningly at mosquitoes as they walked outside. "Remember what I told you," she called as they started down the narrow road, Diana with one arm around Ariel's shoulder. "Meditation and nettle tea. And patience."

"Patience," Ariel murmured; but nobody heard.

ELIZABETH HAND

◆ ◆ ◆

THE WEEKS PASSED. The weather was unusually clear and warm, Mars Hill bereft of the cloak of mist and fog that usually covered it in August. Martin Dionysos took the *Wendameen* out nearly every afternoon, savoring the time alone, the hours spent fighting wind and waves—antagonists he felt he could win against.

"It's the most perfect summer we've ever had," Gary Bonetti said often to his friend. *Too* often, Martin thought bitterly. Recently, Martin was having what Jason called Millennial Thoughts, seeing ominous portents in everything from the tarot cards he dealt out to stricken tourists on Wednesday nights to the pattern of kelp and maidenhair left on the gravel beach after one of the summer's few storms. He had taken to avoiding Ariel, a move that filled him with self-loathing, for all that he told himself that he still needed time to grieve for John before giving himself over to another death. But it wasn't that, of course. Or at least it wasn't *only* that. It was fear, *The* Fear. It was listening to his own heart pounding as he lay alone in bed at night, counting the beats, wondering at what point it all began to break down, at what point It would come to take him.

So he kept to himself. He begged off going on the colony's weekly outing to the little Mexican restaurant up the road. He even stopped attending the weekly readings in the chapel. Instead, he spent his evenings alone, writing to friends back in the Bay Area. After drinking coffee with Jason every morning he'd turn away.

"I'm going to work now," he'd announce, and Jason would nod and leave to find Moony, grateful, his father thought, for the opportunity to escape.

Millennial Thoughts.

Martin Dionysos had given over a corner of his cottage's living room to a studio. There was a tiny drafting table, his portable computer, an easel, stacks of books; the week's forwarded offerings of *Out!* and *The Advocate* and *Q* and *The Bay Weekly*, and, heaped on an ancient stained Windsor chair, the usual pungent mess of oils and herbal decoctions that he used in his work. Golden morning light streamed through the wide mullioned windows, smelling of salt and the diesel fumes from Diana's ancient Volvo. On the easel a large unprimed canvas rested, somewhat unevenly due to the cant of a floor slanted enough that you could drop a marble in the kitchen and watch it roll slowly but inexorably to settle in the left-hand corner of the living room. Gary Bonetti claimed that it wasn't that all of the cottages on Mars Hill were built by incompetent architects. It was the magnetic pull of the ocean just meters away; was the imperious reins of the East, of the Moon, of the magic charters of the Otherworld, that made it impossible to find any two corners that were plumb. Martin and the others laughed at Gary's pronouncement, but John had believed it.

John. Martin sighed, stirred desultorily at a coffee can filled with linseed oil and turpentine, then rested the can on the windowsill. For a long time he had been so caught up with the sad and harrowing and noble and disgusting details of John's dying that he had been able to forestall thinking about his own diagnosis. He had been grateful, in an awful way, that there had been something so horrible, so unavoidably and demandingly *real*, to keep him from succumbing to his own despair.

But all that was gone now. John was gone. Before John's death, Martin had always had a sort of unspoken, formless belief in an afterlife. The long shadow cast by a 1950s Catholic boyhood, he guessed. But when John died, that small hidden solace had died, too. There was nothing there. No vision of a beloved waiting for him on the other side. Not even a body moldering within a polished mahogany casket. Only ashes, ashes; and his own death waiting like a small patient vicious animal in the shadows.

"Shit," he said. He gritted his teeth. This was how it happened to Ariel. She gave in to despair, or dreams, or maybe she just pretended it would go away. She'd be lucky now to last out the summer. At the thought a new wave of grief washed over him, and he groaned.

"Oh, shit, shit, shit," he whispered. With watering eyes he reached for the can full of primer on the sill. As he did so, he felt a faint prickling go through his fingers, a sensation of warmth that was almost painful. He swore under his breath and frowned. A tiny stab of fear lanced through him. Inexplicable and sudden pain, wasn't that the first sign of some sort of degeneration? As his fingers tightened around the coffee can, he looked up. The breath froze in his throat and he cried aloud, snatching his hand back as though he'd been stung.

They were there. Dozens of Them, a horde of flickering golden spots so dense They obliterated the wall behind Them. Martin had seen Them before, but never so close, never so many. He gasped and staggered back, until he struck the edge of the easel and sent the canvas clattering to the floor. They took no notice, instead followed him like a swarm of silent hornets. And as though They were hornets, Martin shouted and turned to run.

Only he could not. He was blinded, his face seared by a terrible heat. They were everywhere, enveloping him in a shimmering cocoon of light and warmth, Their fierce radiance burning his flesh, his eyes, his throat, as though he breathed in liquid flame. He shrieked, batting at the air, and then babbling fell back against the wall. As They swarmed over him he felt Them, not as you feel the sun but as you feel a drug or love or anguish, filling him until he moaned and sank to the floor. He could feel his skin burning and erupting, his bones turning to ash inside him. His insides knotted, cramping until he thought he would faint. He doubled over, retching, but only a thin stream of spittle ran down his chin. An explosive burst of pain raced through him. He opened his mouth to scream, the sound so thin it might have been an insect whining. Then there was nothing but light, nothing but flame; and Martin's body unmoving on the floor.

•◆•

MOONY WAITED UNTIL late afternoon, but Jason never came. Hours earlier, Moony had glanced out the window of her cottage and seen Gary Bonetti running up the hill to Martin's house, followed minutes later by the panting figure of Mrs. Grose. Jason she didn't see at all. He must have never left his cottage that morning, or else left and returned by the back door.

Something had happened to Martin. She knew that as soon as she saw Gary's stricken face. Moony thought of calling Jason, but did not. She did nothing, only paced and stared out the window at Jason's house, hoping vainly to see someone else enter or leave. No one did.

Ariel had been sleeping all day. Moony avoided even walking past her mother's bedroom, lest her own terror wake her. She was afraid to leave the cottage, afraid to find out the truth. Cold dread stalked her all afternoon as she waited for something—an ambulance, a phone call, anything—but nothing happened. Nobody called, nobody came. Although once, her nostrils filled with the acrid smell of cigarette smoke, and she felt Jason there. Not Jason himself, but an overwhelming sense of terror that she knew came from him, a fear so intense that she drew her breath in sharply, her hand shooting out to steady herself against the door. Then the smell of smoke was gone.

"Jason?" she whispered, but she knew he was no longer thinking of her. She stood with her hand pressed against the worn silvery frame of the screen door. She kept expecting Jason to appear, to explain things. But there was nothing. For the first time all summer, Jason seemed to have forgotten her. Everyone seemed to have forgotten her.

That had been hours ago. Now it was nearly sunset. Moony lay on her towel on the gravel beach, swiping at a mosquito and staring up at the cloudless sky, blue skimmed to silver as the sun melted away behind Mars Hill. What a crazy place this was. Someone gets sick, and instead of dialing 911 you send for an obese old fortuneteller. The thought made her stomach churn; because of course that's what her mother had done. Put her faith in fairydust and crystals instead of physicians and chemo. Abruptly Moony sat up, hugging her knees.

"Damn," she said miserably

She'd put off going home, half-hoping, half-dreading that someone would find her and tell her what the hell was going on. Now it was obvious that she'd have to find out for herself. She threw her towel into her bag, tugged on a hooded pullover and began to trudge back up the hill.

On the porches of the other cottages she could see people stirring. Whatever had happened, obviously none of them had heard yet. The new lesbian couple from Burlington sat facing each other in matching wicker armchairs, eyes closed and hands extended. A few houses on, Shasta Daisy sat on the stoop of her tiny Queen Anne Victorian, sipping a wine cooler, curled sheets of graph paper littering the table in front of her.

"Where's your mom?" Shasta called.

Moony shrugged and wiped a line of sweat from her cheek. "Resting, I guess."

"Come have a drink." Shasta raised her bottle. "I'll do your chart."

Moony shook her head. "Later. I got to get dinner."

"Don't forget there's a moon circle tonight," said Shasta. "Nine thirty at the gazebo."

"Right." Moony nodded, smiling glumly as she passed. What a bunch of kooks. At least her mother would be sleeping and not wasting her time conjuring up someone's aura between wine coolers.

But when she got home, no one was there. She called her mother's name as the screen door banged shut behind her, waited for a reply but there was none. For an instant a terrifying surge raced through her: something else had happened, her mother lay dead in the bedroom…

But the bedroom was empty, as were the living room and bathroom and anyplace else where Ariel might have chosen to die. The heady scent of basil filled the cottage, with a fainter hint of marijuana. When Moony finally went into the kitchen, she found the sink full of sand and half-rinsed basil leaves. Propped up on the drainboard was a damp piece of paper towel with a message spelled out in runny magic marker.

> Moony: Went to
> Chapel Moon circle at 9:30
> Love love love Mom

"Right," Moony said, disgusted. She crumpled the note and threw it on the floor. "Way to go, Mom."

Marijuana, moon circle, astrological charts. Fucking *idiots*. All of a sudden she was filled with rage, at her mother and Jason and Martin and all the rest. Why weren't there any *doctors* here? Or lawyers, or secretaries, or anyone with half a brain, enough at least to take some responsibility for the fact that there were sick people here, people who were *dying* for Christ's sake and what was anyone doing about it? What was *she* doing about it?

"I've had it," she said aloud. "I have *had* it." She spun around and headed for the front door, her long hair an angry black blur around her grim face. "Amanda Rheining, you are going to the hospital. *Now.*"

She strode down the hill, ignoring Shasta's questioning cries. The gravel bit into her bare feet as she rounded the turn leading to the chapel. From here she could glimpse the back door of Jason and Martin's cottage. As Moony hurried past a stand of birches, she glimpsed Diana standing by the door, one hand resting on its crooked wooden frame. She was gazing out at the Bay with a rapt expression that might have been joy or exhausted grief, her hair gilded with the dying light.

For a moment Moony stopped, biting her lip. Diana at least might understand. She could ask Diana to come and help her force Ariel to go to the hospital. It would be like the intervention they'd done with Diana's ex-husband. But that would mean going to Martin's cottage, and confronting whatever it was that waited inside. Besides, Moony knew that no one at Mars Hill would ever force Ariel to do something she didn't want to do; even live. No. It was up to her to save her mother: herself, Maggie Rheining. Abruptly she turned away.

Westering light fell through the leaves of the ancient oak that shadowed the weathered gray chapel. The lupines and tiger lilies had faded with the dying summer. Now violet plumes of liatris sprang up around the chapel door beside unruly masses of sweet-smelling phlox and glowing clouds of asters. Of course no one ever weeded or thinned out the garden. The flowers choked the path leading to the door, so that Moony had to beat away a nest of bees and lacewings and pale pink moths like rose petals, all of them rising from the riot of blossoms and then falling in a softly moving skein about the girl's shoulders as she walked. Moony cursed and slashed at the air, heedless of a luna moth's drunken somersault above her head, the glimmering wave of fireflies that followed her through the twilight.

At the chapel doorway Moony stopped. Her heart was beating hard, and she spat and brushed a liatris frond from her mouth. From inside she could hear a low voice; her mother's voice. She was reciting the verse that, over the years, had become a sort of blessing for her, a little mantra she chanted and whispered summer after summer, always in hopes of summoning Them—

"With this field-dew consecrate
Every fairy take his gait
And each several chamber bless,
through this palace, with sweet peace;
Ever shall in safety rest,
and the owner of it blest."

At the sound, Moony felt her heart clench inside her. She moved until her face pressed against the ancient gray screen sagging within its doorframe. The screen smelled heavily of dust; she pinched her nose to keep from sneezing. She gazed through the fine moth-pocked web as though through a silken scrim or the Bay's accustomed fog.

Her mother was inside. She stood before the wooden altar, pathetic with its faded burden of wilting flowers and empty bottles and Jason's cigarette butts scattered across the floor. From the window facing the Bay, lilac-colored light flowed into the room, mingling with the shafts of dusty gold falling from the casements set high within the opposing wall. Where the light struck the floor a small bright pool had formed. Ariel was dancing slowly in and out of this, her thin arms raised, the long heavy sweep of her patchwork skirt sliding back and forth to reveal her slender legs and bare feet shod with a velvety coat of dust. Moony could hear her reciting Shakespeare's fairies' song again, and a line from Julian of Norwich that Diana had taught her:

All will be well, and all will be well, and all manner of things will well.

And suddenly the useless purity of Ariel's belief overwhelmed Moony. A stoned forty-three-year-old woman with breast cancer and a few weeks left to live, dancing inside a ruined chapel singing to herself. Tears filled Moony's eyes, fell and left a dirty streak against the screen. She drew a deep breath, fighting the wave of grief and despair, and pushed against the screen to enter. When she raised her head again, Ariel had stopped.

At first Moony thought her mother had seen her. But no. Ariel was staring straight ahead at the altar, her head cocked to one side as though listening. So intent was she that Moony stiffened as well, inexplicably frightened. She glanced over her shoulder, but of course there was no one there. But it was too late to keep her heart from pounding. She closed her eyes, took a deep breath and turned, stepping over the sill toward Ariel.

"Mom," Moony called softly. "Mom, I'm—"

Moony froze. In the center of the chapel her mother stood, arms writhing as she held them above her head, long hair whipping across her face. She was on fire. Flickers of gold and crimson along her arms and chest, lapped at her throat and face and set runnels of light flaming across her clothes. Moony could hear shrieking, could see her tearing at her breast as she tried to rip away the burning fabric. With a howl Moony stumbled across room—not thinking, hardly even seeing her as she lunged to grab Ariel and pull her down.

"*Mom!*"

But before she could reach Ariel she tripped, smashed onto the uneven floor. Groaning she rolled over and tried to get back up. An arm's-length away, her mother flailed, her voice given over now to a high shrill keening, her flapping arms still raised above her head. And for the first time Moony realized that there was no real heat, no flames. No smoke filled the little room. The light that streamed through the picture window was clear and bright as dawn.

Her mother was not on fire. She was with Them.

They were everywhere, like bees swarming across a bank of flowers. Radiant beads of gold and argent covered Ariel until Moony no longer saw her mother, but only the blazing silhouette of a woman, a numinous figure that sent a prismatic aurora rippling across the ceiling. Moony fell back, horrified, awe-struck. The figure continued its bizarre dance, hands lifting and falling as though reaching for something that was being pulled just out of reach. She could hear her mother's voice, muted now to a soft repetitive cry—*uh, uh!*—and a very faint clear tone, like the sustained note of a glass harmonica.

'Jesus," Moony whispered, then yelled, "*Jesus!* Stop it, *stop*—"

But They didn't stop; only moved faster and faster across Ariel's body until her mother was nothing but a blur, a chrysalis encased in glittering pollen, a burning ghost. Moony's breath scraped against her throat. Her hands clawed at her knees, the floor, her own breasts, as her mother kept on with that soft moaning and the sound of the Light Children filled the chapel the way wine fills a glass.

And then gradually it all began to subside. Gradually the glowing sheath fell from her mother, not fading so much as *thinning*, the way Moony had once read the entrance to a woman's womb will thin as its burden wakes to be born. The chiming noise died away There was only a faint high echo in Moony's ears. Violet light spilled from the high windows, a darker if weaker wine. Ariel sprawled on the dusty floor, her arms curled up against her chest like the dried hollow limbs of an insect, scarab or patient mantis. Her mouth was slack, and the folds of tired skin around her eyes. She looked inutterably exhausted, but also somehow at peace. With a cold stab like a spike driven into her breast, Moony knew that this was how Ariel would look in death; knew that this was how she looked, now; knew that she was dead.

But she wasn't. As Moony watched, her mother's mouth twitched. Then Ariel sneezed, squeezing her eyes tightly. Finally she opened them to gaze at the ceiling. Moony stared at her, uncomprehending. She began to cry, sobbing so loudly that she didn't hear what her mother was saying, didn't hear Ariel's hoarse voice whispering the same words over and over and over again—

"*Thank you, thank you, thank you!*—"

But Moony wasn't listening. And only in her mother's own mind did Ariel herself ever again hear Their voices. Like an unending stream of golden coins being poured into a well, the eternal and incomprehensible echo of Their reply—

"*You are Welcome.*"

• ◆ •

THERE MUST HAVE been a lot of noise. Because before Moony could pull herself together and go to her mother, Diana was there, her face white but her eyes set and in control, as though she were an ambulance driver inured to all kinds of terrible things. She took Ariel in her arms and got her to her feet. Ariel's head flopped to one side, and for a moment Moony thought she'd slide to the floor again. But then she seemed to rally. She blinked, smiled fuzzily at her daughter and Diana. After a few minutes, she let Diana walk her to the door. She shook her head gently but persistently when her daughter tried to help.

"You can follow us, darling," Diana called back apologetically as they headed down the path to Martin's cottage. But Moony made no move to follow. She only watched in disbelief—*I can follow you? Of course I can, asshole!*—and then relief, as the two women lurched safely through the house's crooked door.

Let someone else take care of her for a while, Moony thought bitterly. She shoved her hands into her pockets. Her terror had turned to anger. Now, perversely, she needed to yell at someone. She thought briefly of following her mother; then of finding Jason. But really, she knew all along where she had to go.

• ◆ •

MRS. GROSE SEEMED surprised to see her (*Ha!* thought Moony triumphantly; what kind of psychic would be *surprised?*). But maybe there was something about her after all. Because she had just made a big pot of chamomile tea, heavily spiked with brandy, and set out a large white plate patterned with alarmingly lifelike butterflies and bees, the insects seeming to hover intently beside several slabs of cinnamon-fragrant zucchini bread.

"They just keep *mul*tiplying." Mrs. Grose sighed so dramatically that Moony thought she must be referring to the bees, and peered at them again to make sure they weren't real. "Patricia—you know, that nice lady with the lady friend?—she says, *pick* the flowers, so I pick them but I still have too many squashes. Remind me to give you some for your mother."

At mention of her mother, Moony's anger melted away. She started to cry again.

"My darling, what is it?" cried Mrs. Grose. She moved so quickly to embrace Moony that a soft-smelling pinkish cloud of face powder wafted from her cheeks onto the girl's. "Tell us darling, tell us—"

Moony sobbed luxuriously for several minutes, letting Mrs. Grose stroke her hair and feed her healthy sips of tepid brandy-laced tea. Mrs. Grose's pug wheezed anxiously at his mistress's feet and struggled to climb into Moony's lap. Eventually he succeeded. By then, Moony had calmed down enough to tell the aged woman what had happened, her rambling narrative punctuated by hiccuping sobs and small gasps of laughter when the dog lapped excitedly at her teacup.

"Ah *so*," said Mrs. Grose, when she first understood that Moony was talking about the Light Children. She pressed her plump hands together and raised her tortoiseshell eyes to the ceiling. "They are having a busy day."

Moony frowned, wiping her cheeks. As though They were like the people who collected the trash or turned the water supply off at the end of the summer. But then Moony went on talking, her voice growing less tremulous as the brandy kicked in. When she finished, she sat in somewhat abashed silence and stared at the teacup she held in her damp hand. Its border of roses and cabbage butterflies took on a flushed glow from Mrs. Grose's paisley-draped Tiffany lamps. Moony looked uneasily at the door. Having confessed her story she suddenly wanted to flee, to check on her mother; to forget the whole thing. But she couldn't just take off. She cleared her throat, and the pug growled sympathetically.

"*Well*," Mrs. Grose said at last. "I see I will be having lots of company this winter."

Moony stared at her uncomprehending. "I mean, your mother and Martin will be staying on," Mrs. Grose explained, and sipped her tea. Her cheeks like the patterned porcelain had a febrile glow, and her eyes were so bright that Moony wondered if she was very drunk. "So at last! there will be enough of us here to really talk about it, to *learn*—"

"Learn what?" demanded Moony. Confusion and brandy made her peevish. She put her cup down and gently shoved the pug from her lap. "I mean, what happened? *What is going on?*"

"Why, it's Them, of course," Mrs. Grose said grandly, then ducked her head, as though afraid she might be overheard and deemed insolent. "We are so *fortunate*—you are so fortunate, my dear, and your darling mother! And Martin, of course—this is a wonderful time for us, a blessed, blessed time!" At Moony's glare of disbelief she went on, "You understand, my darling—They have come, They have *greeted* your mother and Martin, it is a very exciting thing, very rare—only a very few of us—"

Mrs. Grose preened a little before going on, "—and it is always so wonderful, so miraculous, when another joins us—and now suddenly we have *two!*"

Moony stared at her, her hands opening and closing in her lap. "But what *happened?*" she cried desperately. "What *are* They?"

Mrs. Grose shrugged and coughed delicately. "What are They," she repeated. "Well, Moony, that is a very good question." She heaved back onto the couch and sighed. "What are They? I do not know."

At Moony's rebellious glare she added hastily, "Well, many things, of course, we have thought They were many things, and They might be any of these or all of them or—well, none, I suppose. Fairies, or little angels of Jesus, or tree spirits—that is what a dear friend of mine believed. And some sailors thought They were will-o-the-wisps, and let's see, Miriam Hopewell, whom you don't remember but was *another* very dear friend of mine, God rest her soul, Miriam thought They came from flying saucers."

At this Moony's belligerence crumpled into defeat. She recalled the things she had seen on her mother—*devouring* her it seemed, setting her aflame—and gave a small involuntary gasp.

"But why?" she wailed. "I mean, *why?* Why should They care? What can They possibly get from us?"

Mrs. Grose enfolded Moony's hand in hers. She ran her fingers along Moony's palm as though preparing for a reading, and said, "Maybe They get something They don't have. Maybe we *give* Them something."

"But what?" Moony's voice rose, almost a shriek. "What?"

"Something They don't have," Mrs. Grose repeated softly. "Something everybody else has, but They don't—

Our deaths."

Moony yanked her hand away. "Our *deaths?* My mother like, sold her soul, to—to—"

"You don't understand, darling." Mrs. Grose looked at her with mild, whiskey-colored eyes. "They don't want us to die. They want our *deaths.* That's why we're still at Mars Hill, me and Gary and your mother and Martin. As long as we stay here, They will keep them for us—our sicknesses, our destinies. It's something They don't have." Mrs. Grose sighed, shaking her head. "I guess They just get lonely, or bored of being immortal. Or whatever it is They are."

That's right? Moony wanted to scream. *What the hell are They?* But she only said, "So as long as you stay here you don't die? But that doesn't make any sense—I mean, John died, he was here—"

Mrs. Grose shrugged. "He left. And They didn't come to him, They never greeted him…

"Maybe he didn't know—or maybe he didn't want to stay. Maybe he didn't want to live. Not everybody does, you know. I don't want to live forever—" She sighed melodramatically, her bosom heaving. "But I just can't seem to tear myself away."

She leaned over to hug Moony. "But don't worry now, darling. Your mother is going to be *okay*. And so is Martin. And so are you, and all of us. We're safe—"

Moony shuddered. "But I can't stay here! I have to go back to school, I have a life—"

"Of course you do, darling! We all do! *Your* life is out there—" Mrs. Grose gestured out the window, wiggling her fingers toward where the cold blue waters of the Bay lapped at the gravel. "And ours is here." She smiled, bent her head to kiss Moony so that the girl caught a heavy breath of chamomile and brandy. "Now you better go, before your mother starts to worry."

Like I was a goddamn kid, Moony thought, but she felt too exhausted to argue. She stood, bumping against the pug. It gave a muffled bark, then looked up at her and drooled apologetically. Moony leaned down to pat it and took a step toward the door. Abruptly she turned back.

"Okay," she said. "Okay. Like, I'm going. I understand, you don't know about these—about all this—I mean I know you've told me everything you can. But I just want to ask you one thing—"

Mrs. Grose placed her teacup on the edge of the coffee table and waved her fingers, smiling absently. "Of course, of course, darling. Ask away."

"How old are you?"

Mrs. Grose's penciled eyebrows lifted above mild surprised eyes. "How old am I? One doesn't *ask* a lady such things, darling. But—" She smiled slyly, leaning back and folding her hands upon her soft bulging stomach. "If I'd been a man and had the vote, it would have gone to Mr. Lincoln."

Moony nodded, just once, her breath stuck in her throat. Then she fled the cottage.

◆ ◆ ◆

IN BANGOR, THE doctor confirmed that the cancer was in remission.

"It's incredible." She shook her head, staring at Ariel's test results before tossing them ceremoniously into a wastebasket. "I would say the phrase 'A living miracle' is not inappropriate here. Or voodoo, or whatever it is you do there at Mars Hill."

She waved dismissively at the open window, then bent to retrieve the tests. "You're welcome to get another opinion. I would advise it, as a matter of fact."

"Of course," Ariel said. But of course she wouldn't, then or ever. She already knew what the doctors would tell her.

There was some more paperwork, a few awkward efforts by the doctor to get Ariel to confess to some secret healing cure, some herbal remedy or therapy practiced by the kooks at the spiritualist community. But finally they were done. There was nothing left to discuss, and only a Blue Cross number to be given to the receptionist. When the doctor stood to walk with Ariel to the door, her eyes were too bright, her voice earnest and a little shaky as she said, "And look: whatever you were doing, Ms. Rising—howling at the moon, whatever—you just keep on doing it. Okay?"

"Okay," Ariel smiled, and left.

"You really can't leave, now," Mrs. Grose told Martin and Ariel that night. They were all sitting around a bonfire on the rocky beach, Diana and Gary singing "Sloop John B" in off-key harmony, Rvis and Shasta Daisy and the others disemboweling leftover lobster bodies with the remorseless patience of raccoons. Mrs. Grose spread out the fingers of her right hand and twisted a heavy filigreed ring on her pinkie, her lips pursed as she regarded Ariel. "*You* shouldn't have gone to Bangor, that was *very foolish*," she said, frowning. "In a few months, maybe you can go with Gary to the Beach Store. *Maybe*. But no further than that."

Moony looked sideways at her mother, but Ariel only shook her head. Her eyes were luminous, the same color as the evening sky above the Bay.

"Who would want to leave?" Ariel said softly. Her hand crept across the pebbles to touch Martin's. As Moony watched them she felt again that sharp pain in her heart, like a needle jabbing her. She would never know exactly what had happened to her mother, or to Martin. Jason would tell her nothing. Nor would Ariel or anyone else. But there they were, Ariel and Martin sitting cross-legged on the gravel strand, while all around them the others ate and drank and sang as though nothing had happened at all; or as though whatever *had* occurred had been decided on long ago. Without looking at each other Martin and her mother smiled, Martin somewhat wryly Mrs. Grose nodded.

"That's right," the old woman said. When she tossed a stone into the bonfire an eddy of sparks flared up. Moony jumped, startled, and looked up into the sky. For an instant she held her breath, thinking, *At last!*—it was Them and all would be explained. The Fairy King would offer his benediction to the united and loving couples; the dour Puritan would be avenged, the Fool would sing his sad sweet song and everyone would wipe away happy tears.

But no. The sparks blew off into ashes, filling the air with a faint smell of incense. When she turned back to the bonfire, Jason was holding out a flaming marshmallow on a stick, laughing, and the others had segued into a drunken rendition of "Leaving on a Jet Plane."

"Take it, Moony," he urged her, the charred mess slipping from the stick. "Eat it quick, for luck."

She leaned over until it slid onto her tongue, a glowing coal of sweetness and earth and fire; and ate it quick, for luck.

◆ ◆ ◆

LONG AFTER MIDNIGHT they returned to their separate bungalows. Jason lingered with Moony by the dying bonfire, stroking her hair and staring at the lights of Dark Harbor. There was the crunch of gravel behind them. He turned to see his father, standing silhouetted in the soft glow of the embers.

"Jason," he called softly. "Would you mind coming back with me? I—there's something we need to talk about."

Jason gazed down at Moony. Her eyes were heavy with sleep, and he lowered his head to kiss her, her mouth still redolent of burnt sugar. "Yeah, okay," he said, and stood. "You be okay, Moony?"

Moony nodded, yawning. "Sure." As he walked away, Jason looked back and saw her stretched out upon the gravel beach, arms outspread as she stared up at the three-quarter moon riding close to the edge of Mars Hill.

"So what's going on?" he asked his father when they reached the cottage. Martin stood at the dining room table, his back to Jason. He picked up a small stack of envelopes and tapped them against the table, then turned to his son.

"I'm going back," he said. "Home. I got a letter from Brandon today"—Brandon was his agent—"there's going to be a show at the Frick Gallery and a symposium. They want me to speak."

Jason stared at him, uncomprehending. His long pale hair fell into his face, and he pushed it impatiently from his eyes. "But—you can't," he said at last. "You'll die. You can't leave here. That's what Adele said. You'll *die*."

Martin remained silent, before replacing the envelopes and shaking his head. "We don't know that. Even before, we—I—didn't know that. Nobody knows that, ever."

Jason stared at him in disbelief. His face grew flushed as he said, "But you can't! You're sick—shit, Dad, look at John, you can't just—"

His father pursed his lips, tugged at his ponytail. "No, Jason, I can." Suddenly he looked surprised, a little sheepish even, and said more softly. "I mean, I *will*. There's too much for me to give up, Jason. Maybe it sounds stupid, but I think it's important that I go back. Not right away. I think I'll stay on for a few weeks, maybe until the end of October. You know, see autumn in New England and all. But after that—well, there's work for me to do at home, and—"

Jason's voice cracked as he shook his head furiously. "Dad. No. You'll—you'll die."

Martin shrugged. "I might. I mean, I guess I will, sometime. But—well, everybody dies." His mouth twisted into a smile as he stared at the floor. "Except Mrs. Grose."

Jason continued to shake his head. "But—you saw Them—They came, They must've done *something*—"

Martin looked up, his eyes feverishly bright. "They did. That's why I'm leaving. Look, Jason, I can't explain, all right? But what if you had to stay here, instead of going on to Bowdoin? What if Moony left, and everyone else—would you stay at Mars Hill? *Forever?*"

Jason was silent. Finally, "I think you should stay," he said, a little desperately. "Otherwise whatever They did was wasted."

Martin shook his head. His hand closed around a tube of viridian on the table and he raised it, held it in front of him like a weapon. His eyes glittered as he said, "Oh, no, Jason. Not wasted. Nothing is wasted, not ever." And tilting his head he smiled, held out his arm until his son came to him and Martin embraced him, held him there until Jason's sobs quieted, and the moon began to slide behind Mars Hill.

◆ ◆ ◆

JASON DROVE MOONY to the airport on Friday. Most of his things already had been shipped from San Francisco to Bowdoin College, but Moony had to return to Kamensic Village and the Loomises, to gather her clothes and books for school and make all the awkward explanations and arrangements on her own. Friends and relations in New York had been told that Ariel was undergoing some kind of experimental therapy, an excuse they bought as easily as they'd bought most of Ariel's other strange ideas. Now Moony didn't want to talk to anyone else on the phone. She didn't want to talk to anyone at all, except for Jason.

"It's kind of on the way to Brunswick," he explained when Diana protested his driving Moony. "Besides, Diana, if you took her she'd end up crying the whole way. This way I can keep her intact at least until the airport."

Diana gave in, finally. No one suggested that Ariel drive.

"Look down when the plane flies over Mars Hill," Ariel said, hugging her daughter by the car. "We'll be looking for you."

Moony nodded, her mouth tight, and kissed her mother. "You be okay," she whispered, the words lost in Ariel's tangled hair.

"I'll be okay" Ariel said, smiling.

Behind them Jason and Martin embraced. "If you're still here, I'll be up Columbus Weekend," said Jason. "Maybe sooner if I run out of money."

Martin shook his head. "If you run out of money you better go see your mother."

It was only twenty minutes to the airport. "Don't wait," Moony said to Jason, as the same woman who had taken her ticket loaded her bags onto the little Beechcraft. "I mean it. If you do, I'll cry and I'll kill you."

Jason nodded. "Righto. We don't want any bad publicity. *'Noted Queer Activist's Son Slain by Girlfriend at Local Airport. Wind Shear Is Blamed.'*"

Moony hugged him, drew away to study his face. "I'll call you in the morning."

He shook his head. "Tonight. When you get home. So I'll know you got in safely. 'Cause it's dangerous out there." He made an awful face, then leaned over to kiss her. "Ciao, Moony"

"Ciao, Jason."

She could feel him watching her as she clambered into the little plane, but she didn't look back. Instead she smiled tentatively at the few other passengers—a businessman with a tie loose around his neck, two middleaged women with L.L. Bean shopping bags—and settled into a seat by the window.

During takeoff she leaned over to see if she could spot Jason. For an instant she had a flash of his car, like a crimson leaf blowing south through the darkening green of pines and maples. Then it was gone.

Trailers of mist whipped across the little window. Moony shivered, drew her sweatshirt tight around her chest. She felt that beneath her everything she had ever known was shrinking, disappearing, swallowed by golden light; but somehow it was okay. As the Beechcraft banked over

Penobscot Bay she pressed her face close against the glass, waiting for the gap in the clouds that would give her a last glimpse of the gray and white cottages tumbling down Mars Hill, the wind-riven pier where her mother and Martin and all the rest stood staring up into the early autumn sky, tiny as fairy people in a child's book. For an instant it seemed that something hung over them, a golden cloud like a September haze. But then the blinding sun made her glance away. When she looked down again the golden haze was gone. But the others were still there, waving and calling out soundlessly until the plane finally turned south and bore her away, away from summer and its silent visitors—her mother's cancer, Martin's virus, the Light Children and Their hoard of stolen sufferings—away, away, away from them all, and back to the welcoming world.

Pavane for a Prince of the Air

WHEN I came back from visiting my family at Christmas, Tina's message was on the answering machine. I hadn't even taken my coat off, just dumped a suitcase on the floor as the kids ran past and I punched the play button. The voice was so faint I had to play it back three times to decipher parts of it, and then another two times to make sure it was Tina's voice at all; and finally one last time to convince myself that this was real, this was happening, this was how one part of my life was going to play out.

Carrie, it's Tina. Something really, really bad has happened. Cal's in the hospital, he got sick the day after Christmas. He has brain cancer. I'm taking him home tonight, I'll call you later.

I had seen them three days before. Everything was fine then.

Click.

• ◆ •

THIS WAS WHAT was supposed to happen: me and Tina and Cal had been talking off and on for years about buying land, starting a commune, maybe here in Maine or up in Nova Scotia, someplace where we and a few of our friends could live together as we got older. The getting older part hadn't started yet, of course, not in earnest. Tina and I were the same age, forty-two, Cal had ten years on us, and most of our friends fell into the same demographic, skewing a few years older or younger but with the same dazed, weathered look of people whose party-barge ran aground while they were sleeping, and who now found themselves wandering about onshore, looking for fellow survivors, bits of sea wrack to salvage, anyone got some smoke? Boisterously or apologetically middle-aged, their appetites—for sex, drugs, booze, music, magic, general larking about—tempered by time but not diminished, not extinguished, no, not yet.

Yet.

I wrote a story about these people, I have written a lot of stories about them. In the stories things happen. People get sick but magic saves them, or else the world ends but then everyone dies anyway, which makes it easier, not so much to clean up. But no matter what happens in the stories, when they were finished, I could call them, Cal and Tina, on the phone and we could have dinner, they could smoke pot and I could drink red wine and we could watch a movie, something about King Arthur or pirates, something with Uma Thurman or Johnny Depp in it. Then we'd go home and the next day we'd talk on the phone and make plans for next time.

Then this happened.

• ◆ •

I NEVER FOUND out exactly what kind of brain cancer it was. Cal and Tina were not the sort of people who remembered and reported details from the oncology reports. I was going to find out what kind, only it all came down so fast, it was like a freak storm, spring snow, thunder in December; and pretty soon it was obvious that knowing what kind wouldn't make any difference.

It was lung cancer that metastasized to the brain. Cal had been having headaches for the last few weeks, but figured it was pressure from work—he was designing sets for an independent film, an adaptation of an early Stephen King story scheduled to begin shooting in Bangor right after New Year's. The day after Christmas, Cal felt so nauseated he could do nothing but lie down with a towel covering his eyes; it finally

PAVANE FOR A PRINCE OF THE AIR

got so bad Tina took him to the ER, fearing it was food poisoning. The ER doctor thought it might be meningitis, and ordered a CAT scan. The CAT scan showed it wasn't meningitis but a constellation of small black stars, the largest slowly going nova, engulfing his optic nerve.

Tina didn't bring him home that night. They were at the hospital for two more days. I spent that time in bed, too stunned to do anything but down valerian capsules and Nyquil, trying to be anything but awake. Robert took care of the kids. As I slept I realized I had been dreaming this for the past year or more, recurring dreams with an urgency attached to my finding Cal, to seeing him as soon as I could. After waking from these dreams I called him and Tina, making arrangements to get together, dinners at their place where Cal made enchiladas with tomatillo sauce, dinners where Tina and my daughter sat in a corner whispering while Cal told me stories about his years with the Merry Pranksters in San Francisco, his stint as one of the first people to deal LSD, flying coast-to-coast with vials and blotters of Owsley acid, selling to rock bands and socialites and university professors. He told me about his years in Nepal, where he'd seen the corpse of a young man burning on a pyre on the rock-strewn road outside Katmandu. He and his first wife lived ten miles outside the city; they would walk back and forth every day, buying and trading rugs, temple bells, cakes of hashish, statues of demons and gods, prayer wheels. Later they moved back to Austin, where Cal sold antiquities and cocaine to private collectors and rock bands. That was where he'd met Tina. She was twenty-three and working at a radio station. He was thirty-three and called the station incessantly, to request "Tupelo Honey." Three months later they got married and moved to live on a wooden sailboat in Maine.

"I'm having a hard time adjusting to this," he whispered when I finally saw him, when Tina finally brought him home from the hospital in Bangor. There were tears in his eyes. He wore what he always wore, an extravagantly embroidered shirt and bell-bottoms, wool or denim depending on the time of year, wool now, a week after Christmas. His hands were on his knees, the skin asphalt-grey and stretched so that as I lay my hand on his I could feel bone and vein and muscle beneath, sharp as the tines of a rake. "Those doctors, they looked at me. Fifty-two, no kids, a man, cigarettes. They said all they could do was check me in. They said I should just check in and stay there till I die."

I grabbed his shoulders and hugged him. "I'm right here. We're all going to be here. We'll all help."

Tina told me later that she had already made the arrangements with the hospice in Ellsworth, for nurses to come check him daily. Cal would not go back to the hospital. They had no health insurance. There would be no chemo or radiation treatments, no second opinion. They would try other things. I told her about someone I knew, a nutritionist who worked with cancer patients. Tina had heard of an alternative treatment made from Venus Fly Trap. It was only available in Germany; when Cal felt better they were going to Germany to try it.

"He doesn't want to do anything," Tina whispered when Cal went to the bathroom. He was throwing up a lot, from the tumor's pressure on the optic nerve. It was like being seasick twenty-four hours a day. "I can't push him, it's not my decision." Her voice was breaking with anger. "It's his life and he has to make his own decision."

"What about some sort of operation?" I asked. "Wouldn't that relieve the pressure, at least?"

She shook her head. "A long time ago a shaman told Cal never to let anyone cut him. He won't have any surgery."

So that was that. In the meantime, the phone rang nonstop and the machine picked up the messages, hours worth of messages: from other pagans, massage therapists, nurses, acupuncturists, carpenters, boat-builders, filmmakers, lapsed Episcopalians from the Unitarian Church where Cal and Tina performed solstice rituals.

"I can help," I said. I had cared for terminally ill people, and lived with my grandmothers when they were dying. "I know how to do this."

"We're going to need you, Carrie," she said. "All of you. Probably very soon."

PAVANE FOR A PRINCE OF THE AIR

It happened fast. For two weeks I helped out when I could, driving Cal to a dentist appointment, staying with him while Tina was at her job as an assistant to a documentary filmmaker. He couldn't drive anymore.

"He can't be left alone. He has seizures. Kenny and Lisa next door can come over if you have to leave."

Outside it was snowing. For the last few years we'd had little or no snow, only ice storms. This winter it snowed, it seemed to snow every day. Sometimes I had to leave Cal because school was canceled and I had to go meet my kids; I'd call Kenny and Lisa and they would come and sit with him, keep the woodstove going, roll him joints and cigarettes. He had a medical prescription for marijuana, something that he and Tina were gleefully triumphant about. Marijuana, laetrile, apricot kernels. I wondered what would happen if I got stopped by the police, driving around with Cal next to me smoking a joint.

"Do you carry your doctor's note with you?" I asked.

"Always." He laughed but very quietly, so he wouldn't start to cough. That was one of the things you had to get used to, laughing was like talking for Cal, he always laughed, stoned or not. Now he was so quiet.

During one snowstorm while he could still talk we sat and he saved my book. He always helped me, reading my books and telling me, usually too late, what I'd done wrong. He was an avid and acute reader, loved heroic fantasy and Arthurian epics. My own books were too dark for his taste but he read them because he loved me.

"The last one was really good, Carrie. But it's sort of the same, isn't it? You have the plucky heroine and her cynical best friend sidekick and the blood sacrifice."

"And sex," said Tina. "Don't forget the sex."

"And sex. But they're always so young. You should write about grownups now, Carrie."

I hadn't written much for months. I was depressed, battling the black dog for the hundredth time. It was only in the weeks before Christmas that I'd started to feel better.

Still, in the past I'd always managed to write, even through the worst parts. But since last summer this novel felt dead. The voices in my head had gone silent, and more terrible than any despair or fear was the discovery, day after day, that they would no longer speak to me.

"I need you to help me with my book, Cal." We were sitting in their living room, Tina putting on boots and parka and funny Laplander hat, getting ready to leave. "You too, Tina."

She smiled. "Cal will be better than I am."

All three of us knew this was something for Cal, something for him to look forward to: he loved talking about writing, about stories, about magicians and shamans and drugs.

I ran my hands through my hair. "I'm completely stalled. I'll tell you the story, okay, Cal? I'll tell you what I've done so far. All the elements are there but I don't know what to do with them, I can't see it anymore."

He could see it. While the snow fell outside and the wind hammered the windows and Tina drove to an appointment in Skowhegan, I sat and told Cal my story, and he fixed it. He blinked a lot because his eyes hurt, but he laughed too, and paced back and forth like he used to. For a few hours we talked, me spinning my story and Cal smoothing it out. By the time the call came that school had been canceled, again, we had finished.

"You're amazing." I hugged him and we both laughed. "You're a miracle worker. You saved my ass."

"I'm really glad, Carrie." He smiled, tired but happy. I helped him back into his chair.

"Robert's been trying to help me too, he's been trying but it's different, he has a different point of view."

Cal smiled again. "He doesn't believe in it."

"That's right." I hugged and kissed him goodbye. "Jesus, Cal, thank you. I'll be back tomorrow—"

I could never say, to him or Tina, that I didn't believe in it, either. But that night I dreamed I was in the city, in a vast apartment building that's a frequent site for my dreams; and there I met all the characters

PAVANE FOR A PRINCE OF THE AIR

from my books, the characters and the people they were based on, coming by to say hello like guests at a party, a few of them introducing their real-life counterparts to me. When I woke the structure of my novel was as clear to me as if I had been given a map.

So I'm not sure what I believe in anymore.

• ◆ •

CAL AND TINA believed in everything. Fairies, elves, spirits of earth air water fire; Tibetan gods, Minoan sea goddesses, totemic animals, reincarnation, Iroquois spirits. Their names for each other were Fox and Wolf; when they were married, nineteen years before, it was a marriage by capture, with Tina and her attendants dressed as sprites and Cal and his men like Fafhrd and the Grey Mouser. Their house was a renovated barn filled with masks they'd made, columns and porticos and temples from sets Cal had built, Tina's galaxies of scarves and capes and hats, posters from Grateful Dead shows they'd attended over the course of decades. Cal's canvases covered the walls, and the gorgeous leather bags they made and sold, with Tina's elaborate beadwork and braiding and Cal's painting and leatherwork. There were papier-mâché skeletons everywhere, crowned with paper roses; animal skulls on ribboned standards; grinning Day of the Dead figures holding chalices and hash pipes between bony fingers. The cats prowled among them, and slept beneath daturas drooping with waxy white blossoms, or alongside the marijuana plants growing in plastic pots by the big picture window, or in the tiny head-crunching loft above Cal and Tina's bed.

That was where I slept. After the first two weeks there was a small group of us who took turns staying over, two or even three at a time, so we could spell each other during the night. I was usually there for two nights a week; Robert took care of the children.

Cal and Tina's friend Loki often stayed over with me. Loki was unusually quiet, for a friend of theirs; wore chinos and polo shirts or, sometimes, a very old faded *Star Wars* T-shirt. He lived forty-five minutes away, in Rockland, where he worked as a paralegal. A few mornings a week before work he would drive over and take their laundry home with him, wash and dry it, and then return it that evening, sometimes staying overnight. I knew Loki from the elaborate solstice and equinoctial rituals Cal and Tina had staged over the years, where Loki wore an otter's mask he had made, and his usual beige pants and topsiders.

When Loki and I stayed over we didn't talk much. He was strong and serious but occasionally laughed unexpectedly; he was very fond of the cats. I wasn't as useful as I wanted to be. I wasn't a masseuse, like Luna, or strong, like Loki, although I had a strong stomach. I showed Loki how to give Cal morphine injections, after the hospice nurse taught me; then how to administer the morphine IV, morphine suppositories, morphine spikes, morphine pump.

"You know, I could get you a job down on Fifty-Second Street," another friend, Jerry, remarked one day. We laughed: Jerry and his wife, Pansy, laughed a lot. They stayed over together, and in the morning when I arrived they'd report on the previous night and show me the yellow legal pad where we kept track of Cal's injections, meds, liquid intake.

"Tina still hasn't slept," Pansy whispered hoarsely. She ran a greenhouse in Verona and looked like a flower herself, slender with huge violet-circled eyes, fine silvery hair, voice husky from sleeplessness and pot smoke. "See if you can get her to sleep."

"We can't," said Jerry. He was a boatbuilder who'd helped make the pagan standards that he and Pansy had put out on the porch, to billow in the winter wind. "She's getting kinda crazed."

"The nurse says if she doesn't sleep she'll have no strength left for when he goes." Pansy's eyes were bloodshot; she fingered a little leather bag around her neck, an amulet made by Cal with loons painted on it. "See if you can get her to sleep."

For five weeks that was my job: getting Cal and Tina to sleep. The morphine made Cal restless, struggling reflexively to rise from the futon, but he was too weak and dizzy to stand. If there was no one there to catch him he would fall, and did, lacerating his skull; or else he would have seizures. The medication to control these would knock him out for five or six hours, but Tina didn't like to give it to him. She was afraid he would die in his sleep; she was afraid to sleep herself, thinking he would die then. I would practically force her onto the futon beside him, tucking the two of them in, Cal unconscious, Tina wild-eyed and speaking slowly, purposefully, crazily, like a child with night terrors. Sometimes she would read to him, from Hans Christian Andersen. He would say, "I love you, Fox," she would say, "I love you, Little Wolf," and curl around him like a cat. He couldn't move by himself; she would lift her head every few minutes, checking that he was breathing and then looking around until she saw me, sitting in a chair and reading old issues of *Vogue*. A few times I got her to go up to the loft, where she finally would pass out for an hour, maybe two, before climbing back down the ladder again. Several times we had to contact the hospice nurse who was on call, to come help when an IV popped out, or to talk us through the process of administering a new type of painkiller—opium suppositories, the morphine pump. The morphine continued to make Cal restless; he hadn't eaten for ten days, was taking in very little fluid, but he still tried to stand and walk to the bathroom. He couldn't walk, of course, and what water he did drink he would vomit up again within an hour, along with black bile.

One night while Tina was in the loft sleeping I read aloud to Cal, "The Seven Swans," from the Brothers Grimm. As I read his eyes flickered, so sunken in his white face they were like marbles buried in the snow.

"That's nice, Carrie," he whispered when I'd finished. "Thank you."

It was the last time he said my name. Afterwards, as he slept, I read "The Juniper Tree."

• ◆ •

MEANWHILE, MARLENE GATHERED all the bones, tied them up in her silk kerchief and carried them outside. There she wept bitter tears and buried the bones beneath the juniper tree. But as she put them there, she suddenly felt relieved and stopped crying. That was when the juniper tree began to sway, its branches moving as though they were clapping. At the same time smoke came out of the tree, and a flame that seemed to be burning. Then a beautiful bird flew out of the fire and began to sing, the most beautiful song she had ever heard…

• ◆ •

WHEN I FINISHED "The Juniper Tree" I started on the book of pagan death rituals that I found in the living room, alongside articles on cancer therapy and acupuncture left by Luna and Pansy. I prayed that up in the loft Tina was sleeping. But every time Cal stirred she would peer down, and I despaired of her ever resting at all. If Tina slept for two hours it was a triumph. I would always pass out before dawn and feel like Peter in Gethsemane, waking to the sound of Tina ringing a pair of piercingly clear Tibetan temple bells as she stood before the window facing the sun, reciting an incantation.

> Spirits of the East, of water and sky and starlight, I welcome you.
> Spirits of the West, land of fire and the dying sun, I welcome you.
> Spirits of the North, hear us…

• ◆ •

AS THE WEEKS passed, Cal grew frailer and weaker, though his hands when I helped him to stand were painfully strong, fingers like claws digging into my arm. There were always people around now, sometimes only two or three of us; at other times the house was full, like a party. Cal's ex-wife Yala came from Vermont and stayed for three weeks. Some cousins and an elderly aunt flew in from Texas and stayed for several days. That was the last time I saw Cal really happy, just beaming with delight, his eyes widening behind the morphine cloud when he saw them walking slowly towards him, like people on the moon.

"Hey Cal, you ol' peckerwood!" Cousin Bub shouted, and Cal laughed and fell into his arms, really fell, Bub yelping as he caught him. "Hooboy, too much of that reefer, huh!"

Before Cal got sick, their house had always seemed like backstage at Mardi Gras, masks and marijuana smoke, patchouli and the Neville

PAVANE FOR A PRINCE OF THE AIR

Brothers or Joe Ely blasting from the speakers. But as the weeks passed it became more and more like a cave. The windows were covered with scarves and Tibetan hangings. Tiny blue Christmas lights blinked on the ceiling like phosphorescent insects; there were votive candles burning everywhere, in blue glasses and on plates, lined up in front of the corner altar where statues of goddesses and wolves and foxes peered out from thickets of ivy and datura blossoms. The smell of marijuana grew choking; sage and juniper burned in ashtrays and abalone shells, so that there was a constant sweet blue fume. When I smoothed out the bedclothes I found crystals the size of my fist beneath Cal's pillow, amethyst and rose quartz, and necklaces of red thread. The music was soft Japanese flute music, the shakuhachi flutes that Cal loved and played himself. We got in the habit of always whispering, of touching each other as we passed, not so much for solace but as though finding our way in the dark. On the futon Cal lay, eyes closed, breathing softly, and sometimes it seemed he did not breathe at all. He did not speak anymore, or wake. He smelled of marijuana and sweat, a harsh strong smell scarcely obviated by sponge baths and lavender oil and aloe ointment for his bedsores. His auburn hair lay in two long unraveling braids upon his breast, his hands and arms were curled like ferns. He had always worn gorgeous heathen jewelry, of bone and ivory and silver, Celtic torques and lunulas, wristbands wide and weighty as manacles, strings of turquoise and lapis lazuli, earrings and dragon pendants and bones threaded in his hair and beard. On his finger he wore a heavy gold ring with a dragon on it, from Nepal.

But little by little the jewelry had been removed, to make it easier to probe veins for the IV, to get him in and out of his clothes, to turn him so the bedsores would not get worse. He seemed to have only two modes of being now, anguish or unconsciousness. He was on eight different kinds of morphine, but when he was awake none of them really cut the pain. I became obsessed with giving him shots, and later with the morphine IV. I could not bear to see him, that beautiful face twisted in pain, the way he whispered *Oh, Oh, oh fuck,* too weak to even turn his head, too weak, almost, to blink.

Someone asked me once, someone who didn't know Cal, "Have you thought of, you know?" Meaning, had I thought of killing him, of ending that interminable unendurable pain.

No, I said, never; and did not say what I *did* think, the impossible bargains I made at three o' clock in the morning with the pagan deities flitting about the room: what I would give up to save him, which digits, which hand, which leg; eyesight, the power of speech, an ear; two; my tongue.

• ◆ •

ONE DAY WHEN only Tina and I were home, a woman named Deirdre came. Deirdre was a friend of Luna's. Neither Tina nor I knew her.

"Are you a massage therapist?" I asked.

"No." Deirdre was my age, beautifully dressed in stark clothes, black soft trousers, white silk shirt, her dark hair sleek and expensively cut. She had strong patrician features and wore no makeup; her eyes were pale blue and sharply intelligent. "I'm a holistic advisor and a clairvoyant. I help people make transitions from one life-stage to the next. I can see their auras, and help them through the Seven Gates. I'm going to do some work with Cal. But I think Tina is the one who needs some help," she added softly. Her voice was calm, reassuring yet businesslike; she reminded me of the midwife who had delivered my children. "She looks exhausted."

"She is. She won't sleep. She hasn't slept for days." I didn't say that Tina seemed almost demented from sleeplessness and grief. She paced around the house, her long dark hair loose or hidden beneath one of her Laplander hats, a syringe in her hand or a mug of tea or a joint. Right now she was carrying an eagle feather and an abalone shell with juniper burning in it; she was fanning the smoke, moving quickly from corner to corner and returning again and again to Cal's motionless figure, wafting smoke over his face as she chanted.

"I'll work with her," said Deirdre. "But I'll see Cal first."

For over an hour she knelt on the floor behind Cal, cradling his head in her hands. Shakuhachi flute music played softly, incense burned, the cats crept across the beams overhead and light snow fell outside. I felt as though I had been here all my life; that life had shrunk and tightened like a telescoping lens to this pinpoint of being, Tina in the shower, myself doing the dishes and picking up newspapers and feeding the woodstove, a woman kneeling with a dying man's head in her hands, her eyes closed and her lips moving silently. When at last she finished, Deirdre stood, stretching, then came into the kitchen where Tina and I were drinking green tea.

"How is he?" asked Tina. Her eyes were huge and black, her wet hair neatly brushed and hanging down her back. "Is he still here? Is he still here?"

"He's here," said Deirdre. She smiled. She looked tired but peaceful, her face unlined, unmarked by her travels. When she looked at you, you felt as though she were shining a flashlight into your eyes. "He hasn't left. I've gone with him, we walked through all the gates but the last one. He's been there before—"

"He has!" Tina nodded urgently. "He has, lots of times—he's not afraid of dying, he's done it before and he's never been afraid! That's why I'm so confused—I think it's the morphine, he can't remember what he's supposed to do."

"That could be. He's worried about you. He doesn't want to leave you."

"I know!" Tina wailed. "I know, I know—but I don't want him to stay because of me, not if it's his time! But I don't want him to go, and he knows, and I'm afraid I'm confusing him, I'm keeping him when it's his time to go—"

She began to cry. Deirdre put her arms around her. She stared past Tina's shoulder into my eyes and I felt as though I had walked in on a mother nursing her child. "That's right, that's right, let it out, let it go. You're mad, aren't you? You're so angry at him—"

"I am, I am! It wasn't supposed to be like this! We did everything we could! We did everything! There's no time—it happened so fast, it wasn't supposed to be this fast—he's gone and I'll be alone, I don't know how to do anything, I just wanted to be able to make love to him again, I want to fight and have him make dinner for me, oh Little Wolf, Little Wolf—"

She began to sob, wrenchingly. I turned and tiptoed into the back room, where Cal and Tina's clothes hung on racks and were stacked in neatly folded piles; a hippie queen and king's ransom in brocade and velvet and hand-embroidered cowboy shirts. From the next room I could hear Tina's grief rushing out like water into a pool, Deirdre's soft voice comforting her and calling out loudly, encouragingly when Tina's sorrow choked into rage. Now and then I peeked through the India-print curtain, and these glimpses underscored the sense of watching someone give birth: the screaming, the agony, the constant strong presence of a woman who held you and talked you through it. The same knowledge of an inevitable outcome; the same exhaustion afterwards, when I finally came back out to hug both of them. There was even a sort of terrible joy, a radiance in Tina's face as she held me and the tears came again as I stared over her shoulder at Deirdre, so calm and strong. And I was helpless to do anything at all.

Tina went back to sit with Cal, kneeling to wipe his forehead with a washcloth. I walked Deirdre to the door, watching as she pulled on boots and coat and scarf.

"What can I do?" I asked. "For Tina? What can I do?"

"I know you want to make everything better, Carrie. I know you want to help her, and that's really good, she needs someone to take care of her. But you need to be open with your own grieving, and let Tina see that. Show her it's okay that she feels this way."

Deirdre's gaze met mine and I knew she saw right through me. I could only grieve like a teenager, alone in my room at night. At the benefit concert where famous and near-famous and formerly famous singers and musicians raised money for Cal's medical expenses, I sat in the front row and clenched my jaws so hard I had a headache. But I would not cry.

"And see if you can get her to sleep," Deirdre finished. She touched my hand and I nodded.

"Right," I said. I went back inside and watched Tina, curled up beside her husband with the cats sleeping at their feet, like Hansel and Gretel, Jorinda and Joringel, all those lost children. I stayed until Luna arrived for her night shift, and then drove home through the snow, not crying then either because I didn't want to go off the road; not crying until I woke up in the middle of the night from a dream where Cal was hugging me, strong and straight as ever. It was only a dream, but for a little while, at least, he had been there. And I was able to cry.

◆ ◆ ◆

THINGS STARTED HAPPENING even faster then. Or rather, things stopped happening. Cal's periods of lucidity and consciousness became fewer and fewer. The hospice nurses told us it was only a matter of a day or two; but in fact it was nine days. Deirdre came again, and I listened as she and Tina discussed Cal's silent journeying.

"I know he'll come back, but will I know him?" One of the nurses had managed to get Tina to take some sleeping pills. She was sleeping as many as four hours a night now, and seemed less manic. "Do you think he might actually become a wolf? Or another person, do you think he might be a person? Maybe I could find him and we could do this all again? Will I recognize him? Will I *know* him?"

"No one knows." Deirdre leaned against the kitchen counter, sipping green tea. "I think it's partly a matter of luck and partly a matter of being in the right place at the right time. You just never know. But if you're mindful, if you're aware and consciously looking for him, you might find him sooner rather than later."

"I hope so," Tina said fervidly. "Oh god, I hope so."

There was a constant stream of people in and out of the house. Some stayed all day, talking quietly, taking turns to sit at Cal's side, stroking his head, chanting in low voices or kneeling with eyes closed and hands upturned. Praying, I guess, or looking for those seven gates, tapping into some secret stream of healing energy that evaded me. We stacked firewood, folded clothes, washed dishes, fed cats; unpacked groceries and heated the huge vats of chowder Lisa brought from next door.

I continued to drop by once and occasionally twice a day, if I wasn't staying over. Pansy was often there, and I'd kneel beside her and Tina, the three of us gently stroking Cal's face while Tina read from Lorca's poems. I could hardly bear to touch Cal, I was so afraid I might hurt or wake him; but he seemed very far away now. He lay curled upon his side, shrunken, his arms held close to his chest; he looked like a praying mantis, with his eyes so deep set and his limbs withered. It was two weeks since he had eaten anything at all, and then only a few bites of applesauce. Always wiry, he now seemed insubstantial as one of the delicate papier-mâché figures in the room around him, skeletons wearing crowns of roses, a steer's skull ringed round with dried blossoms. I would close my eyes and try to find him, try to see the gates that Deirdre had described. I would picture Cal and Tina walking in a field of bluebonnets, their long hair streaming, or imagine mountains and Cal flying above them, not a wolf but an eagle.

Be there now, I thought, trying to make it real, to scale my own stony disbelief and somehow give him peace. *Be there.*

But still he would twitch and moan, so softly it was like a sigh. His skin was oily with sweat; Tina had washed and braided his hair, but reddish strands had come loose and stuck damply to his forehead. Each time I left I would kiss him, murmuring, *I love you, Cal, I love you.* It would be hours before the scent of his dying left my skin, the smell of candle wax and incense, marijuana, sweat, the heavy odor of farewell he exhaled.

We began to make plans for what happened next, what happened after. That was how we said it. Weeks before, Tina had asked me if I would make arrangements for cremation.

"Cal wants to be burned on a bonfire here in the woods," she told me. "Can you see if we can do that?"

"Sure," I said.

I went outside, huddled in my parka against heavy blowing snow, and in the middle of the dirt road hung out for a while with some of the other people caught between arriving and leaving.

"You're taking care of the cremation?" asked Jorge. He was one of Cal's oldest friends, lived just a few miles down Route 52. He stopped by every day, bringing carafes of coffee and fresh donuts from town, but he wouldn't stay inside. His inside expression was distant, almost bored, as though he were listening to radio reports of bad news far away. But once outside again he grew animated and could give way to worry and, sometimes, anger. "Tina said she asked you…"

"Yeah. But I'm pretty sure the whole Darth Vader trip is totally illegal."

Jorge laughed. "I figured. Larry and Paul want to build a coffin shaped like a boat, and then just push it into the harbor."

"I'm pretty sure that's illegal, too."

◆ ◆ ◆

LARRY AND PAUL did end up making the coffin, a beautiful thing of dovetailed pine and maple and very old, hand-hammered nails. They painted it with runes and sacred symbols, Tibetan prayers and, on its sides, two enormous Argus eyes, like those on ancient Greek triremes. The coffin was immense, nearly seven feet long; but I'd made sure we'd gotten the correct dimensions from the crematorium, so that we'd be certain it would fit into the retort.

Previously, my only knowledge of cremation came from having watched *Jules and Jim* numerous times, taking especial note of those scenes at the end showing the lovers' coffins disappearing into the furnace. But that week I got to be on a first-name basis with the crematorium staff. Tina wanted to keep Cal's body at home for forty-eight hours after he died, and then arrange for our own transportation to the crematory facility in Lewiston, more than three hours away. To do this involved a draconian process of obtaining death certificates and medical examiner's reports, notarized forms from doctors, county clerks, the hospice. A Burial Transport Permit was needed, and a permit for the Disposition of Human Remains. Certain lines of the forms could only be handwritten in black ink. While being transported, the body could never be in public view. I spent hours and hours on the telephone sorting all this out and discussing the more salient aspects of cremation with Mr. Brusher, the crematorium director.

Mr. Brusher was polite, patient, and professionally dubious about the prospect of the bereaved, non-professionals all, performing the pagan duty of driving a corpse in an old red International pickup truck to his crematorium. He had a pleasantly oleaginous voice and seemed to enjoy discussing his work. After he had spent six or seven hours advising me on how best to obtain the proper papers, his tone became one of furtive and confiding amusement.

"The most *efficient* thing to do, Miss Waverley, would be to contact us as soon as possible, after the death has occurred. That way we can make certain we schedule you for the appropriate time.

"Between you and me," he added, giving a soft apologetic snort of laughter, "this has been a very *high volume* week. Mmm. You understand. And you see, we need time in between to thoroughly clean out the retort. *Some* people—"

He lowered his voice conspiratorially. "—*some* people, when they bring the casket in, can be quite distressed when they first see the interior of the retort. Because *occasionally* there is something left over, we do our best to clean it *thoroughly* but *sometimes* there might be a little piece of bone, or metal. Teeth. And this can be upsetting."

I knew he was trying to talk me out of doing any of this ourselves. I was not afraid of bones, although I was worried about Tina. Apart from any visceral shock or fear, there probably was some pagan proscription against somebody else's Judeo-Christian bones being included with your loved one's.

So I spared her the more graphic details provided by Mr. Brusher. I wished I could spare her all of them. Still, she would not be dissuaded; she had a kind of moral strength that was almost nunlike in its purity and the unwavering belief that she was doing the one true right thing.

Which, of course, she was. I could only watch, my chest aching as she braided and rebraided her husband's hair, dampened his cracked lips with a washcloth or her own mouth, kissed his forehead and hands and the staved-in curve of his shoulder blades. And I did what I could to prepare for Death, to lay down a paper trail, or at least provide a sort of map that would indicate where the paper trail would be. I was very, very organized.

But when I was in my own home, I would wake in the middle of the night and lie there for hours in a cold sweat. What terrified me was something so banal I was ashamed to even speak it aloud: I could not bear the thought of Cal's body being burned; of all that beauty, his long red hair and Viking jewelry, his gorgeous clothes and long slender fingers heavy with rings—of all that being consigned to the air.

And that was how I thought of it, not of smoke or ash or flame but of air and nothingness, an eternal blue sweep of sky and Cal nowhere to be seen. I had studied archaeology in college and always loved bones, fragments of stone and crushed beads, the patterns of livelihood and ritual that you could discern within a cubic yard of rich humus and potsherds, tibia and skulls and broken glass. I had no belief in resurrection beyond this.

But when I thought of that beautiful casket, painstakingly made and carved by men who loved their friend, and of my friend within it with all his treasure laid upon his breast—when I thought of that, I imagined Cal as a prince of the earth, one who might be found a thousand years hence, buried in a rocky northern graveyard. And when he was discovered, by archaeologists to whom he would be as remote as Scythian horselords were to me—why then he would live again! Cal would be a mystery, but he would be known. He would be alive, and not forgotten, even if no one knew his name; even if no one understood the meaning of the tattoos upon his wrists or the runestones he carried in a leather bag at his side.

But if all of that were consigned to the air there would be nothing that remained of my friend; nothing at all.

• ◆ •

CAL DIED EARLY on Thursday evening, during a snowstorm. I wasn't there; I would be snowed in with my children for the next forty-eight hours, and so I missed everything I had tried to plan for so diligently. Tina was there, of course, in the next room, talking to Leenamarie, the

Wiccan priestess who would oversee the death rites. Later, Tina told me about everything.

"I walked back into the room and without even looking at him, I knew he was gone. I just knew. I walked over and looked at him. Then I went into the kitchen. I picked up a bowl, that heavy blue glass bowl? And I smashed it into the sink. I was screaming at the top of my lungs.

'You bastard, you sonofabitch, I spent the last two months never leaving you and now you go? Now *you go?'*

"I don't know what Leenamarie thought. Then I looked down at my hand. I hadn't felt anything when I smashed the bowl, but I was bleeding, like, a lot. And I thought, Hmmm. I better get a grip on this."

Within a few hours, the tribe had gathered around her. Tina and Leenamarie and Luna washed Cal's body and anointed it; Tina braided his hair, snipping a single long plait and putting it on the altar, to keep. They dressed him in his nineteenth-century naval captain's uniform, the one he had worn when he was Captain Ahab one Hallowe'en, and laid him out on a makeshift table made from planks and sawhorses, in the keeping room out back. It was so cold there that your fingers and nose grew numb within minutes, but everyone took turns keeping a vigil by his body. The men prepared a huge bonfire in the field behind the woods, and as the snow fell Leenamarie led a mooncircle out there, with dozens of friends chanting, singing, howling like wolves as the storm subsided and the full moon rose above the trees. Inside, Tina sat on a stool in the kitchen while her friend Doreen shaved her head. Doreen worked as a veterinary assistant; she used sheep shears on Tina, and then a series of disposable razors until her skull was smooth and yellow as a monk's. Afterward, Tina showed me a series of pictures, the women seeming never to change position, save their eyes and mouths, which were twisted between hysterical laughter and ravaged weeping. It was like some weird time-lapse film that recorded emotion and not movement.

"He looked so beautiful, Carrie." There were photographs of Cal, too; Tina made a little album of them. "He lost that old-man look and he looked the way he used to, the way he did when we first met. He was so beautiful, I couldn't stop touching him. I just kept going back into the back room and touching his face.

"But then, after about thirty-six hours, he changed. It happened really suddenly. And I went back into the house and said, 'Dead Body! Get him out of here!'"

• ♦ •

THE NIGHT THAT Cal died, I had a dream about him. In my dream I was calling Tina on the phone, but Cal answered, his voice as strong and full of laughter as it had been once, three months gone by, oh so long ago. That was my only knowledge of his presence, his voice, and it filled me with an overwhelming mix of confusion and joy—had there, after all, been a mistake?

But no: even in my dream I couldn't let go of the facts.

"Cal," I said. "Aren't you—"

I stopped. I didn't want to embarrass him by pointing out he was a ghost.

"No, Carrie." He sounded amused, slightly annoyed, the way he'd sounded when we'd argued about politics during the Gulf War. "No, Carrie. I'm still here. I'm right here, Carrie. I'm here."

I woke, feeling not frightened but bemused and oddly exhilarated, which I guess was the closest I ever came to experiencing some kind of faith.

• ♦ •

EARLY FRIDAY MORNING I had called Mr. Brusher and informed him of the time of Cal's death, and told him when to expect the little procession of pickups and old four-wheel-drive Subarus and Saabs.

"The widow is aware that, after forty-eight hours, the body will start to—decay?"

"Yes, she is." I had been warned about this by the hospice nurses, too; one of them advised me that we should all put Noxzema around and inside our nostrils. "They'll be there Saturday afternoon."

Saturday morning they put Cal into his coffin. They laid him upon a bed of marijuana, tucking it around his thin shoulders and wasted legs, and then filled his pockets with semi-precious stones, agates and Maine tourmaline, jade from Nepal and Indian cinnabar. Tina slipped coins into his pockets, and hand-rolled cigarettes, a six-ounce green glass bottle of Coca-Cola, a Defenders of Wildlife coffee mug with wolves on it. In one hand she put the last of the Owsley acid he'd hung onto since his days of dealing it thirty years before. His paints went into the casket, and his pastels; his shakuhachi flute and the new hand-beaded moccasins that were a Christmas present he'd never been able to wear. He wore most of his jewelry, save a few pieces that Tina had decided to keep; and so the casket was made that much heavier by golden rings and thick silver bracelets embossed with dragons and waves, his ivory torque, the yards and yards of Tibetan necklaces strung with little brass and bronze and copper and silver and jade dragons. Tina placed one of his painted and embroidered leather bags beside him. Inside were his well-worn tarot deck and favorite books—Howard Pyle's *King Arthur and the Knights of the Round Table,* the Rockwell Kent *Moby Dick,* paperbacks of Dostoevsky and Tolstoy. Another leather bag held his runestones. Last of all, on his breast there was an exquisite wooden model of a Viking ship under full sail.

She had color photographs of all this, too, and when I saw them I thought how Cal truly did look like a pagan prince, a shaman and not a man who had been born in Dimebox, Texas, fifty-two years before.

◆ ◆ ◆

AND SO I missed the cremation. They drove in a little caravan to Lewiston, Cal's casket inside Jorge's old pickup truck, a big blue tarp covering it and a Tibetan silk painting like a flag draped across the tarp. During that weekend I continued to speak to Tina several times a day. I finally saw her the day after the cremation.

"I missed you so much, Carrie," she said. She was dressed all in black, black linen tunic and loose black trousers, a star-spangled black scarf around her neck. "I wished you'd been there, it felt so wrong you weren't there."

"I know," I said, and held her for a long time. She looked exhausted but beautiful, her gaunt face even more striking now that her head was shaved. "I'm sorry, I—"

"But I have something I'd like for you to do. I have Cal's ashes and I'd like to sift through them with you."

"Sure," I said. I had wondered about this. Mr. Brusher had asked me whether the widow would like the remains crushed.

"Most people do," he said. "But it takes a few extra hours, and we need to schedule that time in. Can you let me know?"

This was one command decision I was not prepared to make. I hadn't even mentioned it to Tina, but now I learned that she had not opted to do what most people would have done.

"Sure," I told her. Of course. It would be an honor.

"Okay." She turned and picked up a little book from the coffee table. There was a largish cardboard carton there as well, sealed with tape and with Cal's name and address written on it in magic marker. Someone had drawn swirly moons and stars on the box in red and gold glitter ink. Tina ignored the box and opened the little book, flipping quickly through it. "Next Tuesday, nothing will be in retrograde, after—hmm, let's see, twelve forty-seven p.m. Can you come then?"

"Sure. I'll take you to lunch first, how's that?"

So our date was set, as though we were going to Belfast to have a manicure from the woman who used only non-toxic, vegetable-based nail products. That night, when I told Robert about what I was going to do, he frowned and shook his head.

"This sounds a bit dangerous to me. Psychologically risky, I mean."

"For Tina, you mean?"

"Well, yes. And you. There's no cultural safety net for this sort of thing, Carrie."

I nodded again but said nothing. But I thought, it was like everything else Cal and Tina and their friends did, part of their crazy-beautiful patchwork of belief. Magic mushrooms, shamans giving medical advice, moonrise and silver temple bells at dawn. Seat-of-the-pants religion: but who was I, a non-believer, to say it was wrong? I went into another room and put on the radio. Yet another DJ on the little local station was doing a tribute show for Cal, a scratchy vinyl recording of an old old song, a woman's husky vibrato and in the background noisy echoing feedback—

> But Magic is no instrument
> Magic is the end.

• ◆ •

THE FOLLOWING TUESDAY I picked up Tina, and we went to have an early lunch in town. We both ordered the same thing, Japanese somen noodles with fresh ginger and garlic. We spoke about how she and Cal had first met, about all the e-mails she'd received from friends all over the world, all the letters. Afterwards we drove around for a little while, to give Tina a chance to talk more, I thought. But then I glanced at the clock on the dashboard of the old Saab and remembered that nothing would be in retrograde until close to one o'clock. At twelve forty-five we were driving back down the dirt road to Tina's house, dodging frost heaves and patches of black ice, listening to Cab Calloway on the radio.

"Well," she said when we finally pulled into the driveway. "Here we are."

Inside, I boiled water for tea, while Tina prepared a space in the living room. First she laid a white sheet on the floor atop the old kilim rug. Then she set down four candles in star-shaped glass holders, one at each corner of the sheet. In the middle she set the cardboard carton and a pair of scissors. At the edge of the sheet were dozens of containers—cookie tins, beautiful blown-glass decanters, tiny glass and metal vials, antique silver urns from Nepal, carved wooden boxes, terracotta pots with lids. There were also several boxes of Ziploc bags in varying sizes.

"I'm going to bury some of his ashes in the backyard," said Tina. "Along with whatever else we find."

PAVANE FOR A PRINCE OF THE AIR

The rest she was going to take with her on a months-long pilgrimage, first across the United States, then to Europe, India, and Nepal: all the places Cal had ever lived, all the places they had ever visited together, all the places they had planned to go. She would scatter his ashes everywhere, and bury some of whatever else we found in Dimebox, Chaco Canyon, on the road outside Katmandu.

"Well," Tina said at last. She seemed edgy, anxious to start but also uneasy: the first time in all the weeks of Cal's dying that I had seen her actually fearful about something. Outside the sun was shining; a sudden thaw had melted most of the snow over the last few days, and on the maple trees tiny red buds were swelling. "I guess we should begin. Do you need to go to the bathroom or anything?"

I said no. We walked into the living room, set down our tea mugs. Tina went back and got the cardboard box from the coffee table and carried it to the white sheet laid out on the floor. She put the box in its center, then performed the ritual of charging the circle, lighting each of the four candles in turn and making a little recitation as she rang the silvery Tibetan temple bells.

"Spirits of the West, of Fire and—no, wait. I think East is Fire—"

She began again, while I knelt and listened. I knew that once the circle was charged we were not supposed to leave it; only children and cats could pass through a charged circle without disrupting the force, or something. When Tina was finished she knelt opposite me, her glasses glinting in the candlelight.

"Well," she said.

She took the scissors and slit open the heavy tape on the cardboard carton. Inside was a bag of heavy clear plastic, its sides opaque with grey dust. There was a twist tie at the top; Tina undid this and set it aside, then unfolded the plastic and smoothed it down over the sides of the box.

"*Oh, wow*," she breathed. "*Oh, wow*."

I gazed down and felt every hair on my body lift. I have never experienced anything like it. Tina's hands hovered above the bag's opening, then dipped down and into what the carton held. "Oh, oh, Little Wolf, my Little Wolf…"

"Jesus," I whispered; then slipped my hand inside.

It was not ashes, of course. Even ashes are not technically ashes, but a gritty substance more like kitty litter or medium-fine gravel.

What the box contained was not that at all, but bones. Most of them burned or broken up, but nearly all immediately recognizable. A forensic anthropologist would have been able to piece some of them together to form part of an arm, or hand; ribcage and spine and shoulder blade. Everything was covered with a fine layer of ash, pale-grey, almost white. I picked up a slender bone the length of my hand, hollow, like a bone flute, set it to one side and filled my palm with soft dust and shattered tibia, a lovely wing-shaped fragment of vertebra.

"Look," murmured Tina. Her eyes were huge, transfixed; she held up the tiny intact figure of a dragon, its ruby eyes winking as she rubbed the ash from them.

"That's amazing," I said, shaking my head. "Look—"

I let the fine ash trickle through my fingers, then plucked a curved smooth shard of green glass from my palm. "The Coke bottle!"

Tina nodded. She rubbed at her glasses, leaving a smear of ash; then said, "I'm going to get some bandannas, so we don't breathe this in—"

She stood, moving her hands back and forth above a candle as she recited the words that would let her leave the circle. She returned a few minutes later, closed the circle again and handed me a bright-red kerchief. I cleaned my glasses with it, then tied it over my mouth and bent back over the box. Very carefully, I began taking handfuls of what was inside and laying it on the sheet in front of me. Without discussing it, we began sorting everything in small heaps splayed in a long sweep across the white sheet. Larger bones here; glass there, melted blobs from the Coke bottle; here unidentifiable bits of charred and twisted metal.

What was extraordinary was not just how many things could be identified, but how many had not been destroyed by the incandescent heat of the furnace. We found Cal's gold-rimmed spectacles, the frames bent but the glass intact. We found dozens of tiny animal figurines of bronze and silvery metal, and the twin circlets of steel which were part of his leather bag. There were shards of semi-precious stone, and the wire that had formed the rigging of the Viking ship. There were the runestones, some of them split in two; only those that Cal had painted himself, with tiny V-shaped symbols and letters, still retained their color and whatever arcane meaning he had charged them with. As the hours passed the piles in front of us grew larger, and Tina began to make another series of orderly heaps, objects that she would keep, ultimately placing them on the little corner shrine where incense and candles burned round the clock.

"What do you think these are?" I asked, holding up a small, smooth cylinder. It was grey-white, the same color as the ashes. I had quite a little pile of them.

"Bones?"

"No. I think they're his pastels."

"That's it!" Tina picked one up and turned it to the light. "The color got all burned away..."

We found the metal ferrules from his paintbrushes, scores of beads and other remnants of jewelry. Tina was dismayed and surprised that none of his heavy bracelets or torques had survived, save for a tiny bit of silvery filigree, melted and charred like burned lace. Amazingly, we did find several small pieces of cloth that had somehow come through unscathed, dark wool soft and worn as felt, a shred of leather. And there was his wolf coffee mug, in three pieces, and a triangular piece of scorched paper, the corner of a page from one of the paperbacks.

He set out on his, it read.

Hours passed. I felt as though I had slipped through a crack in time, my back bent as I sifted and sorted and held fragments of bone before the candle-flame, enacting some nameless ritual that women had performed for a thousand thousand years, before ritual had a name; before women did. The world smelled of ash—it would take more than a faded red bandanna to keep that from me—of scorched metal and bone. My fingers felt as though they were gloved in something at once soft and slightly abrasive, the inside of an animal skin perhaps, or feathers. The sun had gone down, the room around us was growing almost too dark for us to see what we were doing; but we were almost done. In front of me was the pile of bones. Tina had a long line of smaller heaps beside her, jewelry and runestones and metal and tiny figurines. The only bones she had put aside were those of Cal's skull, which were larger than most of the others. There was a surprising number of these; I think you could probably have pieced his entire skull back together, like one of those ancient figures in a barrow, their skeletons dusted with ochre and pollen.

But at last, nothing remained in the box but very fine white ash. Tina looked around, dazed, at everything that surrounded us, bones and charred metal, a soft sifting of grey veiling her face.

"Carrie. You must want something. What would you like to have?"

I sat back on my heels, gazing at her and then at the orderly piles that surrounded us. "You choose for me," I said. "I will take this—"

I picked up the slender hollow bone I had first seen, cupped it in my hand. "And some of his pastels."

"Okay." Tina frowned studiously, then reached over and plucked the two metal rings that had come from Cal's leather bag. "And here—"

She placed them in my hand. They felt warm, as though they still held some of the retort's heat and flame. I put them, along with the bone and the pastels, into the leather bag Cal had made for me years before. "Thank you, Tina," I said, and leaned across the grey-streaked sheet to embrace her.

"I guess I better start putting this into the containers." She smiled weakly as she withdrew from me. She pushed at the kerchief covering her shaven skull, and I saw where dark ashy fingerprints covered her forehead. "God, I had no idea there would be so much. I hope I have enough to hold everything..."

As it turned out, she didn't. After she had filled as many containers as she could, sorting them out as to what would go to Texas, what would remain here in the woods behind the house, what would go to England, to India, to Nepal; after all that, enough remained that I filled several large Ziploc bags with the smallest fragments of bone, and several more with ashes.

"Well," Tina said at last. She looked exhausted, more in the grips of some intense hallucinogen than grief; and I imagined I must look exactly the same. "I guess we'd better stop."

I stood, my back aching, as she walked around the perimeter of the white sheet, reciting the words that would open the circle to us once more. Against one wall was the cardboard box, filled now with sealed Ziploc bags, and the dozens of containers that held Cal's remains. When Tina was finished, I picked up the white sheet and folded it, then walked out onto the back porch. The wind tugged at the sheet as I opened it and shook it out, and at that moment I felt how strange all this was, how I might have been shaking out a white tablecloth but instead was consigning the last of my friend to the cold night air.

Later, after I had kissed Tina goodbye and made plans to see her before she left on her pilgrimage, I went home. The taste of ash was in my mouth, not a bitter or horrible taste at all but warm, pleasantly acrid. When I got home I checked on the children and Robert, the three of them already asleep, then went into the bathroom and lit a series of votive candles in red glasses. I undressed, my clothes powdery with white dust, and took a bath and drank half a bottle of red wine as I soaked in the tub. When I slept that night I had no dreams that I could recall, no mystic voices or faces greeting me. But neither did I wake and lie for hours in the dark, haunted by the thought of empty blue air, of silence and the sound of the wind.

• ◆ •

IT IS NEARLY two months now since Cal died. Just this morning I got another postcard from Tina, from Venice this time—a place Cal had never visited, but where the two of them had planned to go on their twenty-fifth wedding anniversary. She loved the city so much she was staying longer than she had planned, after having dropped some of his ashes into the Grand Canal; but she would be leaving within the week, with Tangiers her next stop. She couldn't wait to see me again, to tell me about all of her adventures: she had seen some amazing things, really unbelievable stuff, and of course she was always looking for Cal, always keeping her eyes and mind opened, so that she would recognize him when they met again.

Here in Maine spring has come earlier than usual, the snow melt deepening the lakes and rivers, the daffodils already starting to bloom even though it's only the second week of April, far too early for northern New England, the earliest spring I can remember. Outside the earth smells sweet, almost perfumed, bacteria thriving in the warm moist soil and the lake releasing its muddy hyacinth scent.

Last week, a bird appeared at the window where I work. I was hunched over my computer, writing, my back to the glass, when I heard a soft insistent tapping. When I turned I saw a tiny brown bird on the sill outside. As I stared it began to peck at the glass, gently but without stopping, like a thrush cracking a snail on a stone.

"Hello," I said. I sat and watched it for several minutes, expecting it to fly away, but it did not. I finally turned back to my computer, but the bird remained where it was, still tapping at the window.

"What're you doing?" I asked it. "Hmm? You want to see me?"

Moving slowly, I opened the window, letting in the cool April air, the faintest whiff of narcissus. To my surprise the bird did not fly away, but instead hopped onto the inside sill. It cocked its head and stared at me; I stared back, then laughed.

"Hey, what're you doing?" I held my hand out. The bird looked at my finger but would not step onto it. Neither did it fly away. Instead, it turned and began hopping along the sill, stopping to examine the things I have there: an old magic-lantern slide of Red Riding Hood and the Big Bad Wolf, a photograph of Robert and the children; Cal's bone, his pastels, the two steel rings from his leather bag, the small reddish curl of braid that Tina had given me the day I drove her to the airport. The bird looked at all of these, then turned and flew back outside.

PAVANE FOR A PRINCE OF THE AIR

It comes every day now and stays, watching me. I looked it up in my nature guides, going from one to another until I found the right description: the European wren, *troglodytes troglodytes,* a diminutive brown bird with white bars on its wings and breast, native to western Europe and the British Isles, but not North America. I called my friend Lucy, who writes the wildlife column for our local paper, and asked if she had ever heard of anyone seeing a European wren in Maine before. She had not, and when she posed the question to her readers, none of them had, either.

Still, the bird is here. I researched it online, and in some books of folklore I have, and learned that the European wren is the bird that was the subject of the annual wren hunt, an ancient pre-Christian ritual of death and resurrection, still practiced in obscure parts of Ireland and the Isle of Man. It is a creature known for its cheer and its valor, its bravery suiting a bird of far greater size; and also for its song, which is piercingly sweet and flutelike, carrying for miles on a clear day.

I can attest to this, writing as I do while the bird sits on the sill behind me and watches me work, as it plucks the last strands of Cal's hair from the braid and flies off to build its nest, somewhere in the rowan tree outside. There it sings, its voice rising and drowning out the songs of redwing blackbirds and chickadees, northern loons and kingfishers and the tapping of my fingers on the keyboard. It sings, day after day after day, and sometimes into the night as well. I never cease to marvel at the sound.

The Bacchae

SHE GOT into the elevator with him, the young woman from down the hall, the one he'd last seen at the annual Coop Meeting a week before. Around her shoulders hung something soft that brushed his cheek as Gordon moved aside to let her in: a fur cape, or pelt, or no, something else. The flayed skin of an animal, an animal that when she shouldered past him to the corner of the elevator proved to be her Rottweiler, Leopold. He could smell it now: the honeyed stench of uncured flesh, a pink and scarlet veil still clinging to the pelt's ragged fringe of coarse black hair. It had left a crimson streak down the back of her skirt, and stippled her legs with pink rosettes.

Gordon got off at the next floor and ran all the way down the hall. When he got into his own apartment he locked and chained the door behind him. For several minutes he stood there panting, squinting out the peephole until he saw her turn the corner and head for her door. It still clung to her shoulders, stiff front legs jouncing against the breast of her boiled-wool suit jacket. After the door closed behind her Gordon walked into the kitchen, poured himself a shot of Jameson's, and stood there until the trembling stopped.

Later, after he had changed and poured himself several more glasses of whisky, he saw on the news that the notorious Debbie DeLucia had been found not guilty of the murder of the young man she claimed had assaulted her in a parking garage one evening that summer. The young man had been beaten severely about face and chest with one of Ms. DeLucia's high-heeled shoes. When he was found by the parking lot attendant most of his hair was missing. Gordon switched off the television when it displayed photographs of these unpleasantries followed by shots of a throng of cheering women outside the courthouse. That evening he had difficulty falling asleep.

• ◆ •

HE WOKE IN the middle of the night. Moonlight flooded the room, so brilliant it showed the tiny pointed feathers poking through his down comforter. Rubbing his eyes Gordon sat up, tugged the comforter around his shoulders against the room's chill. He peered out at a full moon, not silver nor even the sallow gold he had seen on summer nights but a color he had never glimpsed in the sky before, a fiery bronze tinged with red.

"Jeez," Gordon said to himself, awed. He wondered if this had something to do with the solar shields tearing, the immense satellite-borne sails of mylar and solex that had been set adrift in the atmosphere to protect the cities and farmlands from ultraviolet radiation. But you weren't supposed to be able to see the shields. Certainly Gordon had never noticed any difference in the sky, although his friend Olivia claimed she could tell they were there. Women were more sensitive to these things than men, she had told him with an accusing look. There was a luminous quality to city light that had formerly been sooty and gray at best, and the air now had a russet tinge. Wonderful for outdoor setups—Olivia was a noted food photographer—or would be save for the odd bleeding of colors that appeared during developing, winesap apples touched with violet, a glass of Semillon shot with sparks of emerald, the parchment crust of an aged Camembert taking on an unappetizing salmon glow.

It would be the same change in the light that made the moon bleed, Gordon decided. And now he had noticed it, even though he wasn't supposed to be sensitive to these things. What did that mean, he wondered? Maybe it was better not to notice, or to pretend he had seen nothing,

THE BACCHAE

no sanguine moon, no spectral colors in a photograph of a basket of eggs. Strange and sometimes awful things happened to men these days. Gordon had heard of some of these on television, but other tales came from friends, male friends. Near escapes recounted in low voices at the gym or club, random acts of violence spurred by innocent offers of help in carrying groceries, the act of holding a door open suddenly seen as threatening. Women friends, even relatives, sisters and daughters refusing to accompany family on trips to the city. An exodus of wives and children to the suburbs, from the suburbs to the shrinking belts of countryside ringing the megalopolis. And then, husbands and fathers disappearing during weekend visits with the family in exile. Impassive accounts by the next of kin of mislaid directions, trees where there had never been trees before. Evidence of wild animals, wildcats or coyotes perhaps, where nothing larger than a squirrel had been sighted in fifty years.

Gordon laughed at these tales at first. Until now. He pulled a feather from the bed-ticking and stroked his chin thoughtfully before tossing it away. It floated down, a breath of tawny mist. Gordon determinedly pulled the covers over his head and went back to sleep.

He was reading the paper in the kitchen next morning, a detailed account of Ms. DeLucia's trial and a new atrocity. Three women returning late from a nightclub had been harassed by a group of teenage boys, some of them very young. It was one of the young ones the women had killed, turning on the boys with a ferocity the newspaper described as "demonic." Gordon turned to the section that promised full photographic coverage and shuddered. Hastily he put aside the paper and crossed the room to get a second cup of coffee. How could a woman, even three women, be strong enough to do that? He recalled his neighbor down the hall. Christ. He'd take the fire stairs from now on, rather than risk seeing her again. He let his breath out in a low whistle and stirred another spoonful of white powder into his cup.

As he turned to go back to the table he noticed the MESSAGE light blinking on his answering machine. Odd. He hadn't heard the phone ring during the night. He sipped his coffee and played back the tape.

At first he thought there was nothing there. Dead silence, a wrong number. Then he heard faint sounds, a shrill creaking that he recognized as crickets, a katydid's resolute twang, and then the piercing, distant wail of a whippoorwill. It went on for several minutes, all the way to the end of the message tape. Nothing but night sounds, insects and a whippoorwill, once a sharp yapping that, faint as it was, Gordon knew was not a dog but a fox. Then abrupt silence as the tape ended. Gordon started, spilling coffee on his cuff, and swearing rewound the tape while he went to change shirts.

Afterward he played it back. He could hear wind in the trees, leaves pattering as though struck by a soft rain. Had Olivia spent the night in the country? No: they had plans for tonight, and there was no country within a day's drive in any direction from here. She wouldn't have left town on a major shoot without letting him know. He puzzled over it for a long while, playing back the gentle pavane of wind and tiny chiming voices, trying to discern something else there, breathing or muted laughter or a screen door banging shut, anything that might hint at a caller. But there was nothing, nothing but crickets and whippoorwills and a solitary vixen barking at the moon. Finally he left for work.

◆ ◆ ◆

IT WAS THE sort of radiant autumn day when even financial analysts wax rapturous over the color of the sky—in this case a startling electric blue, so deep and glowing Gordon fancied it might leave his fingers damp if he reached to touch it, like wet canvas. He skipped his lunchtime heave at the gym. Instead he walked down to Lafayette Park, filling his pockets with the polished fruit of horse-chestnuts and wondering why it was the leaves no longer turned colors in the fall, only darkened to sear crisps and then clogged the sewers when they fell, a dirty brown porridge.

In the park he sat on a bench. There he ate a stale ersatz croissant and shied chestnuts at the fearless squirrels. A young woman with two small children stood in the middle of a circle of dun-colored grass, sowing crusts of bread among a throng of bobbing pigeons. One of the children pensively

THE BACCHAE

chewed a white crescent. She squealed when a dappled white bird flew up at her face, dropped the bread as her mother laughed and took the children's hands, leading them back to the bench across from Gordon's. He smiled, conspiratorially tossed the remains of his lunch onto the grass, and watched it disappear beneath a mass of iridescent feathers.

A shadow sped across the ground. For an instant it blotted out the sun and Gordon looked up, startled. He had an impression of something immense, immense and dark and moving very quickly through the bright clear air. He recalled his night-time thoughts, had a delirious flash of insight: it was one of the shields torn loose, a ragged gonfalon of Science's floundering army. The little girl shrieked, not in fear but pure excitement. Gordon stood, ready to run for help; saw the woman, the children's mother, standing opposite him pointing at the grass and shouting something. Beside her the two children watched motionless, the little girl clutching a heel of bread.

In the midst of the feeding pigeons a great bird had landed, mahogany wings beating the air as its brazen feathers flashed and it stabbed, snakelike, at the smaller fowl. Its head was perfectly white, the beak curved and as long as Gordon's hand. Again and again that beak gleamed as it struck ferociously, sending up a cloud of feathers gray and pink and brown as the other birds scattered, wings beating feebly as they tried to escape. As Gordon watched blood pied the snowy feathers of the eagle's neck and breast until it was dappled white and red, then a deeper russet. Finally it glowed deep crimson. Still it would not stop its killing. And it seemed the pigeons could not flee, only fill the air with more urgent twittering and, gradually, silence. No matter how their wings flailed it was as though they were stuck in birdlime, or one of those fine nets used to protect winter shrubs.

Suddenly the eagle halted, raised its wings protectively over the limp and thrashing forms about its feet. Gordon felt his throat constrict. He had jammed his hands in his pockets and now closed them about the chestnuts there, as though to use them as weapons. Across the grass the woman stood very still. The wind lifted her hair across her face like a banner. She did not brush it away, only stared through it to where the eagle waited, not eating, not moving, its baleful golden eye gazing down at the fluttering ruin of feather and bone.

As her mother stared the little girl broke away, ran to the edge of the ruddy circle where the eagle stood. It had lifted one clawed foot, thick with feathers, and shook it. The girl stopped and gazed at the sanguine bird. Carelessly she tossed away her heel of bread, wiped her hand and bent to pluck a bloodied feather from the ground. She stared at it, marveling, then pensively touched it to her face and hand. It left a rosy smear across one cheek and wrist and she laughed in delight. She glanced around, first at her mother and brother, then at Gordon.

The eyes she turned to him were ice-blue, wondering but fear-less; and absolutely, ruthlessly indifferent.

• ◆ •

HE TOLD OLIVIA about it that evening.

"I don't see what's so weird," she said, annoyed. It was intermission of the play they had come to see: Euripides' "The Bacchae" in a new translation. Gordon was unpleasantly conscious of how few men there were at the performance, the audience mostly composed of women in couples or small groups, even a few mothers with children, boys and girls who surely were much too young for this sort of thing. He and Olivia stood outside on the theater balcony over-looking the river. "Eagles kill things, that's what they're made for."

"But here? In the middle of the city? I mean, where did it come from? I thought they were extinct."

All about them people strolled beneath the sulfurous crime-lights, smoking cigarettes, pulling coats tight against the wind, exclaiming at the full moon. Olivia leaned against the railing and stared up at the sky, smiling slightly. She wore ostrich cowboy boots with steel toes and tapped them rhythmically against the cement balcony. "I think you just don't like it when things don't go as you expect them to. Even if it's the way things really are supposed to be. Like an eagle killing pigeons."

THE BACCHAE

He snorted but said nothing. Beside him Olivia tossed her hair back. Thick and lustrous dark-brown hair, like a caracal's pelt, hair that for years had been unfashionably long. Though lately it seemed that more women wore it the way she did, loose and long and artlessly tangled. As she pulled a lock away from her throat he saw something there, a mark upon her shoulder like a bruise or scrape.

"What's that?" he wondered, moving the collar of her jacket so he could see better.

She smiled, arching her neck. "Do you like it?"

He touched her shoulder, wincing. "Jesus, what the hell did you do? Doesn't it hurt?"

"A little." She shrugged, turned so that the jaundiced spotlight struck her shoulder and he could see better. A pattern of small incisions had been sliced into her skin, forming the shape of a crescent, or perhaps a grin. Blood still oozed from a few of the cuts. In the others ink or colored powder had been rubbed so that the little moon, if that's what it was, took on the livid shading of a bruise or orchid: violet, verdigris, citron yellow. From each crescent tip hung a gold ring smaller than a teardrop.

"But why?" He suddenly wanted to tear off her jacket and blouse, search the rest of her to see what other scarifications might be hiding here. "Why?"

Olivia smiled, stared out at the river moving in slow streaks of black and orange beneath the sullen moon. "A melted tiger," she said softly.

"What?" The electronic ping of bells signaled the end of intermission. Gordon grasped her elbow, overwhelmed by an abrupt and unfathomable fear. He recalled the moon last night, not crescent but swollen and blood-tinged as the scar on her shoulder. "What did you say?"

A woman passing them turned to stare in disapproval at his shrill voice. Olivia slipped from him as though he were a stranger crowding a subway door. "Come on," she said gently, brushing her hair from her face. She flashed him a smile as she adjusted her blouse to hide the scar. "We'll miss the second act." He followed her without another word.

• ◆ •

AFTER THE SHOW they walked down by the river. Gordon couldn't shake a burgeoning uneasiness, a feeling he might have called terror were it not that the word seemed one he couldn't apply to his own life, this measured round of clocks and stocks and evenings on the town. But he didn't want to say anything to Olivia, didn't want to upset her; more than anything he didn't want to upset her.

She was flushed with excitement, smoking cigarette after cigarette and tossing each little brand into the moonlit water snaking sluggishly beside them.

"Wonderful, just wonderful! The *Post* really did it justice, for a change." She stooped to pluck something from the mucky shadows and grimaced in distaste. "Christ. Their fucking beer cans—"

She glared at Gordon as though he had tossed it there. Smiling wanly he took it from her hand and carried it in apology. "I don't know," he began, and stopped. They had almost reached the Memorial Bridge. A path curved up through the tangled grasses toward the roadway, a path choked with dying goldenrod and stunted asters and Queen Anne's Lace that he suspected should not be such a luminous white, almost greenish in the moonlight. Shreds of something silver clung to the stunted limbs of low-growing shrubs. The way they fluttered in the cold wind made him think again of the atmospheric shields giving way, leaving the embarrened earth beneath them vulnerable and soft as the inner skin of some smooth green fruit. He squinted, trying to see exactly what it was that trembled from the branches. His companion sighed loudly and pointedly where she waited on the path ahead of him. Gordon turned from the shrubs and walked more quickly to join her.

"We should probably get up on the street," he said a little defensively.

Olivia made a small sound showing annoyance. "I'm tired of goddam streets. It's so peaceful here..."

He nodded and walked on beside her. A little ways ahead of them the bridge reared overhead, the ancient iron fretwork shedding green

THE BACCHAE

and russet flakes like old bark. Its crumbling concrete piers were lost in the blackness beneath the great struts and supports. The river disappeared and then materialized on the other side, black and gold and crimson, the moon's reflection a shimmering arrow across its surface. Gordon shivered a little. It reminded him of the stage set they had just left, all stark blacks and browns and greens. Following a new fashion for realism in the theater there had been a great deal of stage blood that had fairly swallowed the monolithic pillars and bound the proscenium with bright ribbons.

"I thought it was sort of gruesome," he said at last. He walked slowly now, reluctant to reach the bridge. In his hand the beer can felt gritty and cold, and he thought of tossing it away. "I mean the way the king's own mother killed him. Ugh." The scene had been very explicit. Even though warned by the *Post* critic Gordon had been taken aback. He had to close his eyes once. And then he couldn't block out their voices, the sound of knife ripping flesh (and how had they done that so convincingly?), the women chanting *Evohe! Evohe!*, which afterwards Olivia explained as roughly meaning "O ecstasy" or words to that effect. When he asked her how she knew that she gave him a cross look and lit another cigarette.

No wonder the play was so seldom revived. "Don't you think we should go back? I mean, it's not very safe here at night."

"Huh." Olivia had stopped a few feet back. He turned and saw that she didn't seem to have heard him. She squatted at the river's edge, staring intently at something in the water.

"What is it?" He stood behind her, trying to see. The water smelled rank, not the brackish reek of rotting weeds and rich mud but a chemical smell that made his nostrils burn. The ruddy light glinted off Olivia's hair, touched her steel boot-tips with bronze. In the water in front of her a fish swam lethargically on its side, sides striped with scales of brown and yellow. Its mouth gaped open and closed and its gills showed an alarming color, bright pink like the inside of a wound.

"Ah," Olivia was murmuring. She put her hand into the water and lifted the fish upon it. It curled delicately within her palm, its fins stretching open like a butterfly warming to the sun as the water dripped heavily from her fingers. It took him a moment to realize it had no eyes.

"Poor thing," he said; then added, "I don't think you should touch it, Olivia. I mean, there's something wrong with it—"

"Of course there's something wrong with it," Olivia spat, so vehemently that he stepped backward. The mud smelled of ammonia where his heels slipped through it. "It's dying, poisoned, everything's been poisoned—"

"Well, then for Christ's sake drop it, Olivia, what's the sense in *playing* with it—"

Hissing angrily she slid her hand back through the water. The fish vanished beneath the surface and floated up again a foot away, fins fluttering pathetically. Olivia wiped her hand on her trousers, heedless of the dark stain left upon the silk.

"I wasn't playing with it," she announced coldly, shaking her head so that her jacket slipped to one side and he glimpsed the gold rings glinting from her shoulder. "You don't care, do you, you don't even notice anymore what's happened. There'd be nothing left at all if it was up to people like you—"

He swore in aggravation as she stormed off in the direction of the bridge, then hurried after her. Muck covered his shoes and he stumbled upon another cache of beer cans. When he looked up again he saw Olivia standing at the edge of the bridge's shadow, hands clenched at her sides as she confronted two tall figures.

"Oh, fuck," Gordon breathed. He felt sick with apprehension but hurried on, finally to stand beside her. "Hey!" he said loudly, pulling at Olivia's arm.

She stood motionless. One of the men held something small and dark at his side, a gun, the other wore a tan trenchcoat and looked calmly back and forth, as though preparing to cross a busy street. Before Gordon could take another breath the second man was shoving at his chest. Gordon shouted and struck at him, his hand flailing harmlessly against the man's coat. His other hand tightened around the beer can

THE BACCHAE

and he felt a sudden warm rush of pain as the metal sliced through his palm. He glanced down at his hand, saw blood streaming down his wrist and staining the white cuff of his shirt. He stared in disbelief, heard a thudding sound and then a moan. Then running, stones rattling down the grassy slope.

The man in the trenchcoat was gone. The other, the man with the gun, lay on the ground at the river's edge. Olivia was kicking him in the head, over and over, her boots scraping through the mud and gravel when they missed him and sending up a spume of gritty water. The gun was nowhere to be seen. Olivia paused for an instant. Gordon could hear her breathing heavily, saw her wipe her hands upon her trousers as she had when she freed the dying perch. "Olivia," he whispered. She grunted to herself, not hearing him, not looking; and suddenly he was terrified that she *would* look and see him there watching her. He stepped backwards, and as he did so she glanced up. For an instant she was silhouetted against the glimmering water, her white face spattered with mud, hair a coppery nimbus about her shoulders. Behind her the moon shone brilliantly, and on the opposite shore he could see the glittering lights of the distant airfield. It did not seem that she saw him at all. After a moment she looked down and began to kick again, more powerfully, and this time she would bring her heel back down across the man's back until Gordon could hear a crackling sound. He looked on, paralyzed, his good hand squeezing tighter and tighter about the wrist of his bleeding hand as she went on and on and on. One of her steel boot-tips tore through his shoulder and the man screamed. Gordon could see one side of his face caved in like a broken gourd, dark and shining as though water pooled in its ragged hollows. Olivia bent and lifted something dark and heavy from the shallow water. Gordon made a whining noise in his throat and ran away, up the hill to where the crimelights cast wavering shadows through the weeds. Behind him he heard a dull crash and then silence.

• ♦ •

A CROWD HAD gathered in front of his apartment building when he finally got there. He shoved a bill at the cab driver and stumbled from the car. "Oh, no," he said out loud as the cab drove off, certain the crowd had something to do with Olivia and the man by the river: policemen, reporters, ambulances.

But it didn't have anything to do with that after all. There was music, cheerful music pouring from a player set inside one of the ground floor windows. Suddenly Gordon remembered talk of this at the Coop meeting last week: a party, an opportunity for the tenants to get to know one another. It had been his neighbor's idea, the one with the dog. Someone had strung Christmas lights from another window, and several people had set up barbecues on the gray front lawn. Flames leaped from the grills, making the shadows dance so it was impossible to determine how many people were actually milling about. Quite a few, Gordon thought. He smelled roasting meat, bitter woodsmoke with the unpleasant reek of paint in it—were they burning *furniture?*—and a strange sweetish scent, herbs or perhaps marijuana. The pain in his hand had dulled to a steady throbbing. When he looked down he closed his eyes for a few seconds and grit his teeth. There was so much blood.

"Hi!" a voice cried. He opened his eyes to see the woman from down the hall. She was no longer wearing her Rottweiler, nor the expensively tailored suits she usually favored. Instead she wore faded jeans and the kind of extravagantly beaded and embroidered tunic Gordon associated with his parents' youth. These and the many jingling chains and jewels that hung from her ears and about her wrists and ankles (she was barefoot, in spite of the cool evening) gave her a gypsy air. In the firelight he could see that her face sans makeup was childishly freckled. She looked very young and very happy.

"Mm, hi," Gordon mumbled, moving his bloodsoaked arm from her sight. "A block party." He tried to keep his tone polite but uninterested as he pushed through the crowd of laughing people, but the young woman followed him, grinning.

THE BACCHAE

"Isn't it great? You should come down, bring something to throw on the grill or something to drink, we're running out of hooch—"

She laughed, raising a heavy crystal wineglass and gulping from it something that was a deep purplish color and slightly viscous, certainly not wine. When she lowered the goblet he saw there was a small crack along its rim. This had cut the girl's upper lip which spun a slender filament of blood down across her chin. She didn't notice and threw her arm around his shoulders. "Promise you'll come back, mmmm? We need more guys so we can *dance* and stuff, there's just never enough guys anymore—"

She whirled away drunkenly, swinging her arms out like a giddy spinning child. Whether purposely or not the goblet flew from her hand and shattered on the broken concrete sidewalk. A cheer went up from the crowd. Someone turned the music up louder. A number of people by the glowing braziers seemed to be dancing as the girl was, drunkenly, merrily, arms outstretched and hair flying. Gordon heard the tinkling report of another glass breaking, then another; then the sharper crash of what might have been a window. He put his face down and fairly ran through the swarm to the front door, which had been propped open with an old stump overgrown with curling ivy. The neatly lettered sign warning against strangers and open doors had been yanked from the doorframe and lay in a twisted mass on the steps inside. Gordon kicked it aside and fled down the hall to the firestairs.

There were people in the stairwell, sitting or lying on the steps in drunken twos and threes. One couple had shed their clothes and stood grunting and heaving in the darkened corner near the fire extinguisher. Gordon averted his eyes, stepping carefully among the others. A small pile of twigs had been ignited on the floor and sweet-smelling smoke trailed upward through the dimness. And other things were scattered upon the steps: branches of fir-trees scenting the air with balsam, sheaves of goldenrod, empty wine bottles. One of these clattered underfoot, nearly tripping him. Gordon looked over his shoulder to see it roll downstairs, bumping the head of a woman passed out near the bottom and then spinning across the floor, finally coming to rest beside the couple in the corner. No one noticed it; no one noticed Gordon as he flung open the door to the fifth floor and ran to his apartment.

He walked numbly through the kitchen. The answering machine blinked. Mechanically he reset it as he passed, paused between the kitchen and living room as the tape began. A sound of wind filled the room, wind and the rustle of many feet in dead leaves. Gordon swallowed, pressed his shaking hands together as the tape played on behind him. The wind grew louder, then softer, swelled and whispered. And all the while he heard beneath the faint staticky recording the ceaseless passage of many feet, and sometimes voices, murmurous and laughing, eerie and wild as the wind itself. The tape ended. The apartment was silent save for the dull insistent clicking of the answering machine begging to be switched off, that and the muffled sound of laughter from outside.

Gordon stepped warily into the next room. He had forgotten to leave a light on. But it was not dark: moonlight flooded the space, glimmering across the dark wooden floor, making the shadowed bulk of armchairs and sofa and electronic equipment seem black and strange and ominous. On the sill of the picture window that covered an entire wall the moonlight gleamed upon one of his treasures, a fish of handblown Venetian glass, hundreds of years old. Its mauve and violet swirls glowed in the milky light, its gaping mouth and crystalline eyes reminding him of the perch he had seen earlier, eyeless, dying. He stepped across the living room and stood there at the window staring down at the glass fish. And suddenly his head hurt, his chest felt heavy and cold. Looking at the glass fish he was filled with a dull puzzling ache, as though he were trying to remember a dream. He pondered how he had come to have such a thing, why it was that this marvel of spun glass and pastel coloring had ever meant more to him than a blind perch struggling through the poisonous river. His hand traced the delicate filigree of its spines. They felt cold, burning cold in the cloudy light spilling through the window.

◆ ◆ ◆

THE BACCHAE

THERE WAS A knock at the door. Gordon started, as though he had been asleep, then crossed the darkened room. Through the peephole he saw Olivia, her hair atangle, a streak of black across one cheek. Her expression was oddly calm and untroubled in the carmine glare of the EXIT light. He tightened his hand about the doorknob, biting his lip against the pain that shot up through his arm as he did so. He wondered dully how she had gotten into the building, then remembered the chaos outside. Anyone could come in; even a woman who had seemingly just kicked a man to death by the polluted river. Perhaps it was like this all across the city, perhaps doors that had been locked since the riots had this evening suddenly sprung open.

"Gordon," Olivia commanded, her voice muffled by the heavy door that separated them. He was not surprised to feel the knob twist beneath his throbbing palm, or see the door swing inward to bump against his toe. Olivia slipped in, and with her a breath of incense-smelling smoke, the muted clamor of voices and laughter and pulsing music.

"Where'd you go?" she asked, smiling. He noticed that behind her the door had not quite closed. He reached to push it shut but before he could grasp it she took him by the hand, the one that hurt. Grunting softly with pain he turned from the door to follow her into the living room.

"What's happening?" he whispered. "Olivia, what is it?" Without speaking she pulled him to the floor beside her, still smiling. She pulled his jacket from him, then his shoes and trousers and finally his blood-stained shirt. He reached to remove her blouse but Olivia pushed him away ungently, so that he cried out. As she moved above him his hand began to bleed again, leaving dark petals across her blouse and arms. The pain was so intense that he moaned, tried in vain to slow her but she only tightened her grip about his upper arm, tossing her hair back so that it formed a dark haze against the window's milky light. The blouse slipped from her shoulder and he could see the scars there, the little golden rings against her skin, drops of blood like rain flashing across her throat. Behind her the moon shone, bloated and sanguine. He could hear voices chanting counterpoint to the blood thudding in his temples. It took him a long time to catch his breath afterward. Olivia had bitten him on the shoulder, hard enough to bruise him. The pain coupled with that from his cut hand had suddenly made everything very intense, made him cry out loudly and then fall back hard against the cold floor as Olivia slipped from him. Now only the pain was left. He rubbed his shoulder ruefully. "Olivia? Are you angry?" he asked. She stood impassively in front of the window. The torn blouse had slipped from her shoulder. She had kicked her silk trousers beneath the sofa but pulled her boots back on, and moonlight glinted off the two wicked metal points. She seemed not to have heard him, so he repeated her name softly.

"Mmmm?" she said, distracted. She stared up at the sky, then leaned forward and opened the casement. Cold air flooded the room, and a brighter, colder light as well, as though the glass had ceased to filter out the lunar brilliance. Gordon shivered and groped for his shirt.

"Look at them," whispered Olivia. He got unsteadily to his feet and stood beside her, staring down at the sidewalk. Small figures capered across the broken tarmac, forms made threatening by the lurid glow of myriad bonfires that had sprung up across the dead gray lawn. He heard music, too, not music from the radio or stereo but a crude raw sound, thrumming and beating as of metal drums, voices howling and forming words he could not quite make out, an unknown name or phrase—

"*Evohe*," whispered Olivia. The face she turned to him was white and merciless, her eyes inflamed. "*Evohe*."

"What?" said Gordon. He stepped backwards and stumbled on one of his shoes. When he righted himself and looked up he saw that there were other people in the room, other women, three four six of them, even more it seemed, slipping silently through the door that Olivia had left open behind her. They filled the small apartment with a cloying smell of smoke and burning hair, some of them carrying smoking sticks, others leather pocketbooks or scorched briefcases. He recognized many of them: though their hair was matted and wild, their clothes torn: dresses or suits ripped so that their breasts were exposed and he could

THE BACCHAE

see where the flesh had been raked by their own fingernails, leaving long wavering scars like signatures scratched in blood. Two of them were quite young and naked and caressed each other laughing, turning to watch him with sly feral eyes. Several of the older women had golden rings piercing their breasts or the frail web of flesh between their fingers. One traced a cut that ran down her thigh, then lifted her bloodied finger to her lips as though imploring Gordon to keep a secret. He saw another gray-haired woman whom he had greeted often at the newsstand where they both purchased the *Wall Street Journal*. She seemingly wore only a furtrimmed camel's-hair coat. Beneath its soft folds Gordon glimpsed an undulating pattern of green and gray and gold. As she approached him she let the coat fall away and he saw a snake encircling her throat, writhing free to slide down between her breasts and then to the floor at Gordon's feet. He shouted and turned to flee.

Olivia was there, Olivia caught him and held him so tightly that for a moment he imagined she was embracing him, imagined the word she repeated was his name, spoken more and more loudly as she held him until he felt the breath being crushed from within his chest. But it was not his name, it was another name, a word like a sigh, like the whisper of a thought coming louder and louder as the others took it up and they were chanting now:

"*Evohe, evohe...*"

As he struggled with Olivia they fell upon him, the woman from the newsstand, the girl from down the hall now naked and laughing in a sort of grunting chuckle, the two young girls encircling him with their slender cool arms and giggling as they kissed his cheeks and nipped his ears. Fighting wildly he thrashed until his head was free and he could see beyond them, see the open window behind the writhing web of hair and arms and breasts, the moon blazing now like a mad watchful eye above the burning canyons. He could see shreds of darkness falling from the sky, clouds or rain or wings, and he heard faintly beneath the shrieks and moans and panting voices the wail of sirens all across the city. Then he fell back once more beneath them.

There was a tinkling crash. He had a fleeting glimpse of some-thing mauve and lavender skidding across the floor, then cried out as he rolled to one side and felt the glass shatter beneath him, the slivers of breath-spun fins and gills and tail slicing through his side. He saw Olivia, her face serene, her liquid eyes full of ardor as she turned to the girl beside her and took from her something that gleamed like silver in the moonlight, like pure and icy water, like a spear of broken glass. Gordon started to scream when she knelt between his thighs. Before he fainted he saw against the sky the bloodied fingers of eagle's wings, blotting out the face of a vast triumphant moon.

Cleopatra Brimstone

H ER EARLIEST memory was of wings. Luminous red and blue, yellow and green and orange; a black so rich it appeared liquid, edible. They moved above her and the sunlight made them glow as though they were themselves made of light, fragments of another, brighter world falling to earth about her crib. Her tiny hands stretched upwards to grasp them but could not: they were too elusive, too radiant, too much of the air.

Could they ever have been real?

For years she thought she must have dreamed them. But one afternoon when she was ten she went into the attic, searching for old clothes to wear to a Halloween party. In a corner beneath a cobwebbed window she found a box of her baby things. Yellow-stained bibs and tiny fuzzy jumpers blued from bleaching, a much-nibbled stuffed dog that she had no memory of whatsoever.

And at the very bottom of the carton, something else. Wings flattened and twisted out of shape, wires bent and strings frayed: a mobile. Six plastic butterflies, colors faded and their wings giving off a musty smell, no longer eidolons of Eden but crude representations of monarch, zebra swallowtail, red admiral, sulphur, an unnaturally elongated hairskipper and *Agrias narcissus*. Except for the *narcissus*, all were common New World species that any child might see in a suburban garden. They hung limply from their wires, antennae long since broken off; when she touched one wing it felt cold and stiff as metal.

The afternoon had been overcast, tending to rain. But as she held the mobile to the window, a shaft of sun broke through the darkness to ignite the plastic wings, blood-red, ivy-green, the pure burning yellow of an August field. In that instant it was as though her entire being was burned away, skin hair lips fingers all ash; and nothing remained but the butterflies and her awareness of them, orange and black fluid filling her mouth, the edges of her eyes scored by wings.

• ◆ •

AS A GIRL she had always worn glasses. A mild childhood astigmatism worsened when she was thirteen: she started bumping into things, and found it increasingly difficult to concentrate on the entomological textbooks and journals that she read voraciously. Growing pains, her mother thought; but after two months, Jane's clumsiness and concomitant headaches became so severe that her mother admitted that this was perhaps something more serious, and took her to the family physician.

"Jane's fine," Dr. Gordon announced after peering into her ears and eyes. "She needs to see the ophthalmologist, that's all. Sometimes our eyes change when we hit puberty." He gave her mother the name of an eye doctor nearby.

Her mother was relieved, and so was Jane—she had overhead her parents talking the night before her appointment, and the words *CAT scan* and *brain tumor* figured in their hushed conversation. Actually, Jane had been more concerned about another odd physical manifestation, one which no one but herself seemed to have noticed. She had started menstruating several months earlier: nothing unusual in that. Everything she had read about it mentioned the usual things—mood swings, growth spurts, acne, pubic hair.

But nothing was said about eyebrows. Jane first noticed something strange about hers when she got her period for the second time. She had

CLEOPATRA BRIMSTONE

retreated to the bathtub, where she spent a good half-hour reading an article in *Nature* about Oriental Ladybug swarms. When she finished the article, she got out of the tub, dressed and brushed her teeth, then spent a minute frowning at the mirror.

Something was different about her face. She turned sideways, squinting. Had her chin broken out? No; but something had changed. Her hair color? Her teeth? She leaned over the sink until she was almost nose-to-nose with her reflection.

That was when she saw that her eyebrows had undergone a growth spurt of their own. At the inner edge of each eyebrow, above the bridge of her nose, three hairs had grown remarkably long. They furled back towards her temple, entwined in a sort of loose braid. She had not noticed them sooner because she seldom looked in a mirror, and also because the odd hairs did not arch above the eyebrows, but instead blended in with them, the way a bittersweet vine twines around a branch. Still, they seemed bizarre enough that she wanted no one, not even her parents, to notice. She found her mother's eyebrow tweezers, neatly plucked the six hairs and flushed them down the toilet. They did not grow back.

At the optometrist's, Jane opted for heavy tortoiseshell frames rather than contacts. The optometrist, and her mother, thought she was crazy, but it was a very deliberate choice. Jane was not one of those homely B movie adolescent girls, driven to Science as a last resort. She had always been a tomboy, skinny as a rail, with long slanted violet-blue eyes; a small rosy mouth; long, straight black hair that ran like oil between her fingers; skin so pale it had the periwinkle shimmer of skim milk.

When she hit puberty, all of these conspired to beauty. And Jane hated it. Hated the attention, hated being looked at, hated that other girls hated her. She was quiet, not shy but impatient to focus on her schoolwork, and this was mistaken for arrogance by her peers. All through high school she had few friends. She learned early the perils of befriending boys, even earnest boys who professed an interest in genetic mutations and intricate computer simulations of hive activity. Jane could trust them not to touch her, but she couldn't trust them not to fall in love. As a result of having none of the usual distractions of high school—sex, social life, mindless employment—she received an Intel/Westinghouse Science Scholarship for a computer-generated schematic of possible mutations in a small population of viceroy butterflies exposed to genetically engineered crops. She graduated in her junior year, took her scholarship money, and ran.

She had been accepted at Stanford and MIT, but chose to attend a small, highly prestigious women's college in a big city several hundred miles away. Her parents were apprehensive about her being on her own at the tender age of seventeen, but the college, with its elegant, cloister-like buildings and lushly wooded grounds, put them at ease. That and the dean's assurances that the neighborhood was completely safe, as long as students were sensible about not walking alone at night. Thus mollified, and at Jane's urging—she was desperate to move away from home—her father signed a very large check for the first semester's tuition. That September she started school.

She studied entomology, spending her first year examining the genitalia of male and female Scarce Wormwood Shark Moths, a species found on the Siberian steppes. Her hours in the zoology lab were rapturous, hunched over a microscope with a pair of tweezers so minute they were themselves like some delicate portion of her specimen's physiognomy. She would remove the butterflies' genitalia, tiny and geometrically precise as diatoms, and dip them first into glycerine, which acted as a preservative, and next into a mixture of water and alcohol. Then she observed them under the microscope. Her glasses interfered with this work—they bumped into the microscope's viewing lens—and so she switched to wearing contact lenses. In retrospect, she thought that this was probably a mistake.

At Argus College she still had no close friends, but neither was she the solitary creature she had been at home. She respected her fellow students, and grew to appreciate the company of women. She could go for days at a time seeing no men besides her professors or the commuters driving past the school's wrought-iron gates.

CLEOPATRA BRIMSTONE

And she was not the school's only beauty. Argus College specialized in young women like Jane: elegant, diffident girls who studied the burial customs of Mongol women or the mating habits of rare antipodean birds; girls who composed concertos for violin and gamelan orchestra, or wrote computer programs that charted the progress of potentially dangerous celestial objects through the Oort Cloud. Within this educational greenhouse, Jane was not so much orchid as sturdy milkweed blossom. She thrived.

Her first three years at Argus passed in a bright-winged blur with her butterflies. Summers were given to museum internships, where she spent months cleaning and mounting specimens in solitary delight. In her senior year Jane received permission to design her own thesis project, involving her beloved Shark Moths. She was given a corner in a dusty anteroom off the Zoology Lab, and there she set up her microscope and laptop. There was no window in her corner, indeed there was no window in the anteroom at all, though the adjoining lab was pleasantly old-fashioned, with high arched windows set between Victorian cabinetry displaying lepidoptera, neon-carapaced beetles, unusual tree fungi and (she found these slightly tragic) numerous exotic finches, their brilliant plumage dimmed to dusty hues. Since she often worked late into the night, she requested and received her own set of keys. Most evenings she could be found beneath the glare of the small halogen lamp, entering data into her computer, scanning images of genetic mutations involving female Shark Moths exposed to dioxin, corresponding with other researchers in Melbourne and Kyoto, Siberia and London.

The rape occurred around ten o'clock one Friday night in early March. She had locked the door to her office, leaving her laptop behind, and started to walk to the subway station a few blocks away. It was a cold clear night, the yellow glow of the crime lights giving dead grass and leafless trees an eerie autumn shimmer. She hurried across the campus, seeing no one, then hesitated at Seventh Street. It was a longer walk, but safer, if she went down Seventh Street and then over to Michigan Avenue. The shortcut was much quicker, but Argus authorities and the local police discouraged students from taking it after dark. Jane stood for a moment, looking across the road to where the desolate park lay; then, staring resolutely straight ahead and walking briskly, she crossed Seventh and took the shortcut.

A crumbling sidewalk passed through a weedy expanse of vacant lot, strewn with broken bottles and the spindly forms of half a dozen dusty-limbed oak trees. Where the grass ended, a narrow road skirted a block of abandoned row houses, intermittently lit by crime lights. Most of the lights had been vandalized, and one had been knocked down in a car accident—the car's fender was still there, twisted around the lamppost. Jane picked her way carefully among shards of shattered glass, reached the sidewalk in front of the boarded-up houses and began to walk more quickly, towards the brightly lit Michigan Avenue intersection where the subway waited.

She never saw him. He was *there*, she knew that; knew he had a face, and clothing; but afterwards she could recall none of it. Not the feel of him, not his smell; only the knife he held—awkwardly, she realized later, she probably could have wrested it from him—and the few words he spoke to her. He said nothing at first, just grabbed her and pulled her into an alley between the row houses, his fingers covering her mouth, the heel of his hand pressing against her windpipe so that she gagged. He pushed her onto the dead leaves and wads of matted wind-blown newspaper, yanked her pants down, ripped open her jacket and then tore her shirt open. She heard one of the buttons strike brick and roll away. She thought desperately of what she had read once, in a Rape Awareness brochure: not to struggle, not to fight, not to do anything that might cause her attacker to kill her.

Jane did not fight. Instead, she divided into three parts. One part knelt nearby and prayed the way she had done as a child, not intently but automatically, trying to get through the strings of words as quickly as possible. The second part submitted blindly and silently to the man in the alley. And the third hovered above the other two, her hands wafting slowly up and down to keep her aloft as she watched.

CLEOPATRA BRIMSTONE

"Try to get away," the man whispered. She could not see him or feel him though his hands were there. "Try to get away."

She remembered that she ought not to struggle, but from the noise she made and the way he tugged at her, she realized that was what aroused him. She did not want to anger him; she made a small sound deep in her throat and tried to push him from her chest. Almost immediately he groaned, and seconds later rolled off her. Only his hand lingered for a moment upon her cheek. Then he stumbled to his feet—she could hear him fumbling with his zipper—and fled.

The praying girl and the girl in the air also disappeared then. Only Jane was left, yanking her ruined clothes around her as she lurched from the alley and began to run, screaming and staggering back and forth across the road, towards the subway.

• ◆ •

THE POLICE CAME, an ambulance. She was taken first to the police station and then to the City General Hospital, a hellish place, starkly lit, with endless underground corridors that led into darkened rooms where solitary figures lay on narrow beds like gurneys. Her pubic hair was combed and stray hairs placed into sterile envelopes; semen samples were taken, and she was advised to be tested for HIV and other diseases. She spent the entire night in the hospital, waiting and undergoing various examinations. She refused to give the police or hospital staff her parents' phone number, or anyone else's. Just before dawn they finally released her, with an envelope full of brochures from the local rape crisis center, New Hope for Women, Planned Parenthood, and a business card from the police detective who was overseeing her case. The detective drove her to her apartment in his squad car; when he stopped in front of her building, she was suddenly terrified that he would know where she lived, that he would come back, that he had been her assailant.

But, of course, he had not been. He walked her to the door and waited for her to go inside. "Call your parents," he said right before he left.

"I will."

She pulled aside the bamboo window shade, watching until the squad car pulled away. Then she threw out the brochures she'd received, flung off her clothes, and stuffed them into the trash. She showered and changed, packed a bag full of clothes and another of books. Then she called a cab. When it arrived, she directed it to the Argus campus, where she retrieved her laptop and her research on Tiger Moths, then had the cab bring her to Union Station.

She bought a train ticket home. Only after she arrived and told her parents what had happened did she finally start to cry. Even then, she could not remember what the man had looked like.

◆ ◆ ◆

SHE LIVED AT home for three months. Her parents insisted that she get psychiatric counseling and join a therapy group for rape survivors. She did so, reluctantly, but stopped attending after three weeks. The rape was something that had happened to her, but it was over.

"It was fifteen minutes out of my life," she said once at group. "That's all. It's not the rest of my life."

This didn't go over very well. Other women thought she was in denial; the therapist thought Jane would suffer later if she did not confront her fears now.

"But I'm not afraid," said Jane.

"Why not?" demanded a woman whose eyebrows had fallen out.

Because lightning doesn't strike twice, Jane thought grimly, but she said nothing. That was the last time she attended group.

That night her father had a phone call. He took the phone and sat at the dining table, listening; after a moment stood and walked into his study, giving a quick backward glance at his daughter before closing the door behind him. Jane felt as though her chest had suddenly frozen: but after some minutes she heard her father's laugh: he was not, after all, talking to the police detective. When after half an hour he returned, he gave Jane another quick look, more thoughtful this time.

"That was Andrew." Andrew was a doctor friend of his, an Englishman. "He and Fred are going to Provence for three months. They were wondering if you might want to housesit for them."

"In *London?*" Jane's mother shook her head. "I don't think—"

"I said we'd think about it."

"*I'll* think about it," Jane corrected him. She stared at both her parents, absently ran a finger along one eyebrow. "Just let me think about it."

And she went to bed.

◆ ◆ ◆

SHE WENT TO London. She already had a passport, from visiting Andrew with her parents when she was in high school. Before she left, there were countless arguments with her mother and father, and phone calls back and forth to Andrew. He assured them that the flat was secure, there was a very nice reliable older woman who lived upstairs, that it would be a good idea for Jane to get out on her own again.

"So you don't get gun-shy," he said to her one night on the phone. He was a doctor, after all: a homeopath not an allopath, which Jane found reassuring. "It's important for you to get on with your life. You won't be able to get a real job here as a visitor, but I'll see what I can do."

It was on the plane to Heathrow that she made a discovery. She had splashed water onto her face, and was beginning to comb her hair when she blinked and stared into the mirror.

Above her eyebrows, the long hairs had grown back. They followed the contours of her brow, sweeping back towards her temples; still entwined, still difficult to make out unless she drew her face close to her reflection and tilted her head just so. Tentatively she touched one braided strand. It was stiff yet oddly pliant; but as she ran her finger along its length a sudden *surge* flowed through her. Not an electrical shock: more like the thrill of pain when a dentist's drill touches a nerve, or an elbow rams against a stone. She gasped; but immediately the pain was gone. Instead there was a thrumming behind her forehead, a spreading warmth that trickled into her throat like sweet syrup. She opened her mouth, her gasp turning into an uncontrollable yawn, the yawn into a spike of such profound physical ecstasy that she grabbed the edge of the sink and thrust forward, striking her head against the mirror. She was dimly aware of someone knocking at the lavatory door as she clutched the sink and, shuddering, climaxed.

"Hello?" someone called softly. "Hello, is this occupied?"

"Right out," Jane gasped. She caught her breath, still trembling; ran a hand across her face, her fingers halting before they could touch the hairs above her eyebrows. There was the faintest tingling, a temblor of sensation that faded as she grabbed her cosmetic bag, pulled the door open and stumbled back into the cabin.

◆ ◆ ◆

ANDREW AND FRED lived in an old Georgian row house just north of Camden Town, overlooking the Regent's Canal. Their flat occupied the first floor and basement; there was a hexagonal solarium out back, with glass walls and heated stone floor, and beyond that a stepped terrace leading down to the canal. The bedroom had an old wooden four-poster piled high with duvets and down pillows, and French doors that also opened onto the terrace. Andrew showed her how to operate the elaborate sliding security doors that unfolded from the walls, and gave her the keys to the barred window guards.

"You're completely safe here," he said, smiling. "Tomorrow we'll introduce you to Kendra upstairs, and show you how to get around. Camden market's just up that way, and *that* way—"

He stepped out onto the terrace, pointing to where the canal coiled and disappeared beneath an arched stone bridge, "—that way's the Regent's Park Zoo. I've given you a membership—"

"Oh! Thank you!" Jane looked around delighted. "This is *wonderful*."

"It is." Andrew put an arm around her and drew her close. "You're going to have a wonderful time, Jane. I thought you'd like the zoo—there's a new exhibit there, 'The World Within' or words to that effect—it's about insects. I thought perhaps you might want to volunteer there—they have an active docent program, and you're so knowledgeable about that sort of thing."

"Sure. It sounds great—really great." She grinned and smoothed her hair back from her face, the wind sending up the rank scent of stagnant water from the canal, the sweetly poisonous smell of hawthorn blossom. As she stood gazing down past the potted geraniums and Fred's rosemary trees, the hairs upon her brow trembled, and she laughed out loud, giddily, with anticipation.

• ◆ •

FRED AND ANDREW left two days later. It was enough time for Jane to get over her jet lag and begin to get barely acclimated to the city, and to its smell. London had an acrid scent: damp ashes, the softer underlying fetor of rot that oozed from ancient bricks and stone buildings, the thick vegetative smell of the canal, sharpened with urine and spilled beer. So many thousands of people descended on Camden Town on the weekend that the tube station was restricted to incoming passengers, and the canal path became almost impassable. Even late on a weeknight she could hear voices from the other side of the canal, harsh London voices echoing beneath the bridges or shouting to be heard above the din of the Northern Line trains passing overhead.

Those first days Jane did not venture far from the flat. She unpacked her clothes, which did not take much time, and then unpacked her collecting box, which did. The sturdy wooden case had come through the overseas flight and customs seemingly unscathed, but Jane found herself holding her breath as she undid the metal hinges, afraid of what she'd find inside.

"*Oh!*" she exclaimed. Relief, not chagrin: nothing had been damaged. The small glass vials of ethyl alcohol and gel shellac were intact, as were the pillboxes where she kept the tiny #2 pins she used for mounting. Fighting her own eagerness she carefully removed packets of stiff archival paper, a block of styrofoam covered with pinholes; two bottles of clear Maybelline nail polish and a small container of Elmer's Glue; more pillboxes, empty, and empty gelatine capsules for very small specimens; and last of all a small glass-fronted display box, framed in mahogany and holding her most precious specimen: a hybrid *Celerio harmuthi Kordesch*, the male crossbreed of a Spurge and an Elephant Hawkmoth. As long as the first joint of her thumb, it had the hawkmoth's typically streamlined wings but exquisitely delicate coloring, fuchsia bands shading to a soft rich brown, its thorax thick and seemingly feathered. Only a handful of these hybrid moths had ever existed, bred by the Prague entomologist Jan Pokorny in 1961; a few years afterward, both the Spurge Hawkmoth and the Elephant Hawkmoth had become extinct.

Jane had found this one for sale on the Internet three months ago. It was a former museum specimen and cost a fortune; she had a few bad nights, worrying whether it had actually been a legal purchase. Now she held the display box in her cupped palms and gazed at it raptly. Behind her eyes she felt a prickle, like sleep or unshed tears; then a slow thrumming warmth crept from her brows, spreading to her temples, down her neck and through her breasts, spreading like a stain. She swallowed, leaned back against the sofa and let the display box rest back within the larger case; slid first one hand then the other beneath her sweater and began to stroke her nipples. When some time later she came, it was with stabbing force and a thunderous sensation above her eyes, as though she had struck her forehead against the floor.

She had not: gasping, she pushed the hair from her face, zipped her jeans and reflexively leaned forward, to make certain the hawkmoth in its glass box was safe.

• ♦ •

OVER THE FOLLOWING days she made a few brief forays to the newsagent and greengrocer, trying to eke out the supplies Fred and Andrew had left in the kitchen. She sat in the solarium, her bare feet warm against the heated stone floor, and drank chamomile tea or claret, staring down to where the ceaseless stream of people passed along the canal path, and watching the narrow boats as they plied their way slowly between Camden Lock and Little Venice, two miles to the west in Paddington. By the following Wednesday she felt brave enough, and bored enough, to leave her refuge and visit the zoo.

It was a short walk along the canal, dodging bicyclists who jingled their bells impatiently when she forgot to stay on the proper side of the path. She passed beneath several arching bridges, their undersides pleated with slime and moss. Drunks sprawled against the stones and stared at her blearily or challengingly by turns; well-dressed couples walked dogs, and there were excited knots of children, tugging their parents on to the zoo.

Fred had walked here with Jane, to show her the way. But it all looked unfamiliar now. She kept a few strides behind a family, her head down, trying not to look as though she was following them, and felt a pulse of relief when they reached a twisting stair with an arrowed sign at its top.

REGENT'S PARK ZOO

There was an old old church across the street, its yellow stone walls overgrown with ivy; and down and around the corner a long stretch of hedges with high iron walls fronting them, and at last a huge set of gates, crammed with children and vendors selling balloons and banners and London guidebooks. Jane lifted her head and walked quickly past the family that had led her here, showed her membership card at the entrance, and went inside.

She wasted no time on the seals or tigers or monkeys, but went straight to the newly renovated structure where a multicolored banner flapped in the late-morning breeze.

AN ALTERNATE UNIVERSE:
SECRETS OF THE INSECT WORLD

Inside, crowds of schoolchildren and harassed-looking adults formed a ragged queue that trailed through a brightly lit corridor, its walls covered with huge glossy color photos and computer-enhanced images of hissing cockroaches, hellgrammites, morpho butterflies, death-watch beetles, polyphemous moths. Jane dutifully joined the queue, but when the corridor opened into a vast sun-lit atrium she strode off on her own, leaving the children and teachers to gape at monarchs in butterfly cages and an interactive display of honeybees dancing. Instead she found a relatively quiet display at the far end of the exhibition space, a floor-to-ceiling cylinder of transparent net, perhaps six feet in diameter. Inside, buckthorn bushes and blooming hawthorn vied for sunlight with a slender beech sapling, and dozens of butterflies flitted upwards through the new yellow leaves, or sat with wings outstretched upon the beech tree. They were a type of Pieridae, the butterflies known as whites; though these were not white at all. The females had creamy yellow-green wings, very pale, their wingspans perhaps an inch and a half. The males were the same size; when they were at rest their flattened wings were a dull, rather sulphurous color. But when the males lit into the air their wings revealed vivid, spectral yellow undersides. Jane caught her breath in delight, her neck prickling with that same atavistic joy she'd felt as a child in the attic.

"Wow," she breathed, and pressed up against the netting. It felt like wings against her face, soft, webbed; but as she stared at the insects inside her brow began to ache as with migraine. She shoved her glasses onto her nose, closed her eyes and drew a long breath; then took a step away from the cage. After a minute she opened her eyes. The headache had diminished to a dull throb; when she hesitantly touched one eyebrow, she could feel the entwined hairs there, stiff as wire. They were vibrating, but at her touch the vibrations like the headache dulled. She stared at the floor, the tiles sticky with contraband juice and gum; then looked up once again at the cage. There was a display sign off to one side; she walked over to it, slowly, and read.

CLEOPATRA BRIMSTONE
Gonepteryx rhamni cleopatra
This popular and subtly colored species has a range which extends throughout the Northern Hemisphere, with the exception of Arctic regions and several remote islands. In Europe, the

CLEOPATRA BRIMSTONE

brimstone is a harbinger of spring, often emerging from its winter hibernation under dead leaves to revel in the countryside while there is still snow upon the ground.

"I must ask you please not to touch the cages."

Jane turned to see a man, perhaps fifty, standing a few feet away. A net was jammed under his arm; in his hand he held a clear plastic jar with several butterflies at the bottom, apparently dead.

"Oh. Sorry," said Jane. The man edged past her. He set his jar on the floor, opened a small door at the base of the cylindrical cage, and deftly angled the net inside. Butterflies lifted in a yellow-green blur from leaves and branches; the man swept the net carefully across the bottom of the cage, then withdrew it. Three dead butterflies, like scraps of colored paper, drifted from the net into the open jar.

"Housecleaning," he said, and once more thrust his arm into the cage. He was slender and wiry, not much taller than she was, his face hawkish and burnt brown from the sun, his thick straight hair iron-streaked and pulled back into a long braid. He wore black jeans and a dark-blue hooded jersey, with an ID badge clipped to the collar.

"You work here," said Jane. The man glanced at her, his arm still in the cage; she could see him sizing her up. After a moment he glanced away again. A few minutes later he emptied the net for the last time, closed the cage and the jar, and stepped over to a waste bin, pulling bits of dead leaves from the net and dropping them into the container.

"I'm one of the curatorial staff. You American?"

Jane nodded. "Yeah. Actually, I—I wanted to see about volunteering here."

"Lifewatch desk at the main entrance." The man cocked his head towards the door. "They can get you signed up and registered, see what's available."

"No—I mean, I want to volunteer here. With the insects—"

"Butterfly collector, are you?" The man smiled, his tone mocking. He had hazel eyes, deep-set; his thin mouth made the smile seem perhaps more cruel than intended. "We get a lot of those."

Jane flushed. "No. I am not a *collector*," she said coldly, adjusting her glasses. "I'm doing a thesis on dioxin genital mutation in *Cucullia artemisia*." She didn't add that it was an undergraduate thesis. "I've been doing independent research for seven years now." She hesitated, thinking of her Intel scholarship, and added, "I've received several grants for my work."

The man regarded her appraisingly. "Are you studying here, then?"

"Yes," she lied again. "At Oxford. I'm on sabbatical right now. But I live near here, and so I thought I might—"

She shrugged, opening her hands, looked over at him and smiled tentatively. "Make myself useful?"

The man waited a moment, nodded. "Well. Do you have a few minutes now? I've got to do something with these, but if you want you can come with me and wait, and then we can see what we can do. Maybe circumvent some paperwork."

He turned and started across the room. He had a graceful, bouncing gait, like a gymnast or circus acrobat: impatient with the ground beneath him. "Shouldn't take long," he called over his shoulder as Jane hurried to catch up.

She followed him through a door marked AUTHORIZED PERSONS ONLY, into the exhibit laboratory, a reassuringly familiar place with its display cases and smells of shellac and camphor, acetone and ethyl alcohol. There were more cages here, but smaller ones, sheltering live specimens—pupating butterflies and moths, stick insects, leaf insects, dung beetles. The man dropped his net onto a desk, took the jar to a long table against one wall, blindingly lit by long fluorescent tubes. There were scores of bottles here, some empty, others filled with paper and tiny inert figures.

"Have a seat," said the man, gesturing at two folding chairs. He settled into one, grabbed an empty jar and a roll of absorbent paper.

"I'm David Bierce. So where're you staying? Camden Town?"

"Jane Kendall. Yes—"

"The High Street?"

CLEOPATRA BRIMSTONE

Jane sat in the other chair, pulling it a few inches away from him. The questions made her uneasy, but she only nodded, lying again, and said, "Closer, actually. Off Gloucester Road. With friends."

"Mm." Bierce tore off a piece of absorbent paper, leaned across to a stainless steel sink and dampened the paper. Then he dropped it into the empty jar. He paused, turned to her and gestured at the table, smiling. "Care to join in?"

Jane shrugged. "Sure—"

She pulled her chair closer, found another empty jar and did as Bierce had, dampening a piece of paper towel and dropping it inside. Then she took the jar containing the dead brimstones and carefully shook one onto the counter. It was a female, its coloring more muted than the males'; she scooped it up very gently, careful not to disturb the scales like dull green glitter upon its wings, dropped it into the jar and replaced the top.

"Very nice." Bierce nodded, raising his eyebrows. "You seem to know what you're doing. Work with other insects? Soft-bodied ones?"

"Sometimes. Mostly moths, though. And butterflies."

"Right." He inclined his head to a recessed shelf. "How would you label that, then? Go ahead."

On the shelf she found a notepad and a case of Rapidograph pens. She began to write, conscious of Bierce staring at her. "We usually just put all this into the computer, of course, and print it out," he said. "I just want to see the benefits of an American education in the sciences."

Jane fought the urge to look at him. Instead she wrote out the information, making her printing as tiny as possible.

Gonepteryx rhamni cleopatra
UNITED KINGDOM: LONDON
Regent's Park Zoo
Lat/Long unknown
21.IV.2001
D. Bierce
Net/caged specimen

She handed it to Bierce. "I don't know the proper coordinates for London."

Bierce scrutinized the paper. "It's actually the Royal Zoological Park," he said. He looked at her, then smiled. "But you'll do."

"Great!" She grinned, the first time she'd really felt happy since arriving here. "When do you want me to start?"

"How about Monday?"

Jane hesitated: this was only Friday. "I could come in tomorrow—"

"I don't work on the weekend, and you'll need to be trained. Also they have to process the paperwork. Right—"

He stood and went to a desk, pulling open drawers until he found a clipboard holding sheaves of triplicate forms. "Here. Fill all this out, leave it with me and I'll pass it on to Carolyn—she's the head volunteer coordinator. They usually want to interview you, but I'll tell them we've done all that already."

"What time should I come in Monday?"

"Come at nine. Everything opens at ten, that way you'll avoid the crowds. Use the staff entrance, someone there will have an ID waiting for you to pick up when you sign in—"

She nodded and began filling out the forms.

"All right then." David Bierce leaned against the desk and again fixed her with that sly, almost taunting gaze. "Know how to find your way home?"

Jane lifted her chin defiantly. "Yes."

"Enjoying London? Going to go out tonight and do Camden Town with all the yobs?"

"Maybe. I haven't been out much yet."

"Mm. Beautiful American girl, they'll eat you alive. Just kidding." He straightened, started across the room towards the door. "I'll see you Monday then."

He held the door for her. "You really should check out the clubs. You're too young not to see the city by night." He smiled, the fluorescent light slanting sideways into his hazel eyes and making them suddenly glow icy blue. "Bye then."

"Bye," said Jane, and hurried quickly from the lab towards home.

CLEOPATRA BRIMSTONE

◆ ◆ ◆

THAT NIGHT, FOR the first time, she went out. She told herself she would have gone anyway, no matter what Bierce had said. She had no idea where the clubs were; Andrew had pointed out the Electric Ballroom to her, right across from the tube station, but he'd also warned her that was where the tourists flocked on weekends.

"They do a disco thing on Saturday nights—Saturday Night Fever, everyone gets all done up in vintage clothes. Quite a fashion show," he'd said, smiling and shaking his head.

Jane had no interest in that. She ate a quick supper, vindaloo from the take-away down the street from the flat, then dressed. She hadn't brought a huge number of clothes—at home she'd never bothered much with clothes at all, making do with thrift-shop finds and whatever her mother gave her for Christmas. But now she found herself sitting on the edge of the four-poster, staring with pursed lips at the sparse contents of two bureau drawers. Finally she pulled out a pair of black corduroy jeans and a black turtleneck and pulled on her sneakers. She removed her glasses, for the first time in weeks inserted her contact lenses. Then she shrugged into her old, navy peacoat and left.

It was after ten o'clock. On the canal path, throngs of people stood, drinking from pints of canned lager. She made her way through them, ignoring catcalls and whispered invitations, stepping to avoid where kids lay making out against the brick wall that ran alongside the path, or pissing in the bushes. The bridge over the canal at Camden Lock was clogged with several dozen kids in mohawks or varicolored hair, shouting at each other above the din of a boom box and swigging from bottles of Spanish champagne.

A boy with a champagne bottle leered, lunging at her.

"'Ere, sweetheart, 'ep youseff—"

Jane ducked, and he careered against the ledge, his arm striking brick and the bottle shattering in a starburst of black and gold.

"Fucking cunt!" he shrieked after her. "Fucking bloody *cunt!*"

People glanced at her, but Jane kept her head down, making a quick turn into the vast cobbled courtyard of Camden Market. The place had a desolate air: the vendors would not arrive until early next morning, and now only stray cats and bits of windblown trash moved in the shadows. In the surrounding buildings people spilled out onto balconies, drinking and calling back and forth, their voices hollow and their long shadows twisting across the ill-lit central courtyard. Jane hurried to the far end, but there found only brick walls, closed-up shop doors, and a young woman huddled within the folds of a filthy sleeping bag.

"*Couldya—couldya—*" the woman murmured.

Jane turned and followed the wall until she found a door leading into a short passage. She entered it, hoping she was going in the direction of Camden High Street. She felt like Alice trying to find her way through the garden in Wonderland: arched doorways led not into the street but headshops and blindingly lit piercing parlors, open for business; other doors opened onto enclosed courtyards, dark, smelling of piss and marijuana. Finally from the corner of her eye she glimpsed what looked like the end of the passage, headlights piercing through the gloom like landing lights. Doggedly she made her way towards them.

"Ay watchowt watchowt," someone yelled as she emerged from the passage onto the sidewalk, and ran the last few steps to the curb.

She was on the High Street—rather, in that block or two of curving no-man's-land where it turned into Chalk Farm Road. The sidewalks were still crowded, but everyone was heading towards Camden Lock and not away from it. Jane waited for the light to change and raced across the street, to where a cobblestoned alley snaked off between a shop selling leather underwear and another advertising "Fine French Country Furniture."

For several minutes she stood there. She watched the crowds heading toward Camden Town, the steady stream of minicabs and taxis and buses heading up Chalk Farm Road toward Hampstead. Overhead, dull orange clouds moved across a night sky the color of charred wood; there was the steady low thunder of jets circling after takeoff at Heathrow.

At last she tugged her collar up around her neck, letting her hair fall in loose waves down her back, shoved her hands into her coat pockets and turned to walk purposefully down the alley.

Before her the cobblestone path turned sharply to the right. She couldn't see what was beyond, but she could hear voices: a girl laughing, a man's sibilant retort. A moment later the alley spilled out onto a cul-de-sac. A couple stood a few yards away, before a doorway with a small copper awning above it. The young woman glanced sideways at Jane, quickly looked away again. A silhouette filled the doorway; the young man pulled out a wallet. His hand disappeared within the silhouette, re-emerged, and the couple walked inside. Jane waited until the shadowy figure withdrew. She looked over her shoulder, then approached the building.

There was a heavy metal door, black, with graffiti scratched into it and pale blurred spots where painted graffiti had been effaced. The door was set back several feet into a brick recess; there was a grilled metal slot at the top that could be slid back, so that one could peer out into the courtyard. To the right of the door, on the brick wall within the recess, was a small brass plaque with a single word on it.

HIVE

There was no doorbell or any other way to signal that you wanted to enter. Jane stood, wondering what was inside; feeling a small tingling unease that was less fear than the knowledge that even if she were to confront the figure who'd let that other couple inside, she herself would certainly be turned away.

With a *skreek* of metal on stone the door suddenly shot open. Jane looked up, into the sharp, raggedly handsome face of a tall, still youngish man with very short blond hair, a line of gleaming gold beads like drops of sweat piercing the edge of his left jaw.

"Good evening," he said, glancing past her to the alley. He wore a black sleeveless T-shirt with a small golden bee embroidered upon the breast. His bare arms were muscular, striated with long sweeping scars: black, red, white. "Are you waiting for Hannah?"

"No." Quickly Jane pulled out a handful of five-pound notes. "Just me tonight."

"That'll be twenty then." The man held his hand out, still gazing at the alley; when Jane slipped the notes to him he looked down and flashed her a vulpine smile. "Enjoy yourself." She darted past him into the building.

Abruptly it was as though some darker night had fallen. Thunderously so, since the enfolding blackness was slashed with music so loud it was itself like light: Jane hesitated, closing her eyes, and white flashes streaked across her eyelids like sleet, pulsing in time to the music. She opened her eyes, giving them a chance to adjust to the darkness, and tried to get a sense of where she was. A few feet away a blurry greyish lozenge sharpened into the window of a coat-check room. Jane walked past it, towards the source of the music. Immediately the floor slanted steeply beneath her feet. She steadied herself with one hand against the wall, following the incline until it opened onto a cavernous dance floor.

She gazed inside, disappointed. It looked like any other club, crowded, strobe-lit, turquoise smoke and silver glitter coiling between hundreds of whirling bodies clad in candy pink, sky blue, neon red, rainslicker yellow. Baby colors, Jane thought. There was a boy who was almost naked, except for shorts, a transparent water bottle strapped to his chest and long tubes snaking into his mouth. Another boy had hair the color of lime Jell-O, his face corrugated with glitter and sweat; he swayed near the edge of the dance floor, turned to stare at Jane and then beamed, beckoning her to join him.

Jane gave him a quick smile, shaking her head; when the boy opened his arms to her in mock pleading she shouted "No!"

But she continued to smile, though she felt as though her head would crack like an egg from the throbbing music. Shoving her hands into her pockets she skirted the dance floor, pushed her way to the

CLEOPATRA BRIMSTONE

bar and bought a drink, something pink with no ice in a plastic cup. It smelled like Gatorade and lighter fluid. She gulped it down, then carried the cup held before her like a torch as she continued on her circuit of the room. There was nothing else of interest; just long queues for the lavatories and another bar, numerous doors and stairwells where kids clustered, drinking and smoking. Now and then beeps and whistles like birdsong or insect cries came through the stuttering electronic din, whoops and trilling laughter from the dancers. But mostly they moved in near-silence, eyes rolled ceiling-ward, bodies exploding into Catherine wheels of flesh and plastic and nylon, but all without a word.

It gave Jane a headache—a *real* headache, the back of her skull bruised, tender to the touch. She dropped her plastic cup and started looking for a way out. She could see past the dance floor to where she had entered, but it seemed as though another hundred people had arrived in the few minutes since then: kids were standing six-deep at both bars, and the action on the floor had spread, amoeba-like, towards the corridors angling back up towards the street.

"Sorry—"

A fat woman in an Arsenal jersey jostled her as she hurried by, leaving a smear of oily sweat on Jane's wrist. Jane grimaced and wiped her hand on the bottom of her coat. She gave one last look at the dance floor, but nothing had changed within the intricate lattice of dancers and smoke, braids of glow-lights and spotlit faces surging up and down, up and down, while more dancers fought their way to the center.

"Shit." She turned and strode off, heading to where the huge room curved off into relative emptiness. Here, scores of tables were scattered, some overturned, others stacked against the wall. A few people sat, talking; a girl lay curled on the floor, her head pillowed on a Barbie knapsack. Jane crossed to the wall, and found first a door that led to a bare brick wall, then a second door that held a broom closet. The next was dark red, metal, official-looking: the kind of door that Jane associated with school fire drills.

A fire door. It would lead outside, or into a hall that would lead there. Without hesitating she pushed it open and entered. A short corridor lit by EXIT signs stretched ahead of her, with another door at the end. She hurried towards it, already reaching reflexively for the keys to the flat, pushed the door-bar and stepped inside.

For an instant she thought she had somehow stumbled into a hospital emergency room. There was the glitter of halogen light on steel, distorted reflections thrown back at her from curved glass surfaces; the abrasive odor of isopropyl alcohol and the fainter tinny scent of blood, like metal in the mouth.

And bodies: everywhere, bodies, splayed on gurneys or suspended from gleaming metal hooks, laced with black electrical cord and pinned upright onto smooth rubber mats. She stared open-mouthed, neither appalled nor frightened but fascinated by the conundrum before her: how did *that* hand fit *there*, and whose leg was *that*? She inched backward, pressing herself against the door and trying to stay in the shadows—just inches ahead of her ribbons of luminous bluish light streamed from lamps hung high overhead. The chiaroscuro of pallid bodies and black furniture, shiny with sweat and here and there red-streaked, or brown; the mere sight of so many bodies, real bodies—flesh spilling over the edge of tabletops, too much hair or none at all, eyes squeezed shut in ecstasy or terror and mouths open to reveal stained teeth, pale gums—the sheer *fluidity* of it all enthralled her. She felt as she had, once, pulling aside a rotted log to disclose the ant's nest beneath, masses of minute fleeing bodies, soldiers carrying eggs and larvae in their jaws, tunnels spiraling into the center of another world. Her brow tingled, warmth flushed her from brow to breast…

Another world, that's what she had found then; and discovered again now.

"*Out.*"

Jane sucked her breath in sharply. Fingers dug into her shoulder, yanked her back through the metal door so roughly that she cut her wrist against it.

CLEOPATRA BRIMSTONE

"No lurkers, what the fuck—"

A man flung her against the wall. She gasped, turned to run but he grabbed her shoulder again. "Christ, a fucking girl."

He sounded angry but relieved. She looked up: a huge man, more fat than muscle. He wore very tight leather briefs and the same black sleeveless shirt with a golden bee embroidered upon it. "How the hell'd you get in like *that*?" he demanded, cocking a thumb at her.

She shook her head, then realized he meant her clothes. "I was just trying to find my way out."

"Well you found your way in. In like fucking Flynn." He laughed: he had gold-capped teeth, and gold wires threading the tip of his tongue. "You want to join the party, you know the rules. No exceptions."

Before she could reply he turned and was gone, the door thudding softly behind him. She waited, heart pounding, then reached and pushed the bar on the door.

Locked. She was out, not in; she was nowhere at all. For a long time she stood there, trying to hear anything from the other side of the door, waiting to see if anyone would come back looking for her. At last she turned, and began to find her way home.

◆ ◆ ◆

NEXT MORNING SHE woke early, to the sound of delivery trucks in the street and children on the canal path, laughing and squabbling on their way to the zoo. She sat up with a pang, remembering David Bierce and her volunteer job; then recalled this was Saturday not Monday.

"Wow," she said aloud. The extra days seemed like a gift.

For a few minutes she lay in Fred and Andrew's great four-poster, staring abstractedly at where she had rested her mounted specimens atop the wainscoting—the hybrid hawkmoth; a beautiful Honduran owl butterfly, *Caligo atreus*; a mourning cloak she had caught and mounted herself years ago. She thought of the club last night, mentally retracing her steps to the hidden back room; thought of the man who had thrown her out, the interplay of light and shadow upon the bodies pinned to mats and tables. She had slept in her clothes; now she rolled out of bed and pulled her sneakers on, forgoing breakfast but stuffing her pocket with ten- and twenty-pound notes before she left.

It was a clear cool morning, with a high pale-blue sky and the young leaves of nettles and hawthorn still glistening with dew. Someone had thrown a shopping cart from the nearby Sainsbury's into the canal; it edged sideways up out of the shallow water, like a frozen shipwreck. A boy stood a few yards down from it, fishing, an absent, placid expression on his face.

She crossed over the bridge to the canal path and headed for the High Street. With every step she took the day grew older, noisier, trains rattling on the bridge behind her and voices harsh as gulls rising from the other side of the brick wall that separated the canal path from the street.

At Camden Lock she had to fight her way through the market. There were tens of thousands of tourists, swarming from the maze of shops to pick their way between scores of vendors selling old and new clothes, bootleg CDs, cheap silver jewelry, kilims, feather boas, handcuffs, cellphones, mass-produced furniture and puppets from Indonesia, Morocco, Guyana, Wales. The fug of burning incense and cheap candles choked her; she hurried to where a young woman was turning samosas in a vat of sputtering oil, and dug into her pocket for a handful of change, standing so that the smells of hot grease and scorched chickpea batter cancelled out patchouli and Caribbean Nights.

"Two, please," Jane shouted.

She ate and almost immediately felt better, then walked a few steps to where a spike-haired girl sat behind a table covered with cheap clothes made of ripstock fabric in Jell-O shades.

"Everything five pounds," the girl announced. She stood, smiling helpfully as Jane began to sort through pairs of hugely baggy pants. They were cross-seamed with velcro and deep zippered pockets. Jane held up a pair, frowning as the legs billowed, lavender and green, in the wind.

"It's so you can make them into shorts," the girl explained. She stepped around the table and took the pants from Jane, deftly tugging at the legs so that they detached. "See? Or a skirt." The girl replaced the pants, picked up another pair, screaming orange with black trim, and a matching windbreaker. "This color would look nice on you."

"Okay." Jane paid for them, waited for the girl to put the clothes in a plastic bag. "Thanks."

"Bye now."

She went out into High Street. Shopkeepers stood guard over the tables spilling out from their storefronts, heaped with leather clothes and souvenir T-shirts: MIND THE GAP, LONDON UNDERGROUND, shirts emblazoned with the Cat in the Hat toking on a cheroot. THE CAT IN THE HAT SMOKES BLACK. Every three or four feet someone had set up a boom box, deafening sound-bites of salsa, techno, "The Hustle," Bob Marley, "Anarchy in the UK," Radiohead. On the corner of Inverness and High Street a few punks squatted in a doorway, looking over the postcards they'd bought. A sign in the smoked-glass window said ALL HAIRCUTS TEN POUNDS, MEN WOMEN CHILDREN.

"Sorry," one of the punks said, as Jane stepped over them and into the shop.

The barber was sitting in an old-fashioned chair, his back to her, reading the *Sun*. At the sound of her footsteps he turned, smiling automatically. "Can I help you?"

"Yes please. I'd like my hair cut. All of it."

He nodded, gesturing to the chair. "Please."

Jane had thought she might have to convince him that she was serious. She had beautiful hair, well below her shoulders—the kind of hair people would kill for, she'd been hearing that her whole life. But the barber just hummed and chopped it off, the *snick snick* of his shears interspersed with kindly questions about whether she was enjoying her visit and his account of a vacation to Disney World ten years earlier.

"Dear, do we want it shaved or buzz-cut?"

In the mirror a huge-eyed creature gazed at Jane, like a tarsier or one of the owlish caligo moths. She stared at it, entranced, then nodded.

"Shaved. Please."

When he was finished she got out of the chair, dazed, and ran her hand across her scalp. It was smooth and cool as an apple. There were a few tiny nicks that stung beneath her fingers. She paid the barber, tipping him two pounds. He smiled and held the door open for her.

"Now when you want a touchup, you come see us, dear. Only five pounds for a touchup."

She went next to find new shoes. There were more shoe shops in Camden Town than she had ever seen anywhere in her life; she checked out four of them on one block before deciding on a discounted pair of twenty-hole black Doc Martens. They were no longer fashionable, but they had blunted steel caps on the toes. She bought them, giving the salesgirl her old sneakers to toss into the waste bin. When she went back onto the street it was like walking in wet cement—the shoes were so heavy, the leather so stiff that she ducked back into the shoe shop and bought a pair of heavy wool socks and put them on. She returned outside, hesitating on the front step before crossing the street and heading in the direction of Chalk Farm Road. There was a shop here that Fred had shown her before he left.

"Now, that's where you get your fetish gear, Jane," he said, pointing to a shop window painted matte black. THE PLACE, it said in red letters, with two linked circles beneath. Fred had grinned and rapped his knuckles against the glass as they walked by. "I've never been in, you'll have to tell me what it's like." They'd both laughed at the thought.

Now Jane walked slowly, the wind chill against her bare skull. When she could make out the shop, sun glinting off the crimson letters and a sad-eyed dog tied to a post out front, she began to hurry, her new boots making a hollow thump as she pushed through the door.

There was a security gate inside, a thin, sallow young man with dreadlocks nodding at her silently as she approached.

CLEOPATRA BRIMSTONE

"You'll have to check that." He pointed at the bag with her new clothes in it. She handed it to him, reading the warning posted behind the counter.

SHOPLIFTERS WILL BE BEATEN,
FLAYED, SPANKED, BIRCHED, BLED
AND THEN PROSECUTED
TO THE FULL EXTENT OF THE LAW

The shop was well lit. It smelled strongly of new leather and coconut oil and pine-scented disinfectant. She seemed to be the only customer this early in the day, although she counted seven employees, manning cash registers, unpacking cartons, watching to make sure she didn't try to nick anything. A CD of dance music played, and the phone rang constantly.

She spent a good half hour just walking through the place, impressed by the range of merchandise. Electrified wands to deliver shocks, things like meat cleavers made of stainless steel with rubber tips. Velcro dog collars, Velcro hoods, black rubber balls and balls in neon shades, a mat embedded with three-inch spikes that could be conveniently rolled up and came with its own lightweight carrying case. As she wandered about, more customers arrived, some of them greeting the clerks by name, others furtive, making a quick circuit of the shelves before darting outside again. At last Jane knew what she wanted. A set of wristcuffs and one of anklecuffs, both of very heavy black leather with stainless steel hardware; four adjustable nylon leashes, also black, with clips on either end that could be fastened to cuffs or looped around a post; a few spare S-clips.

"That it?"

Jane nodded, and the register clerk began scanning her purchases. She felt almost guilty, buying so few things, not taking advantage of the vast Meccano glory of all those shelves full of gleaming, somber contrivances.

"There you go." He handed her the receipt, then inclined his head at her. "Nice touch, that—"

He pointed at her eyebrows. Jane drew her hand up, felt the long pliant hairs uncoiling like baby ferns. "Thanks," she murmured. She retrieved her bag and went home to wait for evening.

◆ ◆ ◆

IT WAS NEARLY midnight when she left the flat. She had slept for most of the afternoon, a deep but restless sleep, with anxious dreams of flight, falling, her hands encased in metal gloves, a shadowy figure crouching above her. She woke in the dark, heart pounding, terrified for a moment that she had slept all the way through till Sunday night.

But of course she had not. She showered, then dressed in a tight, low-cut black shirt and pulled on her new nylon pants and heavy boots. She seldom wore makeup, but tonight after putting in her contacts she carefully outlined her eyes with black, then chose a very pale lavender lipstick. She surveyed herself in the mirror critically. With her white skin, huge violet eyes and hairless skull, she resembled one of the Balinese puppets for sale in the market—beautiful but vacant, faintly ominous. She grabbed her keys and money, pulled on her windbreaker, and headed out.

When she reached the alley that led to the club, she entered it, walked about halfway, and stopped. After glancing back and forth to make sure no one was coming, she detached the legs from her nylon pants, stuffing them into a pocket, then adjusted the Velcro tabs so that the pants became a very short orange and black skirt. Her long legs were sheathed in black tights. She bent to tighten the laces on her metal-toed boots and hurried to the club entrance.

Tonight there was a line of people waiting to get in. Jane took her place, fastidiously avoiding looking at any of the others. They waited for thirty minutes, Jane shivering in her thin nylon windbreaker, before the door opened and the same gaunt blond man appeared to take their money. Jane felt her heart beat faster when it was her turn, wondering if he would recognize her. But he only scanned the courtyard, and, when the last of them darted inside, closed the door with a booming *clang*.

CLEOPATRA BRIMSTONE

Inside all was as it had been, only far more crowded. Jane bought a drink, orange squash, no alcohol. It was horribly sweet, with a bitter, curdled aftertaste. Still, it had cost two pounds: she drank it all. She had just started on her way down to the dance floor when someone came up from behind to tap her shoulder, shouting into her ear.

"Wanna?"

It was a tall, broad-shouldered boy a few years older than she was, perhaps twenty-four, with a lean ruddy face, loose shoulder-length blond hair streaked green, and deep-set, very dark blue eyes. He swayed dreamily, gazing at the dance floor and hardly looking at her at all.

"Sure," Jane shouted back. He looped an arm around her shoulder, pulling her with him; his striped V-necked shirt smelled of talc and sweat. They danced for a long time, Jane moving with calculated abandon, the boy heaving and leaping as though a dog was biting at his shins.

"You're beautiful," he shouted. There was an almost imperceptible instant of silence as the DJ changed tracks. "What's your name?"

"Cleopatra Brimstone."

The shattering music grew deafening once more. The boy grinned. "Well, Cleopatra. Want something to drink?"

Jane nodded in time with the beat, so fast her head spun. He took her hand and she raced to keep up with him, threading their way toward the bar.

"Actually," she yelled, pausing so that he stopped short and bumped up against her. "I think I'd rather go outside. Want to come?"

He stared at her, half-smiling, and shrugged. "Aw right. Let me get a drink first—"

They went outside. In the alley the wind sent eddies of dead leaves and newspaper flying up into their faces. Jane laughed, and pressed herself against the boy's side. He grinned down at her, finished his drink, and tossed the can aside, then put his arm around her. "Do you want to go get a drink, then?" he asked.

They stumbled out onto the sidewalk, turned and began walking. People filled the High Street, lines snaking out from the entrances of pubs and restaurants. A blue glow surrounded the streetlights, and clouds of small white moths beat themselves against the globes; vapor and banners of grey smoke hung above the punks blocking the sidewalk by Camden Lock. Jane and the boy dipped down into the street. He pointed to a pub occupying the corner a few blocks up, a large old green-painted building with baskets of flowers hanging beneath its windows and a large sign swinging back and forth in the wind: THE END OF THE WORLD. "In there, then?"

Jane shook her head. "I live right here, by the canal. We could go to my place if you want. We could have a few drinks there."

The boy glanced down at her. "Aw right," he said—very quickly, so she wouldn't change her mind. "That'd be aw right."

It was quieter on the back street leading to the flat. An old drunk huddled in a doorway, cadging change; Jane looked away from him and got out her keys while the boy stood restlessly, giving the drunk a belligerent look.

"Here we are," she announced, pushing the door open. "Home again, home again."

"Nice place." The boy followed her, gazing around admiringly. "You live here alone?"

"Yup." After she spoke Jane had a flash of unease, admitting that. But the boy only ambled into the kitchen, running a hand along the antique French farmhouse cupboard and nodding.

"You're American, right? Studying here?"

"Uh huh. What would you like to drink? Brandy?"

He made a face, then laughed. "Aw right! You got expensive taste. Goes with the name, I'd guess." Jane looked puzzled, and he went on, "Cleopatra—fancy name for a girl."

"Fancier for a boy," Jane retorted, and he laughed again.

She got the brandy, stood in the living room unlacing her boots. "Why don't we go in there?" she said, gesturing towards the bedroom. "It's kind of cold out here."

The boy ran a hand across his head, his blond hair streaming through his fingers. "Yeah, aw right." He looked around. "Um, that the toilet there?" Jane nodded. "Right back, then…"

CLEOPATRA BRIMSTONE

She went into the bedroom, set the brandy and two glasses on a night table and took off her windbreaker. On another table, several tall candles, creamy white and thick as her wrist, were set into ornate brass holders. She lit these—the room filled with the sweet scent of beeswax—and sat on the floor, leaning against the bed. A few minutes later the toilet flushed and the boy reappeared. His hands and face were damp, redder than they had been. He smiled and sank onto the floor beside her. Jane handed him a glass of brandy.

"Cheers," he said, and drank it all in one gulp.

"Cheers," said Jane. She took a sip from hers, then refilled his glass. He drank again, more slowly this time. The candles threw a soft yellow haze over the four-poster bed with its green velvet duvet, the mounds of pillows, forest-green, crimson, saffron yellow. They sat without speaking for several minutes. Then the boy set his glass on the floor. He turned to face Jane, extending one arm around her shoulder and drawing his face near hers.

"Well then," he said.

His mouth tasted acrid, nicotine and cheap gin beneath the blunter taste of brandy. His hand sliding under her shirt was cold; Jane felt goose pimples rising across her breast, her nipple shrinking beneath his touch. He pressed against her, his cock already hard, and reached down to unzip his jeans.

"Wait," Jane murmured. "Let's get on the bed..."

She slid from his grasp and onto the bed, crawling to the heaps of pillows and feeling beneath one until she found what she had placed there earlier. "Let's have a little fun first."

"*This* is fun," the boy said, a bit plaintively. But he slung himself onto the bed beside her, pulling off his shoes and letting them fall to the floor with a thud. "What you got there?"

Smiling, Jane turned and held up the wrist cuffs. The boy looked at them, then at her, grinning. "Oh ho. Been in the back room, then—"

Jane arched her shoulders and unbuttoned her shirt. He reached for one of the cuffs, but she shook her head. "No. Not me, yet."

"Ladies first."

"Gentleman's pleasure."

The boy's grin widened. "Won't argue with that."

She took his hand and pulled him, gently, to the middle of the bed. "Lie on your back," she whispered.

He did, watching as she removed first his shirt and then his jeans and underwear. His cock lay nudged against his thigh, not quite hard; when she brushed her fingers against it he moaned softly, took her hand and tried to press it against him.

"No," she whispered. "Not yet. Give me your hand."

She placed the cuffs around each wrist, and his ankles, fastened the nylon leash to each one, and then began tying the bonds around each bedpost. It took longer than she had expected; it was difficult to get the bonds taut enough that the boy could not move. He lay there watchfully, his eyes glimmering in the candlelight as he craned his head to stare at her, his breath shallow, quickening.

"There." She sat back upon her haunches, staring at him. His cock was hard now, the hair on his chest and groin tawny in the half-light. He gazed back at her, his tongue pale as he licked his lips. "Try to get away," she whispered.

He moved slightly, his arms and legs a white X against a deep green field. "Can't," he said hoarsely.

She pulled her shirt off, then her nylon skirt. She had nothing on beneath. She leaned forward, letting her fingers trail from the cleft in his throat to his chest, cupping her palm atop his nipple and then sliding her hand down to his thigh. The flesh was warm, the little hairs soft and moist. Her own breath quickened; sudden heat flooded her, a honeyed liquid in her mouth. Above her brow the long hairs stiffened and furled straight out to either side: when she lifted her head to the candlelight she could see them from the corner of her eyes, twin barbs black and glistening like wire.

"You're so sexy." The boy's voice was hoarse. "God, you're—"

She placed her hand over his mouth. "Try to get away," she said, commandingly this time. "*Try to get away.*"

CLEOPATRA BRIMSTONE

His torso writhed, the duvet bunching up around him in dark folds. She raked her fingernails down his chest and he cried out, moaning "Fuck me, God, fuck me…"

"Try to get away."

She stroked his cock, her fingers barely grazing its swollen head. With a moan he came, struggling helplessly to thrust his groin towards her. At the same moment Jane gasped, a fiery rush arrowing down from her brow to her breasts, her cunt. She rocked forward, crying out, her head brushing against the boy's side as she sprawled back across the bed. For a minute she lay there, the room around her seeming to pulse and swirl into myriad crystalline shapes, each bearing within it the same line of candles, the long curve of the boy's thigh swelling up into the hollow of his hip. She drew breath shakily, the flush of heat fading from her brow; then pushed herself up until she was sitting beside him. His eyes were shut. A thread of saliva traced the furrow between mouth and chin. Without thinking she drew her face down to his, and kissed his cheek.

Immediately he began to grow smaller. Jane reared back, smacking into one of the bedposts, and stared at the figure in front of her, shaking her head.

"No," she whispered. "No, no."

He was shrinking: so fast it was like watching water dissolve into dry sand. Man-size, child-size, large dog, small. His eyes flew open and for a fraction of a second stared horrified into her own. His hands and feet slipped like mercury from his bonds, wriggling until they met his torso and were absorbed into it. Jane's fingers kneaded the duvet; six inches away the boy was no larger than her hand, then smaller, smaller still. She blinked, for a heart-shredding instant thought he had disappeared completely.

Then she saw something crawling between folds of velvet. The length of her middle finger, its thorax black, yellow-striped, its lower wings elongated into frilled arabesques like those of a festoon, deep yellow, charcoal black, with indigo eye spots, its upper wings a chiaroscuro of black and white stripes.

Bhutanitis lidderdalii. A native of the eastern Himalayas, rarely glimpsed: it lived among the crowns of trees in mountain valleys, its caterpillars feeding on lianas. Jane held her breath, watching as its wings beat feebly. Without warning it lifted into the air. Jane cried out, falling onto her knees as she sprawled across the bed, cupping it quickly but carefully between her hands.

"Beautiful, beautiful," she crooned. She stepped from the bed, not daring to pause and examine it, and hurried into the kitchen. In the cupboard she found an empty jar, set it down and gingerly angled the lid from it, holding one hand with the butterfly against her breast. She swore, feeling its wings fluttering against her fingers, then quickly brought her hand to the jar's mouth, dropped the butterfly inside and screwed the lid back in place. It fluttered helplessly inside; she could see where the scales had already been scraped from its wing. Still swearing she ran back into the bedroom, putting the lights on and dragging her collection box from under the bed. She grabbed a vial of ethyl alcohol, went back into the kitchen and tore a bit of paper towel from the rack. She opened the vial, poured a few drops of ethyl alcohol onto the paper, opened the jar, and gently tilted it onto its side. She slipped the paper inside, very slowly tipping the jar upright once more, until the paper had settled on the bottom, the butterfly on top of it. Its wings beat frantically for a few moments, then stopped. Its proboscis uncoiled, finer than a hair. Slowly Jane drew her own hand to her brow and ran it along the length of the antennae there. She sat there staring at it until the sun leaked through the wooden shutters in the kitchen window. The butterfly did not move again.

◆ ◆ ◆

THE NEXT DAY passed in a metallic gray haze, the only color the black and saturated yellow of the *lidderdalii*'s wings, burned upon Jane's eyes as though she had looked into the sun. When she finally roused herself, she felt a spasm of panic at the sight of the boy's clothes on the bedroom floor.

CLEOPATRA BRIMSTONE

"Shit." She ran her hand across her head, was momentarily startled to recall she had no hair. "Now what?"

She stood there for a few minutes, thinking, then gathered the clothes—striped V-neck sweater, jeans, socks, jockey shorts, Timberlake knockoff shoes—and dumped them into a plastic Sainsbury's bag. There was a wallet in the jeans pocket. She opened it, gazed impassively at a driver's license—KENNETH REED, WOLVERHAMPTON—and a few five-pound notes. She pocketed the money, took the license into the bathroom and burned it, letting the ashes drop into the toilet. Then she went outside.

It was early Sunday morning, no one about except for a young mother pushing a baby in a stroller. In the neighboring doorway the same drunk old man sprawled, surrounded by empty bottles and rubbish. He stared blearily up at Jane as she approached.

"Here," she said. She bent and dropped the five-pound notes into his scabby hand.

"God bless you, darlin'." He coughed, his eyes focusing on neither Jane nor the notes. "God bless you."

She turned and walked briskly back toward the canal path. There were few waste bins in Camden Town, and so each day trash accumulated in rank heaps along the path, beneath streetlights, in vacant alleys. Street cleaners and sweeping machines then daily cleared it all away again: like elves, Jane thought. As she walked along the canal path she dropped the shoes in one pile of rubbish, tossed the sweater alongside a single high-heeled shoe in the market, stuffed the underwear and socks into a collapsing cardboard box filled with rotting lettuce, and left the jeans beside a stack of papers outside an unopened newsagent's shop. The wallet she tied into the Sainsbury's bag and dropped into an overflowing trash bag outside of Boots. Then she retraced her steps, stopping in front of a shop window filled with tatty polyester lingerie in large sizes and boldly artificial-looking wigs: pink afros, platinum blond falls, black-and-white Cruella de Vil tresses.

The door was propped open; Schubert lieder played softly on 32.

Jane stuck her head in and looked around, saw a beefy man behind the register, cashing out. He had orange lipstick smeared around his mouth and delicate silver fish hanging from his ears.

"We're not open yet. Eleven on Sunday," he said without looking up.

"I'm just looking." Jane sidled over to a glass shelf where four wigs sat on styrofoam heads. One had very glossy black hair in a chin-length flapper bob. Jane tried it on, eyeing herself in a grimy mirror. "How much is this one?"

"Fifteen. But we're not—"

"Here. Thanks!" Jane stuck a twenty-pound note on the counter and ran from the shop. When she reached the corner she slowed, pirouetted to catch her reflection in a shop window. She stared at herself, grinning, then walked the rest of the way home, exhilarated and faintly dizzy.

◆ ◆ ◆

MONDAY MORNING SHE went to the zoo to begin her volunteer work. She had mounted the *Bhutanitis lidderdalii* on a piece of styrofoam with a piece of paper on it, to keep the butterfly's legs from becoming embedded in the styrofoam. She'd softened it first, putting it into a jar with damp paper, removed it and placed it on the mounting platform, neatly spearing its thorax—a little to the right—with a #2 pin. She propped it carefully on the wainscoting beside the hawk-moth, and left.

She arrived and found her ID badge waiting for her at the staff entrance. It was a clear morning, warmer than it had been for a week; the long hairs on her brow vibrated as though they were wires that had been plucked. Beneath the wig her shaved head felt hot and moist, the first new hairs starting to prickle across her scalp. Her nose itched where her glasses pressed against it. Jane walked, smiling, past the gibbons howling in their habitat and the pygmy hippos floating calmly in their pool, their eyes shut, green bubbles breaking around them like little fish. In front of the Insect Zoo a uniformed woman was unloading sacks of meal from a golf cart.

"Morning," Jane called cheerfully, and went inside.

She found David Bierce standing in front of a temperature gauge beside a glass cage holding the hissing cockroaches.

"Something happened last night, the damn things got too cold." He glanced over, handed her a clipboard and began to remove the top of the gauge. "I called Operations but they're at their fucking morning meeting. Fucking computers—"

He stuck his hand inside the control box and flicked angrily at the gauge. "You know anything about computers?"

"Not this kind." Jane brought her face up to the cage's glass front. Inside were half a dozen glossy roaches, five inches long and the color of pale maple syrup. They lay, unmoving, near a glass petri dish filled with what looked like damp brown sugar. "Are they dead?"

"Those things? They're fucking immortal. You could stamp on one and it wouldn't die. Believe me, I've done it." He continued to fiddle with the gauge, finally sighed and replaced the lid. "Well, let's let the boys over in Ops handle it. Come on, I'll get you started."

He gave her a brief tour of the lab, opening drawers full of dissecting instruments, mounting platforms, pins; showed her where the food for the various insects was kept in a series of small refrigerators. Sugar syrup, cornstarch, plastic containers full of smaller insects, grubs and mealworms, tiny gray beetles. "Mostly we just keep on top of replacing the ones that die," David explained, "that and making sure the plants don't develop the wrong kind of fungus. Nature takes her course and we just goose her along when she needs it. School groups are here constantly, but the docents handle that. You're more than welcome to talk to them, if that's the sort of thing you want to do."

He turned from where he'd been washing empty jars at a small sink, dried his hands, and walked over to sit on top of a desk. "It's not terribly glamorous work here." He reached down for a styrofoam cup of coffee and sipped from it, gazing at her coolly. "We're none of us working on our PhDs anymore."

Jane shrugged. "That's all right."

"It's not even all that interesting. I mean, it can be very repetitive. Tedious."

"I don't mind." A sudden pang of anxiety made Jane's voice break. She could feel her face growing hot, and quickly looked away. "Really," she said sullenly.

"Suit yourself. Coffee's over there; you'll probably have to clean yourself a cup, though." He cocked his head, staring at her curiously, then said, "Did you do something different with your hair?"

She nodded once, brushing the edge of her bangs with a finger. "Yeah."

"Nice. Very Louise Brooks." He hopped from the desk and crossed to a computer set up in the corner. "You can use my computer if you need to, I'll give you the password later."

Jane nodded, her flush fading into relief. "How many people work here?"

"Actually, we're short-staffed here right now—no money for hiring and our grant's run out. It's pretty much just me, and whoever Carolyn sends over from the docents. Sweet little bluehairs mostly, they don't much like bugs. So it's providential you turned up, *Jane*."

He said her name mockingly, gave her a crooked grin. "You said you have experience mounting? Well, I try to save as many of the dead specimens as I can, and when there's any slow days, which there never are, I mount them and use them for the workshops I do with the schools that come in. What would be nice would be if we had enough specimens that I could give some to the teachers, to take back to their classrooms. We have a nice website and we might be able to work up some interactive programs. No schools are scheduled today, Monday's usually slow here. So if you could work on some of *those*—" He gestured to where several dozen cardboard boxes and glass jars were strewn across a countertop. "—that would be really brilliant," he ended, and turned to his computer screen.

She spent the morning mounting insects. Few were interesting or unusual: a number of brown hairstreaks, some Camberwell Beauties,

CLEOPATRA BRIMSTONE

three hissing cockroaches, several brimstones. But there was a single *Acherontia atropos*, the Death's head hawkmoth, the pattern of gray and brown and pale yellow scales on the back of its thorax forming the image of a human skull. Its proboscis was unfurled, the twin points sharp enough to pierce a finger: Jane touched it gingerly, wincing delightedly as a pinprick of blood appeared on her fingertip.

"You bring lunch?"

She looked away from the bright magnifying light she'd been using and blinked in surprise. "Lunch?"

David Bierce laughed. "Enjoying yourself? Well, that's good, makes the day go faster. Yes, lunch!" He rubbed his hands together, the harsh light making him look gnomelike, his sharp features malevolent and leering. "They have some decent fish and chips at the stall over by the cats. Come on, I'll treat you. Your first day."

They sat at a picnic table beside the food booth and ate. David pulled a bottle of ale from his knapsack and shared it with Jane. Overhead scattered clouds like smoke moved swiftly southwards. An Indian woman with three small boys sat at another table, the boys tossing fries at seagulls that swept down, shrieking, and made the smallest boy wail.

"Rain later," David said, staring at the sky. "Too bad." He sprinkled vinegar on his fried haddock and looked at Jane. "So did you go out over the weekend?"

She stared at the table and smiled. "Yeah, I did. It was fun."

"Where'd you go? The Electric Ballroom?"

"God, no. This other place." She glanced at his hand resting on the table beside her. He had long fingers, the knuckles slightly enlarged; but the back of his hand was smooth, the same soft brown as the *Acherontia*'s wingtips. Her brows prickled, warmth trickling from them like water. When she lifted her head she could smell him, some kind of musky soap, salt; the bittersweet ale on his breath.

"Yeah? Where? I haven't been out in months, I'd be lost in Camden Town these days."

"I dunno. The Hive?"

She couldn't imagine he would have heard of it—far too old. But he swiveled on the bench, his eyebrows arching with feigned shock. "You went to *Hive*? And they let you in?"

"Yes," Jane stammered. "I mean, I didn't know—it was just a dance club. I just—danced."

"Did you." David Bierce's gaze sharpened, his hazel eyes catching the sun and sending back an icy emerald glitter. "Did you."

She picked up the bottle of ale and began to peel the label from it. "Yes."

"Have a boyfriend, then?"

She shook her head, rolled a fragment of label into a tiny pill. "No."

"Stop that." His hand closed over hers. He drew it away from the bottle, letting it rest against the table edge. She swallowed: he kept his hand on top of hers, pressing it against the metal edge until she felt her scored palm begin to ache. Her eyes closed: she could feel herself floating, and see a dozen feet below her own form, slender, the wig beetle-black upon her skull, her wrist like a bent stalk. Abruptly his hand slid away and beneath the table, brushing her leg as he stooped to retrieve his knapsack.

"Time to get back to work," he said lightly, sliding from the bench and slinging his bag over his shoulder. The breeze lifted his long graying hair as he turned away. "I'll see you back there."

Overhead the gulls screamed and flapped, dropping bits of fried fish on the sidewalk. She stared at the table in front of her, the cardboard trays that held the remnants of lunch, and watched as a yellowjacket landed on a fleck of grease, its golden thorax swollen with moisture as it began to feed.

◆ ◆ ◆

SHE DID NOT return to Hive that night. Instead she wore a patchwork dress over her jeans and Doc Martens, stuffed the wig inside a drawer and headed to a small bar on Inverness Street. The fair day had turned to rain, black puddles like molten metal capturing the amber glow of traffic signals and streetlights.

There were only a handful of tables at Bar Ganza. Most of the customers stood on the sidewalk outside, drinking and shouting to be heard above the sound of wailing Spanish love songs. Jane fought her way inside, got a glass of red wine, and miraculously found an empty stool alongside the wall. She climbed onto it, wrapped her long legs around the pedestal, and sipped her wine.

"Hey. Nice hair." A man in his early thirties, his own head shaven, sidled up to Jane's stool. He held a cigarette, smoking it with quick, nervous gestures as he stared at her. He thrust his cigarette towards the ceiling, indicating a booming speaker. "You like the music?"

"Not particularly."

"Hey, you're American? Me too. Chicago. Good bud of mine, works for Citibank, he told me about this place. Food's not bad. Tapas. Baby octopus. You like octopus?"

Jane's eyes narrowed. The man wore expensive-looking corduroy trousers, a rumpled jacket of nubby charcoal-colored linen. "No," she said, but didn't turn away.

"Me neither. Like eating great big slimy bugs. Geoff Lanning—"

He stuck his hand out. She touched it, lightly, and smiled. "Nice to meet you, Geoff."

For the next half hour or so she pretended to listen to him, nodding and smiling brilliantly whenever he looked up at her. The bar grew louder and more crowded, and people began eyeing Jane's stool covetously.

"I think I'd better hand over this seat," she announced, hopping down and elbowing her way to the door. "Before they eat me."

Geoff Lanning hurried after her. "Hey, you want to get dinner? The Camden Brasserie's just up here—"

"No thanks." She hesitated on the curb, gazing demurely at her Doc Martens. "But would you like to come in for a drink?"

He was very impressed by her apartment. "Man, this place'd probably go for a half mil, easy! That's three quarters of a million American."

He opened and closed cupboards, ran a hand lovingly across the slate sink. "Nice hardwood floors, high speed access—you never told me what you do."

Jane laughed. "As little as possible. Here—"

She handed him a brandy snifter, let her finger trace the top part of his wrist. "You look like kind of an adventurous sort of guy."

"Hey, big adventure, that's me." He lifted his glass to her. "What exactly did you have in mind? Big game hunting?"

"Mmm. Maybe."

It was more of a struggle this time, not for Geoff Lanning but for Jane. He lay complacently in his bonds, his stocky torso wriggling obediently when Jane commanded. Her head ached from the cheap wine at Bar Ganza; the long hairs above her eyes lay sleek against her skull, and did not move at all until she closed her eyes, and, unbidden, the image of David Bierce's hand covering hers appeared.

"Try to get away," she whispered.

"Whoa, Nellie," Geoff Lanning gasped.

"Try to get away," she repeated, her voice hoarser.

"Oh." The man whimpered softly. "Jesus Christ, what—oh my God, what—"

Quickly she bent and kissed his fingertips, saw where the leather cuff had bitten into his pudgy wrist. This time she was prepared when with a keening sound he began to twist upon the bed, his arms and legs shriveling and then coiling in upon themselves, his shaved head withdrawing into his tiny torso like a snail within its shell.

But she was not prepared for the creature that remained, its feathery antennae a trembling echo of her own, its extraordinarily elongated hind spurs nearly four inches long.

"*Oh,*" she gasped.

She didn't dare touch it until it took to the air: the slender spurs fragile as icicles, scarlet, their saffron tips curling like Christmas ribbon, its large delicate wings saffron with slate-blue and scarlet eyespots, and spanning nearly six inches. A Madagascan Moon Moth,

CLEOPATRA BRIMSTONE

one of the loveliest and rarest silk moths, and almost impossible to find as an intact specimen.

"What do I do with you, what do I do?" she crooned as it spread its wings and lifted from the bed. It flew in short sweeping arcs; she scrambled to blow out the candles before it could near them. She pulled on her kimono and left the lights off, closed the bedroom door and hurried into the kitchen, looking for a flashlight. She found nothing, but recalled Andrew telling her there was a large torch in the basement.

She hadn't been down there since her initial tour of the flat. It was brightly lit, with long neat cabinets against both walls, a floor-to-ceiling wine rack filled with bottles of claret and vintage burgundy, compact washer and dryer, small refrigerator, buckets and brooms waiting for the cleaning lady's weekly visit. She found the flashlight sitting on top of the refrigerator, a container of extra batteries beside it. She switched it on and off a few times, then glanced down at the refrigerator and absently opened it.

Seeing all that wine had made her think the little refrigerator might be filled with beer. Instead it held only a long plastic box, with a red lid and a red biohazard sticker on the side. Jane put the flashlight down and stooped, carefully removing the box and setting it on the floor. A label with Andrew's neat architectural handwriting was on the top.

DR. ANDREW FILDERMAN
ST. MARTIN'S HOSPICE

"Huh," she said, and opened it.

Inside there was a small red biohazard waste container, and scores of plastic bags filled with disposable hypodermics, ampules, and suppositories. All contained morphine at varying dosages. Jane stared, marveling, then opened one of the bags. She shook half a dozen morphine ampules into her palm, carefully reclosed the bag, put it back into the box, and returned the box to the refrigerator. Then she grabbed the flashlight and ran upstairs.

It took her a while to capture the moon moth. First she had to find a killing jar large enough, and then she had to very carefully lure it inside, so that its frail wing spurs wouldn't be damaged. She did this by positioning the jar on its side and placing a gooseneck lamp directly behind it, so that the bare bulb shone through the glass. After about fifteen minutes, the moth landed on top of the jar, its tiny legs slipping as it struggled on the smooth curved surface. Another few minutes and it had crawled inside, nestled on the wad of tissues Jane had set there, moist with ethyl alcohol. She screwed the lid on tightly, left the jar on its side, and waited for it to die.

◆ ◆ ◆

OVER THE NEXT week she acquired three more specimens. *Papilio demetrius*, a Japanese swallowtail with elegant orange eyespots on a velvety black ground; a scarce copper, not scarce at all, really, but with lovely pumpkin-colored wings; and *Graphium agamemnon*, a Malaysian species with vivid green spots and chrome-yellow strips on its somber brown wings. She'd ventured away from Camden Town, capturing the swallowtail in a private room in an SM club in Islington and the *Graphium agamemnon* in a parked car behind a noisy pub in Crouch End. The scarce copper came from a vacant lot near the Tottenham Court Road tube station very late one night, where the wreckage of a chain link fence stood in for her bedposts. She found the morphine to be useful, although she had to wait until immediately after the man ejaculated before pressing the ampule against his throat, aiming for the carotid artery. This way the butterflies emerged already sedated, and in minutes died with no damage to their wings. Leftover clothing was easily disposed of, but she had to be more careful with wallets, stuffing them deep within rubbish bins, when she could, or burying them in her own trash bags and then watching as the waste trucks came by on their rounds.

In South Kensington she discovered an entomological supply store. There she bought more mounting supplies, and inquired casually as to whether the owner might be interested in purchasing some specimens.

He shrugged. "Depends. What you got?"

"Well, right now I have only one *Argema mittrei*." Jane adjusted her glasses and glanced around the shop. A lot of morphos, an Atlas moth: nothing too unusual. "But I might be getting another, in which case…"

"Moon moth, eh? How'd you come by that, I wonder?" The man raised his eyebrows, and Jane flushed. "Don't worry, I'm not going to turn you in. Christ, I'd go out of business. Well, obviously I can't display those in the shop, but if you want to part with one, let me know. I'm always scouting for my customers."

She began volunteering three days a week at the insect zoo. One Wednesday, the night after she'd gotten a gorgeous *Urania leilus*, its wings sadly damaged by rain, she arrived to see David Bierce reading that morning's *Camden New Journal*. He peered above the newspaper and frowned.

"You still going out alone at night?"

She froze, her mouth dry; turned and hurried over to the coffeemaker. "Why?" she said, fighting to keep her tone even.

"Because there's an article about some of the clubs around here. Apparently a few people have gone missing."

"Really?" Jane got her coffee, wiping up a spill with the side of her hand. "What happened?"

"Nobody knows. Two blokes reported gone, family frantic, sort of thing. Probably just runaways. Camden Town eats them alive, kids." He handed the paper to Jane. "Although one of them was last seen near Highbury Fields, some sex club there."

She scanned the article. There was no mention of any suspects. And no bodies had been found, although foul play was suspected. ("*Ken would never have gone away without notifying us or his employer…*")

Anyone with any information was urged to contact the police.

"I don't go to sex clubs," Jane said flatly. "Plus those are both guys."

"Mmm." David leaned back in his chair, regarding her coolly. "You're the one hitting Hive your first weekend in London."

"It's a *dance* club!" Jane retorted. She laughed, rolled the newspaper into a tube, and batted him gently on the shoulder. "Don't worry. I'll be careful."

David continued to stare at her, hazel eyes glittering. "Who says it's you I'm worried about?"

She smiled, her mouth tight as she turned and began cleaning bottles in the sink.

It was a raw day, more late November than mid-May. Only two school groups were scheduled; otherwise the usual stream of visitors was reduced to a handful of elderly women who shook their heads over the cockroaches and gave barely a glance to the butterflies before shuffling on to another building. David Bierce paced restlessly through the lab on his way to clean the cages and make more complaints to the Operations Division. Jane cleaned and mounted two stag beetles, their spiny legs pricking her fingertips as she tried to force the pins through their glossy chestnut-colored shells. Afterwards she busied herself with straightening the clutter of cabinets and drawers stuffed with requisition forms and microscopes, computer parts and dissection kits.

It was well past two when David reappeared, his anorak slick with rain, his hair tucked beneath the hood. "Come on," he announced, standing impatiently by the open door. "Let's go to lunch."

Jane looked up from the computer where she'd been updating a specimen list. "I'm really not very hungry," she said, giving him an apologetic smile. "You go ahead."

"Oh, for Christ's sake." David let the door slam shut as he crossed to her, his sneakers leaving wet smears on the tiled floor. "That can wait till tomorrow. Come on, there's not a fucking thing here that needs doing."

"But—" She gazed up at him. The hood slid from his head; his gray-streaked hair hung loose to his shoulders, and the sheen of rain on his sharp cheekbones made him look carved from oiled wood. "What if somebody comes?"

"A very nice docent named Mrs. Eleanor Feltwell is out there, *even as we speak*, in the unlikely event that we have a single visitor."

CLEOPATRA BRIMSTONE

He stooped so that his head was beside hers, scowling as he stared at the computer screen. A lock of his hair fell to brush against her neck. Beneath the wig her scalp burned, as though stung by tiny ants; she breathed in the warm acrid smell of his sweat and something else, a sharper scent, like crushed oak-mast or fresh-sawn wood. Above her brows the antennae suddenly quivered. Sweetness coated her tongue like burnt syrup. With a rush of panic she turned her head so he wouldn't see her face.

"I—I should finish this—"

"Oh, just *fuck* it, Jane! It's not like we're *paying* you. Come on, now, there's a good girl—"

He took her hand and pulled her to her feet, Jane still looking away. The bangs of her cheap wig scraped her forehead and she batted at them feebly. "Get your things. What, don't you ever take days off in the States?"

"All right, all right." She turned and gathered her black vinyl raincoat and knapsack, pulled on the coat and waited for him by the door. "Jeez, you must be hungry," she said crossly.

"No. Just fucking bored out of my skull. Have you been to Ruby in the Dust? No? I'll take you then, let's go—"

The restaurant was down the High Street, a small, cheerfully claptrap place, dim in the gray afternoon, its small wooden tables scattered with abandoned newspapers and overflowing ashtrays. David Bierce ordered a steak and a pint. Jane had a small salad, nasturtium blossoms strewn across pale green lettuce, and a glass of red wine. She lacked an appetite lately, living on vitamin-enhanced, fruity bottled drinks from the health food store and baklava from a Greek bakery near the tube station.

"So." David Bierce stabbed a piece of steak, peering at her sideways. "Don't tell me you really haven't been here before."

"I haven't!" Despite her unease at being with him, she laughed, and caught her reflection in the wall-length mirror. A thin plain young woman in shapeless Peruvian sweater and jeans, bad haircut and ugly glasses. Gazing at herself she felt suddenly stronger, invisible. She tilted her head and smiled at Bierce. "The food's good."

"So you don't have someone taking you out to dinner every night? Cooking for you? I thought you American girls all had adoring men at your feet. Adoring slaves," he added dryly. "Or slave girls, I suppose. If that's your thing."

"No." She stared at her salad, shook her head demurely and took a sip of wine. It made her feel even more invulnerable. "No, I—"

"Boyfriend back home, right?" He finished his pint, flagged the waiter to order another, and turned back to Jane. "Well, that's nice. That's very nice—for him," he added, and gave a short harsh laugh.

The waiter brought another pint, and more wine for Jane. "Oh really, I better—"

"Just drink it, Jane." Under the table, she felt a sharp pressure on her foot. She wasn't wearing her Doc Martens today but a pair of red plastic jellies. David Bierce had planted his heel firmly atop her toes; she sucked in her breath in shock and pain, the bones of her foot crackling as she tried to pull it from beneath him. Her antennae rippled, then stiffened, and heat burst like a seed inside her.

"Go ahead," he said softly, pushing the wineglass towards her. "Just a sip, that's right—"

She grabbed the glass, spilling wine on her sweater as she gulped at it. The vicious pressure on her foot subsided, but as the wine ran down her throat she could feel the heat thrusting her into the air, currents rushing beneath her as the girl at the table below set down her wineglass with trembling fingers.

"There." David Bierce smiled, leaning forward to gently cup her hand between his. "Now this is better than working. Right, Jane?"

• ◆ •

HE WALKED HER home along the canal path. Jane tried to dissuade him, but he'd had a third pint by then; it didn't seem to make him drunk but coldly obdurate, and she finally gave in. The rain had turned to a fine drizzle, the canal's usually murky water silvered and softly gleaming in the twilight. They passed few other people, and Jane found herself wishing someone else would appear, so that she'd have an excuse to move closer to David Bierce. He kept close to the canal itself, several feet from Jane; when the breeze lifted she could catch his oaky scent again, rising above the dank reek of stagnant water and decaying hawthorn blossom.

They crossed over the bridge to approach her flat by the street. At the front sidewalk Jane stopped, smiled shyly, and said, "Thanks. That was nice."

David nodded. "Glad I finally got you out of your cage." He lifted his head to gaze appraisingly at the row house. "Christ, this where you're staying? You split the rent with someone?"

"No." She hesitated: she couldn't remember what she had told him about her living arrangements. But before she could blurt something out he stepped past her to the front door, peeking into the window and bobbing impatiently up and down.

"Mind if I have a look? Professional entomologists don't often get the chance to see how the quality live."

Jane hesitated, her stomach clenching; decided it would be safer to have him in, rather than continue to put him off.

"All right," she said reluctantly, and opened the door.

"Mmmm. Nice, nice, very nice." He swept around the living room, spinning on his heel and making a show of admiring the elaborate molding, the tribal rugs, the fireplace mantel with its thick ecclesiastical candles and ormolu mirror. "Goodness, all this for a wee thing like you? You're a clever cat, landing on your feet here, Lady Jane."

She blushed. He bounded past her on his way into the bedroom, touching her shoulder; she had to close her eyes as a fiery wave surged through her and her antennae trembled.

"*Wow*," he exclaimed.

Slowly she followed him into the bedroom. He stood in front of the wall where her specimens were balanced in a neat line across the wainscoting. His eyes were wide, his mouth open in genuine astonishment.

"Are these *yours*?" he marveled, his gaze fixed on the butterflies. "You didn't actually catch them—?"

She shrugged.

"These are incredible!" He picked up the *Graphium agamemnon* and tilted it to the pewter-colored light falling through the French doors. "Did you mount them, too?"

She nodded, crossing to stand beside him. "Yeah. You can tell, with that one—" She pointed at the *Urania leilus* in its oak-framed box. "It got rained on."

David Bierce replaced the *Graphium agamemnon* and began to read the labels on the others.

Papilio demetrius
UNITED KINGDOM: LONDON
Highbury Fields, Islington
7.V.2001
J. Kendall

Loepa katinka
UNITED KINGDOM: LONDON
Finsbury Park
09.V.2001
J. Kendall

Argema mittrei
UNITED KINGDOM: LONDON
Camden Town
13.IV.2001
J. Kendall

He shook his head. "You screwed up, though—you wrote 'London' for all of them." He turned to her, grinning wryly. "Can't think of the last time I saw a moon moth in Camden Town."

She forced a laugh. "Oh—right."

"And, I mean, you can't have actually *caught* them—"

CLEOPATRA BRIMSTONE

He held up the *Loepa katinka*, a butter-yellow Emperor moth, its peacock's-eyes russet and jet-black. "I haven't seen any of these around lately. Not even in Finsbury."

Jane made a little grimace of apology. "Yeah. I meant, that's where I found them—where I bought them."

"Mmmm." He set the moth back on its ledge. "You'll have to share your sources with me. I can never find things like these in North London."

He turned and headed out of the bedroom. Jane hurriedly straightened the specimens, her hands shaking now as well, and followed him.

"Well, Lady Jane." For the first time he looked at her without his usual mocking arrogance, his green-flecked eyes bemused, almost regretful. "I think we managed to salvage something from the day."

He turned, gazing one last time at the flat's glazed walls and highly waxed floors, the imported cabinetry and jewel-toned carpets. "I was going to say, when I walked you home, that you needed someone to take care of you. But it looks like you've managed that on your own."

Jane stared at her feet. He took a step toward her, the fragrance of oak-mast and honey filling her nostrils, crushed acorns, new fern. She grew dizzy, her hand lifting to find him; but he only reached to graze her cheek with his finger.

"Night then, Jane," he said softly, and walked back out into the misty evening.

◆ ◆ ◆

WHEN HE WAS gone she raced to the windows and pulled all the velvet curtains, then tore the wig from her head and threw it onto the couch along with her glasses. Her heart was pounding, her face slick with sweat—from fear or rage or disappointment, she didn't know. She yanked off her sweater and jeans, left them on the living room floor and stomped into the bathroom. She stood in the shower for twenty minutes, head upturned as the water sluiced the smells of bracken and leaf-mold from her skin.

Finally she got out. She dried herself, let the towel drop, and went into the kitchen. Abruptly she was famished. She tore open cupboards and drawers until she found a half-full jar of lavender honey from Provence. She opened it, the top spinning off into the sink, and frantically spooned honey into her mouth with her fingers. When she was finished she grabbed a jar of lemon curd and ate most of that, until she felt as though she might be sick. She stuck her head into the sink, letting water run from the faucet into her mouth, and at last walked, surfeited, into the bedroom.

She dressed, feeling warm and drowsy, almost dreamlike; pulling on red-and-yellow-striped stockings, her nylon skirt, a tight red T-shirt. No bra, no panties. She put in her contacts, then examined herself in the mirror. Her hair had begun to grow back, a scant velvety stubble, bluish in the dim light. She drew a sweeping black line across each eyelid, on a whim took the liner and extended the curve of each antenna until they touched her temples. She painted her lips black as well and went to find her black vinyl raincoat.

It was early when she went out, far too early for any of the clubs to be open. The rain had stopped, but a thick greasy fog covered everything, coating windshields and shop windows, making Jane's face feel as though it were encased in a clammy shell. For hours she wandered Camden Town, huge violet eyes turning to stare back at the men who watched her, dismissing each of them. Once she thought she saw David Bierce coming out of Ruby in the Dust, but when she stopped to watch him cross the street it was not David but someone else. Much younger, his long dark hair in a thick braid, his feet clad in knee-high boots. He crossed the High Street, heading towards the tube station. Jane hesitated, then darted after him.

He went to the Electric Ballroom. Fifteen or so people stood out front, talking quietly. The man she'd followed joined the line, standing by himself. Jane waited across the street, until the door opened and the little crowd began to shuffle inside. After the long-haired young man had entered, she counted to one hundred, crossed the street, paid her cover, and went inside.

CLEOPATRA BRIMSTONE

The club had three levels; she finally tracked him down on the uppermost one. Even on a rainy Wednesday night it was crowded, the sound system blaring Idris Mohammed and Jimmie Cliff. He was standing alone near the bar, drinking bottled water.

"Hi!" she shouted, swaying up to him with her best First Day of School Smile. "Want to dance?"

He was older than she'd thought—thirtyish, still not as old as Bierce. He stared at her, puzzled, then shrugged. "Sure."

They danced, passing the water bottle between them. "What's your name?" he shouted.

"Cleopatra Brimstone."

"You're kidding!" he yelled back. The song ended in a bleat of feedback, and they walked, panting, back to the bar.

"What, you know another Cleopatra?" Jane asked teasingly.

"No. It's just a crazy name, that's all." He smiled. He was handsomer than David Bierce, his features softer, more rounded, his eyes dark brown, his manner a bit reticent. "I'm Thomas Raybourne. Tom."

He bought another bottle of Pellegrino and one for Jane. She drank it quickly, trying to get his measure. When she finished she set the empty bottle on the floor and fanned herself with her hand.

"It's hot in here." Her throat hurt from shouting over the music. "I think I'm going to take a walk. Feel like coming?"

He hesitated, glancing around the club. "I was supposed to meet a friend here..." he began, frowning. "But—"

"Oh." Disappointment filled her, spiking into desperation. "Well, that's okay. I guess."

"Oh, what the hell." He smiled: he had nice eyes, a more stolid, reassuring gaze than Bierce. "I can always come back."

Outside she turned right, in the direction of the canal. "I live pretty close by. Feel like coming in for a drink?"

He shrugged again. "I don't drink, actually."

"Something to eat then? It's not far—just along the canal path a few blocks past Camden Lock—"

"Yeah, sure."

They made desultory conversation. "You should be careful," he said as they crossed the bridge. "Did you read about those people who've gone missing in Camden Town?"

Jane nodded but said nothing. She felt anxious and clumsy—as though she'd drunk too much, although she'd had nothing since the two glasses of wine with David Bierce. Her companion also seemed ill at ease; he kept glancing back, as though looking for someone on the canal path behind them.

"I should have tried to call," he explained ruefully. "But I forgot to recharge my mobile."

"You could call from my place."

"No, that's all right."

She could tell from his tone that he was figuring how he could leave, gracefully, as soon as possible.

Inside the flat he settled on the couch, picked up a copy of *Time Out* and flipped through it, pretending to read. Jane went immediately into the kitchen and poured herself a glass of brandy. She downed it, poured a second one, and joined him on the couch.

"So." She kicked off her Doc Martens, drew her stockinged foot slowly up his leg, from calf to thigh. "Where you from?"

He was passive, so passive she wondered if he would get aroused at all. But after a while they were lying on the couch, both their shirts on the floor, his pants unzipped and his cock stiff, pressing against her bare belly.

"Let's go in there," Jane whispered hoarsely. She took his hand and led him into the bedroom.

She only bothered lighting a single candle, before lying beside him on the bed. His eyes were half-closed, his breathing shallow. When she ran a fingernail around one nipple he made a small surprised sound, then quickly turned and pinned her to the bed.

"Wait! Slow down," Jane said, and wriggled from beneath him. For the last week she'd left the bonds attached to the bedposts, hiding

CLEOPATRA BRIMSTONE

them beneath the covers when not in use. Now she grabbed one of the wristcuffs and pulled it free. Before he could see what she was doing it was around his wrist.

"Hey!"

She dove for the foot of the bed, his leg narrowly missing her as it thrashed against the covers. It was more difficult to get this in place, but she made a great show of giggling and stroking his thigh, which seemed to calm him. The other leg was next, and finally she leapt from the bed and darted to the headboard, slipping from his grasp when he tried to grab her shoulder.

"This is not consensual," he said. She couldn't tell if he was serious or not.

"What about this, then?" she murmured, sliding down between his legs and cupping his erect penis between her hands. "This seems to be enjoying itself."

He groaned softly, shutting his eyes. "Try to get away," she said. "Try to get away."

He tried to lunge upward, his body arcing so violently that she drew back in alarm. The bonds held; he arched again, and again, but now she remained beside him, her hands on his cock, his breath coming faster and faster and her own breath keeping pace with it, her heart pounding and the tingling above her eyes almost unbearable.

"Try to get away," she gasped. "Try to get away—"

When he came he cried out, his voice harsh, as though in pain, and Jane cried out as well, squeezing her eyes shut as spasms shook her from head to groin. Quickly her head dipped to kiss his chest; then she shuddered and drew back, watching.

His voice rose again, ended suddenly in a shrill wail, as his limbs knotted and shriveled like burning rope. She had a final glimpse of him, a homunculus sprouting too many legs. Then on the bed before her a perfectly formed *Papilio krishna* swallowtail crawled across the rumpled duvet, its wings twitching to display glittering green scales amidst spectral washes of violet and crimson and gold.

"Oh, you're beautiful, beautiful," she whispered.

From across the room echoed a sound: soft, the rustle of her kimono falling from its hook as the door swung open. She snatched her hand from the butterfly and stared, through the door to the living room.

In her haste to get Thomas Raybourne inside she had forgotten to latch the front door. She scrambled to her feet, naked, staring wildly at the shadow looming in front of her, its features taking shape as it approached the candle, brown and black, light glinting across his face.

It was David Bierce. The scent of oak and bracken swelled, suffocating, fragrant, cut by the bitter odor of ethyl alcohol. He forced her gently onto the bed, heat piercing her breast and thighs, her antennae bursting out like flame from her brow and wings exploding everywhere around her as she struggled fruitlessly.

"Now. Try to get away," he said.

Ghost Light

I WAS NEVER a fan of Zeke McDermott's music. Too angsty, despite the Tom Waits growl and lumberjack look favored by guys who wouldn't know a maul from a mailbox. But he had buzz—solid Pitchfork rankings, an NPR feature. When McDermott came through last winter, the house was half-full, damn good considering the show had been canceled due to a blizzard then rescheduled for two nights later.

McDermott didn't travel with a road crew. Few solo performers do—that's why places like the Opera House hire guys like me to run lights and sound.

McDermott rode out the storm at the Harbor Inn, in what passes for downtown. That was when he hooked up with Bree. Bree's cute, small and tomboyish, with a fish tattoo on her upper arm, a brookie. I assumed she was gay. I never caught any sexual vibe from her, not so unusual when you consider I'm twice her age, a former roadie who drives to Ellsworth to attend weekly NarcAnon meetings.

Anyway, she met McDermott at the Rum Line. They spent the next three nights together. My place is a few doors down from the Inn; I saw her leaving a couple times. I wasn't stalking her: that's just the kind of thing you notice in a town small as this.

Plus, Bree works for me. She went to Northeastern to study music—she plays mandolin—but moved back home after a year. Money issues. I know her dad and, as a favor, took her under my wing. Taught her the basics of wiring, how to rig the lighting pipes, set up and break down a show.

Bree was good at it. I liked having her around, liked hearing her play the mandolin while I figured out lighting cues. Far as I know, she never slept with the talent till McDermott. Didn't matter to me as long as she did her job.

And all bets are off during a blizzard. She showed up on the afternoon of the rescheduled performance, and we got to work.

McDermott had a strong stage presence. Good-looking enough, with a beard and dark hair, a disarmingly gruff, somewhat theatrical manner at odds with all those heartachey songs. He sat in a chair near the edge of the stage, cradling his Gibson as he sang into a mic that dated to the Nixon era.

His only special request was he wanted a floor lamp within reach. He did this shtick during his closer, something else he copped from Waits: set down his guitar and danced, did this little drunken waltz with the mic, singing as he grabbed onto the lamp like an old-time cartoon drunk. Our lamp had a tasseled shade and had done hard duty in community theater plays for decades. Blue gels in the followspot simulated moonlight; dust in the air glowed like snow. Schmaltzy but effective. He got a standing ovation.

To top it off, he brought Bree and her mandolin onstage for an encore. I don't know if they planned it or not. Not, I think, from the way she blushed. They sang "Shady Grove," the two of them grinning at each other like they'd done this a hundred times.

I know they were together that night—next day was one of the few when Bree showed up late for work. I didn't say anything. She looked happier than I'd ever seen her.

That didn't last. Weeks went by, then months. She never told me, but I knew.

She gained a little weight, then lost it, showed up a few times drunk or stoned. I reamed her out—it wasn't just unprofessional but dangerous. I didn't want one of those pipes falling on me, or her.

GHOST LIGHT

After that I'd still see her at the Rum Line, but she showed up sober. Never heard her play the mandolin again.

A year went by. Come February, McDermott's back. No blizzard this time: freakishly warm weather, no snow, maple sap running. I called McDermott and asked if he wanted anything special.

Nope. Like last year, just a mic and standing lamp close to hand.

Bree laid down spike tape to mark where his chair and mic would go. The lamp we'd used before had been totaled during a production of "Arsenic and Old Lace," so we used the ghost light. Our ghost light was old, like everything else.

Bree measured off from McDermott's chair, set the lamp there. We were good to go.

We didn't sell out, but it was close. Locals remembered last year's show, and the springlike weather brought people from far away as Bangor. Inside, it must've been eighty degrees, worse on stage with the footlights. I'd asked Bree to turn down the heat; either she forgot or so many bodies raised the temp.

Still, McDermott put on a great show. When it came time for his final song, I dimmed everything save that spooky blue followspot. He waltzed around with the mic, sweat streaming down his face: a convincing drunk. Did his little pirouette and grabbed the ghost light.

It looked like part of the act. His head snapped back: he clutched the mic in one hand and the lamp in the other, staggering to the edge of the stage. Some people laughed.

Then he plummeted offstage, pulling mic stand and lamp with him. People screamed. Somebody—Bree, probably—hit the house lights. Somebody else called 911.

Probably he was dead before he hit the floor. From the lighting booth, I could see how his neck torqued as his head struck the stage edge.

I dealt with the cops and EMTs when they arrived, and later with more cops.

So did Bree. Everyone knew me, everyone believed me when I said I'd checked everything beforehand.

The death was ruled accidental. No one blamed me, or Bree, but the Opera House was shuttered afterwards and we had to find other work. Neither of us spoke to any media, though videos of Bree playing with McDermott showed up online, along with footage from his final show.

I know what happened. That old ghost light had a two-prong plug that wasn't polarized like modern ones. If you plugged it into the wall outlet one way, no problem. If you put it in with the prongs reversed, the metal lamp-stand would be live with current. Even that wasn't a problem—unless you grasped the lamp with one hand and something else that was grounded with the other. Like a mic.

Bree knew to plug in the ghost light so it wasn't hot. And I'd checked it, twice. At some point before the performance, she'd gone backstage.

If you brush a hot piece of equipment with your knuckles, you'll get a shock, though not enough to kill you. If you grab it, the live current causes your muscles to contract: you can't let go. Combine that with sweaty hands, a grounded mic, dim stage, and an eight foot drop, and you get Zeke McDermott, RIP.

I never said anything to Bree about it. I assume she had her reasons. She's taken up the mandolin again—I see her sometimes at the Rum Line's open mic night. She's pretty damn good.

The Have-Nots

NOW YOU know Eddie Rule came and took that baby girl three days after she was born.

Actually, his mother took her, Nora Margaret. That was his mother's name, not the girl's. Marched right into that hospital room, Loretta said the nurse was checking her stitches Down There and Nora Margaret marched right in anyway, didn't give a tinker's damn.

I'm taking that baby, she said.

Pardon me? said the nurse. She didn't know Nora Margaret Rule from a hole in the ground.

Excuse *us*, she told the nurse, I think you better go now.

The hell you will, said Loretta; at least now that's what she says she said, but I knew Loretta since fourth grade and she never said a swear in her life 'til she met Eddie Rule, and let me tell you, he was such a goddamn son of a bitch, pardon my French, I would of swore, too.

Now, Alice Jean honey, let me explain something. That shade is just all wrong for you. You're a Summer Rose, remember, you got that blonde hair and blue eyes, you just *have* to go with the Love That Pink. That's the wonder of Mary Rose Cosmetics, everyone gets their own special coordinated color. I think the Salmon Joy is for Erika here, now see the difference?

I thought you would.

Now I'm sorry, I got distracted. But Loretta says now she should of told Nora Margaret off like that, anyhow, swears or not, and I wish she had.

We're married, Loretta said. Ask that nurse, she saw it, Mr. Proctor came down and did it before the baby came. The nurse was gone by then but Loretta showed me the license, it was real all right, she's still got it at home. They wanted to see it for the movie.

Well, you ain't married no more, says Nora Margaret. Loretta told me later, she was surprised a rich lady'd talk like that, but I told her Nora Margaret Rule had no more schooling than my dog King, she just married a rich man is all. Anyway she flaps some thing in front of Loretta's face, Loretta practically went into hysterics then and they called the doctor in. She got them to annex the marriage—

Pardon?

Oh. Well, whatever. Annul it, then, she went to court and had them fix it somehow, said 'cause her son is a Catholic and there was no priest it wasn't a real marriage. Loretta said if you're a Christian how come you're taking my baby and I'm gonna call the police.

Catholic, not Christian, Nora Margaret says, and don't waste your breath, Miss Missy.

Loretta says, It's *Missus*, and Nora Margaret says, Not anymore it ain't. And you know she really did, she took that little baby practically out of her mama's arms and took it away. Paid somebody to adopt it in Richmond and that was the last Loretta saw of it.

Erika, honey, I swear that color takes ten years off your life. Not that you need it. I swear. Alice Jean, don't you think so? I love it that we can compare like this, friends at home. That's why I love Mary Rose Cosmetics, I can come right here to your house with everything and then later, in the middle of the night, you change your mind, why next day I can come right back and you can exchange that Salmon Joy for anything you like.

That Touch of Teal is *very* popular this year, Erika, you just go right ahead and try it. Kind of smudge it around your eyelid like that. There. I sold one to Suzanne Masters last week, she had that Dinner Dance at the Club to go to and it just matched her dress. I told her if I keep going like this, I'm gonna have that Mary Rose Cadillac by the end of summer and drive my kids to school in it.

THE HAVE-NOTS

I haven't forgotten I'm telling about Loretta's Cadillac, Alice Jean. You get too impatient. Let me give you a facial massage and masque, you got that hot water there, Erika? All right. Now this only takes a few minutes but I swear you will feel like a new woman. You need to relax more, Alice Jean.

There. Isn't that nice? I think it smells like that shampoo they use at Fashion Flair.

So that was, what, Nineteen fifty-six? Nineteen fifty-six. Loretta got out of the hospital and I got her a job at the Blue Moon. Now I swear to god every small town and every city I ever lived in had a diner called the Blue Moon. But it wasn't a bad place to work, just not what you'd want to do after you were married for three days to a Catholic whose rude mama came into the hospital and stole your baby and then gave it to a chiropractor and his wife in Richmond. Plus Nora Margaret said she was gonna change the baby's name—

Her name is Eloise, Loretta shouted. Eloise LeMay Rule.

Not anymore it ain't, Nora Margaret yelled back.

So she's gone forever, Eloise or whatever her name was. Eddie Rule is gone, too, his father sent him off to college, some place where they take people even if you got kicked out of high school without graduating and your mother's the kind of person says ain't. But let me tell you, it's an ill wind blows no one any good, 'cause Loretta hasn't seen him since then and that's the best thing ever happened to her. Good riddance to bad rubbish and I mean that. But of course she didn't feel like that then—

I love him, Terry! she'd tell me, and I'd say, Sure, honey, you love him, but he's gone now and don't do you any good to moon over him. We all thought it best not to bring up the baby at all. Nowadays they wouldn't do that, they'd have her going to some kind of Group, like now Loretta's been going to AA, some place where they'd all talk about having their babies taken away. Like when Noreen was on Oprah, they had all these people claimed to have seen him since he died—

Well, all right, Alice Jean, I *am* getting to it. Let me put some more warm water there—

Well, I'm sorry, was that too hot? I'm sorry, honey, I surely am. Erika, see if there's any ice there, will you?

All right. So we're at work one day, this is still at the Blue Moon, and *he* comes in. The Colonel was with him, we recognized the Colonel first 'cause of he's wearing this big hat, but let me tell you, it didn't take us more than a New York second to recognize him. He was famous then but it wasn't like later, he could still walk around like a regular person.

My god he's a handsome man, said Loretta. Sweet Jesus he sure is.

Yup, I said. I was Manageress-in-Training so I had to be more professional, though that was a dead-end job, too. Doing this Mary Rose thing is the best thing ever happened to me, god strike me if that isn't the truth. Erika, if you're still interested you let me know, 'cause I get extra points for signing up new people and it all goes towards the You-Know-What.

The one they had you wouldn't believe. One of the other girls saw it and told us, Look outside, and we did and there it was. Looked like it took up the whole parking lot, and that was before they opened the Piggly Wiggly next door.

Holy cow, said Loretta. That's the biggest goddamn Cadillac I ever saw. Pardon my French, I told you she started talking like that after Eddie. But she was right, it *was* a big car—but you all've seen it, least you saw it the way Loretta had it. Sure you have, oh, Erika honey, thank you—

Alice Jean, I *am* telling it! Here, put this ice there and see if that helps. If it swells up Mary Rose makes this Aloe Vera Nutrifying Lotion, Kenny Junior sunburned himself caddying after school last week and I gave him some and he said it really helped.

So they come in and sit down, I started to give them the booth in the back corner 'cause I thought, well, they're famous, maybe they'd like some privacy, but the Colonel said, No ma'am, we're on vacation, and then *he* said, Put us right here in the front window, it'll be good for business!

Which was just like him, because he meant it to be nice. He always was a nice man and good to his mother, I tell Kenny Junior he should pay attention to that. So anyway I sat them there and since I was in charge I

THE HAVE-NOTS

had Loretta serve them. We were all feeling sorry for her, she just had that dinky little Half-Moon trailer to live in and some people in town thought she was just Bad Luck back in those days, she hadn't had a real date since Eddie left. Though she was really nice looking, she hadn't started drinking yet, not much at least, we used to have rum and Cokes sometimes after work but nobody thought anything of it back then.

The Colonel ordered a ribeye steak sandwich and he got fried chicken. Loretta says she doesn't remember, she was so nervous, but *I* remember. I told the director for the TV movie exactly what they had and even showed her how to set the platter. Just pay me my consulting fee, I told her.

I was only joking, Alice Jean. They're not really going to pay me for it.

Here's that Nutrifying Lotion. It doesn't smell as nice as the other but it sure feels good, doesn't it?

You're welcome, honey. I'm sure sorry about burning you like that.

Well, he said it was the best fried chicken he ever had, and as you know if you read that book his wife wrote about him after he was dead, that man loved fried chicken better than Saint John loved the Lord, even after he got to be so famous he had to have it sent up to him in disguise from Popeye's. And really Loretta did a real nice job, she brought the Colonel extra ketchup without him asking and extra napkins for the fried chicken, because it *was* a little greasy, but good, and she was so cute in that pink uniform and all that when they left he gave her his car. Just like that.

Brand-new Cadillac. They just walked downtown to Don Thomas's dealership and bought another one. Drove by and waved to us on their way out of town.

Well, Loretta just about fainted. He kissed her cheek and the Colonel shook her hand and took a picture. Later Hal Morehead from the *Reporter Dispatch* came and took another picture of her and the car, and WINY made the next day Loretta Dooley Day and played "Hound Dog" and "Love Me Tender" about sixty-three million times, I thought I was going to throw up if I heard that song one more time but it did get the point across. And of course Loretta had to learn to drive, but by then people were starting to show more interest and think maybe she wasn't bad luck after all, the absolute reverse in fact. Don Thomas came over, to see what model Cadillac it was this waitress got tipped with, and after a while he and Loretta started seeing each other. And I got promoted to Manager Full-Time. It was all good for business at the Blue Moon, I can tell you that.

But eventually it all settled down. She was still working at the Blue Moon, 'cause of course it was just a *car*, it wasn't like he gave her a million dollars or something. But she'd drive to work every day and park it out front, and people'd stop by just to see it, and then of course they'd come in to see *her*, and most of the time they'd have something to eat. I always recommended the fried chicken.

After a while Loretta stopped seeing Don Thomas. She found out he wasn't actually divorced from his wife after all, just separated, and his wife told him she was pregnant and Loretta put two and two together and told him he better find somewhere else to eat fried chicken, if he knew what was good for him. It was around then she got this weird idea for finding her daughter again.

Erika, I really do like the way he did your hair this time. Those red streaks really show off your eyes. With that color eye shadow you look like that actress in *Working Girl*. Doesn't she, Alice Jean? You know, what's-her-name's daughter. Kim Novak. The one married to what's-his-name.

Whoever.

So look at this, Loretta tells me one day at work. She'd been off for two days and drove in but I was in the back checking on the freezer 'cause the freon tube seized up, so I didn't see her drive up. Come on out, I want to show you something.

Well, okay, I said. Just a minute; and then I went outside.

And you know, she had just ruined that car.

It was sky-blue and black, that car, I swear it was the prettiest thing on earth. The TV movie director, she wanted to make it pink but I told her, Come on, you think a man like that would drive a *pink* car? Back then you wouldn't be caught dead in a pink car, less you were a fairy.

THE HAVE-NOTS

Pardon me, can't say that anymore. I mean a gay. But *you* know what I mean, right Alice Jean? Back then regular people did *not* drive pink cars around. This one was sky-blue.

Look at this, Erika—Mojave Turquoise! Since you're a Spring Rose you can wear that. Try this tester here. Alice Jean, that blusher takes ten years off your life, I am serious.

Did I tell you what she did?

All right. What she did was this: she spent that whole weekend off putting stuff on her car. I mean, *stuff*—old headlights painted green and blue and orange, rocking horses she took off their rockers and painted like carousel animals, Barbie dolls, you name it. All these old antennas she got at the dump and covered in foil and colored paper and stuck all over the car like—well, like these antennas stuck all over the car. There was even this Virgin Mary thing she put where a hood ornament would go, I think that was because of Eddie being a Catholic and having the marriage canceled. I mean, it looked *awful*. And I said, Loretta honey, what in god's name have you done to your car?

She got kind of defensive. What do you mean? she said.

What do I *mean?* I said. I *mean* why have you made the car that beautiful man gave you look like it belongs in Ripley's Believe It or Not?

It's *my* car, she said. She was mad but she also looked like she might cry. And I already was one girl short because Jocelyn Reny's son Peter, the older one who's at Fort Bragg now, had unexpectedly fallen off the roof of their house and broken his arm and she had to take him to the hospital. So I couldn't afford for Loretta to go home because she was crying because I insulted her car, which looked like a blind person had decorated it.

So I said, Well, it's very interesting Loretta, that's all. It's very unusual.

She smiled then and walked over to it. She'd put a bicycle wheel over the front grill, and stuck these little Troll dolls all around the edge of the wheel so it looked like a wheel with all these Troll things sticking on it. I mean, how she drove that car to work without getting arrested I don't know.

Thank you, she said. She started braiding one of the Trolls' hair. She was always good at things like that. Probably she should of gone to the Academy of Beauty and studied Cosmetology. That's another reason it was so sad about her little girl.

Really, I said. It's very interesting.

I had to think about the customers.

Thank you, she said again, and she adjusted another part of the front, where she had stuck these Rat Fink key chains and a flamingo like we have in our front yard. Thank you, Terry. I put a lot of work into it.

I didn't know what else to say, but I had to say something so we could end this conversation and get back to work. So I said, Well, they're sure gonna see you coming, Loretta, that's for sure.

I know, she said. That's what I want. That's the whole point. And she patted it like it was something she had just won on *Lets Make a Deal* instead of a car you wouldn't want to see clowns climbing out of at the Fork Union Fair.

She said, People'll see me coming and they'll talk about me, and everyone'll know who is in this car. Even if they've never been to this town, even if they're a complete and total stranger, they'll hear about me and know how to find me.

Then without another word she turned around and went inside, like nothing unusual had happened at all.

Well, I'll tell you, everyone in the tri-state area pretty well, *did* know who owned that car already, because even though it had been a couple years now since she got it Loretta was sort of the town drunk and people knew her 'cause of that. And let's face it, a sky-blue Cadillac that the most famous man in the world gave you as a tip, who could forget about *that*? I mean, some people had forgotten, but then they recognized her for the other reason, so one way or the other Loretta Dooley was not exactly sneaking around Black Spot, Virginia, without somebody knowing about it. So I didn't get why she wanted people to see it was her driving this car that looked like a King Kone on wheels, unless

THE HAVE-NOTS

she wanted to give them the chance to see her coming from about three miles away and stay home if they wanted to.

Later I understood better, how she had this kind of daydream that someday her daughter would figure out who her real mother was and start looking for her. And I guess in Loretta's mind somehow her daughter would hear about the story of what happened and come to Black Spot to find her. And then of course once she was here she'd hear about the lady with this famous car, which on top of everything else now it looks like Woolworth's blew up on it. And so that way she'd be able to find her mama. It was kind of a sad thing, to think Loretta had this crazy old idea and thought junking up her nice car would help things along. But I didn't have time to discuss Loretta's problems right then.

Although to tell you the truth, it did seem to cheer her up some. She was lonely a lot, and sort of quiet. Some people thought she was stuck up, because of the Cadillac, but it wasn't that. It was that Nora Margaret Rule took her baby girl and gave her to perfect strangers when she was only three days old. Up until then Loretta was fine as frog hair. And afterwards, well, she wasn't mean or anything. I mean, she was always nice to the customers and me and everybody, it's not like she was *ever* mean. But you could just sort of tell that maybe she felt like the only good thing that was ever going to happen to her already had, and let's face it, living in a rented Half-Moon trailer down on Delbarton and slinging hash at the Blue Moon is not what anyone wants to spend the rest of their life doing, even if you do own a famous Cadillac.

Which, incidentally, by this time was worth about zero money. All that junk she stuck on it weighed it down, and of course kids started trying to pull off the Rat Fink key chains and the baby dolls, and the antennas got snagged on branches and broke off. And to tell you the absolute truth, Loretta's driving wasn't all that great to begin with, so you can just imagine how that poor car looked after a few years.

He would roll over in his grave if he could see what you've done to his nice car, I told her once.

I'd be surprised there was room in his grave for him to turn in, Loretta said. She never forgave him for getting fat and running around on his wife and those other nasty things. Truth was, I think she never forgave him for not coming back and getting her and taking her the hell out of Black Spot.

Besides, why should he care, she sniffled. He never really gave a shit about me. It was just a publicity stunt, like Don said.

She really started crying then. He did tell her that once, Don Thomas did. I thought it was a real mean thing for him to say to her. Loretta is a *very* sensitive person.

Oh, honey, that's not true, I told her. I was trying to fix that damn freezer again and she'd stayed late, to keep me company and also 'cause her license had been suspended and she didn't want Sergeant Merdeck to see her driving. She thought in the dark he wouldn't be able to tell it was her but there was no way you could sneak that thing around, no way. Plus she'd had a few. I didn't say anything, but I could tell.

What?

Well, Alice Jean, all I can say is, if anyone ever had a good reason to drink, it was Loretta Dooley. I know some people do it just for fun. I cut back except for cookouts and parties sometimes. It just *ruins* your skin.

Why, thank you, Erika. I got it last quarter, for being Mary Rose's Most Improved Salesperson in the Southern Mid-Atlantic Area. Ken Senior gave me the gold chain for our anniversary so it's sort of double special. The Mary Rose Cadillac is the same color, only kind of darker, sort of more purple. It's got whitewalls, too. I could have the first one in the Southern Mid-Atlantic, if I get it.

Doesn't that Aloe Vera feel nice, Alice Jean? I keep it in the fridge—makes it sort of a treat to get burned!

Anyway, as I was saying, Loretta was pretty upset that night. I guess it had just all sort of gotten her depressed. It was right after they shut down the Merriam Brick Plant in Petrol, and at the Blue Moon everybody's hours were cut back, not that we were making any money to begin with. That was when I first started thinking about working for

THE HAVE-NOTS

myself. Plus her landlord had given her notice, they were developing that part of Delbarton and he just figured he'd cash in, I guess. But I was only trying to be nice to her, cheer her up.

It's not true, Loretta, I told her. I think he really meant it to be a nice thing. I think he truly appreciated the service you gave him.

Well, you are wrong, Terry Westerburgh, she said. You are wrong, 'cause he just did not give a shit, about me or anyone else. Her eyes got this kind of look sometimes when she was drinking, like if you were made of paper they would just burn you up. She crumpled her Dixie cup and threw it on the floor and said, There are two kinds of people in this world, the Haves and the Have-Nots. And I am a Have-Not, and you know what *he* was.

Well, I got sort of P.O.'d then. I mean, here I was on my hands and knees, trying to fix that damn refrigerator, and it wasn't like Ken didn't have to work nights at Big Jim's Barbeque just so we'd get by, and here she was throwing Dixie cups on the floor like she was the Queen of Sheba.

Now you listen to me, *Miss* Dooley, I said. I was pretty aggravated. He worked for everything he ever got, that man did, he was poor as dirt when he started and until the day he died he never forgot where he came from. *That's* why he gave you that car. But you just go ahead and listen to Don Thomas if you want and see where it gets you.

I see where it got me, she said, too mad herself by now to even care who it was she was talking to, Number One, her oldest friend Terry Westerburgh, Number Two, her boss. It got me a shitty job I can't even work enough hours to make my rent. If I had a place to rent, which I don't.

Well, then you just see if you can find another place where you'll be happier, Miss Potty-mouth, I said, and I slammed the refrigerator shut and stomped out.

I was so mad. I shouldn't have to put up with that kind of talk. That was when I decided I was going to really have my own business someday, not work for some person who owns a diner. Sort of the first step towards working for Mary Rose Cosmetics, only of course I didn't know that then.

Erika honey, I know you would love it. You can set your own hours, sleep late as you want, plus you get all your makeup free! And you-know-who would like *that*!

But you know I felt terrible about five minutes after yelling at her. I went into the back room, but she was gone. I heard her leaving, that poor old car scraping along the ground like some dog that got run over. It's funny but I even had started to like that car in a way. I mean it really *did* get your attention. The kids loved it. We got so we'd save old toys, dolls and things, and parts from Ken's Buick and the lawnmower, and I'd bring them over and give them to Loretta and they'd all end up on her car. She had this giant Mr. Potato Head she put on the roof and these colored tennis balls she stuck on all the antennas and really, it was a hoot. Plus her nephew had rigged up some kind of lights that blinked all around the rearview window and Jocelyn's son Peter gave her this funny moose horn she could honk. It was really from the football team but none of us was supposed to know that.

I went outside but it was too late. I really felt terrible. Like Ann Landers says, you should always make your words sweet, 'cause you never know when you'll have to eat them. If I had to eat my words right then I would have thrown up. And so right then I decided to quit the Blue Moon. If it was making me into this mean unkind person, well, then it wasn't the job for me.

Alice Jean, you should kind of dab that Aloe Vera stuff off now, I think, honey, otherwise your pores turn a funny color. Here, use this—these are specially formulated for removing deep-down dirt and grime. Doesn't it smell refreshing!

Okay, this is the good part now. So Loretta is gone, and I felt real bad. I felt guilty, too, because I knew she'd had a few and all I could think of was her and her famous car going off the bridge into the reservoir. I thought of calling Bud Merdeck but then I thought, well, Loretta's not going to feel any better spending the night in the drunk tank, so I decided I'd go after her. She was supposed to get all moved out the next day, she was supposed to have started packing stuff that night. Her sister was going to let her stay

THE HAVE-NOTS

with her until she found another place. And you know, she really was in a tight spot, because where are you going to find a decent place to live on what you make working fifteen hours a week at the Blue Moon?

So I got in my car and drove to her house. It was dark by then, and a bad night. It had been raining off and on and now it had finally stopped but it was so foggy, I drove with my low beams on the whole way. Once I even slowed down and opened the window and stuck my head out, 'cause I couldn't see otherwise.

You know where she used to live. Where those Hunters Glen condos are now. That used to be all fields, just these three mobile homes that Gus Brinzer used to rent out. Loretta had the nicest one but that's not saying much. After they sold them they found out the Hell's Angels used one of the others to make LSD in.

Well, I finally got there, but there was nobody home. I would've let myself in but when I peeked in the windows I saw all these boxes, and stuff thrown around everywhere, and—well, to tell you the truth, it was a terrible mess. I mean, it looked like the Hell's Angels had been living *there*. And I knew then, things were worse with Loretta than I'd known. I mean, here she was, my oldest friend plus I was her supervisor, but I just had no idea. If I'd known I would've done something, she had a lot of friends, really, but I just had no idea at all.

So I waited outside. There was a kind of metal stairs in front of the trailer but that was broken so I sat on my car. I was there for a long time. It was cold, the fog was real damp and just sank into you after a while. I was starting to worry, too; I mean I was starting to get so worried I was afraid I'd start to scream, thinking of all the horrible things that might've happened to Loretta and I was nasty to her. I was just getting ready to let myself in and call Ken, when I heard somebody walking down the road.

I turned around and it was her. She looked awful, like when you see movies and there's people been in a car wreck. There was no blood or anything but she was wet and her hair was wet and she had mud on her face and oh, I just screamed and ran over and started hugging her.

Loretta, thank god you're all right! What happened?

She made a noise like she was embarrassed and then she started to cry. I wrecked it, she said. I put my arms around her, I didn't even care I had already changed out of my uniform. She said, I went down Lee Highway and rolled it into the reservoir.

Oh, my god! I said. You could have killed yourself, Loretta!

I know, she said. I had to swim out. It's in there so deep they'll never get it out. She really started crying then.

Why'd you do *that*? I said and started crying, too, but I stopped. I only had one clean tissue left, and I gave it to her.

Because it doesn't matter, she said. My whole life and nothing matters. I live *here*—she bent and picked up a rock and threw it and broke a window, I heard it—in this *dump*, and now I don't even live here anymore. I had a husband and a baby for three days, and twenty-seven years ago someone famous gave me a goddamn Cadillac as a tip, and that's it. That's my whole life. That's it, Terry. My whole life is right there.

Well, you know I wished I could of said something to her, but she was right. That was her whole life, right there.

I just wish I could've kept my baby, she said. She was crying so I could hardly hear what she said. If they'd of left me my baby girl I would've felt like I had something. Like you have Ken and Little Kenny. I would have had Eloise.

I started crying again then, too. I mean, god! It was just so *sad*. So then we sat for a little while but we didn't say anything. It was all just too depressing.

But after a while I started to think, Well, we have got to do something, we can't sit here all night in the mud, and I thought maybe I'd call Ken and see was it okay if Loretta came back with me and could stay at our house. I was just thinking of standing up and asking Loretta was it okay if I went inside to use the phone, when we heard it. It had started raining again, a little, and we had sat on that broken step in front of the trailer, 'cause there's an awning there.

Loretta stood up first. Oh, my god, she said. Shit.

THE HAVE-NOTS

I listened and stood, too. Shit, I said.

It was her car. That was obvious, I mean you couldn't mistake that car for anything else in the world. It sounded like it was having trouble getting over the last hill, where it was always overgrown and muddy anyway. And you figure a car that was in the bottom of the reservoir, it probably wouldn't run too well.

Shit, Loretta said again. That's it.

I knew just what she meant. I was thinking that Bud Merdeck had found it somehow and gotten Lynnwood Gentry to tow it out, and now how was Loretta going to pay for it, not to mention they could have arrested her, probably, for rolling a car into the reservoir on purpose. Especially that car.

And then it made this grinding nose, and suddenly it popped over the rise. The headlights were on, at least one of them was. The wheel that used to have the Trolls on it and now had this Big Bird sort of tied to it was all bent up and the antennas were all mashed together. Whoever was driving it tried to honk the moose horn but it hardly made a noise at all. It was just about the saddest car you ever saw.

Loretta and I looked at each other and she rubbed at her face, trying to get some of the mud off.

We better go see who it is, I whispered. If it's Lynnwood I'll call Ken and he'll talk to him.

Thank you, Terry, she said. She knew that was my way of making up with her.

We started walking to the car, slowly because of the rain and it was sloppy going. The car had stopped at the edge of the drive and waited with the motor running. It didn't sound too good either. Maybe better than you'd expect, but it was pretty sad, to think that car had come to this. As we walked up to it the door on the passenger side popped open.

Hello? It was this woman's voice, nobody we knew.

Hi, I said. I stopped, wondering if maybe Lynnwood brought along his girlfriend Donna. He stays at the shop all night sometimes and on weekends she usually keeps him company.

But it wasn't Donna. It wasn't anybody that I recognized at all. This short woman, with dyed blonde hair. She stepped out of the car, jumping over the water. She had on nice clothes, not expensive or designer clothes but like a secretary's clothes, like she hadn't changed from work yet. She had a nice smile, and nice eyes—I know you wouldn't think you'd notice something like that in the dark but I did, I have a good eye for things like that. Mary Rose says that a great saleswoman needs an eye for detail.

Are you—? The woman started to say something, then she turned around and leaned back into the car, like she was asking the driver something. Then she turned around again and said, Is one of you Loretta Dooley?

That's me, said Loretta. She had this squinched-up tone. I knew she was nervous they were going to ask, Have you been drinking?

Instead the girl says, My name is Noreen Marcus.

Marcus? Loretta says.

That's right, says the girl. She glances back at the car, sort of nervously, but then it was like whoever was inside told her it was okay, so she goes on.

Noreen Marcus. My parents are Lowell and Angeline Marcus, in Richmond. I hitchhiked here. This man gave me a ride out by the reservoir. I'm your daughter.

My daughter? Loretta says, and *I'm* saying, Your *who*?

Ye-es—

And the girl stepped forward, holding up her skirt so it wouldn't get wet, and then she looked up, and it was like for the first time she got a good look at Loretta in the headlight. 'Cause she suddenly gave this scream and started laughing, and dropped her purse in the water and ran across and I started running, too, next to Loretta, only then at the last minute I stopped because I thought, Now wait a minute, this is something very special going on here between Loretta and this young woman who is her daughter, and so I stayed and waited a little while until they calmed down.

THE HAVE-NOTS

Well, Alice Jean, I knew it was her because she had Eddie Rule's eyes and his smile. He may have been a poor father but he did have a nice smile.

And so for a little while there was some crying and laughing and you can just imagine how we all felt. And all the while that old car just sat there, though whoever was inside turned the motor off after a while and smoked a cigarette. There was no radio in it but you could hear him sort of humming to himself.

And finally Loretta said, Well, for god's sakes let's go inside, we're getting soaked.

Well, wait a minute while I get my bag, said Noreen.

She went back to the car and stuck her head in and said something to whoever was in there.

Okay, now this is when I got goosebumps.

Because I couldn't hear what he was saying—it was too far away, and it wasn't like I wanted to eavesdrop or anything. I guess I sort of expected it must be old Eddie Rule inside. But now I could definitely hear his voice, and it wasn't Eddie Rule's voice at all. It was—

Well, *you* know whose voice it was.

Loretta knew, too. She stood by me with her arms crossed, shivering, and when she heard him she turned to me and opened her mouth and for a minute there I thought she was going to faint.

Oh, my god, she said, oh, my *god*—

Thank you for the ride, I heard Noreen yelling at him, and I could just barely make out his voice saying something back to her, goodbye I guess, something like that. Then she pulled this suitcase out of the car and stood back while it backed up.

Loretta! I said, elbowing her and then pulling her to me. Loretta, hurry up! Tell him thank you—

And she yelled, Thank you, thank you! and then she started running after the car, yelling and waving like she was crazy. Which we all were by then, all of us yelling and waving at him and laughing like we'd known each other all this time, when it'd really only been, like, five minutes. And the car just kept backing up 'til it got over the top of the hill, and then

I guess he turned it around and drove off. And that was the last time anybody ever saw Loretta's famous Cadillac.

Afterwards we went inside and kind of dried off and then on the way to my house we stopped at Big Jim's and got a half-dozen Specials and went home. The Specials were so Ken Senior wouldn't be too mad about me being out so late.

And so that's how it happened. Next day of course the story got out, because there is no way, just no way, you can keep something like that a secret. Noreen says she thinks it was just a coincidence, she says everybody out here in Black Spot looks like him and who could tell the difference? Plus she said if it was really him wouldn't he have been in a fancy limousine, not some crazy fixed-up car her real mother drove into the reservoir.

But *I* said, Well, that's how you know it was really him. 'Cause it's like Loretta said, there's the Haves and there's the Have-Nots, and if you're a Have-Not you never forget what it's like to be poor and on your own. I mean how could he have sung "Heartbreak Hotel" otherwise? Noreen said, Well, I still have my doubts, but when she and her mama went on Oprah they played it up for all they could, I can tell you that. And like the TV movie director says, it doesn't really matter, does it? Because it's such a good story.

And I mean there's Noreen reunited with Loretta to prove it, not to mention how would you ever get a car like that out of the reservoir, *plus* where is that car now, I ask you? Because I saw it, too, and I hadn't had a thing to drink.

What do I think? Well, Erika honey, I guess it's just one of those things. Strange things happen sometimes and you just got to take the good with the bad, is all. But you won't hear me complaining about how it all turned out, not as long as business stays this good and I get that new Mary Rose Cadillac in the fall, no ma'am.

The Maiden Flight
of McCauley's *Bellerophon*

BEING ASSIGNED to The Head for eight hours was the worst security shift you could pull at the museum. Even now, thirty years later, Robbie had dreams in which he wandered from the Early Flight gallery to Balloons & Airships to Cosmic Soup, where he once again found himself alone in the dark, staring into the bland gaze of the famous scientist as he intoned his endless lecture about the nature of the universe.

"Remember when we thought nothing could be worse than that?" Robbie stared wistfully into his empty glass, then signaled the waiter for another bourbon and Coke. Across the table, his old friend Emery sipped a beer.

"I liked The Head," said Emery. He cleared his throat and began to recite in the same portentous tone the famous scientist had employed. "'Trillions and trillions of galaxies in which our own is but a mote of cosmic dust.' It made you think."

"It made you think about killing yourself," said Robbie. "Do you want to know how many times I heard that?"

"A trillion?"

"Five thousand." The waiter handed Robbie a drink, his fourth. "Twenty-five times an hour, times eight hours a day, times five days a week, times five months."

"Five thousand, that's not so much. Especially when you think of all those trillions of galleries. I mean galaxies. Only five months? I thought you worked there longer."

"Just that summer. It only seemed like forever."

Emery knocked back his beer. "A long time ago, in a gallery far, far away," he intoned, not for the first time.

Thirty years before, the Museum of American Aviation and Aerospace had just opened. Robbie was nineteen that summer, a recent dropout from the University of Maryland, living in a group house in Mount Rainier. Employment opportunities were scarce; making $3.40 an hour as a security aide at the Smithsonian's newest museum seemed preferable to bagging groceries at Giant Food. Every morning he'd punch his time card in the guards' locker room and change into his uniform. Then he'd duck outside to smoke a joint before trudging downstairs for morning meeting and that day's assignments.

Most of the security guards were older than Robbie, with backgrounds in the military and an eye on future careers with the D.C. Police Department or FBI. Still, they tolerated him with mostly good-natured ribbing about his longish hair and bloodshot eyes. All except for Hedge, the security chief. He was an enormous man with a shaved head who sat, knitting, behind a bank of closed-circuit video monitors, observing tourists and guards with an expression of amused contempt.

"What are you making?" Robbie once asked. Hedge raised his hands to display an intricately-patterned baby blanket. "Hey, that's cool. Where'd you learn to knit?"

"Prison." Hedge's eyes narrowed. "You stoned again, Opie? That's it. Gallery Seven. Relieve Jones."

Robbie's skin went cold, then hot with relief when he realized Hedge wasn't going to fire him. "Seven? Uh, yeah, sure, sure. For how long?"

"Forever," said Hedge.

"Oh, man, you got The Head." Jones clapped his hands gleefully when Robbie arrived. "Better watch your ass, kids'll throw shit at you," he said, and sauntered off.

THE MAIDEN FLIGHT OF McCAULEY'S *BELLEROPHON*

Two projectors at opposite ends of the dark room beamed twin shafts of silvery light onto a head-shaped Styrofoam form. Robbie could never figure out if they'd filmed the famous scientist just once, or if they'd gone to the trouble to shoot him from two different angles.

However they'd done it, the sight of the disembodied Head was surprisingly effective: it looked like a hologram floating amid the hundreds of back-projected twinkly stars that covered the walls and ceiling. The creep factor was intensified by the stilted, slightly puzzled manner in which the Head blinked as it droned on, as though the famous scientist had just realized his body was gone, and was hoping no one else would notice. Once, when he was really stoned, Robbie swore that the Head deviated from its script.

"What'd it say?" asked Emery. At the time he was working in the General Aviation Gallery, operating a flight simulator that tourists clambered into for three-minute rides.

"Something about peaches," said Robbie. "I couldn't understand, it sort of mumbled."

Every morning, Robbie stood outside the entrance to Cosmic Soup and watched as tourists streamed through the main entrance and into the Hall of Flight. Overhead, legendary aircraft hung from the ceiling. The 1903 Wright Flyer with its Orville mannequin; a Lilienthal glider; the Bell X-1 in which Chuck Yeager broke the sound barrier. From a huge pit in the center of the Hall rose a Minuteman III ICBM, rust-colored stains still visible where a protester had tossed a bucket of pig's blood on it a few months earlier. Directly above the entrance to Robbie's gallery dangled the Spirit of St. Louis. The aides who worked upstairs in the planetarium amused themselves by shooting paperclips onto its wings.

Robbie winced at the memory. He gulped what was left of his bourbon and sighed. "That was a long time ago."

"Tempus fugit, baby. Thinking of which—" Emery dug into his pocket for a Blackberry. "Check this out. From Leonard."

Robbie rubbed his eyes blearily, then read.

From: l.scopes@MAAA.SI.edu
Subject: Tragic Illness
Date: April 6, 7:58:22 PM EDT
To: emeryubergeek@gmail.com

Dear Emery,

    I just learned that our Maggie Blevin is very ill. I wrote her at Christmas but never heard back. Fuad El-Hajj says she was diagnosed with advanced breast cancer last fall. Prognosis is not good. She is still in the Fayetteville area, and I gather is in a hospice. I want to make a visit though not sure how that will go over. I have something I want to give her but need to talk to you about it.

    L.

"Ahhh." Robbie sighed. "God, that's terrible."
"Yeah. I'm sorry. But I figured you'd want to know."
Robbie pinched the bridge of his nose. Four years earlier, his wife, Anna, had died of breast cancer, leaving him adrift in a grief so profound it was as though he'd been poisoned, as though his veins had been pumped with the same chemicals that had failed to save her. Anna had been an oncology nurse, a fact that at first afforded some meager black humor, but in the end deprived them of even the faintest of false hopes borne of denial or faith in alternative therapies.

There was no time for any of that. Zach, their son, had just turned twelve. Between his own grief and Zach's subsequent acting-out, Robbie got so depressed that he started pouring his first bourbon and coke before the boy left for school. Two years later, he got fired from his job with the County Parks Commission.

He now worked in the shipping department at Small's, an off-price store in a desolate shopping mall that resembled the ruins of a regional airport. Robbie found it oddly consoling. It reminded him of the museum. The same generic atriums and industrial carpeting; the same bleak sunlight filtered through clouded glass; the same vacant-faced people trudging from Dollar Store to SunGlass Hut, the way they'd wandered from the General Aviation Gallery to Cosmic Soup.

"Poor Maggie." Robbie returned the Blackberry. "I haven't thought of her in years."

"I'm going to see Leonard."

"When? Maybe I'll go with you."

"Now." Emery shoved a twenty under his beer bottle and stood. "You're coming with me."

"What?"

"You can't drive—you're snackered. Get popped again, you lose your license."

"Popped? Who's getting popped? And I'm not snackered, I'm—" Robbie thought. "Snockered. You pronounced it wrong."

"Whatever." Emery grabbed Robbie's shoulder and pushed him to the door. "Let's go."

Emery drove an expensive hybrid that could get from Rockville to Utica, New York on a single tank of gas. The vanity plate read MARVO and was flanked by bumper stickers with messages like GUNS DON'T KILL PEOPLE: TYPE 2 PHASERS KILL PEOPLE and FRAK OFF! as well as several slogans that Emery said were in Klingon.

Emery was the only person Robbie knew who was somewhat famous. Back in the early 1980s, he'd created a local-access cable TV show called Captain Marvo's Secret Spacetime, taped in his parents' basement and featuring Emery in an aluminum foil costume behind the console of a cardboard spaceship. Captain Marvo watched videotaped episodes of low-budget 1950s science fiction serials with titles like PAYLOAD: MOONDUST while bantering with his co-pilot, a homemade puppet made by Leonard, named Mungbean.

The show was pretty funny if you were stoned. Captain Marvo became a cult hit, and then a real hit when a major network picked it up as a late-night offering. Emery quit his day job at the museum and rented studio time in Baltimore. He sold the rights after a few years, and was immediately replaced by a flashy actor in Lurex and a glittering robot sidekick. The show limped along for a season then died. Emery's fans claimed this was because their slacker hero had been sidelined.

But maybe it was just that people weren't as stoned as they used to be. These days the program had a surprising afterlife on the internet, where Robbie's son Zach watched it with his friends, and Emery did a brisk business selling memorabilia through his official Captain Marvo website.

It took them nearly an hour to get into D.C. and find a parking space near the Mall, by which time Robbie had sobered up enough to wish he'd stayed at the bar.

"Here." Emery gave him a sugarless breath mint, then plucked at the collar of Robbie's shirt, acid-green with SMALLS embroidered in purple. "Christ, Robbie, you're a freaking mess."

He reached into the back seat, retrieved a black t-shirt from his gym bag. "Here, put this on."

Robbie changed into it and stumbled out onto the sidewalk. It was mid-April but already steamy; the air shimmered above the pavement and smelled sweetly of apple blossom and coolant from innumerable air conditioners. Only as he approached the Museum entrance and caught his reflection in a glass wall did Robbie see that his t-shirt was emblazoned with Emery's youthful face and foil helmet above the words O CAPTAIN MY CAPTAIN.

"You wear your own t-shirt?" he asked as he followed Emery through the door.

"Only at the gym. Nothing else was clean."

They waited at the security desk while a guard checked their IDs, called upstairs to Leonard's office, signed them in and took their pictures before finally issuing each a Visitor's Pass.

"You'll have to wait for Leonard to escort you upstairs," the guard said.

THE MAIDEN FLIGHT OF McCAULEY'S *BELLEROPHON*

"Not like the old days, huh, Robbie?" Emery draped an arm around Robbie and steered him into the Hall of Flight. "Not a lot of retinal scanning on your watch."

The museum hadn't changed much. The same aircraft and space capsules gleamed overhead. Tourists clustered around the lucite pyramid that held slivers of moon rock. Sunburned guys sporting military haircuts and tattoos peered at a mockup of an F-15 flight deck. Everything had that old museum smell: soiled carpeting, machine oil, the wet-laundry odor wafting from steam tables in the public cafeteria.

But The Head was long gone. Robbie wondered if anyone even remembered the famous scientist, dead for many years. The General Aviation Gallery, where Emery and Leonard had operated the flight simulators and first met Maggie Blevin, was now devoted to Personal Flight, with models of jetpacks worn by alarmingly lifelike mannequins.

"Leonard designed those." Emery paused to stare at a child-sized figure who seemed to float above a solar-powered skateboard. "He could have gone to Hollywood."

"It's not too late."

Robbie and Emery turned to see their old colleague behind them.

"Leonard," said Emery.

The two men embraced. Leonard stepped back and tilted his head. "Robbie. I wasn't expecting you."

"Surprise," said Robbie. They shook hands awkwardly. "Good to see you, man."

Leonard forced a smile. "And you."

They headed toward the staff elevator. Back in the day, Leonard's hair had been long and luxuriantly blond. It fell unbound down the back of the dogshit-yellow uniform jacket, designed to evoke an airline pilot's, that he and Emery and the other General Aviation aides wore as they gave their spiel to tourists eager to yank on the controls of their Link Trainers. With his patrician good looks and stern gray eyes, Leonard was the only aide who actually resembled a real pilot.

Now he looked like a cross between Obi-Wan Kenobi and Willie Nelson. His hair was white, and hung in two braids that reached almost to his waist. Instead of the crappy polyester uniform, he wore a white linen tunic, a necklace of unpolished turquoise and coral, loose black trousers tucked into scuffed cowboy boots, and a skull earring the size of Robbie's thumb. On his collar gleamed the cheap knock-off pilot's wings that had once adorned his museum uniform jacket. Leonard had always taken his duties very seriously, especially after Margaret Blevin arrived as the museum's first Curator of Proto-Flight. Robbie's refusal to do the same, even long after he'd left the museum himself, had resulted in considerable friction between them over the intervening years.

Robbie cleared his throat. "So, uh. What are you working on these days?" He wished he wasn't wearing Emery's idiotic t-shirt.

"I'll show you," said Leonard.

Upstairs, they headed for the old photo lab, now an imaging center filled with banks of computers, digital cameras, scanners.

"We still process film there," Leonard said as they walked down a corridor hung with production photos from *The Day the Earth Stood Still* and *Frau Im Mond*. "Negatives, old motion picture stock—people still send us things."

"Any of it interesting?" asked Emery.

Leonard shrugged. "Sometimes. You never know what you might find. That's part of Maggie's legacy—we're always open to the possibility of discovering something new."

Robbie shut his eyes. Leonard's voice made his teeth ache. "Remember how she used to keep a bottle of Scotch in that side drawer, underneath her purse?" he said.

Leonard frowned, but Emery laughed. "Yeah! And it was good stuff, too."

"Maggie had a great deal of class," said Leonard in a somber tone.

You pompous asshole, thought Robbie.

Leonard punched a code into a door and opened it. "You might remember when this was a storage cupboard."

They stepped inside. Robbie did remember this place—he'd once had sex here with a General Aviation aide whose name he'd long forgotten. It had been a good-sized supply room then, with an odd, sweetish scent from the rolls of film stacked along the shelves.

Now it was a very crowded office. The shelves were crammed with books and curatorial reports dating back to 1981, and archival boxes holding god knows what—Leonard's original government job application, maybe. A coat had been tossed onto the floor in one corner. There was a large metal desk covered with bottles of nail polish, an ancient swivel chair that Robbie vaguely remembered having been deployed during his lunch hour tryst.

Mostly, though, the room held Leonard's stuff: tiny cardboard dioramas, mockups of space capsules and dirigibles. It smelled overpoweringly of nail polish. It was also extremely cold.

"Man, you must freeze your ass off." Robbie rubbed his arms.

Emery picked up one of the little bottles. "You getting a manicurist's license?"

Leonard gestured at the desk. "I'm painting with nail polish now. You get some very unusual effects."

"I bet," said Robbie. "You're, like huffing nail polish." He peered at the shelves, impressed despite himself. "Jeez, Leonard. You made all these?"

"Damn right I did."

When Robbie first met Leonard, they were both lowly GS-1s. In those days, Leonard collected paper clips and rode an old Schwinn bicycle to work. He entertained tourists by making balloon animals. In his spare time, he created Mungbean, Captain Marvo's robot friend, out of a busted lamp and some spark plugs.

He also made strange ink drawings, hundreds of them. Montgolfier balloons with sinister faces; B-52s carrying payloads of soap bubbles; caricatures of the museum director and senior curators as greyhounds sniffing each others' nether quarters.

It was this last, drawn on a scrap of legal paper, which Margaret Blevin picked up on her first tour of the General Aviation Gallery. The sketch had fallen out of Leonard's jacket: he watched in horror as the museum's deputy director stooped to retrieve the crumpled page.

"Allow me," said the woman at the director's side. She was slight, forty-ish, with frizzy red hair and enormous hoop earrings, wearing an indian-print tunic over tight, sky-blue trousers and leather clogs. She snatched up the drawing, stuffed it in her pocket and continued her tour of the gallery. After the deputy director left, the woman walked to where Leonard stood beside his flight simulator, sweating in his polyester jacket as he supervised an overweight kid in a Chewbacca t-shirt. When the kid climbed down, the woman held up the crumpled sheet.

"Who did this?"

The other two aides—one was Emery—shook their heads.

"I did," said Leonard.

The woman crooked her finger. "Come with me."

"Am I fired?" asked Leonard as he followed her out of the gallery.

"Nope. I'm Maggie Blevin. We're shutting down those Link Trainers and making this into a new gallery. I'm in charge. I need someone to start cataloging stuff for me and maybe do some preliminary sketches. You want the job?"

"Yes," stammered Leonard. "I mean, sure."

"Great." She balled up the sketch and tossed it into a wastebasket. "Your talents were being wasted. That looks just like the director's butt."

"If he was a dog," said Leonard.

"He's a son of a bitch, and that's close enough," said Maggie. "Let's go see Personnel."

Leonard's current job description read Museum Effects Specialist, Grade 9, Step 10. For the last two decades, he'd created figurines and models for the museum's exhibits. Not fighter planes or commercial aircraft—there was an entire division of modelers who handled that.

Leonard's work was more rarefied, as evidenced by the dozens of flying machines perched wherever there was space in the tiny room. Rocket ships, bat-winged aerodromes, biplanes and triplanes and saucers, many of them striped and polka-dotted and glazed with, yes, nail polish in circus colors, so that they appeared to be made of ribbon candy.

THE MAIDEN FLIGHT OF McCAULEY'S *BELLEROPHON*

His specialty was aircraft that had never actually flown; in many instances, aircraft that had never been intended to fly. Crypto-aviation, as some disgruntled curator dubbed it. He worked from plans and photographs, drawings and uncategorizable materials he'd found in the archives Maggie Blevin had been hired to organize. These were housed in a set of oak filing cabinets dating to the 1920s. Officially, the archive was known as the Pre-Langley Collection. But everyone in the museum, including Maggie Blevin, called it the Nut Files.

After Leonard's fateful promotion, Robbie and Emery would sometimes punch out for the day, go upstairs and stroll to his corner of the library. You could do that then—wander around workrooms and storage areas, the library and archives, without having to check in or get a special pass or security clearance. Robbie just went along for the ride, but Emery was fascinated by the things Leonard found in the Nut Files. Grainy black-and-white photos of purported UFOs; typescripts of encounters with deceased Russian cosmonauts in the Nevada desert; an account of a Raelian wedding ceremony attended by a glowing crimson orb. There was also a large carton donated by the widow of a legendary rocket scientist, which turned out to be filled with 1950s foot fetish pornography, and 16-millimeter film footage of several Pioneers of Flight doing something unseemly with a spotted pig.

"Whatever happened to that pig movie?" asked Robbie as he admired a biplane with violet-striped ailerons.

"It's been de-accessioned," said Leonard.

He cleared the swivel chair and motioned for Emery to sit, then perched on the edge of his desk. Robbie looked in vain for another chair, finally settled on the floor beside a wastebasket filled with empty nail polish bottles.

"So I have a plan," announced Leonard. He stared fixedly at Emery, as though they were alone in the room. "To help Maggie. Do you remember the *Bellerophon*?"

Emery frowned. "Vaguely. That old film loop of a plane crash?"

"*Presumed* crash. They never found any wreckage, everyone just assumes it crashed. But yes, that was the *Bellerophon*—it was the clip that played in our gallery. Maggie's gallery."

"Right—the movie that burned up!" broke in Robbie. "Yeah, I remember, the film got caught in a sprocket or something. Smoke detectors went off and they evacuated the whole museum. They got all on Maggie's case about it, they thought she installed it wrong."

"She didn't." Leonard said angrily. "One of the tech guys screwed up the installation—he told me a few years ago. He didn't vent it properly, the projector bulb overheated and the film caught on fire. He said he always felt bad she got canned."

"But they didn't fire her for that." Robbie gave Leonard a sideways look. "It was the UFO—"

Emery cut him off. "They were gunning for her," he said. "C'mon, Rob, everyone knew—all those old military guys running this place, they couldn't stand a woman getting in their way. Not if she wasn't Air Force or some shit. Took 'em a few years, that's all. Fucking assholes. I even got a letter-writing campaign going on the show. Didn't help."

"Nothing would have helped." Leonard sighed. "She was a visionary. She *is* a visionary," he added hastily. "Which is why I want to do this—"

He hopped from the desk, rooted around in a corner and pulled out a large cardboard box.

"Move," he ordered.

Robbie scrambled to his feet. Leonard began to remove things from the carton and set them carefully on his desk. Emery got up to make more room, angling himself beside Robbie. They watched as Leonard arranged piles of paper, curling 8x10s, faded blueprints and an old 35mm film viewer, along with several large manila envelopes closed with red string. Finally he knelt beside the box and very gingerly reached inside.

"I think the Lindbergh baby's in there," whispered Emery.

Leonard stood, cradling something in his hands, turned and placed it in the middle of the desk.

"Holy shit." Emery whistled. "Leonard, you've outdone yourself."

Robbie crouched so he could view it at eye level: a model of some sort of flying machine, though it seemed impossible that anyone, even Leonard or Maggie Blevin, could ever have dreamed it might fly. It had a zeppelin-shaped body, with a sharp nose like that of a Lockheed Starfighter, slightly uptilted. Suspended beneath this was a basket filled with tiny gears and chains, and beneath that was a contraption with three wheels, like a velocipede, only the wheels were fitted with dozens of stiff flaps, each no bigger than a fingernail, and even tinier propellers.

And everywhere, there were wings, sprouting from every inch of the craft's body in an explosion of canvas and balsa and paper and gauze. Bird-shaped wings, bat-shaped wings; square wings like those of a box-kite, elevators and hollow cones of wire; long tubes that, when Robbie peered inside them, were filled with baffles and flaps. Ailerons and struts ran between them to form a dizzying grid, held together with fine gold thread and monofilament and what looked like human hair. Every bit of it was painted in brilliant shades of violet and emerald, scarlet and fuchsia and gold, and here and there shining objects were set into the glossy surface: minute shards of mirror or colored glass; a beetle carapace; flecks of mica.

Above it all, springing from the fuselage like the cap of an immense toadstool, was a feathery parasol made of curved bamboo and multi-colored silk.

It was like gazing at the Wright Flyer through a kaleidoscope.

"That's incredible!" Robbie exclaimed. "How'd you do that?"

"Now we just have to see if it flies," said Leonard.

Robbie straightened. "How the hell can that thing fly?"

"The original flew." Leonard leaned against the wall. "My theory is, if we can replicate the same conditions—the *exact same* conditions—it will work."

"But." Robbie glanced at Emery. "The original didn't fly. It crashed. I mean, presumably."

Emery nodded. "Plus there was a guy in it. McCartney—"

"McCauley," said Leonard.

"Right, McCauley. And you know, Leonard, no one's gonna fit in that, right?" Emery shot him an alarmed look. "You're not thinking of making a full-scale model, are you? Because that would be completely insane."

"No." Leonard fingered the skull plug in his earlobe. "I'm going to make another film—I'm going to replicate the original, and I'm going to do it so perfectly that Maggie won't even realize it's *not* the original. I've got it all worked out." He looked at Emery. "I can shoot it on digital, if you'll lend me a camera. That way I can edit it on my laptop. And then I'm going to bring it down to Fayetteville so she can see it."

Robbie and Emery glanced at each other. "Well, it's not completely insane," said Robbie.

"But Maggie knows the original was destroyed," said Emery. "I mean, I was there, I remember—she saw it. We all saw it. She has cancer, right? Not Alzheimer's or dementia or, I dunno, amnesia."

"Why don't you just Photoshop something?" asked Robbie. "You could tell her it was an homage. That way—"

Leonard's glare grew icy. "It is not an homage. I am going to Cowana Island, just like McCauley did, and I am going to recreate the maiden flight of the *Bellerophon*. I am going to film it, I am going to edit it. And when it's completed, I'm going to tell Maggie that I found a dupe in the archives. Her heart broke when that footage burned up. I'm going to give it back to her."

Robbie stared at his shoe, so Leonard wouldn't see his expression. After a moment he said, "When Anna was sick, I wanted to do that. Go back to this place by Mount Washington where we stayed before Zach was born. We had all these great photos of us canoeing there, it was so beautiful. But it was winter, and I said we should wait and go in the summer."

"I'm not waiting." Leonard sifted through the papers on his desk. "I have these—"

He opened a manila envelope and withdrew several glassine sleeves. He examined one, then handed it to Emery.

"This is what survived of the original footage, which in fact was *not* the original footage—the original was shot in 1901, on cellulose nitrate film. That's what Maggie and I found when we first started going through the Nut Files. Only of course nitrate stock is like a ticking time bomb. So the Photo Lab duped it onto safety film, which is what you're looking at."

Emery held the film to the light. Robbie stood beside him, squinting. Five frames, in shades of amber and tortoiseshell, with blurred images that might have been bushes or clouds or smoke damage, for all Robbie could see.

Emery asked, "How many frames do you have?"

"Total? Seventy-two."

Emery shook his head. "Not much, is it? What was it, fifteen seconds?"

"Seventeen seconds."

"Times 24 frames per second—so, out of about 400 frames, that's all that's left."

"No. There was actually less than that, because it was silent film, which runs at more like 18 frames per second, and they corrected the speed. So, about 300 frames, which means we have about a quarter of the original stock." Leonard hesitated. He glanced up. "Lock that door, would you, Robbie?"

Robbie did, looked back to see Leonard crouched in the corner, moving aside his coat to reveal a metal strongbox. He prised the lid from the top.

The box was filled with water—Robbie *hoped* it was water. "Is that an aquarium?" Leonard ignored him, tugged up his sleeves then dipped both hands below the surface. Very, very carefully he removed another metal box. He set it on the floor, grabbed his coat and meticulously dried the lid, then turned to Robbie.

"You know, maybe you should unlock the door. In case we need to get out fast."

"Jesus Christ, Leonard, what is it?" exclaimed Emery. "Snakes?"

"Nope." Leonard plucked something from the box, and Emery flinched as a serpentine ribbon unfurled in the air. "It's what's left of the original footage—the 1901 film."

"That's nitrate?" Emery stared at him, incredulous. "You *are* insane! How the hell'd you get it?"

"I clipped it before they destroyed the stock. I think it's okay—I take it out every day, so the gases don't build up. And it doesn't seem to interact with the nail polish fumes. It's the part where you can actually see McCauley, where you get the best view of the plane. See?"

He dangled it in front of Emery, who backed toward the door. "Put it away, put it away!"

"Can I see?" asked Robbie.

Leonard gave him a measuring look, then nodded. "Hold it by this edge—"

It took a few seconds for Robbie's eyes to focus properly. "You're right," he said. "You can see him—you can see someone, anyway. And you can definitely tell it's an airplane."

He handed it back to Leonard, who fastidiously replaced it, first in its canister and then the water-filled safe.

"They could really pop you for that." Emery whistled in disbelief. "If that stuff blew? This whole place could go up in flames."

"You say that like it's a bad thing." Leonard draped his coat over the strongbox, then started to laugh. "Anyway, I'm done with it. I went into the Photo Lab one night and duped it myself. So I've got that copy at home. And this one—"

He inclined his head at the corner. "I'm going to take the nitrate home and give it a Viking funeral in the back yard. You can come if you want."

"Tonight?" asked Robbie.

"No. I've got to work late tonight, catch up on some stuff before I leave town."

Emery leaned against the door. "Where you going?"

"South Carolina. I told you. I'm going to Cowana Island, and..." Robbie caught a whiff of acetone as Leonard picked up the *Bellerophon*. "I am going to make this thing fly."

◆ ◆ ◆

"HE REALLY IS nuts. I mean, when was the last time he even saw Maggie?" Robbie asked as Emery drove him back to the mall. "I still don't know what really happened, except for the UFO stuff."

"She found out he was screwing around with someone else. It was a bad scene. She tried to get him fired; he went to Boynton and told him Maggie was diverting all this time and money to studying UFOs. Which unfortunately was true. They did an audit, she had some kind of nervous breakdown even before they could fire her."

"What a prick."

Emery sighed. "It was horrible. Leonard doesn't talk about it. I don't think he ever got over it. Over her."

"Yeah, but..." Robbie shook his head. "She must be, what, twenty years older than us? They never would have stayed together. If he feels so bad, he should just go see her. This other stuff is insane."

"I think maybe those fumes did something to him. Nitrocellulose, it's in nail polish, too. It might have done something to his brain."

"Is that possible?"

"It's a theory," said Emery broodingly.

Robbie's house was in a scruffy subdivision on the outskirts of Rockville. The place was small, a bungalow with masonite siding, cracked cinderblock foundation and the remains of a garden that Anna had planted. A green GMC pickup with expired registration was parked in the drive. Robbie peered into the cab. It was filled with empty Bud Light bottles.

Inside, Zach was hunched at a desk beside his friend Tyler, owner of the pickup. The two of them stared intently into a computer screen.

"What's up?" said Zach without looking away.

"Not much," said Robbie. "Eye contact."

Zach glanced up. He was slight, with Anna's thick blonde curls reduced to a buzzcut that Robbie hated. Tyler was tall and gangly, with long black hair and wire-rimmed sunglasses. Both favored tie-dyed t-shirts and madras shorts that made them look as though they were perpetually on vacation.

Robbie went into the kitchen and got a beer. "You guys eat?"

"We got something on the way home."

Robbie drank his beer and watched them. The house had a smell that Emery once described as Failed Bachelor. Unwashed clothes, spilled beer, marijuana smoke. Robbie hadn't smoked in years, but Zach and Tyler had taken up the slack. Robbie used to yell at them but eventually gave up. If his own depressing example wasn't enough to straighten them out, what was?

After a minute, Zach looked up again. "Nice shirt, Dad."

"Thanks, son." Robbie sank into a beanbag chair. "Me and Emery dropped by the museum and saw Leonard."

"Leonard!" Tyler burst out laughing. "Leonard is so fucking sweet! He's, like, the craziest guy ever."

"All Dad's friends are crazy," said Zach.

"Yeah, but Emery, he's cool. Whereas that guy Leonard is just wack."

Robbie nodded somberly and finished his beer. "Leonard is indeed wack. He's making a movie."

"A real movie?" asked Zach.

"More like a home movie. Or, I dunno—he wants to reproduce another movie, one that was already made, do it all the same again. Shot by shot."

Tyler nodded. "Like *The Ring* and *Ringu*. What's the movie?"

"Seventeen seconds of a 1901 plane crash. The original footage was destroyed, so he's going to re-stage the whole thing."

"A plane crash?" Zach glanced at Tyler. "Can we watch?"

"Not a real crash—he's doing it with a model. I mean, I think he is."

"Did they even have planes then?" said Tyler.

"He should put it on Youtube," said Zach, and turned back to the computer

"Okay, get out of there." Robbie rubbed his head wearily. "I need to go online."

The boys argued but gave up quickly. Tyler left. Zach grabbed his cellphone and slouched upstairs to his room. Robbie got another beer, sat at the computer and logged out of whatever they'd been playing, then typed in MCCAULEY BELLEROPHON.

Only a dozen results popped up. He scanned them, then clicked the Wikipedia entry for Ernesto McCauley.

> McCauley, Ernesto (18??—1901) American inventor whose eccentric aircraft, the *Bellerophon*, allegedly flew for seventeens seconds before it crashed during a 1901 test flight on Cowana Island, South Carolina, killing McCauley. In the 1980s, claims that this flight was successful and predated that of the Wright Brothers by two years were made by a Smithsonian expert, based upon archival film footage. The claims have since been disproved and the film record unfortunately lost in a fire. Curiously, no other record of either McCauley or his aircraft has ever been found.

Robbie took a long pull at his beer, then typed in MARGARET BLEVIN.

> Blevin, Margaret (1938—) Influential cultural historian whose groundbreaking work on early flight earned her the nickname "The Magnificent Blevin." During her tenure at the Smithsonian's Museum of American Aeronautics and Aerospace, Blevin redesigned the General Aviation Gallery to feature lesser-known pioneers of flight, including Charles Dellschau and Ernesto McCauley, as well as…

"'The Magnificent Blevin?'" Robbie snorted. He grabbed another beer and continued reading.

> But Blevin's most lasting impact upon the history of aviation was her 1986 bestseller *Wings for Humanity!*, in which she presents a dramatic and visionary account of the mystical aspects of flight, from Icarus to the Wright Brothers and beyond. Its

central premise is that millennia ago a benevolent race seeded the Earth, leaving isolated locations with the ability to engender human-powered flight. "We dream of flight because flight is our birthright," wrote Blevin, and since its publication *Wings for Humanity!* has never gone out of print.

"Leonard wrote this frigging thing!"
"What?" Zach came downstairs, yawning.
"This Wikipedia entry!" Robbie jabbed at the screen. "That book was never a bestseller—she snuck it into the museum gift shop and no one bought it. The only reason it's still in print is that she published it herself."

Zach read the entry over his father's shoulder. "It sounds cool."

Robbie shook his head adamantly. "She was completely nuts. Obsessed with all this New Age crap, aliens and crop circles. She thought that planes could only fly from certain places, and that's why all the early flights crashed. Not because there was something wrong with the aircraft design, but because they were taking off from the wrong spot."

"Then how come there's airports everywhere?"
"She never worked out that part."
"'We must embrace our galactic heritage, the spiritual dimension of human flight, lest we forever chain ourselves to earth,'" Zach read from the screen. "Was she in that plane crash?"

"No, she's still alive. That was just something she had a wild hair about. She thought the guy who invented that plane flew it a few years before the Wright Brothers made their flight, but she could never prove it."

"But it says there was a movie," said Zach. "So someone saw it happen."
"This is Wikipedia." Robbie stared at the screen in disgust. "You can say any fucking thing you want and people will believe it. Leonard wrote that entry, guarantee you. Probably she faked that whole film loop. That's what Leonard's planning to do now—replicate the footage then pass it off to Maggie as the real thing."

Zach collapsed into the bean bag chair. "Why?"

"Because he's crazy, too. He and Maggie had a thing together."

Zach grimaced. "Ugh."

"What, you think we were born old? We were your age, practically. And Maggie was about twenty years older—"

"A cougar!" Zach burst out laughing. "Why didn't she go for you?"

"Ha ha ha." Robbie pushed his empty beer bottle against the wall. "Women liked Leonard. Go figure. Even your Mom went out with him for a while. Before she and I got involved, I mean."

Zach's glassy eyes threatened to roll back in his head. "Stop."

"We thought it was pretty strange," admitted Robbie. "But Maggie was good-looking for an old hippie." He glanced at the Wikipedia entry and did the math. "I guess she's in her seventies now. Leonard's in touch with her. She has cancer. Breast cancer."

"I heard you," said Zach. He rolled out of the beanbag chair, flipped open his phone and began texting. "I'm going to bed."

Robbie sat and stared at the computer screen. After a while he shut it down. He shuffled into the kitchen and opened the cabinet where he kept a quart of Jim Beam, hidden behind bottles of vinegar and vegetable oil. He rinsed out the glass he'd used the night before, poured a jolt and downed it; then carried the bourbon with him to bed.

◆ ◆ ◆

THE NEXT DAY after work, he was on his second drink at the bar when Emery showed up.

"Hey." Robbie gestured at the stool beside him. "Have a seat."

"You okay to drive?"

"Sure." Robbie scowled. "What, you keeping an eye on me?"

"No. But I want you to see something. At my house. Leonard's coming over, we're going to meet there at six-thirty. I tried calling you but your phone's off."

"Oh. Right. Sorry." Robbie signaled the bartender for his tab. "Yeah, sure. What, is he gonna give us manicures?"

"Nope. I have an idea. I'll tell you when I get there, I'm going to Royal Delhi first to get some takeout. See you—"

Emery lived in a big townhouse condo that smelled of Moderately Successful Bachelor. The walls held framed photos of Captain Marvo and Mungbean alongside a lifesized painting of Leslie Nielsen as Commander J.J. Adams.

But there was also a climate-controlled basement filled with Captain Marvo merchandise and packing material, with another large room stacked with electronics equipment—sound system, video monitors and decks, shelves and files devoted to old Captain Marvo episodes and dupes of the Grade Z movies featured on the show.

This was where Robbie found Leonard, bent over a refurbished Steenbeck editing table. "Robbie." Leonard waved, then returned to threading film onto a spindle. "Emery back with dinner?"

"Uh uh." Robbie pulled a chair alongside him. "What are you doing?"

"Loading up that nitrate I showed you yesterday."

"It's not going to explode, is it?"

"No, Robbie, it's not going to explode." Leonard's mouth tightened. "Did Emery talk to you yet?"

"He just said something about a plan. So what's up?"

"I'll let him tell you."

Robbie flushed angrily, but before he could retort there was a knock behind them.

"Chow time, campers." Emery held up two steaming paper bags. "Can you leave that for a few minutes, Leonard?"

They ate on the couch in the next room. Emery talked about a pitch he'd made to revive Captain Marvo in cellphone format. "It'd be freaking perfect, if I could figure out a way to make any money from it."

Leonard said nothing. Robbie noted the cuffs of his white tunic were stained with flecks of orange pigment, as were his fingernails. He looked tired, his face lined and his eyes sunken.

"You getting enough sleep?" Emery asked.

Leonard smiled wanly. "Enough."

Finally the food was gone, and the beer. Emery clapped his hands on his knees, pushed aside the empty plates then leaned forward.

"Okay. So here's the plan. I rented a house on Cowana for a week, starting this Saturday. I mapped it online and it's about ten hours. If we leave right after you guys get off work on Friday and drive all night, we'll get there early Saturday morning. Leonard, you said you've got everything pretty much assembled, so all you need to do is pack it up. I've got everything else here. Be a tight fit in the Prius, though, so we'll have to take two cars. We'll bring everything we need with us, we'll have a week to shoot and edit or whatever, then on the way back we swing through Fayetteville and show the finished product to Maggie. What do you think?"

"That's not a lot of time," said Leonard. "But we could do it."

Emery turned to Robbie. "Is your car road-worthy? It's about twelve hundred miles roundtrip."

Robbie stared at him. "What the hell are you talking about?"

"The *Bellerophon*. Leonard's got storyboards and all kinds of drawings and still frames, enough to work from. The realtor's in Charleston, she said there wouldn't be many people this early in the season. Plus there was a hurricane a couple years ago, I gather the island got hammered and no one's had money to rebuild. So we'll have it all to ourselves, pretty much."

"Are you high?" Robbie laughed. "I can't just take off. I have a job."

"You get vacation time, right? You can take a week. It'll be great, man. The realtor says it's already in the 80s down there. Warm water, a beach—what more you want?"

"Uh, maybe a beach with people besides you and Leonard?" Robbie searched in vain for another beer. "I couldn't go anyway—next week's Zach's spring break."

"Yeah?" Emery shook his head. "So, you're going to be at the store all day, and he'll be home getting stoned. Bring him. We'll put him to work."

Leonard frowned, but Robbie looked thoughtful. "Yeah, you're right. I hadn't thought of that. I can't really leave him alone. I guess I'll think about it."

"Don't think, just do it. It's Wednesday, tell 'em you're taking off next week. They gonna fire you?"

"Maybe."

"I'm not babysitting some—" Leonard started.

Emery cut him off. "You got that nitrate loaded? Let's see it."

They filed into the workroom. Leonard sat at the Steenbeck. The others watched as he adjusted the film on its sprockets. He turned to Robbie, then indicated the black projection box in the center of the deck.

"Emery knows all this, so I'm just telling you. That's a quartz halogen lamp. I haven't turned it on yet, because if the frame was just sitting there it might incinerate the film, and us. But there's only about four seconds of footage, so we're going to take our chances and watch it, once. Maybe you remember it from the gallery?"

Robbie nodded. "Yeah, I saw it a bunch of times. Not as much as The Head, but enough."

"Good. Hit that light, would you, Emery? Everyone ready? Blink and you'll miss it."

Robbie craned his neck, staring at a blank white screen. There was a whir, the stutter of film running through a projector.

At the bottom of the frame the horizon lurched, bright flickers that might be an expanse of water. Then a blurred image, faded sepia and amber, etched with blotches and something resembling a beetle leg: the absurd contraption Robbie recognized as the original *Bellerophon*. Only it was moving—it was flying—its countless gears and propellers and wings spinning and whirring and flapping all at once, so it seemed the entire thing would vibrate into a thousand pieces. Beneath the fuselage, a dark figure perched precariously atop the velocipede, legs like black scissors slicing at the air. From the left corner of the frame leaped a flare of light, like a shooting star or burning firecracker tossed at the pedaling figure. The pilot listed to one side, and—

Nothing. The film ended as abruptly as it had begun. Leonard quickly reached to turn off the lamp, and immediately removed the film from the take-up drive.

Robbie felt his neck prickle—he'd forgotten how weird, uncanny even, the footage was.

"Jesus, that's some bizarre shit," said Emery.

"It doesn't even look real." Robbie watched as Leonard coiled the film and slid it in a canister. "I mean, the guy, he looks fake."

Emery nodded. "Yeah, I know. It looks like one of those old silents, "The Lost World" or something. But it's not. I used to watch it back when it ran a hundred times a day in our gallery, the way you used to watch The Head. And it's definitely real. At least the pilot, McCauley—that's a real guy. I got a big magnifier once and just stood there and watched it over and over again. He was breathing, I could see it. And the plane, it's real too, far as I could tell. The thing I can't figure is, who the hell shot that footage? And what was the angle?"

Robbie stared at the empty screen, then shut his eyes. He tried to recall the rest of the film from when it played in the General Aviation gallery: the swift, jerky trajectory of that eerie little vehicle with its bizarre pilot, a man in a black suit and bowler hat; then the flash from the corner of the screen, and the man toppling from his perch into the white and empty air. The last thing you saw was a tiny hand at the bottom of the frame, then some blank leader, followed by the words THE MAIDEN FLIGHT OF MCCAULEY'S "BELLEROPHON" (1901). And the whole thing began again.

"It was like someone was in the air next to him," said Robbie. "Unless he only got six feet off the ground. I always assumed it was faked."

"It wasn't faked," said Leonard. "The cameraman was on the beach filming. It was a windy day, they were hoping that would help give the plane some lift but there must have been a sudden gust. When the *Bellerophon* went into the ocean, the cameraman dove in to save McCauley. They both drowned. They never found the bodies, or the wreckage. Only the camera with the film."

"Who found it?" asked Robbie.

"We don't know." Leonard sighed, his shoulders slumping. "We don't know anything.

"Not the name of the cameraman, nothing. When Maggie and I ran the original footage, the leader said "Maiden Flight of McCauley's Bellerophon." The can had the date and 'Cowana Island' written on it. So Maggie and I went down there to research it. A weird place.

"Hardly any people, and this was in the summer. There's a tiny historical society on the island, but we couldn't find anything about McCauley or the aircraft. No newspaper accounts, no gravestones. The only thing we did find was in a diary kept by the guy who delivered the mail back then. On May 13, 1901 he wrote that it was a very windy day and two men had drowned while attempting to launch a flying machine on the beach. Someone must have found the camera afterward. Somebody processed the film, and somehow it found its way to the museum."

Robbie followed Leonard into the next room. "What was that weird flash of light?"

"I don't know." Leonard stared out a glass door into the parking lot. "But it's not overexposure or lens flare or anything like that. It's something the cameraman actually filmed. Water, maybe—if it was a windy day, a big wave might have come up onto the beach or something."

"I always thought it was fire. Like a rocket or some kind of flare."

Leonard nodded. "That's what Maggie thought, too. The mailman— mostly all he wrote about was the weather. Which if you were relying on a horse-drawn cart makes sense. About two weeks before he mentioned the flying machine, he described something that sounds like a major meteor shower."

"And Maggie thought it was hit by a meteor?"

"No." Leonard sighed. "She thought it was something else. The weird thing is, a few years ago I checked online, and it turns out there was an unusual amount of meteor activity in 1901."

Robbie raised an eyebrow. "Meaning?"

Leonard said nothing. Finally he opened the door and walked outside. The others trailed after him.

THE MAIDEN FLIGHT OF McCAULEY'S *BELLEROPHON*

They reached the edge of the parking lot, where cracked tarmac gave way to stony ground. Leonard glanced back, then stooped. He brushed away a few stray leaves and tufts of dead grass, set the film canister down and unscrewed the metal lid. He picked up one end of the coil of film, gently tugging until it trailed a few inches across the ground. Then he withdrew a lighter, flicked it and held the flame to the tail of film.

"What the—" began Robbie.

There was a dull *whoosh*, like the sound of a gas burner igniting. A plume of crimson and gold leaped from the canister, writhing in the air within a ball of black smoke. Leonard staggered to his feet, covering his head as he backed away.

"Leonard!" Emery grabbed him roughly, then turned and raced to the house.

Before Robbie could move, a strong chemical stink surrounded him. The flames shrank to a shining thread that lashed at the smoke then faded into flecks of ash. Robbie ducked his head, coughing. He grasped Leonard's arm and tried to drag him away, glanced up to see Emery running toward them with a fire extinguisher.

"Sorry," gasped Leonard. He made a slashing motion through the smoke, which dispersed. The flames were gone. Leonard's face was black with ash. Robbie touched his own cheek gingerly, looked at his fingers and saw they were coated with something dark and oily.

Emery halted, panting, and stared at the twisted remains of the film can. On the ground beside it, a glowing thread wormed toward a dead leaf, then expired in a gray wisp. Emery raised the fire extinguisher threateningly, set it down and stomped on the canister.

"Good thing you didn't do that in the museum," said Robbie. He let go of Leonard's arm.

"Don't think it didn't cross my mind," said Leonard, and walked back inside.

• ◆ •

THEY LEFT FRIDAY evening. Robbie got the week off, after giving his dubious boss a long story about a dying relative down south. Zach shouted and broke a lamp when informed he would be accompanying his father on a trip during his spring vacation.

"With Emery and *Leonard*? Are you fucking *insane*?"

Robbie was too exhausted to fight: he quickly offered to let Tyler come with them. Tyler, surprisingly, agreed, and even showed up on Friday afternoon to help load the car. Robbie made a pointed effort not to inspect the various backpacks and duffel bags the boys threw into the trunk of the battered Taurus. Alcohol, drugs, firearms: he no longer cared.

Instead he focused on the online weather report for Cowana Island. 80 degrees and sunshine, photographs of blue water, white sand, a skein of pelicans skimming above the waves. Ten hours, that wasn't so bad. In another weak moment, he told Zach he could drive part of the way, so Robbie could sleep.

"What about me?" asked Tyler. "Can I drive?"

"Only if I never wake up," said Robbie.

Around six Emery pulled into the driveway, honking. The boys were already slumped in Robbie's Taurus, Zach in front with earbuds dangling around his face and a knit cap pulled down over his eyes, Tyler in the back, staring blankly as though they were already on I-95.

"You ready?" Emery rolled down his window. He wore a blue flannel shirt and a gimme cap that read STARFLEET ACADEMY. In the hybrid's passenger seat, Leonard perused a road atlas. He looked up and shot Robbie a smile.

"Hey, a road trip."

"Yeah." Robbie smiled back and patted the hybrid's roof. "See you."

It took almost two hours just to get beyond the gravitational pull of the Washington Beltway. Farms and forest had long ago disappeared beneath an endless grid of malls and housing developments, many of them vacant. Every time Robbie turned up the radio for a song he liked, the boys complained that they could hear it through their earphones.

THE MAIDEN FLIGHT OF McCAULEY'S *BELLEROPHON*

Only as the sky darkened and Virginia gave way to North Carolina did the world take on a faint fairy glow, distant green and yellow lights reflecting the first stars and a shining cusp of moon. Sprawl gave way to pine forest. The boys had been asleep for hours, in that amazing, self-willed hibernation they summoned whenever in the presence of adults for more than fifteen minutes. Robbie put the radio on, low, searched until he caught the echo of a melody he knew, and then another. He thought of driving with Anna beside him, a restive Zach behind them in his car seat; the aimless trips they'd make until the toddler fell asleep and they could talk or, once, park in a vacant lot and make out.

How long had it been since he'd remembered that? Years, maybe. He fought against thinking of Anna; sometimes it felt as though he fought Anna herself, her hands pummeling him as he poured another drink or staggered up to bed.

Now, though, the darkness soothed him the way those long-ago drives had lulled Zach to sleep. He felt an ache lift from his breast, as though a splinter had been dislodged; blinked and in the rearview mirror glimpsed Anna's face, slightly turned from him as she gazed out at the passing sky.

He started, realized he'd begun to nod off. On the dashboard his fuel indicator glowed red. He called Emery, and at the next exit pulled off 95, the Prius behind him.

After a few minutes they found a gas station set back from the road in a pine grove, with an old-fashioned pump out front and yellow light streaming through a screen door. The boys blinked awake.

"Where are we?" asked Zach.

"No idea." Robbie got out of the car. "North Carolina."

It was like stepping into a twilight garden, or some hidden biosphere at the zoo.

Warmth flowed around him, violet and rustling green, scented overpoweringly of honeysuckle and wet stone. He could hear rushing water, the stirring of wind in the leaves and countless small things—frogs peeping, insects he couldn't identify. A nightbird that made a burbling song. In the shadows behind the building, fireflies floated between kudzu-choked trees like tiny glowing fish.

For an instant he felt himself suspended in that enveloping darkness. The warm air moved through him, sweetly fragrant, pulsing with life he could neither see nor touch. He tasted something honeyed and faintly astringent in the back of his throat, and drew his breath in sharply.

"What?" demanded Zach.

"Nothing." Robbie shook his head and turned to the pump. "Just—isn't this great?"

He filled the tank. Zach and Tyler went in search of food, and Emery strolled over.

"How you holding up?"

"I'm good. Probably let Zach drive for a while so I can catch some Z's."

He moved the car, then went inside to pay. He found Leonard buying a pack of cigarettes as the boys headed out, laden with energy drinks and bags of chips. Robbie slid his credit card across the counter to a woman wearing a tank top that set off a tattoo that looked like the face of Marilyn Manson, or maybe it was Jesus.

"Do you have a restroom?"

The woman handed him a key. "Round back."

"Bathroom's here," Robbie yelled at the boys. "We're not stopping again."

They trailed him into a dank room with gray walls. A fluorescent light buzzed overhead. After Tyler left, Robbie and Zach stood side by side at the sink, trying to coax water from a rusted spigot to wash their hands.

"The hell with it," said Robbie. "Let's hit the road. You want to drive?"

"Dad." Zach pointed at the ceiling. "Dad, look."

Robbie glanced up. A screen bulged from a small window above the sink. Something had blown against the wire mesh, a leaf or scrap of paper. But then the leaf moved, and he saw that it wasn't a leaf at all but a butterfly.

No, not a butterfly—a moth. The biggest he'd ever seen, bigger than his hand. Its fan-shaped upper wings opened, revealing vivid golden eyespots; its trailing lower wings formed two perfect arabesques, all a milky, luminous green.

"A luna moth," breathed Robbie. "I've never seen one."

Zach clambered onto the sink. "It wants to get out—"

"Hang on." Robbie boosted him, bracing himself so the boy's weight wouldn't yank the sink from the wall. "Be careful! Don't hurt it—"

The moth remained where it was. Robbie grunted—Zach weighed as much as he did—felt his legs trembling as the boy prised the screen from the wall then struggled to pull it free.

"It's stuck," he said. "I can't get it—"

The moth fluttered weakly. One wing-tip looked ragged, as though it had been singed.

"Tear it!" Robbie cried. "Just tear the screen."

Zach wedged his fingers beneath a corner of the window frame and yanked, hard enough that he fell. Robbie caught him as the screen tore away to dangle above the sink. The luna moth crawled onto the sill.

"Go!" Zach banged on the wall. "Go on, fly!"

Like a kite catching the wind, the moth lifted. Its trailing lower wings quivered and the eyespots seemed to blink, a pallid face gazing at them from the darkness. Then it was gone.

"That was cool." For an instant, Zach's arm draped across his father's shoulder, so fleetingly Robbie might have imagined it. "I'm going to the car."

When the boy was gone, Robbie tried to push the screen back into place. He returned the key and went to join Leonard, smoking a cigarette at the edge of the woods. Behind them a car horn blared.

"Come on!" shouted Zach. "I'm leaving!"

"Happy trails," said Leonard.

Robbie slept fitfully in back as Zach drove, the two boys arguing about music and a girl named Eileen. After an hour he took over again.

The night ground on. The boys fell back asleep. Robbie drank one of their Red Bulls and thought of the glimmering wonder that had been the luna moth. A thin rind of emerald appeared on the horizon, deepening to copper then gold as it overtook the sky. He began to see palmettos among the loblolly pines and pin oaks, and spiky plants he didn't recognize. When he opened the window, the air smelled of roses, and the sea.

"Hey." He poked Zach, breathing heavily in the seat beside him. "Hey, we're almost there."

He glanced at the directions, looked up to see the hybrid passing him and Emery gesturing at a sandy track that veered to the left. It was bounded by barbed wire fences and clumps of cactus thick with blossoms the color of lemon cream. The pines surrendered to palmettos and prehistoric-looking trees with gnarled roots that thrust up from pools where egrets and herons stabbed at frogs.

"Look," said Robbie.

Ahead of them the road narrowed to a path barely wide enough for a single vehicle, built up with shells and chunks of concrete. On one side stretched a blur of cypress and long-legged birds; on the other, an aquamarine estuary that gave way to the sea and rolling white dunes.

Robbie slowed the car to a crawl, humping across mounds of shells and doing his best to avoid sinkholes. After a quarter-mile, the makeshift causeway ended. An old metal gate lay in a twisted heap on the ground, covered by creeping vines. Above it a weathered sign clung to a cypress.

WELCOME TO COWANA ISLAND

NO DUNE BUGGIES

They drove past the ruins of a mobile home. Emery's car was out of sight. Robbie looked at his cellphone and saw there was no signal. In the back, Tyler stirred.

"Hey Rob, where are we?"

"We're here. Wherever here is. The island."

"Sweet." Tyler leaned over the seat to jostle Zach awake. "Hey, get up."

Robbie peered through the overgrown greenery, looking for something resembling a beach house. He tried to remember which hurricane had pounded this part of the coast, and how long ago. Two years? Five?

The place looked as though it had been abandoned for decades. Fallen palmettos were everywhere, their leaves stiff and reddish-brown, like rusted blades. Some remained upright, their crowns lopped off. Acid-green lizards sunned themselves in driveways where ferns poked through the blacktop. The remains of carports and decks dangled above piles of timber and mold-blackened sheetrock. Now and then an intact house appeared within the jungle of flowering vines.

But no people, no cars except for an SUV crushed beneath a toppled utility pole. The only store was a modest grocery with a brick facade and shattered windows, through which the ghostly outlines of aisles and displays could still be glimpsed.

"It's like *28 Days*," said Zach, and shot a baleful look at his father.

Robbie shrugged. "Talk to the man from the Starfleet Academy."

He pulled down a rutted drive to where the hybrid sat beneath a thriving palmetto. Driftwood edged a path that led to an old wood-frame house raised on stiltlike pilings. Stands of blooming cactus surrounded it, and trees choked with honeysuckle. The patchy lawn was covered with hundreds of conch shells arranged in concentric circles and spirals. On the deck a tattered red whirligig spun in the breeze, and rope hammocks hung like flaccid cocoons.

"I'm sleeping there," said Tyler.

Leonard gazed at the house with an unreadable expression. Emery had already sprinted up the uneven steps to what Robbie assumed was the front door. When he reached the top, he bent to pick up a square of coconut matting, retrieved something from beneath it then straightened, grinning.

"Come on!" he shouted, turning to unlock the door; and the others raced to join him.

• ◆ •

THE HOUSE HAD linoleum floors, sifted with a fine layer of sand, and mismatched furniture—rattan chairs, couches covered with faded barkcloth cushions, a canvas seat that hung from the ceiling by a chain and groaned alarmingly whenever the boys sat in it. The sea breeze stirred dusty white curtains at the windows. Anoles skittered across the floor, and Tyler fled shouting from the outdoor shower, where he'd seen a black widow spider. The electricity worked, but there was no air conditioning and no television; no internet.

"This is what you get for three hundred bucks in the off season," said Emery when Tyler complained.

"I don't get it." Robbie stood on the deck, staring across the empty road to where the dunes stretched, tufted with thorny greenery. "Even if there was a hurricane—this is practically oceanfront, all of it. Where is everybody?"

"Who can afford to build anything?" said Leonard. "Come on, I want to get my stuff inside before it heats up."

Leonard commandeered the master bedroom. He installed his laptop, Emery's camera equipment, piles of storyboards, the box that contained the miniature *Bellerophon*. This formidable array took up every inch of floor space, as well as the surface of a ping pong table.

"Why is there a ping pong table in the bedroom?" asked Robbie as he set down a tripod.

Emery shrugged. "You might ask, why is there not a ping pong table in all bedrooms?"

"We're going to the beach," announced Zach.

Robbie kicked off his shoes and followed them, across the deserted road and down a path that wound through a miniature wilderness of cactus and bristly vines. He felt lightheaded from lack of sleep, and also from the beer he'd snagged from one of the cases Emery had brought. The sand was already hot; twice he had to stop and pluck sharp spurs from his bare feet. A horned toad darted across the path, and a skink with a blue tongue. His son's voice came to him, laughing, and the sound of waves on the shore.

Atop the last dune small yellow roses grew in a thick carpet, their soapy fragrance mingling with the salt breeze. Robbie bent to pluck a handful of petals and tossed them into the air.

"It's not a bad place to fly, is it?"

He turned and saw Emery, shirtless. He handed Robbie a bottle of Tecate with a slice of lime jammed in its neck, raised his own beer and took a sip.

"It's beautiful." Robbie squeezed the lime into his beer, then drank. "But that model. It won't fly."

"I know." Emery stared to where Zach and Tyler leaped in the shallow water, sending up rainbow spray as they splashed each other. "But it's a good excuse for a vacation, isn't it?"

"It is," replied Robbie, and slid down the dune to join the boys.

OVER THE NEXT few days, they fell into an odd, almost sleepless rhythm, staying up till two or three a.m., drinking and talking. The adults pretended not to notice when the boys slipped a Tecate from the fridge, and ignored the incense-scented smoke that drifted from the deck after they stumbled off to bed. Everyone woke shortly after dawn, even the boys. Blinding sunlight slanted through the worn curtains. On the deck where Zack and Tyler huddled inside their hammocks, a treefrog made a sound like rusty hinges. No one slept enough, everyone drank too much.

For once it didn't matter. Robbie's hangovers dissolved as he waded into water warm as blood, then floated on his back and watched pelicans skim above him. Afterward he'd carry equipment from the house to the dunes, where Emery had created a shelter from old canvas deck chairs and bedsheets. The boys helped, the three of them lugging tripods and digital cameras, the box that contained Leonard's model of the *Bellerophon*, a cooler filled with beer and Red Bull.

That left Emery in charge of household duties. He'd found an ancient red wagon half-buried in the dunes, and used this to transport bags of tortilla chips and a cooler filled with Tecate and limes. There was no store on the island save the abandoned wreck they'd passed when they first arrived. No gas station, and the historical society building appeared to be long gone.

But while driving around, Emery discovered a roadside stand that sold homemade salsa in mason jars and sage-green eggs in recycled cardboard cartons. The drive beside it was blocked with a barbed-wire fence and a sign that said BEWARE OF TWO-HEADED DOG.

"You ever see it?" asked Tyler.

"Nope. I never saw anyone except an alligator." Emery opened a beer. "And it was big enough to eat a two-headed dog."

By Thursday morning, they'd carted everything from one end of the island to the other, waiting with increasing impatience as Leonard climbed up and down dunes and stared broodingly at the blue horizon.

"How will you know which is the right one?" asked Robbie.

Leonard shook his head. "I don't know. Maggie said she thought it would be around here—"

He swept his arm out, encompassing a high ridge of sand that crested above the beach like a frozen wave. Below, Tyler and Zach argued over whose turn it was to haul everything uphill again. Robbie shoved his sunglasses against his nose.

"This beach has probably been washed away a hundred times since McCauley was here. Maybe we should just choose a place at random. Pick the highest dune or something."

"Yeah, I know." Leonard sighed. "This is probably our best choice, here."

He stood and for a long time gazed at the sky. Finally he turned and walked down to join the boys.

"We'll do it here," he said brusquely, and headed back to the house.

Late that afternoon they made a bonfire on the beach. The day had ended gray and much cooler than it had been, the sun swallowed in a haze of bruise-tinged cloud. Robbie waded into the shallow water, feeling with his toes for conch shells. Beside the fire, Zach came across a shark's tooth the size of a guitar pick.

"That's probably a million years old," said Tyler enviously.

"Almost as old as Dad," said Zach.

Robbie flopped down beside Leonard. "It's so weird," he said, shaking sand from a conch. "There's a whole string of these islands, but I haven't seen a boat the whole time we've been here."

"Are you complaining?" said Leonard.

"No. Just, don't you think it's weird?"

"Maybe." Leonard tossed his cigarette into the fire.

"I want to stay." Zack rolled onto his back and watched sparks fly among the first stars. "Dad? Why can't we just stay here?"

Robbie took a long pull from his beer. "I have to get back to work. And you guys have school."

"Fuck school," said Zach and Tyler.

"Listen." The boys fell silent as Leonard glared at them. "Tomorrow morning I want to set everything up. We'll shoot before the wind picks up too much. I'll have the rest of the day to edit. Then we pack and head to Fayetteville on Saturday. We'll find some cheap place to stay, and drive home on Sunday."

The boys groaned. Emery sighed. "Back to the salt mines. I gotta call that guy about the show."

"I want to have a few hours with Maggie." Leonard pulled at the silver skull in his ear. "I told the nurse I'd be there Saturday before noon."

"We'll have to leave pretty early," said Emery.

For a few minutes nobody spoke. Wind rattled brush in the dunes behind them. The bonfire leaped then subsided, and Zach fed it a knot of driftwood. An unseen bird gave a piping cry that was joined by another, then another, until their plaintive voices momentarily drowned out the soft rush of waves.

Robbie gazed into the darkening water. In his hand, the conch shell felt warm and silken as skin.

"Look, Dad," said Zach. "Bats."

Robbie leaned back to see black shapes dodging sparks above their heads.

"Nice," he said, his voice thick from drink.

"Well." Leonard stood and lit another cigarette. "I'm going to bed."

"Me too," said Zach.

Robbie watched with mild surprise as the boys clambered to their feet, yawning. Emery removed a beer from the cooler, handed it to Robbie.

"Keep an eye on the fire, compadre," he said, and followed the others.

Robbie turned to study the dying blaze. Ghostly runnels of green and blue ran along the driftwood branch. Salt, Leonard had explained to the boys, though Robbie wondered if that was true. How did Leonard know all this stuff? He frowned, picked up a handful of sand and tossed it at the feeble blaze, which promptly sank into sullen embers.

Robbie swore under his breath. He finished his beer, stood and walked unsteadily toward the water. The clouds obscured the moon, though there was a faint umber glow reflected in the distant waves. He stared at the horizon, searching in vain for some sign of life, lights from a cruiseship or plane; turned and gazed up and down the length of the beach.

Nothing. Even the bonfire had died. He stood on tiptoe and tried to peer past the high dune, to where the beach house stood within the grove of palmettos. Night swallowed everything,

He turned back to the waves licking at his bare feet. Something stung his face, blown sand or maybe a gnat. He waved to disperse it, then froze.

In the water, plumes of light coiled and unfolded, dazzling him. Deepest violet, a fiery emerald that stabbed his eyes; cobalt and a pure blaze of scarlet. He shook his head, edging backward; caught himself and looked around.

He was alone. He turned back, and the lights were still there, just below the surface, furling and unfurling to some secret rhythm.

Like a machine, he thought; some kind of underwater windfarm. A wavefarm?

But no, that was crazy. He rubbed his cheeks, trying to sober up. He'd seen something like this in Ocean City late one night—it was something alive, Leonard had explained, plankton or jellyfish, one of those things that glowed. They'd gotten high and raced into the Atlantic to watch pale-green streamers trail them as they body-surfed.

Now he took a deep breath and waded in, kicking at the waves, then halted to see if he'd churned up a luminous cloud.

Darkness lapped almost to his knees: there was no telltale glow where he'd stirred the water. But a few yards away, the lights continued to turn in upon themselves beneath the surface: scores of fist-sized nebulae, soundless and steady as his own pulse.

He stared until his head ached, trying to get a fix on them. The lights weren't diffuse, like phosphorescence. And they didn't float like jellyfish. They seemed to be rooted in place, near enough for him to touch.

Yet his eyes couldn't focus: the harder he tried, the more the lights seemed to shift, like an optical illusion or some dizzying computer game.

He stood there for five minutes, maybe longer. Nothing changed. He started to back away, slowly, finally turned and stumbled across the sand, stopping every few steps to glance over his shoulder. The lights were still there, though now he saw them only as a soft yellowish glow.

He ran the rest of the way to the house. There were no lights on, no music or laughter.

But he could smell cigarette smoke, and traced it to the deck where Leonard stood beside the rail.

"Leonard!" Robbie drew alongside him, then glanced around for the boys.

"They slept inside," said Leonard. "Too cold."

"Listen, you have to see something. On the beach—these lights. Not on the beach, in the water." He grabbed Leonard's arm. "Like—just come on."

Leonard shook him off angrily. "You're drunk."

"I'm not drunk! Or, okay, maybe I am, a little. But I'm not kidding. Look—"

He pointed past the sea of palmettos, past the dunes, toward the dark line of waves. The yellow glow was now spangled with silver. It spread across the water, narrowing as it faded toward the horizon, like a wavering path.

Leonard stared, then turned to Robbie in disbelief. "You idiot. It's the fucking moon."

Robbie looked up. And yes, there was the quarter-moon, a blaze of gold between gaps in the cloud.

"That's not it." He knew he sounded not just drunk but desperate. "It was *in* the water—"

"Bioluminescence." Leonard sighed and tossed his cigarette, then headed for the door. "Go to bed, Robbie."

Robbie started to yell after him, but caught himself and leaned against the rail. His head throbbed. Phantom blots of light swam across his vision. He felt dizzy, and on the verge of tears.

He closed his eyes; forced himself to breathe slowly, to channel the pulsing in his head into the memory of spectral whirlpools, a miniature galaxy blossoming beneath the water. After a minute he looked out again, but saw nothing save the blades of palmetto leaves etched against the moonlit sky.

• ◆ •

HE WOKE SEVERAL hours later on the couch, feeling as though an ax were embedded in his forehead. Gray light washed across the floor. It was cold; he reached fruitlessly for a blanket, groaned and sat up.

Emery was in the open kitchen, washing something in the sink. He glanced at Robbie then hefted a coffee pot. "Ready for this?"

Robbie nodded, and Emery handed him a steaming mug. "What time is it?'

"Eight, a little after. The boys are with Leonard—they went out about an hour ago. It looks like rain, which kind of throws a monkey wrench into everything. Maybe it'll hold off long enough to get that thing off the ground."

Robbie sipped his coffee. "Seventeen seconds. He could just throw it into the air."

"Yeah, I thought of that too. So what happened to you last night?"

"Nothing. Too much Tecate."

"Leonard said you were raving drunk."

"Leonard sets the bar pretty low. I was—relaxed."

"Well, time to unrelax. I told him I'd get you up and we'd be at the beach by eight."

"I don't even know what I'm doing. Am I a cameraman?"

"Uh uh. That's me. You don't know how to work it, plus it's my camera. The boys are in charge of the windbreak and, I dunno, props. They hand things to Leonard."

"Things? What things?" Robbie scowled. "It's a fucking model airplane. It doesn't have a remote, does it? Because that would have been a g*ood* idea."

Emery picked up his camera bag. "Come on. You can carry the tripod, how's that? Maybe the boys will hand you things, and you can hand them to Leonard."

"I'll be there in a minute. Tell Leonard he can start without me."

After Emery left he finished his coffee and went into his room. He rummaged through his clothes until he found a bottle of Ibuprofen, downed six, then pulled on a hooded sweatshirt and sat on the edge of his bed, staring at the wall.

He'd obviously had some kind of blackout, the first since he'd been fired from the Parks Commission. Somewhere between his seventh beer and this morning's hangover was the blurred image of Crayola-colored pinwheels turning beneath dark water, his stumbling flight from the beach and Leonard's disgusted voice: *You idiot, it's the fucking moon.*

Robbie grimaced. He *had* seen something, he knew that.

But he could no longer recall it clearly, and what he could remember made no sense. It was like a movie he'd watched half-awake, or an accident he'd glimpsed from the corner of his eye in a moving car. Maybe it had been the moonlight, or some kind of fluorescent seaweed.

Or maybe he'd just been totally wasted.

Robbie sighed. He put on his sneakers, grabbed Emery's tripod and headed out.

A scattering of cold rain met him as he hit the beach. It was windy. The sea glinted gray and silver, like crumpled tinfoil. Clumps of seaweed covered the sand, and small round discs that resembled pieces of clouded glass: jellyfish, hundreds of them. Robbie prodded one with his foot, then continued down the shore.

The dune was on the north side of the island, where it rose steeply a good fifteen feet above the sand. Now, a few hours before low tide, the water was about thirty feet away. It was exactly the kind of place you might choose to launch a human-powered craft, if you knew little about aerodynamics. Robbie didn't know much, but he was fairly certain you needed to be higher to get any kind of lift.

Still, that would be for a full-sized craft. For a scale model you could hold in your two cupped hands, maybe it would be high enough. He saw Emery pacing along the water's edge, vidcam slung around his neck. The only sign of the others was a trail of footsteps leading to the dune. Robbie clambered up, using the tripod to keep from slipping on sand the color and texture of damp cornmeal. He was panting when he reached the top.

"Hey Dad. Where were you?"

Robbie smiled weakly as Zach peered out from the windbreak. "I have a sinus infection."

Zach motioned him inside. "Come on, I can't leave this open."

Robbie set down the tripod, then crouched to enter the makeshift tent. Inside, bedsheet walls billowed in the wind, straining at an elaborate scaffold of broom handles, driftwood, the remains of wooden deck chairs. Tyler and Zach sat crosslegged on a blanket and stared at their cellphones.

"You can get a strong signal here," said Tyler. "Nope, it's gone again."

Next to them, Leonard knelt beside a cardboard box. Instead of his customary white tunic, he wore one that was sky-blue, embroidered with yellow birds. He glanced at Robbie, his gray eyes cold and dismissive. "There's only room for three people in here."

"That's okay—I'm going out," said Zach, and crawled through the gap in the sheets. Tyler followed him. Robbie jammed his hands into his pockets and forced a smile.

"So," he said. "Did you see all those jellyfish?"

Leonard nodded without looking at him. Very carefully he removed the *Bellerophon* and set it on a neatly folded towel. He reached into the box again, and withdrew something else. A doll no bigger than his hand, dressed in black frockcoat and trousers, with a bowler hat so small that Robbie could have swallowed it.

"*Voila*," said Leonard.

"Jesus, Leonard." Robbie hesitated, then asked, "Can I look at it?"

To his surprise, Leonard nodded. Robbie picked it up. The little figure was so light he wondered if there was anything inside the tiny suit.

But as he turned it gently, he could feel slender joints under its clothing, a miniature torso. Tiny hands protruded from the sleeves, and it wore minute, highly polished shoes that appeared to be made of black leather. Under the frock coat was a waistcoat, with a watch-chain of gold thread that dangled from a nearly invisible pocket. From beneath the bowler hat peeked a fringe of red hair fine as milkweed down. The cameo-sized face that stared up at Robbie was Maggie Blevin's, painted in hairline strokes so that he could see every eyelash, every freckle on her rounded cheeks.

He looked at Leonard in amazement. "How did you do this?"

"It took a long time." He held out his hand, and Robbie returned the doll. "The hardest part was making sure the *Bellerophon* could carry her weight. And that she fit into the bicycle seat and could pedal it. You wouldn't think that would be difficult, but it was."

"It—it looks just like her." Robbie glanced at the doll again, then said, "I thought you wanted to make everything look like the original film. You know, with McCauley—I thought that was the point."

"The point is for it to fly."

"But—"

"You don't need to understand," said Leonard. "Maggie will."

He bent over the little aircraft, its multi-colored wings and silken parasol bright as a toy carousel, and tenderly began to fit the doll-sized pilot into its seat.

Robbie shivered. He'd seen Leonard's handiwork before, mannequins so realistic that tourists constantly poked them to see if they were alive.

But those were life-sized, and they weren't designed to resemble someone he *knew*. The sight of Leonard holding a tiny Maggie Blevin tenderly, as though she were a captive bird, made Robbie feel lightheaded and slightly sick. He turned toward the tent opening. "I'll see if I can help Emery set up."

Leonard's gaze remained fixed on the tiny figure. "I'll be right there," he said at last.

At the foot of the dune, the boys were trying to talk Emery into letting them use the camera.

"No way." He waved as Robbie scrambled down. "See, I'm not even letting your Dad do it."

"That's because Dad would suck," Zach said as Emery grabbed Robbie and steered him toward the water. "Come on, just for a minute."

"Trouble with the crew?" asked Robbie.

"Nah. They're just getting bored."

"Did you see that doll?"

"The Incredible Shrinking Maggie?" Emery stopped to stare at the dune. "The thing about Leonard is, I can never figure out if he's brilliant or potentially dangerous. The fact that he'll be able to retire with a full government pension suggests he's normal. The Maggie voodoo doll, though…"

He shook his head and began to pace again. Robbie walked beside him, kicking at wet sand and staring curiously at the sky. The air smelled odd, of ozone or hot metal. But it felt too chilly for a thunderstorm, and the dark ridge that hung above the palmettos and live oaks looked more like encroaching fog than cumulus clouds.

"Well, at least the wind's from the right direction," said Robbie.

Emery nodded. "Yeah. I was starting to think we'd have to throw it from the roof."

A few minutes later, Leonard's voice rang out above the wind. "Okay, everyone over here."

They gathered at the base of the dune and stared up at him, his tunic an azure rent in the ominous sky. Between Leonard's feet was a cardboard box. He glanced at it and went on.

"I'm going to wait till the wind seems right, and then I'll yell '*Now!*' Emery, you'll just have to watch me and see where she goes, then do your best. Zach and Tyler—you guys fan out and be ready to catch her if she starts to fall. Catch her *gently*," he added.

"What about me?" called Robbie.

"You stay with Emery in case he needs backup."

"Backup?" Robbie frowned.

"You know," said Emery in a low voice. "In case I need help getting Leonard back to the rubber room."

The boys began to walk toward the water. Tyler had his cellphone out. He looked at Zach, who dug his phone from his pocket.

"Are they *texting* each other?" asked Emery in disbelief. "They're ten feet apart."

"Ready?" Leonard shouted.

"Ready," the boys yelled back.

Robbie turned to Emery. "What about you, Captain Marvo?"

Emery grinned and held up the camera. "I have never been readier."

Atop the dune, Leonard stooped to retrieve the *Bellerophon* from its box. As he straightened, its propellers began turning madly. Candy-striped rotators spun like pinwheels as he cradled it against his chest, his long white braids threatening to tangle with the parasol.

The wind gusted suddenly: Robbie's throat tightened as he watched the tiny black figure beneath the fuselage swung wildly back and forth, like an accelerated pendulum. Leonard slipped in the sand and fought to regain his balance.

"Uh oh," said Emery.

The wind died, and Leonard righted himself. Even from the beach, Robbie could see how his face had gone white.

"Are you okay?" yelled Zach.

"I'm okay," Leonard yelled back.

He gave them a shaky smile, then stared intently at the horizon. After a minute his head tilted, as though listening to something. Abruptly he straightened and raised the *Bellerophon* in both hands. Behind him, palmettos thrashed as the wind gusted.

"*Now!*" he shouted.

Leonard opened his hands. As though it were a butterfly, the *Bellerophon* lifted into the air. Its feathery parasol billowed. Fan-shaped wings rose and fell; ailerons flapped and gears whirled like pinwheels. There was a sound like a train rushing through a tunnel, and Robbie stared open-mouthed as the *Bellerophon* skimmed the air above his head, its pilot pedaling furiously as it headed toward the sea.

Robbie gasped. The boys raced after it, yelling. Emery followed, camera clamped to his face and Robbie at his heels.

"This is fucking incredible!' Emery shouted. "Look at that thing go!"

They drew up a few yards from the water. The Bellerophon whirred past, barely an arm's-length above them. Robbie's eyes blurred as he stared after that brilliant whirl of color and motion, a child's dream of flight soaring just out of reach. Emery waded into the shallows with his camera. The boys followed, splashing and waving at the little plane. From the dune behind them echoed Leonard's voice.

"*Godspeed.*"

Robbie gazed silently at the horizon as the *Bellerophon* continued on, its pilot silhouetted black against the sky, wings opened like sails. Its sound grew fainter, a soft whirring that might have been a flock of birds. Soon it would be gone. Robbie stepped to the water's edge and craned his neck to keep it in sight.

Without warning a green flare erupted from the waves and streamed toward the little aircraft. Like a meteor shooting *upward*, emerald blossomed into a blinding radiance that engulfed the *Bellerophon*. For an instant Robbie saw the flying machine, a golden wheel spinning within a comet's heart.

Then the blazing light was gone, and with it the *Bellerophon*.

Robbie gazed, stunned, at the empty air. After an endless moment he became aware of something—someone—near him. He turned to see Emery stagger from the water, soaking wet, the camera held uselessly at his side.

"I dropped it," he gasped. "When that—whatever the fuck it was, when it came, I dropped the camera."

Robbie helped him onto the sand.

"I felt it." Emery shuddered, his hand tight around Robbie's arm. "Like a riptide. I thought I'd go under."

Robbie pulled away from him. "Zach?" he shouted, panicked. "Tyler, Zach, are you—"

Emery pointed at the water, and Robbie saw them, heron-stepping through the waves and whooping in triumph as they hurried back to shore.

"What happened?" Leonard ran up alongside Robbie and grabbed him. "Did you see that?"

Robbie nodded. Leonard turned to Emery, his eyes wild. "Did you get it? The *Bellerophon*? And that flare? Like the original film! The same thing, the exact same thing!" Emery reached for Robbie's sweatshirt. "Give me that, I'll see if I can dry the camera." Leonard stared blankly at Emery's soaked clothes, the water dripping from the vidcam. "Oh no." He covered his face with his hands. "Oh no..."

"We got it!" Zach pushed between the grownups. "We got it, we got it!" Tyler ran up beside him, waving his cellphone. "Look!"

Everyone crowded together, the boys tilting their phones until the screens showed black.

"Okay," said Tyler. "Watch this." Robbie shaded his eyes, squinting.

And there it was, a bright mote bobbing across a formless gray field, growing bigger and bigger until he could see it clearly—the whirl of wings and gears, the ballooning peacock-feather parasol and steadfast pilot on the velocipede; the swift silent flare that lashed from the water then disappeared in an eyeblink.

"Now watch mine," said Zach, and the same scene played again from a different angle. "Eighteen seconds."

"Mine says twenty," said Tyler. Robbie glanced uneasily at the water. "Maybe we should head back to the house," he said.

Leonard seized Zach's shoulder. "Can you get me that? Both of you? Email it or something?"

"Sure. But we'll need to go where we can get a signal."

"I'll drive you," said Emery. "Let me get into some dry clothes."

He turned and trudged up the beach, the boys laughing and running behind him.

Leonard walked the last few steps to the water's edge, spray staining the tip of one cowboy boot. He stared at the horizon, his expression puzzled yet oddly expectant.

Robbie hesitated, then joined him. The sea appeared calm, green-glass waves rolling in long swells beneath parchment-colored sky. Through a gap in the clouds he could make out a glint of blue, like a noonday star. He gazed at it in silence, and after a minute asked, "Did you know that was going to happen?"

Leonard shook his head. "No. How could I?"

"Then—what was it?" Robbie looked at him helplessly. "Do you have any idea?" Leonard said nothing. Finally he turned to Robbie. Unexpectedly, he smiled.

"I have no clue. But you saw it, right?" Robbie nodded. "And you saw her fly. The *Bellerophon*."

Leonard took another step, heedless of waves at his feet. "She flew." His voice was barely a whisper. "She really flew."

◆ ◆ ◆

THAT NIGHT NOBODY slept. Emery drove Zach, Tyler and Leonard to a Dunkin Donuts where the boys got a cellphone signal and sent their movie footage to Leonard's laptop. Back at the house, he disappeared while the others sat on the deck and discussed, over and over again, what they had seen. The boys wanted to return to the beach, but Robbie refused to let them go. As a peace offering, he gave them each a beer. By the time Leonard emerged from his room with the laptop, it was after three a.m.

He set the computer on a table in the living room. "See what you think." When the others had assembled, he hit Play.

Blotched letters filled the screen: THE MAIDEN FLIGHT OF MCCAULEY'S BELLEROPHON. The familiar tipsy horizon appeared, sepia and amber, silvery flashes from the sea below. Robbie held his breath.

And there was the *Bellerophon* with its flickering wheels and wings propelled by a steadfast pilot, until the brilliant light struck from below and the clip abruptly ended, at exactly seventeen seconds. Nothing betrayed the figure as Maggie rather than McCauley; nothing seemed any different at all, no matter how many times Leonard played it back.

"So that's it," he said at last, and closed his laptop. "Are you going to put it on YouTube?" asked Zach.

"No," he replied wearily. The boys exchanged a look, but for once remained silent. "Well." Emery stood and stretched his arms, yawning. "Time to pack."

Two hours later they were on the road.

The hospice was a few miles outside town, a rambling old white house surrounded by neatly-kept azaleas and rhododendrons. The boys were turned loose to wander the neighborhood. The others walked up to the veranda, Leonard carrying his laptop. He looked terrible, his gray eyes bloodshot and his face unshaved. Emery put an arm over his shoulder and Leonard nodded stiffly.

A nurse met them at the door, a trim blonde woman in chinos and a yellow blouse. "I told her you were coming," she said as she showed them into a sunlit room with wicker furniture and a low table covered with books and magazines. "She's the only one here now, though we expect someone tomorrow."

"How is she?" asked Leonard.

"She sleeps most of the time. And she's on morphine for the pain, so she's not very lucid. Her body's shutting down. But she's conscious."

"Has she had many visitors?" asked Emery.

"Not since she's been here. In the hospital a few neighbors dropped by. I gather there's no family. It's a shame." She shook her head sadly. "She's a lovely woman."

"Can I see her?" Leonard glanced at a closed door at the end of the bright room.

"Of course."

Robbie and Emery watched them go, then settled into the wicker chairs. "God, this is depressing," said Emery.

"It's better than a hospital," said Robbie. "Anna was going to go into a hospice, but she died before she could."

Emery winced. "Sorry. Of course, I wasn't thinking."

"It's okay."

Robbie leaned back and shut his eyes. He saw Anna sitting on the grass with azaleas all around her, bees in the flowers and Zach laughing as he opened his hands to release a green moth that lit momentarily upon her head, then drifted into the sky.

"Robbie." He started awake. Emery sat beside him, shaking him gently. "Hey—I'm going in now. Go back to sleep if you want, I'll wake you when I come out."

Robbie looked around blearily. "Where's Leonard?"

"He went for a walk. He's pretty broken up. He wanted to be alone for a while."

"Sure, sure." Robbie rubbed his eyes. "I'll just wait."

When Emery was gone he stood and paced the room. After a few minutes he sighed and sank back into his chair, then idly flipped through the magazines and books on the table. *Tricycle, Newsweek,* the *Utne Reader*; some pamphlets on end-of-life issues, works by Viktor Frankl and Elizabeth Kubler-Ross.

And, underneath yesterday's newspaper, a familiar sky-blue dust-jacket emblazoned with the garish image of a naked man and woman,

THE MAIDEN FLIGHT OF McCAULEY'S *BELLEROPHON*

hands linked as they floated above a vast abyss, surrounded by a glowing purple sphere. Beneath them the title appeared in embossed green letters.

>Wings for Humanity! The Next Step is OURS!
>by Margaret S. Blevin, PhD

Robbie picked it up. On the back was a photograph of the younger Maggie in a white embroidered tunic, her hair a bright corona around her piquant face. She stood in the Hall of Flight beside a mockup of the Apollo Lunar Module, the Wright Flyer high above her head. She was laughing, her hands raised in welcome. He opened it to a random page.

>...that time has come: With the dawn of the Golden Millennium we will welcome their return, meeting them at last as equals to share in the glory that is the birthright of our species.

He glanced at the frontispiece and title page, and then the dedication.

>*For Leonard, who never doubted*

"Isn't that an amazing book?"

Robbie looked up to see the nurse smiling down at him. "Uh, yeah," he said, and set it on the table.

"It's incredible she predicted so much stuff." The nurse shook her head. "Like the Hubble Telescope, and that caveman they found in the glacier, the guy with the lens? And those turbines that can make energy in the jet stream? I never even heard of that, but my husband said they're real. Everything she says, it's all so hopeful. You know?"

Robbie stared at her, then quickly nodded. Behind her the door opened. Emery stepped out.

"She's kind of drifting," he said.

"Morning's her good time. She usually fades around now." The nurse glanced at her watch, then at Robbie. "You go ahead. Don't be surprised if she nods off."

He stood. "Sure. Thanks."

The room was small, its walls painted a soft lavender-gray. The bed faced a large window overlooking a garden. Goldfinches and tiny green wrens darted between a bird feeder and a small pool lined with flat white stones. For a moment Robbie thought the bed was empty. Then he saw an emaciated figure had slipped down between the white sheets, dwarfed by pillows and a bolster.

"Maggie?"

The figure turned its head. Hairless, skin white as paper, mottled with bruises like spilled ink. Her lips and fingernails were violet; her face so pale and lined it was like gazing at a cracked egg. Only the eyes were recognizably Maggie's, huge, the deep slatey blue of an infant's. As she stared at him, she drew her wizened arms up, slowly, until her fingers grazed her shoulders. She reminded Robbie disturbingly of a praying mantis.

"I don't know if you remember me." He sat in a chair beside the bed. "I'm Robbie. I worked with Leonard. At the museum."

"He told me." Her voice was so soft he had to lean close to hear her. "I'm glad they got here. I expected them yesterday, when it was still snowing."

Robbie recalled Anna in her hospital bed, doped to the gills and talking to herself. "Sure," he said.

Maggie shot him a glance that might have held annoyance, then gazed past him into the garden. Her eyes widened as she struggled to lift her hand, fingers twitching. Robbie realized she was waving. He turned to stare out the window, but there was no one there.

Maggie looked at him, then gestured at the door. "You can go now," she said. "I have guests."

"Oh. Yeah, sorry."

He stood awkwardly, then leaned down to kiss the top of her head. Her skin was smooth and cold as metal. "Bye, Maggie."

At the door he looked back, and saw her gazing with a rapt expression at the window, head cocked slightly and her hands open, as though to catch the sunlight.

• ◆ •

TWO DAYS AFTER they got home, Robbie received an email from Leonard.

Dear Robbie,

Maggie died this morning. The nurse said she became unconscious early yesterday, seemed to be in pain but at least it didn't last long. She had arranged to be cremated. No memorial service or anything like that. I will do something, probably not till the fall, and let you know.

Yours, Leonard

Robbie sighed. Already the week on Cowana seemed long ago and faintly dreamlike, like the memory of a childhood vacation. He wrote Leonard a note of condolence, then left for work.

Weeks passed. Zach and Tyler posted their clips of the *Bellerophon* online. Robbie met Emery for drinks every week or two, and saw Leonard once, at Emery's Fourth of July barbecue. By the end of summer, Tyler's footage had been viewed 347,623 times, and Zach's 347,401. Both provided a link to the Captain Marvo site, where Emery had a free download of the entire text of *Wings for Humanity!* There were now over a thousand Google hits for Margaret Blevin, and Emery added a *Bellerophon* t-shirt to his merchandise: organic cotton with a silkscreen image of the baroque aircraft and its bowler-hatted pilot.

Early in September, Leonard called Robbie.

"Can you meet me at the museum tomorrow, around eight-thirty? I'm having a memorial for Maggie, just you and me and Emery. After hours, I'll sign you in."

"Sure," said Robbie. "Can I bring something?"

"Just yourself. See you then."

He drove in with Emery. They walked across the twilit Mall, the museum a white cube that glowed against a sky swiftly darkening to indigo. Leonard waited for them by the side door. He wore an embroidered tunic, sky-blue, his white hair loose upon his shoulders, and held a cardboard box with a small printed label.

"Come on," he said. The museum had been closed since five, but a guard opened the door for them. "We don't have a lot of time."

Hedges sat at the security desk, bald and even more imposing than when Robbie last saw him, decades ago. He signed them in, eying Robbie curiously then grinning when he read his signature.

"I remember you—Opie, right?"

Robbie winced at the nickname, then nodded. Hedges handed Leonard a slip of paper. "Be quick."

"Thanks. I will."

They walked to the staff elevator, the empty museum eerie and blue-lit. High above them the silent aircraft seemed smaller than they had been in the past, battered and oddly toylike. Robbie noticed a crack in the Gemini VII space capsule, and strands of dust clinging to the Wright Flyer. When they reached the third floor, Leonard led them down the corridor, past the Photo Lab, past the staff cafeteria, past the library where the Nut Files used to be.

Finally he stopped at a door near some open ductwork. He looked at the slip of paper Hedges had given him, punched a series of numbers into the lock, opened it then reached in to switch on the light. Inside was a narrow room with a metal ladder fixed to one wall.

"Where are we going?" asked Robbie.

"The roof," said Leonard. "If we get caught, Hedges and I are screwed. Actually, we're all screwed. So we have to make this fast."

He tucked the cardboard box against his chest, then began to climb the ladder. Emery and Robbie followed him to a small metal platform and another door. Leonard punched in another code and pushed it open. They stepped out into the night.

It was like being atop an ocean liner. The museum's roof was flat, nearly a block long. Hot air blasted from huge exhaust vents, and Leonard motioned the others to move away, toward the far end of the building.

The air was cooler here, a breeze that smelled sweet and rainwashed, despite the cloudless sky. Beneath them stretched the Mall, a vast green gameboard, with the other museums and monuments huge gamepieces, ivory and onyx and glass. The spire of the Washington Monument rose in the distance, and beyond that the glittering reaches of Roslyn and Crystal City

"I've never been here," said Robbie, stepping beside Leonard. Emery shook his head. "Me neither."

"I have," said Leonard, and smiled. "Just once, with Maggie."

Above the Capitol's dome hung the full moon, so bright against the starless sky that Robbie could read what was printed on Leonard's box.

MARGARET BLEVIN.

"These are her ashes." Leonard set the box down and removed the top, revealing a ziplocked bag. He opened the bag, picked up the box again and stood. "She wanted me to scatter them here. I wanted both of you to be with me."

He dipped his hand into the bag and withdrew a clenched fist; held the box out to Emery, who nodded silently and did the same; then turned to Robbie.

"You too," he said.

Robbie hesitated, then put his hand into the box. What was inside felt gritty, more like sand than ash. When he looked up, he saw that Leonard had stepped forward, head thrown back so that he gazed at the moon. He drew his arm back, flung the ashes into the sky and stooped to grab more.

Emery glanced at Robbie, and the two of them opened their hands.

Robbie watched the ashes stream from between his fingers, like a flight of tiny moths. Then he turned and gathered more, the three of them tossing handful after handful into the sky.

When the box was finally empty Robbie straightened, breathing hard, and ran a hand across his eyes. He didn't know if it was some trick of the moonlight or the freshening wind, but everywhere around them, everywhere he looked, the air was filled with wings.

Eat the Wyrm

JOHAN HAD been telling me about Solopgang ever since I arrived in Greenland.

"It's not on the way to anyplace, so you have to make a special pilgrimage. Maybe we can go after the SIKON conference." *Nothing's on the way to anyplace in Greenland*, I wanted to say, but what was the point? Solopgang was legendary in the way things are, or used to be, in Greenland—famous to fifteen people. The name was Danish for "sunrise." The guy who ran it, Kurt Gunderson, had knocked around the country for a few years as a corporate geologist before lighting out for the territory and, in one of the country's more improbable reinventions, becoming a grower and distiller of mescal. I'm not much of a drinker, but I used to have a taste for tequila. Not a very elevated taste—Cuervo Gold was about as far as it reached. But after the SIKON conference, where I spent three futile days discussing core samples and how to downplay the dangers of nuclear contamination as the ice sheet melted, exposing the waste stored there decades earlier, I was ready for a pilgrimage. Let's go, I texted Johan. He picked me up on Friday. It took us three days to reach Ipat-kitak, on the northeast coast. We stayed in rentals the first two nights, corrugated buildings that in the US might have been used for storing cannibalized lawnmowers or refrigerators too heavy to be lugged to the dump. The morning of the third day we left our SUV in the lee of an immense spar of black rock, and hiked the remainder of the way.

The views were spectacular, black crags and that endless stretch of indigo water, the luminous cerulean of melting icebergs igniting to gold as the sun rose, the blue heart of a dying flame. The air had a raw, stony smell I've only experienced in the Greenland wilderness, untainted by the stink of fuel and rotting fish and burning tires that hangs over the larger settlements; a stink recently grown more corrosive as reps from corporations and nations crowded the villages in the grab for mineral rights as the icecap disappeared.

"Can't we just stay here?" I asked on the third night, when we pitched a tent beneath the rusting hulk of an abandoned transport vehicle.

"Maybe Kurt will let us stay with him." Johan rolled over in his sleeping bag, opened the tent flap so he could light a cigarette. "We can tend his greenhouse."

"Greenland greenhouse. That's an oxymoron."

Johan nodded. "Oxymoron would have been a good name for the bar."

During the Cold War, Ipatkitak had been the site of a small US air base. Military detritus was everywhere, strewn across the barren rocks like the wreckage of some long-ago plane crash. Shattered windshields, husks of Jeeps and trailers, tires as big as a wading pool. Kurt's homestead was still half a day's trek from here. We left early the next morning and arrived before noon, just as a cold fog settled in, obscuring the surrounding plain and the distant sweep of jagged mountains.

"Welcome!"

Kurt strode from a small Quonset hut that appeared to float on the rocky plain, a black bubble. He was short for a Dane, dark-haired, not blond, with a graying beard and round tinted eyeglasses. He looked like a benign if earnest Trotskyite. "Johan, great to see you! And Emma, so glad we finally meet. Come, you can put your things inside, then we can head over to Solopgang. It's only a minute's walk that way."

He gestured vaguely at the thickening fog as we followed him into the Quonset hut. Half an hour later, we ventured back out. I'd been hoping to fortify myself with some food before we turned to the business of sampling Kurt's booze, but Johan was too impatient.

"We've come eight hundred miles for a drink. I want that drink."

Kurt nodded, and we followed him to another Quonset hut, smaller, its round windows brilliantly lit from within. Solar panels and propane tanks and several generators littered the rocky ground. A polar bear hide dangled from a flagpole, its jaws rattling in the wind. Above the hut's entrance hung a hand-carved wooden sign, the letters picked out in crimson paint.

SOLOPGANG

Kurt held the door for us as we stepped inside, blasted by a wave of heat so intense that immediately I began to sweat. I blinked, blinded by banks of growlights suspended from the domed ceiling and arranged along the perimeter off the space. I felt as though we'd stepped onstage, at the mercy of hundreds of spotlights, or into the loading bay of a UFO.

"My god, Emma, look at all this!" Johan cried.

The room was filled with huge, spiky plants, some nearly as tall as I was, their thick blade-shaped leaves shading from periwinkle blue to a green so rich and dark the leaves might have been carved from malachite. I inhaled deeply, my nostrils stung by the heat and also the slightly acrid scent of the agave plants; it was as though their leaves had been singed.

I turned to Kurt, who had stopped to stroke a long stalk that held a creamy agave blossom. "How can you possibly keep them warm enough in winter?"

He shrugged. "That's my secret, right? But very strange things are happening around here. Everywhere, I think. Did you hear they found an arm on the Garm glacier? Thousands of years old, they think, like the Ice Man. Tattoos on the hand and part of a sleeve made from sealskin. But only the arm. What do you think happened to the rest of him?"

I laughed. "They'll find him when the rest of the glacier melts."

"No, the ice everywhere near him is gone. They searched and searched and they found nothing. I think something ate him. Okay, this way."

I'd expected Solopgang to bear at least a cursory resemblance to an actual bar or restaurant. While it didn't cost as much as climbing Everest, or dinner at a Michelin-starred place, I'd heard you could rack up a hefty bar tab.

But the space Kurt ushered us into was a narrow annex with walls of unpainted plywood. The cement floor was sticky. There were no windows. Strings of white LEDs drooped from nails in the wood, illuminating a rectangular table with a battered red formica top, and six metal folding chairs. Beside the door someone had scrawled on a piece of cardboard with a Sharpie.

Eat the wyrm.

"Have a seat," said Kurt. He walked to a small metal cabinet, opened it and withdrew a bottle and three glass tumblers. "We'll start with this."

"No." Johan shook his head, then pointed at the sign by the door. "We want to taste it."

Kurt hesitated, set the bottle and tumblers back on the shelf and walked towards us, pulling out a mobile. Johan did the same with his phone. After a brief exchange of information and shadow currency, Kurt nodded.

"Right back," he said, and headed into the greenhouse. I sat on one of the rickety chairs next to Johan.

"I've never done that," I said, staring at the hand-lettered sign. "Eat the worm. Have you?"

"Yeah, sure. It's not a big deal—in Mexico, they eat caterpillars, you know? This is very different. Five K it cost, but it'll be worth it." A few minutes later Kurt returned. He settled at the table, and placed two small bottles in front of us, each stoppered with a cork.

Carefully he removed the corks.

There you go," he said.

At first I thought they were made of the same kind of glass they used for old Coke bottles, that diffuse green-blue color that always reminded me of a hurricane sky.

But when I gingerly picked up mine, I saw that the glass was clear. The strange glaucous hue came from the liquid inside. Something floated at the bottom of the glass.

No, didn't float—swam. I gazed at it, my neck prickling: a creature roughly the size and length of my pinkie finger, shimmering and pulsating, its sinuous motion causing it to flicker dull orange, then the brilliant acid green of Vasoline glass.

I drew the bottle closer to my face, hardly daring to breathe. The little creature writhed, coiling and uncoiling so that it was difficult to count its legs. *Six*, I thought. A rippling scarlet fringe surrounded its thumbnail-sized head, the same color as its eyes. There were four of them.

I glanced at Johan. He'd already brought the glass to his lips, eyes shining and his cheeks pink with excitement.

"Skol," he said, raising his tumbler to me and downing the mescal in a gulp. I watched him, my mouth dry, as he and Kurt both turned to me expectantly. I drew the bottle to my lips, caught a faint odor of sulfur and an even fainter hint of putrefying meat. I closed my eyes.

"Skol," I said, and drank.

Fire.

EVERYBODY GATHER round. Hold hands. Whose turn is it? Mine? Okay.

So a poet, a fireman, a director and a magician all walk into a bar.

Okay, obviously I know this is not a bar. I'm changing some of the details cause it's my turn to tell our story, okay? I know that. We all know that. It's just, that's how a lot of stories start, people walking into a bar. Jokes.

I know, none of this is funny, but what else are we going to do? Food's gone, enough water for what, another day? If we all just take sips. Can people even live on such a small amount of water? With the fire just…

I know, right, I'll stop. Back to the story. Five random people walk into a bar. A couple of them know each other from the hiking trail or before. The poet, she had a book won some prize, I can't remember the name. I know, it's sweet. She's an amazing cook, too, that's her day job, she's a chef in this great place in Telluride. And it's actually a firefighter, not a fireman. Definitely not a fire*man*. *She* is a firefighter, we all know what a badass, right? Right! Like would we even have survived here for the last three days without her?

Yeah, I know. Really, thank you, Marina.

Please don't everyone start to cry—*lo siento*, please, I'm sorry, I'm sorry. Can I just start over?

So they all walk into a bar, only it's not a bar. There's a standup comic too, and a rocket scientist. Cause like how great is that, you know how everyone always says, "I'm not a rocket scientist?" He *is* a rocket scientist! Robert, how's that imaginary escape pod coming? The imaginary flame retardant one that'll fly us all back to Denver or wherever the hell they said people would be safe?

Okay, I get it. Also not funny. You're killing me. Talk about a tough crowd.

So a poet, a firefighter, a nuclear physicist guy, a director—right, a documentarian, not a regular filmmaker—and an illusionist, and a standup comic all walk into a bar. Whew! Got one right. They're all on a hike, they all started off before the fire got out of control and became a, whatever they call it.

Right—a megafire. Thanks, Marina.

So they're on a hike and like a thousand other idiots—ten thousand, a hundred thousand, I don't know how many—they're outside and get cut off by the fire. The mega—

Yeah. okay. *The fire event.* I'm fine with calling it that, Lula. Fire event, very nice. That's why it's good to have a poet. They're hiking, though they didn't all start out together, they just end up in the same place.

But not the firefighter, she's not hiking. She's working here. And no, it's not a bar, I think we can all agree on that. It's a fire tower and a fire research station on top of Mount Reynolds, ten thousand five hundred and forty seven feet—is that above sea level? I never get that, like do we measure from the beach somewhere a thousand miles away or from the ground up?

All I know is, it was a fucking hike to get here. I've never been so exhausted in my life, and I was on a whole season of *Who Wants to Marry My Mom?* If that show had worked out, probably I wouldn't be here now. Maybe I wouldn't have gone on that stupid retreat in the middle of the woods in the middle of fucking nowhere, Colorado. Maybe things would have been better, maybe not. These days, *quién sabe?*

No, I absolutely would not be here now. I'd be back East with Reuben and Peter and Lou, I'd be with my kids, my family…

――― **FIRE.** ―――

Lo siento, sorry. You are my family now, I know that. We all know that. *Lo siento*. Just so hard, you know? To…

All right, if you're my family—who gets to be Uncle Al?

Yo, thanks, Jeff. Didn't know there was any of that left. Who here thought we'd be having whatever they call it, communion with Jim Beam, when the water ran out? When the water *almost* ran out. Jeff, you're recording all this, right?

I can't say it enough, Jeff really is a genius. When we were hiking up here I thought he was crazy, half the filmmakers I know, they're all about big cameras and shit, big crews. Not Jeff. Just the smartphone, but a fuckload more backup chargers than I've ever seen. We passed Lula and Hermanos on the trail, if I'd known she was a cook—*and a poet!*—and he was a magician I would have stuck with them. In case, you know, she might have made us Thanksgiving dinner and he could have teleported us all somewhere to eat it. Turkey and pecan pie, what I wouldn't—

Right, yeah, sorry again. No food talk. But remember the first day we were up here—I can say this, right?—remember the first day, those lights in the sky? They were so beautiful and scary, me and Marina saw them and I'll admit, I was scared. I thought it was some kind of drones. Bad drones, the kind the terrorists used to start the fires. But I was hoping maybe they were the other kind, the ones they used to fight the LA megafire last year. They worked then, right? I thought maybe they were sending them here. But Marina said no, she'd trained in using them. This must be another kind of drone. So I was kind of nervous, yeah, I was scared.

Then it turns out it wasn't drones but birds, that whole flock of birds on fire—hundreds and hundreds. I know everybody saw them, once they got close. Jeff got that amazing footage. That noise.

And it was horrible when they came down. That smell. But we ate, right? I'm not talking about food here, I'm talking about something else—

I don't know what I'm talking about. Just, birds on fire from the sky. And we at least got to eat. You'd think there'd be all kinds of animals ran up here the way we did, to escape. Like that scene in *Bambi*, remember that? Scared the shit out of me when I was a kid. But at least we could've eaten them.

Jeff, any more of that? Just a—

Thanks. If nothing else, it's good to be someplace where bourbon is a major food group.

So Jeff thought the smoke was getting worse before I did, when we were first hiking here, I mean. We left before dawn, just taking a hike. It seemed like a good idea, why we were here. I saw the news, they said it was far away, or it seemed far away, just not that far away, I guess, or not far enough away. A different state, maybe. I thought the smoke might have drifted from somewhere else, another one of those places where everyone wants to live. Or used to. The mountains, the desert, it's so beautiful. Who wouldn't want to live here, right? Or at least visit. Do your poet magician movie thing. Your nuclear physicist thing. Second home, whatever.

Yeah, you all get it. I know you all get it. Actually, I smelled it first, even before Jeff noticed it. I even said something about no smoking on the trail, no cigarettes or campfires—even I knew about that. I don't smoke anyway, and I've never started a campfire in my life.

But the smell. It was crazy. You all remember it, right? Lula, how did you describe it yesterday when it was your turn?

Like smoke exhaling itself, thrice burnt—that's good, Lula. Why you're the poet.

After a while, I didn't even notice I was breathing it in. But I couldn't smell anything else. I think all the receptors in my nostrils got burned out by the smoke. Which, being around Jeff three days with no bathing facilities, is not such a bad thing.

Yeah bra, I love you too.

I know the smoke thing's different for people with asthma, Hermanos. I wasn't forgetting that. But the respirator helps, right? I wish there were enough for everyone but it's good to take turns. Everyone takes turns with whatever's left. Which isn't much.

———— FIRE. ————

No, I won't shut up about it. I'm not done yet. This is *my* version of the story. This is why it's great we have different people ended up here. People from the artist colony, Lula and Hermanos. Hermanos, it's incredible what you're doing. Have you guys seen it? You really have to—Marina, is it okay if we open the safe room and go down? Right now? Cause I don't think everyone has seen it, just me and Marina and him. Would that be okay with you, Hermanos? Marina? Yeah? That would be amazing! Thanks, Marina!

Just everyone be really careful going down the stairs. It's cooler here, even with the a/c dead. Concrete bunker. Also, this is why it's good to have the rocket scientist around, to handle those solar panels if we ever—

Yeah, well, I know there's not enough sun because of the smoke. And I know the light batteries are almost dead. I thought we weren't going to discuss that now? Plus it's my turn, and I definitely do not want to discuss it.

So it's kind of dark down here and I know we can't waste the batteries or the lanterns. But. I think we should see what Hermanos did with his turn. Cause he couldn't talk with the asthma and all. Wearing the respirator.

Thanks, Marina—I should just get a tattoo that says that. *Thanks Marina*. Because, if like you're going to be trapped on a mountain for the firepocalypse, you want to be with the beautiful firefighter, right?

The beautiful, brilliant, *innovative* firefighter! You said it, Robert, not me! How did we get so lucky? Work with what you got, right?

Can you hand me that flashlight, please?

Isn't this amazing? Hermanos, this is just such a fucking amazing thing, I can't even say it. Every wall, he covered every wall. The one thing all this charcoal is good for—you can draw with it! I never even knew that.

Isn't it amazing? This is like, you see those cave paintings and you think, how did this last for a hundred thousand years? Or however many years—ten thousand, I dunno. Maybe some guy painted them when no one was looking during the World Cup. I never actually saw one, just pictures and that 3D movie. Point is, it lasted all that time.

So Hermanos is a magician—an illusionist, yeah—and I hope maybe you can figure out a way to do some of that shit for us. Maybe disappear us from here back home. That would be nice.

But the fact is, he's an artist, too, and he drew all this, and I just think it's fucking amazing. Like someday in ten thousand years, someone will find this bunker and see it and they'll understand what happened. A picture story without words. Maybe Jeff's batteries will last ten thousand years and they can watch it on his phone. Cause there sure as shit ain't gonna be anything left out there to show them what happened.

Yeah okay, okay, I'm sorry, *lo siento*. I should get a tattoo with that, too, right? *I'm sorry* in every language. Hermanos, could you do that? It would be cool if we could all get matching tattoos.

Look, I really *am* sorry. Really. Aw, Jeff, come on. Marina, I know. I said I'm sorry. Lula. I know we all feel the same way. We just show it different.

This is me. I'm sorry this is me. But that's why it's good we have everyone else.

Yeah, I'd like to stay down here too. It's definitely cooler. Not like we're missing much up there.

I did go up to the tower really early this morning, while it was still dark. No, I was with Marina, I didn't break any goddam rules. Robert was there too. Not that I could understand what he was saying. Physics, that should be a language, too.

It *is* a language? Yeah? How do you say "I'm sorry" in physics?

Anyway, it was strange. In the day everything's all hazed out by the smoke. Looks like fucking Mordor out there. At night it does too, but you can see the fire better in the dark.

Can you even tell anymore if it's day or night? If this keeps up. I wonder about that sometimes. Anyway we're up there on the tower and it's night, it's dark, you can't see anything, *really* can't see anything

——— FIRE. ———

because of the smoke, so no stars, I don't even know if you could ever see lights here from houses or something, because the whole three days I've been here it's just smoke.

Marina? Before, could you see lights?

So okay, some, but not now. Not this morning. No moon, *nada, oscura*, no nothing. Just dark.

Except for, up there on the tower, if you turned in a circle, you could see the fire, this ring of fire. Shut up, I hate that song. Jeff, serious, bra, shut up. A perfect ring of fire, *so perfect*—it was beautiful, I couldn't make this up. You could see it moving but it was like someone had designed it, like a special effects. Like Marina says, fire is a living thing—that's what it was like. A living thing. Only so big, you can't imagine any living thing could be that big. Huge. *Enorme. Vasto.*

And it's here. It's right here. Right there.

No, I won't. I haven't finished yet. Let me finish.

Thanks.

This is the other thing, we were out there watching and eventually it got light. Sunrise only no sun, it just got light. Lighter. All you could see was smoke and you could definitely smell it more, I could smell it more—everyone did, I know. You couldn't see the fire so much but I assume it's there, right, Marina?

Look, there's no point, we can't fucking pretend! And it's my fucking turn. And the thing is, as it got light—lighter—Marina and Robert and me looked at the sky and we saw clouds. Big clouds, far away but dark, not those other clouds that are just the smoke and dust. Real clouds. And the wind, you all felt the wind, right? I know it's hot, we all get that, but it's wind. You could feel it now, if we were outside. Dr. Science there, he can tell you, wind means a front coming in. A front.

I don't know what kind of front. Santa Ana? I know it's the wrong time of year but now we get those crazy winds all the time. Yeah, see, Marina says the same thing, and that's like her *job*. But we don't know what kind. It could be, it could be it's just blowing towards us, all of it, and—

But it could be, maybe, maybe it's rain. Those kind of clouds, tell them what they are, Robert.

Mammatus, right. Mammatus clouds. Big thunderstorms, they can be part of a severe storm, with rain, maybe. Rain, real rain, a ton of rain...

Right? Right? Maybe? Yeah.

Can we go up back there to the fire tower, Marina? All of us? It'll be dark soon but if we go up now it'll be easier on the steps. Then everyone could see what I was talking about. The way it looks at night, the fire. I think everyone should see it, I think everyone might want to see it. So afterwards you can say you saw it, maybe. And if not, just so we can all see it together.

Yeah, we can have a vote. I don't think we should leave anyone behind—that's not for me to decide, we all need to—okay, that's cool, everyone says yes. Marina, you can do the honors? And Robert, you and me, we can go at the end, in case anyone needs—yeah, it's a long freaking way, you will definitely get winded, Lula. It's fine with me if you keep those things on, you and Hermanos. I know it's my turn but I'll wait cause I want you to see up there. And you need them more than I do. Especially now. Too bad we don't have spacesuits. Spacesuits to breathe. But thank god we have two respirators. Thank god for the U.S. Fire Service. Thank god for Marina.

Jeff, you got that one charger left, right? Now's the time, bra. Maybe. Roll 'em!

It does smell different up here, right? Right? I bet you can smell it even with those respirators on. The smoke but something else, I think maybe there's something else. Something not smoke.

Did you see that? Did anyone see that? Was it, do you think—lightning? Yeah? Maybe? Maybe.

Yeah, I know it could be a goddamn terrorist drone. But it also could be lightning. So it could, something could happen. Rain. It might happen, is all I'm saying.

Anyway, we're all here. It's like a movie, here we all are, the fuck we would ever know each other but here we are. I wonder if anyone else...

FIRE.

Okay. Okay. That's it for me. Thanks—really, thank you. You don't know what it's like—but of course you do. I know you do. Even Jeff. So okay, I'm done. I'm done. So.

Everyone gather round. Everyone hold hands.

Whose turn is it?

The Lost Domain—
Three Story Variations

Echo

THIS IS not the first time this has happened. I've been here every time it has. Always I learn about it the same way, a message from someone five hundred miles away, a thousand, comes flickering across my screen. There's no TV here on the island, and the radio reception is spotty: the signal comes across Penobscot Bay from a tower atop Mars Hill, and any kind of weather—thunderstorms, high winds, blizzards—brings the tower down. Sometimes I'm listening to the radio when it happens, music playing, Nick Drake, a promo for the Common Ground Country Fair; then a sudden soft explosive hiss like damp hay falling onto a bonfire. Then silence.

Sometimes I hear about it from you. Or, well, I don't actually hear anything: I read your messages, imagine your voice, for a moment neither sardonic nor world-weary, just exhausted, too fraught to be expressive. Words like feathers falling from the sky, black specks on blue.

The Space Needle. Sears Tower. LaGuardia Airport. Golden Gate Bridge. The Millennium Eye. The Bahrain Hilton. Sydney, Singapore, Jerusalem.

Years apart at first; then months; now years again. How long has it been since the first tower fell? When did I last hear from you?

I can't remember.

• ◆ •

THIS MORNING I took the dog for a walk across the island. We often go in search of birds, me for my work, the wolfhound to chase for joy. He ran across the ridge, rushing at a partridge that burst into the air in a roar of copper feathers and beech leaves. The dog dashed after her fruitlessly, long jaw sliced open to show red gums, white teeth, a panting unfurled tongue.

"Finn!" I called and he circled round the fern brake, snapping at bracken and crickets, black splinters that leapt wildly from his jaws. "Finn, get back here."

He came. Mine is the only voice he knows now.

• ◆ •

THERE WAS A while when I worried about things like food and water, whether I might need to get to a doctor. But the dug well is good. I'd put up enough dried beans and canned goods to last for years, and the garden does well these days. The warming means longer summers here on the island, more sun; I can grow tomatoes now, and basil, scotch bonnet peppers, plants that I never could grow when I first arrived. The root cellar under the cottage is dry enough and cool enough that I keep all my medications there, things I stockpiled back when I could get over to Ellsworth and the mainland—albuterol inhalers, alprazolam, amoxicillin, Tylenol and codeine, ibuprofen, aspirin; cases of food for the wolfhound. When I first put the solar cells up, visitors shook their heads: not enough sunny days this far north, not enough light. But that changed too as the days got warmer.

Now it's the wireless signal that's difficult to capture, not sunlight. There will be months on end of silence and then it will flare up again, for days or even weeks, I never know when. If I'm lucky, I patch into it then sit there, waiting, holding my breath until the messages begin to scroll across the screen, looking for your name. I go downstairs to my office every day, like an angler going to shore, casting my line though I know the weather's wrong, the currents too strong, not enough wind or too much, the power grid like the Grand Banks scraped barren by decades

THE LOST DOMAIN—THREE STORY VARIATIONS

of trawlers dragging the bottom. Sometimes my line would latch onto you: sometimes, in the middle of the night, it would be the middle of the night where you were, too, and we'd write back and forth. I used to joke about these letters going out like messages in bottles, not knowing if they would reach you, or where you'd be when they did.

London, Paris, Petra, Oahu, Moscow. You were always too far away. Now you're like everyone else, unimaginably distant. Who would ever have thought it could all be gone, just like that? The last time I saw you was in the hotel in Toronto, we looked out and saw the spire of the CN Tower like Cupid's arrow aimed at us. You stood by the window and the sun was behind you and you looked like a cornstalk I'd seen once, burning, your gray hair turned to gold and your face smoke.

I can't see you again, you said. Deirdre is sick and I need to be with her.

I didn't believe you. We made plans to meet in Montreal, in Halifax, Seattle. Grey places; after Deirdre's treatment ended. After she got better.

But that didn't happen. Nobody got better. Everything got worse.

In the first days I would climb to the highest point on the island, a granite dome ringed by tamaracks and hemlock, the grey stone covered with lichen, celadon, bone-white, brilliant orange: as though armfuls of dried flowers had been tossed from an airplane high overhead. When evening came the aurora borealis would streak the sky, crimson, emerald, amber, as though the sun were rising in the west, in the middle of the night, rising for hours on end. I lay on my back wrapped in an old Pendleton blanket and watched, the dog Finn stretched out alongside me. One night the spectral display continued into dawn, falling arrows of green and scarlet, silver threads like rain or sheet lightning racing through them. The air hummed, I pulled up the sleeve of my flannel shirt and watched as the hairs on my arm rose and remained erect; looked down at the dog, awake now, growling steadily as it stared at the trees edging the granite, its hair on end like a cat's. There was nothing in the woods, nothing in the sky above us. After perhaps thirty minutes I heard a muffled sound to the west, like a far-off sonic boom; nothing more.

♦ ♦ ♦

AFTER TORONTO WE spoke only once a year; you would make your annual pilgrimage to mutual friends in Paris and call me from there. It was a joke, that we could only speak like this.

I'm never closer to you than when I'm in the seventh arrondissement at the Bowlses', you said.

But even before then we'd seldom talked on the phone. You said it would destroy the purity of our correspondence, and refused to give me your number in Seattle. We had never seen that much of each other anyway, a handful of times over the decades. Glasgow once, San Francisco, a long weekend in Liverpool, another in New York. Everything was in the letters; only of course they weren't actual letters but bits of information, code, electrical sparks; like neurotransmitters leaping the chasm between synapses. When I dreamed of you, I dreamed of your name shining in the middle of a computer screen like a ripple in still water. Even in dreams I couldn't touch you: my fingers would hover above your face and you'd fragment into jots of grey and black and silver. When you were in Basra I didn't hear from you for months. Afterward you said you were glad; that my silence had been like a gift.

♦ ♦ ♦

FOR A WHILE, the first four or five years, I would go down to where I kept the dinghy moored on the shingle at Amonsic Cove. It had a little two-horsepower engine that I kept filled with gasoline, in case I ever needed to get to the mainland.

But the tides are tricky here, they race high and treacherously fast in the Reach; the *Ellsworth American* used to run stories every year about lobstermen who went out after a snagged line and never came up, or people from away who misjudged the time to come back from their picnic on Egg Island, and never made it back. Then one day I went down to check on the dinghy and found the engine gone. I walked the length of the beach two days running at low tide, searching for it, went out as far as I could on

THE LOST DOMAIN—THREE STORY VARIATIONS

foot, hopping between rocks and tidal pools and startling the cormorants where they sat on high boulders, wings held out to dry like black angels in the thin sunlight. I never found the motor. A year after that the dinghy came loose in a storm and was lost as well, though for months I recognized bits of its weathered red planking when they washed up onshore.

• ◆ •

THE BOOK I was working on last time was a translation of Ovid's *Metamorphosis*. The manuscript remains on my desk beside my computer, with my notes on the nymph "whose tongue did not still when others spoke," the girl cursed by Hera to fall in love with beautiful, brutal Narkissos. He hears her pleading voice in the woods and calls to her, mistaking her for his friends.

But it is the nymph who emerges from the forest. And when he sees her Narkissos strikes her, repulsed; then flees. *Emoriar quam sit tibi copia nostri!* he cries; and with those words condemns himself.

Better to die than be possessed by you.

And see, here is Narkissos dead beside the woodland pool, his hand trailing in the water as he gazes at his own reflection. Of the nymph,

> She is vanished, save for these:
> her bones and a voice that
> calls out amongst the trees.
> Her bones are scattered in the rocks.
> She moves now in the laurels and beeches,
> she moves unseen across the mountaintops.
> You will hear her in the mountains and wild places,
> but nothing of her remains save her voice,
> her voice alone, alone upon the mountaintop.

• ◆ •

SEVERAL MONTHS AGO, midsummer, I began to print out your letters. I was afraid something would happen to the computer and I would lose them forever. It took a week, working off and on. The printer uses a lot of power and the island had become locked in by fog; the rows of solar cells, for the first time, failed to give me enough light to read by during the endless grey days, let alone run the computer and printer for more than fifteen minutes at a stretch. Still, I managed, and at the end of a week held a sheaf of pages. Hundreds of them, maybe more; they made a larger stack than the piles of notes for Ovid.

I love the purity of our relationship, you wrote from Singapore. *Trust me, it's better this way. You'll have me forever!*

There were poems, quotes from Cavafy, Sappho, Robert Lowell, W.S. Merwin. *It's hard for me to admit this, but the sad truth is that the more intimate we become here, the less likely it is we'll ever meet again in real life.* Some of the letters had my responses copied at the beginning or end,—imploring, fractious—; lines from other poems, songs.

> Swept with confused alarms of
> I long and seek after
> You can't put your arms around a memory.

• ◆ •

THE FIRST TIME, air traffic stopped. That was the eeriest thing, eerier than the absence of lights when I stood upon the granite dome and looked westward to the mainland. I was used to the slow constant flow overhead, planes taking the Great Circle Route between New York, Boston, London, Stockholm, passing above the islands, Labrador, Greenland, grey space, white. Now, day after day after day the sky was empty. The tower on Mars Hill fell silent. The dog and I would crisscross the island, me throwing sticks for him to chase across the rocky shingle, the wolfhound racing after them and returning tirelessly, over and over.

After a week the planes returned. The sound of the first one was like an explosion after that silence, but others followed, and soon enough I grew accustomed to them again. Until once more they stopped.

THE LOST DOMAIN—THREE STORY VARIATIONS

I wonder sometimes, How do I know this is all truly happening? Your letters come to me, blue sparks channeled through sunlight; you and your words are more real to me than anything else. Yet how real is that? How real is all of this? When I lie upon the granite I can feel stone pressing down against my skull, the trajectory of satellites across the sky above me a slow steady pulse in time with the firing of chemical signals in my head. It's the only thing I hear, now: it has been a year at least since the tower at Mars Hill went dead, seemingly for good.

• ◆ •

ONE AFTERNOON, A long time ago now, the wolfhound began barking frantically and I looked out to see a skiff making its way across the water. I went down to meet it: Rick Osgood, the part-time constable and volunteer fire chief from Mars Hill.

"We hadn't seen you for a while," he called. He drew the skiff up to the dock but didn't get out. "Wanted to make sure you were okay."

I told him I was, asked him up for coffee but he said no. "Just checking, that's all. Making a round of the islands to make sure everyone's okay."

He asked after the children. I told him they'd gone to stay with their father. I stood waving, as he turned the skiff around and it churned back out across the dark water, a spume of black smoke trailing it. I have seen no one since.

• ◆ •

THREE WEEKS AGO I turned on the computer and, for the first time in months, was able to patch into a signal and search for you. The news from outside was scattered and all bad. Pictures, mostly; they seem to have lost the urge for language, or perhaps it is just easier this way, with so many people so far apart. Some things take us to a place where words have no meaning. I was readying myself for bed when suddenly there was a spurt of sound from the monitor. I turned and saw the screen filled with strings of words. Your name: they were all messages from you. I sat down elated and trembling, waiting as for a quarter-hour they cascaded from the sky and moved beneath my fingertips, silver and black and grey and blue. I thought that at last you had found me; that these were years of words and yearning, that you would be back. Then, as abruptly as it had begun, the stream ceased; and I began to read.

They were not new letters; they were all your old ones, decades-old, some of them. 2009, 2007, 2004, 2001, 1999, 1998, 1997, 1996. I scrolled backwards in time, a skein of years, words; your name popping up again and again like a bright bead upon a string. I read them all, I read them until my eyes ached and the floor was pooled with candle wax and broken light bulbs. When morning came I tried to tap into the signal again but it was gone. I go outside each night and stare at the sky, straining my eyes as I look for some sign that something moves up there, that there is something between myself and the stars. But the satellites too are gone now, and it has been years upon years since I have heard an airplane.

• ◆ •

IN FALL AND winter I watch those birds that do not migrate. Chickadees, nuthatches, ravens, kinglets. This last autumn I took Finn down to the deep place where in another century they quarried granite to build the Cathedral of Saint John the Divine. The quarry is filled with water, still and black and bone-cold. We saw a flock of wild turkeys, young ones; but the dog is so old now he can no longer chase them, only watch as I set my snares. I walked to the water's edge and gazed into the dark pool, saw my face reflected there but there is no change upon it, nothing to show how many years have passed for me here, alone. I have burned all the empty crates and cartons from the root cellar, though it is not empty yet. I burn for kindling the leavings from my wood bench, the hoops that did not curve properly after soaking in willow-water, the broken dowels and circlets. Only the wolfhound's grizzled muzzle tells me how long it's been since I've seen a human face. When I dream of you now I see a smooth stretch of water with only a few red leaves upon its surface.

We returned from the cottage, and the old dog fell asleep in the late afternoon sun. I sat outside and watched as a downy woodpecker,

THE LOST DOMAIN—THREE STORY VARIATIONS

picus pubescens, crept up one of the red oaks, poking beneath its soft bark for insects. They are friendly birds, easy to entice, sociable; unlike the solitary wrynecks they somewhat resemble. The wrynecks do not climb trees but scratch upon the ground for the ants they love to eat. "Its body is almost bent backward," Thomas Bewick wrote over two hundred years ago in his *History of British Birds,* "whilst it writhes its head and neck by a slow and almost involuntary motion, not unlike the waving wreaths of a serpent. It is a very solitary bird, never being seen with any other society but that of its female, and this is only transitory, for as soon as the domestic union is dissolved, which is in the month of September, they retire and migrate separately."

It was this strange involuntary motion, perhaps, that so fascinated the ancient Greeks. In Pindar's fourth Pythian Ode, Aphrodite gives the wryneck to Jason as the magical means to seduce Medea, and with it he binds the princess to him through her obsessive love. Aphrodite of many arrows: she bears the brown-and-white bird to him, "the bird of madness," its wings and legs nailed to a four-spoked wheel.

> And she shared with Jason
> the means by which a spell
> might blaze and burn Medea,
> burning away all love she had for her family
> a fire that would ignite her mind, already aflame
> so that all her passion turned to him alone.

The same bird was used by the nymph Simaitha, abandoned by her lover in Theokritos's Idyll: pinned to the wooden wheel, the feathered spokes spin above a fire as the nymph invokes Hecate. The isle is full of voices: they are all mine.

• ◆ •

YESTERDAY THE WOLFHOUND died, collapsing as he followed me to the top of the granite dome. He did not get up again, and I sat beside him, stroking his long grey muzzle as his dark eyes stared into mine and, at last, closed. I wept then as I didn't weep all those times when terrible news came, and held his great body until it grew cold and stiff between my arms. It was a struggle to lift and carry him, but I did, stumbling across the lichen-rough floor to the shadow of the thin birches and tamaracks overlooking the Reach. I buried him there with the others, and afterward lit a fire.

◆ ◆ ◆

THIS IS NOT the first time this has happened. There is an endless history of forgotten empires, men gifted by a goddess who bears arrows, things in flight that fall in flames. Always, somewhere, a woman waits alone for news. At night I climb alone to the highest point of the island. There I make a little fire and burn things that I find on the beach and in the woods. Leaves, bark, small bones, clumps of feathers, a book. Sometimes I think of you and stand upon the rock and shout as the wind comes at me, cold and smelling of snow. A name, over and over and over again.

Farewell, Narkissos said, and again Echo sighed and whispered Farewell.

―――― THE LOST DOMAIN—THREE STORY VARIATIONS ――――

The Saffron Gatherers

HE HAD almost been as much a place to her as a person; the lost domain, the land of heart's desire. Alone at night she would think of him as others might imagine an empty beach, blue water; for years she had done this, and fallen into sleep.

She flew to Seattle to attend a symposium on the Future. It was a welcome trip—on the East Coast, where she lived, it had rained without stopping for thirty-four days. A meteorological record, now a tired joke: only six more days to go! Even Seattle was drier than that.

She was part of a panel discussion on natural disasters and global warming. Her first three novels had presented near-future visions of apocalypse; she had stopped writing them when it became less like fiction and too much like reportage. Since then she had produced a series of time-travel books, wish-fulfillment fantasies about visiting the ancient world. Many of her friends and colleagues in the field had turned to similar themes, retro, nostalgic, historical. Her academic background was in classical archaeology; the research was joyous, if exhausting. She hated to fly, the constant round of threats and delay. The weather and concomitant poverty, starvation, drought, flooding, riots—it had all become so bad that it was like an extreme sport now, to visit places that had once unfolded from one's imagination in the brightly colored panoramas of 1920s postal cards. Still she went, armed with eyeshade, earplugs, music, and pills that put her to sleep. Behind her eyes, she saw Randall's arm flung above his head, his face half-turned from hers on the pillow. Fifteen minutes after the panel had ended she was in a cab on her way to SeaTac. Several hours later she was in San Francisco.

He met her at the airport. After the weeks of rain back East and Seattle's muted sheen, the sunlight felt like something alive, clawing at her eyes. They drove to her hotel, the same place she always stayed; like something from an old B-movie, the lobby with its ornate cast-iron stair-rail, the narrow front desk of polished walnut; clerks who all might have been played by the young Peter Lorre. The elevator with its illuminated dial like a clock that could never settle on the time; an espresso shop tucked into the back entrance, no bigger than a broom closet.

Randall always had to stoop to enter the elevator. He was very tall, not as thin as he had been when they first met, nearly twenty years earlier. His hair was still so straight and fine that it always felt wet, but the luster had faded from it: it was no longer dark-blond but grey, a strange dusky color, almost blue in some lights, like pale, damp slate. He had grey-blue eyes; a habit of looking up through downturned black lashes that at first had seemed coquettish. She had since learned it was part of a deep reticence, a detachment from the world that sometimes seemed to border on the pathological. You might call him an agoraphobe, if he had stayed indoors.

But he didn't. They had grown up in neighboring towns in New York, though they only met years later, in D.C. When the time came to choose allegiance to a place, she fled to Maine, with all those other writers and artists seeking a retreat into the past; he chose Northern California. He was a journalist, a staff writer for a glossy magazine that only came out four times a year, each issue costing as much as a bottle of decent sémillon. He interviewed scientists engaged in paradigm-breaking research, Nobel Prize-winning writers; poets who wrote on their own skin and had expensive addictions to drugs that subtly altered their personalities, the tenor of their words, so that each new book or online publication seemed to have been written by another person. Multiple Poets' Disorder, Randall had tagged this, and the term stuck; he was the sort of writer who coined phrases. He had a curved mouth, beautiful long fingers. Each time he used a pen, she was surprised again to recall that he was left-handed. He collected incunabula—*Ars oratoria*, Jacobus Publicus's disquisition on the art of memory; the *Opera Philosophica of Seneca*, containing the first written account of an earthquake; Pico della Mirandola's *Hetaplus*—as well as manuscripts. His apartment was filled with quarter-sawn oaken barrister's bookcases, glass fronts bright as mirrors, holding manuscript binders, typescripts, wads of foolscap bound in leather. By the window

THE LOST DOMAIN—THREE STORY VARIATIONS

overlooking the bay, a beautiful old mapchest of letters written by Neruda, Beckett, Asaré. There were signed broadsheets on the walls, and drawings, most of them inscribed to Randall. He was two years younger than she was. Like her, he had no children. In the years since his divorce, she had never heard him mention his former wife by name.

The hotel room was small and stuffy. There was a wooden ceiling fan that turned slowly, barely stirring the white curtain that covered the single window. It overlooked an airshaft. Directly across was another old building, a window that showed a family sitting at a kitchen table, eating beneath a fluorescent bulb.

"Come here, Suzanne," said Randall. "I have something for you."

She turned. He was sitting on the bed—a nice bed, good mattress and expensive white linens and duvet—reaching for the leather mailbag he always carried to remove a flat parcel.

"Here," he said. "For you."

It was a book. With Randall it was always books. Or expensive tea: tiny, neon-colored foil packets that hissed when she opened them and exuded fragrances she could not describe, dried leaves that looked like mouse droppings, or flower petals, or fur; leaves that, once infused, tasted of old leather and made her dream of complicated sex.

"Thank you," she said, unfolding the mauve tissue the book was wrapped in. Then, as she saw what it was, "Oh! Thank you!"

"Since you're going back to Thera. Something to read on the plane."

It was an oversized book in a slipcase: the classic edition of *The Thera Frescoes*, by Nicholas Spirotiadis, a volume that had been expensive when first published, twenty years earlier. Now it must be worth a fortune, with its glossy thick photographic paper and fold-out pages depicting the larger murals. The slipcase art was a detail from the site's most famous image, the painting known as *The Saffron Gatherers*. It showed the profile of a beautiful young woman dressed in an elaborately patterned tiered skirt and blouse, her head shaven save for a serpentine coil of dark hair, her brow tattooed. She wore hoop earrings and bracelets, two on her right hand, one on her left. Bell-like tassels hung from her sleeves. She was plucking the stigma from a crocus blossom. Her fingernails were painted red.

Suzanne had seen the original painting a decade ago, when it was easier for American researchers to gain access to the restored ruins and the National Archaeological Museum in Athens. After two years of paperwork and bureaucratic wheedling, she had just received permission to return.

"It's beautiful," she said. It still took her breath away, how modern the girl looked, not just her clothes and jewelry and body art but her expression, lips parted, her gaze at once imploring and vacant: the fifteen-year-old who had inherited the earth.

"Well, don't drop it in the tub." Randall leaned over to kiss her head. "That was the only copy I could find on the Net. It's become a very scarce book."

"Of course," said Suzanne, and smiled.

"Claude is going to meet us for dinner. But not till seven. Come here—"

They lay in the dark room. His skin tasted of salt and bitter lemon; his hair against her thighs felt warm, liquid. She shut her eyes and imagined him beside her, his long limbs and rueful mouth; opened her eyes and there he was, now, sleeping. She held her hand above his chest and felt heat radiating from him, a scent like honey. She began to cry silently.

His hands. That big rumpled bed. In two days she would be gone, the room would be cleaned. There would be nothing to show she had ever been here at all.

◆ ◆ ◆

THEY DROVE TO an Afghan restaurant in North Beach. Randall's car was older, a second-generation hybrid; even with the grants and tax breaks, a far more expensive vehicle than she or anyone she knew back east could ever afford. She had never gotten used to how quiet it was.

Outside, the sidewalks were filled with people, the early evening light silvery-blue and gold, like a sun shower. Couples arm-in-arm,

THE LOST DOMAIN—THREE STORY VARIATIONS

children, groups of students waving their hands as they spoke on their cell phones, a skateboarder hustling to keep up with a pack of parkour.

"Everyone just seems so much more absorbed here," she said. Even the panhandlers were antic.

"It's the light. It makes everyone happy. Also the drugs they put in our drinking water." She laughed, and he put his arm around her.

Claude was sitting in the restaurant when they arrived. He was a poet who had gained notoriety and then prominence in the late 1980s with the *Hyacinthus Elegies*, his response to the AIDS epidemic. Randall first interviewed him after Claude received his MacArthur Fellowship. They subsequently became good friends. On the wall of his flat, Randall had a hand-written copy of the second elegy, with one of the poet's signature drawings of a hyacinth at the bottom.

"Suzanne!" He jumped up to embrace her, shook hands with Randall then beckoned them both to sit. "I ordered some wine. A good cab I heard about from someone at the gym."

Suzanne adored Claude. The day before she left for Seattle, he'd sent flowers to her, a half-dozen delicate *narcissus serotinus*, with long white narrow petals and tiny yellow throats. Their sweet scent perfumed her entire small house. She'd e-mailed him profuse but also wistful thanks—they were such an extravagance, and so lovely; and she had to leave before she could enjoy them fully. He was a few years younger than she was, thin and muscular, his face and skull hairless save for a wispy black beard. He had lost his eyebrows during a round of chemo and had feathery lines, like antennae, tattooed in their place and threaded with gold beads. His chest and arms were heavily tattooed with stylized flowers, dolphins, octopi, the same iconography Suzanne had seen in Akrotiri and Crete; and also with the names of lovers and friends and colleagues who had died. Along the inside of his arms you could still see the stippled marks left by hypodermic needles—they looked like tiny black beads worked into the pattern of waves and swallows—and the faint white traces of an adolescent suicide attempt. His expression was gentle and melancholy, the face of a tired ascetic, or a benign Antonin Artaud.

"I should have brought the book!" Suzanne sat beside him, shaking her head in dismay. "This beautiful book that Randall gave me—Spirotiadis's Thera book?"

"No! I've heard of it, I could never find it. Is it wonderful?"

"It's gorgeous. You would love it, Claude."

They ate, and spoke of his collected poetry, forthcoming next winter; of Suzanne's trip to Akrotiri. Of Randall's next interview, with a woman on the House Committee on Bioethics who was rumored to be sympathetic to the pro-cloning lobby, but only in cases involving "only" children—no siblings, no twins or multiples—who died before age fourteen.

"Grim," said Claude. He shook his head and reached for the second bottle of wine. "I can't imagine it. Even pets..."

He shuddered, then turned to rest a hand on Suzanne's shoulder. "So: back to Santorini. Are you excited?"

"I am. Just seeing that book, it made me excited again. It's such an incredible place—you're there, and you think, What could this have been? If it had survived, if it all hadn't just gone *bam*, like that—"

"Well, then it would really have gone," said Randall. "I mean, it would have been lost. There would have been no volcanic ash to preserve it. All your paintings, we would never have known them. Just like we don't know anything else from back then."

"We know some things," said Suzanne. She tried not to sound annoyed—there was a lot of wine, and she was jet-lagged. "Plato. Homer..."

"Oh, them," said Claude, and they all laughed. "But he's right. It would all have turned to dust by now. All rotted away. All one with Baby Jesus, or Baby Zeus. Everything you love would be buried under a Tradewinds Resort. Or it would be like Athens, which would be even worse."

"Would it?" She sipped her wine. "We don't know that. We don't know what it would have become. This—"

She gestured at the room, the couple sitting beneath twinkling rose-colored lights, playing with a digital toy that left little chattering faces in the air as the woman switched it on and off. Outside, dusk and neon. "It might have become like this."

"This." Randall leaned back in his chair, staring at her. "Is this so wonderful?"

"Oh yes," she said, staring back at him, the two of them unsmiling. "This is all a miracle."

He excused himself. Claude refilled his glass and turned back to Suzanne. "So. How are things?"

"With Randall?" She sighed. "It's good. I dunno. Maybe it's great. Tomorrow—we're going to look at houses."

Claude raised a tattooed eyebrow. "Really?"

She nodded. Randall had been looking at houses for three years now, ever since the divorce.

"Who knows?" she said. "Maybe this will be the charm. How hard can it be to buy a house?"

"In San Francisco? Doll, it's easier to win the stem cell lottery. But yes, Randall is a very discerning buyer. He's the last of the true idealists. He's looking for the eidos of the house. Plato's eidos, not Socrates'," he added. "Is this the first time you've gone looking with him?"

"Yup."

"Well. Maybe that is great," he said. "Or not. Would you move out here?"

"I don't know. Maybe. If he had a house. Probably not."

"Why?"

"I don't know. I guess I'm looking for the eidos of something else. Out here, it's just too…"

She opened her hands as though catching rain. Claude looked at her quizzically.

"Too sunny?" he said. "Too warm? Too beautiful?"

"I suppose. The land of the lotus-eaters. I love knowing it's here, but." She drank more wine. "Maybe if I had more job security."

"You're a writer. It's against nature for you to have job security."

"Yeah, no kidding. What about you? You don't ever worry about that?"

He gave her his sweet sad smile and shook his head. "Never. The world will always need poets. We're like the lilies of the field."

"What about journalists?" Randall appeared behind them, slipping his cell phone back into his pocket. "What are we?"

"Quackgrass," said Claude.

"Cactus," said Suzanne.

"Oh, gee. I get it," said Randall. "Because we're all hard and spiny and no one loves us."

"Because you only bloom once a year," said Suzanne.

"When it rains," added Claude.

"That was my realtor." Randall sat and downed the rest of his wine. "Sunday's open house day. Two o'clock till four. Suzanne, we have a lot of ground to cover."

He gestured for the waiter. Suzanne leaned over to kiss Claude's cheek.

"When do you leave for Hydra?" she asked.

"Tomorrow."

"Tomorrow!" She looked crestfallen. "That's so soon!"

"'The beautiful life was brief,'" said Claude, and laughed. "You're only here till Monday. I have a reservation on the ferry from Piraeus, I couldn't change it."

"How long will you be there? I'll be in Athens Tuesday after next, then I go to Akrotiri."

Claude smiled. "That might work. Here—"

He copied out a phone number in his careful, calligraphic hand. "This is Zali's number on Hydra. A cell phone, I have no idea if it will even work. But I'll see you soon. Like you said—"

He lifted his thin hands and gestured at the room around them, his dark eyes wide. "This is a miracle."

Randall paid the check and they turned to go. At the door, Claude hugged Suzanne. "Don't miss your plane," he said.

"Don't wind her up!" said Randall.

"Don't miss yours," said Suzanne. Her eyes filled with tears as she pressed her face against Claude's. "It was so good to see you. If I miss you, have a wonderful time in Hydra."

"Oh, I will," said Claude. "I always do."

THE LOST DOMAIN—THREE STORY VARIATIONS

• ◆ •

RANDALL DROPPED HER off at her hotel. She knew better than to ask him to stay; besides, she was tired, and the wine was starting to give her a headache.

"Tomorrow," he said. "Nine o'clock. A leisurely breakfast, and then…"

He leaned over to open her door, then kissed her. "The exciting new world of California real estate."

Outside, the evening had grown cool, but the hotel room still felt close: it smelled of sex, and the sweetish dusty scent of old books. She opened the window by the airshaft and went to take a shower. Afterwards she got into bed, but found herself unable to sleep.

The wine, she thought; always a mistake. She considered taking one of the anti-anxiety drugs she carried for flying, but decided against it. Instead she picked up the book Randall had given her.

She knew all the images, from other books and websites, and the island itself. Nearly four thousand years ago, now; much of it might have been built yesterday. Beneath fifteen feet of volcanic ash and pumice, homes with ocean views and indoor plumbing, pipes that might have channeled steam from underground vents fed by the volcano the city was built upon. Fragments of glass that might have been windows, or lenses. The great pithoi that still held food when they were opened millennia later. Great containers of honey for trade, for embalming the Egyptian dead. Yellow grains of pollen. Wine.

But no human remains. No bones, no grimacing tormented figures as were found beneath the sand at Herculaneum, where the fishermen had fled and died. Not even animal remains, save for the charred vertebrae of a single donkey. They had all known to leave. And when they did, their city was not abandoned in frantic haste or fear. All was orderly, the pithoi still sealed, no metal utensils or weapons strewn upon the floor, no bolts of silk or linen; no jewelry.

Only the paintings, and they were everywhere, so lovely and beautifully wrought that at first the excavators thought they had uncovered a temple complex.

But they weren't temples: they were homes. Someone had paid an artist, or teams of artists, to paint frescoes on the walls of room after room after room. Sea daffodils, swallows; dolphins and pleasure boats, the boats themselves decorated with more dolphins and flying seabirds, golden nautilus on their prows. Wreaths of flowers. A shipwreck. Always you saw the same colors, ochre-yellow and ferrous red; a pigment made by grinding glaucophane, a vitreous mineral that produced a grey-blue shimmer; a bright pure French blue. But of course it wasn't French blue but Egyptian blue—Pompeiian blue—one of the earliest pigments, used for thousands of years; you made it by combining a calcium compound with ground malachite and quartz, then heating it to extreme temperatures.

But no green. It was a blue and gold and red world. Not even the plants were green.

Otherwise, the paintings were so alive that, when she'd first seen them, she half-expected her finger would be wet if she touched them. The eyes of the boys who played at boxing were children's eyes. The antelopes had the mad topaz glare of wild goats. The monkeys had blue fur and looked like dancing cats. There were people walking in the streets. You could see what their houses looked like, red brick and yellow shutters.

She turned towards the back of the book, to the section on Xeste 3. It was the most famous building at the site. It contained the most famous paintings—the woman known as the "Mistress of Animals." "The Adorants," who appeared to be striding down a fashion runway. "The Lustral Basin."

The saffron gatherers.

She gazed at the image from the East Wall of Room Three, two women harvesting the stigma of the crocus blossoms. The flowers were like stylized yellow fireworks, growing from the rocks and also appearing in a repetitive motif on the wall above the figures, like the fleur-de-lis patterns on wallpaper. The fragments of painted plaster had been meticulously restored; there was no attempt to fill in what was missing, as had been done at Knossos under Sir Arthur Evans' supervision to sometimes cartoonish effect.

THE LOST DOMAIN—THREE STORY VARIATIONS

None of that had been necessary here. The fresco was nearly intact. You could see how the older woman's eyebrow was slightly raised, with annoyance or perhaps just impatience, and count the number of stigmata the younger acolyte held in her outstretched palm.

How long would it have taken for them to fill those baskets? The crocuses bloomed only in autumn, and each small blossom contained just three tiny crimson threads, the female stigmata. It might take 100,000 flowers to produce a half-pound of the spice.

And what did they use the spice for? Cooking; painting; a pigment they traded to the Egyptians for dyeing mummy bandages.

She closed the book. She could hear distant sirens, and a soft hum from the ceiling fan. Tomorrow they would look at houses.

• ◆ •

FOR BREAKFAST THEY went to the Embarcadero, the huge indoor market inside the restored ferry building that had been damaged over a century before, in the 1906 earthquake. There was a shop with nothing but olive oil and infused vinegars; another that sold only mushrooms, great woven panniers and baskets filled with tree-ears, portobellos, fungus that looked like orange coral; black morels and matsutake and golden chanterelles.

They stuck with coffee and sweet rolls, and ate outside on a bench looking over the bay. A man threw sticks into the water for a pair of black labs; another man swam along the embankment. The sunlight was strong and clear as gin, and nearly as potent: it made Suzanne feel lightheaded and slightly drowsy, even though she had just gotten up.

"Now," said Randall. He took out the newspaper, opened it to the real estate section, and handed it to her. He had circled eight listings. "The first two are in Oakland; then we'll hit Berkeley and Kensington. You ready?"

They drove in heavy traffic across the Oakland-Bay bridge. To either side, bronze water that looked as though it would be too hot to swim in; before them the Oakland Hills, where the houses were ranged in undulating lines like waves. Once in the city they began to climb in and out of pocket neighborhoods poised between the arid and the tropic. Bungalows nearly hidden beneath overhanging trees suddenly yielded to bright white stucco houses flanked by aloes and agaves. It looked at once wildly fanciful and comfortable, as though all urban planning had been left to Dr. Seuss.

"They do something here called 'staging,'" said Randall as they pulled behind a line of parked cars on a hillside. A phalanx of realtors' signs rose from a grassy mound beside them. "Homeowners pay thousands and thousands of dollars for a decorator to come in and tart up their houses with rented furniture and art and stuff. So, you know, it looks like it's worth three million dollars."

They walked to the first house, a Craftsman bungalow tucked behind trees like prehistoric ferns. There was a fountain outside, filled with koi that stared up with engorged silvery eyes. Inside, exposed beams and dark hardwood floors so glossy they looked covered with maple syrup. There was a grand piano, and large framed posters from Parisian cafés—Suzanne was to note a lot of these as the afternoon wore on—and much heavy dark Mediterranean-style furniture, as well as a few early Mission pieces that might have been genuine. The kitchen floors were tiled. In the master bath, there were mosaics in the sink and sunken tub.

Randall barely glanced at these. He made a beeline for the deck. After wandering around for a few minutes, Suzanne followed him.

"It's beautiful," she said. Below, terraced gardens gave way to stepped hillsides, and then the city proper, and then the gilded expanse of San Francisco Bay, with sailboats like swans moving slowly beneath the bridge.

"For four million dollars, it better be," said Randall.

She looked at him. His expression was avid, but it was also sad, his pale eyes melancholy in the brilliant sunlight. He drew her to him and gazed out above the treetops, then pointed across the blue water.

"That's where we were. Your hotel, it's right there, somewhere." His voice grew soft. "At night it all looks like a fairy city. The lights, and the bridges… You can't believe that anyone could have built it."

THE LOST DOMAIN—THREE STORY VARIATIONS

He blinked, shading his eyes with his hand, then looked away. When he turned back his cheeks were damp.

"Come on," he said. He bent to kiss her forehead. "Got to keep moving."

They drove to the next house, and the next, and the one after that. The light and heat made her dizzy, and the scents of all the unfamiliar flowers, the play of water in fountains and a swimming pool like a great turquoise lozenge. She found herself wandering through expansive bedrooms with people she did not know, walking in and out of closets, bathrooms, a sauna. Every room seemed lavish, the air charged as though anticipating a wonderful party, tables set with beeswax candles and bottles of wine and crystal stemware. Countertops of hand-thrown Italian tiles; globular cobalt vases filled with sunflowers, another recurring motif.

But there was no sign of anyone who might actually live in one of these houses, only a series of well-dressed women with expensively restrained jewelry who would greet them, usually in the kitchen, and make sure they had a flyer listing the home's attributes. There were plates of cookies, banana bread warm from the oven. Bottles of sparkling water and organic lemonade.

And, always, a view. They didn't look at houses without views. To Suzanne, some were spectacular; others, merely glorious. All were more beautiful than anything she saw from her own windows or deck, where she looked out onto evergreens and grey rocks and, much of the year, snow.

It was all so dreamlike that it was nearly impossible for her to imagine real people living here. For her, a house had always meant a refuge from the world; the place where you hid from whatever catastrophe was breaking that morning.

But now she saw that it could be different. She began to understand that, for Randall at least, a house wasn't a retreat. It was a way of engaging with the world; of opening himself to it. The view wasn't yours. You belonged to it, you were a tiny part of it, like the sailboats and the seagulls and the flowers in the garden; like the sunflowers on the highly polished tables.

You were part of what made it real. She had always thought it was the other way around.

"You ready?" Randall came up behind her and put his hand on her neck. "This is it. We're done. Let's go have a drink."

On the way out the door he stopped to talk to the agent.

"They'll be taking bids tomorrow," she said. "We'll let you know on Tuesday."

"Tuesday?" Suzanne said in amazement when they got back outside. "You can do all this in two days? Spend a million dollars on a house?"

"Four million," said Randall. "This is how it works out here. The race is to the quick."

She had assumed they would go to another restaurant for drinks and then dinner. Instead, to her surprise, he drove to his flat. He took a bottle of Pommery Louise from the refrigerator and opened it, and she wandered about examining his manuscripts as he made dinner. At the Embarcadero, without her knowing, he had bought chanterelles and morels, imported pasta colored like spring flowers, arugula and baby tatsoi. For dessert, orange-blossom custard. When they were finished, they remained out on the deck and looked at the bay, the rented view. Lights shimmered through the dusk. In a flowering quince in the garden, dozens of hummingbirds droned and darted like bees, attacking each other with needle beaks.

"So." Randall's face was slightly flushed. They had finished the champagne, and he had poured them each some cognac. "If this happens—if I get the house. Will you move out here?"

She stared down at the hummingbirds. Her heart was racing. The quince had no smell, none that she could detect, anyway; yet still they swarmed around it. Because it was so large, and its thousands of blossoms were so red. She hesitated, then said, "Yes."

He nodded and took a quick sip of cognac. "Why don't you just stay, then? Till we find out on Tuesday? I have to go down to San Jose early tomorrow to interview this guy, you could come and we could go to that place for lunch."

THE LOST DOMAIN—THREE STORY VARIATIONS

"I can't." She bit her lip, thinking. "No... I wish I could, but I have to finish that piece before I leave for Greece."

"You can't just leave from here?"

"No." That would be impossible, to change her whole itinerary. "And I don't have any of my things—I need to pack, and get my notes... I'm sorry."

He took her hand and kissed it. "That's okay. When you get back."

That night she lay in his bed as Randall slept beside her, staring at the manuscripts on their shelves, the framed lines of poetry. His breathing was low, and she pressed her hand against his chest, feeling his ribs beneath the skin, his heartbeat. She thought of canceling her flight; of postponing the entire trip.

But it was impossible. She moved the pillow beneath her head, so that she could see past him, to the wide picture window. Even with the curtains drawn you could see the lights of the city, faraway as stars.

Very early next morning he drove her to the hotel to get her things and then to the airport.

"My cell will be on," he said as he got her bag from the car. "Call me down in San Jose, once you get in."

"I will."

He kissed her and for a long moment they stood at curbside, arms around each other.

"Book your ticket back here," he said at last, and drew away. "I'll talk to you tonight."

She watched him go, the nearly silent car lost among the taxis and limousines, then hurried to catch her flight. Once she had boarded she switched off her cell, then got out her eyemask, earplugs, book, water bottle. She took one of her pills. It took twenty minutes for the drug to kick in, but she had the timing down pat: the plane lifted into the air and she looked out her window, already feeling not so much calm as detached, mildly stoned. It was a beautiful day, cloudless; later it would be hot. As the plane banked above the city she looked down at the skein of roads, cars sliding along them like beads or raindrops on a string.

The traffic crept along 280, the road Randall would take to San José. She turned her head to keep it in view as the plane leveled out and began to head inland.

Behind her a man gasped, then another. Someone shouted. Everyone turned to look out the windows.

Below, without a sound that she could hear above the jet's roar, the city fell away. Where it met the sea the water turned brown then white then turgid green. A long line of smoke arose—no not smoke, Suzanne thought, starting to rise from her seat; dust. No flames, none that she could see; more like a burning fuse, though there was no fire, nothing but white and brown and black dust, a pall of dust that ran in a straight line from the city's tip north to south, roughly tracking along the interstate. The plane continued to pull away, she had to strain to see it now, a long green line in the water, the bridges trembling and shining like wires. One snapped then fell, another, miraculously, remained intact. She couldn't see the third bridge. Then everything was green crumpled hillsides, vineyards, distant mountains.

People began to scream. The pilot's voice came on, a blaze of static then silence. Then his voice again, not calm but ordering them to remain so. A few passengers tried to clamber into the aisles but flight attendants and other passengers pulled or pushed them back into their seats. She could hear someone getting sick in the front of the plane. A child crying. Weeping, the buzz and bleat of cell phones followed by repeated commands to put them all away.

Amazingly, everyone did. It wasn't a terrorist attack. The plane, apparently, would not plummet from the sky, but everyone was too afraid that it might to turn their phones back on.

She took another pill, frantic, fumbling at the bottle and barely getting the cap back on. She opened it again, put two, no three, pills into her palm and pocketed them. Then she flagged down one of the flight attendants as she rushed down the aisle.

"Here," said Suzanne. The attendant's mouth was wide, as though she were screaming; but she was silent. "You can give these to them—"

Suzanne gestured towards the back of the plane, where a man was repeating the same name over and over and a woman was keening. "You can take one if you want, the dosage is pretty low. Keep them. Keep them."

The flight attendant stared at her. Finally she nodded as Suzanne pressed the pill bottle into her hand.

"Thank you," she said in a low voice. "Thank you so much, I will."

Suzanne watched her gulp one pink tablet, then walk to the rear of the plane. She continued to watch from her seat as the attendant went down the aisle, furtively doling out pills to those who seemed to need them most. After about twenty minutes, Suzanne took another pill. As she drifted into unconsciousness she heard the pilot's voice over the intercom, informing the passengers of what he knew of the disaster. She slept.

The plane touched down in Boston, greatly delayed by the weather, the ripple effect on air traffic from the catastrophe. It had been raining for thirty-seven days. Outside, glass-green sky, the flooded runways and orange cones blown over by the wind. In the plane's cabin the air chimed with the sound of countless cell phones. She called Randall, over and over again; his phone rang but she received no answer, not even his voice mail.

Inside the terminal, a crowd of reporters and television people awaited, shouting questions and turning cameras on them as they stumbled down the corridor. No one ran; everyone found a place to stand, alone, with a cell phone. Suzanne staggered past the news crews, striking at a man who tried to stop her. Inside the terminal there were crowds of people around the TV screens, covering their mouths at the destruction. A lingering smell of vomit, of disinfectant. She hurried past them all, lurching slightly, feeling as though she struggled through wet sand. She retrieved her car, joined the endless line of traffic and began the long drive back to that cold green place, trees with leaves that had yet to open though it was already almost June, apple and lilac blossoms rotted brown on their drooping branches.

It was past midnight when she arrived home. The answering machine was blinking. She scrolled through her messages, hands shaking. She listened to just a few words of each, until she reached the last one.

A blast of static, satellite interference; then a voice. It was unmistakably Randall's.

She couldn't make out what he was saying. Everything was garbled, the connection cut out then picked up again. She couldn't tell when he'd called. She played it over again, once, twice, seven times, trying to discern a single word, something in his tone, background noise, other voices: anything to hint when he had called, from where.

It was hopeless. She tried his cell phone again. Nothing.

She stood, exhausted, and crossed the room, touching table, chairs, countertops, like someone on a listing ship. She turned on the kitchen faucet and splashed cold water onto her face. She would go online and begin the process of finding numbers for hospitals, the Red Cross. He could be alive.

She went to her desk to turn on her computer. Beside it, in a vase, were the flowers Claude had sent her, a half-dozen dead narcissus smelling of rank water and slime. Their white petals were wilted, and the color had drained from the pale yellow cups.

All save one. A stem with a furled bloom no bigger than her pinkie, it had not yet opened when she'd left. Now the petals had spread like feathers, revealing its tiny yellow throat, three long crimson threads. She extended her hand to stroke first one stigma, then the next, until she had touched all three; lifted her hand to gaze at her fingertips, golden with pollen, and then at the darkened window. The empty sky, starless. Beneath blue water, the lost world.

―――― THE LOST DOMAIN—THREE STORY VARIATIONS ――――

Kronia

"Nothing sorts out memories from ordinary moments It is only later that they claim remembrance, when they show their scars."

Chris Marker, "La Jetée"

WE NEVER meet. Not never, fleetingly: five times in the last eighteen years. The first time I don't recall; you say it was late spring, a hotel bar. But I see you entering a restaurant five years later, stooping beneath the lintel behind our friend Andrew. You don't remember that.

We grew up a mile apart. The road began in Connecticut and ended in New York. A dirt road when we moved in, we both remember that; it wasn't paved till much later. We rode our bikes back and forth. We passed each other fifty-seven times. We never noticed. I fell once, rounding that curve by the golf course, a long scar on my leg now from ankle to knee, a crescent colored like a peony. Grit and sand got beneath my skin, there was blood on the bicycle chain. A boy with glasses stopped his bike and asked was I okay. I said yes, even though I wasn't. You rode off. I walked home, most of the mile, my leg black, sticky with dirt, pollen, deerflies. I never saw the boy on the bike again.

We went to different schools. But in high school we were at the same party. Your end, Connecticut. How did I get there? I have no clue. I knew no one. A sad fat girl's house, a girl with red kneesocks, beanbag chairs. She had one album: The Shaggs. More sad girls, a song called Foot Foot. You stood by a table and ate pretzels and drank so much Hi-C you threw up. I left with my friends. We got stoned in the car and drove off. A tall boy was puking in the azaleas out front.

Wonder what he had? I said.

Another day. The New Canaan Bookstore, your end again. I was looking at a paperback book.

That's a good book, said a guy behind me. My age, sixteen or seventeen. Very tall, springy black hair, wire-rimmed glasses. You like his stuff?

I shook my head. No, I said. I haven't read it. I put the book back. He took it off the shelf again. As I walked off I heard him say Time Out of Joint.

We went to college in the same city. The Metro hadn't opened yet. I was in Northeast, you were in Northwest. Twice we were on the same bus going into Georgetown. Once we were at a party where a guy threw a drink in my face.

Hey! yelled my boyfriend. he dumped his beer on the guy's head.

You were by the table again, watching. I looked over and saw you laugh. I started laughing too, but you immediately looked down then turned then walked away.

Around that time I first had this dream. I lived in the future. My job was to travel through time, hunting down evildoers. I kept running into the same man, my age, dark-haired, tall. Each time I saw him my heart lurched. We kissed furtively, beneath a table while bullets zipped overhead, beside a waterfall in Hungary. For two weeks we hid in a shack in the Northwest Territory, our radio dying, waiting to hear that the first wave of fallout had subsided. A thousand years, back and forth, the world reshuffled. Our child was born, died, grew old, walked for the first time. Sometimes your hair was grey, sometimes black. Once your glasses shattered when a rock struck them. You still have the scar on your cheek. Once I had an abortion. Once the baby died. Once you did. That was just a dream.

You graduated and went to the Sorbonne for a year to study economics. I have never been to France. I got a job at NASA collating photographs of spacecraft. You came back and started working for the newspaper. Those years, I went to the movies almost every night. Flee the sweltering heat, sit in the Biograph's crippling seats for six hours, Pasolini, Fellini, Truffaut, Herzog, Weir. "La Jetée," a lightning bolt: an illuminated moment when a woman's black-and-white face moves in

THE LOST DOMAIN—THREE STORY VARIATIONS

the darkness. A tall man sat in front of me and I moved to another seat so I could see better; he turned and I glimpsed your face. Unrecognized: I never knew you. Later in the theater's long corridor you hurried past me, my head bent over an elfin spoonful of coke.

Other theaters. We didn't meet again when we sat through "Berlin Alexanderplatz," though I did read your review. "Our Hitler" was nine hours long; you stayed awake, I fell asleep halfway through the last reel, curled on the floor, but after twenty minutes my boyfriend shook me so I wouldn't miss the end.

How could I have missed you then? The theater was practically empty.

I moved far away. You stayed. Before I left the city I met your colleague Andrew: we corresponded. I wrote occasionally for your paper. You answered the phone sometimes when I called there.

You say you never did.

But I remember your voice: you sounded younger than you were, ironic, world-weary. A few times you assigned me stories. We spoke on the phone. I knew your name.

At some point we met. I don't remember. Lunch, maybe, with Andrew when I visited the city? A conference?

You married and moved three thousand miles away. E-mail was invented. We began to write. You sent me books.

We met at a conference: we both remember that. You stood in a hallway filled with light, midday sun fogging the windows. You shaded your eyes with your hand, your head slightly downturned, your eyes glancing upward, your glasses black against white skin. Dark eyes, dark hair, tall and thin and slightly stooped. You were smiling; not at me, at someone talking about about the mutability of time. Abruptly the sky darkened, the long rows of windows turned to mirrors. I stood in the hallway and you were everywhere, everywhere.

You never married. I sent you books.

I had children. I never wrote you back.

You travelled everywhere: Paris, Beirut, London, Cairo, Tangier, Cornwall, Fiji. You sent me postcards. I never left this country.

I was living in London with my husband and children when the towers fell. I emailed you. You wrote back:

Oh sure, it takes a terrorist attack to hear from you!

I was here alone on the mountain when I found out. A brilliant cloudless day, the loons calling outside my window. I have no TV; I was online when a friend emailed me:

Terrorism. An airplane flew into the World Trade center. Bombs. Disaster.

I tried to call my partner but the phone lines went down. I drove past the farmstand where I buy tomatoes and basil and stopped to see if anyone knew what had happened. A van was there with DC plates: the woman inside was talking on a cell phone and weeping. Her brother worked in one of the towers: he had rung her to say he was safe. Then the second tower fell. He had just rung back to say he was still alive. When the phone lines were restored that night I wrote you.
You didn't write back. I never heard from you again.
I was in New York. I had gone to Battery Park. I had never been there before. The sun was shining. You never heard from me again.
I had no children. At the National zoo, I saw a tall man walking hand in hand with a little girl. She turned to stare at me: grey eyes, glasses, wispy dark hair. She looked like me.
Two years ago you came to see me here on the lake. We drank two bottles of champagne. We stayed up all night talking. You slept on the couch. When I said goodnight, I touched your forehead. I had never touched you before. You flinched.
Once in 1985 we sat beside each other on the Number 80 bus from North Capitol Street. Neither of us remembers that.
I was fifteen years old, riding my bike on that long slow curve by the golf course. The Petro Oil truck went by, too fast, and I lost my balance

THE LOST DOMAIN—THREE STORY VARIATIONS

and went careening into the stone wall. I fell and blacked out. When I opened my eyes a tall boy with glasses knelt beside me, so still he was like a black and white photograph. A sudden flicker: for the first time he moved. He blinked, dark eyes, dark hair. It took a moment for me to understand he was talking to me.

"Are you okay?" he pointed to my leg. "You're bleeding. I live just down there—"

He pointed to the Connecticut end of the road.

He hid my ruined bike in the ferns. "Come on."

You put your arm around me and we walked very slowly to your house. A plane flew by overhead. This is how we met.

Near Zennor

HE FOUND the letters inside a round metal candy tin, at the bottom of a plastic storage box in the garage, alongside strings of outdoor Christmas lights and various oddments his wife had saved for the yard sale she'd never managed to organise in almost thirty years of marriage. She'd died suddenly, shockingly, of a brain aneurysm, while planting daffodil bulbs the previous September.

Now everything was going to Goodwill. The house in New Canaan had been listed with a realtor; despite the terrible market, she'd reassured Jeffrey that it should sell relatively quickly, and for something close to his asking price.

"It's a beautiful house, Jeffrey," she said, "not that I'm surprised." Jeffrey was a noted architect: she glanced at him as she stepped carefully along a flagstone path in her Louboutin heels. "And these gardens are incredible."

"That was all Anthea." He paused beside a stone wall, surveying an emerald swathe of new grass, small exposed hillocks of black earth, piles of neatly-raked leaves left by the crew he'd hired to do the work that Anthea had always done on her own. In the distance, birch trees glowed spectral white against a leaden February sky that gave a twilit cast to midday. "She always said that if I'd had to pay her for all this, I wouldn't have been able to afford her. She was right."

He signed off on the final sheaf of contracts and returned them to the realtor. "You're in Brooklyn now?" she asked, turning back toward the house.

"Yes. Green Park. A colleague of mine is in Singapore for a few months, he's letting me stay there till I get my bearings."

"Well, good luck. I'll be in touch soon." She opened the door of her Prius and hesitated. "I know how hard this is for you. I lost my father two years ago. Nothing helps, really."

Jeffrey nodded. "Thanks. I know."

He'd spent the last five months cycling through wordless, imageless night terrors from which he awoke gasping; dreams in which Anthea lay beside him, breathing softly then smiling as he touched her face; nightmares in which the neuroelectrical storm that had killed her raged inside his own head, a flaring nova that engulfed the world around him and left him floating in an endless black space, the stars expiring one by one as he drifted past them.

He knew that grief had no target demographic, that all around him versions of this cosmic reshuffling took place every day. He and Anthea had their own shared experience years before, when they had lost their first and only daughter to sudden infant death syndrome. They were both in their late thirties at the time. They never tried to have another child, on their own or through adoption. It was as though some psychic house fire had consumed them both: it was a year before Jeffrey could enter the room that had been Julia's, and for months after her death neither he nor Anthea could bear to sit at the dining table and finish a meal together, or sleep in the same bed. The thought of being that close to another human being, of having one's hand or foot graze another's and wake however fleetingly to the realisation that this too could be lost—it left both of them with a terror that they had never been able to articulate, even to each other.

Now as then, he kept busy with work at his office in the city, and dutifully accepted invitations for lunch and dinner there and in New Canaan. Nights were a prolonged torment: he was haunted by the realisation that Anthea been extinguished, a spent match pinched between one's fingers. He thought of Houdini, arch-rationalist of another century who desired proof of a spirit world he desperately wanted to believe in.

Jeffrey believed in nothing, yet if there had been a drug to twist his neurons into some synaptic impersonation of faith, he would have taken it.

For the past month he'd devoted most of his time to packing up the house, donating Anthea's clothes to various charity shops, deciding what to store and what to sell, what to divvy up among nieces and nephews, Anthea's sister, a few close friends. Throughout he experienced grief as a sort of low-grade flu, a persistent, inescapable ache that suffused not just his thoughts but his bones and tendons: a throbbing in his temples, black sparks that distorted his vision; an acrid chemical taste in the back of his throat, as though he'd bitten into one of the pills his doctor had given him to help him sleep.

He watched as the realtor drove off soundlessly, returned to the garage and transferred the plastic bin of Christmas lights into his own car, to drop off at a neighbour's the following weekend. He put the tin box with the letters on the seat beside him. As he pulled out of the driveway, it began to snow.

• ♦ •

THAT NIGHT, HE sat at the dining table in the Brooklyn loft and opened the candy tin. Inside were five letters, each bearing the same stamp: RETURN TO SENDER. At the bottom of the box was a locket on a chain, cheap gold-coloured metal and chipped red enamel circled by tiny fake pearls. He opened it: it was empty. He examined it for an engraved inscription, initials, a name, but there was nothing. He set it aside and turned to the letters.

All were postmarked 1971—February, March, April, July, end of August—all addressed to the same person at the same address, carefully spelled out in Anthea's swooping, schoolgirl's hand.

Mr. Robert Bennington,
Trawraethun Farm,
Padwithiel,
Cornwall.

Love letters? He didn't recognise the name. Anthea would have been thirteen in February; her birthday was in May. He moved the envelopes across the table, as though performing a card trick. His heart pounded, which was ridiculous. He and Anthea had told each other about everything—three-ways at university, coke-fuelled orgies during the 1980s, affairs and flirtations throughout their marriage.

None of that mattered now; little of it had mattered then. Still, his hands shook as he opened the first envelope. A single sheet of onionskin was inside. He unfolded it gingerly and smoothed it on the table.

His wife's handwriting hadn't changed much in forty years. The same cramped cursive, each *i* so heavily dotted in black ink that the pen had almost poked through the thin paper. Anthea had been English, born and raised in North London. They'd met at the University of London, where they were both studying, and moved to New Canaan after they'd married. It was an area that Sarah had often said reminded her of the English countryside, though Jeffrey had never ventured outside London, other than a few excursions to Kent and Brighton. Where was Padwithiel?

21 February, 1971

Dear Mr. Bennington,

My name is Anthea Ryson...

And would a thirteen-year-old girl address her boyfriend as 'Mr.,' even forty years ago?

...I am thirteen-years-old and live in London. Last year my friend Evelyn let me read Still the Seasons *for the first time and since then I have read it two more times, also* Black Clouds Over Bragmoor *and* The Second Sun. *They are my favourite books! I keep looking for more but the library here doesn't have them. I have asked and they said I should try the shops but*

that is expensive. My teacher said that sometimes you come to schools and speak, I hope some day you'll come to Islington Day School. Are you writing more books about Tisha and the great Battle?

I hope so, please write back! My address is 42 Highbury Fields, London NW1.

Very truly yours,
Anthea Ryson

Jeffrey set aside the letter and gazed at the remaining four envelopes. *What a prick*, he thought. He never even wrote her back. He turned to his laptop and googled Robert Bennington.

Robert Bennington (1932-), British author of a popular series of children's fantasy novels published during the 1960s known as 'The Sun Battles'. Bennington's books rode the literary tidal wave generated by J.R.R. Tolkien's work, but his commercial and critical standing were irrevocably shaken in the late 1990s, when he became the centre of a drawn-out court case involving charges of paedophilia and sexual assault, with accusations lodged against him by several girl fans, now adults. One of the alleged victims later changed her account, and the case was eventually dismissed amidst much controversy by child advocates and women's rights groups. Bennington's reputation never recovered: school libraries refused to keep his books on their shelves. All of his novels are now out of print, although digital editions (illegal) can be found, along with used copies of the four books in the 'Battles' sequence...

Jeffrey's neck prickled. The court case didn't ring a bell, but the books did. Anthea had thrust one upon him shortly after they first met.

"These were my *favourites*." She rolled over in bed and pulled a yellowed paperback from a shelf crowded with textbooks and Penguin editions of the mystery novels she loved. "I must have read this twenty times."

"Twenty?" Jeffrey raised an eyebrow.

"Well, maybe seven. A *lot*. Did you ever read them?"

"I never even heard of them."

"You have to read it. Right now." She nudged him with her bare foot. "You can't leave here till you do."

"Who says I want to leave?" He tried to kiss her but she pushed him away.

"Uh uh. Not till you read it. I'm serious!"

So he'd read it, staying up till 3:00 a.m., intermittently dozing off before waking with a start to pick up the book again.

"It gave me bad dreams," he said as grey morning light leaked through the narrow window of Anthea's flat. "I don't like it."

"I know." Anthea laughed. "That's what I liked about them—they always made me feel sort of sick."

Jeffrey shook his head adamantly. "I don't like it," he repeated.

Anthea frowned, finally shrugged, picked up the book and dropped it onto the floor. "Well, nobody's perfect," she said, and rolled on top of him.

A year or so later he did read *Still the Seasons*, when a virus kept him in bed for several days and Anthea was caught up with research at the British Library. The book unsettled him deeply. There were no monsters *per se*, no dragons or Nazgûl or witches. Just two sets of cousins, two boys and two girls, trapped in a portal between one of those grim post-war English cities, Manchester or Birmingham, and a magical land that wasn't really magical at all but even bleaker and more threatening than the council flats where the children lived.

Jeffrey remembered unseen hands tapping at a window, and one of the boys fighting off something invisible that crawled under the bedcovers and attacked in a flapping wave of sheets and blankets. Worst of all was the last chapter, which he read late one night and could never recall clearly, save for the vague, enveloping dread it engendered, something he had never encountered before or since.

Anthea had been right—the book had a weirdly visceral power, more like the effect of a low-budget, black-and-white horror movie than a children's fantasy novel. How many of those grown-up kids now knew their hero had been a paedophile?

Jeffrey spent a half-hour scanning articles on Bennington's trial, none of them very informative. It had happened over a decade ago; since then there'd been a few dozen blog posts, pretty equally divided between *Whatever happened to...?* and excoriations by women who themselves had been sexually abused, though not by Bennington.

He couldn't imagine that had happened to Anthea. She'd certainly never mentioned it, and she'd always been dismissive, even slightly callous, about friends who underwent counselling or psychotherapy for childhood traumas. As for the books themselves, he didn't recall seeing them when he'd sorted through their shelves to pack everything up. Probably they'd been donated to a library book sale years ago, if they'd even made the crossing from London.

He picked up the second envelope. It was postmarked 'March 18, 1971'. He opened it and withdrew a sheet of lined paper torn from a school notebook.

Dear Rob,

Well, we all got back on the train, Evelyn was in a lot of trouble for being out all night and of course we couldn't tell her aunt why, her mother said she can't talk to me on the phone but I see her at school anyway so it doesn't matter. I still can't believe it all happened. Evelyn's mother said she was going to call my mother and Moira's but so far she didn't. Thank you so much for talking to us. You signed Evelyn's book but you forgot to sign mine. Next time!!!

Yours sincerely your friend,
Anthea

Jeffrey felt a flash of cold through his chest. *Dear Rob, I still can't believe it all happened.* He quickly opened the remaining envelopes, read first one then the next and finally the last.

12 April 1971

Dear Rob,

Maybe I wrote down your address wrong because the last letter I sent was returned. But I asked Moira and she had the same address and she said her letter wasn't returned. Evelyn didn't write yet but says she will. It was such a really, really great time to see you! Thank you again for the books, I thanked you in the last letter but thank you again. I hope you'll write back this time, we still want to come back on holiday in July! I can't believe it was exactly one month ago we were there.

Your friend,
Anthea Ryson

July 20, 1971

Dear Rob,

Well I still haven't heard from you so I guess you're mad maybe or just forgot about me, ha ha. School is out now and I was wondering if you still wanted us to come and stay? Evelyn says we never could and her aunt would tell her mother but we could hitch-hike, also Evelyn's brother Martin has a caravan and he and his girlfriend are going to Wales for a festival and we thought they might give us a ride partway, he said maybe they would. Then we could hitch-hike the rest. The big news is Moira ran away from home and they called the POLICE. Evelyn said she went without us to see you and she's really mad. Moira's boyfriend Peter is mad too.

    If she is there with you is it okay if I come too? I could come alone without Evelyn, her mother is a BITCH.

Please please write!
Anthea (Ryson)

Dear Rob,

    I hate you. I wrote FIVE LETTERS including this one and I know it is the RIGHT address. I think Moira went to your house without us. FUCK YOU Tell her I hate her too and so does Evelyn. We never told anyone if she says we did she is a LIAR.

FUCK YOU FUCK YOU FUCK YOU

    Where a signature should have been, the page was ripped and blotched with blue ink—Anthea had scribbled something so many times the pen tore through the lined paper. Unlike the other four, this sheet was badly crumpled, as though she'd thrown it away then retrieved it. Jeffrey glanced at the envelope. The postmark read 'August 28'. She'd gone back to school for the fall term, and presumably that had been the end of it.

    Except, perhaps, for Moira, whoever she was. Evelyn would be Evelyn Thurlow, Anthea's closest friend from her school days in Islington. Jeffrey had met her several times while at university, and Evelyn had stayed with them for a weekend in the early 1990s, when she was attending a conference in Manhattan. She was a flight-test engineer for a British defence contractor, living outside Cheltenham; she and Anthea would have hour-long conversations on their birthdays, for several years planning a dream vacation together to someplace warm—Greece or Turkey or the Caribbean.

Jeffrey had e-mailed her about Anthea's death, and they had spoken on the phone—Evelyn wanted to fly over for the funeral but was on deadline for a major government contract and couldn't take the time off.

"I so wish I could be there," she'd said, her voice breaking. "Everything's just so crazed at the moment. I hope you understand…"

"It's okay. She knew how much you loved her. She was always so happy to hear from you."

"I know," Evelyn choked. "I just wish—I just wish I'd been able to see her again."

Now he sat and stared at the five letters. The sight made him feel lightheaded and slightly queasy: as though he'd opened his closet door and found himself at the edge of a precipice, gazing down some impossible distance to a world made tiny and unreal. Why had she never mentioned any of this? Had she hidden the letters for all these years, or simply forgotten she had them? He knew it wasn't rational; knew his response derived from his compulsive sense of order, what Anthea had always called his architect's left brain.

"Jeffrey would never even try to put a square peg into a round hole," she'd said once at a dinner party. "He'd just design a new hole to fit it."

He could think of no place he could fit the five letters written to Robert Bennington. After a few minutes, he replaced each in its proper envelope and stacked them atop each other. Then he turned back to his laptop, and wrote an e-mail to Evelyn.

• ◆ •

HE ARRIVED IN Cheltenham two weeks later. Evelyn picked him up at the train station early Monday afternoon. He'd told her he was in London on business, spent the preceding weekend at a hotel in Bloomsbury and wandered the city, walking past the building where he and Anthea had lived right after university, before they moved to the U.S.

NEAR ZENNOR

It was a relief to board the train and stare out the window at an unfamiliar landscape, suburbs giving way to farms and the gently rolling outskirts of the Cotswolds.

Evelyn's husband, Chris, worked for one of the high-tech corporations in Cheltenham; their house was a rambling, expensively renovated cottage twenty minutes from the congested city centre.

"Anthea would have loved these gardens," Jeffrey said, surveying swathes of narcissus already in bloom, alongside yellow primroses and a carpet of bluebells beneath an ancient beech. "Everything at home is still brown. We had snow a few weeks ago."

"It must be very hard, giving up the house." Evelyn poured him a glass of Medoc and sat across from him in the slate-floored sunroom.

"Not as hard as staying would have been," Jeffrey raised his glass. "To old friends and old times."

"To Anthea," said Evelyn.

They talked into the evening, polishing off the Medoc and starting on a second bottle long before Chris arrived home from work. Evelyn was florid and heavy-set, her unruly raven hair long as ever and braided into a single plait, thick and grey-streaked. She'd met her contract deadline just days ago, and her dark eyes still looked hollowed from lack of sleep. Chris prepared dinner, lamb with fresh mint and new peas; their children were both off at university, so Jeffrey and Chris and Evelyn lingered over the table until almost midnight.

"Leave the dishes," Chris said, rising. "I'll get them in the morning." He bent to kiss the top of his wife's head, then nodded at Jeffrey. "Good to see you, Jeffrey."

"Come on." Evelyn grabbed a bottle of Armagnac and headed for the sunroom. "Get those glasses, Jeffrey. I'm not going in till noon. Project's done, and the mice will play."

Jeffrey followed her, settling onto the worn sofa and placing two glasses on the side-table. Evelyn filled both, flopped into an armchair and smiled. "It *is* good to see you."

"And you."

He sipped his Armagnac. For several minutes they sat in silence, staring out the window at the garden, narcissus and primroses faint gleams in the darkness. Jeffrey finished his glass, poured another, and asked, "Do you remember someone named Robert Bennington?"

Evelyn cradled her glass against her chest. She gazed at Jeffrey for a long moment before answering. "The writer? Yes. I read his books when I was a girl. Both of us did—me and Anthea."

"But—you knew him. You met him, when you were thirteen. On vacation or something."

Evelyn turned, her profile silhouetted against the window. "We did," she said at last, and turned back to him. "Why are you asking?"

"I found some letters that Anthea wrote to him. Back in 1971, after you and her and a girl named Moira saw him in Cornwall. Did you know he was a paedophile? He was arrested about fifteen years ago."

"Yes, I read about that. It was a big scandal." Evelyn finished her Armagnac and set her glass on the table. "Well, a medium-sized scandal. I don't think many people even remembered who he was by then. He was a cult writer, really. The books were rather dark for children's books."

She hesitated. "Anthea wasn't molested by him, if that's what you're asking about. None of us were. He invited us to tea—we invited ourselves, actually, he was very nice and let us come in and gave us Nutella sandwiches and tangerines."

"Three little teenyboppers show up at his door, I bet he was very nice," said Jeffrey. "What about Moira? What happened to her?"

"I don't know." Evelyn sighed. "No one ever knew. She ran away from home that summer. We never heard from her again."

"Did they question him? Was he even taken into custody?"

"Of course they did!" Evelyn said, exasperated. "I mean, I don't know for sure, but I'm certain they did. Moira had a difficult home life, her parents were Irish and the father drank. And a lot of kids ran away back then, you know that—all us little hippies. What did the letters say, Jeffrey?"

NEAR ZENNOR

He removed then from his pocket and handed them to her. "You can read them. He never did—they all came back to Anthea. Where's Padwithiel?"

"Near Zennor. My aunt and uncle lived there, we went and stayed with them during our school holidays one spring." She sorted through the envelopes, pulled out one and opened it, unfolding the letter with care. "February twenty-first. This was right before we knew we'd be going there for the holidays. It was my idea. I remember when she wrote this—she got the address somehow, and that's how we realised he lived near my uncle's farm. Padwithiel."

She leaned into the lamp and read the first letter, set it down and continued to read each of the others. When she was finished, she placed the last one on the table, sank back into her chair and gazed at Jeffrey.

"She never told you about what happened."

"You just said that nothing happened."

"I don't mean with Robert. She called me every year on the anniversary. March 12." She looked away. "Next week, that is. I never told Chris. It wasn't a secret, we just—well, I'll just tell you.

"We went to school together, the three of us, and after Anthea sent that letter to Robert Bennington, she and I cooked up the idea of going to see him. Moira never read his books—she wasn't much of a reader. But she heard us talking about his books all the time, and we'd all play these games where we'd be the ones who fought the Sun Battles. She just did whatever we told her to, though for some reason she always wanted prisoners to be boiled in oil. She must've seen it in a movie.

"Even though we were older now, we still wanted to believe that magic could happen like in those books—probably we wanted to believe it even more. And all that New Agey, hippie stuff, Tarot cards and Biba and 'Ride a White Swan'—it all just seemed like it could be real. My aunt and uncle had a farm near Zennor, my mother asked if we three could stay there for the holidays and Aunt Becca said that would be fine. My cousins are older, and they were already off at university. So we took the train and Aunt Becca got us in Penzance.

"They were turning one of the outbuildings into a pottery studio for her, and that's where we stayed. There was no electricity yet, but we had a kerosene heater and we could stay up as late as we wanted. I think we got maybe five hours sleep the whole time we were there." She laughed. "We'd be up all night, but then Uncle Ray would start in with the tractors at dawn. We'd end up going into the house and napping in one of my cousin's beds for half the afternoon whenever we could. We were very grumpy houseguests.

"It rained the first few days we were there, just pissing down. Finally one morning we got up and the sun was shining. It was cold, but we didn't care—we were just so happy we could get outside for a while. At first we just walked along the road, but it was so muddy from all the rain that we ended up heading across the moor. Technically it's not really open moorland—there are old stone walls criss-crossing everything, ancient field systems. Some of them are thousands of years old, and farmers still keep them up and use them. These had not been kept up. The land was completely overgrown, though you could still see the walls and climb them. Which is what we did.

"We weren't that far from the house—we could still see it, and I'm pretty sure we were still on my uncle's land. We found a place where the walls were higher than elsewhere, more like proper hedgerows. There was no break in the wall like there usually is, no gate or old entryway. So we found a spot that was relatively untangled and we all climbed up and then jumped to the other side. The walls were completely overgrown with blackthorn and all these viney things. It was like Sleeping Beauty's castle—the thorns hurt like shit. I remember I was wearing new boots and they got ruined, just scratched everywhere. And Moira tore her jacket and we knew she'd catch grief for that. But we thought there must be something wonderful on the other side—that was the game we were playing, that we'd find some amazing place. Do you know *The Secret Garden?* We thought it might be like that. At least I did."

"And was it?"

Evelyn shook her head. "It wasn't a garden. It was just this big overgrown field. Dead grass and stones. But it was rather beautiful in a bleak way. Ant laughed and started yelling 'Heathcliff, Heathcliff!' And it was warmer—the walls were high enough to keep out the wind, and there were some trees that had grown up on top of the walls as well. They weren't in leaf yet, but they formed a bit of a windbreak.

"We ended up staying there all day. Completely lost track of the time. I thought only an hour had gone by, but Ant had a watch, at one point she said it was past three and I was shocked—I mean, really shocked. It was like we'd gone to sleep and woken up, only we weren't asleep at all."

"What were you doing?"

Evelyn shrugged. "Playing. The sort of let's-pretend game we always did when we were younger and hadn't done for a while. Moira had a boyfriend, Ant and I really *wanted* boyfriends—mostly that's what we talked about whenever we got together. But for some reason, that day Ant said 'Let's do Sun Battles,' and we all agreed. So that's what we did. Now of course I can see why—I've seen it with my own kids when they were that age, you're on the cusp of everything, and you just want to hold on to being young for as long as you can.

"I don't remember much of what we did that day, except how strange it all felt. As though something was about to happen. I felt like that a lot, it was all tied in with being a teenager; but this was different. It was like being high, or tripping, only none of us had ever done any drugs at that stage. And we were stone-cold sober. Really all we did was wander around the moor and clamber up and down the walls and hedgerows and among the trees, pretending we were in Gearnzath. That was the world in *The Sun Battles*—like Narnia, only much scarier. We were mostly just wandering around and making things up, until Ant told us it was after three o'clock.

"I think it was her idea that we should do some kind of ritual. I know it wouldn't have been Moira's, and I don't think it was mine. But I knew there was going to be a full moon that night—I'd heard my uncle mention it—and so we decided that we would each sacrifice a sacred thing, and then retrieved them all before moonrise. We turned our pockets inside-out looking for what we could use. I had a comb, so that was mine—just a red plastic thing, I think it cost ten pence. Ant had a locket on a chain from Woolworths, cheap but the locket part opened.

"And Moira had a pencil. It said RAVENWOOD on the side, so we called the field Ravenwood. We climbed up on the wall and stood facing the sun, and made up some sort of chant. I don't remember what we said. Then we tossed our things onto the moor. None of us threw them far, and Ant barely tossed hers—she didn't want to lose the locket. I didn't care about the comb, but it was so light it just fell a few yards from where we stood. Same with the pencil. We all marked where they fell—I remember mine very clearly, it came down right on top of this big flat stone.

"Then we just left. It was getting late, and cold, and we were all starving—we'd had nothing to eat since breakfast. We went back to the house and hung out in the barn for a while, and then we had dinner. We didn't talk much. Moira hid her jacket so they couldn't see she'd torn it, and I took my boots off so no one would see how I'd got them all mauled by the thorns. I remember my aunt wondering if we were up to something, and my uncle saying what the hell could we possibly be up to in Zennor? After dinner we sat in the living room and waited for the sun to go down, and when we saw the moon start to rise above the hills, we went back outside.

"It was bright enough that we could find our way without a torch—a flashlight. I think that must have been one of the rules, that we had to retrieve our things by moonlight. It was cold out, and none of us had dressed very warmly, so we ran. It didn't take long. We climbed back over the wall and then down onto the field, at the exact spot where we'd thrown our things.

"They weren't there. I knew exactly where the rock was where my comb had landed—the rock was there, but not the comb. Ant's locket had landed only a few feet past it, and it wasn't there either. And Moira's pencil was gone, too."

"The wind could have moved them," said Jeffrey. "Or an animal."

"Maybe the wind," said Evelyn. "Though the whole reason we'd stayed there all day was that there was no wind—it was protected, and warm."

"Maybe a bird took it? Don't some birds like shiny things?"

"What would a bird do with a pencil? Or a plastic comb?"

Jeffrey made a face. "Probably you just didn't see where they fell. You thought you did, in daylight, but everything looks different at night. Especially in moonlight."

"I knew where they were." Evelyn shook her head and reached for the bottle of Armagnac. "Especially my comb. I have that engineer's eye, I can look at things and keep a very precise picture in my mind. The comb wasn't where it should have been. And there was no reason for it to be gone, unless…"

"Unless some other kids had seen you and found everything after you left," said Jeffrey.

"No." Evelyn sipped her drink. "We started looking. The moon was coming up—it rose above the hill, and it was very bright. Because it was so cold there was hoarfrost on the grass, and ice in places where the rain had frozen. So all that reflected the moonlight. Everything glittered. It was beautiful, but it was no longer fun—it was scary. None of us was even talking; we just split up and criss-crossed the field, looking for our things.

"And then Moira said, 'There's someone there,' and pointed. I thought it was someone on the track that led back to the farmhouse—it's not a proper road, just a rutted path that runs alongside one edge of that old field system. I looked up and yes, there were three people there—three torches, anyway. Flashlights. You couldn't see who was carrying them, but they were walking slowly along the path. I thought maybe it was my uncle and two of the men who worked with him, coming to tell us it was time to go home. They were walking from the wrong direction, across the moor, but I thought maybe they'd gone out to work on something. So I ran to the left edge of the field and climbed up on the wall."

She stopped, glancing out the window at the black garden, and finally turned back. "I could see the three lights from there," she said.

"But the angle was all wrong. They weren't on the road at all—they were in the next field, up above Ravenwood. And they weren't flashlights. They were high up in the air, like this—"

She set down her glass and got to her feet, a bit unsteadily, extended both her arms and mimed holding something in her hands. "Like someone was carrying a pole eight or ten feet high, and there was a light on top of it. Not a flame. Like a ball of light…"

She cupped her hands around an invisible globe the size of a soccer ball. "Like that. White light, sort of foggy. The lights bobbed as they were walking."

"Did you see who it was?"

"No. We couldn't see anything. And, this is the part that I can't explain—it just felt bad. Like, horrible. Terrifying."

"You thought you'd summoned up whatever it was you'd been playing at." Jeffrey nodded sympathetically and finished his drink. "It was just marsh gas, Ev. You know that. Will o' the wisp, or whatever you call it here. They must get it all the time out there in the country. Or fog. Or someone just out walking in the moonlight."

Evelyn settled back into her armchair. "It wasn't," she said. "I've seen marsh gas. There was no fog. The moon was so bright you could see every single rock in that field. Whatever it was, we all saw it. And you couldn't hear anything—there were no voices, no footsteps, nothing. They were just there, moving closer to us—slowly," she repeated, and moved her hand up and down, as though calming a cranky child. "That was the creepiest thing, how slowly they just kept coming."

"Why didn't you just run?"

"Because we couldn't. You know how kids will all know about something horrible, but they'll never tell a grown-up? It was like that. We knew we had to find our things before we could go.

"I found my comb first. It was way over—maybe twenty feet from where I'd seen it fall. I grabbed it and began to run across the turf, looking for the locket and Moira's pencil. The whole time the moon was rising, and that was horrible too—it was a beautiful clear night, no

NEAR ZENNOR

clouds at all. And the moon was so beautiful, but it just terrified me. I can't explain it."

Jeffrey smiled wryly. "Yeah? How about this: three thirteen-year-old girls in the dark under a full moon, with a very active imagination?"

"Hush. A few minutes later Moira yelled: she'd found her pencil. She turned and started running back toward the wall, I screamed after her that she had to help us find the locket. She wouldn't come back. She didn't go over the wall without us, but she wouldn't help. I ran over to Ant but she yelled at me to keep searching where I was. I did, I even started heading for the far end of the field, toward the other wall—where the lights were.

"They were very close now, close to the far wall I mean. You could see how high up they were, taller than a person. I could hear Moira crying, I looked back and suddenly I saw Ant dive to the ground. She screamed 'I found it!' and I could see the chain shining in her hand.

"And we just turned and hightailed it. I've never run so fast in my life. I grabbed Ant's arm, by the time we got to the wall Moira was already on top and jumping down the other side. I fell and Ant had to help me up, Moira grabbed her and we ran all the way back to the farm and locked the door when we got inside.

"We looked out the window and the lights were still there. They were there for hours. My uncle had a Border Collie, we cracked the door to see if she'd hear something and bark but she didn't. She wouldn't go outside, though—we tried to get her to look and she wouldn't budge."

"Did you tell your aunt and uncle?"

Evelyn shook her head. "No. We stayed in the house that night, in my cousin's room. It overlooked the moor, so we could watch the lights. After about two hours they began to move back the way they'd come—slowly, it was about another hour before they were gone completely. We went out next morning to see if there was anything there—we took the dog to protect us."

"And?"

"There was nothing. The grass was all beat down, as though someone had been walking over it, but probably that was just us."

She fell silent. "Well," Jeffrey said after a long moment. "It's certainly a good story."

"It's a true story. Here, wait."

She stood and went into the other room, and Jeffrey heard her go upstairs. He crossed to the window and stared out into the night, the dark garden occluded by shadow and runnels of mist, blueish in the dim light cast from the solarium.

"Look. I still have it."

He turned to see Evelyn holding a small round tin box. She withdrew a small object and stared at it, placed it back inside and handed the box to him. "My comb. There's some pictures here too."

"That box." He stared at the lid, blue enamel with the words ST. AUSTELL CANDIES: FUDGE FROM REAL CORNISH CREAM stamped in gold above the silhouette of what looked like a lighthouse beacon. "It's just like the one I found, with Anthea's letters in it."

Evelyn nodded. "That's right. Becca gave one to each of us the day we arrived. The fudge was supposed to last the entire two weeks, and I think we ate it all that first night."

He opened the box and gazed at a bright-red plastic comb sitting atop several snapshots; dug into his pocket and pulled out Anthea's locket.

"There it is," said Evelyn wonderingly. She took the locket and dangled it in front of her, clicked it open and shut then returned it to Jeffrey. "She never had anything in it that I knew. Here, look at these."

She took back the tin box. He sat, waiting as she sorted through the snapshots then passed him six small black-and-white photos, each time-stamped OCTOBER 1971.

"That was my camera. A Brownie." Evelyn sank back into the armchair. "I didn't finish shooting the roll till we went back to school."

There were two girls in most of the photos. One was Anthea, apple-cheeked, her face still rounded with puppy fat and her brown hair longer than he'd ever seen it; eyebrows unplucked, wearing baggy bell-bottom jeans and a white peasant shirt. The other girl was taller, sturdy but long-limbed, with long, straight blonde hair and a broad, smooth forehead, elongated eyes and a wide mouth bared in a grin.

"That's Moira," said Evelyn.

"She's beautiful."

"She was. We were the ugly ducklings, Ant and me. Fortunately I was taking most of the photos, so you don't see me except in the ones Aunt Becca took."

"You were adorable." Jeffrey flipped to a photo of all three girls laughing and feeding each other something with their hands, Evelyn still in braces, her hair cut in a severe black bob. "You were all adorable. She's just—"

He scrutinised a photo of Moira by herself, slightly out of focus so all you saw was a blurred wave of blonde hair and her smile, a flash of narrowed eyes. "She's beautiful. Photogenic."

Evelyn laughed. "Is that what you call it? No, Moira was very pretty, all the boys liked her. But she was a tomboy like us. Ant was the one who was boy-crazy. Me and Moira, not so much."

"What about when you saw Robert Bennington? When was that?"

"The next day. Nothing happened—I mean, he was very nice, but there was nothing strange like that night. Nothing *untoward*," she added, lips pursed. "My aunt knew who he was—she didn't know him except to say hello to at the post office, and she'd never read his books. But she knew he was the children's writer, and she knew which house was supposed to be his. We told her we were going to see him, she told us to be polite and not be a nuisance and not stay long.

"So we were polite and not nuisances, and we stayed for two hours. Maybe three. We trekked over to his house, and that took almost an hour. A big old stone house. There was a standing stone and an old barrow nearby, it looked like a hayrick. A fogou. He was very proud that there was a fogou on his land—like a cave, but man-made. He said it was three thousand years old. He took us out to see it, and then we walked back to his house and he made us Nutella sandwiches and tangerines and Orange Squash. We just walked up to his door and knocked—*I* knocked, Ant was too nervous and Moira was just embarrassed. Ant and I had our copies of *The Second Sun*, and he was very sweet and invited us in and said he'd sign them before we left."

"Oh, sure—'Come up and see my fogou, girls.'"

"No—he wanted us to see it because it gave him an idea for his book. It was like a portal, he said. He wasn't a dirty old man, Jeffrey! He wasn't even that old—maybe forty? He had long hair, longish, anyway—to his shoulders—and he had cool clothes, an embroidered shirt and corduroy flares. And pointy-toed boots—blue boots, bright sky-blue, very pointy toes. That was the only thing about him I thought was odd. I wondered how his toes fit into them—if he had long pointy toes to go along with the shoes." She laughed. "Really, he was very charming, talked to us about the books but wouldn't reveal any secrets—he said there would be another in the series but it never appeared. He signed our books—well, he signed mine, Moira didn't have one and for some reason he forgot Ant's. And eventually we left."

"Did you tell him about the lights?"

"We did. He said he'd heard of things like that happening before. That part of Cornwall is ancient, there are all kinds of stone circles and menhirs, cromlechs, things like that."

"What's a cromlech?"

"You know—a dolmen." At Jeffrey's frown she picked up several of the snapshots and arranged them on the side table, a simple house of cards: three photos supporting a fourth laid atop them. "Like that. It's a kind of prehistoric grave, made of big flat stones. Stonehenge, only small. The fogou was a bit like that. They're all over West Penwith—that's where Zennor is. Alaister Crowley lived there, and D.H. Lawrence and his wife. That was years before Robert's time, but he said there were always stories about odd things happening. I don't know what kind of things—it was always pretty boring when I visited as a girl, except for that one time."

Jeffrey made a face. "He was out there with a flashlight, Ev, leading you girls on."

"He didn't even know we were there!" protested Evelyn, so vehemently that the makeshift house of photos collapsed. "He looked genuinely startled when we knocked on his door—I was afraid he'd yell at us to leave. Or, I don't know, have us arrested. He said that field had a name. It was a funny word, Cornish. It meant something, though of course I don't remember what. A lake, maybe, though there was no lake there, no water at all."

She stopped and leaned toward Jeffrey. "Why do you care about this, Jeffrey? *Did* Anthea say something?"

"No. I just found those letters, and..."

He lay his hands atop his knees, turned to stare past Evelyn into the darkness, so that she wouldn't see his eyes welling. "I just wanted to know. And I can't ask her."

Evelyn sighed. "Well, there's nothing to know, except what I told you. We went back once more—we took torches this time, and walking sticks and the dog. We stayed out till 3:00 a.m. Nothing happened except we caught hell from my aunt and uncle because they heard the dog barking and looked in the barn and we were gone.

"And that was the end of it. I still have the book he signed for me. Ant must have kept her copy—she was always mad he didn't sign it."

"I don't know. Maybe. I couldn't find it. Your friend Moira, you're not in touch with her?"

Evelyn shook her head. "I told you, she disappeared—she ran away that summer. There were problems at home, the father was a drunk and maybe the mother, too. We never went over there—it wasn't a welcoming place. She had an older sister but I never knew her. Look, if you're thinking Robert Bennington killed her, that's ridiculous. I'm sure her name came up during the trial, if anything had happened we would have heard about it. An investigation."

"Did you tell them about Moira?"

"Of course not. Look, Jeffrey—I think you should forget about all that. It's nothing to do with you, and it was all a long time ago. Ant never cared about it—I told her about the trial, I'd read about it in

The Guardian, but she was even less curious about it than I was. I don't even know if Robert Bennington is still alive. He'd be an old man now."

She leaned over to take his hand. "I can see you're tired, Jeffrey. This has all been so awful for you, you must be totally exhausted. Do you want to just stay here for a few days? Or come back after your meeting in London?"

"No—I mean, probably not. Probably I need to get back to Brooklyn. I have some projects I backburnered, I need to get to them in the next few weeks. I'm sorry, Ev."

He rubbed his eyes and stood. "I didn't mean to hammer you about this stuff. You're right—I'm just beat. All this—" He sorted the snapshots into a small stack, and asked, "Could I have one of these? It doesn't matter which one."

"Of course. Whichever, take your pick."

He chose a photo of the three girls, Moira and Evelyn doubled over laughing as Anthea stared at them, smiling and slightly puzzled.

"Thank you, Ev," he said. He replaced each of Anthea's letters into its envelope, slid the photo into the last one, then stared at the sheaf in his hand, as though wondering how it got there. "It's just, I dunno. Meaningless, I guess; but I want it to mean something. I want *something* to mean something."

"Anthea meant something." Evelyn stood and put her arms around him. "Your life together meant something. And your life now means something."

"I know." He kissed the top of her head. "I keep telling myself that."

◆ ◆ ◆

EVELYN DROPPED HIM off at the station the next morning. He felt guilty, lying that he had meetings back in London, but he sensed both her relief and regret that he was leaving.

"I'm sorry about last night," he said as Evelyn turned into the parking lot. "I feel like the Bad Fairy at the christening, bringing up all that stuff."

NEAR ZENNOR

"No, it was interesting." Evelyn squinted into the sun. "I hadn't thought about any of that for awhile. Not since Ant called me last March."

Jeffrey hesitated, then asked, "What do you think happened? I mean, you're the one with the advanced degree in structural engineering."

Evelyn laughed. "Yeah. And see where it's got me. I have no idea, Jeffrey. If you ask me, logically, what do I think? Well, I think it's just one of those things that we'll never know what happened. Maybe two different dimensions overlapped—in superstring theory, something like that is theoretically possible, a sort of duality."

She shook her head. "I know it's crazy. Probably it's just one of those things that don't make any sense and never will. Like how did Bush stay in office for so long?"

"That I could explain." Jeffrey smiled. "But it's depressing and would take too long. Thanks again, Ev."

They hopped out of the car and hugged on the curb. "You should come back soon," said Ev, wiping her eyes. "This is stupid, that it took so long for us all to get together again."

"I know. I will—soon, I promise. And you and Chris, come to New York. Once I have a place, it would be great."

He watched her drive off, waving as she turned back onto the main road; went into the station and walked to a ticket window.

"Can I get to Penzance from here?"

"What time?"

"Now."

The station agent looked at her computer. "There's a train in about half-an-hour. Change trains in Plymouth, arrive at Penzance a little before four."

He bought a first-class, one-way ticket to Penzance, found a seat in the waiting area, took out his phone and looked online for a place to stay near Zennor. There wasn't much—a few farmhouses designed for summer rentals, all still closed for the winter. An inn that had in recent years been turned into a popular gastropub was open; but even now, the first week of March, they were fully booked. Finally he came upon a B&B called Cliff Cottage in a neighbouring village just two miles away. There were only two rooms, and the official opening date was not until the following weekend, but he called anyway.

"A room?" The woman who answered sounded tired but friendly. "We're not really ready yet, we've been doing some renovations and—"

"All I need is a bed," Jeffrey broke in. He took a deep breath. "The truth is, my wife died recently. I just need some time to be away from the rest of the world and…"

His voice trailed off. He felt a pang of self-loathing, playing the pity card; listened to a long silence on the line before the woman said, "Oh, dear, I'm so sorry. Well, yes, if you don't mind that we're really not up and running. The grout's not even dry yet in the new bath. Do you have a good head for heights?"

"Heights?"

"Yes. Vertigo? Some people have a very hard time with the driveway. There's a two night minimum for a stay."

Jeffrey assured her he'd never had any issues with vertigo. He gave her his credit card info, rang off and called to reserve a car in Penzance.

He slept most of the way to Plymouth, exhausted and faintly hungover. The train from Plymouth to Penzance was nearly empty. He bought a beer and a sandwich in the buffet car, and went to his seat. He'd bought a novel in London at Waterstones, but instead of reading gazed out at a landscape that was a dream of books he'd read as a child—granite farmhouses, woolly-coated ponies in stone paddocks; fields improbably green against lowering grey sky, graphite clouds broken by blades of golden sun, a rainbow that pierced a thunderhead then faded as though erased by some unseen hand. Ringnecked pheasants, a running fox. More fields planted with something that shone a startling goldfinch-yellow. A silvery coastline hemmed by arches of russet stone. Children wrestling in the middle of an empty road. A woman walking with head bowed against the wind, hands extended before her like a diviner.

NEAR ZENNOR

Abandoned mineshafts and slagheaps; ruins glimpsed in an eye-flash before the train dove into a tunnel; black birds wheeling above a dun-coloured tor surrounded by scorched heath.

And, again and again, groves of gnarled oaks that underscored the absence of great forests in a landscape that had been scoured of trees thousands of years ago. It was beautiful yet also slightly disturbing, like watching an underpopulated, narratively fractured silent movie that played across the train window.

The trees were what most unsettled Jeffrey: the thought that men had so thoroughly occupied this countryside for so long that they had flensed it of everything—rocks, trees, shrubs all put to some human use so that only the abraded land remained. He felt relieved when the train at last reached Penzance, with the beachfront promenade to one side, glassy waves breaking on the sand and the dark towers of St. Michael's Mount suspended between aquamarine water and pearly sky.

He grabbed his bag and walked through the station, outside to where people waited on the curb with luggage or headed to the parking lot. The clouds had lifted: a chill steady wind blew from off the water, bringing the smell of salt and sea wrack. He shivered and pulled on his wool overcoat, looking around for the vehicle from the rental car company that was supposed to meet him.

He finally spotted it, a small white sedan parked along the sidewalk. A man in a dark blazer leaned against the car, smoking and talking to a teenage boy with dreadlocks and rainbow-knit cap and a somewhat older woman with matted dark-blonde hair.

"You my ride?" Jeffrey said, smiling.

The man took a drag from his cigarette and passed it to the woman. She was older than Jeffrey had first thought, in her early thirties, face seamed and sun-weathered and her eyes bloodshot. She wore tight flared jeans and a fuzzy sky-blue sweater beneath a stained Arsenal windbreaker.

"Spare anything?" she said as he stopped alongside the car. She reeked of sweat and marijuana smoke.

"Go on now, Erthy," the man said, scowling. He turned to Jeffrey. "Mr. Kearin?"

"That's me," said Jeffrey.

"Gotta 'nother rollie, Evan?" the woman prodded.

"Come on, Erthy," said the rainbow-hatted boy. He spun and began walking toward the station. "Peace, Evan."

"I apologise for that," Evan said as he opened the passenger door for Jeffrey. "I know the boy, his family's neighbours of my sister's."

"Bit old for him, isn't she?" Jeffrey glanced to where the two huddled against the station wall, smoke welling from their cupped hands.

"Yeah, Erthy's a tough nut. She used to sleep rough by the St. Erth train station. Only this last winter she's taken up in Penzance. Every summer we get the smackhead hippies here, there's always some poor souls who stay and take up on the street. Not that you want to hear about that," he added, laughing as he swung into the driver's seat. "On vacation?"

Jeffrey nodded. "Just a few days."

"Staying here in Penzance?"

"Cardu. Near Zennor."

"Might see some sun, but probably not till the weekend."

◆ ◆ ◆

HE ENDED UP with the same small white sedan. "Only one we have, this last minute," Evan said, tapping at the computer in the rental office. "But it's better really for driving out there in the countryside. Roads are extremely narrow. Have you driven around here before? No? I would strongly recommend the extra damages policy…"

It had been decades since Jeffrey had been behind the wheel of a car in the U.K. He began to sweat as soon as he left the rental car lot, eyes darting between the map Evan had given him and the GPS on his iPhone. In minutes the busy roundabout was behind him; the car crept up a narrow, winding hillside, with high stone walls to either side that swiftly gave way to hedgerows bordering open farmland. A brilliant yellow field proved to be planted with daffodils, their constricted

NEAR ZENNOR

yellow throats not yet in bloom. After several more minutes, he came to a crossroads.

Almost immediately he got lost. The distances between villages and roads were deceptive: what appeared on the map to be a mile or more instead contracted into a few hundred yards, or else expanded into a series of zigzags and switchbacks that appeared to point him back toward Penzance. The GPS directions made no sense, advising him to turn directly into stone walls or gated driveways or fields where cows grazed on young spring grass. The roads were only wide enough for one car to pass, with tiny turnouts every fifty feet or so where one could pull over, but the high hedgerows and labyrinthine turns made it difficult to spot oncoming vehicles.

His destination, a village called Cardu, was roughly seven miles from Penzance; after half-an-hour, the odometer registered that he'd gone fifteen miles, and he had no idea where he was. There was no cell phone reception. The sun dangled a hand's-span above the western horizon, staining ragged stone outcroppings and a bleak expanse of moor an ominous reddish-bronze, and throwing the black fretwork of stone walls into stark relief. He finally parked in one of the narrow turnouts, sat for a few minutes staring into the sullen blood-red eye of the sun, and at last got out.

The hedgerows offered little protection from the harsh wind that raked across the moor. Jeffrey pulled at the collar of his wool coat, turning his back to the wind, and noticed a small sign that read PUBLIC FOOTPATH. He walked over and saw a narrow gap in the hedgerow, three steps formed of wide flat stones. He took the three in one long stride and found himself at the edge of an overgrown field, similar to what Evelyn had described in her account of the lights near Zennor. An ancient-looking stone wall bounded the far edge of the field, with a wider gap that opened to the next field and what looked like another sign. He squinted, but couldn't make out what it read, and began to pick his way across the turf.

It was treacherous going—the countless hummocks hid deep holes, and more than once he barely kept himself from wrenching his ankle. The air smelled strongly of raw earth and cow manure. As the sun dipped lower, a wedge of shadow was driven between him and the swiftly darkening sky, making it still more difficult to see his way. But after a few minutes he reached the far wall, and bent to read the sign beside the gap into the next field.

CAS CIRCLE

He glanced back, saw a glint of white where the rental car was parked, straightened and walked on.

There was a footpath here. Hardly a path, really; just a trail where turf and bracken had been flattened by the passage of not-many feet. He followed it, stopping when he came to a large upright stone that came up his waist. He looked to one side then the other and saw more stones, forming a group more ovoid than circular, perhaps thirty feet in diameter. He ran his hand across the first stone—rough granite, ridged with lichen and friable bits of moss that crumbled at his touch.

The reek of manure was fainter here: he could smell something fresh and sweet, like rain, and when he looked down saw a silvery gleam at the base of the rock. He crouched and dipped his fingers into a tiny pool, no bigger than his shoe. The water was icy cold, and even after he withdrew his hand, the surface trembled.

A spring. He dipped his cupped palm into it and sniffed warily, expecting a foetid whiff of cow muck.

But the water smelled clean, of rock and rain. Without thinking he drew his hand to his mouth and sipped, immediately flicked his fingers to send glinting droplets into the night.

That was stupid, he thought, hastily wiping his hand on his trousers. *Now I'll get dysentery. Or whatever one gets from cows.*

He stood there for another minute, then turned and retraced his steps to the rental car. He saw a pair of headlights approaching and flagged down a white delivery van.

"I'm lost," he said, and showed the driver the map that Evan had given him.

"Not too lost." The driver perused the map, then gave him directions. "Once you see the inn you're almost there."

NEAR ZENNOR

Jeffrey thanked him, got back into the car and started to drive. In ten minutes he reached the inn, a rambling stucco structure with a half-dozen cars out front. There was no sign identifying Cardu, and no indication that there was anything more to the village than the inn and a deeply rutted road flanked by a handful of granite cottages in varying states of disrepair. He eased the rental car by the mottled grey buildings, to where what passed for a road ended; bore right and headed down a cobblestoned, hairpin drive that zigzagged along the cliff-edge.

He could hear but could not see the ocean, waves crashing against rocks hundreds of feet below. Now and then he got a skin-crawling glimpse of immense cliffs like congealed flames—ruddy stone, apricot-yellow gorse, lurid flares of orange lichen all burned to ash as afterglow faded from the western sky.

He wrenched his gaze back to the narrow strip of road immediately in front of him. Gorse and brambles tore at the doors; once he bottomed out, then nosed the car across a water-filled gulley that widened into a stream that cascaded down the cliff to the sea below.

"Holy fucking Christ," he said, and kept the car in first gear. In another five minutes he was safely parked beside the cottage, alongside a small sedan.

"We thought maybe you weren't coming," someone called as Jeffrey stepped shakily out onto a cobblestone drive. Straggly rosebushes grew between a row of granite slabs that resembled headstones. These were presumably to keep cars from veering down an incline that led to a ruined outbuilding, a few faint stars already framed in its gaping windows. "Some people, they start down here and just give up and turn back."

Jeffrey looked around, finally spotted a slight man in his early sixties standing in the doorway of a grey stone cottage tucked into the lee of the cliff. "Oh, hi. No, I made it."

Jeffrey ducked back into the car, grabbed his bag and headed for the cottage.

"Harry," the man said, and held the door for him.

"Jeffrey. I spoke to your wife this afternoon."

The man's brow furrowed. "Wife?" He was a head shorter than Jeffrey, clean-shaven, with a sun-weathered face and sleek grey-flecked, dark-brown hair to his shoulders. A ropey old cable knit sweater hung from his lank frame.

"Well, someone. A woman."

"Oh. That was Thomsa. My sister." The man nodded, as though this confusion had never occurred before. "We're still trying to get unpacked. We don't really open till this weekend, but…"

He held the door so Jeffrey could pass inside. "Thomsa told me of your loss. My condolences."

Inside was a small room with slate floors and plastered walls, sparely furnished with a plain deal table and four chairs intricately carved with Celtic knots; a sideboard holding books and maps and artfully mismatched crockery; large gas cooking stove and a side table covered with notepads and pens, unopened bills, and a laptop. A modern cast-iron wood-stove had been fitted into a wide, old-fashioned hearth. The stove radiated warmth and an acrid, not unpleasant scent, redolent of coalsmoke and burning sage. Peat, Jeffrey realised with surprise. There was a closed door on the other side of the room, and from behind this came the sound of a television. Harry looked at Jeffrey, cocking an eyebrow.

"It's beautiful," said Jeffrey.

Harry nodded. "I'll take you to your room," he said.

Jeffrey followed him up a narrow stair beneath the eaves, into a short hallway flanked by two doors. "Your room's here. Bath's down there, you'll have it all to yourself. What time would you like breakfast?"

"Seven, maybe?"

"How about seven-thirty?"

Jeffrey smiled wanly. "Sure."

The room was small, white plaster walls and a window-seat overlooking the sea, a big bed heaped with a white duvet and myriad pillows, corner wardrobe carved with the same Celtic knots as the chairs below. No TV or radio or telephone, not even a clock. Jeffrey unpacked his bag and checked his phone for service: none.

NEAR ZENNOR

He closed the wardrobe, looked in his backpack and swore. He'd left his book on the train. He ran a hand through his hair, stepped to the window-seat and stared out.

It was too dark now to see much, though light from windows on the floor below illuminated a small, winding patch of garden, bound at the cliff-side by a stone wall. Beyond that there was only rock and, far below, the sea. Waves thundered against the unseen shore, a muted roar like a jet turbine. He could feel the house around him shake.

And not just the house, he thought; it felt as though the ground and everything around him trembled without ceasing. He paced to the other window, overlooking the drive, and stared at his rental car and the sedan beside it through a freize of branches, a tree so contorted by wind and salt that the limbs only grew in one direction. He turned off the room's single light, waited for his eyes to adjust; stared back out through one window, and then the other.

For as far as he could see, there was only night. Ghostly light seeped from a room downstairs onto the sliver of lawn. Starlight touched on the endless sweep of moor, like another sea unrolling from the line of cliffs brooding above black waves and distant headlands. There was no sign of human habitation: no distant lights, no street-lamps, no cars, no ships or lighthouse beacons: nothing.

He sank onto the window seat, dread knotting his chest. He had never seen anything like this—even hiking in the Mojave Desert with Anthea ten years earlier, there had been a scattering of lights sifted across the horizon and satellites moving slowly through the constellations. He grabbed his phone, fighting a cold, black solitary horror. There was still no reception.

He put the phone aside and stared at a framed sepia-tinted photograph on the wall: a three masted schooner wrecked on the rocks beneath a cliff he suspected was the same one where the cottage stood. Why was he even here? He felt as he had once in college, waking in a strange room after a night of heavy drinking, surrounded by people he didn't know in a squalid flat used as a shooting gallery. The same sense that he'd been engaged in some kind of psychic somnambulism, walking perilously close to a precipice.

Here, of course he actually *was* perched on the edge of a precipice. He stood and went into the hall, switching on the light; walked into the bathroom and turned on all the lights there as well.

It was almost as large as his bedroom, cheerfully appointed with yellow and blue towels piled atop a wooden chair, a massive porcelain tub, hand-woven yellow rugs and a fistful of daffodils in a cobalt glass vase on a wide windowsill. He moved the towels and sat on the chair for a few minutes, then crossed to pick up the vase and drew it to his face.

The daffodils smelled sweetly, of overturned earth warming in the sunlight. Anthea had loved daffodils, planting a hundred new bulbs every autumn; daffodils and jonquil and narcissus and crocuses, all the harbingers of spring. He inhaled again, deeply, and replaced the flowers on the sill. He left a light on beside the sink, returned to his room and went to bed.

• ◆ •

HE WOKE BEFORE seven o'clock. Thin sunlight filtered through the white curtains he'd drawn the night before, and for several minutes he lay in bed, listening to the rhythmic boom of surf on the rocks. He finally got up, pulled aside the curtain and looked out.

A line of clouds hung above the western horizon, but over the headland the sky was pale blue, shot with gold where the sun rose above the moor. Hundreds of feet below Jeffrey's bedroom, aquamarine swells crashed against the base of the cliffs and swirled around ragged granite pinnacles that rose from the sea, surrounded by clouds of white seabirds. There was a crescent of white sand, and a black cavern-mouth gouged into one of the cliffs where a vortex rose and subsided with the waves.

The memory of last night's horror faded: sunlight and wheeling birds, the vast expanse of air and sea and all but treeless moor made him feel exhilarated. For the first time since Anthea's death, he had a premonition not of dread but of the sort of exultation he felt as a teenager, waking in his boyhood room in early spring.

He dressed and shaved—there was no shower, only that dinghy-sized tub, so he'd forgo bathing till later. He waited until he was certain he heard movement in the kitchen, and went downstairs.

"Good morning." A woman who might have been Harry's twin leaned against the slate sink. Slender, small-boned, with straight dark hair held back with two combs from a narrow face, brown-eyed and weathered as her brother's. "I'm Thomsa."

He shook her hand, glanced around for signs of coffee then peered out the window. "This is an amazing place."

"Yes, it is," Thomsa said evenly. She spooned coffee into a glass cafetière, picked up a steaming kettle and poured hot water over the grounds. "Coffee, right? I have tea if you prefer. Would you like eggs? Some people have all sorts of food allergies. Vegans, how do you feed them?" She stared at him in consternation, turned back to the sink, glancing at a bowl of eggs. "How many?"

The cottage was silent, save for the drone of a television behind the closed door and the thunder of waves beating against the cliffs. Jeffrey sat at a table set for one, poured himself coffee and stared out to where the moor rose behind them. "Does the sound of the ocean ever bother you?" he asked.

Thomsa laughed. "No. We've been here thirty-five years, we're used to that. But we're building a house in Greece, in Hydra, that's where we just returned from. There's a church in the village and every afternoon the bells ring, I don't know why. At first I thought, isn't that lovely, church bells! Now I'm sick of them just wish they'd just shut up."

She set a plate of fried eggs and thick-cut bacon in front of him, along with slabs of toasted brown bread and glass bowls of preserves, picked up a mug and settled at the table. "So are you here on holiday?"

"Mmm, yes." Jeffrey nodded, his mouth full. "My wife died last fall. I just needed to get away for a bit."

"Yes, of course. I'm very sorry."

"She visited here once when she was a girl—not here, but at a farm nearby, in Zennor. I don't know the last name of the family, but the woman was named Becca."

"Becca? Mmmm, no, I don't think so. Maybe Harry will know."

"This would have been 1971."

"Ah—no, we didn't move here till '75. Summer, us and all the other hippie types from back then." She sipped her tea. "No tourists around this time of year. Usually we don't open till the second week in March. But we don't have anyone scheduled yet, so." She shrugged, pushing back a wisp of dark hair. "It's quiet this time of year. No German tour buses. Do you paint?"

"Paint?" Jeffrey blinked. "No. I'm an architect, so I draw, but mostly just for work. I sketch sometimes."

"We get a lot of artists. There's the Tate in St. Ives, if you like modern architecture. And of course there are all the prehistoric ruins—standing stones, and Zennor Quoit. There are all sorts of legends about them, fairy tales. People disappearing. They're very interesting if you don't mind the walk."

"Are there places to eat?"

"The inn here, though you might want to stop in and make a booking. There's the pub in Zennor, and St. Ives of course, though it can be hard to park. And Penzance."

Jeffrey winced. "Not sure I want to get back on the road again immediately."

"Yes, the drive here's a bit tricky, isn't it? But Zennor's only two miles, if you don't mind walking—lots of people do, we get hikers from all over on the coastal footpath. And Harry might be going out later, he could drop you off in Zennor if you like."

"Thanks. Not sure what I'll do yet. But thank you."

He ate his breakfast, making small talk with Thomsa and nodding at Harry when he emerged and darted through the kitchen, raising a hand as he slipped outside. Minutes later, Jeffrey glimpsed him pushing a wheelbarrow full of gardening equipment.

NEAR ZENNOR

"I think the rain's supposed to hold off," Thomsa said, staring out the window. "I hope so. We want to finish that wall. Would you like me to make more coffee?"

"If you don't mind."

Jeffrey dabbed a crust into the blackcurrant preserves. He wanted to ask if Thomsa or her brother knew Robert Bennington, but was afraid he might be stirring up memories of some local scandal, or that he'd be taken for a journalist or some other busybody. He finished the toast, thanked Thomsa when she poured him more coffee, then reached for one of the brochures on the sideboard.

"So does this show where those ruins are?"

"Yes. You'll want the ordnance map. Here—" She cleared the dishes, gathered a map and unfolded it. She tapped the outline of a tiny cove between two spurs of land. "We're here."

She traced one of the spurs, lifted her head to stare out the window to a grey-green spine of rock stretching directly to the south. "That's Gurnard's Head. And there's Zennor Head—"

She turned and pointed in the opposite direction, to a looming promontory a few miles distant, and looked back down at the map. "You can see where everything's marked."

Jeffrey squinted to make out words printed in a tiny, Gothic font. TUMULI, STANDING STONE, HUT CIRCLE, CAIRN. "Is there a fogou around here?"

"A fogou?" She frowned slightly. "Yes, there is—out toward Zennor, across the moor. It's a bit of a walk."

"Could you give me directions? Just sort of point the way? I might try and find it—give me something to do."

Thomsa stepped to the window. "The coastal path is there—see? If you follow it up to the ridge, you'll see a trail veer off. There's an old road there, the farmers use it sometimes. All those old fields run alongside it. The fogou's on the Golovenna Farm, I don't know how many fields back that is. It would be faster if you drove toward Zennor then hiked over the moor, but you could probably do it from here. You'll have to find an opening in the stone walls or climb over—do you have hiking shoes?" She looked dubiously at his sneakers. "Well, they'll probably be all right."

"I'll give it a shot. Can I take that map?"

"Yes, of course. It's not the best map—the Ordnance Survey has a more detailed one, I think."

He thanked her and downed the rest of his coffee, went upstairs and pulled a heavy woollen sweater over his flannel shirt, grabbed his cell phone and returned downstairs. He retrieved the map and stuck it in his coat pocket, said goodbye to Thomsa rinsing dishes in the sink, and walked outside.

The air was warmer, almost balmy despite a stiff wind that had torn the line of clouds into grey shreds. Harry knelt beside a stone wall, poking at the ground with a small spade. Jeffrey paused to watch him, then turned to survey clusters of daffodils and jonquils, scores of them scattered across the terraced slopes among rocks and apple trees. The flowers were not yet in bloom, but he could glimpse sunlit yellow and orange and saffron petals swelling within the green buds atop each slender stalk.

"Going out?" Harry called.

"Yes." Jeffrey stooped to brush his fingers across one of the flowers. "My wife loved daffodils. She must have planted thousands of them."

Harry nodded. "Should open in the next few days. If we get some sun."

Jeffrey waved farewell and turned to walk up the drive.

In a few minutes, the cottage was lost to sight. The cobblestones briefly gave way to cracked concrete, then a deep rut that marked a makeshift path that led uphill, toward the half-dozen buildings that made up the village. He stayed on the driveway, and after another hundred feet reached a spot where a narrow footpath meandered off to the left, marked by a sign. This would be the path that Thomsa had pointed out.

He shaded his eyes and looked back. He could just make out Cliff Cottage, its windows a flare of gold in the sun. He stepped onto the trail, walking with care across loose stones and channels where water raced

NEAR ZENNOR

downhill, fed by the early spring rains. To one side, the land sheared away to cliffs and crashing waves; he could see where the coastal path wound along the headland, fading into the emerald crown of Zennor Head. Above him, the ground rose steeply, overgrown with coiled ferns, newly-sprung grass, thickets of gorse in brilliant, sun-yellow bloom where bees and tiny, orange butterflies fed. At the top of the incline, he could see the dark rim of a line of stone walls. He stayed on the footpath until it began to bear toward the cliffs, then looked for a place where he could break away and make for the ancient fields. He saw what looked like a path left by some kind of animal and scrambled up, dodging gorse, his sneakers sliding on loose scree, until he reached the top of the headland.

The wind here was so strong he nearly lost his balance as he hopped down into a grassy lane. The lane ran parallel to a long ridge of stone walls perhaps four feet high, braided with strands of rusted barbed wire. On the other side, endless intersections of yet more walls divided the moor into a dizzyingly ragged patchwork: jade-green, beryl, creamy yellow; ochre and golden amber. Here and there, twisted trees grew within sheltered corners, or rose from atop the walls themselves, gnarled branches scraping at the sky. High overhead, a bird arrowed toward the sea, and its plaintive cry rose above the roar of wind in his ears.

He pulled out the map, struggling to open it in the wind, finally gave up and shoved it back into his pocket. He tried to count back four fields, but it was hopeless—he couldn't make out where one field ended and another began.

And he had no idea what field to start with. He walked alongside the lane, away from the cottage and the village of Cardu, hoping he might find a gate or opening. He finally settled on a spot where the barbed wire had become engulfed by a protective thatch of dead vegetation. He clambered over the rocks, clutching desperately at dried leaves as the wall gave way beneath his feet and nearly falling onto a lethal-looking knot of barbed wire. Gasping, he reached the top of the wall, flailed as wind buffeted him then crouched until he could catch his breath.

The top of the wall was covered with vines, grey and leafless, as thick as his fingers and unpleasantly reminiscent of veins and arteries. This serpentine mass seemed to hold the stones together, though when he tried to step down the other side, the rocks once again gave way and he fell into a patch of whip-like vines studded with thorns the length of his thumbnail. Cursing, he extricated himself, his chinos torn and hands gouged and bloody, and staggered into the field.

Here at least there was some protection from the wind. The field sloped slightly uphill, to the next wall. There was so sign of a gate or breach. He shoved his hands into his pockets and strode through knee-high grass, pale-green and starred with minute, yellow flowers. He reached the wall and walked alongside it. In one corner several large rocks had fallen. He hoisted himself up until he could see into the next field. It was no different from the one he'd just traversed, save for a single massive evergreen in its centre.

Other than the tree, the field seemed devoid of any vegetation larger than a tussock. He tried to peer into the field beyond, and the ones after that, but the countryside dissolved into a glitter of green and topaz beneath the morning sun, with a few stone pinnacles stark against the horizon where moor gave way to sky.

He turned and walked back, head down against the wind; climbed into the first field and crossed it, searching until he spied what looked like a safe place to gain access to the lane once more. Another tangle of blackthorn snagged him as he jumped down and landed hard, grimacing as a thorn tore at his neck. He glared at the wall, then headed back to the cottage, picking thorns from his overcoat and jeans.

He was starving by the time he arrived at the cottage, also filthy. It had grown too warm for his coat; he slung it over his shoulder, wiping sweat from his cheeks. Thomsa was outside, removing a shovel from the trunk of the sedan.

"Oh, hello! You're back quickly!"

He stopped, grateful for the wind on his overheated face. "Quickly?"

NEAR ZENNOR

"I thought you'd be off till lunchtime. A few hours, anyway?"

"I thought it *was* lunchtime." He looked at his watch and frowned. "That can't be right. It's not even ten."

Thomsa nodded, setting the shovel beside the car. "I thought maybe you forgot something." She glanced at him, startled. "Oh my. You're bleeding—did you fall?"

He shook his head. "No, well, yes," he said sheepishly. "I tried to find that fogou. Didn't get very far. Are you sure it's just ten? I thought I was out there for hours—I figured it must be noon, at least. What time did I leave?"

"Half-past nine, I think."

He started to argue, instead shrugged. "I might try again. You said there's a better map from the Ordnance Survey? Something with more details?"

"Yes. You could probably get it in Penzance—call the bookstore there if you like, phone book's on the table."

He found the phone book in the kitchen and rang the bookshop. They had a copy of the Ordnance map and would hold it for him. He rummaged on the table for a brochure with a map of Penzance, went upstairs to spend a few minutes washing up from his trek, and hurried outside. Thomsa and Harry were lugging stones across the grass to repair the wall. Jeffrey waved, ducked into the rental car and crept back up the drive toward Cardu.

In broad daylight it still took almost ten minutes. He glanced out to where the coastal footpath wound across the top of the cliffs, could barely discern a darker trail leading to the old field systems, and, beyond that, the erratic cross-stitch of stone walls fading into the eastern sky. Even if he'd only gone as far as the second field, it seemed impossible that he could have hiked all the way there and back to the cottage in half-an-hour.

The drive to Penzance took less time than that; barely long enough for Jeffrey to reflect how unusual it was for him to act like this, impulsively, without a plan. Everything an architect did was according to plan. Out on the moor and gorse-grown cliffs, the strangeness of the immense, dour landscape had temporarily banished the near-constant presence of his dead wife. Now, in the confines of the cramped rental car, images of other vehicles and other trips returned, all with Anthea beside him. He pushed them away, tried to focus on the fact that here at last was a place where he'd managed to escape her; and remembered that was not true at all.

Anthea had been here, too. Not the Anthea he had loved but her mayfly self, the girl he'd never known; the Anthea who'd contained an entire secret world he'd never known existed. It seemed absurd, but he desperately wished she had confided in him about her visit to Bennington's house, and the strange night that had preceded it. Evelyn's talk of superstring theory was silly—he found himself sympathising with Moira, content to let someone else read the creepy books and tell her what to do. He believed in none of it, of course. Yet it didn't matter what he believed, but whether Anthea had, and why.

Penzance was surprisingly crowded for a weekday morning in early March. He circled the town's winding streets twice before he found a parking space, several blocks from the bookstore. He walked past shops and restaurants featuring variations on themes involving pirates, fish, pixies, sailing ships. As he passed a tattoo parlour, he glanced into the adjoining alley and saw the same rainbow-hatted boy from the train station, holding a skateboard and standing with several other teenagers who were passing around a joint. The boy looked up, saw Jeffrey and smiled. Jeffrey lifted his hand and smiled back. The boy called out to him, his words garbled by the wind, put down his skateboard and did a headstand alongside it. Jeffrey laughed and kept going.

There was only one other customer in the shop when he arrived, a man in a business suit talking to two women behind the register.

"Can I help you?" The older of the two women smiled. She had close-cropped red hair and fashionable eyeglasses, and set aside an iPad as Jeffrey approached.

"I called about an Ordnance map?"

"Yes. It's right here."

NEAR ZENNOR

She handed it to him, and he unfolded it enough to see that it showed the same area of West Penwith as the other map, enlarged and far more detailed.

The woman with the glasses cocked her head. "Shall I ring that up?"

Jeffrey closed the map and set it onto the counter. "Sure, in a minute. I'm going to look around a bit first."

She returned to chatting. Jeffrey wandered the shop. It was small but crowded with neatly-stacked shelves and tables, racks of maps and postcards, with an extensive section of books about Cornwall—guidebooks, tributes to Daphne du Maurier and Barbara Hepworth, DVDs of *The Pirates of Penzance* and *Rebecca*, histories of the mines and glossy photo volumes about surfing Newquay. He spent a few minutes flipping through one of these, and continued to the back of the store. There was an entire wall of children's books, picture books near the floor, chapter books for older children arranged alphabetically above them. He scanned the Bs, and looked aside as the younger woman approached, carrying an armful of calendars.

"Are you looking for something in particular?"

He glanced back at the shelves. "Do you have anything by Robert Bennington?"

The young woman set the calendars down, ran a hand along the shelf housing the Bs; frowned and looked back to the counter. "Rose, do we have anything by Robert Bennington? It rings a bell but I don't see anything here. Children's writer, is he?" she added, turning to Jeffrey.

"Yes. *The Sun Battles*, I think that's one of them."

The other customer nodded goodbye as Rose joined the others in the back.

"Robert Bennington?" She halted, straightening a stack of coffee table books, tapped her lower lip then quickly nodded. "Oh yes! The fantasy writer. We did have his books—he's fallen out of favour." She cast a knowing look at the younger clerk. "He was the child molester."

"Oh, right." The younger woman made a face. "I don't think his books are even in print now, are they?"

— 341 —

"I don't think so," said Rose. "I'll check. We could order something for you, if they are."

"That's okay—I'm only here for a few days."

Jeffrey followed her to the counter and waited as she searched online.

"No, nothing's available." Rose shook her head. "Sad bit of business, wasn't it? I heard something recently, he had a stroke I think. He might even have died, I can't recall now who told me. He must be quite elderly, if he's still alive."

"He lived around here, didn't he?" said Jeffrey.

"Out near Zennor, I think. He bought the old Golovenna Farm, years ago. We used to sell quite a lot of his books—he was very popular. Like the *Harry Potter* books now. Well, not that popular." She smiled. "But he did very well. He came in here once or twice, it must be twenty years at least. A very handsome man. Theatrical. He wore a long scarf, like Doctor Who. I'm sure you could find used copies online, or there's a second-hand bookstore just round the corner—they might well have something."

"That's all right. But thank you for checking."

He paid for the map and went back out onto the sidewalk. It was getting on to noon. He wandered the streets for several minutes looking for a place to eat, settled on a small, airy Italian restaurant where he had grilled sardines and spaghetti and a glass of wine. Not very Cornish, perhaps, but he promised himself to check on the pub in Zennor later.

The Ordnance map was too large and unwieldy to open at his little table, so he stared out the window, watching tourists and women with small children in tow as they popped in and out of the shops across the street. The rainbow-hatted boy and his cronies loped by, skateboards in hand. Dropouts or burnouts, Jeffrey thought; the local constabulary must spend half its time chasing them from place to place. He finished his wine and ordered a cup of coffee, gulped it down, paid the check, and left.

A few high white clouds scudded high overhead, borne on a steady wind that sent up flurries of grit and petals blown from ornamental cherry trees. Here in the heart of Penzance, the midday sun was almost hot: Jeffrey hooked his coat over his shoulder and ambled back to his car. He paused to glance at postcards and souvenirs in a shop window, but could think of no one to send a card to. Evelyn? She'd rather have something from Zennor, another reason to visit the pub.

He turned the corner, had almost reached the tattoo parlour when a plaintive cry rang out.

"Have you seen him?"

Jeffrey halted. In the same alley where he'd glimpsed the boys earlier, a forlorn figure sat on the broken asphalt, twitchy fingers toying with an unlit cigarette. Erthy, the woman who'd been at the station the day before. As Jeffrey hesitated she lifted her head, swiped a fringe of dirty hair from her eyes and stumbled to her feet. His heart sank as she hurried toward him, but before he could flee she was already in his face, her breath warm and beery. "Gotta light?"

"No, sorry," he said, and began to step away.

"Wait—you're London, right?"

"No, I'm just visiting."

"No—I saw you."

He paused, thrown off-balance by a ridiculous jolt of unease. Her eyes were bloodshot, the irises a peculiar marbled blue like flawed bottle-glass, and there was a vivid crimson splotch in one eye, as though a capillary had burst. It made it seem as though she looked at him sideways, even though she was staring at him straight on.

"You're on the London train!" She nodded in excitement. "I need to get back."

"I'm sorry." He spun and walked off as quickly as he could without breaking into a run. Behind him he heard footsteps, and again the same wrenching cry.

"Have you seen him?"

He did run then, as the woman screamed expletives and a shower of gravel pelted his back.

He reached his rental car, his heart pounding. He looked over his shoulder, jumped inside and locked the doors before pulling out into the street. As he drove off, he caught a flash in the rear-view mirror of the woman sidling in the other direction, unlit cigarette still twitching between her fingers.

◆ ◆ ◆

WHEN HE ARRIVED back at the cottage, he found Thomsa and Harry sitting at the kitchen table, surrounded by the remains of lunch, sandwich crusts and apple cores.

"Oh, hello." Thomsa looked up, smiling, and patted the chair beside her. "Did you go to The Tinners for lunch?"

"Penzance." Jeffrey sat and dropped his map onto the table. "I think I'll head out again, then maybe have dinner at the pub."

"He wants to see the fogou," said Thomsa. "He went earlier but couldn't find it. There is a fogou, isn't there, Harry? Out by Zennor Hill?"

Jeffrey hesitated, then said, "A friend of mine told me about it—she and my wife saw it when they were girls."

"Yes," said Harry after a moment. "Where the children's writer lived. Some sort of ruins there, anyway."

Jeffrey kept his tone casual. "A writer?"

"I believe so," said Thomsa. "We didn't know him. Someone who stayed here once went looking for him, but he wasn't home—this was years ago. The old Golovenna Farm."

Jeffrey pointed to the seemingly random network of lines that covered the map, like crazing on a piece of old pottery. "What's all this mean?"

Harry pulled his chair closer and traced the boundaries of Cardu with a dirt-stained finger. "Those are the field systems—the stone walls."

"You're kidding." Jeffrey laughed. "That must've driven someone nuts, getting all that down."

"Oh, it's all GPS and satellite photos now," said Thomsa. "I'm sorry I didn't have this map earlier, before you went for your walk. "

"It'll be on this survey." Harry angled the map so the sunlight illuminated the area surrounding Cardu. "This is our cove, here…"

They pored over the ordnance survey. Jeffrey pointed at markers for hut circles and cairns, standing stones and tumuli, all within a handspan of Cardu, as Harry continued to shake his head.

NEAR ZENNOR

"It's this one, I think," Harry said at last, and glanced at his sister. He scored a square half-inch of the page with a blackened fingernail, minute Gothic letters trapped within the web of field systems.

CHAMBERED CAIRN

"That looks right," said Thomsa. "But it's a ways off the road. I'm not certain where the house is—the woman who went looking for it said she roamed the moor for hours before she came on it."

Jeffrey ran his finger along the line marking the main road. "It looks like I can drive to here. If there's a place to park, I can just hike in. It doesn't look that far. As long as I don't get towed."

"You shouldn't get towed," said Thomsa. "All that land's part of Golovenna, and no one's there. He never farmed it, just let it all go back to the moor. You'd only be a mile or so from Zennor if you left your car. They have musicians on Thursday nights, some of the locals come in and play after dinner."

Jeffrey refolded the map. When he looked up, Harry was gone. Thomsa handed him an apple.

"Watch for the bogs," she said. "Marsh grass, it looks sturdy but when you put your foot down it gives way and you can sink under. Like quicksand. They found a girl's body ten years back. Horses and sheep, too." Jeffrey grimaced and she laughed. "You'll be all right—just stay on the footpaths."

He thanked her, went upstairs to exchange his overcoat for a windbreaker, and returned to his car. The clouds were gone: the sun shone high in a sky the summer blue of gentians. He felt the same surge of exultation he'd experienced that morning, the sea-fresh wind tangling the stems of daffodils and iris, white gulls crying overhead. He kept the window down as he drove up the twisting way to Cardu, and the honeyed scent of gorse filled the car.

The road to Zennor coiled between hedgerows misted green with new growth and emerald fields where brown-and-white cattle grazed. In the distance a single tractor moved so slowly across a black furrow that Jeffrey could track its progress only by the skein of crows that followed it, the birds dipping then rising like a black thread drawn through blue cloth.

Twice he pulled over to consult the map. His phone didn't work here—he couldn't even get the time, let alone directions. The car's clock read 14:21. He saw no other roads, only deeply-rutted tracks protected by stiles, some metal, most of weathered wood. He tried counting stone walls to determine which marked the fields Harry had said belonged to Golovenna Farm, and stopped a third time before deciding the map was all but useless. He drove another hundred feet, until he found a swathe of gravel between two tumbledown stone walls, a rusted gate sagging between them. Beyond it stretched an overgrown field bisected by a stone-strewn path.

He was less than a mile from Zennor. He folded the map and jammed it into his windbreaker pocket along with the apple, and stepped out of the car.

The dark height before him would be Zennor Hill. Golovenna Farm was somewhere between there and where he stood. He turned slowly, scanning everything around him to fix it in his memory: the winding road, intermittently visible between walls and hedgerows; the ridge of cliffs falling down to the sea, book-ended by the dark bulk of Gurnards Head in the south-west and Zennor Head to the north-east. On the horizon were scattered outcroppings that might have been tors or ruins or even buildings. He locked the car, checked that he had his phone, climbed over the metal gate and began to walk.

The afternoon sun beat down fiercely. He wished he'd brought a hat, or sunglasses. He crossed the first field in a few minutes, and was relieved to find a break in the next wall, an opening formed by a pair of tall, broad stones. The path narrowed here, but was still clearly discernible where it bore straight in front of him, an arrow of new green grass flashing through ankle-high turf overgrown with daisies and fronds of young bracken.

The ground felt springy beneath his feet. He remembered Thomsa's warning about the bogs, and glanced around for something he might use as a walking stick. There were no trees in sight, only wicked-looking thickets of blackthorn clustered along the perimeter of the field.

He found another gap in the next wall, guarded like the first by two broad stones nearly as tall as he was. He clambered onto the wall, fighting to open his map in the brisk wind, and examined the survey, trying to find some affinity between the fields around him and the crazed pattern on the page. At last he shoved the map back into his pocket, set his back to the wind and shaded his eyes with his hand.

It was hard to see—he was staring due west, into the sun—but he thought he glimpsed a black bulge some three or four fields off, a dark blister within the haze of green and yellow. It might be a ruin, or just as likely a farm or outbuildings. He clambered down into the next field, crushing dead bracken and shoots of heather; picked his way through a breach where stones had fallen and hurried until he reached yet another wall.

There were the remnants of a gate here, a rusted latch and iron pins protruding from the granite. Jeffrey crouched beside the wall to catch his breath. After a few minutes he scrambled to his feet and walked through the gap, letting one hand rest for an instant upon the stone. Despite the hot afternoon sun it felt cold beneath his palm, more like metal than granite. He glanced aside to make sure he hadn't touched a bit of rusted hardware, but saw only a boulder seamed with moss.

The fields he'd already passed through had seemed rank and overgrown, as though claimed by the wilderness decades ago. Yet there was no mistaking what stretched before him as anything but open moor. Clumps of gorse sprang everywhere, starbursts of yellow blossom shadowing pale-green ferns and tufts of dogtooth violets. He walked cautiously—he couldn't see the earth underfoot for all the new growth—but the ground felt solid beneath mats of dead bracken that gave off a spicy October scent. He was so intent on watching his step that he nearly walked into a standing stone.

He sucked his breath in sharply and stumbled backward. For a fraction of a second he'd perceived a figure there, but it was only a stone, twice his height and leaning at a forty-five degree angle, so that it pointed toward the sea. He circled it, then ran his hand across its granite flank, sun-warmed and furred with lichen and dried moss. He kicked at the thatch of ferns and ivy that surrounded its base, stooped and dug his hand through the vegetation, until his fingers dug into raw earth.

He withdrew his hand and backed away, staring at the ancient monument, at once minatory and banal. He could recall no indication of a standing stone between Cardu and Zennor, and when he checked the map he saw nothing there.

But something else loomed up from the moor a short distance away—a house. He headed toward it, slowing his steps in case someone saw him, so that they might have time to come outside.

No one appeared. After five minutes he stood in a rutted drive beside a long, one-storey building of grey stone similar to those he'd passed on the main road; slate-roofed, with deep small windows and a wizened tree beside the door, its branches rattling in the wind. A worn hand-lettered sign hung beneath the low eaves: GOLOVENNA FARM.

Jeffrey looked around. He saw no car, only a large plastic trash bin that had blown over. He rapped at the door, waited then knocked again, calling out a greeting. When no one answered he tried the knob, but the door was locked.

He stepped away to peer in through the window. There were no curtains. Inside looked dark and empty, no furniture or signs that someone lived here, or indeed if anyone had for years. He walked round the house, stopping to look inside each window and half-heartedly trying to open them, without success. When he'd completed this circuit, he wandered over to the trash bin and looked inside. It too was empty.

He righted it, then stood and surveyed the land around him. The rutted path joined a narrow, rock-strewn drive that led off into the moor to the west. He saw what looked like another structure not far from where the two tracks joined, a collapsed building of some sort.

He headed towards it. A flock of little birds flittered from a gorse bush, making a sweet high-pitched song as they soared past him, close enough that he could see their rosy breasts and hear their wings beat against the wind. They settled on the ruined building, twittering companionably as he approached, then took flight once more.

It wasn't a building but a mound. Roughly rectangular but with rounded corners, maybe twenty feet long and half again as wide; as tall as he was, and so overgrown with ferns and blackthorn that he might have mistaken it for a hillock. He kicked through brambles and clinging thorns until he reached one end, where the mound's curve had been sheared off.

Erosion, he thought at first; then realised that he was gazing into an entryway. He glanced behind him before drawing closer, until he stood knee-deep in dried bracken and whip-like blackthorn.

In front of him was a simple doorway of upright stones, man-high, with a larger stone laid across the tops to form a lintel. Three more stones were set into the ground as steps, descending to a passage choked with young ferns and ivy mottled black and green as malachite.

Jeffrey ducked his head beneath the lintel and peered down into the tunnel. He could see nothing but vague outlines of more stones and straggling vines. He reached to thump the ceiling to see if anything moved.

Nothing did. He checked his phone—still no signal—turned to stare up into the sky, trying to guess what time it was. He'd left the car around two thirty, and he couldn't have been walking for more than an hour. Say it was four o'clock, to be safe. He still had a good hour-and-a-half to get back to the road before dark.

He took out the apple Thomsa had given him and ate it, dropped the core beside the top step; zipped his windbreaker and descended into the passage.

He couldn't see how long it was, but he counted thirty paces, pausing every few steps to look back at the entrance, before the light faded enough that he needed to use his cell phone for illumination. The walls glittered faintly where broken crystals were embedded in the granite, and there was a moist, earthy smell, like a damp cellar. He could stand upright with his arms outstretched, his fingertips grazing the walls to either side. The vegetation disappeared after the first ten paces, except for moss, and after a few more steps there was nothing beneath his feet but bare earth. The walls were of stone, dirt packed between them and hardened by the centuries so that it was almost indistinguishable from the granite.

He kept going, glancing back as the entryway diminished to a bright mouth, then a glowing eye, and finally a hole no larger than that left by a finger thrust through a piece of black cloth.

A few steps more and even that was gone. He stopped, his breath coming faster, then walked another five paces, the glow from his cell phone a blue moth flickering in his hand. Once again he stopped to look back.

He could see nothing behind him. He shut off the cell phone's light, experimentally moved his hand swiftly up and down before his face; closed his eyes then opened them. There was no difference.

His mouth went dry. He turned his phone on, took a few more steps deeper into the passage before halting again. The phone's periwinkle glow was insubstantial as a breath of vapour: he could see neither the ground beneath him nor the walls to either side. He raised his arms and extended them, expecting to feel cold stone beneath his fingertips.

The walls were gone. He stepped backward, counting five paces, and again extended his arms. Still nothing. He dropped his hands and began to walk forward, counting each step—five, six, seven, ten, thirteen—stopped and slowly turned in a circle, holding the phone at arm's-length as he strove to discern some feature in the encroaching darkness. The pallid-blue gleam flared then went out.

He swore furiously, fighting panic. He turned the phone on and off, to no avail; finally shoved it into his pocket and stood, trying to calm himself.

It was impossible that he could be lost. The mound above him wasn't that large, and even if the fogou's passage continued for some distance underground, he would eventually reach the end, at which point he could turn around and painstakingly wend his way back out again. He tried to recall something he'd read once, about navigating the maze at Hampton Court—always keep your hand on the left-hand side of the hedge. All he had to do was locate a wall, and walk back into daylight.

He was fairly certain that he was still facing the same way as when he had first entered. He turned, so that he was now facing where the doorway should be, and walked, counting aloud as he did. When he reached one hundred he stopped.

There was no way he had walked more than a hundred paces into the tunnel. Somehow, he had gotten turned around. He wiped his face, slick and chill with sweat, and breathed deeply, trying to slow his racing heart. He heard nothing, saw nothing save that impenetrable darkness. Everything he had ever read about getting lost advised staying put and waiting for help; but that involved being lost above ground, where someone would eventually find you. At some point Thomsa and Harry would notice he hadn't returned, but that might not be till morning.

And who knew how long it might be before they located him? The thought of spending another twelve hours or more here, motionless, unable to see or hear, or touch anything save the ground beneath his feet, filled Jeffrey with such overwhelming horror that he felt dizzy.

And that was worst of all: if he fell, would he even touch the ground? He crouched, felt an absurd wash of relief as he pressed his palms against the floor. He straightened, took another deep breath and began to walk.

He tried counting his steps, as a means to keep track of time, but before long a preternatural stillness came over him, a sense that he was no longer awake but dreaming. He pinched the back of his hand, hard enough that he gasped. Yet still the feeling remained, that he'd somehow fallen into a recurring dream, the horror deadened somewhat by a strange familiarity. As though he'd stepped into an icy pool, he stopped, shivering, and realised the source of his apprehension.

It had been in the last chapter of Robert Bennington's book, *The Sun Battles*; the chapter that he'd never been able to recall clearly. Even now it was like remembering something that had happened *to* him, not something he'd read: the last of the novel's four children passing through a portal between one world and another, surrounded by utter darkness and the growing realisation that with each step the world around her was disintegrating and that she herself was disintegrating as well, until the book ended with her isolated consciousness fragmented into incalculable motes within an endless, starless void.

The terror of that memory jarred him. He jammed his hands into his pockets and felt his cell phone and the map, his car keys, some change. He walked more quickly, gazing straight ahead, focused on finding the spark within the passage that would resolve into the entrance.

After some time his heart jumped—it was there, so small he might have imagined it, a wink of light faint as a clouded star.

But when he ran a few paces he realised it was his mind playing tricks on him. A phantom light floated in the air, like the luminous blobs behind one's knuckled eyelids. He blinked and rubbed his eyes: the light remained.

"Hello?" he called, hesitating. There was no reply.

He started to walk, but slowly, calling out several times into the silence. The light gradually grew brighter. A few more minutes and a second light appeared, and then a third. They cast no glow upon the tunnel, nor shadows: he could see neither walls nor ceiling, nor any sign of those who carried the lights. All three seemed suspended in the air, perhaps ten feet above the floor, and all bobbed slowly up and down, as though each was borne upon a pole.

Jeffrey froze. The lights were closer now, perhaps thirty feet from where he stood.

"Who is it?" he whispered.

He heard the slightest of sounds, a susurrus as of escaping air. With a cry he turned and fled, his footsteps echoing through the passage. He heard no sounds of pursuit, but when he looked back, the lights were still there, moving slowly toward him. With a gasp he ran harder, his chest aching, until one foot skidded on something and he fell. As he scrambled back up, his hand touched a flat smooth object; he grabbed it and without thinking jammed it into his pocket, and raced on down the tunnel.

And now, impossibly, in the vast darkness before him he saw a jot of light that might have been reflected from a spider's eye. He kept going. Whenever he glanced back, he saw the trio of lights behind him.

They seemed to be more distant now. And there was no doubt that the light in front of him spilled from the fogou's entrance—he could see the outlines of the doorway, and the dim glister of quartz and mica in the walls to either side. With a gasp he reached the steps, stumbled up them and back out into the blinding light of afternoon. He stopped, coughing and covering his eyes until he could see, then staggered back across first one field and then the next, hoisting himself over rocks heedless of blackthorns tearing his palms and clothing, until at last he reached the final overgrown tract of heather and bracken, and saw the white roof of his rental car shining in the sun.

He ran up to it, jammed the key into the lock and with a gasp fell into the driver's seat. He locked the doors, flinching as another car drove past, and finally looked out the window.

To one side was the gate he'd scaled, with field after field beyond; to the other side the silhouettes of Gurnard's Head and its sister promontory. Beyond the fields, the sun hung well above the lowering mass of Zennor Hill. The car's clock read 15:23.

He shook his head in disbelief: it was impossible he'd been gone for scarcely an hour. He reached for his cell phone and felt something in the pocket beside it—the object he'd skidded on inside the fogou.

He pulled it out. A blue metal disc, slightly flattened where he'd stepped on it, with gold-stamped words above a beacon.

ST. AUSTELL CANDIES: FUDGE FROM REAL CORNISH CREAM

He turned it over in his hands and ran a finger across the raised lettering.

Becca gave one to each of us the day we arrived. The fudge was supposed to last the entire two weeks, and I think we ate it all that first night.

The same kind of candy tin where Evelyn had kept her comb and Anthea her locket and chain. He stared at it, the tin bright and enamel glossy-blue as though it had been painted yesterday. Anyone could have a candy tin, especially one from a local company that catered to tourists.

After a minute he set it down, took out his wallet and removed the photo Evelyn had given him: Evelyn and Moira doubled-up with laughter as Anthea stared at them, slightly puzzled, a half-smile on her face as though trying to determine if they were laughing at her.

He gazed at the photo for a long time, returned it to his wallet, then slid the candy lid back into his pocket. He still had no service on his phone.

• ◆ •

HE DROVE VERY slowly back to Cardu, nauseated from sunstroke and his terror at being underground. He knew he'd never been seriously lost—a backwards glance as he fled the mound reassured him that it hadn't been large enough for that.

Yet he was profoundly unnerved by his reaction to the darkness, the way his sight had betrayed him and his imagination reflexively dredged up the images from Evelyn's story. He was purged of any desire to remain another night at the cottage, or even in England, and considered checking to see if there was an evening train back to London.

But by the time he edged the car down the long drive to the cottage, his disquiet had ebbed somewhat. Thomsa and Harry's car was gone. A stretch of wall had been newly repaired, and many more daffodils and narcissus had opened, their sweet fragrance following him as he trudged to the front door.

Inside he found a plate with a loaf of freshly-baked bread and some local blue cheese, beside it several pamphlets with a yellow Sticky note.

NEAR ZENNOR

Jeffrey—

Gone to see a play in Penzance. Please turn off lights downstairs. I found these books today and thought you might be interested in them.

Thomsa

He glanced at the pamphlets—another map, a flyer about a music night at the pub in Zennor, a small paperback with a green cover—crossed to the refrigerator and foraged until he found two bottles of ale. Probably not proper B&B etiquette, but he'd apologise in the morning.

He grabbed the plate and book and went upstairs to his room. He kicked off his shoes, groaning with exhaustion, removed his torn windbreaker and regarded himself in the mirror, his face scratched and flecked with bits of greenery.

"What a mess," he murmured, and collapsed onto the bed.

He downed one of the bottles of ale and most of the bread and cheese. Outside, light leaked from a sky deepening to ultramarine. He heard the boom and sigh of waves, and for a long while he reclined in the window-seat and stared out at the cliffs, watching as shadows slipped down them like black paint. At last he stood and got some clean clothes from his bag. He hooked a finger around the remaining bottle of ale, picked up the book Thomsa had left for him, and retired to the bathroom.

The immense tub took ages to fill, but there seemed to be unlimited hot water. He put all the lights on and undressed, sank into the tub and gave himself over to the mindless luxury of hot water and steam and the scent of daffodils on the windowsill.

Finally he turned the water off. He reached for the bottle he'd set on the floor and opened it, dried his hands and picked up the book. A worn paperback, its creased cover showing a sweep of green hills topped by a massive tor, with a glimpse of sea in the distance.

ELIZABETH HAND

OLD TALES FOR NEW DAYS
BY ROBERT BENNINGTON

Jeffrey whistled softly, took a long swallow of ale and opened the book. It was not a novel but a collection of stories, published in 1970—Cornish folktales, according to a brief preface, 'told anew for today's generation'. He scanned the table of contents—'Pisky-Led', 'Tregeagle and the Devil', 'Jack the Giant Killer'—then sat up quickly in the tub, spilling water as he gazed at a title underlined with red ink: 'Cherry of Zennor'. He flipped through the pages until he found it.

> Sixteen-year-old Cherry was the prettiest girl in Zennor, not that she knew it. One day while walking on the moor she met a young man as handsome as she was lovely.
> "Will you come with me?" he asked, and held out a beautiful lace handkerchief to entice her. "I'm a widower with an infant son who needs tending. I'll pay you better wages than any man or woman earns from here to Kenidjack Castle, and give you dresses that will be the envy of every girl at Morvah Fair."
> Now, Cherry had never had a penny in her pocket in her entire young life, so she let the young man take her arm and lead her across the moor...

There were no echoes here of *The Sun Battles*, no vertiginous terrors of darkness and the abyss; just a folk tale that reminded Jeffrey a bit of 'Rip Van Winkle', with Cherry caring for the young son and, as the weeks passed, falling in love with the mysterious man.

Each day she put ointment on the boy's eyes, warned by his father never to let a drop fall upon her own. Until of course one day she couldn't resist doing so, and saw an entire host of gorgeously-dressed men and women moving through the house around her, including her mysterious employer and a beautiful woman who was obviously his

NEAR ZENNOR

wife. Betrayed and terrified, Cherry fled; her lover caught up with her on the moor and pressed some coins into her hand.

"You must go now and forget what you have seen," he said sadly, and touched the corner of her eye. When she returned home she found her parents dead and gone, along with everyone she knew, and her cottage a ruin open to the sky. Some say it is still a good idea to avoid the moors near Zennor.

Jeffrey closed the book and dropped it on the floor beside the tub. When he at last headed back down the corridor, he heard voices from the kitchen, and Thomsa's voice raised in laughter. He didn't go downstairs; only returned to his room and locked the door behind him.

• ◆ •

HE LEFT EARLY the next morning, after sharing breakfast with Thomsa at the kitchen table.

"Harry's had to go to St. Ives to pick up some tools he had repaired." She poured Jeffrey some more coffee and pushed the cream across the table toward him. "Did you have a nice ramble yesterday and go to the Tinners?"

Jeffrey smiled but said nothing. He was halfway up the winding driveway back to Cardu before he realised he'd forgotten to mention the two bottles of ale.

He returned the rental car then got a ride to the station from Evan, the same man who'd picked him up two days earlier.

"Have a good time in Zennor?"

"Very nice," said Jeffrey.

"Quiet this time of year." Evan pulled the car to the curb. "Looks like your train's here already."

Jeffrey got out, slung his bag over his shoulder and started for the station entrance. His heart sank when he saw two figures arguing on the sidewalk a few yards away, one a policeman.

"Come on now, Erthy," he said, glancing as Jeffrey drew closer. "You know better than this."

"Fuck you!" she shouted, and kicked at him. "Not my fucking name!"

"That's it."

The policeman grabbed her wrist and bent his head to speak into a walkie-talkie. Jeffrey began to hurry past. The woman screamed after him, shaking her clenched fist. Her eye with its bloody starburst glowed crimson in the morning sun.

"London!" Her voice rose desperately as she fought to pull away from the cop. "London, please, take me—"

Jeffrey shook his head. As he did, the woman raised her fist and flung something at him. He gasped as it stung his cheek, clapping a hand to his face as the policeman shouted and began to drag the woman away from the station.

"London! *London!*"

As her shrieks echoed across the plaza, Jeffrey stared at a speck of blood on his finger. Then he stooped to pick up what she'd thrown at him: a yellow pencil worn with toothmarks, its graphite tip blunted but the tiny, embossed black letters still clearly readable above the ferrule.

RAVENWOOD.

The Owl Count

In mid-march, Louis's childhood friend Eric died of a cerebral aneurysm after being in a coma for nine days. The memorial was in the small Vermont town where they'd grown up together. Louis drove there from northern Maine, spent the night at a friend's house after the service, and left again the next morning.

It was late afternoon when he got back home, to a few inches of new snow. He went inside and fired up the woodstove, sorted through the few items of mail that had arrived since he'd left, grabbed a beer from the fridge and checked his mobile. There he found a text message from his old friend Yvette, with the subject line **OWL COUNT**.

> **Looks like the best night will be tonight or Monday. Moon is just past full now. Will be cold but I'm afraid if we don't get out this week we'll miss the chance because of weather.**

Louis stared out at the bare trees silhouetted against the dusk. After a moment he wrote, **just returned from a funeral in vermont, can do it tomorrow maybe**

Immediately she replied: **No, supposed to snow early tomorrow. Need to go tonight.**

Louis swore softly, then sighed. **ok what time**

Will pick you up @ 11:30. See you then!

He finished his beer and reheated some soup for dinner, checked the temperature and weather: twenty-eight degrees, cloudy, not much wind. Heavy snow predicted but not till morning. Not an ideal night, at least as far as Louis was concerned—it was way too cold.

But the owls wouldn't care, and neither would Yvette. Like Louis, she was widowed. Her husband, Buddy, had been Louis's close friend, a game warden who'd been two months from retirement when he had a heart attack while searching for a snowmobiler who'd gone missing up by Greenville. Louis always felt like he'd taken Buddy's death harder than Yvette. Not true, he knew that; it was just Yvette's way. Her composure and oddly fatalistic good humor remained unshaken by death, war, the slow decay of the wilderness where they lived. And now, her own illness.

Louis's wife, Sheila, had died within a year of Buddy. That was over a decade ago. The plastic bins full of medications she'd been prescribed in her last months were still jammed onto the floor of the bedroom closet where her winter coats, flannel shirts, and snowmobiling gear continued to hang alongside Louis's own. Like Yvette—like everyone—he'd been downsized from his teaching job when their university rolled over to the AI modules. Since then he'd gotten by the same way his Maine ancestors had a century earlier. Barter and scavenging; hunting and fishing; coaxing pumpkins, squash, beans, onions, garlic, Jacob's cattle beans from the stony soil and longer growing season that was one of the few enduring benefits of the so-called lost winters.

"You can grow tomatoes in Maine now!" Yvette always marveled.

"Yeah, but not potatoes," Louis would retort. The mutated potato bugs had seen to that.

He washed his soup bowl and spoon, went outside to bring in more firewood. If it really did snow the next day, he'd be too tired from the owl count to bother in the morning. He drank another beer, set the alarm for 11 P.M., four hours from now, and went to bed.

He woke when the phone rang. Yvette again. He looked blearily at the time and groaned. "Jesus, you couldn't let me sleep another fifteen minutes?"

THE OWL COUNT

"I was afraid you wouldn't wake up!"

Louis had never overslept for the owl count, but he knew that wasn't the issue. Yvette was too excited to wait. "Well, give me a few minutes. I need some coffee."

"I have coffee."

"I give up. See you when you get here."

He heated water for the coffee and dressed. Thermal long underwear, a pair of wool hunting pants that had been his father's, a rag wool sweater and another that Sheila had knit for him. Two pairs of wool socks, old insulated Bean boots. Most years, he and Yvette didn't hear any owls. But it was guaranteed that they'd freeze as they waited in hopes of doing so.

He'd just finished gulping down the coffee when Yvette's headlights cut through the darkness outside the kitchen window. She left the car idling and entered without knocking. Louis held up his coffee mug. "Want some?"

Yvette perched on the arm of the chair beside the woodstove. With her green snowpants, oversized black boots and red parka, its pointed hood pulled up so that wispy white curls framed her face, she resembled a garden gnome. She glanced at the coffee mug and shook her head.

"I'm all set," she said. She watched Louis with the avid expression of a dog awaiting a walk. He grabbed gloves and knit cap, pulled on his own parka; shoved his mobile in a pocket and stuck another log in the wood stove.

"Okay," he said.

Yvette hopped up and hurried outside. Louis followed, the snow soft beneath his boots. He got into her old Subaru, where she handed him a clipboard.

"And there's more coffee." She pointed at a thermos on the floor, put the car into gear, and gingerly pulled out onto the road. "I'm so excited!" she exclaimed, and grinned.

Louis had joined the owl count twenty-six years earlier, when Yvette's former owling partner moved back to Florida. Back then, the program was administered by a Maine college that had received a grant to do a study of the state's owl population. The top data sheet on Louis's clipboard dated to that time.

> We seek to establish owl presence across our landscape, to estimate population and density for common Maine owls, and to detect changes in distribution or density perhaps related to human influences...

Data was collected by teams of volunteers across Maine between early March and mid-April—breeding season. They monitored five owl species—short- and long-eared owls, saw-whet owls, barred owls, great horned owls. The project ended years ago, but Yvette and Louis had continued to go out nearly every spring since. This was Yvette's idea, of course, but except for that year when Sheila had finally gone into hospice in Bangor, Louis accompanied Yvette every time, including the March night only weeks after Buddy's death.

The Subaru jounced down the rutted drive to the road as Yvette downshifted to avoid potholes and frost heaves. Louis's car was a hybrid, nearly as old as Yvette's Subaru, but it didn't fare as well in winter. He stuck the clipboard on the floor and reached to turn down the heat. Yvette's car reeked of dog and scorched engine oil—the head gasket leaked, so she had to top off the oil every other day, from a stockpile she'd traded for with gallons of tomato sauce and some de-worming medicine with a 2007 expiration date. Her dog, Wilmer, was back at the house. The only time he didn't accompany Yvette was during the owl count.

"Damn!" Yvette slapped the steering wheel and Louis looked at her in alarm. Yvette never swore. "I forgot to check if there's batteries in the CD player! Do you have any?"

"At the house, maybe." He twisted to look into the back seat, piled with outdoor gear and blankets covered in dog hair, and snaked out his arm to retrieve the portable boom box, a decrepit piece of outmoded technology that Yvette coddled as though it had been one of her

THE OWL COUNT

wheezing dogs. She'd bought it specifically for the owl count. That must have been more than thirty years ago, when CDs were already being phased out.

As far as Louis knew, she never used it for any other purpose—he'd never seen a single other CD in her house. Some nights during the summer, she'd play the owl call CD on the deck of her house up on Flywheel Mountain, watching as the owls appeared ghostlike from the darkness above her head. A practice the Owl Monitoring Program had strictly warned against, back in the day, but the study had ended so long ago, who was possibly left to care? Certainly Yvette had seen and heard more owls during these forbidden sessions than they ever had during the owl count.

He peered through the CD player's smudged plastic window and saw the disk. Did she ever even remove it? Probably not. He hit play, watched as the disc began to spin. "It's working," he said.

"Thank god."

The car juddered as she steered it onto Route 217, one of the secondary roads that threaded through this part of the Allagash territory. Yvette had meticulous directions for the owl count—the exact mileage between each stop; numbers on utility poles and mailboxes; descriptions of unusual trees or rocks; notes for other landmarks. Once upon a time, there had been sporting camps here, then family-friendly resorts, then a few glampsites, a fairly desperate and frankly insane attempt on the part of entrepreneurs from away that failed almost overnight. As the timber companies went under, most of their holdings went to the state, but with no demand for paper, building materials, or recreation, the land had reverted to wilderness. A new and different kind of wilderness: the nature of the boreal forest changed as conifers and evergreens adapted to the longer growing season or, in many cases, died.

Someone from away might not notice the difference. Looking out the window of the Subaru, Louis still saw the black encroaching walls to either side of the narrow road, the trees closer to the broken tarmac with each passing season. He rolled down the window—even with the heat off, the car was stifling. Cold air rushed in, balsam and the pissy scent of cat spruce, along with a more forbidding, granitic scent that he knew presaged snow.

"It feels like it could be a real storm," he said, cradling the boom box in his lap.

"I know." Yvette sounded triumphant. "That's why I wanted to go tonight. Can you see the Gazetteer back there? Grab it, will you? I want to head up to the Araweag."

"Really?" The Araweag was paper mill land, or had been before it was clearcut long ago. Now it was boggy, impenetrable thickets of speckled alder and blackberry crowding the wetland.

"I want to try something different. Miriam Rogers told me her son was hunting moose up there and saw a great horned owl. Hunting, in daylight."

"The owl or Miriam's son?"

"The owl. He watched it swoop down on a snowshoe hare. Poor bunny."

"A snowshoe hare? In broad daylight?"

"That's why I want to go."

"If the owls are hunting in daytime, why would we hear them now?"

Yvette swatted him. "Just tell me how far it is."

He opened the glove compartment so he could read by its light, flipped through the Gazetteer until he found the right page. "Twenty miles, maybe? Bad roads, though. Some may not be opened anymore."

"Let's stay on 217. Make a few of the old stops first."

Louis nodded. He closed the glove compartment and tossed the Gazetteer onto the floor behind his seat, swigged a mouthful of tepid coffee from the thermos and closed his eyes.

"I'm sorry about your friend," Yvette said. "It was your friend, right?"

Louis didn't open his eyes. Yvette had mild dementia that manifested mostly as forgetfulness. "Thanks."

"After Buddy died," she went on cheerfully, "someone told me I should watch for signs. Lori, she's the massage therapist used to live at Stone Farm. She told me if I wanted a sign from Buddy, I should close my eyes and count to three. When I opened them, the first three things I saw, that would be the sign."

THE OWL COUNT

"Did you ever see anything?"

"Just the dogs."

Eyes shut, Louis thought of Eric, the last time they'd met. Walking along the Battenkill, the river where as boys they'd fished for brownies and brookies: once one of the world's great trout streams, now nothing but a stony track that resembled an ancient Roman road winding through the Vermont woods. When he opened his eyes, he saw only his own reflection in the black glass of the Subaru's passenger window.

When they used to do the owl count, she'd put a big cardboard sign that read OWL MONITORING PROJECT on the dashboard. In those days, more vehicles were on the road. Not many, especially in the middle of the night, but there'd been a few times when people slowed or even stopped. Always men, they often seemed to have been drinking, another reason Louis liked to accompany Yvette. Once a state trooper had approached them—someone had noticed the parked Subaru and phoned dispatch. The policeman had been bemused, even more so when Yvette played him some of the owl calls.

"Well, just be careful you don't run out of gas," he'd finally said. "Cold out here."

It had been years since they'd seen another car or pickup at night, but Louis felt the familiar frisson as they pulled over beside their first landmark, a Bangor Hydro power pole that hadn't been live since 2023. A small piece of metal stamped 141A was nailed to the pole, but Louis had long since learned to identify it by the surrounding fields: once farmland, now overgrown with highbush blueberry and sumac.

In daylight, you could spot the centuries-old clapboard farmhouse in the distance. When he and Yvette had first done the count, lights shone from one or two of its windows and dogs barked, alerting the household to interlopers in the road, but no one had ever come out to investigate. Louis heard the old man who'd lived there wandered off one night a few summers ago. His body was never found. Now Louis could barely make out the house, ghostly white against the black trees.

Yvette asked, "Did you check the volume?"

Louis reached again for the boom box. He switched it to the radio, reflexively turning the dial. Nothing but static until he hit the Christian music station out of Houlton, one of the few remaining stations in operation and the only one with a signal strong enough to be heard up here. Louis adjusted the volume, grimacing, and quickly switched the player back to CD mode.

"Did you bring extra batteries?"

Louis shook his head. "I told you, no."

"Oh," said Yvette. She turned the car off and stared at the steering column with vague interest, as though she'd never seen one before. "I didn't hear you."

"That's okay." Louis often wondered if her forgetfulness might be an evolutionary advantage. If you couldn't recall the world as it had once been, you couldn't miss it.

Though the evolutionary benefits diminished once you factored in things like forgetting to eat, or misplacing the car keys while you were out in the middle of the night in sub-zero weather. He slid the key from the ignition and pocketed it.

Yvette smiled. "I didn't forget the key."

Louis smiled back. "Neither did I." He turned on the dashboard light, fumbled a pen from his parka pocket as he balanced the clipboard on his knees, turning from the first data sheet to the one beneath.

MOMP 2012 MAINE OWL MONITORING PROGRAM

MAINE AUDUBON AND THE MAINE DEPARTMENT OF INLAND FISHERIES AND WILDLIFE

He filled in the date and time, ignored the other blank spaces— *Observer, Route Code, Observer Email/Phone Number, Assistant's Name*—and began to fill in the information for Stop 1:

Time (military): 0027, Temp: 28F, Cloud Cover: 40%

For Wind he circled the appropriate numerical Beaufort Wind Code, guessing it was a 2 *[4-7 mph, slight breeze, wind felt on face, leaves rustle]*, even though there were no leaves to rustle. He glanced outside

THE OWL COUNT

and saw spruce boughs rippling, changed the 2 to a 3 *[gentle breeze, leaves and small twigs in motion]*. He notated Noise and Precipitation in the same way, circling 0 for Precipitation *[note that survey should not be conducted if precipitation is a 3 or above]* and 1 for Noise *[relatively quiet]*, even though when he cracked the window, it was pretty much silent outside.

For Snow Cover he circled C *[complete]*. For Frogs: Yes/No, *No*. He left Car Count and Plane Count blank. He couldn't remember when he'd last seen or heard a plane. He filled in the Playback info from memory—*Boom Box, High Volume, Memorex, Audible at 1/10 mile*—and left the Comments section blank, for now.

"Ready?" asked Yvette.

"Almost." He turned to the next sheet, scrawled in the date, his name and Yvette's, the name of the township. He didn't bother with the odometer reading, but looked outside once more before filling in the stop and habitat descriptions: *Pole 141 A, Overgrown fields and abandoned house to right of road, woods to L.* "Okay, let's go."

He set the clipboard on the floor, opened his door, and stepped outside. Yvette turned off the dashboard light, grabbed the boom box and did the same. "Not that cold," she said.

Louis gave a noncommittal nod. It didn't feel that cold, but he knew how it worked, especially with snow in the forecast. No fear of frostbite, but the humidity would seep through your parka and gloves and cap: if you didn't keep moving, within a short while your blood would seem to cool and thicken, your bones to feel as though they held ice instead of marrow.

And you weren't supposed to move, not once the playback started. Yvette set the boom box onto the rust-pocked hood of the old car, pointing it towards the distant empty house across the fields. That overgrown swathe would still be ideal habitat for owls and their prey—voles and whitefooted mice, rabbits and snowshoe hare, smaller winter birds like chickadees that would be sleeping now but might be caught at dawn or dusk if they stirred.

He leaned against the car, letting his eyes adjust to the darkness, his ears to the silence. His breath clouded the air as he tipped his head back and saw a few stars pricking through the haze. *Cloud cover only 30%*, he thought, but that wouldn't last. A few feet away, Yvette's pose mirrored his own, but her eyes were closed. Not sleeping: listening intently. He squeezed his own eyes shut, his head still uptilted.

Everything sounded the same: white pine needles a susurrus like waves on the shore; the skreek of spruce branches rubbing together; a noise like knuckles cracking that might be a deer moving through the woods. He recalled what Yvette had said about watching for signs, held his breath, counted to three, and opened his eyes.

For a split second he thought he saw another pair of eyes gazing into his, then realized they were stars, momentarily dazzling in a gap of clouds that moved swiftly across the sky. The wind carried a faint scent of crushed bracken and balsam. Almost certainly a deer had left its bed, awakened by their presence. He looked over his shoulder and saw Yvette watching him, her hand on the boom box. She raised her eyebrows. He nodded, she nodded back then pushed *Play*.

The owl call sequence began with a low electronic beep, followed by the first track: two minutes of silence. During that time, Louis's hearing grew more acute, the rustling of trees amplified so that he could distinguish between individual branches as they rubbed together, some high, others closer to the ground. After two minutes, Track Two kicked in—the call of a short-eared owl: a series of short, breathy hoots, repeated twice, then another two minutes of silence.

Louis held his breath, straining to hear a reply. Many years ago, he had seen a short-eared owl in daylight, skimming above a field, its yellow eyes bright as traffic lights, tiny tufted ears nowhere in evidence. He saw or heard nothing now. The next call was the long-eared owl's: a single, rather toneless hoot, repeated several times, each after a few seconds' interval, followed by the two minute silence.

Only now it wasn't so silent. Tiny things stirred nearby—small birds fluttering nervously in the lower branches of the spruce trees.

THE OWL COUNT

Mice skittered across the dead leaves that had rucked up against the trees trunks to provide shelter from the snow. Squeaks and rustlings, a swift settling back into a new, more watchful silence.

The saw-whet owl was next. Its breathy piping cry grew gradually louder, paused then repeated. Louis had seen one of these, too, improbably perched upon his bulkhead one late-spring morning. It looked like a toy, small enough to fit into his cupped palm, with enormous orange eyes that, when it blinked, gave it the appearance of a sleepy child. Louis had longed to pick it up, it looked so utterly helpless and soft. When he went to check on it an hour later, it was gone. He hoped it hadn't fallen prey to some larger owl or eagle. He cocked his head, hoping to hear a response in the silence that followed.

Again, he heard nothing but wind in the trees. Like him, the birds and mice were holding their breaths. He glanced at Yvette and saw her staring raptly into the sky above the field, her gaze flicking back and forth. Was she watching something? He squinted, but could make out only darkness seeded by a handful of stars.

Two tracks left. The barred owl came first, the owl they were most likely to hear, with its distinctive demand *Who cooks for you? Who cooks for you?* followed by a six-minute silence—barred owls sometimes took longer to reply.

This was the most difficult part of each stop. Six minutes could be an agony, if you were cold and unable to move. The frigid air crept up from his frozen feet: he felt immobilized, his legs encased in ice as though he were trapped in one of those fairy tales where people turned into statues. He no longer felt his fingers in his gloves. He tensed his muscles, fighting the urge to shiver, when fainter than the sound of his own breath, an answering call echoed from somewhere far off in the black woods that surrounded the overgrown fields.

Who cooks for you? Who cooks for you?

Elation flooded him, he glanced at Yvette and saw her grinning like a madwoman. He strained to hear another call but none came. The long silence broke with the final track, the great horned owl's loud, increasingly threatening *Who? Who?? WHO???*

Its cry died off into the sound of wind rattling the aster stalks. Louis tilted his head slightly, mentally counting down the remaining seconds; and stiffened.

Something was walking across the snow. Furtively: it paused before its feet broke through the frozen surface, a sound like a boot crunching shattered glass.

Heat flashed through Louis's body, terror and adrenaline. He looked at Yvette and saw her eyes widening, not in fear but wonder. He turned to see what she gazed at, detected nothing at first but then caught a glimpse of a dark blur at the edge of the field, maybe twenty yards away. In an eyeblink it had disappeared into the trees.

An electronic beep signaled the end of the owl call sequence. Louis grabbed the boom box. He and Yvette jumped backed into the car, slamming the doors closed behind them. Louis locked his, leaned over and did the same to Yvette's.

"Did you see that?" she asked, eyes so wide she looked like an owl herself.

"I don't know." He set the boom box at his feet—it felt cold as a block of ice—yanked off his gloves and blew on his fingers as Yvette turned the ignition. "What was it?"

"I don't know." Hands gripping the wheel, she craned her neck to peer past him, to where the black line of spruce and pine gave way to the long white expanse broken by brambles, stands of dead aster and milkweed. "It looked like a person."

"It can't have been a person," Louis said, even though his thumping heart suggested that's exactly what he believed. "A deer, probably."

"It was upright." Yvette stared outside for another minute before she sighed, turned on the headlights, and began to drive, very very slowly, continuing to look out the passenger side of the windshield. "Did you see it? Tall and kind of stooped. It might have been a bear."

"Bears don't walk upright. Not in winter, anyway. They're hibernating."

"But you saw it, right?"

He shrugged, unwilling to look at her. "I don't know," he repeated. "I saw something—I *think* I saw something. I definitely heard something.

THE OWL COUNT

I thought it was a deer. That noise their hooves make when they break through the crust."

"Deer don't walk upright."

"Then it was a person."

Now he did meet Yvette's gaze. They grimaced in unison.

"That's not good," she said. "They could freeze."

"Do you think we should go back?"

"No." They both laughed, and Yvette added, "Maybe we should go back? What if it's someone who's lost?"

"No one's lost." Louis removed his knit cap and pressed his hands against his ears to warm them. As heat flooded the car, and him, his fear abated. "It was probably a deer. I mean, it could have been an owl—I just saw it from the corner of my eye. You heard that barred owl, right?"

"Yes! *'Who cooks for you?'*" Yvette hooted, and laughed again. "Did you write it down?"

Louis shook his head. He retrieved the clipboard and pen, using his mobile as a flashlight as he scrawled *Barred owl*. He couldn't recall the last time they'd heard an owl respond to the CD when they were out in the field like this—four or five years? Yet he heard plenty of owls when he was at home, barred owls and the occasional great horned owl, and he and Yvette had even sighted them a few times when they were driving along the owl count route. Maybe there were simply fewer owls than there used to be, along with everything else. Fewer bats, fewer nightjars, fewer bugs, fewer bees.

Fewer people, too, since the last few outbreaks, though it was hard to think of that as a bad thing. Friends of his in the warden service said that wildlife populations appeared to be rebounding, not just deer and moose but apex predators and omnivores. Black bears and coyotes; mountain lions and wolves, whose existence the state's Department of Inland Fisheries and Wildlife had a decades-long policy of denying, despite numerous sightings. The last confirmed wolf in Maine had been shot dead in Ellsworth in the 1990s, but Louis knew people who'd seen them, reliable witnesses—hunters, trappers, loggers, fishermen. The wolves came down from Quebec. No one knew if there were enough in Maine for a breeding population. Funding for that sort of study had disappeared long ago.

Yvette longed to see a bear or wolf. Louis was content to think that they were out there at a safe distance from his home. Hearing a family of coyotes erupt into howls in the middle of the night, fifty feet from his driveway, could be hair-rising enough.

"What's the next stop?" he asked.

"Deadman's Curve."

After about five miles, Yvette pulled the car over again, this time along a heavily wooded stretch. The road here hadn't been plowed, but wind had scoured most of the snow from the broken blacktop. A decaying mobile home stood a dozen yards from the road, its roof and walls collapsed to expose clouds of soggy pink fiberglass insulation shredded Tyvek and splintered beams, like some immense piece of roadkill.

As Louis stepped out of the car, he recoiled from the odor of mildew and an overpowering reek of rodent urine, along with the stink of something dead, a rat or scavenging fox or coyote. He pulled his scarf up to cover his face as Yvette motioned him back into the car, and they pulled up farther along the road, out of sight of the trailer.

"Whew. That was bad." He stepped outside cautiously, pressing his scarf against his nose so he could breathe in the reassuring scents of damp wool and woodsmoke. "It's better here."

Yvette nodded. She looked drifty, like maybe she couldn't quite remember where they were, or why, but when she saw Louis watching her she smiled and set the boom box on the car's hood. For a minute they stood without speaking. Louis lowered his scarf and breathed in tentatively, catching only the faintest whiff of mildew.

Not far from the road, on the same side as the ruined trailer, a stream ran through the woods. A small stream—with his long legs, he could have jumped across it without much effort—yet deep enough that it hadn't frozen. No one had bothered to trim the trees here for ages—while most of the power poles remained standing, the power companies

THE OWL COUNT

had long ago stopped maintaining them. As a result, the oaks and maple and birch had grown unchecked, their branches nearly meeting above the road to form a ragged net in which a few stars gleamed like trapped minnows. In the darkness, the little stream sounded startlingly loud, more like a torrent than a brook.

"Ready?"

He turned back to Yvette, nodding, and she pressed Play.

The owls' mournful liturgy repeated itself as before, alternating between silence and melancholy summons, its only response a fretful twittering from above that Louis recognized as a red squirrel's alarm. The cold seemed more penetrating here; because of the tangle of branches over the road, Louis thought, then realized that was ridiculous. There was no sun. It must be getting onto 2 A.M.

He cursed himself for not bringing along a thermos of hot coffee. He knew better than to ask Yvette to abort the trip: she might forget what day, or even year, it was, but the owl count was sacrosanct. As the great horned owl's cry faded into the final, silent track, Louis didn't bother to suppress a yawn. He rubbed his arms, noting that Yvette remained stock-still, her hood's pointed tip silhouetted against the trees like a spearpoint. The rushing stream sounded so loud he wondered if they'd missed the beep signaling the end of the call sequence.

But then he heard the soft *beep*. Immediately he turned to open the car door. As he did, an explosive sound echoed from the woods directly behind them. Louis shouted: he stared into the trees, then at Yvette where she stood and gazed open-mouthed at him. He heard splashing, a huffing noise that turned into a strangled grunt as something crashed through the underbrush. An overpowering fecal odor filled his nostrils, rot and shit but also sweat, a smell he'd never encountered that was somehow, horribly recognizable.

"Get in!" he gasped at Yvette, but she'd already grabbed the boom box and was back in the car. Louis flung the door open and saw her fumbling for the keys—she'd forgotten again and left them in the ignition. He got inside and locked the door, shouted at Yvette to do the same. The

Subaru's engine rumbled and the car shot forward, fishtailing across the slick road then straightening as Yvette hunched over the steering wheel.

"That was a bear!" She sounded exultant.

Louis said nothing, tried to slow his breath enough to speak without his voice breaking. "The fuck it was," he said at last. He pulled off his gloves, hands shaking, and turned to look through the rear window. The car's brake lights cast a dull crimson glow across skeletal birch trees and a fallen evergreen bough that Yvette had somehow avoided. "It sounded huge."

"Bears are huge. It could've been a moose. Or a beaver."

Louis snorted, but she was right. The sound of a beaver slapping its tail on the water in warning could reverberate like a thunderclap. "There's no pond back there, just that stream."

"Maybe it runs into a pond nearby. Check the Gazetteer."

Louis shook his head impatiently—he felt at once irritated and frightened—but he picked up the Gazetteer and found the corresponding map among its frayed pages. "Nope. No pond."

Yvette slowed the car to a crawl, its studded tires grinding over the snow. "There should be a turn in the next few miles. For the Araweag—I think it's on the left. Can you check for that?"

"You still want to go?"

"I thought we decided."

"Yeah, but. That thing…"

"I know!" Her cheeks were flushed, excitement more than cold, he suspected. "See if you can find that turn."

A glance at the open Gazetteer on his lap showed the township, a formless green space threaded by streams that connected myriad small ponds, lakes, and wetlands. Broken stitches indicated a seasonal road, which these days meant an impassable one. Before he could voice a perfectly reasonable excuse for not going there—they'd get stuck, run out of gas and not be found until spring, besides which there was just as much likelihood of hearing owls right here on the old route as in the Araweag—Yvette brought up the single unreasonable one.

THE OWL COUNT

"Are you scared?"

He took a deep breath. "Not really. Just—that noise, it spooked me. And the smell? Did you smell it?"

"I did." Yvette wrinkled her nose. "Phew! Like when my septic field overflows every year."

Yvette's septic field hadn't flooded in decades—she'd switched to a composting toilet, like nearly everyone else, as the grid became unreliable. Louis knew it would be pointless to remind her of this. She'd laugh and say *Oh right, I forgot.* Then forget it all over again, just as she'd done with the car keys. He cleared his window, the glass already steaming up, stared out at the shifting cross-hatch of black and gray-white. Trees, rocks, snowdrifts, trees.

"It smelled worse than that," he said. "Like…"

"It could have been a moose. It sounded big."

Louis nodded, frowning. He picked up the thermos, took a swig of cold coffee then offered it the Yvette, who shook her head. "Whatever it was, it smelled like it had rolled in something dead," he said. "Like a dog does. And what was that noise? It sounded like an entire tree came down."

"Like I said, moose."

"A moose doesn't knock down trees."

"Well, it's not the same thing we heard at the first stop, whatever it was." Yvette tugged her hood from her face. "It's four miles from there to that old trailer. Nothing goes that fast. Maybe an owl," she added after a moment's thought. "Horned owls, they're fast."

Yvette turned the wipers on. It had started to snow, tiny dry flakes, the kind that normally blow off the windshield but they weren't driving fast enough for that. She hunched over the steering wheel, scanning the road. "I think there's a sign—didn't there used to be a sign?"

"I don't remember." Louis didn't bother to keep the irritation from his tone. He peeled off his gloves and closed his eyes for a moment, imagining himself back at home in bed, warm and asleep. Then he remembered Eric was dead. He was old enough now that grief had become a near-constant presence, a prolonged dull ache rather than the piercing anguish he'd experienced when he was younger. The aftermath of his wife's death was like a raging virus that left him sickened and weak for several years, a virus that could be reawakened by stress, or sunrise, or a scent. You don't recover from grief, he'd learned, it can't be cured; it only appears to go into remission, to flare up, not as intensely perhaps but retaining its nightmarish power, with the next death.

He had not even begun to mourn Eric. He thought again of that last time, just over a year ago, the two of them leaving the dried-up Battenkill to hike up a ski trail, a broad swathe of young beech and sugar maple that had sprung up when the ski mountain closed early in the century. Eric white-haired but hale, more so than Louis, who'd had to stop often to catch his breath, holding on to young birch trees that showered them with autumn leaves like a rain of new pennies.

"They found a mastodon in the Mastigouche," Eric had told him, and Louis laughed.

"That sounds like a song," he said, and began to warble. "Mastodon, in the Mastigooooche..."

"No, really—there was a landslide, and they found its tusks in the rubble. Like in Siberia, where they keep mining mammoth ivory where the permafrost used to be."

He started as Yvette nudged him, looked up to see her grinning at him. "I know," she said. "It was the agropelter!" She pronounced the word with a slight lilt and the accent on the final syllable, the way her Quebecois grandmother would have. *Agre'peltay.*

Louis made a face. "Well, I hope not," he said, and they laughed. Yvette's great-grandfather had been a trucker who worked the Golden Road, the hundred-mile-long, mostly unpaved track that ran from the old paper mill in Millinocket to the Quebec border, and her great-great-grandfather had worked in Canadian logging camps. Yvette's grandmother claimed he had hundreds of stories about the terrible things that could happen in the north woods, but the only one

THE OWL COUNT

Yvette recalled was about the agropelter. Half human, half ape, the agropelter sat in treetops and hurled rocks and branches at unsuspecting woodsman, sometimes killing them.

"Sounds like a bad excuse for knocking someone off with an axe," Louis had remarked the first time Yvette recounted the legend.

Now he checked the time: 2:17. "Getting late," he said. "And it's starting to snow. We're supposed to call it off if it snows."

"Who's going to check? And it's not snowing now," she added. Which was true, the sifting flakes had stopped. "You came, why did you come if you didn't want to?"

"I needed to be distracted." That sounded cruel, she might not even remember his best friend had died. "Because of Eric."

"Of course," she said, her customary briskness softened. "I remember." She grasped his hand and squeezed it. "I'm so sorry, Louis."

"Thank you."

"You know, when Buddy died, my friend Lori told me if I ever wanted a sign from him, I should just close my eyes. The first three things I saw when I opened them, those would be the sign."

"Yes, you told me that."

"Oh, sorry!" she said without embarrassment. "I keep forgetting."

He turned away, recalling how Sheila during her illness had joked that whatever he did after she died, he shouldn't marry Yvette. "Not a chance," he'd told her, and that had never changed. His eyes stung and he closed them, thinking this time of Sheila, not Eric; opened them and gazed at his bare hands, the red knuckles swollen and fingers twisted from Depuytens contracture.

He leaned over to check the gas gauge. A quarter tank, enough to get home. He wondered when and where she'd been able to last fill the tank. Bangor, probably, which meant she'd used up a considerable amount of fuel driving home afterwards. He looked in the back seat again, reached into the heap of dog-hair-covered fabric, rummaged around till he found a zipper, and pulled at it. A sleeping bag emerged, trailing a chewed-up leash.

"There might still be some of those handwarmers," said Yvette. "Poke around, see if you can find them."

"That's okay. I was looking for a weapon, actually. In case it tries to eat us."

"Very funny. They only eat owls, my Gran said. And woodpeckers."

"Well, we're safe, then. The turn looks to be about eight miles, on the left. You remembered that fine."

The car inched along, Yvette downshifting as they crept over knee-high frost heaves and avoiding potholes large enough to swallow a bicycle. Intermittent gusts of snow would cloud the air then just as swiftly disappear, the tiny flakes not big enough to constitute a squall. The real snow wouldn't start until morning. If it looked like it would come down sooner, they'd simply turn around.

They drove in silence, interrupted only when one of them pointed out a former stop—the flat boulder overlooking a bog, the sweeping vista where they'd once heard two great horned owls—or when they spotted something. A fox crossing leisurely in front of them; a snowshoe hare sprinting off in alarm, its long hind feet kicking up feathers of snow; a pair of tufted ears like devil horns above glowing green eyes, barely visible in the underbrush.

"Bobcat!" said Louis.

"Lynx!" cried Yvette in triumph.

"Oh, come on, how could you tell?"

"It was bigger than a bobcat."

"It was there for two seconds!"

Yvette pursed her lips in a smug smile. "I just know."

Louis unzipped his parka as the car grew overheated, the doggie smell vying with the faint, scorched-sugar scent of antifreeze that seeped from the vents. "You have a radiator leak," he said.

"I know. Bob Marsh said he'd fix it, come spring."

Louis checked the odometer, trying to figure out how much farther it was to the turn. They'd been driving for at least twenty minutes, a long time to cover only eight miles, even in the middle of the night, even on these roads.

THE OWL COUNT

"Do you think we missed it?" he asked. "The sign could be gone. That old access road could be completely overgrown by now."

Yvette's brow creased. "I hope not. Let's give it another few minutes."

A few minutes became ten—Louis clocked the time. He couldn't do anything else with his mobile, even back in the early part of the century, there hadn't been service here.

"Look."

Yvette inclined her head to the left, where a twisted metal pole jutted toward the road at a thirty degree angle. Atop it dangled a small green sign so rusted Louis could barely read it. FR 2973, a fire road.

"Huh. I haven't seen one of those for years." Once ubiquitous, these numerical signs designated seasonal or little-used roads. The numbering system had disappeared when towns had to conform to Emergency 911 standards, meaning all roads needed an actual name. Despite the warmth, Louis shivered. He peered into the darkness past the twisted pole. "Can we even get down there?"

"I'll just turn in, we can park and walk a bit if the snow's not too deep."

Louis ran his hands across his knees but said nothing. His knees ached, his back. The Depuytens contracture in his right hand made it hard to move his fingers in the chill. He'd dressed for cold, not for trudging through deep snow.

But the old fire road, while overgrown and snow-covered, still showed signs of use. He saw snowmobile tracks veering across the broad path, along with those of another vehicle, a small Snocat, probably. Someone poaching firewood, now that the territory was basically no-man's-land. A few inches of snow had fallen since anyone had last been here—judging by the crust, at least a week ago—but not enough to impede walking.

He zipped up his parka, watched as Yvette made the turn and drove several yards. He winced as the old Subaru jolted over a buried rock and bottomed out. "Maybe this is far enough?"

Yvette nodded and brought the car to an abrupt stop, forgetting to take it out of gear. Louis's skull banged against the headrest. *"Ow!"*

"Sorry!" Yvette clapped her hands to her face. She began to laugh, then reached to touch Louis's neck, gently. "We don't have to stay long. Miriam's son saw a great horned owl here. He was hunting, moose I think. I would love to see another one of those. The owl, I mean. Or the moose."

"I would rather not see a moose at night," said Louis, gingerly rubbing the back of his neck. "Not if it's going to knock a tree on my head."

"That wasn't a moose. Bear," said Yvette.

She pulled up her hood and stepped out of the car without the boom box. Louis considered leaving it inside—maybe she'd forget the reason they were here, and they could just head home. But then she turned and pointed at it. He tucked it under one arm and joined her, stumping through the snow and halting in front of the car.

Shreds of grey lichen littered the snow, and the dark scales of pine cones resembling fingernail clippings, which fell where red squirrels had fed in the trees overhead. Balsam and pine resin scented the air, rather than pissy cat spruce and crushed bracken. Even though the road was only a few yards off, he felt as though with a few steps, he'd traversed a hundred years, backwards or forwards, to a moment when his presence was as inconsequential as a thread of reindeer moss.

He found the thought oddly comforting. Perhaps this was how Yvette felt all the time. He set the boom box on the hood, tugged his knit cap snugly over his ears, pulled up his hood and stared at the sky.

Far above him, a gap in the clouds revealed stars so brilliant he imagined he heard them crackling in the frigid air. The night seemed absolutely still—he felt no wind on his cheeks, and the jagged black evergreens that scraped the horizon appeared not to move.

And yet he did hear something. A faint, nearly subliminal sound like static, a noise he could imagine accompanying the prickles that presaged the agonizing leg cramps that woke him some nights. He cocked his head, trying to figure out if he was imagining it and, if not, where it came from; glanced over to see Yvette looking at him, eyebrows raised. Within moments her expression altered, from perplexity to alarm to

THE OWL COUNT

outright horror. He opened his mouth to ask *What?* Then he heard the same thing.

He thought it was the wind at first: a low rumbling that lasted mere seconds before it stopped. In the near-silence he heard Yvette's breathing and his own, a frantic rustling in a tree overhead. He exhaled shakily, caught his breath sharply when the sound recurred—louder this time, closer, rising then fading into a long echo that, after several moments, died away completely.

And, after another few moments, resumed. The cry rose, not the yodeling ululation of a coyote or wolf, both of which he knew: something deeper, more sustained and resonant. It died away before recurring a fourth time, much louder, so close that the hairs on his neck and arms and scalp rose, as from nearby lightning. Sensation flooded him, an emotion he had never experienced before: a horror so all-encompassing his stomach convulsed. His arms grew limp, his knees buckled and he slumped against the car's hood, gloved fingers sliding across the smooth metal as he tried to grab it.

The sound faded. Silence surrounded him, long enough that his gasps subsided and he drew a shuddering breath, wiping tears onto his sleeve. He struggled to stand upright, bracing himself against the car, and cried aloud when the sound came again, from not more than twenty feet away. Loud enough now that he could detect within the deafening bellow a grinding anguish, physical pain and also a deeper torment, as the cry exploded into a thunderous roar. His ears ached but he could clearly hear as it crashed through the trees, not blindly but with steady purpose, pausing between each step as though ensuring the ground would bear its weight. A shrill piping sounded in his ears, the saw-whet owl he thought with desperate calm, before recognizing his own scream. The roar came again and with it a wave of heat.

He gagged as that smell of fecal rot overwhelmed him. A tree crashed down, pine needles and splinters of wood stabbed his cheek and his vision blurred as blood washed across one eye. Soft feathers brushed his face, or fur, he could no longer distinguish between what was his skin, his body inside his layers of clothing, his scalp or neck or toes. His feet disappeared, the ground beneath them. With a moan he slanted his gaze sideways, searching for Yvette in the maelstrom of snow and broken bark, hair, blood, bone and feathers.

He saw only a smudge of red, the tip of her parka's hood. He tried to breathe but found his mouth sealed shut by the wind; tasted blood, he'd bitten his tongue. He thought of Yvette, of Sheila in bed beside him, of Eric walking next to him as they traced the lost Battenkill.

He closed his eyes, counted to three. *Who cooks for you?* he thought, and opened them.

The Least Trumps

IN THE Lonely House there is a faded framed *Life* magazine article from almost half a century ago, featuring a color photograph of a beautiful woman with close-cropped blonde hair and rather sly grey eyes, wide crimson-lipsticked mouth, a red-and-white striped bateau-neck shirt. The woman is holding a large magnifying lens and examining a very large insect, a plastic scientific model of a common black ant, *Lasius niger*, posed atop a stack of children's picture books. Each book displays the familiar blocky letters and illustrated image that has been encoded into the dreamtime DNA of generations of children: that of a puzzled-looking, goggle-eyed ant, its antennae slightly askew as though trying, vainly, to tune into the signal from some oh-so-distant station.

Wise Aunt or Wise Ant? reads the caption beneath the photo. *Blake E. Tun Examines a Friend.*

The woman is the beloved children's book author and illustrator, Blake Eleanor Tun, known to her friends as Blakie. The books are the six classic *Wise Ant* books, in American and English editions and numerous translations—*Wise Ant, Brave Ant, Curious Ant, Formi Sage, Weise Ameise, Una Ormiga Visionaria*. In the room behind Blakie, you can just make out the figure of a toddler, out-of-focus as she runs past. You can see the child's short blonde hair cut in a pageboy, and a tiny hand that the camera records as a mothlike blur. The little girl with the Prince

Valiant haircut, identified in the article as Miss Tun's adopted niece, is actually Blakie's illegitimate daughter, Ivy Tun. That's me.

Here in her remote island hidey-hole, the article begins, *Eleanor Blake Tun brings to life an imaginary world inhabited by millions.*

People used to ask Blakie why she lived on Aranbega. Actually, just living on an island wasn't enough for my mother. The Lonely House stood on an islet in Green Pond, so we lived on an island on an island.

"Why do I live here? Because enchantresses always live on islands," she'd say, and laugh. If she fancied the questioner she might add, "Oh, *you* know. Circe, Calypso, the Lady in the Lake—"

Then she'd give her, or very occasionally him, one of her mocking sideways smiles, lowering her head so that its fringe of yellow hair would fall across her face, hiding her eyes so that only the smile remained.

"The smile on the face of the tiger," Katherine told me once when I was a teenager. "Whenever you saw that smile of hers, you'd know it was only a matter of time."

"Time till what?" I asked.

But by then her attention had already turned back to my mother: the sun to Katherine's gnomon, the impossibly beautiful bright thing that we all circled, endlessly.

Anyway, I knew what Blakie's smile meant. Her affairs were notorious even on the island. For decades, however, they were carefully concealed from her readers, most of whom assumed (as they were meant to) that Blake E. Tun was a man—that *Life* magazine article caused quite a stir among those not already in the know. My mother was Blakie to me as to everyone else. When I was nine she announced that she was not my aunt but my mother, and produced a birth certificate from a Boston hospital to prove it.

"No point in lying. It would however be more *convenient* if you continued to call me Blakie." She stubbed out her cigarette on the sole of her tennis shoe and tossed it over the railing into Green Pond. "But it's no one's business who you are. Or who I am in relation to you, for that matter."

THE LEAST TRUMPS

And that was that. My father was not a secret kept from me; he just didn't matter that much, not in Blakie's scheme of things. The only thing she ever told me about him was that he was very young.

"Just a boy. Not much older than you are now, Ivy," which at the time was nineteen. "Just a kid."

"Never knew what hit him," agreed my mother's partner Katherine, as Blakie glared at her from across the room.

It never crossed my mind to doubt my mother, just as it never crossed my mind to hold her accountable for any sort of duplicity she may have practiced, then or later. The simple mad fact was that I adored Blakie. Everyone did. She was lovely and smart and willful and rich, a woman who believed in seduction not argument; when seduction failed, which was rarely, she was not above abduction, of the genteel sort involving copious amounts of liquor and the assistance of one or two attractive friends.

The *Wise Ant* books she had written and illustrated when she was in her twenties. By her thirtieth birthday they had made her a fortune. Blakie had a wise agent named Letitia Thorne and a very wise financial adviser named William Dunlap, both of whom took care that my mother would never have to work again unless she wanted to.

Blakie did not want to work. She wanted to seduce Dunlap's daughter-in-law, a twenty-two-year-old Dallas socialite named Katherine Mae Moss. The two women eloped to Aranbega, a rocky spine of land some miles off the coast of Maine. There they built a fairytale cottage in the middle of a lake, on a tamarack-and-fern-covered bump of rock not much bigger than the Bambi Airstream trailer they'd driven up from Texas. The cottage had two small bedrooms, a living room and dining nook and wraparound porch overlooking the still, silvery surface of Green Pond. There was a beetle-black cast-iron Crawford woodstove for heat and cooking, kerosene lanterns, and a small red hand-pump in the slate kitchen sink. No electricity; no telephone. Drinking water was pumped up from the lake. Septic and grey water disposal was achieved through an ancient holding tank that was emptied once a year.

They named the cottage The Lonely House, after the tiny house where Wise Ant lived with her friends Grasshopper and Bee. Here they were visited by Blakie's friends, artistic sorts from New York and Boston, several other writers from Maine; and by Katherine's relatives, a noisy congeries of cattle heiresses, disaffected oil men and Ivy League dropouts, first-wave hippies and draft dodgers, all of whom took turns babysitting me when Blakie took off for Crete or London or Taos in pursuit of some new *amour*. Eventually of course Katherine would find her and bring her home: as a child I imagined my mother engaged in some world-spanning game of hide-and-seek, where Katherine was always It. When the two of them returned to the Lonely House, there would always be a prize for me as well. A rainbow map of California, tie-dyed on a white bedsheet; lizard-skin drums from Angola; a Meerschaum pipe carved in the likeness of Richard Nixon.

"You'll never have to leave here to see the world, Ivy," my mother said once, after presenting me with a Maori drawing, on bark, of a stylized honeybee. "It will all come to you, like it all came to me."

My mother was thirty-seven when I was born, old to be having a baby, and paired in what was then known as a Boston marriage. She and Katherine are still together, two old ladies now living in a posh assisted-living community near Rockland, no longer scandalizing anyone. They've had their relationship highlighted in an episode of *This American Life*, and my mother is active in local liberal causes, doing benefit readings of *The Vagina Monologues* and signings of *Wise Ant* for the Rockland Domestic Abuse Shelter. Katherine reconciled with her family and inherited a ranch near Goliad, where they still go sometimes in the winter. *The Wise Ant* books are now discussed within the context of mid-century American Lesbian Literature, a fact which annoys my mother no end.

"I wrote those books for children," she cries whenever the topic arises. "They are *children's books*," as though someone had confused the color of her mailbox, red rather than black. "For God's sake."

Of course Wise Ant will never be anything more than her antly self—wise, brave, curious, kind, noisy, helpful—just as Blakie at eighty-two

THE LEAST TRUMPS

remains beautiful, maddening, forgetful, curious, brave; though seldom, if ever, quiet. We had words when I converted the Lonely House to solar power—

"You're spoiling it. It was never *intended* to have electricity—"

Blakie and Katherine were by then well-established in their elegant cottage at Penobscot Fields. I looked at the room around me—Blakie's study, small but beautifully appointed, with a Gustav Stickley lamp that she'd had rewired by a curator at the Farnsworth, her laptop screen glowing atop a quartersawn oak desk, and Bose speakers and miniature CD console.

"You're right," I said. "I'll just move in here with you."

"That's not the—"

"Blakie. I need electricity to work. The generator's too noisy, my customers don't like it. And expensive. I have to work for a living—"

"You don't have to—"

"I *want* to work for a living." I paused, trying to calm myself. "Look, it'll be fun—doing the wiring and stuff. I got all these photovoltaic cells, when it's all set up you'll see. It'll be great."

And it was. The cottage is south-facing: two rows of cells on the roof, a few extra batteries boxed-in under the porch, a few days spent wiring and I was set. I left the bookshelves in the living room, mostly my books now, and a few valuable first editions that I'd talked Blakie into leaving. Eliot's *Four Quartets* and some Theodore Roethke; *Gormenghast*; a Leonard Baskin volume signed *For Blakie*. One bedroom I kept as my own, with a wide handcrafted oak cupboard bed, cleverly designed to hold clothes beneath and more books all around. At the head of the bed were those I loved best, a set of all six *Wise Ant* books and the five volumes of Walter Burden Fox's unfinished *Five Windows One Door* sequence.

The other bedroom became my studio. I set up a drafting table and autoclave and light box, a shelf with my ultrasonic cleaner and driclave. On the floor was an additional power unit just for my machine and equipment; a tool bench holding soldering guns, needle bars and jigs; a tall stainless steel medicine cabinet with enough disinfectant and bandages and gloves and hemostats to outfit a small clinic; an overhead cabinet with my inks and pencils and acetates. Empty plastic caps await the colored inks that fill the machine's reservoir. A small sink drains into a special tank that I bring to the Rockland dump once a month, when everyone else brings in their empty paint cans. A bookshelf holds albums filled with pictures of my own work and some art books—Tibetan stuff, pictures from Chauvet Cavern, Japanese woodblock prints.

But no flash sheets; no framed flash art; no fake books. If a customer wants flash, they can go to Rockland or Bangor. I do only my own designs. I'll work with a customer, if she has a particular image in mind, or come up with something original if she doesn't. But if somebody has her heart set on a prancing unicorn, or Harley flames, or Mister Natural, or a Grateful Dead logo, I send her elsewhere.

This doesn't happen much. I don't advertise. All my business is word of mouth, through friends or established customers, a few people here on Aranbega. But mostly, if someone wants me to do her body work, she *really* has to want me, enough to fork out sixty-five bucks for the round-trip ferry and at least a couple hundred for the tattoo, and three hundred more for the Aranbega Inn if she misses the last ferry, or if her work takes more than a single day. Not to mention the cost of a thick steak dinner afterwards, and getting someone else to drive her home. I don't let people stay at the Lonely House, unless it's someone I've known for a long time, which usually means someone I was involved with at some point, which usually means she wouldn't want to stay with me in any case. Sue is an exception, but Sue is seeing someone else now, one of the other occupational therapists from Penobscot Fields, so she doesn't come over as much as she used to.

That suits me fine. My customers are all women. Most of them are getting a tattoo to celebrate some milestone, usually something like finally breaking with an abusive boyfriend, leaving a bad marriage, coming to grips with the aftermath of a rape. Breast cancer survivors—I do a lot of breast work—or tattoos to celebrate coming out, or giving birth.

THE LEAST TRUMPS

Sometimes anniversaries. I get a lot of emotional baggage dumped in my studio, for hours or days at a time; it always leaves when the customers do, but it pretty much fulfills my need for any kind of emotional connection, which is pretty minimal anyway.

And, truth to tell, it fulfills most of my sexual needs too; at least any baseline desire I have for physical contact. My life is spent with skin: cupping a breast in my hand, pulling the skin taut between my fingers while the needle etches threadlike lines around the aureole, tracing yellow above violet veins, turning zippered scars into coiled serpents, an explosion of butterfly wings, flames or phoenixes rising from a puckered blue-white mound of flesh; or drawing secret maps, a hidden cartography of grottoes and ravines, rivulets and waves lapping at beaches no bigger than the ball of my thumb; the ball of my thumb pressed there, index finger there, tissue film of latex between my flesh and hers, the hushed drone of the machine as it chokes down when the needle first touches skin and the involuntary flinch that comes, no matter how well she's prepared herself for this, no matter how many times she's lain just like this, paper towels blotting the film of blood that wells, nearly invisible, beneath the moving needle bar's tip, music never loud enough to drown out the hum of the machine. Hospital smells of disinfectant, blood, antibacterial ointment, latex.

And sweat. A stink like scorched metal: fear. It wells up the way blood does, her eyes dilate and I can smell it, even if she doesn't move, even if she's done this enough times to be as controlled as I am when I draw the needle across my own flesh: she's afraid, and I know it, needle-flick, soft white skin pulled taut, again, again, between my fingers.

I don't want a lot of company, after a day's work.

◆ ◆ ◆

I KNEW SOMETHING was going to happen the night before I found the Trumps. Sue teases me, but it's true, I can tell when something is going to happen. A feeling starts to swell inside me, as though I'm being blown up like a balloon, my head feels light and somehow cold, there are glittering things at the edges of my eyes. And sure enough, within a day or two someone turns up out of the blue, or I get a letter or e-mail from someone I haven't thought of in ten years. Whenever I see something—a mink, a yearling moose, migrating elvers—I just know.

I shouldn't even tell Sue when it happens. She says it's just a manifestation of my disorder, like a migraine aura.

"Take your fucking medicine, Ivy. It's an early warning system: take your Xanax!"

Rationally I can understand that, rationally I know she's right. That's all it is, a chain of neurons going off inside my head, like a string of firecrackers with a too-short fuse. But I can never explain to her the way the world looks when it happens, that green glow in the sky not just at twilight but all day long, the way I can see the stars sometimes at noon, sparks in the sky.

I was outside the Lonely House, cutting some flowers to take to Blakie. Pink and white cosmos; early asters, powder-blue and mauve; white sweet-smelling phlox, their stems slightly sticky, green aphids like minute beads of dew beneath the flower-heads. From the other shore a chipmunk gave its warning *cheeet.* I looked up, and there on the bank a dozen yards away sat a red fox. It was grinning at me, I could see the thin black rind of its gums, its yellow eyes shining as though lit from within by candles. It sat bolt upright and watched me, its white-tipped brush twitching like a cat's.

I stared back, my arms full of asters. After a moment I said, "Hello there. Hello. What are you looking for?"

I thought it would lope off then, the way foxes do; but it just sat and continued to watch me. I went back to gathering flowers, putting them into a wooden trug and straightening to gaze back at the shore. The fox was still there, yellow eyes glinting in the late-summer light. Abruptly it jumped to its feet. It looked right at me, cocking its head like a dog waiting to be walked.

It barked—a shrill, bone-freezing sound, like a child screaming. I felt my back prickle; it was still watching me, but there was something

THE LEAST TRUMPS

distracted about its gaze, and I saw its ears flatten against its narrow skull. A minute passed. Then, from away across Cameron Mountain there came an answer, another sharp yelp, higher-pitched and ending in a sort of yodeling wail. The fox turned so quickly it seemed to somersault through the low grass, and arrowed up the hillside towards the birch grove. In a moment it was gone. There was only the frantic chatter of red squirrels in the woods and, when I drew the dory up on the far shore a quarter-hour later, a musky sharp smell like crushed grapes.

• ♦ •

I GOT THE last ferry over to Port Symes, me and a handful of late-season people from away, sunburned and loud, waving their cellphones over the rail as they tried to pick up a signal from one of the towers on the mainland.

"We'll *never* get a reservation," a woman said accusingly to her husband. "I *told* you to have Marisa do it before she left—"

At Port Symes I hopped off before any of them, heading for where I'd left Katherine's car parked by an overgrown bank of dog roses. The roses were all crimson hips and thorns by now, the dark-green leaves already burning to yellow; there were yellow beech leaves across the car's windshield, and as I drove out onto the main road I saw acorns like thousands of green-and-bronze marbles scattered across the gravel road. Summer lingers for weeks on the islands, trapped by pockets of warmer air, soft currents and grey fog holding it fast till mid-October some years. Here on the mainland it was already autumn.

The air had a keen winey scent that reminded me of the fox. As I headed down the peninsula towards Rockland I caught the smell of burning leaves, the dank odor of smoke snaking through a chimney that had been cold since spring. The maples were starting to turn, pale gold and pinkish red. There had been a lot of rain in the last few weeks; one good frost would set the leaves ablaze. On the seat beside me Blakie's flowers sat in their mason jar, wrapped in a heavy towel; one good frost and they might be the last ones I'd pick this year.

I got all the way to the main road before the first temblors of panic hit. I deliberately hadn't taken my medication—it made me too sleepy, I couldn't drive and Sue would have had to meet me at the ferry, I would be asleep before we got to her place. The secondary road ended; there was a large green sign with arrows pointing east and west.

THOMASTON

OWLS HEAD

ROCKLAND

I turned right, towards Rockland. In the distance I could see the slate-colored reach of Penobscot Bay, a pine-pointed tip of land protruding into the waters, harsh white lights from Rockland Harbor; miles and miles off a tiny smudge like a thumbprint upon the darkening sky.

Aranbega. I was off island.

The horror comes down, no matter how I try to prepare myself for it, no matter how many times I've been through it: an incendiary blast of wind, the feeling that an iron helmet is tightening around my head. I began to gasp, my heart starting to pound and my entire upper body going cold. Outside was a cool September twilight, the lights of the strip malls around Rockland starting to prick through the gold-and-violet haze, but inside the car the air had grown black, my skin icy. There was a searing fire in my gut. My T-shirt was soaked through. I forced myself to breathe, to remember to exhale; to think *You're not dying, nobody dies of this, it will go, it will go...*

"Fuck." I clutched the steering wheel and crept past the Puffin Stop convenience store, past the Michelin tire place, the Dairy Queen; through one set of traffic lights, a second. *You won't die, nobody dies of this; don't look at the harbor.*

I tried to focus on the trees—two huge red oaks, there, you could hardly see where the land had been cleared behind them to make way for a car wash. *It's just a symptom, you're reacting to the symptoms, nobody dies of this, nobody.* At a stop sign I grabbed my cell phone and called Sue.

THE LEAST TRUMPS

"I'm by the Rite-Aid." *Don't look at the Rite-Aid.* "I'll be there, five minutes—"

An SUV pulled up behind me. I dropped the phone, feeling like I was going to vomit; turned sharply onto the side street. My legs shook so I couldn't feel the pedals under my feet. *How can I drive if my legs are numb?*

The SUV turned in behind me. My body trembled, I hit the gas too hard and my car shot forward, bumping over the curb then down again. The SUV veered past, a great grey blur, its lights momentarily blinding me. My eyes teared and I forced my breath out in long hoots, and drove the last few hundred feet to Sue's house.

She was in the driveway, still holding the phone in one hand.

"Don't," I said. I opened the car door and leaned out, head between my knees, waiting for the nausea to pass. When she came over I held my hand up and she stopped, but I heard her sigh. From the corner of my eye I could see the resigned set to her mouth, and that her other hand held a prescription bottle.

◆ ◆ ◆

ALWAYS BEFORE WHEN I came over to visit my mother, I'd stay with Sue and we'd sleep together, comfortably, not so much for old time's sake as to sustain some connection at once deeper and less enduring than talk. Words I feel obliged to remember, skin I can afford to forget. A woman's body inevitably evokes my own small, wet mouth, my own breath, my own legs, breasts, arms, shoulders, back. Even after Sue started seeing someone else, we'd ease into her wide bed with its wicker headboard, cats sliding to the floor in a grey heap like discarded laundry, radio playing softly, *Tea and oranges, so much more.*

"I think you'd better stay on the couch," Sue said that night. "Lexie isn't comfortable with this arrangement, and…"

She sighed, glancing at my small leather bag, just big enough to hold a change of underwear, hairbrush, toothbrush, wallet, a battered paperback of *Lorca in New York*. "I guess I'm not either. Anymore."

I felt my mouth go tight, stared at the mason jar full of flowers on the coffee table.

"Yup," I said.

I refused to look at her. I wouldn't give her the satisfaction of seeing how I felt.

But of course Sue wouldn't be gleeful, or vindictive. She'd just be sad, maybe mildly annoyed. I was the one who froze and burned; I was the one who scarred people for a living.

"It's fine," I said after a minute, and looking at her smiled wryly. "I have to get up early anyway."

She looked at me, not smiling, dark-brown eyes creased with regret. *What a waste*, I could hear her thinking. *What a lonely wasted life.*

• ◆ •

I THINK THE world is like this: beautiful, hard, cold, unmoving. Oh, it turns, things change—clouds, leaves, the ground beneath the beech trees grows thick with beechmast and slowly becomes black fragrant earth ripe with hellgrammites, millipedes, nematodes, deer mice. Small animals die, we die; a needle moves across honey-colored skin and the skin turns black, or red, or purple. A freckle or a mole becomes an eye; given enough time an eye becomes an earthworm.

But change, the kind of change Sue believes in—Positive Change, Emotional Change, Cultural Change—I don't believe in that. When I was young, I thought the world *was* changing: there was a time, years-long, when the varicolored parade of visitors through the Lonely House made me believe that the world Outside must have changed its wardrobe as well, from sere black suits and floral housedresses to velvet capes and scarlet morning coats, armies of children and teenagers girding themselves for skirmish in embroidered pants, feathered headdresses, bare feet, bare skin. I dressed myself as they did—actually, they dressed *me*, as Blakie smoked and sipped her whiskey sour, and Katherine made sure the bird feeders and wood box were full. And one day I went out to see the world.

THE LEAST TRUMPS

It was only RISD—the Rhode Island School of Design—and it should have been a good place, it should have been a Great Place for me. David Byrne and a few other students were playing at someone's house, other students were taking off for Boston and New York, squatting in Alphabet City in burned-out tenements with a toilet in the kitchen, getting strung out, but they were doing things, they were having adventures, hocking bass guitars for Hasselblad cameras, learning how to hold a tattoo machine in a back room on St. Mark's Place, dressing up like housewives and shooting five hours of someone lying passed out in bed while a candle flickered down to a shiny red puddle and someone else laughed in the next room. It didn't look like it at the time, but you can see it now, when you look at their movies and their photographs and their vinyl 45s and their installations: it didn't seem so at the time, but they were having a life.

I couldn't do that. My problem, I know. I lasted a semester, went home for Christmas break and never went back. For a long time it didn't matter—maybe it never mattered—because I still had friends, people came to see me even when Blakie and Katherine were off at the ranch, or bopping around France. Everyone's happy to have a friend on an island in Maine. So in a way it was like Blakie had told me long ago: the world *did* come to me.

Only of course I knew better.

• ◆ •

SATURDAY WAS SUE'S day off. She'd been at Penobscot Fields for eleven years now and had earned this, a normal weekend; I wasn't going to spoil it for her. I got up early, before seven, fed the cats and made myself coffee, then went out.

I walked downtown. Rockland used to be one the worst-smelling places in the United States: there was a chicken processing plant, fish factories, the everyday reek and spoils of a working harbor. That's all changed, of course. Now there's a well-known museum, and tourist boutiques have filled up the empty storefronts left when the factories shut down. Only the sardine processing plant remains, down past the Coast Guard station on Tilson Avenue; when the wind is off the water you can smell it, a stale odor of fishbones and rotting bait that cuts through the scents of fresh-roasted coffee beans and car exhaust.

Downtown was nearly empty. A few people sat in front of Second Read, drinking coffee. I went inside and got coffee and a croissant, walked back onto the sidewalk, and wandered down to the waterfront. For some reason seeing the water when I'm on foot usually doesn't bother me. There's something about being in a car, or a bus, something about moving, the idea that there's *more* out there, somewhere; the idea that Aranbega is floating in the blue pearly haze and I'm here, away: disembodied somehow, like an astronaut untethered from a capsule, floating slowly beyond that safe closed place, unable to breathe and everything gone to black, knowing it's just a matter of time.

But that day, standing on the dock with the creosote-soaked wooden pilings beneath my sneakers, looking at orange peels bobbing in the black water and gulls wheeling overhead—that day I didn't feel bad at all. I drank my coffee and ate my croissant, tossed the last bit of crust into the air, and watched the gulls veer and squabble over it. I looked at my watch. A little before eight, still too early to head to Blakie's. She liked to sleep in, and Katherine enjoyed the peace and quiet of a morning.

I headed back towards Main Street. There was some early morning traffic now, people heading off to do their shopping at Shaw's and Wal-Mart. On the corner I waited for the light to change, glanced at a storefront and saw a sign taped to the window.

ST. BRUNO'S EPISCOPAL CHURCH
ANNUAL RUMMAGE SALE
SATURDAY SEPTEMBER 7
8:00 A.M.-3:00 P.M.
LUNCH SERVED FROM 11:30

THE LEAST TRUMPS

Penobscot Fields had once been the lupine-strewn meadow behind St. Bruno's; proximity to the church was one of the reasons Blakie and Katherine had first signed on to the retirement community. I wasn't a churchgoer, but during the summer I was an avid haunter of yard sales in the Rockland area. You don't get many of them after Labor Day, but the rummage sale at St. Bruno's almost makes up for it. I made sure I had my wallet and checkbook in my bag, then hurried to get there before the doors opened.

There was already a line. I recognized a couple of dealers, a few regulars who smiled or nodded at me. St. Bruno's is a late-nineteenth century neo-gothic building, designed in the late Arts and Crafts style by Halbert Liston: half-timbered beams, local dove-grey fieldstone, slate shingles on the roof. The rummage sale was not in the church, of course, but the adjoining parish house. It had whitewashed walls rather than stone, the same half-timbered upper story, etched with arabesques of dying clematis and sere Virginia creeper. In the door was a diamond-shaped window through which a worried elderly woman peered out every few minutes.

"Eight o'clock!" someone called good-naturedly from the front of the line. Bobby Day, the greying hippie who owned a used bookstore in Camden. "Time to go!"

From inside, the elderly woman gave one last look at the crowd, then nodded. The door opened; there was a surge forward, laughter and excited murmurs, someone crying "Marge, look out! Here they come!" Then I was inside.

Long tables of linens and clothing were at the front of the hall, surrounded by women with hands already full of flannel sheets and crewel-work. I scanned these quickly, then glanced at the furniture. Nice stuff—a Morris chair and old oak settle, some wicker, a flax wheel. Episcopalians always have good rummage sales, better quality than Our Lady of the Harbor or those off-brand churches straggling down towards Warren.

But the Lonely House was already crammed with my own nice stuff, besides which it would be difficult to get anything back to the island. So I made my way to the rear of the hall, where Bobby Day was going through boxes of books on the floor. We exchanged hellos, Bobby smiling but not taking his eyes from the books; in deference to him I continued on to the back corner. An old man wearing a canvas apron with a faded silhouette of St. Bruno on it stood over a table covered with odds and ends.

"This is whatever didn't belong anywhere else," he said. He waved a hand at a hodgepodge of beer steins, Tupperware, mismatched silver, shoeboxes overflowing with candles, buttons, mason-jar lids. "Everything's a dollar."

I doubted there was anything there worth fifty cents, but I just nodded and moved slowly down the length of the table. A chipped Poppy Trails bowl and a bunch of ugly glass ashtrays. Worn Beanie Babies with the tags clipped off. A game of Twister. As I looked, a heavyset woman barreled up behind me. She had a rigidly unsmiling face and an overflowing canvas bag: I caught glints of brass and pewter, the telltale dull green glaze of a nice Teco pottery vase. A dealer. She avoided my gaze, her hand snaking out to grab something I'd missed, a tarnished silver flask hidden behind a stack of plastic Easter baskets.

I tried not to grimace. I hated dealers and their greedy bottom-feeder mentality. By this afternoon she'd have polished the flask and stuck a seventy-five-dollar price tag on it. I moved quickly to the end of the table. I could see her watching me whenever my hand hovered above something; once I moved on she'd grab whatever I'd been examining, give it a cursory glance before elbowing up beside me once more. After a few minutes I turned away, was just starting to leave when my gaze fell upon a swirl of violet and orange tucked within a Pyrex dish.

"Not sure what that is," the old man said as I pried it from the bowl. Beside me the dealer watched avidly. "Lady's scarf, I guess."

It was a lumpy packet a bit larger than my hand, made up of a paisley scarf that had been folded over several times to form a thick square, then wrapped and tightly knotted around a rectangular object. The cloth was frayed, but it felt like fine wool. There was probably

THE LEAST TRUMPS

enough of it to make a nice pillow cover. Whatever was inside felt compact but also slightly flexible; it had a familiar heft as I weighed it in my palm.

An oversized pack of cards. I glanced up to see the dealer watching me with undisguised impatience.

"I'll take this," I said, and handed the old man a dollar. "Thanks."

A flicker of disappointment across the dealer's face. I smiled at her, enjoying my mean little moment of triumph, and left.

Outside the parish hall a stream of people were headed for the parking lot, carrying lamps and pillows and overflowing plastic bags. The church bell tolled eight thirty. Blakie would just be getting up. I killed a few more minutes by wandering around the church grounds, past a well-kept herb garden and stands of yellow chrysanthemums. Behind a neatly trimmed hedge of boxwood I discovered a statue of St. Bruno himself, standing watch over a granite bench. Here I sat with my paisley-wrapped treasure, and set about trying to undo the knot.

For a while I thought I'd have to just rip the damn thing apart, or wait till I got to Blakie's to cut it open. The cloth was knotted so tightly I couldn't undo it, and the paisley had gotten wet at some point then shrunk—it was like trying to pick at dried plaster, or Sheetrock.

But gradually I managed to tease one corner of the scarf free, tugging it gently until, after a good ten minutes, I was able to undo the wrappings. A faint odor wafted up, the vanilla-tinged scent of pipe tobacco. There was a greasy feel to the frayed cloth, sweat, or maybe someone had dropped it on the damp grass. I opened it carefully, smoothing its folds till I could finally see what was tucked inside.

It was a large deck of cards, bound with a rubber band. The rubber band fell to bits when I tried to remove it, and something fluttered onto the bench. I picked it up: a scrap of paper with a few words scrawled in pencil.

The least trumps.

I frowned. The Greater Trumps, those were the picture cards that made up the Major Arcana in a tarot deck—the Chariot, the Magician, the Empress, the Hierophant. Eight or nine years ago I had a girlfriend with enough New Age tarots to channel the entire Order of the Golden Dawn. Marxist tarots, lesbian tarots, African, Zen, and Mormon tarots; Tarots of the Angels, of Wise Mammals, poisonous snakes and smiling madonni; Aleister Crowley's tarot, and Shirley MacLaine's; the dread Feminist Tarot of the Cats. There were twenty-two Major Arcana cards, and the lesser trumps were analogous to the fifty-two cards in an ordinary deck, with an additional four representing knights.

But the least trumps? The phrase stabbed at my memory, but I couldn't place it. I stared at the scrap of paper with its rushed scribble, put it aside and examined the deck.

The cards were thick, with the slightly furry feel of old pasteboard. Each was printed with an identical and intricate design of spoked wheels, like old-fashioned gears with interlocking teeth. The inks were primitive, too-bright primary colors, red and yellow and blue faded now to periwinkle and pale rose, a dusty gold like smudged pollen. I guessed they dated to the early or mid-nineteenth century. The images had the look of old children's picture books from that era, at once vivid and muted, slightly sinister, as though the illustrators were making a point of not revealing their true meaning to the casual viewer. I grinned, thinking of how I'd wrested them from the clutches of an antiques dealer, then turned them over.

The cards were all blank. I shook my head, fanning them out on the bench before me. A few of the cards had their corners neatly clipped, but others looked as though they had been bitten off in tiny crescent-shaped wedges. I squinted at one, trying to determine if someone had peeled off a printed image. The surface was rough, flecked with bits of darker grey and black, or white, but it didn't seem to have ever had anything affixed to it. There was no trace of glue or spirit gum that I could see, no jots of ink or colored paper.

THE LEAST TRUMPS

A mistake, then. The deck had obviously been discarded by the printer. Not even a dealer would have been able to get more than a couple of bucks for it.

Too bad. I gathered the cards into a stack, and started wrapping the scarf around them when I noticed that one card was thicker than the rest. I pulled it out: not a single card after all but two that had become stuck together. I set the rest of the deck aside, safe within the paisley shroud; then gingerly slid my thumbnail between the stuck cards. It was like prising apart sheets of mica—I could feel where the pasteboard held fast towards the center, but if I pulled at it too hard or too quickly the cards would tear.

But very slowly, I felt the cards separate. Maybe the warmth of my touch helped, or the sudden exposure to air and moisture. For whatever reason, the cards suddenly slid apart so that I held one in each hand.

"Oh."

I cried aloud, they were that wonderful. Two tiny, brilliantly inked tableaux like medieval tapestries, or paintings by Brueghel glimpsed through a rosace window. One card was awhirl with minute figures, men and women but also animals, dogs dancing on their hind legs, long-necked cranes, and crabs that lifted clacking claws to a sky filled with pennoned airships, exploding suns, a man being carried on a litter, and a lash-fringed eye like a greater sun gazing down upon them all. The other card showed only the figure of a naked man, kneeling so that he faced the viewer, but with head bowed so that you saw only his broad back, a curve of neck like a quarter-moon, a sheaf of dark hair spilling to the ground before him. The man's skin was painted in gold leaf; the ground he knelt upon was the dreamy green of old bottle-glass, the sky behind him crocus-yellow, with a tinge upon the horizon like the first flush of sun, or the protruding tip of a finger. As I stared at them I felt my heart begin to beat, too fast too hard but not with fear this time, not this time.

The Least Trumps. The term was used, just once, in the first chapter of the unfinished, final volume of *Five Windows One Door*. I remembered it suddenly, the way you recall something from early childhood, the smell of marigolds towering above your head, a blue plush dog with one glass eye, thin sunlight filtering through a crack in a frosted glass cold frame. My mouth filled with liquid and I tasted sour cherries, salt and musk, the first time my tongue probed a girl's cunt. A warm breeze stirred my hair. I heard distant laughter, a booming bass-note that resolved into the echo of a church clock tolling nine.

◆ ◆ ◆

ONLY WHEN HE was certain that Mabel had fallen fast asleep beside him would Tarquin remove the cards from their brocade pouch, her warm limbs tangled in the stained bedcovers where they emitted a smell of yeast and limewater, the surrounding room suffused with twilight so that when he held the cards before her mouth, one by one, he saw how her breath brought to life the figures painted upon each, as though she breathed upon a winter windowpane where frost-roses bloomed: Pavell Saved From Drowning, The Bangers, One Leaf Left, Hermalchio and Lachrymatory, Villainous Saltpetre, The Ground-Nut, The Widower: all the recusant figures of the Least Trumps quickening beneath Mabel's sleeping face.

◆ ◆ ◆

EVEN NOW THE words came to me by heart. Sometimes, when I couldn't fall asleep, I would lie in bed and silently recite the books from memory, beginning with Volume One, *The First Window: Love Plucking Rowan Berries,* with its description of Mabel's deflowering that I found so tragic when I first read it. Only later in my twenties, when I read the books for the fifth or seventh time, did I realize the scene was a parody of the seduction scene in *Rigoletto.* In this way Walter Burden Fox's books eased my passage into the world, as they did in many others. Falling in love with fey little Clytie Winton then weeping over her death; making my first forays into sex when I masturbated to the memory of Tarquin's mad brother Elwell taking Mabel as she slept; realizing, as I read of Mabel's great love affair with the silent film actress Nola Flynn, that there were words to describe what I did sometimes with my own friends, even if those words had a lavender must of the attic to them: *tribadism, skylarking, sit Venus in the garden with Her Gate unlocked.*

My mother never explained any of this to me: sex, love, suffering, patience. Probably she assumed that her example alone was enough, and for another person it might well have been. But I never saw my mother unhappy, or frightened. My first attack came not long after Julia Sa'adah left me. Julia who inked my life Before and After; and while at the time I was contemptuous of anyone who suggested a link between the two events, breakup and crackup, I can see now that it was so. In Fox's novels, love affairs sometimes ended badly, but for all the lessons his books held, they never readied me for the shock of being left.

That was more than eleven years ago. I still felt the aftershocks, of course. I still dream about her: her black hair, so thick it was like oiled rope streaming through my fingers; her bronzey skin, its soft glaucous bloom like scuppernongs; the way her mouth tasted. Small mouth, smaller than my own, cigarettes and wintergreen, tea oil, coriander seed. The dream is different each time, though it always ends the same way, it ends the way it ended: Julia looking at me as she packs up her Rockland studio, arms bare so I can see my own apprentice work below her elbow, vine leaves, stylized knots. My name there, and hers, if you knew where to look. Her face sad but amused as she shakes her head. "You never happened, Ivy."

"How can you *say* that?" This part never changes either, though in my waking mind I say a thousand other things. "Six years, how can you fucking *say* that?"

She just shakes her head. Her voice begins to break up, swallowed by the harsh buzz of a tattoo machine choking down; her image fragments, hair face eyes breasts tattoos spattering into bits of light, jabs of black and red. The tube is running out of ink. "That's not what I mean. You just don't get it, Ivy. *You* never happened. *You.* Never. Happened."

Then I wake and the panic's full-blown, like waking into a room where a bomb's exploded. Only there's no bomb. What's exploded is all inside my head.

It was years before anyone figured out how it worked, this accretion of synaptic damage, neuronal misfirings, an overstimulated fight-or-flight response; the way one tiny event becomes trapped within a web of dendrites and interneurons and triggers a cascade of cortisol and epinephrine, which in turns wakes the immense black spider that rushes out and seizes me so that I see and feel only horror, only dread, the entire world poisoned by its bite. There is no antidote—the whole disorder is really just an accumulation of symptoms, accelerated pulse-rate, racing heartbeat, shallow breathing. There is no cure, only chemicals that lull the spider back to sleep. It may be that my repeated tattooing of my own skin has somehow oversensitized me, like bad acupuncture, caused an involuntary neurochemical reaction that only makes it worse.

No one knows. And it's not something Walter Burden Fox ever covered in his books.

I stared at the illustrated cards in my hands. Fox had lived not far from here, in Tenants Harbor. My mother knew him years before I was born. He was much older than she was, but in those days—this was long before e-mail and cheap long distance servers—writers and artists would travel a good distance for the company of their own kind, and certainly a lot further than from Tenants Harbor to Aranbega Island. It was the first time I can remember being really impressed by my mother, the way other people always assumed I must be. She had found me curled up in the hammock, reading *Love Plucking Rowan Berries.*

"You're reading Burdie's book." She stooped to pick up my empty lemonade glass.

I corrected her primly. "It's by Walter Burden Fox."

"Oh, I know. Burdie, that's what he liked to be called. His son was Walter too. Wally, they called him. I knew him."

Now, behind me, St. Bruno's bell rang the quarter-hour. Blakie would be up by now, waiting for my arrival. I carefully placed the two cards with their fellows inside the paisley scarf, put the bundle inside my bag, and headed for Penobscot Fields.

THE LEAST TRUMPS

• ◆ •

BLAKIE AND KATHERINE were sitting at their dining nook when I let myself in. Yesterday's *New York Times* was spread across the table, and the remains of breakfast.

"Well," my mother asked, white brows raised above calm grey eyes as she looked at me. "Did you throw up?"

"Oh, hush, you," said Katherine.

"Not this time." I bent to kiss my mother, then turned to hug Katherine. "I went to the rummage sale at St. Bruno's, that's why I'm late."

"Oh, I meant to give them my clothes!" Katherine stood to get me coffee. "I brought over a few boxes of things, but I forgot the clothes. I have a whole bag, some nice Hermes scarves, too."

"You shouldn't give those away." Blakie patted the table, indicating where I should sit beside her. "That consignment shop in Camden gives us good credit for them. I got this sweater there." She touched her collar, dove-grey knit, three pearl buttons. "It's lamb's wool. Bergdorf Goodman. They closed ages ago. Someone must have died."

"Oh hush," said Katherine. She handed me a coffee mug. "Like we need credit for *clothes*."

"Look," I said. "Speaking of scarves—"

I pulled the paisley packet from the purse, clearing a space amidst the breakfast dishes. For a fraction of a second Blakie looked surprised; then she blinked, and along with Katherine leaned forward expectantly. As I undid the wrappings the slip of paper fell onto the table beside my mother's hand. Her gnarled fingers scrabbled at the table, finally grabbed the scrap.

"I can't read this," she said, adjusting her glasses as she stared and scowled. I set the stack of cards on the scarf, then slid them all across the table. I had withheld the two cards that retained their color; now I slipped them into my back jeans pocket, carefully, so they wouldn't get damaged. The others lay in a neat pile before my mother.

"'The Least Trumps.'" I pointed at the slip of paper. "That's what it says."

She looked at me sharply, then at the cards. "What do you mean? It's a deck of cards."

"What's written on the paper. It says, 'The Least Trumps.' I don't know if you remember, but there's a scene in one of Fox's books, the first one? The Least Trumps is what he calls a set of tarot cards that one of the characters uses." I edged over beside her, and pointed at the bit of paper she held between thumb and forefinger. "I was curious if you could read that. Since you knew him? I was wondering if you recognized it. If it was his handwriting."

"Burdie's?" My mother shook her head, drew the paper to her face until it was just a few inches from her nose. It was the same pose she'd assumed when pretending to gaze at Wise Ant through a magnifying glass for *Life* magazine, only now it was my mother who looked puzzled, even disoriented. "Well, I don't know. I don't remember."

I felt a flash of dread, that now of all times would be when she started to lose it, to drift away from me and Katherine. But no. She turned to Katherine and said, "Where did we put those files? When I was going through the letters from after the war. Do you remember?"

"Your room, I think. Do you want me to get them?"

"No, no..." Blakie waved me off as she stood and walked, keeping her balance by touching chair, countertop, wall on the way to her study.

Katherine looked after her, then at the innocuous shred of paper, then at me. "What is it?" She touched one unraveling corner of the scarf. "Where did you get them?"

"At the rummage sale. They were wrapped up in that, I didn't know what they were till I got outside and opened it."

"Pig in a poke." Katherine winked at me. She still had her silvery hair done every Thursday, in the whipped-up spray-stiffened bouffant of her Dallas socialite days—not at the beauty parlor at the retirement center, either, but the most expensive salon in Camden. She had her nails done too, even though her hands were too twisted by arthritis to wear the bijoux rings she'd always favored, square-cut diamonds and aquamarines and the emerald my mother had given her when they first met. "I'm surprised you bought a pig in a poke, Ivy Bee."

THE LEAST TRUMPS

"Yeah. I'm surprised too."

"Here we are." My mother listed back into the room, settling with a thump in her chair. "Now we can see."

She jabbed her finger at the table, where the scrap of paper fluttered like an injured moth, then handed me an envelope. "Open that, please, Ivy dear. My hands are so clumsy now."

It was a white, letter-sized envelope, unsealed, tipsy typed address.

Miss Blakie Tun,
The Lonely House,
Aranbega Island, Maine.

Before Zip Codes, even, one faded blue four-cent stamp in one corner. The other corner with the typed return address. W. B. Fox, Sand Hill Road, T. Harbor, Maine.

"Look at it!" commanded Blakie.

Obediently I withdrew the letter, unfolded it, and scanned the handwritten lines, front and back, until I reached the end. Blue ink, mouse-tail flourish on the final *e*. *Very Fondly Yours, Burdie.*

"I think it's the same writing." I scrutinized the penmanship, while trying not to actually absorb its content. Which seemed dull in any case, something about a dog, and snow, and someone's car getting stuck, and *Be glad when summer's here, at least we can visit again.*

Least. I picked up the scrap of paper to compare the two words.

"You know, they *are* the same," I said. There was something else, too. I brought the letter to my face and sniffed it. "And you know what else? I can smell it. It smells like pipe tobacco. The scarf smells like it, too."

"Borkum Riff." My mother made a face. "Awful sweet stuff, I couldn't stand it. So."

She looked at me, grey eyes narrowed, not sly but thoughtful. "We were good friends, you know. Burdie. Very loveable man."

Katherine nodded. "Fragile."

"Fragile. He would have made a frail old man, wouldn't he?" She glanced at Katherine—two strong old ladies—then at me. "I remember how much you liked his books. I'm sorry now we didn't write to each other more, I could have given you his letters, Ivy. He always came to visit us, once or twice a year. In the summer."

"But not after the boy died," said Katherine.

My mother shook her head. "No, not after Wally died. Poor Burdie."

"Poor Wally," suggested Katherine.

It was why Fox had never completed the last book of the quintet. His son had been killed in the Korean War. I knew that; it was one of the only really interesting, if tragic, facts about Walter Burden Fox. There had been one full-length biography, written in the 1970s, when his work achieved a minor cult status boosted by the success of Tolkien and Mervyn Peake, a brief vogue in those days for series books in uniform paperback editions. *The Alexandria Quartet, Children of Violence, A Dance to the Music of Time. Five Windows One Door* had never achieved that kind of popularity, of course, despite the affection for it held by figures like Anais Nin, Timothy Leary, and Virgil Thomson, themselves eclipsed now by brighter, younger lights.

Fox died in 1956. I hadn't been born yet. I could never have met him.

Yet, in a funny way, he made me who I am—well, maybe not *me* exactly. But he certainly changed the way I thought about the world; made it seem at once unabashedly romantic and charged with a sense of imminence, as ripe with possibility as an autumn orchard is ripe with fruit. Julia and I were talking once about the 1960s—she was seven years older than me, and had lived through them as an adult, communes in Tennessee, drug dealing in Malibu, before she settled down in Rockland and opened her tattoo studio.

She said, "You want to know what the sixties were about, Ivy? The sixties were about *It could happen.*"

And that's what Fox's books were like. They gave me the sense that there was someone leaning over my shoulder, someone whispering *It could happen.*

THE LEAST TRUMPS

So I suppose you could say that Walter Burden Fox ruined the real world for me, when I didn't find it as welcoming as the one inhabited by Mabel and Nola and the Sienno brothers. Could there ever have been a real city as marvelous as his imagined Newport? Who would ever choose to bear the weight of this world? Who would ever want to?

Still, that was my weakness, not his. The only thing I could really fault him for was his failure to finish that last volume. But, under the circumstances, who could blame him for that?

"So these are his cards? May I?" Katherine glanced at me. I nodded, and she picked up the deck tentatively, turned it over, and gave a little gasp. "Oh! They're blank—"

She looked embarrassed and I laughed. "Katherine! *Now* look what you've done!"

"But were they like this when you got them?" She began turning the cards over, one by one, setting them out on the table as though playing an elaborate game of solitaire. "Look at this! They're every single one of them blank. I've never seen such a thing."

"All used up," said Blakie. She folded the scarf and pushed it to one side. "You should wash that, Ivy. Who knows where it's been."

"Well, where *has* it been? Did he go to church there? St. Bruno's?"

"I don't remember." Blakie's face became a mask: as she had aged, Circe became the Sphinx. She was staring at the cards lying face-up on the table. Only of course there were no faces, just a grid of grey rectangles, some missing one or two corners or even three corners. My mother's expression was watchful but wary; she glanced at me, then quickly looked away again. I thought of the two cards in my back pocket but said nothing. "His wife died young, he raised the boy alone. He wanted to be a writer too, you know. Probably they just ended up in someone's barn."

"The cards, you mean," Katherine said mildly. Blakie looked annoyed. "There. That's all of them."

"How many are there?" I asked. Katherine began to count, but Blakie said, "Seventy-three."

"Seventy-three?" I shook my head. "What kind of deck uses seventy-three cards?"

"Some are missing, then. There's only seventy." Katherine looked at Blakie. "Seventy-three? How do you know?"

"I just remember, that's all," my mother said irritably. She pointed at me. "You should know. You read all his books."

"Well." I shrugged and stared at the bland pattern on the dining table, then reached for a card. The top right corner was missing; but how would you know it was the top? "They were only mentioned once. As far as I recall, anyway. Just in passing. Why do you think the corners are cut off?"

"To keep track of them." Katherine began to collect them back into a pile. "That's how card cheats work. Take off a little teeny bit, just enough so they can tell when they're dealing 'em out. Which one's an ace, which one's a trey."

"But these are all the same," I said. "There's no point to it."

Then I noticed Blakie was staring at me. Suddenly I began to feel paranoid, like when I was a teenager out getting high, walking back into the Lonely House and praying she wouldn't notice how stoned I was. I felt like I'd been lying, although what had I done, besides stick two cards in my back pocket?

But then maybe I was lying when I said there was no point; maybe I was wrong. Maybe there *was* a point. If two of the cards had a meaning, maybe they all did; even if I had no clue what their meaning was. Even if nobody had a clue: they still might mean something.

But what? It was like one of those horrible logic puzzles—you have one boat, three geese, one fox, an island: how do you get all the geese onto the island without the fox eating them? Seventy-three cards: seventy that Katherine had counted, the pair in my back pocket; where was the other one?

I fought an almost irresistible urge to reveal the two picture cards I'd hidden. Instead I looked away from my mother, and saw that now Katherine was staring at me, too. It was a moment before I realized she

THE LEAST TRUMPS

was waiting for the last card, the one that was still in my hand. "Oh. Thanks—"

I gave it to her, she put it on top of the stack, turned and gave the stack to Blakie, who gave it to me. I looked down at the cards and felt that cold pressure starting to build inside my head, helium leaking into my brain, something that was going to make me float away, talk funny.

"Well." I wrapped the cards in the paisley scarf. It still smelled faintly of pipe tobacco, but now there was another scent too, mother's Chanel N°5. I stuck the cards in my bag, turned back to the dining table. "What should we do now?"

"I don't have a clue," said my mother, and gave me the smile of an octogenarian tiger. "Ivy? You decide."

• ◆ •

JULIA'S FATHER WAS Egyptian, a Coptic diplomat from Cairo. Her mother was an artist manqué from a wealthy Boston family that had a building at Harvard named for it. Her father, Narouz, had been married and divorced four times; Julia had a much younger half-brother and several half-sisters. The brother died in a terrorist attack in Egypt in the early nineties, a year or so before she left me. After her mother's death from cancer the same year, Julia refused to have anything else to do with Narouz or his extended family. A few months later, she refused to have anything to do with me as well.

Julia claimed that *Five Windows One Door* could be read as a secret text of ancient Coptic magic; that there were meanings encoded within the characters' ceaseless and often unrequited love affairs, that the titles of Nola Flynn's silent movies corresponded to oracular texts in the collections of the Hermitage and the Institut Francais d'Archeologie Orientale in Cairo; that the scene in which Tarquin sodomizes his twin is in fact a description of a ritual to leave a man impotent and protect a woman from sexual advances. I asked her how such a book could possibly be conceived and written by a middle-aged inhabitant of Maine, in the middle of the twentieth century.

Julia just shrugged. "That's why it works. Nobody knows. Look at Lorca."

"Lorca?" I shook my head, trying not to laugh. "What, was he in Maine, too?"

"No. But he worked in the twentieth century."

That was almost the last thing Julia Sa'adah ever said to me. This is another century. Nothing works anymore.

• ♦ •

I CAUGHT AN earlier ferry back than I'd planned. Katherine was tired; I had taken her and my mother to lunch at the small café they favored, but it was more crowded than usual, with a busload of blue-haired leaf-peepers from Newburyport who all ordered the specials so that the kitchen ran out and we had to eat BLTs.

"I just hate that." Blakie glowered at the table next to us, four women the same age as she was, scrying the bill as though it were tea-leaves. "Look at them, trying to figure out the tip! Fifteen percent, darling," she said loudly. "Double the tax and add one."

The women looked up. "Oh, thank you!" one said. "Isn't it pretty here?"

"I wouldn't know," said Blakie. "I'm blind."

The woman looked shocked. "Oh, hush, you," scolded Katherine. "She is not," but the women were already scurrying to leave.

I drove them back to their tidy modern retirement cottage, the made-for-TV version of the Lonely House.

"I'll see you next week," I said, after helping them inside. Katherine kissed me and made a beeline for the bathroom. My mother sat on the couch, waiting to catch her breath. She had congestive heart disease, payback for all those years of smoking Kents and eating heavily marbled steaks.

"You could stay here if you wanted," she said, and for almost the first time I heard a plaintive note in her voice. "The couch folds out."

I smiled and hugged her. "You know, I might do that. I think Sue wants a break from me. For a little while."

THE LEAST TRUMPS

For a moment I thought she was going to say something. Her mouth pursed and her grey eyes once again had that watchful look. But she only nodded, patting my hand with her strong cold one, then kissed my cheek, a quick furtive gesture like she might be caught.

"Be careful, Ivy Bee," she said. "Goodbye."

On the ferry I sat on deck. There were only a few other passengers. I had the stern to myself, a bench sheltered by the engine house from spray and chill wind. The afternoon had turned cool and grey. There was a bruised line of clouds upon the horizon, violet and slate-blue; it made the islands look stark as a Rockwell Kent woodblock, the pointed firs like arrowheads.

It was a time of day, a time of year, I loved; one of the only times when things still seemed possible to me. Something about the slant of the late year's light, the sharp line between shadows and stones, as though if you slid your hand in there you'd find something unexpected.

It made me want to work.

I had no customers lined up that week. Idly I ran my right hand along the top of my left leg, worn denim and beneath it muscle, skin. I hadn't worked on myself for a while. That was one of the first things I learned when I was apprenticed to Julia: a novice tattoo artist practices on herself. If you're right-handed, you do your left arm, your left leg; just like a good artist makes her own needles, steel flux and solder, jig and needles, the smell of hot tinning fluid on the tip of the solder gun. That way people can see your work. They know they can trust you.

The last thing I'd done was a scroll of oak leaves and eyes, fanning out above my left knee. My upper thigh was still taut white skin. I was thin and rangy like my mother had been, too fair to ever have tanned. I flexed my hand, imagining the weight of the machine, its pulse a throbbing heart. As I stared at the ferry's wake, I could see the lights of Rockland Harbor glimmer then disappear into the growing dusk. When I stuck my head out to peer towards the bow, I saw Aranbega rising from the Atlantic, black firs and granite cliffs buffed to pink by the failing sun.

I stood, keeping my balance as I gently pulled the two cards from my back pocket. I glanced at both, then put one into my wallet, behind my driver's license; sat and examined the other, turning so that the wall of the engine house kept it safe from spray. It was the card that showed only the figure of a kneeling man. A deceptively simple form, a few fluid lines indicating torso, shoulders, offertory stance—that crescent of bare neck, his hands half-hidden by his long hair.

Why did I know it was a man? I'm not sure. The breadth of his shoulders, maybe; maybe some underlying sense that any woman in such a position would be inviting disaster. This figure seemed neither resigned nor abdicating responsibility. He seemed to be waiting.

It was amazing, how the interplay of black and white and a few drops of gold leaf could conjure up an entire world. Like Pamela Colman Smith's designs for the Waite tarot—the High Priestess, the King of Wands—or a figure that Julia had shown me once. It was from a facsimile edition of a portfolio of Coptic texts on papyrus, now in the British Library. There were all kinds of spells—

> For I am having a clash with a headless dog, seize him
> when he comes. Grasp this pebble with both your hands,
> flee eastward to your right, while you journey on up.

> A stinging ant: In this way, while it is still fresh, burn it,
> grind it with vinegar, put it with incense. Put it on eyes
> that have discharge. They will get better.

The figure was part of a spell to obtain a good singing voice. Julia translated the text for me as she had the others:

> Yea, yea, for I adjure you in the name of the seven letters
> that are tattooed on the chest of the father, namely
> AAAAAAAA, EEEEEEE, EEEEEEE, IIIIIII,
> OOOOOOO, UUUUUUU, OOOOOOO. Obey
> my mouth, before it passes and another one comes in its
> place! Offering: wild frankincense; wild mastic; cassia.

THE LEAST TRUMPS

The Coptic figure that accompanied the text had a name: DAVITHEA RACHOCHI ADONIEL. It looked nothing like the figure on the card in front of me; it was like something you'd see scratched on the wall of a cave.

Yet it had a name. And I would never know the name of this card.

But I would use it, I decided. *The least trumps.* Beneath me the ferry's engine shifted down, its dull steady groan deepening as we drew near Aranbega's shore. I slid the card into the Lorca book I'd brought, stuffed it into my bag, and waited to dock.

• ◆ •

I'D LEFT MY old GMC pickup where I always did, parked behind the Island General Store. I went inside and bought a sourdough baguette and a bottle of Toquai. I'd gotten a taste for the wine from Julia; now the store ordered it especially for me, though some of the well-heeled summer people bought it as well.

"Working tonight?" said Mary, the store's owner.

"Yup."

Outside it was full dusk. I drove across the island on the rugged gravel road that bisected it into north and south, village and wild places. To get to Green Pond you drive off the main road, following a rutted lane that soon devolves into what resembles a washed-out streambed. Soon this rudimentary road ends, at the entrance to a large grove of hundred-and-fifty-year-old pines. I parked here and walked the rest of the way, a quarter-mile beneath high branches that stir restlessly, making a sound like the sea even on windless days. The pines give way to birches, ferns growing knee-high in a spinney of trees like bones. Another hundred feet and you reach the edge of Green Pond, before you the Lonely House rising on its grey islet, a dream of safety. Usually this was when the last vestiges of fear would leave me, blown away by the cool wind off the lake and the sight of my childhood home, my wooden dory pulled up onto the shore a few feet from where I stood.

But tonight the unease remained. Or no, not unease exactly; more a sense of apprehension that, very slowly, resolved into a kind of anticipation. But anticipation of what? I stared at the Lonely House with its clumps of asters and yellow coneflowers, the ragged garden I deliberately didn't weed or train. Because I wanted the illusion of wilderness, I wanted to pretend I'd left something to chance. And suddenly I wanted to see something else.

If you walk to the other side of the small lake—I hardly ever do—you find that you're on the downward slope of a long boulder-strewn rise, a glacial moraine that eventually plummets into the Atlantic Ocean. Scattered white pines and birches grow here, and ancient white oaks, some of the very few white oaks left in the entire state, in fact, the rest having been harvested well over a century before, as masts for the great schooners. The lesser trees—red oaks, mostly, a few sugar maples—have been cut, for the Lonely House's firewood and repairs, so that if you stand in the right place you can actually look down the entire southeastern end of the island and see the ocean: scumbled grey cliffs and beyond that nothing, an unbroken darkness that might be fog, or sea, or the end of the world.

The right place to see this is from an outcropping of granite that my mother named The Ledges. On a foggy day, if you stand there and look at the Lonely House, you have an illusion of gazing from one sea-island to another. If you turn, you see only darkness. The seas are too rough for recreational sailors; far from the major shipping lanes; too risky for commercial fishermen. The entire Grand Banks fishery has been depleted, so that you can stare out for hours or maybe even days and never see a single light, nothing but stars and maybe the blinking red eye of a distant plane flying the Great Circle Route to Gander or London.

It was a vista that terrified me, though I would dutifully point it out to first-time visitors, showing them where they could sit on The Ledges.

"On a clear day you can see Ireland," Katherine used to say, the joke being that on a Maine island you almost never had a clear day.

This had not been a clear day, of course, and, with evening, high grey clouds had come from the west. Only the easternmost horizon held

THE LEAST TRUMPS

a pale shimmer of blue-violet, lustrous as the inner curve of a mussel shell. Behind me the wind moved through the old pines, and I could hear the high rustling of the birch leaves. Not so far off a fox barked. The sound made my neck prickle.

But I'd left a single light on inside the Lonely House, and so I focused on that, walking slowly around the perimeter of Green Pond with the little beacon always at the edge of my vision, until I reached the far side, the eastern side. Ferns crackled underfoot; I smelled the sweet odor of dying bracken, and bladderwrack from the cliffs far below. The air had the bite of rain to it, and that smell you get sometimes, when a low pressure system carries the reek of places much farther south—a soupy thick smell, like rotting vegetation, mangroves or palmettos. I breathed it in and thought of Julia, and realized that for the first time in years, an hour had gone by and I had not thought about her at all. From the trees on the other side of Green Pond the fox barked again, even closer this time.

For one last moment I stood, gazing at The Ledges. Then I turned and walked back to where my dory waited, clambered in and rowed myself home.

◆ ◆ ◆

THE TATTOO TOOK me till dawn to finish. Once inside the Lonely House I opened the bottle of Toquai, poured myself a glassful and drank it. Then I went to retrieve the card, stuck inside that decrepit New Directions paperback in my bag. The book was the only thing of Julia's I had retained. She'd made a point of going through every single box of clothes and books I'd packed, through every sagging carton of dishware, and removed anything that had been hers. Anything we'd purchased together, anything that it had been her idea to buy. So that by the time she was done, it wasn't just like I'd never happened. It was like she'd never happened, either.

Except for this book. I found it a few months after the breakup. It had gotten stuck under the driver's seat of my old Volvo, wedged between a broken spring and the floor. In all the years I'd been with Julia, I'd never read it, or seen her reading it. But just a few weeks earlier I started flipping through the pages, casually, more to get the poet's smell than to actually understand him. Now I opened the book to the page where the card was stuck, and noticed several lines that had been highlighted with yellow marker.

> *The* duende, *then, is a power and not a construct, is a struggle and not a concept. That is to say, it is not a question of aptitude, but of a true and viable style—of blood, in other words; of creation made act.*

A struggle not a concept. I smiled, and dropped the book on the couch; took the card and went into my studio to work.

I spent over an hour just getting a feel for the design, trying to copy it freehand onto paper before giving up. I'm a good draftsman but one thing I've learned over the years is that the simpler a good drawing appears to be, the more difficult it is to copy. Try copying one of Picasso's late minotaur drawings and you'll see what I mean. Whoever did the design on this particular card probably wasn't Picasso; but the image still defeated me. There was a mystery to it, a sense of waiting that was charged with power; like that D. H. Lawrence poem, *those who have not exploded.* I finally traced it on my light board, the final stencil image exactly the same size as that on the card, outlined in black hectograph ink.

Then I prepped myself. My studio is as sterile as I can make it. There's no carpet on the bare wood floor, which I scrub every day. Beneath a blue plastic cover, the worktable is white Formica, so blood or dirt shows, or spilled ink. I don't bother with an apron or gloves when I'm doing myself, and between the lack of protection and a couple of glasses of Toquai, I always get a slightly illicit-feeling buzz. I feel like I'm pulling something over, even though there's never anyone around but myself. I swabbed the top of my thigh with 70 percent alcohol, used a new, disposable razor to shave it, swabbed it again, dried it with sterile gauze soaked in more alcohol. Then I coated the shaved skin with betadine, tossing the used gauze into a small metal biohazard bin.

I'd already set up my inks in their plastic presterilized caps—black; yellow and red to get the effect of gold leaf; white. I got ready to apply the stencil, rubbing a little bit of stick deodorant onto my skin, so that the ink would adhere, then pressing the square of stenciled paper and rubbing it for thirty seconds. Then I pulled the paper off. Sometimes I have to do this more than once, if the customer's skin is rough, or the ink too thick. This time, though, the design transferred perfectly.

I sat for a while, admiring it. From my angle, the figure was upside down—I'd thought about that, whether I should just say the hell with it and do it so I'd be the only one who'd ever see it properly. But I decided to go with convention, so that now I'd be drawing a reverse of what everyone else would see. I'm a bleeder, so I had a good supply of vaseline and paper towels at hand. I went into the living room and knocked back one last glass of Toquai, returned to the studio, switched on my machine, and went at it.

I did the outlines first. There's always this *frisson* when the needles first touch my own skin, sterilized metal skimming along the surface so that it burns, as though I'm running a flame-tipped spike along my flesh. Before Julia did my first tattoo I'd always imagined the process would be like pricking myself with a needle, a series of fine precise jabs of pain.

It's not like that at all. It's more like carving your own skin with the slanted nib of a razor-sharp calligraphy pen, or writing on flesh with a soldering iron. The pain is excruciating, but contained: I look down at the vibrating tattoo gun, its tip like a wasp's sting, and see beneath the needle a flowing line of black ink, red weeping from the black: my own blood. My left hand holds the skin taut—this also hurts like hell—while my right fingers manipulate the machine and the wad of paper towel that soaks up blood as the needle moves on, its tip moving in tiny circles, being careful not to press too hard, so it won't scab. I trace a man's shoulders, a crescent that becomes a neck, a skull's crown above a single thick line that signals a cascade of hair. Then down and up to outline his knees, his arms.

When the pain becomes too much I stop for a bit, breathing deeply. Then I smooth vaseline over the image on my thigh, take a bit of gauze and clean the needle tip of blood and ink. After twenty minutes or so of being scarred with a vibrating needle your endorphins kick in, but they don't block the pain; they merely blur it, so that it diffuses over your entire body, not just a few square inches of stretched skin burning like a fresh brand. It's perversely like the aftermath of a great massage, or great sex: exhausting, unbearable, exhilarating. I finished the outline and took a break, turning on the radio to see if WERU had gone off the air. Two or three nights a week they sign off at midnight, but Saturdays sometimes the DJ stays on.

This was my lucky night. I turned the music up and settled back into my chair. My entire leg felt sore, but the outline looked good. I changed the needle tip and began to do the shading, the process that would give the figure depth and color. The tip of the needle tube is flush against my skin, but only for an instant; then I flick it up and away. This way the ink is dispersed beneath the epidermis, deepest black feathering up to create grey.

It takes days and days of practice before you get this technique down, but I had it. When I was done edging the figure's hair, I cleaned and changed the needle tube again, mixing gamboge yellow and crimson until I got just the hue I wanted, a brilliant tigerlily orange. I sprayed the tattoo with disinfectant, gave it another swipe of vaseline, then went to work with the orange. I did some shading around the man's figure, until it looked even better than the original, with a numinous glow that made it stand out from the other designs around it.

It was almost two more hours before I was done. At the very last I put in a bit of white, a few lines here and there, ambient color, really, the eye didn't register it as white but it charged the image with a strange, almost eerie brilliance. White ink pigment is paler than human skin; it

THE LEAST TRUMPS

changes color the way skin does, darkening when exposed to the sun until it's almost indistinguishable from ordinary flesh tone.

But I don't spend a lot of time outside: inks don't fade much on my skin. When I finally put down the machine, my hand and entire right arm ached. Outside, rain spattered the pond. The wind rose, and moments later I heard droplets lashing the side of the house. A barred owl called its four querulous notes. From my radio came a low steady hum of static. I hadn't even noticed when the station went off the air. Soon it would be five A.M., and the morning DJ would be in. I cleaned my machine and work area quickly, automatically; washed my tattoo, dried it and covered the raw skin with antibacterial ointment, and finally taped on a Telfa bandage. In a few hours, after I woke, I'd shower and let the warm water soften the bandage until it slid off. Now I went into the kitchen, stumbling with fatigue and the post-orgasmic glow I get from working on myself.

I'd remembered to leave out a small porterhouse steak to defrost. I heated a cast-iron skillet, tossed the steak in and seared it, two minutes on one side, one on the other. I ate it standing over the sink, tearing off meat still cool and bloody in the center. There's some good things about living alone. I knocked back a quart of skim milk, took a couple of ibuprofen and a high-iron formula vitamin, went to bed, and passed out.

• ◆ •

THE CENTRAL CONCEIT of *Five Windows One Door* is that the same story is told and retold, with constantly shifting points of view, abrupt changes of narrator, of setting, of a character's moral or political beliefs. Even the city itself changed, so that the bistro frequented by Nola's elderly lover Hans Liep was sometimes at the end of Tufnell Street; other times it could be glimpsed in a cul-de-sac near the Boulevard El-Baz. There were madcap scenes in which Shakespearean plot reversals were enacted—the violent reconciliation between Mabel and her father; Nola Flynn's decision to enter a Carmelite convent after her discovery of the blind child Kelson; Roberto Metropole's return from the dead; even the reformation of the incomparably wicked Elwell, who, according to the notes discovered after Fox's death, was to have married Mabel and fathered her six children, the eldest of whom grew up to become Amantine, Popess of Tuckahoe and the first saint to be canonized in the Reformed Catholic Church.

Volume five, *Ardor ex Cathedra*, was unfinished at the time of Fox's death. He had completed the first two chapters, and in his study was a box full of hand-drawn genealogical charts and plot outlines, character notes, a map of the city, even names for new characters—Billy Tyler, Gordon MacKenzie-Hart, Paulette Houdek, Ruben Kirstein. Fox's editor at Griffin/Sage compiled these remnants into an unsatisfactory final volume that was published a year after Fox died. I bought a copy, but it was a sad relic, like the blackened lump of glass that is all that remains of a stained-glass window destroyed by fire. Still, I kept it with its brethren on a bookshelf in my bedroom, the five volumes in their uniform dust jackets, scarlet letters on a brilliant indigo field with the author's name beneath in gold.

• ◆ •

I DREAMED I heard the fox barking, or maybe it really was the fox barking. I turned, groaning as my leg brushed against the bedsheet. The bandage had fallen off while I slept. I groped under the covers till I found it, a clump of sticky brown gauze and I tossed it on the floor, sat up and rubbed my eyes. It was morning. My bedroom window was blistered with silvery light, the glass flecked with rain. I looked down at my thigh. The tattoo had scabbed over, but not much. The figure of the kneeling man was stark and precise, its orange nimbus glazed with clear fluid. I got up and limped into the bathroom, sat on the edge of the tub and laved my thigh tenderly, warm water washing away dead skin and dried blood. I patted it dry and applied another thin layer of antibiotic ointment, and headed for the kitchen to make coffee.

The noise came again—not barking at all but something tapping against a window. It took me a minute to figure out what it was: the basket the Lonely House used as a message system. Blakie had devised it

THE LEAST TRUMPS

forty years ago, a pulley and old-fashioned clothesline, strung between the Lonely House and a birch tree on the far shore. A small wicker basket hung from the line, with a plastic zip lock bag inside it, and inside the bag magic markers and a notepad. Someone could write a note on shore then send the basket over; it would bump against the front window, alerting us to a visitor. A bit more elegant than standing onshore and shouting, it also gave the Lonely House's inhabitants the chance to hide, if we weren't expecting anyone.

I couldn't remember the last time someone had used it. I had a cell phone now, and customers made appointments months in advance. I'd almost forgotten the clothesline was there.

I went to the front window and peered out. Fog had settled in during the night; on the northern side of the island the foghorn moaned. No one would be leaving Aranbega today. I could barely discern the other shore, thick grey mist striated with white birch trees. I couldn't see anyone.

But sure enough, there was the basket dangling between the window and the front door. I opened the window and stuck my hand out, brushing aside a mass of cobwebs strung with dead crane flies and mosquitoes to get at the basket. Inside was the zip lock bag and the notebook, the latter pleached with dark green threads. I grimaced as I pulled it out, the pages damp and molded into a block of viridian pulp.

But stuck to the back of the notebook was a folded square of yellow legal paper. I unfolded it and read the message written in strong square letters.

Ivy—

Christopher Sa'adah here, I'm staying in Aran. Harbor, stopped by to say hi. You there? Call me @ 462-1117. Hope you're okay.

C.

I stared at the note for a full minute. Thinking, this is a mistake, this is a sick joke, someone trying to torment me about Julia. Christopher was dead. Nausea washed over me, that icy chill like a shroud, my skin clammy and the breath freezing in my lungs.

"Ivy? You there?"

I rested my hand atop the open window and inhaled deeply. "Christopher." I shook my head, gave a gasping laugh. "Jesus—"

I leaned out the open window. "Christopher?" I shouted. "Is that really you?"

"It's really me," a booming voice yelled back.

"Hold on! I'll get the dory and come right over—"

I ran into the bedroom and pulled on a pair of loose cutoffs and faded T-shirt, then hurried outside. The dory was where I'd left it, pulled up on shore just beyond the fringe of cattails and bayberries. I pushed it into the lake, a skein of dragonflies rising from the dark water to disappear in the mist. There was water in the boat, dead leaves that nudged at my bare feet; I grabbed the oars and rowed, twenty strong strokes that brought me to the other shore.

"Ivy?"

That was when I saw him, a tall figure like a shadow breaking from the fog thick beneath the birches. He was so big that I had to blink to make sure that this, too, wasn't some trick of the mist: a black-haired, bearded man, strong enough to yank one of the birch saplings up by the roots if he'd wanted to. He wore dark-brown corduroys, a flannel shirt and brown Carhart jacket, heavy brown work boots. His hair was long and pushed back behind his ears; his hands were shoved in his jacket pockets. He was a bit stooped, his shoulders raised in a way that made him look surprised, or unsure of himself. It made him look young, younger than he really was; it made him look like Christopher, Julia's thirteen-year-old brother.

He wasn't thirteen any more. I did the math quickly, bringing the boat round and grabbing the wet line to toss on shore. Christopher was Narouz Sa'adah's son by his third wife. He was eighteen years younger than Julia; that would make him eleven years younger than me, which would make him—

"Little Christopher!" I looked up at him from the dory, grinning. "How the hell old are you?"

He shrugged, leaned down to grab the end of the line and loop it around the granite post at the shoreline. He took out a cigarette and lit it, inhaled rapidly—nervously, I see now—and let his arm dangle so that the smoke coiled up around his wrist.

"I'm thirty-four." He had an almost comically basso voice that echoed across Green Pond like the foghorn. An instant later I heard a loon give its warning cry. Christopher dropped his cigarette and stubbed it out, cocking his head towards the dory. "Is that the same boat you used to have?"

"Sure is." I hopped into the water, wincing at the cold, then waded to shore. "Jesus. Little Christopher. I can't believe it's you. You—Christ! I—well, I thought you were dead!"

"I got better." He stared down at me and for the first time smiled, his teeth still a little crooked and nicotine-stained, not Julia's teeth at all: his face completely guileless, close-trimmed black beard, long hair falling across tawny eyes. "After the bombing? I was in hospital for a long time, outside Cairo. It wasn't just you—everyone thought I was dead. My father finally tracked me down and brought me back to Washington. I think you and Julia had broken up by then."

I just stared at him. I felt dizzy: even though it was a small piece of the world, of history, it meant everything was different. Everything was changed. I blinked and looked away from him, saw the birch leaves spinning in the breeze, pale gold and green, goldenrod past its prime, tall stalks of valerian with their flower-heads blown to brown vein. I looked back at Christopher: everything was the same.

He said, "I can't believe it's you either, Ivy."

I threw my arms around him. He hugged me awkwardly—he was so much bigger than I was!—and started laughing in delight. "Ivy! I walked all the way over here! From the village, I'm staying at the Inn. That lady at the General Store?"

"Mary?"

"Right, Mary—she remembered me, she said you still lived here—"

"Why didn't you call?"

He looked startled. "You have a phone?"

"Of course I have a phone! Actually, it's a cell phone, and I only got it a year ago, after they put up a tower over on Blue Hill." I drew away from him, balancing on my heels to make myself taller. "Jeez, you're all growed up, Christopher. I'm trying to think, when was the last time I saw you—"

"Twelve years ago. I was just starting grad school in Cairo. I came to see you and Julia in Rockland before I left. Remember?"

I tried, but couldn't; not really. I'd never known him well. He'd been a big ungainly teenager, extremely quiet and sitting at the edges of the room, where he always seemed to be listening carefully to everything his older sister or her friends said. He'd grown up in D.C. and Cairo, but he spent his summers in the States. I first met him when he was twelve or thirteen, a gangly kid into Dungeons & Dragons and Star Wars, who'd recently read Tolkien and had just started on Terry Brooks.

"Jesus, don't read *that*," I'd said, snatching away *The Sword of Shannara* and shoving my own copy of *Love Plucking Rowan Berries* into his big hands. For a moment he looked hurt. Then, "Thanks," he said, and gave me that sweet slow smile. He spent the rest of that summer in our apartment overlooking Rockland Harbor, hunched into a wicker chair on the decrepit back deck as he worked his way through *Sybylla and the Summer Sky*, *Mellors' Plasma Bistro*, *Love Regained in Idleness*, and finally the tattered remnants of *Ardor ex Cathedra*.

"Of course I remember," I said. I swiped at a mosquito, looked up and grinned. "Gosh. You were still a kid then. How're you doing? *What are you doing?* Are you married?"

"Divorced." He raised his arms, yawning, and stretched. His silhouette blotted out the grey sky, the blurred shapes of trees and boulders. "No kids, though. I'm at the Center for Remote Sensing at B.U., coordinating a project near the Chephren Quarries, in the Western Desert. Upper Egypt."

THE LEAST TRUMPS

He dropped his arms and looked down at me again. "So Ivy—would you—how'd you feel about company? I could use a cup of coffee. We can walk back to town if you want. Have a late lunch. Or early dinner."

"Christ, no." I glanced at my raw tattoo. "I should clean that again, before I do anything. And I haven't even had breakfast yet."

"Really? What were you doing? I mean, are you with a customer or something?"

I shook my head. "I was up all night, doing this—" I splayed my fingers above the figure on my thigh. "What time is it, anyway?"

He looked at his watch. "Almost four."

"Almost *four?*" I grabbed his hand and twisted it to see his wristwatch. "I don't believe it! How could I, I—" I shivered. "I slept through the whole day."

Christopher stared at me curiously. I was still holding his wrist, and he turned his hand, gently, his fingers brushing mine. "You okay, Ivy? Did I get you in the middle of something? I can come back—"

"I don't know." I shook my head and withdrew my hand from his; but slowly, so I wouldn't hurt his feelings. "I mean no, I'm fine, just—"

I looked at my thigh. A thread of blood ran down my leg, and as I stared a damselfly landed beneath the tattoo, its thorax a metallic blue needle, wings invisible against my skin. "I was up all night, doing that—"

I pointed at the kneeling man; only from my angle he wasn't kneeling but hanging suspended above my knee, like a bat. "I—I don't think I finished until five o'clock this morning. I had no idea it was so late—"

I could hear the panic in my own voice. I took a deep breath, trying to keep my tone even; but Christopher just put one hand lightly on my shoulder and said, "Hey, it's okay. I really can come back. I just wanted to say hi."

"No. Wait." I counted ten heartbeats, twelve. "I'm okay. I'll be okay. Just, can you row us back?"

"Sure." He stooped to grab a leather knapsack leaning against a tree. "Let's go."

With Christopher in it, the dory sat a good six inches lower in the water, and it took a little longer with him rowing. Halfway across the brief stretch of pond I finally asked him.

"How is Julia?"

My voice was shaky, but he didn't seem to notice. "I don't know. One of my sisters talked to her about five years ago. She was in Toronto, I think. No one's heard from her." He strained at the oars, then glanced at me measuringly. "I never really knew her, you know. She was so much older. I always thought she was kind of a bitch, to tell you the truth. The way she treated you—it made me uncomfortable."

I was silent. My leg ached from the tattoo, searing pain like a bad sunburn. I focused on that, and after a few minutes I could bear to talk.

"Sorry," I said. The dory ground against the shore of the islet. The panic was receding; I could breathe again. "I get these sometimes. Panic attacks. Usually it's not at home, though, only when I go off island."

"That's no fun." Christopher gave me an odd look. Then he clambered out and helped me pull the dory into the reeds. He followed me through the overgrown stands of phlox and aster, up the steps and into the Lonely House. The floor shuddered at his footsteps. I closed the door, looked up at him, and laughed.

"Boy, you sure fill this place up—watch your head, no, wait—"

Too late. As he turned he cracked into a beam. He clutched his head, grimacing. "Shit—I forgot how small this place is—"

I led him to the couch. "Here, sit—I'll get some ice."

I hurried into the kitchen and pulled a tray from the freezer. I was still feeling a little wonky. For about twenty-four hours after you get tattooed, it's like you're coming down with the flu. Your body's been pretty badly treated; your entire immune system fires up, trying to heal itself. I should have just crawled back into bed. Instead I called, "You want something to drink?"

I walked back in with a bowl of ice and a linen towel. Christopher was on the sofa, yanking something from his knapsack.

"I brought this." He held up a bottle of tequila. "And these—"

THE LEAST TRUMPS

He reached into the knapsack again and pulled out three limes. They looked like oversized marbles in his huge hand. "I remember you liked tequila."

I smiled vaguely. "Did I?" It had been Julia who liked tequila, going through a quart every few days in the summer months. I sat beside him on the couch, wrapped the ice in the towel, and held it out. He lowered his head, childlike; and after a moment I very gently touched it. His hair was thick and coarse, darker than his sister's; when I extended my fingers I felt his scalp, warm as though he'd been sitting in the sun all day. "You're hot," I said softly, and felt myself flush. "I mean your head—your skin feels hot. Like heatstroke."

He kept his head lowered, saying nothing. His long hair grazed the top of my thigh. He reached to take my hand, and his was so much bigger, it was as though my own hand was swallowed in a heated glove, his palm calloused, fingertips smooth and hard, soft hairs on the back of his wrist. I said nothing. I could smell him, an acrid smell, not unpleasant but strange; he smelled of limes and sweat, and raw earth, stones washed by the sea. My mouth was dry, and as I moved to place the ice-filled towel on his brow I felt his hand slip from mine, to rest upon the couch between us.

"There." I could feel my heart racing, the frantic thought *It's just a symptom, there's nothing to be scared of, it's just a symptom, it's just—*

"Christopher," I said thickly. "Just—sit. For a minute."

We sat. My entire body felt hot, and damp; I was sweating now myself, not cold anymore, my heartbeat slow and even. From outside came the melancholy sound of the foghorn, the ripple of rain across the lake. The room around us was full of that strange, translucent green light you get here sometimes: being on an island, on an island suspended in fog, droplets of mist and sea and rain mingling to form a shimmering glaucous veil. Outside the window the world seemed to tremble and break apart into countless motes of silver, steel-grey, emerald, then cohere again into a strangely solid-looking mass. As though someone had tossed a stone into a viscous pool, or probed a limb with a needle:

that sense of skin breaking, parting then closing once more around the wound, the world, untold unseen things flickering and diving, ganglia, axons, otters, loons. A bomb goes off, and it takes twelve years to hear its explosion. I lifted my head and saw Christopher watching me. His mouth was parted, his amber eyes sad, almost anguished.

"Ivy," he said. When his mouth touched mine I flinched, not in fear but in shock at how much bigger it was than my own, than Julia's, any woman's. I had not touched a man since I was in high school; and that was a boy, boys. I had never kissed a man. His face was rough; his mouth tasted bitter, of nicotine and salt. And blood, too—he'd bitten his lip from nervousness, my tongue found the broken seam just beneath the hollow of his upper lip, the hollow hidden beneath soft hair, not rough as I had thought it would be, and smelling of some floral shampoo.

It was like nothing I had imagined—and I *had* imagined it, of course. I'd imagined everything, before I fell in love with Julia Sa'adah. I'd fallen in love with *her*—her soul, her *duende*, she would have called it—but in a way it had almost nothing to do with her being another woman. I'd seen movies, porn films even, lots of them, watching with Julia and some of her wilder friends, the ones who were bisexual, or beyond bisexual, whatever that might be; read magazines, novels, pornography, glanced at sites online; masturbated to dim images of what it was like, what I thought it might be like. Even watched once as a couple we knew went at it in our big untidy bed, slightly revved-up antics for our benefit I suspect, a lot of whimpering and operatic sound effects.

This was nothing like that. This was slow, almost fumbling; even formal. He seemed afraid, or maybe it was just that he couldn't believe it, that it wasn't real to him, yet.

"I was always in love with you." He was lying beside me on the couch; not a lot of room left for me, but his broad arm kept me from rolling off. Our shirts were stuffed behind our heads for pillows, I still wore my cut-offs, and he still had his corduroy jeans on. We hadn't gotten further than this. On the floor beside us was the half-empty bottle

THE LEAST TRUMPS

of tequila, Christopher's pocketknife, and the limes, cloven in two so that they looked like enormous green eyes. He was tracing the designs on my body: the full sleeve on my left arm, Chinese water-dragons, stylized waves, all in shades of turquoise and indigo and green. Green is the hardest ink to work with—you mix it with white, the white blends into your skin tone, you don't realize the green pigment is there and you overdo, going over and over until you scar. I'd spent a lot of time with green when I started out; yellow too, another difficult pigment.

"You are so beautiful. All this—" His finger touched coils of vines, ivy that thrust from the crook of my elbow and extended up to my shoulder. His own body was unblemished, as far as I could see. Skin darker than Julia's, shading more to olive than bronze; an almost hairless chest, dappled line of dark hair beneath his navel. He tapped the inside of my elbow, tender soil overgrown with leaves. "That must have hurt."

I shrugged. "I guess. You forget. All you remember afterwards is how intense it was. And then you have these—"

I ran my hand down my arm, turned to sit up. "This is what I did last night." I flexed my leg, pulled up the edge of my shorts to better expose the new tattoo. "See?"

He sat up, ran a hand through his black hair, then leaned forward to examine it. His hair spilled down from his forehead; he had one hand on my upper thigh, the other on his own knee. His broad back was to me, olive skin, a paler crescent just above his shoulders where his neck was bent: a scar. There were others, jagged smooth lines, some deep enough to hide a fingertip. Shrapnel, or glass thrown off by the explosion. His long hair grazed my leg, hanging down like a dark waterfall.

I swallowed, my gaze flicking from his back to what I could glimpse of my tattoo, a small square of flesh framed between his arms, his hair, the ragged blue line of my cut-offs. A tall man, leaning forward so that his hair fell to cover his face. A waterfall. A curtain. Christopher lifted his head to stare at me.

A veil, torn away.

"Shit," I whispered. "Shit, shit—"

I pushed away from him and scrambled to my feet. "What? What is it?" He looked around as though expecting to see someone else in the room with us. "Ivy—"

He tried to grasp me but I pulled away, grabbing my T-shirt from the couch and pulling it on. "Ivy! What happened?" His voice rose, desperate; I shook my head, then pointed at the tattoo.

"This—" He looked at the tattoo, then at me, not comprehending. "That image? I just found it yesterday. On a card. This sort of tarot card, this deck. I got it at a rummage sale—"

I turned and ran into my studio. Christopher followed.

"Here!" I darted to my work table and yanked off the protective blue covering. The table was empty. "It was here—"

I whirled, went to my light table. Acetates and sheets of rag paper were still strewn across it, my pencils and inks were where I'd left them. A dozen pages with failed versions of the card were scattered across the desk, and on the floor. I grabbed them, holding up each sheet and shaking it as though it were an envelope, as though something might fall out. I picked up the pages from the floor, emptied the stainless steel wastebasket and sifted through torn papers and empty ink capsules. Nothing.

The card was gone.

"Ivy?"

I ignored him and ran back into the living room. "Here!" I yanked the paisley-wrapped deck from my purse. "It was like this, it was one of these—"

I tore the scarf open. The deck was still there. I let the scarf fall and fanned the cards out, face-down, a rainbow arc of labyrinthine wheels; then twisted my hand to show the other side.

"They're blank," said Christopher.

I nodded. "That's right. They're all blank. Only there was one—last night—"

I pointed at the tattoo. "That design. There was one card with that design. I copied it. It was with me in the studio, I had it on my drafting table. I ended up tracing it for the stencil."

THE LEAST TRUMPS

"And now you can't find it."

I shook my head. "No. It's gone." I let my breath out in a long low whoosh. I felt sick at my stomach, but it was more like sea-sickness than panic, a nausea I could override if I wanted to. "It's— I won't find it. It's just gone."

My eyes teared. Christopher stood beside me, his face dark with concern. After a minute he said, "May I?"

He held out his hand, and I nodded and gave him the cards. He rifled through them, frowning. "Are they all like this?"

"All except two. There's another one—" I gestured at my purse. "I put it aside. I got them at the rummage sale at St. Bruno's yesterday. They were—"

I stopped. Christopher was still examining the cards, holding them up to the light as though that might reveal some hidden pattern. I said, "You read Walter Burden Fox, right?"

He glanced up at me. "Sure. *Five Windows One Door?* You gave it to me, remember? That first summer I stayed with you down at that place you had by the water. I loved those books." His tone softened; he smiled, a sweet, sad half-smile, and held the cards up as though to show a winning hand. "That really changed my life, you know. After I read them; when I met you. That's when I decided to become an archaeologist. Because they were—well, I don't know how to explain it—"

He tapped the cards thoughtfully against his chin. "I loved those books so much. I couldn't believe it, when I got to the end? That he never finished them. I used to think, if I had only one wish, it would be that somehow he finished that last book. Like maybe if his son hadn't died, or something. Those books just amazed me!"

He shook his head, still marveling. "They made me think how the world might be different than what it is; what we think it is. That there might be things we still don't know, even though we think we've discovered everything. Like the work I do? We scan all these satellite images of the desert, and we can see where ancient sites were, under the sand; under the hills. Places so changed by wind erosion you would never think anything else was ever there—but there were temples and villages, entire cities! Empires! Like in the third book, when you read it and find out there's this whole other history to everything that happened in the first two. The entire world is changed."

The entire world is changed. I stared at him, then nodded. "Christopher—these cards are from his books. The last one. 'The least trumps.' When I got them, there was a little piece of paper—"

My gaze dropped to the floor. The scrap was there, by Christopher's bare foot. I picked up the scrap and handed it to him. "'The least trumps.' It's in the very first chapter of the last book, the one he never finished. Mabel's in bed with Tarquin and he takes out this deck of cards. He holds them in front of her, and when she breathes on them it somehow makes them come alive. There's an implication that everything that happened before has to maybe do with the cards. But he died before he ever got to that part."

Christopher stared at the fragment of paper. "I don't remember," he said at last. He looked at me. "You said there's one other card. Can I see it?"

I hesitated, then went to get my bag. "It's in here."

I took out my wallet. Everything around me froze; my hand was so numb I couldn't feel it when I slid my finger behind my license. I couldn't feel it, it wasn't there at all—

But it was. The wallet fell to the floor. I stood and held the card in both hands. The last one: the least trump. The room around me was grey, the air motionless. In my hands a lozenge of spectral color glimmered and seemed to move. There were airships and flaming birds, two old women dancing on a beach, an exploding star above a high-rise building. The tiny figure of a man wasn't being carried in a litter, I saw now, but lying in a bed borne by red-clad women. Above them all a lash-fringed eye stared down.

I blinked and rubbed my eye; then gave the card to Christopher. When I spoke my voice was thick. "I—I forgot it was so beautiful. That's it. The last one."

THE LEAST TRUMPS

He walked over to the window, leaned against the wall and angled the card to catch the light. "Wow. This is amazing. Was the other one like it? All this detail—"

"No. It was much simpler. But it was still beautiful. It makes you realize how hard it is, drawing something that simple."

I looked down at my leg and smiled wryly. "But you know, I think I got it right."

For some minutes he remained by the window, silent. Suddenly he looked up. "Could you do this, Ivy? On me?"

I stared at him. "You mean a tattoo?" He nodded, but I shook my head. "No. It's far too intricate. It would take days, something like that. Days, just to make a decent stencil. The tattoo would probably take a week, if you were going to do it right."

"This, then." He strode over to me, pointing to the sun that was an eye. "Just that part, there—could you do just that? Like maybe on my arm?"

He flexed his arm, a dark sheen where the bicep rose, like a wave. "Right there—"

I ran my hand across the skin appraisingly. There was a scar, a small one; I could work around it, make it part of the design. "You should think about it. But yeah, I could do it."

"I have thought about it. I want you to do it. Now."

"Now?" I looked at the window. It was getting late; light was leaking from the sky, everything was fading to lavender-grey, twilight. The fog was coming in again, pennons of mist trailing above Green Pond. I could no longer see the far shore. "It's kind of late…"

"Please." He stood above me; I could feel the heat radiating from him, see the card glinting in his hand like a shard of glass. "Ivy—"

His deep voice dropped, a whisper I felt more than heard. "I'm not my sister. I'm not Julia. Please."

He touched the outer corner of my eye, where it was still damp. "Your eyes are so blue," he said. "I forgot how blue they are."

We went into the studio. I set the card on the light table, with the deck beside it, used a loupe to get a better look at the image he wanted.

It would not be so hard to do, really, just that one thing. I sketched it a few times on paper, finally turned to where Christopher sat waiting in the chair beside my work table.

"I'm going to do it freehand. I usually don't, but this is pretty straightforward, and I think I can do it. You sure about this?"

He nodded. He looked a little pale, there beneath the bright lights I work under, but when I walked over to him he smiled. "I'm sure."

I prepped him, swabbing the skin then shaving his upper arm twice, to make sure it was smooth enough. I made sure my machine was thoroughly cleaned, and set up my inks. Black; cerulean and cobalt; Spaulding and Rogers Bright Yellow.

"Ready?"

He nodded, and I set to.

It took about four hours, though I pretty much lost track of the time. I did the outline first, a circle. I wanted it to look very slightly uneven, like this drawing by Odilon Redon I liked—you can see how the paper absorbed his ink, it made the lines look powerful, like black lightning. After the circle was done I did the eye inside it, a half-circle of white, because in the card the eye is looking down, at the world beneath it. Then I did the flattened ovoid of the pupil. Then the flickering lashes all around it. Christopher didn't talk. Sweat ran in long lines from beneath his arms; he swallowed a lot, and sometimes closed his eyes. There was so much muscle beneath his skin that it was difficult to keep it taut—no fat, and the skin wasn't loose enough—so I had to keep pulling it tight. I knew it hurt.

"That's it, take a deep breath. I can stop, if you need to take a break. I need to take a break, anyway."

But I didn't. My hand didn't cramp up; there was none of that fuzzy feeling that comes after holding a vibrating machine for hours at a stretch. Now and then Christopher would shift in his chair, never very much. Once I moved to get a better purchase on his arm, sliding my knee between his legs: I could feel his cock, rigid beneath his corduroys, and hear his breath catch.

THE LEAST TRUMPS

He didn't bleed much. His olive skin made the inks seem to glow, the blue-and-gold eye within its rayed penumbra, wriggling lines like cilia. At the center of the pupil was the scar. You could hardly see it now, it looked like a shadow, the eye's dark heart.

"There." I drew back, shut the machine off and nestled it in my lap. "It's finished. What do you think?"

He pulled his arm towards him, craning his head to look. "Wow. It's gorgeous." He looked at me and grinned ecstatically. "It's fucking gorgeous."

"All right then." I stood and put the machine over by the sink, turned to get some bandages. "I'll just clean it up, and then—"

"Not yet. Wait, just a minute. Ivy."

He towered above me, his long hair lank and skin sticky with sweat, pink fluid weeping from beneath the radiant eye. When he kissed me I could feel his cock against me, heat arcing above my groin. His leg moved, it rubbed against my tattoo and I moaned but it didn't hurt, I couldn't feel it, anything at all, just heat everywhere now, his hands tugging my shirt off then drawing me into the bedroom.

Not like Julia. His mouth was bigger, his hands; when I put my arms around him my fingers scarcely met, his back was so broad. The scars felt smooth and glossy; I thought they would hurt if I touched them but he said no, he liked my fingernails against them, he liked to press my mouth against his chest, hard, as I took his nipple between my lips, tongued it then held it gently between my teeth, the aureole with its small hairs radiating beneath my mouth. He went down on me and that was different too, his beard against the inside of my thighs, his tongue probing deeper; my fingers tangled in his hair and I felt his breath on me, his tongue still inside me when I came. He kissed me and I tasted myself, held his head between my hands, his beard wet. He was laughing. When he came inside me he laughed again, almost shouted; then collapsed alongside me.

"Ivy. Ivy—"

"Shhh." I lay my palm against his face and kissed him. The sheet between us bore the image of a blurred red sun. "Christopher."

"Don't go." His warm hand covered my breast. "Don't go anywhere."

I laughed softly. "Me? I never go anywhere."

We slept. He breathed heavily, but I was so exhausted I passed out before I could shift towards my own side of the bed. If I dreamed, I don't remember; only knew when I woke that everything was different, because there was a man in bed beside me.

"Huh." I stared at him, his face pressed heavily into the pillow. Then I got up, as quietly as I could. I tiptoed into the bathroom, peed, washed my face and cleaned my teeth. I thought of making coffee, and peered into the living room. Outside all was still fog, dark-grey, shredded with white to mark the wind's passing. The clock read six thirty. I turned and crept back to the bedroom.

Christopher was still asleep. I sat on the edge of the bed, languidly, and let my hand rest upon my tattoo. Already it hurt less; it was healing. I looked up at the head of the bed, where my mother's books were, and Walter Burden Fox's. The five identical dust jackets, deep blue, with their titles and Fox's name in gold letters.

Something was different. The last volume, the one completed posthumously by Fox's editor, with the spine that read *Ardor ex Cathedra *Walter Burden Fox*.

I yanked it from the shelf, holding it so the light fell on the spine.

Ardor ex Cathedra *Walter Burden Fox & W.F. Fox

My heart stopped. Around me the room was black. Christopher moved on the bed behind me, yawning. I swallowed, leaning forward until my hands rested on my knees as I opened the book.

ARDOR EX CATHEDRA

By Walter Burden Fox
Completed by Walter F. Fox

─── **THE LEAST TRUMPS** ───

"No," I whispered. Frantically I turned to the end, the final twenty pages that had been nothing but appendices and transcriptions of notes.

Chapter Seventeen: The Least Trumps.

I flipped through the pages in disbelief, and yes, there they were, new chapter headings, every one of them—

Pavell Saved From Drowning. One Leaf Left. Hermalchio and Lachrymatory. Villainous Saltpetre. The Scars. The Radiant Eye. I gasped, so terrified my hands shook and I almost dropped it, turning back to the frontispiece.

Completed by Walter F. Fox.

I went to the next page—the dedication.

To the memory of my father

I cried out. Christopher sat up, gasping. "What is it? Ivy, what happened—"

"The book! It's different!" I shook it at him, almost screaming. "He didn't die! The son—he finished it, it's all different! *It's changed.*"

He took the book from me, blinking as he tried to wake up. When he opened it I stabbed the frontispiece with my finger.

"There! See—it's all changed. *Everything has changed.*"

I slapped his arm, the raw image that I'd never cleaned, never bandaged. "Hey! Stop—Ivy, stop—"

I started crying, sat on the edge of the bed with my head in my hands. Behind me I could hear him turning pages. Finally he sighed, put a hand on my shoulder and said, "Well, you're right. But—well, couldn't it be a different edition? Or something?"

I shook my head. Grief filled me, and horror: something deeper than panic, deeper even than fear. "No," I said at last. My voice was hoarse. "It's the book. It's everything. We changed it, somehow—the card—"

I stood and walked into my studio, slowly, as though I were drunk. I put the light on and looked at my work table.

"There," I said dully. In the middle of the table, separate from the rest of the deck, was the last card. It was blank. "The last one. The last trump. Everything is different."

I turned to stare at Christopher. He looked puzzled, concerned but not frightened. "So?" He shook his head, ventured a small smile. "Is that bad? Maybe it's a good book."

"That's not what I mean." I could barely speak. "I mean, everything will be different. Somehow. Even if it's just in little ways—it won't be what it was—"

Christopher walked into the living room. He looked out the window, then went to the door and opened it. A bar of pale gold light slanted into the room and across the floor, to end at my feet. "Sun's coming up." He stared at the sky, shading his hands. "The fog is lifting. It'll be nice, I think. Hot though."

He turned and looked at me. I shook my head. "No. No. I'm not going out there."

Christopher laughed, then gave me that sad half-smile. "Ivy—"

He walked over to me and tried to put his arms around me, but I pushed him away and walked into the bedroom. I began pulling on the clothes I'd worn last night. "No. No. Christopher—I can't. I won't."

"Ivy." He watched me, then shrugged and came into the room and got dressed, too. When he was done, he took my hand.

"Ivy, listen." He pulled me to his side, with his free hand pointed at the book lying on the bed. "Even if it *is* different—even if *everything* is different—why does that have to be so terrible? Maybe it's not. Maybe it's better."

I began to shake my head, crying again. "No no no…"

"Look—"

Gently he pulled me into the living room. Full sun was streaming through the windows now; outside, on the other side of Green Pond, a deep-blue sky glowed above the green treetops. There was still mist

THE LEAST TRUMPS

close to the ground but it was lifting. The pines moved in the wind, and the birches; I heard a fox barking, no not a fox: a dog. "Look," Christopher said, and pointed at the open front door. "Why don't we do this, you come with me, I'll stay right by you—shit, I'll *carry* you if you want—we'll just go look, okay?"

I shook my head, No; but when he eased slowly through the door I followed, his hand tight around mine but not too tight: I could slip free if I wanted. He wouldn't keep me. He wouldn't make me go.

"Okay," I whispered. I shut my eyes then opened them. "Okay, okay."

Everything looked the same. A few more of the asters had opened, deep mauve in the misty air. One tall yellow coneflower was still in bloom. We walked through them, to the shore, to the dory. There were dragonflies and damselflies inside it, and something else. A butterfly, brilliant orange edged with cobalt blue, its wings fringed, like an eye. We stepped into the boat and the butterfly lifted into the air, hanging between us then fluttering across the water, towards the western shore. My gaze followed it, watching as it rose above The Ledges then continued down the hillside.

"I've never been over there," said Christopher. He raised one oar to indicate where the butterfly had gone. "What's there?"

"You can see." It hurt to speak, to breathe; but I did it. I didn't die. You can't die, from this. "Katherine—she always says you can see Ireland from there, on a clear day."

"Really? Let's go that way, then."

He rowed to the farther shore. Everything looked different, coming up to the bank; tall blue flowers like irises, a yellow sedge that had a faint fragrance like lemons. A turtle slid into the water, its smooth black carapace spotted with yellow and blue. As I stepped onto the shore I saw something like a tiny orange crab scuttling into the reeds.

"You all right?" Christopher cocked his head and smiled. "Brave little ant. Brave Ivy."

I nodded. He took my hand, and we walked down the hillside. Past The Ledges, past some boulders I had never even known were there, through a stand of trees like birches only taller, thinner, their leaves round and shimmering, silver-green. There was still a bit of fog here but it was lifting, I felt it on my legs as we walked, a damp cool kiss upon my left thigh. I looked over at Christopher, saw a golden rayed eye gazing back at me, a few flecks of dried blood beneath. Overhead, the trees moved and made a high rustling sound in the wind. The ground beneath us grew steeper, the clefts between rocks overgrown with thick masses of small purple flowers. I had never known anything to bloom so lushly, this late in the year. Below us I could hear the sound of waves, not the crash and violent roar of the open Atlantic but a softer sound; and laughter, a distant voice that sounded like my mother's. The fog was almost gone but I still could not glimpse the sea; only through the moving scrim of leaves and mist a sense of vast space, still dark because the sun had not struck it yet in full, pale grey-blue, not empty at all, not anymore. There were lights everywhere, gold and green and red and silver, stationary lights and lights that wove slowly across the lifting veil, as through wide streets and boulevards, haloes of blue and gold hanging from ropes across a wide sandy shore.

"There," said Christopher, and stopped. "There, do you see?"

He turned and smiled at me, reached to touch the corner of my eye, blue and gold; then pointed. "Can you see it now?"

I nodded. "Yeah. Yeah, I do."

The laughter came again, louder this time. Someone calling a name. The trees and grass shivered as a sudden brilliance overtook them, the sun breaking at last from the mist behind me.

"Come on!" said Christopher, and turning he sprinted down the hill. I took a deep breath, looked back at what was behind us. I could just see the grey bulk of The Ledges, and beyond them the thicket of green and white and grey that was the Lonely House. It looked like a picture from one of my mother's books, a crosshatch hiding a hive, a honeycomb; another world. "Ivy!"

Christopher's voice echoed from not very far below me. "Ivy, you have to see this!"

"Okay," I said, and followed him.

Illyria

ROGAN AND I were cousins; our fathers were identical twins. Rogan was the youngest of six boys, I the youngest of six girls. Growing up, there were always jokes about this symmetry, even though everyone in the Tierney clan bred prolifically—there were twenty-six first cousins, divided among five families.

Still, only Rogan and I were ever called kissing cousins, despite the fact that our older brothers and sisters were also paired off, age-wise, as neatly as if our parents had timed their conjugal relations so that their children would all be born within a few days of each other, and Rogan and I actually on the same day. I arrived in the early morning, Rogan moments before midnight. Later, when we were adolescents, the facts of our birth (we always thought of it as *our* birth) conveniently fulfilled our need to find meaning in everything about ourselves.

So Rogan was darkness, I was light, and over the years the metaphor was extended to include just about every doomy literary reference you can imagine—Caliban and Ariel, Peter Pan and Wendy, Heathcliff and Cathy, Abelard and Heloise, Tristan and Iseult, Evnissyen and Nissyen…

You get the idea.

Ours had been a noted theatrical clan, a line of performers stretching back to Shakespeare's day. Our great-grandmother was the once-famous actress Madeline Armin Tierney. I was her namesake. Yeats was rumored to have written his poem "The Last Stone of Carrowkeel" for Madeline, and our aunt Kate claimed that the character of Caitilin Ni Murrachu in James Stephens's *The Crock of Gold* was inspired by her, as well.

But the family forsook the stage. Madeline gave up acting when she married. Her children and grandchildren regarded the theater with a mixture of bemusement and condescension, fear and guilt, the same emotions stirred by the even rarer mention of sex.

Only Aunt Kate dwelled on this abandonment with grim persistence.

"Like cutting down a tree in its prime," she'd tell Rogan and me, the only two who ever listened. "Nothing good ever comes of that. Never ever ever."

There were remnants of family history scattered throughout our homes at Arden Terrace. Framed billets advertising performances by Edwin Booth or Otis Skinner or Charlotte Cushman, with various Tierneys in supporting roles. Peter Pangloss in *The Heir at Law,* Madame Trentoni in *Captain Jinks;* the Fool, Hermione, Dogberry. A lurid painting of a nameless ancestor as one of the witches in *Macbeth.* Mother-of-pearl opera glasses, silver spoons engraved with obscure jokes: "To His Highness from a Rogue."

We retained theatrical superstitions, as well, unmoored from their element and thus meaningless. Peacock feathers were banned from all our homes. It was considered lucky for a cat to sleep on one of our parochial school uniforms. In the carriage house where Madeline once stored her tattered scripts, and where Aunt Kate now lived, a ghost light burned in an upper window, a forty-watt bulb in a floor lamp without a shade. Our attics were full of ruined costumes, tattered moth's-wings of burned velvet and lace that had been court gowns; crinolines reduced to hoops of whalebone; black satin disks that, when smacked upon a cousin's unsuspecting head, burgeoned into top hats; lady's gloves that still smelled like the ladies who had last worn them; sinister puppets and jointed dolls used as models for the wardrobe mistress; old photos of Fairhaven, the island in Maine where Madeline had kept a summer home.

But most of the photographs of Madeline had ended up in Aunt Kate's house. Faded silver-print and sepia images, water damaged or foxed with mold. Still, you could see how striking she'd been, with large, very pale eyes that looked ghostly in black-and-white, a high forehead and thick dark hair, melancholy mouth, and the faintest constellation of freckles across her apple cheeks. She was piquant rather than pretty; yet there was also something unsettling in her looks, though maybe that was just the old-fashioned photography. All the pictures seemed slightly out of focus.

And I could never imagine her eyes having a color. Were they blue? Gray? Green?

They looked like ice. I couldn't imagine her ever crying.

Fey, said Aunt Kate whenever she mentioned her. A word I didn't understand, especially when she added, "You look like her, Maddy."

Because I was ugly. Really ugly; everyone thought so. Crooked buckteeth and glasses, upturned nose, bad skin. The grown-ups called me Skinny Wretch—fondly, but still. Only Aunt Kate would look at me and shake her head, sitting at her dressing table surrounded by her beautiful clothes, Pucci dresses, Betsey Johnson shifts, Yves Saint Laurent blouses transparent as a screen door. On her right hand she wore a ring that had belonged to my great-grandmother, with an emerald roughly the shape and size of a cat's eye.

"You're beautiful, Maddy. Those legs? Just you wait. And when your braces come off? And the glasses? *Glamorous.* You're going to be so *glamorous—*"

And she'd give me a special bar of soap from France, or astringent ointment from London that smelled like coal smoke. "Just you wait."

At my age, my great-grandmother was already beautiful. By the time she was sixteen, she was famous. As a girl, Madeline created unforgettable portrayals of Rosalind, Juliet, Titania, Perdita, and especially Viola, as well as less memorable turns in works like *Storming Castle Dora* and *The Blue-Footed Boy.*

"Unforgettable." That was the word attached to Madeline throughout her career, in every torn clipping I ever read, every review of every performance, every stagy publicity photo that appeared as ancient and remote to me as a stone tablet. Madeline's Unforgettable Cleopatra. Her Unforgettable Viola. Her Unforgettable Series of Unforgettable Triumphs, Never to Be Forgotten.

Only, of course, it's all forgotten now. It was all forgotten then, since none of our parents had ever known Madeline as anything but a fractious old woman holed up in Fairview, her decaying Yonkers mansion. Even in her dotage she was too self-absorbed to pay much attention to her own five children, let alone her grandchildren.

But she'd made a good marriage to a wealthy developer named Rosco O'Meara, a man who anticipated the late-twentieth-century vogue for gated communities by nearly a century. They had five children, all of whom retained Madeline's maiden name. Almost unheard-of at the time, but Madeline belonged to a dynasty, and she was determined it would live on. Her twin brothers, also noted thespians, died of misadventure and left no children. She was the last of her line.

In the early 1900s, Rosco built Arden Terrace, a speculative venture consisting of a score of expansive Shingle-style and Tudor and Gothic homes, along with carriage houses, guesthouses, and various outbuildings, in a huge cul-de-sac overlooking the Hudson River. Artists flocked there from the city—North Yonkers was an exurb in those days, with fields and woodlands and bald eagles nesting along the river—and Arden Terrace became an enclave of successful writers and actors and editors, doctors and lawyers and a stockbroker.

Lovely and otherworldly as Arden Terrace was, it was also vulnerable. When the stock market crashed in 1929, no fewer than seven residents killed themselves, including Madeline's husband. Not, however, Madeline, who seemed to have absorbed the cumulative resilience and resourcefulness of all those plucky heroines she'd once played (her sole substantial flop was as Juliet) and who during the Depression bought up, one by one, all the houses surrounding her own. Her children ended up living in those homes, like hermit crabs scuttling into empty shells; and then *their* children, Madeline's grandchildren; and finally my own generation of kids.

ILLYRIA

By which time Arden Terrace resembled some mad architectural folly spread out across one of the more desirable pieces of real estate in the city. Year after year, the Hudson River moved slowly, far below the turrets and balconies of our ersatz fortress; the tulip trees shed their yellow leaves; and snow covered the slate roofs of the carriage houses and guest cottages where the oldest Tierneys now lived. When summer came, the cul-de-sac was taken over by an occupying army of children in Keds and dungarees and striped shirts from John Wanamaker. Rock and roll blared from upstairs bedrooms, while a legion of mothers and aunts and grandmothers sat on Fairview's immense porch, talking and smoking and drinking whiskey sours as they watched the sun set over the Palisades.

Rogan's father and mine grew up in Fairview, along with their sisters. Later, Rogan's father inherited the mansion—he was the older twin by twelve minutes—and Rogan grew up there. My father moved into the house across the street, a less grand Queen Anne home that still had five bathrooms, exorbitant for the time, and six bedrooms.

That was where I grew up. Though the truth was, I spent as much time at Rogan's home as my own, and nearly as much time where our other cousins lived. During the day we all attended St. Brendan's School, several blocks away, up a winding hill shaded by old apartment buildings and elm trees, all now long gone. Every afternoon we raced home and changed from our uniforms into what were then called play clothes—a misnomer, since our after-school activities were more like the extended rehearsal for a street-theater production of *Lord of the Flies*. We moved from house to house to house like invading army ants. We devoured everything we could find, terrorized the youngest children, raided toy chests and attics, crowded into basement rec rooms to watch *Star Trek* and *Superman*, stole each other's record albums and baseball cards and Barbie clothes, gave too much food to goldfish and dogs that were not our own—all until we were driven back outside by irate adults.

Whereupon we'd move next door, or across the road, or down to the woods overlooking the river, and the whole cycle would begin again.

And Rogan?

There was never a time when I did not know Rogan.

We were the youngest in our generation of cousins. As the youngest girl, I wasn't coddled; mostly tolerated by my sisters and ignored by our parents.

But as the youngest boy, Rogan was bullied and beaten and tormented, relentlessly, cruelly; almost absently.

"Why?" I once demanded of Rogan's brother Michael. I'd jumped onto him from a first-floor balcony at my house when I saw him pounding Rogan on the lawn below. Michael grabbed me and tossed me onto the early-spring grass as though I were a burr that had stuck to him, and not a gangly fourteen-year-old girl with glasses. Rogan ran off, his face crimson with tears. I stumbled to my feet and shouted at Michael, "Why can't you just leave him alone?"

"What?" Michael looked at me, his blue eyes grave with astonishment. I might have asked him why we had to eat or drink or attend Mass on Sundays. "Because he'd be *spoiled*."

Spoiled. It was the worst thing you could be. Only children were spoiled, not that we knew any. Aunt Kate, who'd never married and who had kept her looks, along with a pied-à-terre in Greenwich Village—she was spoiled. Younger siblings by definition were spoiled, since in some obscure way they'd spoiled the paradise occupied by their older brothers and sisters, simply by being born.

So it went without saying that Rogan and I were in danger of being the most spoiled of all. What made it worse was that Rogan had trouble at school. We were in the same class. He was smart but fidgety, the nuns would yell at him for daydreaming, he couldn't focus on homework.

I helped him, reading books out loud, the two of us taking turns; not just schoolbooks but the books we read for fun. In eighth grade that year we'd read *Macbeth*, and at home Rogan and I did all the different parts, Rogan the men, me the women.

And this, too, was considered some obscure betrayal by our brothers and sisters. Since our parents couldn't be trusted to do anything, it was up to our siblings and cousins to make sure we didn't end up flouncing along North Broadway in our underwear, disgracing the rest of the clan. I had my share of black eyes and bruises, but most of these came from defending Rogan. I can see now that much of what he endured was probably the result of rampant, if unspoken, homophobia in a large family of boys and the larger tribe of male cousins. Gays weren't invented yet, not in North Yonkers anyway. You were a guy, or you were a faggot.

The irony, of course, was that Rogan wasn't gay. He was in love with me, as I was with him.

And that was maybe the only thing worse than being gay.

No one had ever heard of DNA back then, not in my family anyway, and our grasp of genetics was practically nonexistent. But, because our fathers were identical twins, their children had all been told—warned—that we were closer than the other cousins.

"More like stepchildren," said Aunt Dita.

"Half-brothers and -sisters," my mother corrected her.

"Kissing cousins," said Aunt Roz. That would be the cue for everyone to cast a cold eye upon Rogan and me.

Now I waited till Michael turned to look for his brother, then I darted up behind him and kicked him squarely in the back of the knee. Michael shouted in pain and crumpled to the grass, his arm lashing out to grab me.

But I was already gone.

I knew where Rogan was—beneath Fairview. A labyrinth of storerooms, root cellars, garden rooms, and disused workshops tunneled under my great-grandmother's house. Once, they'd been tended by a small army of servants and gardeners. For the last fifty years, they'd pretty much fallen into decay. All the doors and stairways that led to the upper house had been boarded up.

Now, the only entrance was behind a thick curtain of wisteria that hung from the great porch above. You had to know where it was—a gap in the wooden trellis that peeled from the house like a scab from a wound. The wisteria looked beautiful, blade-shaped leaves and clusters of blossoms like grapes made of blue tissue. But the flowers smelled horrible, like rotting meat, and they drew clouds of greenflies and bluebottles.

Rogan wasn't afraid of the flies and wisteria. He wasn't afraid of anything.

But I was. I took a deep breath and pinched my nose, closed my eyes and shoved aside the moving tangle of leaves, and ducked inside.

Beneath the porch, it was dim and cool and smelled of earth and old paint. A harlequin pattern of sunlight filtered through the trellis, pied with the shadows of leaves and vines. There were clay pots and rusted garden tools underfoot; also large black beetles and yellow- or blue-spotted salamanders that looked like lost toys. There were brown recluse spiders, too, which various elderly aunts claimed had caused the deaths of careless servants in an earlier day; cave crickets; and, flanking the small raised doorway that led into a dark anteroom, a half dozen plaster leprechauns that my grandfather had brought back from one of his yearly trips to Connemara. The leprechauns were the size of small children, and painted in too-bright colors—bottle-green jackets, scarlet caps, yellow belt buckles. Most of the paint had gone from their faces, which gave them the eerie look of grave monuments.

I was afraid of them, too.

Rogan knew that. And so he waited, as always, squatting inside the doorway with one hand already outstretched to pull me up beside him. I flapped my hand at the ground, scattering invisible bugs, then sat.

"Thanks," said Rogan.

He reached into a niche between two wallboards where we kept a candle in a blue glass holder and a box of matches, lit the candle, and set it back in the wall. The unsteady light washed over him and I stared, as always; unembarrassed because we were alone, and it was dark. And it was Rogan.

He was so beautiful. I never understood why it wasn't spoken: that he was the most beautiful boy you had ever seen. Or maybe it was only

ILLYRIA

me who felt that. The Tierneys were all tall, and our hair was brown or fair or tawny, and we all had deep-blue eyes. There hadn't been a Tierney with anything but blue eyes in five hundred years, my father said. All of the Tierney boys were handsome in a bluff, clean-shaven Hyannisport way, and most of the girls were pretty.

Rogan looked like he'd fallen from a painting.

He was tall like the rest of us, with long legs, long arms, square sturdy hands. His hair was reddish-gold, fine as a baby's hair, and he grew it as long as he could until his father dragged him to the barber up in Getty Square. He had high cheekbones in a feline face—not like a house cat's; more a cougar or lynx, something strong and furtive and quick. His nose was like mine, although it had been broken more than once. His mouth was wide and surprisingly delicate, the only thing about him that might have seemed girlish. Until he smiled, and showed narrow white teeth that were also like an animal's. He had huge, deep-set eyes—wary eyes, which made it slightly alarming when he suddenly turned them on you—and they weren't Tierney blue but a true aquamarine, the palest blue-green, changeable as sea-water in sunlight or cloud.

But the most striking thing about him was the way he moved. Gracefully—sensually, I would have said if I were older—but also with this strange lightness, almost an unease; as though he had trouble getting his footing. His arms moved as if drawing patterns in the air; he'd tilt his head sometimes like he heard something. Even his furtive gaze wasn't sly but oddly watchful.

Yet it wasn't a vigilance that protected him from his brothers or his father, and it was also completely unconscious—I knew because I watched him constantly, had been watching him for as long as I could remember, and maybe for longer.

Once I eavesdropped, unseen, as Aunt Kate and my mother discussed him. The two of them didn't like each other: my mother was suspicious of her sister-in-law's oddly ageless beauty, her chic black gamine hair and expensive clothes, and, it was whispered, her wealthy lovers.

"Fey," Aunt Kate said. She twisted her emerald ring as though it hurt her finger. "Rogan's fey." My mother must have made a face, because Aunt Kate went on, annoyed. "That's *not* what it means."

I heard my mother draw on her cigarette. "All I can say is, if I ever had a red-headed child, I'd strangle it."

Now, watching Rogan, all I wanted to do was touch him. Instead I clutched my own skinny thighs and looked at him sideways, while he held up the match and watched it burn to his fingertips. Finally he tossed the match aside.

"Listen," he said.

I cocked my head. "I don't hear anything."

"No, idiot—listen to *me*. My voice. Listen to me talking. Talking talking talking. Hear it?"

I did. "Wow," I said. "It broke!"

"Yeah. And listen to *this*—"

He put his hands on his knees and leaned forward, his face jutting into the darkness until I could no longer see it. He began to sing.

"When all beside a vigil keep,
The West's asleep, the West's asleep…"

My flesh crawled. I knew the song from one of my father's Clancy Brothers records. "The West's Awake."

"And long a brave and haughty race
Honoured and sentinelled the place.
Sing, Oh! not e'en their sons' disgrace
Can quite destroy their glory's trace…"

I had never heard it sung like this. I had never heard *anything* sung like this, or heard a guy's voice remotely sound like this. It wasn't even singing; more a sustained wail, Rogan's mouth somehow shaping words that seemed to claw against the voice that formed them. He was *keening,* in a tenor so pure and wild and primal that it didn't even sound like music: it was like being burned by a song. It was like hearing something die.

> "But hark! a voice like thunder spake,
> The West's awake! The West's awake..."

His voice rose to a falsetto, then fell. It held the last notes for so long that I couldn't tell when they faded into an echo, until the echo itself dropped into silence and Rogan sank back into the half-light beside me.

"Holy cow." I was crying—when had I started to cry?—not just my face wet but my hands, my shirt, my jeans. "Rogan, that—"

I stopped. His chin was tucked against his chest, his hands clutching his head as he rocked back and forth, mouth bared in a grimace as he moaned something over and over again, words I couldn't understand. I didn't even know if they *were* words. He looked ghastly, unearthly; like a picture I had once seen of a body trapped in a lava flow. I stared, too terrified to move, until he turned toward me and I saw his eyes, his own face streaked with tears; and suddenly I understood what he was saying—

"I made that—I made that—I made that—"

I grabbed him, hugging him to my skinny chest as we both began to laugh hysterically.

"That was me!" He almost shrieked, and I covered his mouth with my hand, still laughing. "That was *me!*"

"Shut up! Rogan, shhh—"

He bit my finger. I yelped and snatched my hand back, then fell on him. He held me so hard I punched him.

"You're choking me!"

He relaxed his hold. I rubbed my face against his shirt to dry my tears, then pressed my fist against his chest. His heart pounded so hard it was like another fist hammered inside him and I splayed my fingers, imagining I could hold it, like a baseball, or a stone. He smelled as he always did, of detergent and sweat, his mother's Chanel No. 5, and dirt and chalk dust.

But he smelled of something else, too. He smelled the way his brothers did, and my older boy cousins; their tree-house smell, sweetish and rank, slightly ammoniacal; at once green and earthen. No one had told me what that smell was, and nobody ever would.

But I knew.

"Maddy," he whispered.

He ran his finger along my chapped lips, then lightly tapped the wires of my braces. I took off my glasses as he tilted his head and brought his mouth close, rubbing his lips across mine. His breath was warm and sour. I stroked his hair, tentatively, drew my hand down to cup his ear then touched his cheek, the line of his jaw. He'd always felt like me, smooth and clean. I had never noticed hair on his face but I felt it now, his skin damp and slightly abraded, like touching a cat's tongue. He angled himself so that he was on top of me and gently pushed me down, so that we were lying face-to-face.

We stayed like that forever, breathing, sometimes moving. I felt as though my clothes had disappeared, and my skin; as though my bones had uncurled like ferns to twine with his. Finally he stirred and touched my face.

"Where are your glasses?"

We sat up. The candle had burned out. The dark underground room felt warmer than it had earlier, and it no longer smelled like dirt and earthworms. It smelled like Rogan. It smelled like us.

"It will all be different now," he said. His tone absent, as though reciting something he only half remembered. "Will you help me with that stuff for math?"

"Sure," I said, and scrambled after him to head back outside.

◆ ◆ ◆

ROGAN WAS RIGHT: it was different. Not all at once, and not immediately.

But the world changed, everything about us changed. Everything about me, certainly.

ILLYRIA

The school year ended. It was the summer before high school. Early in July my braces came off. After that I refused to get my hair cut in the ghastly pixie cut I'd had since I was two years old. The stuff Aunt Kate gave me for my skin began to work. My face cleared up.

And I started to wean myself from my glasses, using them only to read, or when my parents were around. The rest of the time I kept them in an ugly orange case in my pocket, until the day that I forgot the case in my room.

"Maddy." My mother frowned when she saw me at breakfast. "Where are your glasses? You didn't lose them?"

I took a deep breath. "I don't need them anymore."

My mother made the face she made at dinner when someone said they weren't hungry.

"I really don't," I said quickly. "I can read fine. Aunt Kate said you should take me to see Dr. Gordon and he'll tell you."

"Aunt Kate." My mother glowered. But she did take me to see Dr. Gordon.

And it was true, Dr. Gordon said I didn't need my glasses. Someday I would, when I was older, but for now, as long as I didn't get headaches, I could do without them.

"Hooray!" said Rogan. He had grown two more inches, and was now a full head taller than me. "You look a *lot* better."

Aunt Kate regarded me more measuringly.

"I'll take you to my salon." She rubbed the ends of my hair between her fingers and grimaced. "Alain will know what to do about this."

The next time she went into the city, I went with her. My hair was trimmed, not cut, by Alain, a man who wore one chandelier earring and motorcycle boots.

"Beautiful eyes," he said. He glanced at my aunt in the mirror. "How old?"

"She'll be fifteen in October."

"Ohhhh." He smiled at me and arched his eyebrows rakishly. "You're in high school!"

"In the fall," I said.

He nodded, bending to snip my bangs. "Boyfriend?"

I looked up to see Aunt Kate staring back at me from the mirror, the blue Tierney eyes brilliant and faintly threatening in that elegant, ageless face.

"No," she said.

When Alain was finished, Aunt Kate paid him, then took me to lunch at O'Neals' Baloon.

"Good," she said. She watched approvingly as I ate my hot fudge sundae. "This will grow out nicely, Maddy. You look very glamorous."

Rogan had changed as well. He wasn't just taller—his voice had grown, too. At night I'd listen as he stepped onto the tiny balcony outside his room and sang "Wild Horses" in that eerie keening tenor. When he stopped, we'd double over laughing as all the Tierney dogs began to howl, followed by a chorus of angry grown-ups yelling at them to shut up.

In July Rogan joined the choir at St. Brendan's. Not the children's choir, which was all girls—not me, I couldn't sing—but the grown-up choir, which sang at ten thirty High Mass. Our fathers attended Mass on Saturday afternoon so they could play golf on Sunday morning. Our mothers and siblings went to twelve o'clock Mass on Sunday, for those laggards who slept late. Aunt Kate only went at Christmas and Easter.

But I'd walk up with Rogan and sit in the middle of the church (High Mass was never crowded) and listen, bewitched, as his voice soared through the vaulted space, chanting the *Kyrie* and *Te Deum* and *Gloria in excelsis.* It made my flesh crawl. Not just me: I could see other members of the congregation shift uncomfortably in their pews, Tierney great-uncles and -aunts and the Connells' grandparents all staring fixedly at their missalettes until old Monsignor Burke sang the Recessional in his quavering voice, and the Mass was ended.

Only Mrs. Rossi, our diminutive school secretary, seemed to feel as I did. Once she waited with me outside the church for Rogan to come down from the choir loft.

"That was so beautiful, Rogan," she whispered as the rest of the congregation hurried to their cars. "You should be singing at St. Patrick's Cathedral."

Rogan waited till she left, then made a face.

"Another church? Screw that," he said, and we walked home.

Back on Arden Terrace, we hung out with kids from school who came down from Mile Square Road. Our siblings and cousins were all in high school now, or college. One of Aunt Trixie's boys had joined the military. My oldest sister, Brigid, was engaged. Occasionally Michael would pound Rogan, or try to, but Rogan was bigger now. After a while Michael lost interest in the sport and, concomitantly, in Rogan himself. We weren't watched as closely as we once were. When our parents went out to dinner at the club, Rogan and I were left alone.

Or sort of alone. My sisters, perversely, paid more attention to me now than when I was younger; a chilly feminine vigilance to ensure I did nothing to embarrass them, especially with Rogan.

So he and I would engineer games of hide-and-seek with the kids from Mile Square Road, and *then* disappear. We'd hide beneath the porch at Fairview, and forgo the candle to lie in the dark with Rogan on top of me. We'd hold each other and pretend we'd been shipwrecked.

"I can't breathe," Rogan would whisper as he clutched me. Sometimes he'd pinch my nostrils shut. "You can't breathe, your mouth is filled with water..."

We knew we weren't drowning. We knew what we were doing, even though I never quite had a word for it, Rogan's smell and breath and our hearts hammering as we moved, the raw feel of my groin rubbed beneath layers of cotton and denim. Afterward we'd lie on the cold earth and talk and listen to the voices of the others outside as they looked for us, excited then laughing then irritated then bored and finally, as the summer wore toward fall, angry and obdurate. The day came when Rogan called and asked Ookie Connell to come over. I could tell by Rogan's face that the answer was no, and when he put the phone down he shrugged.

"What?" I asked.

"He says if we have a baby it'll be retarded."

In September we started high school. The only two classes we had together were English and Latin. For the latter, Sister Mary Clark made a point of separating us.

"But I help him," I protested. "I help him concentrate."

"I'm sure you do." Sister Mark Clark had taught two generations of Tierneys. She liked my sisters, and she liked me. She was a bony, raw-faced woman who still wore a habit and laughed a lot, though her eyes were long and bright as a knife. "Rogan needs to concentrate by himself. He can't rely on you, Madeline. He has to do his own work."

"He does! He—"

She grabbed my elbow and pinched it hard. "I want you over here."

She guided me to the other side of the classroom. I sat, scowling, as Sister Mary Clark started back across the room. Abruptly she stopped and turned to me. Her eyes narrowed.

"Madeline, where are your glasses?"

I stared back. "I don't need them anymore."

She looked at me, then at Rogan watching me from the other side of the room. He flushed, and her gaze hardened.

"Do not peer too close," she said, deliberately misquoting Pindar. "Everyone, get out yesterday's homework."

A few weeks later we were walking home from school. It was the end of September, a Friday afternoon. Rogan wore a battered fatigue coat over his uniform; I wore his brown corduroy jacket, too big for me. Several other kids from school walked near us. Their voices dropped as they passed. Ookie Connell said something I couldn't hear, and the others laughed.

"I quit the choir," Rogan said as we started down the hill toward Arden Terrace, walking along the curb so we could kick through drifts of leaves.

"How come?"

"Old Mrs. Connell complained." He shook his head, his red-gold hair spilling to his collar. "She said my singing distracted her."

I laughed. "Distracted! Can she even hear you?"

But Rogan didn't smile.

"She's a bitch." He glanced back to make sure the others were gone, then leaned down to touch his head to mine. "This friend of Michael's, Derek, he was over last night. He's in a band. He told me I should come hear them. He said maybe I could sing with them sometime."

"Really?" I smiled, but felt a twinge of unease. I didn't recognize it as jealousy. "Where do they play?"

"I dunno. Someplace in Ardsley. Listen, I want to show you something. When you come over. I found a place."

A place. I knew what that meant. When summer ended, our spot beneath the porch grew cold and overrun with beetles. Field mice sought shelter against the coming winter, and hibernating bats.

"The isle is sinking into the ice," I'd warned Rogan as we lay there in the chilly dark. "We must seek safe harbor, or drown."

"There is no safe harbor," he'd said, and kissed me till I couldn't breathe.

Now I slowed to look at him. The worn fatigue coat made him seem older—a beautiful stranger, like someone on an album cover. His hair was the same color as the maple leaves, his cheeks were reddened from the cold. His eerie eyes caught the cloudless sweep of sky and glowed a startling, mineral blue.

"Is it a good place?" I asked.

Rogan grinned. "It's a *great* place. Wait'll you see it."

When we reached Arden Terrace I went home and changed. My sisters were out. My mother had taken a job in the women's department at Wanamaker's and wouldn't be home till dinnertime. I grabbed my Latin text and went across the street to Rogan's house, to pretend to do homework.

Rogan's father, like mine, was a successful stockbroker, but he always said there wasn't enough money in the world to maintain Fairview. Everywhere shingles were missing. Paint flaked from the balconies on the upper floors. The great porch sagged where it overlooked the Hudson, its wicker furniture unsprung and its balustrades devoured by carpenter ants.

Inside, the house was cold and smelled of stale cigarette smoke and dust. Rogan's mother, too, had taken a job. Autumn leaves had blown across the antique Caucasian carpets. There were semicircles of ash in front of the fireplaces; in the kitchen and bathrooms, sinks bore serpentine trails of rust beneath their faucets.

But on the third floor, where Rogan slept, little had changed. Adults ventured there seldom, chiefly to complain or enact justice: it had the austere air of benign neglect associated with a lakeside home in the off-season. Rogan's brothers Michael and Thomas had the two bedrooms overlooking the front of the house. As usual, they were off with their girlfriends. Rogan stood on the landing, waiting for me.

"Greetings, fair Amazon." He swept out his arm in welcome. "Come into the parlor."

Once his room had been the nursery. It was a wide, sunlit space that occupied nearly half of the third floor, with a row of windows that looked straight across the river, though when you gazed out you mostly saw unbroken sky. It should have seemed cheerful and bright.

Instead, the room felt empty and exposed, even desolate. Temporary quarters, despite Rogan's having lived there his entire life. A sink stood in one corner, an institutional relic of nursery life, and next to it the door that opened onto a tiny morning balcony, big enough for just one person. There were alcoves filled with moldering books and Samuel French scripts that had been defaced by mice. Rag rugs covered the floor. A creepy archaeology of wallpaper peeled in layers from the walls—fox hunters, lurid pink lilacs, Humpty Dumpty.

A bunged-up kitchen table served as desk, and there were two spindly chairs that had been painted meat-red. Beneath the windows stood a very beautiful hand-carved cradle, rumored to have belonged to one of Madeline's twin brothers. Rogan used it as a hamper. A wooden hatbox hid his cigarettes. In the middle of the room was an immense theatrical trunk, its brass fittings black with age, where he kept his clothes. You could just make out the name stenciled on its top in faint white letters.

ILLYRIA

MADELINE ARMIN TIERNEY

I used to wonder why the trunk was here, rather than in Aunt Kate's carriage house. That was until Rogan and I attempted to move it. It wouldn't budge, not even when we enlisted Michael's help.

"Jesus, what's in there? Rocks?" Michael complained, wiping sweat from his lip.

"Uh-uh. Just this—"

Rogan tossed a pair of socks at him. The two ended up scuffling on the floor, until my uncle pounded upstairs and cracked their heads together. Before he went back down he gave the trunk a baleful glance, then looked darkly at Rogan.

"Next time it'll be *you* in there," he said.

Rogan slept in a wrought-iron bed against one wall. There was a bookshelf beside it, and next to that a small door that opened into a long, low, paneled space that was half closet, half attic. It was crammed with boxes of toy machine guns and water pistols, old Halloween noisemakers and masks, crepe-paper streamers and piles of *The Saturday Evening Post*, tinsel garland, and compacts of greasepaint and rouge. Glitter had sifted over everything, like silver dust. It smelled like Christmas, of cloves and balsam.

"Come here, Maddy." Rogan took my hand and drew me to him. "Come and see..."

He stepped to the wall, opened the door to the little attic, and ducked inside, stooping so he wouldn't graze his head against the ceiling. I followed.

"Wait—stay there for a minute," he said. Carefully he stepped between cartons of wigs and old magazines, until he reached the end of the narrow space. He pulled out a flashlight and switched it on, then gestured at the door behind me. "Close that, then come over here. Try not to knock anything over."

I shut the door and joined him in the back of the room. "What is it?"

We stood side by side, backs bent, between boxes of Shiny Brite Christmas ornaments. Directly in front of us, more cartons were stacked against the wall.

"Take this," Rogan commanded. He handed me the flashlight, then knelt. Very gingerly he began to pull the pile of boxes toward him, wedging himself against the stack so that they moved as one and didn't topple over. "Now look. Do you see it?"

He leaned back and shone the flashlight on the wall.

Where the boxes had been was another door. Barely three feet high and not as wide, with a simple latch and hinges that had darkened to the same oaky color as the walls.

"Wow," I breathed. "How'd you find it?"

"Just poking around the other night. There's stuff in here, I swear no one's touched it since Madeline died." Rogan grinned. "No one knows about it but us. Here—"

He undid the latch and pulled the door open, took the flashlight and shone it inside, then motioned at me.

"Go in," he urged. "I fixed it up. Go on, I'm right behind you."

I squatted, got onto my hands and knees, and crawled inside. I could see nothing clearly, but a moment later Rogan's head bumped against me.

"Keep going," he said. "Once you get all the way in you can kneel; just watch your head. But it's bigger than you think."

I laughed in delight, my heart beating fast, and crawled into the near-darkness. Something soft was under me; the flashlight moved wildly as Rogan turned and pulled the door closed behind us. I heard the soft *thhkkk* of a match being struck, and then Rogan lit a candle and set it into a blue glass he'd stolen from church.

"That's not safe," I said.

Rogan snorted and turned off the flashlight.

"Voilà," he said.

We were in a passage under the eaves. To one side, the ceiling slanted down to the floor. On the other side was a fretwork of wood and plaster lath. The wavering blue candlelight made it seem as though this wall was snow covered and moonlit. A neat pallet of Hudson Bay blankets lay on the floor, along with an ashtray and a pack of cigarettes.

Also several books, including the copy of *Tales from Shakespeare* that had once been Madeline's but which I had claimed years before, only to have it disappear.

"Hey!" I grabbed the book and stared at the cover in disbelief, then smacked Rogan with it. "You stole this!"

"Yeah, but I gave it back." He flopped onto the blankets. "What do you think?"

"It's amazing." I lay beside him and stared at the ceiling. "It's like being in a boat."

"That's right." He turned toward me. "It's the boat that saved us from drowning."

He kissed me, his mouth so much bigger than mine, and his hands; everything. When I grasped his shoulders it was like grabbing onto a ladder: I clambered on top of him and he slipped his hands beneath my flannel shirt.

"It's warm here," he whispered. "We can be warm."

We took our shirts off, and for the first time drew ourselves together skin to skin, breast to breast. His flesh was as white and smooth as my own, all but hairless; his nipples small and flat above the long hollow of his waist and his hip bone's sharp rise; his mouth bittersweet with nicotine and toothpaste. Everywhere I touched him was like finding myself in the dark. Rogan's hands moved where mine would move. His murmurs echoed my own. The space around us was another, warmer skin, its reek of sex and sweat cut with the chalky scent of plaster and that intense, oddly evanescent balsam smell. We kept our jeans on, striving together until first Rogan came and then I did, straddling his thigh.

Afterward we lay entwined. Small moons quivered all around us, blue and gold and silver, as the candle guttered in its glass.

"Shhh," I said, though neither of us had spoken. "Listen." I pressed my hand on Rogan's mouth and whispered, "Do you hear?"

"Mice," said Rogan. "They're everywhere."

"That's not mice."

From behind the wall came a faint tapping. Not scrabbling or scratching; more rhythmic. I sat up, my sweat cooling, and cocked my head.

"It's there." I touched the wall with the flat of my hand—warily, as though it might burn me. "Can't you hear it?"

It sounded like drumming fingernails. Or sleet, if sleet could fall inside a house.

Yet the sky had been cloudless.

Rogan yawned. "It's mice, Maddy."

The thought of mice made my bare flesh prickle. I snatched up my flannel shirt and started to pull it on.

"Hey!" Rogan tugged my sleeve. "Don't do that! I was looking."

"I'm cold. Well, not cold, but I don't want mice crawling on me."

"How about this?"

He pulled me toward him. I smacked him, not hard, and pretended to struggle. He pinned me to the floor, I kicked at the blankets as he laughed and tickled me.

"Rogan! Don't—"

I kicked again. My aim went wild and my foot connected with the wall. I felt the wood buckle.

Then, alarmingly, the wall pushed back.

"Shit." With all my strength I pushed Rogan away. "Damn it, look. I broke something."

One of the wood panels had come loose and fallen onto the blankets, leaving a gap as wide as my hand. I nudged the board with my foot, then froze.

From inside the wall, light glimmered. Neither cold blue candle-flame nor an electric bulb; more like starlight, fractured and wavering yet also warm, as though embers had rained from the rafters. For an instant the rhythmic tapping fell silent. Then it started up again, louder now that the wall had been breached.

And I could hear something else besides that soft strange pattering—a susurrus, sweet and high-pitched, like the sound that hunting swallows

ILLYRIA

made in the twilight above Fairview's lawns. I leaned, breathless, toward the opening. Rogan did the same. His arm circled me as our faces drew within inches of the gap.

"Oh, Maddy," he breathed. "Oh, Maddy, look."

Inside the wall was a toy theater, made of folded paper and gilt cardboard and scraps of brocade and lace. Curtains of scarlet tissue shrouded the proscenium. The stage floor was mottled yellow and green, as though to suggest a field starred with flowers. Thumbnail-sized masks of Comedy and Tragedy hung from the proscenium arch, beneath a frieze of Muses that looked as though it had been painted with a single hair. Columns no bigger than a pencil rose to either side, and a dizzyingly intricate arrangement of trompe l'oeil cutouts and folded paper walls and arches made it seem as though the stage receded endlessly, into topiary gardens and ruined statuary, a fallen tower and snow-peaked mountains and, most distant of all, a beach of golden sand with a ruined ship silhouetted against a wintry sun. A row of tiny footlights burned at the edge of the apron, each light the size of a glowing match-head, and there were loops of colored string that hung from the flies, so the curtains could be raised and flats or scrims lowered.

There was even an orchestra pit.

But no orchestra. No actors or stage manager or director.

And no audience, save for Rogan and me. We craned our necks, trying to see it all.

We couldn't. The opening was too small.

And the toy theater, tiny as it was, was too big. Rogan shook his head and gazed at me questioningly.

"Mice," I said.

We both started laughing, our voices edging into hysteria. Rogan finally drew a shuddering breath and wiped his eyes. "How the hell did they get that in there?"

"Jesus, I have no idea." I rubbed my neck. "*Who* put it there? That's what I want to know."

"Maybe they just stuck it inside. Or, you know, built it in pieces then assembled it."

I gave him a dubious look. "How?"

"I dunno. How do they put ships in bottles? Maybe it was like that."

We both turned and peered back inside. The eerie rustling and tapping continued unabated, though nothing moved save the shadows cast by the diminutive footlights.

"There's lights in there," I said flatly. "Those little lights? How come it doesn't burn down? *Who lit them?*"

Abruptly I felt sick. Rogan grew pale. He bit his lip, then reached to thrust his hand through the opening.

"Don't!" I stopped him, gasping, and shook my head. "Don't."

"Why not?" demanded Rogan. But he sat up, crossed his arms, and stared at me. "Is it—"

"I don't know what it is. But."

I grabbed the fallen board and started to angle it back into place, then hesitated. Without looking at each other, we lowered our heads once more.

It was all still there, the picture-frame proscenium and paint-spattered floor, gilt-and-cardboard mountains and tissue curtains and rows of paper columns stretching to an impossible distance beneath an impossible sunrise. For a long time we gazed at it, our cheeks touching, until finally I drew away.

"We should go." I felt a sudden pang. "If someone found it…"

We looked at each other, our hair tangled, Rogan still shirtless. He nodded.

Silently I replaced the panel, making certain we could remove it next time. Rogan blew out the candle and switched on his flashlight. We dressed; I grabbed my copy of *Tales from Shakespeare*, and we crept into the attic storeroom. I helped Rogan move the stacked boxes back into place against the wall, then followed him into his bedroom.

We didn't talk about what we had seen. I felt exalted but also subdued, near tears. Rogan went to the window and stared at the sky, twilit now, the sun a red disk above the Palisades and a shimmering strand of lights poised between the hill where Fairview stood and the nebulous glow of Manhattan, ten miles downriver.

"It looks so far away," he said at last.

I crossed to stand beside him. "It's not, really."

For a few minutes we remained there, watching until the sun disappeared behind the cliffs and the sky darkened to indigo. From a room below a television droned. I could smell roasting chicken and hear Michael talking on the phone. Rogan looked at me and smiled ruefully.

"Latin?" he asked.

We got our textbooks and went downstairs.

I STAYED FOR dinner that night. Michael was there—he was a high school senior that fall—and Thomas, who commuted to his first year at Fordham. And Aunt Pat, who'd arrived home from her job at Gimbels to get the chicken and potatoes in the oven. She was slight and briskly cheerful, her fair hair streaked with gray, her skin taut and lined from smoking.

"Your mom says you're doing well with all your classes," she said as she handed me the string beans.

"Yeah, pretty well, I guess."

"Not like Knucklehead here." She looked fondly at her youngest son. "See if you can get it to rub off on him, will you, Maddy?"

Michael made a crude face. "That shouldn't be too hard."

Rogan kicked him under the table. "You—"

Just then we all heard the front door open. Aunt Pat raised her eyebrows but said nothing. The rest of us straightened in our chairs, even Thomas, who had grown a beard when he started college and had yet to shave it. I paid great interest to my chicken, as I listened to the familiar sound of a briefcase being dropped, the door to the hall closet opening and closing, and then my uncle Richard's tread across the foyer and into the dining room, a heavier echo of my own father's footsteps.

"Hello, everyone."

It was a big doorway, but my uncle filled it. Neither he nor my father was particularly tall. Both scanted six feet, both were wiry though strongly built, broad-shouldered, long-legged, with light-brown hair barely thinning from their foreheads.

But, as the older twin, my uncle seemed to have absorbed the greater psychic mass. He was a bit grayer than my father, more worn about the face—like Aunt Pat, he was a heavy smoker—and more choleric. Seeing both twins in a crowded room, you might be hard put at first to tell them apart.

But inevitably, your gaze would be drawn to my uncle. Even in daylight he appeared to stand half-shadowed, and no matter how animated he was, you were always conscious of something waiting, a coiled anticipation. It was only as I grew older that I realized this sense of expectation didn't come from my uncle himself. It emanated from his children. Being in a room with his sons was like standing in a pen crammed with nervous horses. Their fear was palpable, and their mute hatred; their love.

The older boys all resembled him. Only Rogan was different, with his flaming hair and uncanny sea-foam eyes. He looked like me, and like my father; as though the strange displacement that gave my uncle his somber weight cast a bright aura around his youngest child. In a crowded room with Rogan and me, you would always look at Rogan first.

"How was your day?" asked Aunt Pat.

"It was fine." My uncle bent to kiss the top of her head, then set a big hand on my shoulder. "Hi, Maddy. You setting a good example for these reprobates?"

"Trying to." I smiled weakly.

"Michael, you take care of those gutters like I asked you?"

Michael nodded, staring at his plate. "Yup."

"Good." My uncle's gaze barely touched the other boys as he turned to go upstairs to change. "I'll be down in a minute. Make me a drink, will you, Pat?" When he could be heard in the hall above us, everyone began to eat again.

ILLYRIA

I left soon after, not waiting for Uncle Richard to return, or for dessert. When I looked at Rogan across the table, I felt as though I must give off sparks.

And as I stood to go, I saw Michael staring at me.

"Make sure she rubs off on you," he called as Rogan walked me to the porch.

"Fuck you," said Rogan under his breath. Once we were outside, he bumped his forehead against mine. "Hey, I'll see you tomorrow, okay?"

"Okay," I said. "That was amazing. Up there…"

I tilted my head toward the upper stories.

Rogan grinned. "It was incredible." He looked the way he did on Christmas morning.

He went back inside, and I headed up the winding driveway. I'd gone about halfway when someone called out.

"Maddy!"

I turned. At the bottom of the hill, where the drive wound down to the carriage house, Aunt Kate stood and beckoned to me. "Come here!"

I lifted my hand in a wave and walked down to meet her, my shoulders hunched against the chill night wind. Aunt Kate looked beautiful and exotic as always, in green lizard-skin boots and a russet swing coat, her cheeks pink with cold and a paisley scarf loosely knotted around her neck. Someone was with her, a tall figure I didn't recognize; a man.

No surprise there. Aunt Kate had never married, but she had a lot of male friends. This caused great consternation among her family, especially the women, who took it as a personal affront that Kate had a (presumably) active sex life, as well as an intellectual one. None of her friends were stockbrokers or lawyers or doctors, which might have made their presence slightly more palatable, or at least comprehensible; and most of them appeared to fall under some vaguely defined rubric that identified them as artists of one sort or another: men who had too much hair or none at all, men who gave a blank look when someone brought up the Mets, but who had visited slightly louche destinations, Tangiers or Nepal or London or San Francisco. They had often read the same books as Rogan and me and, despite the disparity in our ages, sometimes listened to the same music.

This man, though, didn't look like the others. He was tall and thin, with a long, angular, ascetic face, and black hair cut very short. He wore a pinstriped suit, with a white shirt open at the neck. No tie. I slowed my steps.

But then Aunt Kate grasped the man's arm with one hand, her emerald ring glinting in the darkness; and with her other hand grabbed mine.

"So this is her?" The man looked at me and smiled. His dark eyes were kind, and amused. "The famous Madeline."

"Peter, I'd like you to meet my niece. Maddy, this is my friend Peter Sullivan. He's going to be teaching you."

"Uh, hi." We shook hands. I looked around, embarrassed and somewhat suspicious. A teacher?

"Next month I'll be teaching at St. Brendan's," explained Mr. Sullivan. "English. Taking over for Sister Alberta. You know she has breast cancer?"

I shook my head, as disconcerted by the realization that nuns could get cancer as that I had just heard a man utter the word *breast*.

"Oh, jeez. That's terrible," I said, then hastily added, "I mean that she's sick, not that you're a teacher."

"Madeline is *extremely talented*," said Aunt Kate. I blushed, though I was pleased. I was accustomed to hearing my parents say those words in the same tone they used to describe Ookie Connell—*He's a little slow.* "She and my nephew Rogan."

Mr. Sullivan cocked his head at Fairview. "Is he the one I hear singing?"

Aunt Kate nodded. "Yes, that's Rogan."

I stared at the ground, then glanced uneasily at Rogan's house.

Of course I knew people had heard Rogan sing. At night, he leaned out the window on purpose so his voice would carry. He'd sung at church.

ILLYRIA

Yet, somehow, I'd never thought that a *stranger* might hear him; someone who might, however remotely, matter in the world beyond Arden Terrace.

"He has an extraordinary voice," Mr. Sullivan went on. "Does he take lessons?"

"No, they won't train them," said Aunt Kate. She might have been referring to dogs that weren't housebroken.

Mr. Sullivan turned to me again. "What about you? Do you sing?"

He looked so open and encouraging that I felt a sudden desolation. As though everything good that had happened in my life was all a mistake—Rogan, outgrowing my glasses, being smart at schoolwork. Even the memory of what we'd seen earlier in the hidden attic; even the memory of Rogan himself, his taste, his hands, and his warmth and his soft skin…it all seemed distant and unreal. As though I'd opened a wonderful present, only to be told it was meant for one of my older, prettier sisters, and not for me.

"No," I said. "I can't sing."

Mr. Sullivan shrugged. "Hey, singing isn't everything." He smiled again.

Aunt Kate touched his arm. "You go on in. I need to talk with Maddy for a minute."

"Nice to meet you, Maddy," he said, and went into the carriage house.

"Come with me," my aunt said. "I left some things in the car."

I went with her into the garage beneath the carriage house, where her red Mustang was parked. She opened the back of the car, reached in, and handed me a bag from Gristede's, then gathered her purse and another grocery bag. "Just bring that up for me, thanks. Did you have dinner yet?"

"Yeah, with Rogan and everybody."

Aunt Kate wrinkled her nose. "Roast chicken?"

"It was good."

"It's the only thing they ever eat."

"They have turkey at Thanksgiving."

Aunt Kate sighed. "That's just a big chicken."

We walked out of the garage and climbed the rickety stairway up to the carriage house door. In the uppermost window shone the ghost light that my aunt kept burning, day or night. Above Fairview a full moon was just beginning to rise. Aunt Kate stopped, halfway up the steps, and looked at me.

"Listen, Maddy. I have something to tell you. I got tickets to take you and Rogan to see *Two Gentlemen of Verona*."

I looked at her blankly. "Who?"

"The play," she said. "By Shakespeare. A musical version; it's supposed to be very good."

"A play?"

"Yes. A play. On Broadway. It's at the St. James Theatre. Your birthdays are next week, I thought this would be fun."

I had never seen a play. Neither had Rogan. Nor, as far as I know, had any of our siblings or cousins. There had always been trips to the city, for baseball games and the circus and the Thanksgiving Day Parade, Christmas windows at Macy's, Radio City Music Hall and the Rockettes, Easter Mass at St. Patrick's Cathedral.

But a play?

"Really?" I said. "Me and Rogan?"

"Yes, really." She sounded angry. "And I haven't told your parents yet, so don't mention it until I've had the chance."

"I won't, I swear. Really?" I shook my head, then laughed. "I can't believe it."

"Neither can I."

She turned once more, her boots clattering up the stairs. At the top, she stopped again.

In the brilliant moonlight her face looked drawn, even gaunt. There were glints of silver at the roots of her sleek black hair. The beringed hands holding the Gristede's bag were crisscrossed with blue veins, and beneath the skin the bones of her fingers looked clawlike.

I had never before thought about how old she was, or even how she was related to me. She was a Tierney by birth. But she wasn't my father's sister, and she had never seemed old enough to be a great-aunt, like Aunt Margaret or Aunt Bella.

But now she looked old. Not ancient; just worn and tired. And resolute.

"Thank you, Maddy." She set her bag down outside the door, then reached for mine. "We have tickets for next Friday. I'll talk to everyone over the weekend."

"What if they say no?"

"I'll kidnap you." She smiled. "But they won't. Just don't make a big deal out of it, all right?"

"*They're* the ones who make a big deal out of it." I kicked at a step and looked back at Fairview. "Why? Why is it such a big goddamn deal? Why do they even care?"

Aunt Kate hesitated.

"They don't care," she finally said. "You know why? Because they have no talent. None of them—none of Madeline's children. Or, well, maybe they did, and she was just so vain and selfish she never encouraged any of them. She was insufferable. And once she stopped acting, all she cared about was money. After Rosco died, during the Depression—all she did was buy up real estate. Like it mattered—"

She gestured fiercely at Madeline's mansion. "As though any of this mattered. This—*stuff.* But that was all her children cared about. And when their children were born, your father and Richard and the rest, their parents never encouraged them, either. Rogan's father, Richard—he had a beautiful voice. Did you know that?"

I blinked in surprise. "No."

"Of course not." Aunt Kate laughed bitterly. "How would you? He never sang; it died on the vine. All those children, all those cousins—just like you and all your cousins, Maddy—and there was Richard with this voice. I used to listen to him—he'd sing when he was in the bathroom, it was the only place anyone was ever alone. 'Where or When…'"

She rubbed her eyes. "He never knew I was there. And after a little while I never heard him sing again."

"Did they—do something to him?"

"No, of course not." She shrugged dismissively. "But talent—if you don't encourage it, if you don't train it, it dies. It might run wild for a little while, but it will never mean anything. Like a wild horse. If you don't tame it and teach it to run on a track, to pace itself and bear a rider, it doesn't matter how fast it is. It's useless. And this family?"

She crossed her arms and stared at Fairview. "They have no use for 'useless.' If you can't make money, forget it."

"But actors make money. Madeline was famous. People on Broadway—they make money."

"That's not what your father or your uncle would call money, Maddy. Chump change. But it's not the money that matters. They lost faith. Madeline lost faith, and so the rest of them never had any."

She turned to gaze to where the woods crept up against the edge of the lawn—thin birches and sumac and a few old elm trees, all leafless now and black against the violet sky—then lifted her face toward the moon.

"You could say there were religious differences," she said.

The door opened, and Mr. Sullivan peered out. "Do you need help bringing things in?"

Aunt Kate shook her head. "Thank you, Peter, no. We were just saying good-bye."

She stepped inside with the groceries.

"I'll see you in a few weeks, Maddy," said Mr. Sullivan, and he closed the door.

I walked slowly back to my house. A light was on in Rogan's window, and I tried to hear his voice in my head, to will him to appear and sing.

But even in my imagination I couldn't give voice to anything that sounded like him. I reached the street and saw my own house, its windows bright and the television blaring from the living room, my mother calling upstairs to my sister. I pulled Rogan's jacket tight around me and went home.

• ♦ •

ILLYRIA

ROGAN CALLED ME early the next morning. "I'm not gonna be around this weekend." He sounded bereft. "I have to go with my parents to see John at Holy Cross. We won't be back till tomorrow night."

"Oh, God." I stretched the phone cord as far as it would go and looked out the front window, down to his house. "Are you downstairs?"

"Yeah." There was a fitful motion in a dark window. "Can you see me?"

"Yeah." I told him about going to the theater with Aunt Kate. "You think they'll say yes?"

"Yours probably will."

This was true. My parents' attitude in most things was one of benign neglect. Or perhaps it was just fatigue, spiking into occasional rages of guilt-fueled retribution for minor infractions, a bad grade, or the expression of an imprudent political view.

"Well, maybe she'll tell them first. That'd make it easier for you."

"Maybe." He sounded grim. "I gotta go. I'll call you when I get back."

I spent the day in a funk. The weather was glorious; my friend Nancy called to see if I wanted to go shopping but I said no. All I could think of was Rogan, all I *wanted* to think of was Rogan, and what we'd seen in the secret attic above Fairview. I paced the house, restless and angry, avoiding my mother (who would have put me to work) and picking fights with my sisters, until late afternoon when my father returned home from playing golf.

"I'm going to five o'clock Mass." He announced this every Saturday as though it were news. "Anyone want to come?"

"I will."

My father looked at me with mild surprise. Since Rogan had stopped singing in church, I attended the sloths' Mass at noon on Sunday. "Well, get ready," he said.

An idea had come to me. I sat in church and worked out the details, then rode home with my father.

"Rogan went with Uncle Richard and Aunt Pat to see John at college," I said.

My father looked absently out the car window. "Yes, I know."

I made my voice sound as casual as possible. "Do you know if Michael and Thomas went?"

"No, I don't, dear." My father frowned. "Well, yes, they might have. I think they did; I think Pat said they were going to stay with the Garlands."

I nodded, holding my breath in case he wondered why I'd asked. But he said nothing more.

Early Sunday morning my father went to play golf again. I slouched around the house till my mother and sisters left for church. Then I pulled on Rogan's jacket and hurried across the street to Fairview. I walked as quickly as I could down the drive, hoping I wouldn't run into my aunt. Not that she would have questioned why I was there, or cared.

But I didn't want to see anyone. I darted onto the porch, pulled open the great oaken front door, and slipped into the foyer, closing the door carefully behind me.

It was the first time I'd ever been in Fairview when no one was home. The rugs and old furniture made it look more like a shabby museum than a house where people lived. Golden sun streamed through the downstairs windows, but did nothing to warm the place. It was spooky and silent and cold. I felt uneasy, even frightened, with none of the exhilaration I felt when Rogan and I did something forbidden. I stood at the foot of the broad curved staircase, shivering, and watched my breath cloud the air.

"Hello?" I called out softly. No one was there.

I went upstairs. When I reached the third floor my anxiety faded somewhat, though as I walked into Rogan's room, I didn't feel the relief I'd expected. Without him, the old nursery looked impossibly, almost cruelly barren and sad. It was even colder than downstairs. There was a glass of water next to the unmade bed, a flashlight, a notebook I prodded with my foot. Rogan's school clothes were strewn across the floor, corduroy trousers and a new jacket, dirty socks and T-shirts.

I picked up a flannel shirt and brought it to my face. It smelled of Rogan, smoky, slightly acrid. It smelled warm. I removed my jacket and my own shirt, and pulled on his. I closed the door to his room, got the flashlight and turned it on, and went into the outer attic.

I stepped gingerly between cardboard boxes until I reached the back wall. I balanced the flashlight as best I could, then began to pull out the stack of cartons. Once or twice it nearly toppled onto me, and I swore under my breath until I could get everything back into place. Finally I moved the cartons enough that I could unlatch the hidden door and open it enough for me to slip inside. I pulled the door closed behind me and shone the flashlight across the narrow space.

Everything was as we'd left it, blankets in disarray and the few books scattered. The loose board hadn't budged. I leaned the flashlight against the door, knelt, and folded the blankets and stacked the books; retrieved the flashlight and turned it off, and sat cross-legged in the darkness.

Silence. I held my breath as long as I could, and listened. But there was still nothing.

"Rogan," I whispered.

I lay down on the blankets, pulled up the flannel shirt until it covered my face. I breathed in his scent, squeezed my eyes tightly shut even though there was nothing to see. I found the place where the blankets still smelled of us, murmured his name, and tried to bring back the sound of Rogan singing, his voice strung between us like the glimmering thread that stretched from Arden Terrace to the city. Only the faintest echo of it came to me; but when it did, there was an instant when I imagined I saw Rogan moving beneath me, darker even than the room, darker than anything; the shadow of the song.

I shuddered and lay without moving, my tear-streaked face pressed against his shirt. Minutes passed. I listened to my heartbeat slow. Then I heard another sound.

It was the same rhythmic tapping I'd heard the other day with Rogan, the same oddly surging whistle, like wind or waves. I pulled my shirt down, wriggled forward until I could touch the wall. I pried my fingers under the board until it came loose, set it down, and looked through the opening.

At first I thought my vision was blurred. The toy theater was exactly where I'd last seen it—perhaps four inches from the wall, lit by those same unearthly footlights.

But now the stage seemed distorted and unsteady, as if it were underwater. I rubbed my eyes, squinting to get a better view, then sucked my breath in.

Snow was falling. Not everywhere. Only behind the proscenium, on the tiny stage itself.

Not real snow. Fake snow.

And not white but silver and palest blue, finer than any glitter I had ever seen, finer than salt or powder, like something that would flake from the most microscopic shining matter you could imagine: glitter's glitter. It sifted onto the stage floor and whirled in tiny eddies, as though stirred by tiny unseen feet, and where it fell too near the footlights there were infinitesimal flares of gold and scarlet, and the most delicate fragrance, roses mingled with scorched sugar.

I stared at it entranced, barely registering the shift in light toward the back of the stage where the topiary trees, now crystalline and opal-colored, gave way to knife-edged mountains and a snow-covered beach beneath a night sky, with a full moon snared in the rigging of a spectral shipwreck and a fluttering shadow like a moth's moving slowly, as though injured, across the white dunes. All the while the tapping continued, and that soft insistent whistle, like a steady indrawn breath.

Without thinking, I lifted my hand and extended it through the gap in the wall. I stretched it toward the stage just beyond the apron, until my fingers gleamed silver-blue in the footlights. I felt no cold, no heat. Just a faint tingling like a mild electrical shock, as though hair-sized needles stabbed my fingertips. I waited to see if anything changed, if something noticed my intrusion.

Nothing did. The fake snow fell and drifted and whirled. The weird noises didn't stop.

Finally I withdrew my hand. It was unmarked, and felt no different when I rubbed it against my cheek.

ILLYRIA

But suddenly I felt scared—that I *didn't* feel anything. That something so strange and inexplicable could leave no lasting mark, no trace that I had encountered it at all: not a scratch, not a shift in body temperature, nothing but a fleeting memory of sound and light and motion.

I shoved the board back into place, then scrambled in the dark for the flashlight. I stumbled back into the outer attic, knocked over a carton, and sat, heart hammering, as I listened for a shout of discovery from below.

But the house remained empty. I lurched from the attic into Rogan's room and blinked, shocked to see that it was still daylight.

The alarm clock read 1:05. I tore off his flannel shirt and flung it onto the floor, pulled my own shirt back on, and grabbed my jacket and fled downstairs. I ran into no one in the house, no one outside, and no one when I got back to my house.

◆ ◆ ◆

"YOUR AUNT KATE wants to take you to see a show," my mother announced at dinner that night.

I feigned surprise. "A show?"

She nodded. "A Broadway show. Something by Shakespeare. *The Merchant of Venice*, I think."

I caught myself before I corrected her. "Can I go?"

"I don't see why not. It's for your birthday. And it's Friday, so it's not a school night. She wanted to take Rogan, too, I think. Hal? Is it all right with you?"

She looked at my father. He swallowed his mouthful of baked potato, then said, "Yes, Kate mentioned it. She said she'd take you to dinner at Rosoff's beforehand."

I said, "That'll be fun."

"Make sure you wear something nice," said my mother.

I didn't get a chance to talk to Rogan until the following afternoon. It was our fifteenth birthday, but we'd already decided not to make a big deal out of it. Nobody else was, except for Aunt Kate. He was waiting for me in the school parking yard.

"Wait'll you see what I got," he said as we walked down the hill toward Arden Terrace. "Un-fucking-believable. In-fucking-credible."

"What?"

"John gave me his old sound system. He has a new roommate this year, this guy Jeff. He's got an amazing stereo so John said I could have his."

"For your birthday?"

"Nah, he didn't even remember that till I told him. But isn't that cool?"

I smiled. "It's great."

"And dig this—this guy Jeff, he gave me a bunch of albums. I listened to some last night. It's wild stuff, Maddy."

He swayed back and forth, singing snatches of a song I didn't recognize. He laughed. "Man, I am *so* psyched."

We reached the bottom of the hill and turned down the road that led to Arden Terrace. Acorns rolled underfoot, hidden by the yellow leaves banked against the curb. Rogan grabbed a handful and tossed them across the road.

"Did Aunt Kate talk to your parents?" I said.

"Not yet."

"Maybe she did today."

"Maybe," he said, unconcerned.

We reached Fairview. I still hadn't told him about sneaking into the attic the day before. Upstairs, Rogan kicked at the door to Michael's room, to make sure no one was inside.

"Come here," said Rogan, and pulled me to him. We kissed in the hallway, then went into Rogan's room and closed the door. "Check this out, Maddy."

The turntable sat on the floor by the wall. Rogan began sorting through a small pile of records beside it.

"Here," he said.

He put the record on the turntable and handed me the sleeve. It showed a cartoon of a subway entrance, with pink smoke welling up from the black tunnel.

"What—"

Rogan put his hand over my mouth. "Shhh. Listen."

He played me two songs about a girl named Jane.

"That's us, Maddy," he said when the songs were over. "Our lives were saved by rock and roll."

I gave him a funny look. "That's more like your life. I can't sing."

"It's both of us." He grabbed my arm and dragged me toward the attic door. "Come on, Mad-girl—"

Afterward we lay side by side in the dark. Rogan pried the board loose and we gazed at the glimmering stage, our own tiny cosmos. There was no snow this time. Wherever the stage was, whatever it was supposed to represent, it seemed to be the middle of the night. The footlights cast a flickering cobalt glow across the stage.

I told Rogan what I had seen the day before. Snow; a full moon.

"Do you think there's anyone there?" he wondered, and stroked my back. "That we can't see?"

"I don't know."

I touched my fingers to his lips, then kissed him. I was afraid to guess at what might be there, beyond the tiny stage; afraid to give a name to what we saw there, just as I couldn't give a name to what I felt for my cousin.

Magic; love.

Endless longing; a face you'd known since childhood, since birth almost; a body that moved as though it were your own. These were things you never spoke of, things you never hoped for; things you could never admit to. Things you'd die for, and die of.

"Rogan," I whispered.

"What?" He turned to me, and his eyes gleamed peacock-blue in the footlights. "Maddy? Why are you crying?"

"Nothing. Rogan." He put his arms around me and I trembled. "Just you."

♦ ♦ ♦

ROGAN'S PARENTS DIDN'T make a big deal over him going to the play.

"They didn't care," he said a few days later. "They're going out Friday anyway. All they said was don't get lost in the city."

"Maybe because it's Aunt Kate? Or Shakespeare?"

"Yeah, maybe." He sounded unconvinced.

After school on Friday we changed for the theater. I wore a long granny skirt and embroidered blouse and a macramé vest, and my new Frye boots. Rogan put on a clean flannel shirt and a different corduroy jacket than the one he'd worn to school that day.

We walked together from Fairview down the drive to Aunt Kate's house. It felt different: the two of us together in the waning daylight, wearing what passed for nice clothes, with a common destination and our parents' approval. Inside the carriage house, Aunt Kate hurried about, looking for her purse, the tickets, her expensive lipstick. She looked elegant—glamorous—in black velvet cigarette pants and a cream-colored silk blouse, a cropped bolero jacket. She wore no jewelry other than her emerald ring. Suddenly she stopped and stared at me.

"Maddy." Her eyes narrowed. "Don't you have a coat?"

I shrugged. "Just that yellow one. It didn't really go."

Aunt Kate winced. "That thing from Sears? You're right. That's an awful coat."

She stood, thinking; then turned and ran upstairs. Minutes later she returned, holding what looked like a blanket.

"Here." She opened the door, walked out onto the top of the stairs, and shook the blanket vigorously. "This has been in storage all these years, I just had it dry-cleaned this summer. See if it fits."

She stepped back inside and handed it to me. Not a blanket but a long cape, of royal-blue velvet lined with white satin, with three gold buttons at the top to fasten it.

"That was your great-grandmother's opera cape," Aunt Kate said as I pulled it on. "Madeline used to wear it after every performance. Wait—"

ILLYRIA

She adjusted it over my shoulders, then buttoned it. "Those are real gold. Wow. Maddy! It fits. It looks *great*. Utterly glamorous. Go look at yourself," she urged.

I walked into the living room and stood before the big old mirror there. Someone else stared back, me but not me. The deep-blue velvet made my hair look glossy chestnut, not mousy. My eyes seemed to have darkened as well, to midnight blue or indigo. I put my arm out and whirled, the folds rippling around me like waves.

"Holy Batcape, Batman," said Rogan.

I turned to him. "What do you think? Am I glamorous?"

"It looks fantastic. Can I try it on?"

"No," said Aunt Kate. "We need to go, the train's in twenty minutes. Come on—"

Rosoff's, the restaurant where we ate, was warm and wood paneled, crowded with theatergoers and filled with Broadway memorabilia—ancient photographs, old etchings, framed faded *Playbills*.

"It's like eating in my house," said Rogan. I couldn't tell if this was a complaint or not. "Better food, though."

He'd ordered the chicken.

After dinner we walked to the St. James Theatre. Our seats were Orchestra, Row E, Center.

"This is where the drama critics always sit," Aunt Kate explained. "Best seats in the house. You're close enough to see the actors sweat and spit when they talk."

Rogan laughed. "Hey, *that's* glamorous."

"It's work, Rogan." Aunt Kate delicately balanced her *Playbill* on a velvet-clad knee. "If the actors are good enough, you don't mind seeing their sweat."

"What about their spit?" asked Rogan. "Do I have to like their spit, too?"

Aunt Kate frowned and began to read her program. Rogan and I did the same.

"Hey." He jabbed a finger at the cast list. "The guy who wrote this is the same guy who wrote *Hair!* Maybe they'll take their clothes off."

We looked at Aunt Kate with renewed admiration.

The play was perfect. How could it have been otherwise? It was the first one either of us had ever seen, barring school productions at Christmas and St. Patrick's Day. The script was bowdlerized Shakespeare, the music cheerful and relentlessly contemporary. There were Black people in the cast, and Puerto Ricans—an astonishing revelation—also sexual innuendos that seemed to be inherent to the original play.

Our admiration for Aunt Kate, and Shakespeare, became immeasurable.

After the play, we spilled onto the street with throngs of happily chattering people. I felt not just exhilarated but exalted, the way I did when Rogan sang. He sang now, a tune from the show he'd already memorized, walking along Broadway and turning on his heels, his voice rising above the crowd in a charmed, eerie falsetto. People looked at him in wonder and delight, his beautiful face and long hair, eyes closed as he walked backward, certain somehow that he wouldn't fall.

We talked about the play the whole way back on the train, then in Aunt Kate's car.

"I don't want it to stop," said Rogan as we walked out of the garage beneath her carriage house. He didn't sound disappointed, but anguished. "Why does it have to end?"

Aunt Kate dropped her keys into her purse. "Well, it doesn't. I got tickets next week for *Butley*."

Rogan and I looked at each other, then burst out laughing.

"Thank you!"

"Jesus, Aunt Kate, really?"

"Shhh!" She cut us off sternly. "Hush. I haven't spoken to them yet. But yes. Good night, Rogan."

She kissed him, then beckoned at me. "Come upstairs, Maddy. That cape stays here."

I waved good-bye at Rogan. His voice echoed through the chill air until he entered Fairview, and the autumn night grew silent.

ILLYRIA

Inside I took off the cape and gave it back to my aunt, who folded it carefully then went upstairs. I stood in the living room, alone, and looked at the framed photographs of my great-great-grandmother on the wall. Madeline as Rosalind, her hair cropped short so she resembled a sly boy; Madeline as Gwendolen in *The Importance of Being Earnest*, a wicked glint in her eye as she pretended to read her diary. Madeline as Anya in *The Cherry Orchard*; as Mrs. Pinchwife, Cordelia, and Cleopatra, and the title character in *Major Barbara*.

She looked different in each picture. Recognizably herself yet somehow, remarkably, older or younger or cunning or heartbroken by turns. Her adult career had been prolific but short-lived. The pictures displayed an eternal ingenue, an eternal boy-girl: Rosalind and Viola but never Hedda Gabler; never Lady Macbeth. There were no photographs of her as an old woman.

I turned and slowly walked over to the mirror. Whatever enchantment I had felt or carried earlier when I'd worn the cape and sat inside the theater was gone now. I looked like an ordinary fifteen-year-old girl wearing new boots that were already scuffed, and clothes from Sears and Gimbels.

"Okay, that's squared away," called Aunt Kate. "We can get it out again next weekend."

I looked over to see my aunt coming down the stairs.

"I'm not glamorous," I said. I didn't feel sad, just resigned. "Rogan is more glamorous than I am. Everyone is."

My aunt walked over to stand beside me at the mirror. She pulled a stray wisp of hair behind my ear and stared at our reflections.

"Rogan's not glamorous."

"How can you even say that?" I looked away so she wouldn't see tears in my eyes. "He's so beautiful. And what you said about talent—he has that *voice...*"

"No, Maddy. Beauty isn't glamour. It's not the same thing at all." She stroked my hair. "Do you know what *glamour* means?"

"Beautiful." I spat the word. "Perfect, talented—"

"That's not what it means, Madeline." She shook her head. "*Glamour*—it has the same root as the word *grammar*. It is a kind of knowledge, of learning. That means it's something that can be taught. It can be learned."

She put her hands on my shoulders and straightened them. "Your great-great-grandmother wasn't beautiful, Maddy."

"Gee, thanks. Since I'm supposed to *look* like her."

"You're actually much prettier than she was," said Aunt Kate. "You have beautiful eyes, your skin's cleared up. And you're taller. She was quite petite; these days you need to be tall. And your teeth are much better—she never had her teeth fixed."

"That's not grammar," I said sullenly. "None of that is stuff I learned."

"No. But you can learn other things. Words, how to speak and walk. How to make your voice carry. Diction."

"That sounds horrible."

"Think of it like this: you're building a house, a beautiful house, a little bit at a time out of all these things—your voice, your body, your memory, how you move. If you do it right, if you put all the elements together, something happens. Something comes to live in that space you've made, inside you. Then you go onstage and people see it. They see you, but they also see this other—thing—that you've created. That you've built, that you're inside of."

"Oh, right," I said. "Like now I'm a goddamn carpenter."

She laughed. "It's like Latin, Maddy. That's grammar, too. But you studied it and learned it and now you're good at it. Your mind is attuned to it. *You* have a *gift*." She turned me so that I looked at her squarely. "You have talent."

"Not like Rogan."

"Rogan is talented, yes." She sounded impatient. "But the tail wags the dog with him."

"I don't even know what means."

She sighed. "It's late. You'd better get home; we need to stay in everyone's good graces."

I walked to the door, contrite. "Thanks, Aunt Kate. It was great—it was the best time I ever had."

"It's only going to get better," she said, and kissed me good night.

At home I went into the living room and found the enormous old dictionary that had been my grandfather's. I opened it to *glamour* and read a definition similar to what Aunt Kate had told me; but also something else.

A corruption of GRAMMAR, meaning GRAMARYE.
1. An enchantment or spell; an illusion of beauty.

I set the book down and looked out the window. In Aunt Kate's carriage house a single lamp burned, and in Rogan's window as well. Ghost lights; gramarye.

I turned the light off in the living room and went upstairs to bed.

◆ ◆ ◆

WE DIDN'T JUST see *Butley*. Over the next few weeks, Rogan and I saw *Pippin* and *Measure for Measure* and *A Streetcar Named Desire* and *Jumpers* and *A Little Night Music*. We went on Friday nights, and sometimes Saturday, and even weekend matinees. A few times Mr. Sullivan accompanied us, along with Aunt Kate.

This was embarrassing at first, and neither Rogan nor I ever mentioned it to our parents. We still couldn't figure out what had happened—did Aunt Kate lie to them? Had they undergone some weird middle-aged conversion? Had they all gone senile?

But, no, Aunt Kate made no secret of what we were doing. She asked for permission each time, always announcing we'd go to Rosoff's first for dinner, or for lunch if it was a matinee. Our parents remained as intransigent as ever otherwise; Rogan's even more so, as his grades, never good, had gotten worse. He'd snuck off twice to hang out with the band fronted by his brother's friend Derek, something I got furious about when he told me.

"They'll kill you if they find out." We were in the secret attic, naked. Rogan had gotten some condoms from Derek, which was how I came to learn about the band rehearsals. "That is so stupid, Rogan."

"Don't you start." He drew away from me. "Stupid. I know, I'm a fucking retard."

"Shut up." I pulled him back toward me and kissed him. His mouth was liquid, his breath pungent with hashish: another gift from Derek. "Don't ever say that. You're brilliant."

It had become more difficult for us to get time together alone—we were with Aunt Kate most of our free time. And my parents made it clear that they didn't want me constantly at Fairview.

"I want you to spend time with your friends," my mother said.

"Rogan's my friend."

My mother gave me a keen look. "He's your cousin, Maddy." I knew it was a warning.

Now, in the attic, I rolled on top of him. My head bumped the ceiling, and plaster fragments rained onto us.

"Be careful," murmured Rogan. "Let's look…"

He gently tugged the board loose so we could peer inside the wall. It never changed—or no, the stage changed every time we looked at it, the footlights glimmering green or cobalt or vermilion, the backdrops shifting as well to signal dawn, or late afternoon, midsummer or deepest winter. Sometimes it snowed; sometimes by some trick of the light the stage seemed slashed with rain or sleet. Once we heard odd chirping strings, like a cricket orchestra, and once a crackling that I realized must be the rattle of a tiny thunder sheet.

But the toy theater itself never changed. The proscenium with its paired masks and delicate frieze of languid Muses; the gauzy red curtains, bound in place with gilt thread—day to day, week to week, all remained unaltered. The invisible audience rustled and sighed, the invisible actors moved, if they moved at all, in steps unknown to my cousin and me.

It was late October. One Monday we arrived at school to find that Mr. Sullivan was now an English teacher. Sister Alberta had gone into St. Joseph's Hospital for treatment.

ILLYRIA

"Will she be back?" a girl asked.

Mr. Sullivan smiled wistfully. "I don't know. I hope so."

"I don't," said another girl, and everyone laughed.

Immediately, Mr. Sullivan became an object of much speculation. He was handsome, though maybe not as good-looking as Mr. Becker, who also taught English, and who was rumored to smoke pot.

But Mr. Sullivan was mysterious. He had been in the seminary—why hadn't Rogan and I known that?—and he'd also been an actor, with a small recurring part as Dr. Burke on *One Life to Live.* He'd been in a commercial for Irish Spring soap, a commercial that still aired and which I'd seen at least a dozen times.

"Why didn't you tell us?" demanded Rogan after class one day, when Mr. Sullivan admitted that, yes, that was him in the commercial, him in the boat, wearing a tweed walking cap and speaking with a brogue so patently false I was ashamed for him.

"You didn't ask," said Mr. Sullivan mildly. "And I can't play favorites in school."

We'd noted that already, when we tried in vain to get him to change the curriculum for Freshman English.

"These books," said Rogan. He began to tick them off on his fingers. *"Billy Budd. The Catcher in the Rye. A Separate Peace. Romeo and Juliet. Lord of the Flies.* Every single ninth-grade book, everyone dies! It's depressing."

Mr. Sullivan tipped his head. "Good point. But you still have to read them."

"Why?" Rogan stared at him challengingly, almost belligerently. "Can you give me one good goddamn reason why?"

"Enough," snapped Mr. Sullivan. "Everyone, get out your copies of *The Diary of Anne Frank.*"

Rogan's defiance bled into our trips to the city as well. We were with Aunt Kate on the train back home after seeing *The Country Wife.* Aunt Kate was seated, reading *The New Yorker.* Rogan and I were goofing around, swinging on the poles by the train doors. As the train approached the 125th Street Station, a small group of people gathered around us, waiting to get out.

The train stopped. The little crowd stepped out onto the platform. So did Rogan.

I gaped in disbelief. He took a step backward, grinning broadly, and as the doors closed gave me a little wave and mouthed *Bye-bye*.

"Holy shit," I said.

The train pulled out of the station. Aunt Kate looked up, eyebrows raised. "What?"

"Rogan." I pointed uselessly at the platform disappearing behind us. "He—"

I collapsed, laughing hysterically, onto the floor of the train.

Aunt Kate was not amused. "That brainless idiot," she fumed, nostrils white with rage. "Getting off in *Harlem* in the *middle of the night?*"

"It's only eleven," I protested. She looked daggers at me.

"Don't you say a word. Did you put him up to it?"

"No!"

At the next stop she dragged me from the train onto the platform. We waited, hardly speaking, for the next southbound train. It was a short distance between Melrose and 125th Street, but there were few trains that late at night. I began to grow anxious.

"Should we call the police?" I asked.

"And say what? That there's a white boy wandering around Harlem?"

By the time we got a train and it stopped at 125th Street, nearly an hour had passed. Aunt Kate grabbed me again and yanked me onto the platform.

There, sitting sheepishly on a bench, was Rogan. Beside him sat a tall black woman, dressed as elegantly as my aunt, her hands crossed resolutely on one knee as she stared straight ahead. I couldn't tell if she was a young woman whose hair had turned prematurely white, or an old woman who had drunk from the same Fountain of Youth as Aunt Kate.

ILLYRIA

As my aunt approached her, the woman stood. "I take it this is your young man?" Aunt Kate nodded. "I found him roaming the street like a chicken with its head cut off."

The woman gave Rogan a severe look, then lightly cuffed his long red hair. "Better for him if that *was* cut off. He said he was interested in the night life."

She and Aunt Kate regarded each other measuringly. I felt the same jaw-dropping disbelief as when Rogan had stepped from the carriage: this woman and my aunt *knew each other.*

But then a voice boomed across the platform, announcing the arrival of the next northbound train.

"Thank you very much," said Aunt Kate. She nodded respectfully.

"I'm just glad I happened by," the woman said. She waited until the train stopped at the platform, smiled, and left.

Aunt Kate pointed at Rogan. "You. Stand up and get on that train. No more nonsense."

"Did you see anything?" I whispered to Rogan as the train pulled away.

"Not really. A little." He turned to stare longingly at the streets below us, desolate and windswept, a few solitary figures hurrying along the sidewalk. "It was cool. Next time I'm staying."

The announcement for the school play went up the following Monday. Rogan and I were walking down the hall, when we saw a few people gathered in front of the bulletin board outside the English Department.

"Bad news, bro," someone said to Rogan. "It's not a musical."

I glanced at Rogan. His jaw tightened, his face froze into a mask of resignation and suppressed anger so intense that, without thinking, I touched his arm. He shrugged me off and pushed through the group to look at the audition sheet.

St. Brendan's Sock & Buskin Club
Annual Play Tryouts for
TWELFTH NIGHT, or What You Will
by William Shakespeare

Friday, November 12, 3:00
See Mr. Sullivan for details

"*Twelfth Night.*" I felt a swell of excitement, despite Rogan's disappointment. "That's the one about the twins."

"Shakespeare," said Rogan in disgust. "Who the hell does Shakespeare in high school?"

"But you like Shakespeare." I looked at him as though he'd forgotten my name. "That's why you stole my book!"

"*Romeo and Juliet.* I fucking hate that play."

"This isn't *Romeo and Juliet.* This is the one with the twins—"

"They all have twins," said Rogan. But he sounded less dismissive. "*Twelfth Night* is the shipwreck, right?"

I nodded, and his expression softened. He glanced around to make sure no one saw, then touched my hand. "Yeah, I remember. I always liked that one."

"Twins." My excitement deepened. "Rogan, we could be the main parts! Because we really could *be* twins, they wouldn't have to make us up, we already look alike—"

"Yeah, yeah, you're right." He nodded thoughtfully. "That could be cool. You'd have to get your hair cut. And do something about the color…"

The bell rang. The corridor filled with students rushing to class.

"We should practice," I said. "For the audition. I'll find a copy at my house or your place. There has to be one somewhere."

"Yeah, well, good luck finding anything in that shithole," he said. "I gotta go."

That afternoon I ransacked my house for a copy of the play. We only knew the story from Madeline's old edition of *Tales from Shakespeare*, with Arthur Rackham's pretty, fairy-tale evocations of winsome lovers and thwarted rulers.

The copy I eventually found seemed a relic from another world entirely: a once-sturdy, extremely ugly high school edition that had once belonged to my father, with cursory annotations to the text explaining the action though not the more unsavory jokes. The book had a pukey green cover and no illustrations, save a black-and-white frontispiece of a mincing, Mephistophelean figure in a stiff ruff and pointy shoes. Malvolio, I guessed, the vain Puritanical steward who becomes the victim of a cruel practical joke. Someone—my father?—had defaced the picture, adding glasses, a Hitler mustache, and buckteeth.

But the text seemed complete, as far as I could tell. At least there was no mention of it having been abridged or modified for a young audience. I skipped through the opening pages to Viola's first lines.

Act I, Scene 2
Enter Viola, a Captain, and Sailors

Viola: *What country, friends, is this?*
Captain: *This is Illyria, lady.*
Viola: *And what should I do in Illyria?*
My brother, he is in Elysium.

"'My brother, he is in Elysium...'"

I read the lines aloud; then went back to the beginning and read it all through, straight to the end. When I was finished, I went across the street to Fairview. Michael was downstairs, his lanky form folded into an armchair, eating a bowl of cereal and watching TV.

"Hey, Maddy," he said without glancing at me. "If you're looking for Rogan, he's not here. He went over to Derek's to practice."

"He did?"

Something in my tone made him look up. "He'll be back. Pretty soon, probably. Derek said he had to do something at five. You want me to tell him you came by?"

"No. I guess I'll just wait. If you think he'll be here." I held up the book. "We were going to practice for the play tryouts. The auditions are Friday."

Michael dug into his Cap'n Crunch. "Oh, yeah. I heard everyone's bummed it's not a musical. That new guy, Sullivan. Breaking with tradition. I didn't think Rogan was going to try out; I felt kinda bad for him. Since they weren't doing a musical. I know he really wanted to sing. He would've gotten the lead, too, whatever they did. He's got such a fucking amazing voice."

A sort of darkness swept over me. I felt cold and dizzy, as though I'd arrived someplace for a big party, only to find I'd gotten the date wrong and missed it, everything had happened weeks before, and I'd never even known.

"You want something to eat?" Michael held out the box of Cap'n Crunch. "You look kinda weird."

"I'm okay."

Rogan arrived half an hour later. He looked happy and wind-blown, sweeping into the house in a flurry of dead leaves.

"Hey, Mad-girl." He grinned when he saw me. I could smell smoke on him, cigarettes and marijuana. The uncanny blue-green eyes were bloodshot. "Whatcha doing?"

I gave him a wan smile and held up the book. "I thought maybe we could rehearse?"

"Oh, yeah. Right. I meant to tell you, the guys wanted to practice, we're doing some new stuff. But we can do it now if you want. That okay?"

He tipped his head to make sure Michael wasn't paying attention, then rubbed my arm. "Come on, let's go to my room."

Upstairs we read the entire play. Rogan took all the male parts. I took the female ones, and gave perfunctory readings to everyone save Viola. I was surprised at how easily Rogan handled all the lines, not just Sebastian's.

"I thought you hated Shakespeare," I said.

"Just *Romeo and Juliet*. This one's pretty funny."

We stopped often, to peruse the facile annotations and try to imagine what the stage directions would be.

ILLYRIA

"This is, like, a dirty joke." Rogan tapped the page where Malvolio read aloud from a forged love letter, supposedly penned by his employer, Olivia. "'*These be her very c's, her u's, and her t's, and thus makes she her great P 's.*' He's talking about a cunt."

I whacked him with the book.

"Hey, I didn't say it! Shakespeare did."

We reached the end. For a minute, neither of us spoke.

"The girl has the bigger part," Rogan said at last. He didn't look at me. "Viola. The play's really about her. Not Sebastian. The boy twin's hardly onstage at all."

"He's on at the end," I said quickly. "He has that great swordfight where Sebastian wins, where he duels Andrew Aguecheek. All his scenes are just toward the end of the play, that's all."

"I guess," said Rogan.

But we both knew he was right. It was Viola's show, at least the way the words read on the page.

"Come on," I said. "It'd be so great, Rogan, we'd be up there together, it would be like—"

I wanted to say, *It would be like when we're alone.* Like when Rogan murmured, *You can't breathe,* and I couldn't breathe, because desire and arousal choked me, because I breathed nothing but him; he was my air, my element; everything.

But being onstage together wouldn't be like that. How could it? Nothing would ever be like that.

The bleak horror I'd felt earlier returned; the sense that I had somehow missed the real meaning of the world, which everyone but me had always known.

"It would be okay, I guess." Rogan shrugged. He ran his hand along the back of my neck and gave me a sweet, stoned smile. "Hey, don't look like that! I'll do it—we'll do it. You're right, it'll be fun…"

He leaned down to kiss me. I shut my eyes and imagined us in the close darkness of the attic, the toy theater tossing its phantom starlight on our bodies as we moved together, like some strange articulated toy.

"What's going on?"

We sat up so violently our jaws cracked. The copy of *Twelfth Night* spun across the floor, to where Rogan's mother stood in the doorway. She stared at us, mouth pursed between uncertainty and angry disapproval.

"Why is this door closed?" she demanded.

"We're rehearsing." I scrambled to pick up the book and showed it to her. "This play by Shakespeare, the auditions are Friday. We're going to try out for it."

Aunt Pat barely glanced at the book.

"Leave this door open," she said. "Rogan, you need to get ready for dinner."

She stood and waited for me to leave.

"I'll see you tomorrow," I said to Rogan, without meeting his eyes.

"Yeah, see you."

At the bottom of the steps, Aunt Pat stopped. She gave me an icy look.

"You need to find other things to do with yourself, Madeline. You're too old for this. You're both too old for this."

She stared at me until I left.

At dinner I showed the battered copy of *Twelfth Night* to my parents and my sister.

"Do you remember doing that?" I pointed to poor Malvolio's scribbled face.

My father took the book and frowned, riffled the pages, then gave it back to me.

"I'm afraid I don't remember it, dear," he said, in the tone he might use if a small child attempted and failed to tell a joke.

"It's got your name in it."

"Mmm."

While we ate dessert I asked, "Is it okay if I dye my hair?"

"No," said my mother. "Are you out of your mind?"

"Nice try." My sister smirked.

I glared at her and went on. "It's for the play at school. The main parts are twins. Rogan and I are trying out together. If we get it I'll need to look like him."

"Then make him get his hair cut," said my father tersely.

"I won't even do it unless I get the part," I pleaded.

"No," my mother repeated. "Don't ask again."

The auditions were held right after school on Friday. Rogan and I made a few halfhearted attempts to practice lines during the week.

But there was only one afternoon when we had several hours to ourselves, and we spent those hours in the attic.

"That's really stupid," I said when we first crawled in and Rogan lit a cigarette. "Someone could smell it."

"My parents smoke. And no one's home now."

I looked at the overflowing ashtray. "It could start a fire."

Rogan stubbed it out and pulled me to him. "I don't need a cigarette to do that. Come on, they'll be home soon—"

Fear of discovery made the time feel urgent, almost frantic. Even the toy theater seemed irradiated by our anxiety. Its footlights dimmed to a glowering dull red, and indistinct shadows cloaked the topiary trees and faraway shipwreck, as though they had been cursorily sketched onto the backdrop. Rogan lay beside me, his face suspended above mine; but I couldn't see him, only smell him, his breath resinous with marijuana, and hear the broken rhythm of his breathing: silence, then a sound like a sigh, then silence once more.

"Rogan." I pressed my hand to his face and he kissed my palm. "I can hardly see you."

"That's because I'm not really here," he said.

On Friday, I was surprised by how many people showed up for the auditions. There were students scattered all over the auditorium, the usual drama crowd but other people, too. A bunch of girls from different English classes, and quite a few upper-class guys. Everyone I knew liked Mr. Sullivan, but I hadn't realized his popularity extended this far—there was a small cohort of cheerleaders, and two seniors from the football team. I sat near Rogan and several of our friends in the third row. Mr. Sullivan sat in the very front, by himself, with a notebook, a script, and several mimeographed sheets of dialogue.

I assumed Rogan and I would be permitted to audition together. Instead, Mr. Sullivan had all the girls read, one at a time, and then all the boys. The girls were given the same two speeches of Olivia's. In the first, Olivia declared her love for the boy Cesario—actually Viola in disguise—while in the second Olivia berated her drunken uncle Toby, and then fawned over Sebastian, Viola's twin brother, thinking he was Cesario. I listened, and secretly gloated, as the cheerleaders stumbled over the strange words and meanings.

"Mr. Sullivan, this is confusing!" one of them wailed.

"Imagine how confusing it is to Lady Olivia," said Mr. Sullivan.

My turn came. A moonfaced girl with long flaxen hair walked off the stage and handed me a script. I glanced at Rogan.

"Break a leg," he said.

Onstage, a row of lights shone down blindingly. I shielded my eyes and stared out into the auditorium, but could see only vague smears and shadows. Was that Mr. Sullivan? Rogan? When I looked down, the white pages of my script glowed with a diabolical brilliance.

"Whenever you're ready, Madeline."

I nodded and smiled nervously.

*"O, what a deal of scorn looks beautiful
In the contempt and anger of his lip!"*

"Louder," said Mr. Sullivan.

I cleared my throat and began again.

*"O, what a deal of scorn looks beautiful
In the contempt and anger of his lip!
A murd'rous guilt shows not itself more soon
Than love that would seem hid. Love's night is noon."*

The cheerleader was right: it made no sense. My face burned. The words of Olivia's speech began to skitter across the page like insects fleeing a light. I took a deep breath and concentrated on speaking as clearly as I could, on getting through the speech without passing out. When I was finished, I stumbled from the stage and thrust the pages at the next girl, then collapsed into the seat beside Rogan.

"That was horrible," I gasped.

Rogan grinned. "You did great."

The boys' auditions weren't much more impressive than the girls'. Mr. Sullivan gave them the speech that opens the play, Duke Orsino's command, "If music be the food of love, play on!" Their second reading was cobbled together from Orsino's amatory advice to Cesario.

I was disconcerted by how good the two football players sounded, though maybe it was just that their booming voices were more suited to the Duke's admonitory tone. Or maybe it was simply that anything sounded better than my own dismal effort had.

"Rogan?" Mr. Sullivan pointed at my cousin. "You ready?"

Rogan shook his head. "I'm going last."

I looked at him furtively. He was taller than me, of course, but then, Viola's twin brother would have been taller than she was. Our eyes were different colors, but would anyone be able to tell that from the audience?

The main thing was the hair. But surely I could find a wig among Madeline's trappings or in the box of props and costumes stored in a closet at St. Brendan's. Or Mr. Sullivan would buy one.

"Okay, Rogan," said Mr. Sullivan. "You're up."

Rogan went onstage. He moved around, face turned to the light, until he found a spot he liked; then began to read.

"If music be the food of love, play on!
Give me excess of it that, surfeiting,
The appetite may sicken and so die..."

I watched, transfixed. Everyone did.

Because Rogan didn't pronounce the words in a fake English accent or stumble as though they were a foreign language. He read them as though he knew what he was saying. And when it seemed like maybe he didn't, he winged it—he mimed some other, private meaning, looking slyly sideways at the audience and indicating by a gesture or smile that, even if we didn't understand what was going on, *he* did.

Only we *did* understand. I did, anyway, and when I stole a look at the other students, I saw that they did, too. They laughed or stared at Rogan with this odd expression of delight and disbelief, as though they'd just been told school was canceled for the day.

Only Mr. Sullivan didn't seem surprised. He leaned back in his seat, chin in hand and a small, knowing smile on his face, as Rogan straightened and began the Duke's second speech.

> "Come hither, boy. If ever thou shalt love,
> In the sweet pangs of it remember me..."

When he reached the end, Rogan tossed the script pages into the audience, made a mocking bow, and jumped offstage. There were murmurs of approval, and then everyone began to clap and cheer.

"Thank you, Rogan," said Mr. Sullivan, as he'd said to everyone. He looked pleased, but also businesslike. "Thank you all. I'll post the cast list first thing Monday morning."

"Monday?" I said in dismay. "We have to wait till Monday?"

Mr. Sullivan nodded. "Yup. Have a good weekend, everybody."

Several people clustered around Rogan as we left the auditorium.

"Hey, man, that was good." One of the football players pretended to punch Rogan's arm. "Play on!"

"You were really funny." The flaxen-haired girl smiled, then turned to me. "You were good, too, Maddy. See you Monday."

On the way home, I found myself looking at Rogan warily. It was like the day his voice had changed, when I'd first heard him sing in a chilling tenor that had come from—where? The same place this ability to act Shakespeare had come from, obviously.

But when had he learned this? *Had* he learned it? Or was it some bizarre fluke, like his voice?

ILLYRIA

"Did you—did you practice that?" I finally asked him.

"Practice? Yeah, some." He reached into his pocket and took out a pack of cigarettes, glanced around, then lit one. "I read it in front of the mirror in my room. Isn't that what you did?"

"Yeah," I said. But I was lying.

I looked at him again and thought of what Aunt Kate had said about glamour. That it could be taught, and learned. That it wasn't a matter of magic or luck.

"You were better than me," I said at last. "A lot better."

• ◆ •

ON MONDAY I went to school early. Rogan liked to sleep until the last possible second, so I walked up by myself. None of the buses had arrived yet, and only a few of the teachers. I looked for Mr. Sullivan's Dodge Dart but didn't see it in the parking lot. Inside I dumped my stuff in my locker, then with feigned nonchalance strolled to the English Department. The bulletin board was empty, save for an outdated announcement about the school poetry magazine.

I killed time as best I could, drifting around the library where I read old magazines. When I went back to the English Department, a knot of people was crowded around the bulletin board. One of them was Rogan.

"Maddy." He gave me a strained look. "You got your part."

"Really?"

He pointed at the cast list. I slipped through the crowd to stand beside him, and scanned the names on the typesheet.

TWELFTH NIGHT CAST
ORSINO, Duke of Illyria   Kevin Hayes
VIOLA, a shipwrecked lady   Madeline Tierney
SEBASTIAN, twin brother of Viola   Duncan Moss

My mouth went dry. Duncan Moss was a nondescript sophomore with longish brown hair and glasses. He was standing in the crowd, too, and flashed me a happy grin.

Short, I thought with a sick feeling; he was short and had hair the same color as mine. Onstage, without makeup or wigs, we'd look alike.

"Oh. Jeez." I turned to Rogan. "Did you—?"

He gave me a twisted, I-told-you-so smile, then jabbed his thumb at the final name on the list.

FESTE, a clown also called FOOL, Olivia's Jester
Rogan Tierney

"Typecasting," he said. He turned and walked away.

Our first rehearsal was that afternoon. We sat in chairs onstage, where Mr. Sullivan handed each of us a new Penguin paperback edition of the play.

"You can make whatever notes you like in these," he said.

"You mean, like, we can write in the book?" asked Duncan Moss.

"I think it would be a very good idea," said Mr. Sullivan.

We all smiled tentatively. Rogan took out a pen and made a big X on the cover of his paperback. Mr. Sullivan shot him an admonitory look.

"Hey, I'm the fool," said Rogan guilelessly, and everyone laughed.

"The zanies have their own little world, outside the mundane one that we live in, that Olivia and Orsino live in," said Mr. Sullivan later. It was too soon to start any blocking, but he stood and paced the stage, tracing an invisible boundary. "It's not governed by our laws—that's what the holiday of Twelfth Night is all about, a time when the Lord of Misrule takes over and our world is turned upside down. For the play to work, the audience has to completely believe in that other world. They have to look at Viola disguised as a boy named Cesario, and see a boy there, the same boy Olivia is in love with. But they also have to see Viola."

Abruptly he stopped and looked at me expectantly. I gazed at my script, flustered.

"Methinks she is speechless," said Rogan, and everyone laughed again.

ILLYRIA

"It's a balancing act," said Mr. Sullivan. "Acting is a matter of balance. Method actors, they say they lose themselves in a part—but you don't really want to lose yourself, do you?"

I looked up. Mr. Sullivan was still staring at me.

"Because if you really lost yourself," he said in a low voice, "you might not come back."

We finished the read-through, and Mr. Sullivan slapped his book against his knee. "Good job, everyone. We'll meet every day right after school, this week and next. After that we'll start going into night rehearsals."

We all stood to go. Rogan gathered his books and joined me.

"I don't know how you're going to balance *those*." He gazed pointedly down my uniform blouse. "Master Cesario."

"Rogan." Mr. Sullivan came up behind us. "Can you read music?"

"Not really. I fool around with the guitar, but—no."

"That's all right. Here." Mr. Sullivan pulled something from his briefcase and handed it to Rogan. "I want you to listen to this. All the songs marked *Feste?* I want you to learn them."

"Thanks," said Rogan, bemused.

It was a record album titled *Songs from Shakespeare*, illustrated with a dreary-looking bust of Shakespeare. Rogan turned to the back cover. There was a boring description of antique musical instruments, followed by a long list of songs, with play titles and character names beside them.

"Hey." Rogan looked at Mr. Sullivan in surprise. "This is a lot of music."

I peered over his shoulder. The entire second side of the album was taken up with songs from *Twelfth Night,* all of them sung by Feste.

Mr. Sullivan nodded. "It's a part for a singer. A strong singer. See what you can do with it."

He put a hand on Rogan's shoulder and smiled. "I've heard you singing by yourself in your room. I'd like you to sing like that here—"

He gestured at the empty auditorium. "When all those seats are full. Think you can do it?"

Rogan shrugged. "Yeah, sure. I guess."

We walked home. It was too late for us to steal any time alone, so we said good night in the street in front of my house.

"What do you think?" I asked.

"I dunno. I was kind of bummed at first. But now…" He glanced at the record album. "I guess I'll see how this music sounds."

I stood and waited for him to say something about me, about the different voices I'd tried using as Viola—one for when she was a girl, the other for when she was dressed as Cesario. But he just stared at the record.

"Well," he said at last. "I better go put this on. See you."

I had trouble falling asleep that night. I read and reread the play—my scenes, anyway—and tried to make sense of the unfamiliar words and the scrawled notes I'd made of Mr. Sullivan's commentary. In Act III, Viola and the Fool had a scene together. I read her part aloud.

> "So thou mayst say the king lies by a beggar if a beggar dwell near him, or the church stands by thy tabor if thy tabor stand by the church."

I frowned and deciphered my scribbled notes.

Tabor = drum

I tried to imagine Rogan speaking his lines and me responding.

"I warrant thou art a merry fool and carest for nothing."

It was hopeless. I dropped the book and turned off the light, lay in the dark, and thought of Rogan. It felt like weeks since we'd been together in the attic. I tried to dredge up an image of the toy theater, the eerie dance of light upon its arches and tiny stage; I tried to recall Rogan's voice, singing, and imagine his hands on me and not my own.

ILLYRIA

But it didn't work, any of it. I was alone. The room was silent and dark. I could no more fill it with Rogan's face or voice or touch than I could fill it with snow or rain. I had no glamour, no magic; no voice to summon up anything extraordinary, here or onstage.

I had no presence.

I brooded on why Mr. Sullivan had even cast me as Viola. Anna, the flaxen-haired girl, was prettier and at least as good an actress as I was—why hadn't he chosen her?

The only reason I could come up with was that Duncan Moss and I could, in a pinch, at a distance, pass for twins.

That was it. There was no glamour in it. No talent, even. Just cold necessity.

I shivered. I felt light-headed and shaken, as when I first saw the toy theater. I stared at the dark ceiling and remembered Aunt Kate's words.

It's something that can be taught. It can be learned. Words, how to speak and walk. How to make your voice carry. Diction...

I thought of Rogan, how effortless it was for him. All he had to do was say the lines, and people laughed.

The tail wags the dog with him.

I couldn't do that. I was too self-conscious; people would never look at me of their own accord.

But maybe I could *make* them look at me.

You're building a house, a beautiful house, a little bit at a time out of all these things.

I thought of how Rogan moved, of his hands drawing pattern in the air. I thought of how he walked, shoulders canted back slightly, head tilted as though he were trying to listen to some far-off sound. His face raised always to the light; the way he'd stare at you so intently it was like a challenge, even if he said nothing. You take all these little things and you build a house. You build a character, a shell, and if you build it right, something comes to live inside it.

Olivia wasn't in love with Viola. She was in love with a make-believe boy that the grief-stricken Viola had created from the memory of her drowned twin.

"Well, I'll put it on, and I will dissemble myself in't," Feste says as he disguises himself to torment poor Malvolio. *"I would I were the first that ever dissembled in such a gown... The competitors enter."*

I might not possess glamour; I might not be a magician.

But I could learn to be a good carpenter.

And I could learn to be a thief. I reached for my copy of the script, turned the light back on, and began once more to read.

The competitors enter.

◆ ◆ ◆

IT WAS LESS like building a house than colonizing an island, this freakish, lovely, marvelous atoll that rose from the gray wasteland of St. Brendan's High School like some extravagant Atlantis we'd willed into being. All of our previous alliances and identities were tossed aside—jock, freak, egghead, cheerleader, anonymous.

But who or what we became wasn't necessarily reflected by the parts we played in *Twelfth Night*. It really was as if we were castaways, our place in Illyria determined as much by luck and skill—and not necessarily acting ability—as by a shared determination to make the play a success. It was my first full-bore exposure to the virus that is theater, not just watching a show but becoming part of its chemistry, the intricate helices of desire and ambition and love and unrelenting effort involved in producing even a bad play. And we all realized, almost from the very beginning, that our *Twelfth Night* was going to be remarkable.

For one thing, everyone knew their lines in record time. This in itself was unusual—apart from Rogan and myself, the cast had only the most rudimentary prior knowledge of Shakespeare. It really *was* like a virus: the boy playing Sir Toby caught it from Olivia, and Sebastian caught it from me, and Sir Andrew caught it from Maria—you get the picture. In the middle of a rehearsal, an actor would stride onstage and abruptly, as though he or she had been pumped with speed, start riffing on the lines.

ILLYRIA

Sudden meaning tumbled out of seemingly banal or incomprehensible exchanges. Malvolio pulled double and triple entendres from his famous scene with the forged love letter. Olivia didn't just come on to my Viola disguised as Cesario: she began to look suggestively at Maria, too. Backstage, Sir Toby would grab on to one of the heavy ropes that controlled the curtain, twist it around as though he were a kid on a swing, then spin himself dizzy, letting go at the last moment to stagger onstage for his scene in such a convincing display of drunkenness that Mr. Sullivan once checked his breath to make sure he hadn't smuggled a bottle backstage. Sir Andrew and Sebastian engaged in such extended swordplay that by opening night both were covered with cuts and bruises.

As for Feste—well, if there was a Patient Zero in this epidemic, it was Rogan. He didn't just learn his lines with a facility that was unnerving. As with the audition, he somehow intuited what they meant and made the meaning clear to everyone who heard him.

And then there were his songs. At rehearsal a few days after Mr. Sullivan had given him the album of Shakespeare's music, Rogan returned it to him.

Mr. Sullivan frowned. "Did you listen to it?"

"Yeah, I listened to it."

"And?"

Rogan gave him an odd half smile. "It was interesting."

Mr. Sullivan's mouth was tight as he slid the album back into his briefcase. "Places, everyone," he called.

The opening scenes went well, though not spectacularly so.

And then Feste made his first entrance, with Maria.

"O mistress mine, where are you roaming?"

The line was from later in the play—a song, according to the script, though Rogan had only ever spoken the lines in rehearsal. Now he sang them.

We heard him before we saw him, that soaring voice like something you'd hear in a dream or a church or a movie, so high and clear and utterly unexpected that there was muffled laughter, followed by surprised gasps as Rogan walked onstage.

Because of course we'd all heard him sing before, in church or just goofing around at school. But no one, not even me, had ever heard anything like this. He only sang two lines, the sweet falsetto at odds with the feline way he walked, and with his expression as he looked past Maria to where I stood offstage.

"O stay and hear, your true love's coming..."

I tore my gaze from him to look at Mr. Sullivan, seated as usual in the first row. He stared at Rogan blissfully, almost stoned with delight. So, by the end of rehearsal, did everyone else.

I've seen spectacular performances since then—Anthony Hopkins's Broadway debut in *Equus,* Kevin Kline in *On the Twentieth Century,* John Wood in *The Invention of Love*. Rogan's turn as the Clown rivaled all of them.

Everyone in that auditorium felt it: everyone was bewitched. I felt drugged, light-headed with desire and raw adrenaline. Whatever envy I had burned away at the expectation of sharing the stage with him. It was like sex—it *was* sex, magnified somehow and transformed into a vision we could all see, all share in; and there was Rogan, grinning and looking as happy as I'd ever seen him outside of the hidden space in his room.

From that moment on, the production was charmed. Malvolio, who was wonderful to begin with, became a miracle of cunning and pathos and self-love. The pallid, flaxen-haired Olivia was a bombshell. Duncan Moss as Sebastian grew dashing and began to flirt with me. Even the members of the tech club, the usually dour collective of outcasts who toiled at sound and lights and props and costumes, rose to the occasion with uncharacteristic displays of exuberance, going so far as to applaud scenes they'd watched a hundred times.

We all were good. But we took our cues from Rogan. There was a subtle undercurrent to everything Feste said, everything he sang; as if he knew some other, deeper, secret meaning attached to the play, something strange, even supernatural; something the rest of us could never hope to understand, although we drove ourselves crazy trying to.

Especially me.

"*Would not a pair of these have bred, sir?*" Rogan held up a quarter, the payment I'd given Feste so that he'd let Viola pass Olivia's gates.

"*Yes, being kept together and put to use,*" I retorted.

But before I could push my way past him, he sidled up beside me and kissed me, his mouth lingering so that I felt his tongue between my lips.

I stumbled backward, mortified. Offstage someone laughed.

"*I would play Lord Pandarus of Phrygia, sir,*" Rogan went on, "*to bring a Cressida to this Troilus.*"

"That's great, Maddy!" Mr. Sullivan called from his seat in the audience. "Brilliant, Rogan!"

Several of Malvolio's big scenes came soon after this, and neither Rogan nor I was on for a while. I found him backstage and dragged him behind the fire curtain.

"Are you nuts?" I hissed.

"Yes," he whispered. He drew me to him and kissed me again, harder, pulling me so close I could feel his heart pound. "Maddy..."

I trembled so much it hurt to speak. "Rogan—stop. I have to go on."

"My parents are gone tonight. Michael's going to Derek's. Come over afterward."

I nodded, turned, and stumbled off to make my entrance.

That night, lying with Rogan in the attic, I felt nearly delirious with arousal, and what I now know was pure, unchecked joy. I knew it then, too; knew that whatever happiness lay in store for me—vast continents of happiness, I was certain, of which this was only the first glimpse of shore—this would always be what I remembered. My cousin beside me, the toy theater's radiance lapping our bodies in waves of gold and green while phantom lightning flickered in Rogan's eyes and phantom vapor roiled across the tiny stage, all those rustlings and whispers silenced by Rogan's voice, singing softly beside me in the dark.

"When that I was and a little tiny boy,
With hey, ho, the wind and the rain,
A foolish thing was but a toy,
For the rain it raineth every day."

He turned to me and stroked my cheek. "I love you, Maddy."

"I love you, too," I whispered.

It was the first time we had ever spoken it aloud.

It was now the week before Christmas. The show was scheduled to open on January 6, the real Twelfth Night. Everyone connected with the play was practically incandescent with excitement and expectation. The corridors at St. Brendan smelled of roses and burned sugar; the overhead lights hummed with a scintillant, cracked-ice glow. I felt as though I were walking around inside the toy theater; as though it had grown, like the magical stage tree in *The Nutcracker,* to encompass everyone I knew, everything I touched.

On Christmas Eve, the last day of school before Christmas break, and after a rehearsal that went on into the night, we exchanged gifts backstage.

Funny gifts, mostly. Duncan Moss gave me an athletic supporter. Maria furtively slipped Sir Toby a pint of rum. Sir Andrew and I exchanged plastic swords. Mr. Sullivan told us we were all exempted from taking the English exam scheduled for when classes resumed.

"Where's Rogan?" he asked.

I looked around. "He was just here—"

Rogan suddenly materialized, stepping from the shadows onto the stage. "Maddy," he called. "Catch!"

I turned and got hit in the face by a snowball. "Hey!"

"Oops," said Rogan. His face was flushed as he pointed to the fire door. "Everyone! Come here, look—"

We ran to the door, then streamed outside, laughing and shouting in amazement.

"It's snowing!"

---- ILLYRIA ----

None of us had ventured from the auditorium for hours. When school ended, the sky had been gray and the ground barren.

Now a good six inches covered Mr. Sullivan's car and drifted up against the sides of the building and into the unplowed streets beyond. The air was so thick with snow I couldn't tell who stood beside me, Olivia or Sebastian or one of the guys from the tech club.

"Maddy," came a voice at my ear. It was Rogan. He made a slow backward pratfall, until he lay on his back in a snowdrift, grinning like a lunatic. "Merry Christmas."

• ♦ •

THAT YEAR, FOR the first time, Christmas seemed anticlimactic. The usual buzz around the Arden Terrace hive was muted. A lot of the older cousins didn't come home or made only fleeting visits. There was no one younger than Rogan or myself to spur parents to keep up the pretenses of the season, and all the adults seemed more tired, less interested in the holiday than usual: exhausted but also relieved that they didn't have to make the long slog through the Valley of the Shadow of Santa Claus. Mr. Sullivan hadn't called any rehearsals until a few days after Christmas, but the break didn't feel like a treat. It felt like an exile. Not even the modest, but still impressive, pile of presents with my name on them cheered me up, until I got to the large box from Aunt Kate.

"This isn't a new present, Maddy." She sat in the wing chair in our living room, having made the rounds of the other families since early that morning. As usual, we were last on her roster; as usual, she took the whiskey sour my father gave her and sipped it as my sisters and I opened our gifts. "But at least this time I know that it fits."

I opened it, suspicious of the Gimbels logo on the box, then gasped.

"Oh, Aunt Kate." I drew it out, the midnight folds falling about me and exhaling a faint fragrance of camphor and Chanel No. 5 and roses. "Thank you, thank you so much..."

My mother asked, "Is that Madeline's old cape?"

"It is." Aunt Kate sipped her whiskey and watched me. "I took it out of storage a while ago and had it cleaned. I knew it fit—Maddy's worn it before—but I wanted to be sure she'd take good care of it."

"I will," I said as my sisters looked on, unsure whether they should be jealous or not. "You know I will."

Aunt Kate nodded. Her blue agate eyes narrowed.

"You'd better," she said.

A few days later we went back to rehearsing; a few days after that school began once more. I hadn't seen Aunt Kate and Mr. Sullivan together for some time, not since we'd all gone down to the city to see *Jumpers*.

During that last week of rehearsals, she showed up every afternoon. She sat in the very back of the auditorium, where the Tech Club guys hung out when they weren't needed. They had started out as a nerdy bunch, but as the weeks passed a sea change had overtaken them, as well. They started getting high with Rogan in the parking lot before school; they let their hair grow long and began listening to different music. *Tales from Topographic Oceans* gave way to *Transformer* and *Electric Warrior*. The first time I saw Aunt Kate in their midst I felt a stab of panic—embarrassment at having an adult family member intrude upon our hidden world; fear that from this vantage point she'd see the indelible path charting my fall from grace, from earnest, slightly anonymous niece to pot-smoking infidel and incestuous wanton.

But she said nothing. And the tech guys seemed to like her.

Sometimes she'd slip from her row to join Mr. Sullivan, her high heels ticking softly until she sank into the seat beside him. If I were onstage, I'd try not to get flustered, seeing them with their heads together, whispering. If I were backstage I'd peer from behind the curtains and vainly try to decipher what they were saying. Were they happy with the box tree scene? Did Malvolio caper too gaily in his cross-gartered yellow stockings?

Mostly they seemed to focus on Rogan. Mr. Sullivan would lean back, pencil at his lips, with the same stoned smile he had every time my cousin sang. Aunt Kate's expression was more difficult to read: tight-mouthed, keen-eyed, unsmiling; but was it disapproval or sheer amazement?

It could have been either. And I was afraid to ask.

Rogan didn't seem to care. It was all one to him: if the auditorium was empty or if a few parents and students wandered in to watch, if we were in costume or still wore our uniforms, if someone else missed a cue, or if the followspot failed to pick him out from the darkness. Rogan moved and sang and spoke as though it was always opening night.

Until, at last, it was.

On Thursday, we had a spectacularly botched final run-through, upholding the old superstition that a bad dress rehearsal portends a successful show. Sir Toby blew his lines and improvised with a series of obscene couplets and Firesign Theater routines. Andrew Aguecheek's sword poked me squarely in the stomach, knocking the wind from me so I couldn't finish the scene. An amber gel on a followspot melted and the stage reeked of charred plastic. Olivia giggled uncontrollably through her love scenes. I forgot my lines, not once but over and over again. The entire rehearsal felt like the quintessential Actor's Nightmare.

That night Aunt Kate was not in the audience, an absence that should have been a relief but instead struck me as slightly ominous. Rogan sang his final song, *"Hey, ho, the wind and the rain,"* and the stage at last went dark. Mr. Sullivan made us practice a curtain call, and this, too, made me uneasy.

"Don't worry," he assured us. "Tomorrow it will be fine. You'll see. Now everyone go and get a good night's sleep."

Olivia looked stricken. "Don't you have any notes?"

"Yeah," said Rogan. "Tomorrow night, don't fuck up."

Mr. Sullivan smiled. "Get some sleep. Rogan, give your voice a rest. No Rolling Stones, okay? And no cigarettes."

"Yeah, sure," said Rogan.

Outside, in the school parking lot, no one hung around. Mr. Sullivan had already left. The tech guys stayed to clean up the mess left by the burned gel. Toby and Olivia and Fabian and Malvolio and Maria all clambered into Toby's car to get dropped off at their respective homes. Duncan Moss's father picked him up as he always did, along with a few other grumpy-looking parents—the dress rehearsal had run even later than usual.

Rogan and I walked home together. He still wore Feste's makeup, a Pierrot mask of white with two crimson spots on his cheeks. The red had rubbed away from his mouth, but the kohl around his eyes remained, smudged so that his eyes seemed enormous, like those of some nocturnal frog or bush baby. He looked beautiful and deeply, strangely androgynous; unearthly, almost inhuman.

"We should have gotten a ride," I said, shivering.

The previous week's snow had turned into a gunmetal soup of slush and ice. The air was clear and so bitingly cold that Christmas lights and traffic lights and street lamps all seemed to shiver and dance, even though there was no wind. The smoke from Rogan's cigarette clung to us long after he'd tossed the cigarette aside. As we approached Arden Terrace his hand found mine and held it, tightly.

"It'll go well," he said in a soft voice. His hand felt as though it had been carved from granite. "It'll be great, Maddy."

"It'll be the first time we're onstage together," I said. I felt my heart open at the thought. "Everyone will see us. Everyone will hear you."

"They've already heard me," said Rogan.

"But not like this."

"No," he said, and turning to me he smiled.

It was like my own reflection in a black mirror, only a mirror that stripped the flesh from my skull so that what grinned back was not the self I showed the daytime world, not the girl who woke and walked and struggled and laughed but the terrible me, the true me; the mad girl inside Maddy. I stared back at him but said nothing, only clutched his hand even tighter, until it felt as though his fingers cut into mine. For the first time in years, I thought of the word Aunt Kate had always used to describe him—*fey*—and my mother's blunt retort.

___ ILLYRIA ___

If I ever had a red-headed child, I'd strangle it.
"Maddy."

He stopped in the street in front of my house and put his arms around me. Even through our jeans and heavy coats I could feel his cock pressing into my groin. I shut my eyes and tried to summon snow, the icy glitter of footlights, and a sun the size of a thumbprint through pink and amber clouds.

But all I saw was ash and a tangle of broken masts, and all I tasted was smoke, a warm spurt of salt where Rogan's chapped lip split beneath mine and blood stained both our mouths until he pulled away, laughing, and walked down the darkened path toward Fairview.

• ♦ •

THE HOUSE WAS three-quarters full for opening night. My parents were there, and Rogan's; two of my sisters and his brother Michael, as well as Aunt Kate and a thin scattering of aunts and uncles. Aunt Kate had dressed as though we were making our Broadway debut, in her lizard-skin boots and a beautiful, embroidered Russian peasant skirt and blouse of jade-green silk. She sat a few rows behind Mr. Sullivan, near a group of St. Brendan's staff, her hands demurely crossed in her lap and her emerald ring casting a green flare from the overhead lights. There were other parents, of course, and numerous children, siblings of the other cast members; as well as students.

Not just the usual Drama Club boosters, either: there was an impressive, rather intimidating block of football players and assorted jocks, as well as cheerleaders, JV and Varsity, and even a few kids from the local public school.

"Shit!" said Orsino. His eyes had the wild white gleam of a spooked horse's, but he sounded exhilarated. "Look at these people!"

I gritted my teeth and gestured at him to shut up. I was doing my best not to look at anyone. I stood just offstage and stared resolutely at the ropes and suspended weights that held backdrops and curtains in place. I'd peeked out earlier and seen the audience, and now I could hear them, along with the excited whispers and muffled laughter of the other actors around me. I felt so sick I thought I might pass out. I *wanted* to pass out, even though that would mean the show would be canceled.

I no longer cared. The horror I felt every time I looked at the stage, that brightly lit array of furniture and fake shrubs and cardboard scenery, was so intense it overpowered any other emotion.

"Hey, Maddy. You ready?" One of the boys who handled the curtains looked at me in concern. I nodded. "You sure?"

I took a step backward and knocked against the sand-filled canister that was a safeguard against fires; then bent and vomited into it.

"Uh, guess not." The boy grimaced. He pushed the can out of the way and grabbed one of the ropes. A minute later I heard the stage manager's voice.

"Places, everyone."

I wiped my mouth and looked across the stage. In the shadows stood Rogan, clad in his loose white Pierrot tunic and pantaloons, his feet bare, hair a loose halo around a ghostly face. He was singing to himself, soundlessly, staring at the stage floor and moving as though he saw his reflection there and danced with it. After a moment he glanced up and saw me. Very slowly he raised his fingers to his lips and kissed them, then extended his hand to me, palm forward. His head sank to his breast as though he had fallen asleep, so all I saw was that cloud of fiery hair.

"...lights and—*curtain.*"

I waited, mouth dry, through Orsino's opening scene, the welcoming wave of laughter as he paced the stage with a golf club and knocked over the plastic geraniums, one by one. He seemed less lovesick than drug addled.

But the scene worked, just as it had in rehearsal. Better, even.

And faster. Before I could blink, Orsino exited, giddy from the scattered applause that followed him. The lights darkened to red and indigo. Someone shook a thunder sheet. A spotlight flickered. The Captain

ILLYRIA

walked on, a tall blond jock who looked like a rock star in his pseudo-naval costume, along with two sailors. They took their places front and center and gazed expectantly at me in the wings. I drew a shuddering breath and raked my fingers through my hair, then stumbled on to fall at the Captain's feet and gaze up at him imploringly.

"What country, friends, is this?"

"This is Illyria, lady." The Captain looked past me, to where Rogan stood offstage.

"And what should I do in Illyria?" I turned to stare at my cousin, and began to cry. "My brother, he is in Elysium..."

I recall almost nothing else of my performance, though I remembered all my lines, all my entrances. People applauded when I walked offstage. They laughed at the right places. I took my pratfalls during my duel with Sir Andrew and praised the countess so that the very babbling gossip of the air cried out "Olivia."

But it was like being stone-cold drunk in a darkened room. Only when Rogan was on did the stage suddenly seem to shake and blaze, as though lightning struck it: his flaming hair, his white costume irradiated by the followspots, his bare feet kicking up a shining haze of dust and rouge and face powder that followed him like a bright shadow. When he first opened his mouth and sang I heard a gasp go through the audience, as though everyone had at the same instant touched a burning wire.

Then the house fell silent.

It was as though I were alone in the attic. Only now, the toy theater had grown to the size of a real one. I watched my cousin, his slender form pacing in front of the footlights, the scrim behind him backlit so I could see the faintest suggestion of tree limbs and the outlines of a wrecked ship, the moon rising above distant mountains, and the blue shadows of the other actors. His voice echoed from the rafters, so piercing and full of heartbreak I felt as if that burning wire had been thrust into my skull. When he finished, he stepped backward and gave a small, plaintive bow, then straightened as, slowly at first, then with the sudden irrevocable rush of water flooding a broken building, the place erupted into applause.

"Holy fuck," someone behind me breathed.

I couldn't speak. I stood beside the curtain and peeked out into the audience.

People were still applauding—jocks, mostly, all fired up with the beer they'd snuck into the auditorium. I saw Mr. Sullivan with Sister Mary Clark beside him, whispering in his ear. A few rows behind them were my parents and sister, who seemed to have reverted to some sort of racial memory of how to behave at the theater. They held their mimeographed programs and clapped and appeared enthusiastic, if bemused: as though they'd suddenly awakened here, fully dressed, and were trying very hard not to draw attention to themselves.

But Rogan's mother looked strained and unsure how to react. I saw her glance furtively at the people sitting next to her, who beamed and nodded, while Aunt Pat kept her hands poised just above her lap.

Meanwhile, Rogan's father stared stony-eyed at the stage, not even looking at Rogan but beyond him, as though someone else were to blame for what he'd just witnessed. My skin prickled and I took a step backward, then told myself that was stupid, there was no way he could see me through the curtain. I continued to search the audience until I found Aunt Kate.

"Don't miss your cue," someone hissed at me.

I nodded but didn't move. My mouth went dry; I felt as I had in those terrible moments before the curtains first parted.

Because Aunt Kate was weeping. Not wiping at the corners of her eyes, as I'd seen her do during a performance of *King Lear*, or crying demurely as she did at a sad movie, or even staring stoic and wet faced as she did at Tierney funerals.

Now she was bent almost double as her body heaved with sobs. Even from backstage I could see how her face had gone dead white. Her eyes and mouth were red slits, like the openings in a mask. She looked as though she were having a seizure or a heart attack; but

ILLYRIA

before I could move, the stage manager grabbed my arm and pushed me toward the stage.

"For chrissakes, you're *on!*"

It was all a blur after that. Love scene, swordplay, mad scene, reconciliation: all flickered around me, a slide show glimpsed through a fever dream—until the play's last moments.

Everyone exited, save Feste. He stood alone, the stage dark except for a single thin followspot that picked out his face: the white makeup smudged, the rouge gone from his cheeks and lips. Only his eyes were more brilliant than ever, blazing aquamarine as he tilted his chin toward the light and sang.

> *"When that I was and a little tiny boy,*
> *With hey, ho, the wind and the rain,*
> *A foolish thing was but a toy,*
> *For the rain it raineth every day."*

I stood with everyone else backstage and watched. Our curtain calls were forgotten, the audience was forgotten. Rogan himself was gone. There was only song and light, and the dust swirling around him in a nimbus of gold and black. As though he'd given voice to it; as though he'd given voice to all of us, and we would flicker back into darkness when he fell silent.

> *"But when I came, alas, to wive,*
> *With hey, ho, the wind and the rain,*
> *By swaggering could I never thrive,*
> *For the rain it raineth every day."*

I didn't know I was crying, until Malvolio gasped and pulled me to him. Dimly I grew aware of other sounds backstage, muffled sobs and breathing. Someone else put their hands on my shoulders. Not to comfort me; more the way a scared child reaches for an adult in the night.

"A great while ago the world begun,
With hey, ho, the wind and the rain,
But that's all one, our play is done,
And we'll strive to please you every day."

The followspot wavered as Rogan raised his hands. His eyes closed as the last notes echoed through the house. The spotlight went out; the auditorium plunged into darkness. His voice hung there still. I shut my eyes and felt him beside me, felt his mouth on mine and his breath warm against my cheek.

The lights went up in such a sudden blaze that everyone backstage started, then laughed nervously. I blinked and rubbed my eyes.

"Places for curtain call!"

The auditorium remained silent. Then, as the curtain parted, a roar of clapping and shouting and catcalls swept over us.

We all got our applause. Lovers, Puritan, knights and Captain and soldiers and attendants.

But it was Rogan's show. No one had ever doubted that, not since he'd first stepped onstage. He took one bow, then another; the curtains closed, then opened again, and we all ran back out for more calls. When the curtain closed for the last time, the drunken jocks chanted Rogan's name until he stepped out alone, front and center, his costume furred with dust and his golden hair wild around his white face. He stared at the audience, elated, until someone put the house lights on. People shaded their eyes and looked around in confused delight. At last, they began to leave.

Onstage actors ran around breathlessly, kissing and embracing. Sir Andrew and Sebastian clashed swords as Maria and Olivia fell into each other's arms, laughing as they wept.

"You were so good!"

"No, you were so good!"

I went out front to receive congratulations from my parents.

"Very nice, very nice," my father said. He kissed me absently on the forehead. "Do you need a ride home?"

"No, there's a party, I'll get a ride later."

"You did very well, Maddy," said my mother, and she hugged me. "We're very proud of you."

I looked around for Rogan's parents. They stood stiffly with their son a few feet away, none of them talking, though it looked like I might have just missed something, an argument or maybe Rogan's announcement that he'd be at the after party.

"Maddy?"

I turned. Mr. Sullivan grinned at me, Aunt Kate at his side. "You were wonderful—you and Rogan both. Just super."

"Thanks."

"You did a lovely job, darling." Aunt Kate hugged me tightly, then kissed both of my cheeks. "And you—"

She reached out to take Rogan by the hand and pulled him to us. I had a glimpse of my uncle's face, gray and unflinching, before he turned and walked out of the auditorium. Mr. Sullivan grasped Rogan's shoulder.

"You were amazing, Rogan. Just incredible." Mr. Sullivan threw his head back and laughed. "That voice!"

Aunt Kate's nose wrinkled as she stared at the unlit cigarette in Rogan's hand. "That voice isn't going to last very long if Rogan doesn't take care of it."

She smiled; but there was no warmth in the way she gazed at Rogan, even as she ruffled his hair and added, "You gave a hundred percent out there tonight, darling."

His mouth twisted in a smile. "Two hundred percent."

Aunt Kate looked at him as though this were part of some other conversation. "Just make sure you save something for tomorrow, sweetheart," she said lightly. "And Sunday. You have two more performances."

Rogan shrugged. "Hey, I might not be here tomorrow. None of us might." He looked sideways at me and smiled. "You getting a ride with Dunc?"

I nodded.

"Come on, then." He bent to kiss Aunt Kate's cheek, then saluted Mr. Sullivan. "I'll see you tomorrow, Mr. S."

"No cigarettes!" Aunt Kate called after us. "Get a good night's sleep!"

The party was like Christmas, an anticlimax. Still, we all stayed till three o'clock in the morning, getting high and passing around a gallon bottle of Almaden wine. Duncan Moss drove Rogan and me home, dropping us off at the top of Fairview's driveway.

"Fare well, my metal of India," Duncan said, and gave me a sloppy kiss.

"If he has an accident, you'll have to play Viola *and* Sebastian," said Rogan as we watched him drive off.

"Might be an improvement."

Rogan shook his head. "Nothing could be an improvement."

We stood with our arms wrapped around each other, swaying slightly while a moon just past full hung above the Hudson. Our breath formed a white cloud around us; underfoot a brittle layer of ice buckled and cracked.

"This is perfect," whispered Rogan. He buried his face in my hair and kissed my neck. "This, now—tonight—"

"Shhh," I said.

I knew what he was going to say next, knew it as though it were my own name. I kissed his mouth and silenced him, silenced everything except for the steady knocking of our chests, heart to heart, breath to breath, and the January wind blowing cold across Arden Terrace.

• ◆ •

THE AUDITORIUM HAD only been three-quarters full on opening night. Saturday it was packed. The performance was even better than it had been the night before: word of mouth and repeat attendance by the jocks meant that Rogan's every entrance was met with cheers and whistles. He never lost his composure, though the other actors began to improvise, doing funny riffs and playing off the audience as though there were no fourth wall between us.

ILLYRIA

When the last act ended, Rogan received a standing ovation. He accepted it gracefully, beckoning the rest of us to join him onstage and saluting Mr. Sullivan where he sat, fifth row center, with Aunt Kate at his side. Afterward there was another party, a more formal affair thrown by Olivia's parents. Rogan didn't bother to change, but I wore my blue velvet cape. My father picked up Rogan and me before midnight.

"How did it go?" he asked as we climbed into the backseat.

"It went great," I said. Neither my parents nor Rogan's had come to the second performance. As far as I knew, they wouldn't attend the final one, either. "I'm tired, though."

"I'm not surprised." My father glanced at me in the rearview mirror. I thought he was going to say something, but he remained silent until after we dropped off Rogan.

"Aunt Kate came over this afternoon." He pulled the car into the garage and turned the ignition off, so we sat in darkness. "She wanted to talk to your mother and me about something."

He used the tone I'd always imagined a parent might use to announce a divorce or death.

"What?" My heart began to race. Had Aunt Kate blown the whistle on Rogan and me sleeping together? Did she even know? "Did something happen? Is it—"

"We'll talk about it tomorrow."

My father got out of the car. I stared after him, incredulous that he could drop this bomb but not watch it go off. "What do you mean, tomorrow? What happened? Is everyone okay?"

"Everyone's fine. Your mother and I will discuss it with you in the morning, I'm going to bed."

I spent an anxious night, finally resorted to taking a Valium Rogan had gotten from God knows where. Toward morning I fell asleep.

It was noon before I woke. That alone would have signaled that something was afoot—I had never been permitted to sleep that late, even when I was sick with chicken pox.

"Maddy?" I looked up blearily and saw my mother at the foot of my bed. "Aunt Kate's here. Why don't you get up and get dressed."

I took my time, showering and gathering everything I needed for the last show, a four o'clock matinee. If I'd even be allowed to perform in it. I wondered if Rogan had already had his meeting; if he was in my house right now, with Aunt Pat and Uncle Richard and my parents and Aunt Kate, all of them waiting to confront us.

But when I finally went downstairs, my parents and Aunt Kate were sitting cheerfully at the dining table, surrounded by coffee cups and half-finished plates of leftover turkey sandwiches.

"Good morning, Maddy," said Aunt Kate. "Did you get enough sleep?"

I looked at her uneasily. "I think so."

"Sit here, darling."

Aunt Kate pulled out the chair beside her. I sat, picked up a slice of pickle, and ate it.

"I came over yesterday to talk to your parents about something I've been working on for the last few months." Aunt Kate reached for the coffeepot and refilled her cup, held it in both hands so that the steam curled in gray wisps around her face. "I think it's time for you to go to London to study."

To hide my confusion, I took a sip of tepid coffee from someone else's cup. "Study what?"

"Acting. I've arranged for you to have an audition at the National Youth Theatre—they're still on their Christmas break. They rarely see potential students this time of year but I pulled some strings and they've agreed to meet with you. We'll have to get your passport photos immediately, but once that's taken care of we can go down to the city and just stand in line to have it processed. The main thing is that you need two audition pieces, one classical and one contemporary. You'll have to learn the contemporary one quickly. I think Lizzie in *The Rainmaker*. There's a good speech there; you'd do a super job with it."

I was still stuck back on that one word, *London*. "You mean England?"

"Yes." Aunt Kate exchanged a quick look with my parents.

"We'll leave you to discuss this," said my mother. She and my father stood, neither of them smiling, and left the room.

ILLYRIA

I stared at Aunt Kate, bewildered. She might as well have told me we were going to visit Middle-Earth or Mars.

"I don't get it," I said.

For a minute Aunt Kate sat and ran a finger across the face of her emerald ring.

"This is something I've given a great deal of thought to," she said at last. "And for a very long time. You're young, but your great-grandmother was younger than you when she first performed professionally. We can always dance around the age issue a bit if we have to—with the right makeup and clothes you could pass for seventeen. If you do well at the National Youth Theatre—and you will—we can decide whether you should attend RADA or Central—Central School of Speech and Drama. But you'll be working well before then."

"I still don't—this is an acting school? In England?"

Aunt Kate nodded. "In London. I have old friends there. Some of them owe me a favor—not that you wouldn't be accepted on your own merits, but it never hurts to call in a favor."

I gaped at her in disbelief. "My parents—my parents know about this?"

Again she nodded. "I've already told them. I'll make all the arrangements, including tuition payment. And I'll stay with you, for the first few months anyway. I have a friend in Hampstead; we can use his flat while he's in Greece for the winter. After that we'll see what we can do. I have other friends. Highgate, maybe, or Belgravia."

"But." I stared at the table in front of me, the white cups and saucers and half-eaten sandwiches, then looked at my aunt. "Rogan."

Aunt Kate hesitated. "I can only afford tuition for one child."

"But Rogan." My mouth tasted bitter, as though I was going to be sick. "I mean—can't you take both of us?"

"No. Even if I wanted to, I can't afford it. And the school wouldn't look kindly on my taking advantage of them, asking to audition two students."

"But that's crazy." I shook my head so hard it hurt. "Rogan is—he's so much better. You know that, right? It's not just me who thinks so. Everyone does. Even Mr. Sullivan. Everyone!"

My voice rose. I began to cry. "You can't. It's not fair—you know it's not fair—"

"This has nothing to do with fair." Aunt Kate's tone was icy. She turned to avoid my gaze. "Rogan's a loose cannon. What he did in Harlem that night—I'd be chasing all over London after him. His mother says he's taking drugs. And..."

She paused, staring at her hand. "There's very little they could teach him."

"What do you mean? He could do anything! You *know* that—"

Aunt Kate turned toward me. With one swift gesture she pulled the emerald ring from her finger.

"This was my grandmother's." Her voice shook as she thrust the ring within inches of my face. "This was Madeline Tierney's. She gave it to me for safekeeping. It has never belonged to me. Your cousin Rogan—"

She tilted the emerald until sunlight struck it and a green flare leaped from her fingers. Then she raised her hand and, with all her strength, threw the ring across the room. I cried out as it smashed into a cabinet, then dropped to the floor.

"Get it," said Aunt Kate. I shook my head and she repeated the command. "Get it and bring it to me, Madeline."

Crying, I stumbled to retrieve the ring and shoved it blindly at her.

"No," she said.

She grabbed my hand and forced it open and placed the ring in my palm. When I looked down, I saw that the gold setting was damaged. The emerald was intact.

But it was no longer possible to wear the ring.

"It was a gift," said Aunt Kate. "A family heirloom. Just like his voice. You remember that, Madeline."

She stood. From the other room I heard my parents talking. The phone rang.

"Does he know?" I whispered.

"There was never a chance, Maddy. Not for a long time." Aunt Kate drew her hand to her face. Without the ring it seemed tiny, a child's

ILLYRIA

hand and not a woman's. "But no, I haven't said anything to him. I think it would be better coming from you."

"I can't do that," I said. "How can you even think I could do that?"

Aunt Kate looked at me, her blue eyes bright with tears.

"You're an actor, Maddy." She turned to leave. "You'll find a way."

• ◆ •

I GRABBED MY things and fled the house through the back door, so I wouldn't have to face my parents. Rogan and I had planned to walk together to the last show.

But I was only halfway down his driveway when Fairview's front door opened and Rogan's brother Michael stepped out. He looked at me and shook his head, motioning for me to stop, then hurried up the drive to meet me.

"He's not here," he said. His face was flushed; he wore only a T-shirt and rubbed his arms to keep warm. "And if you were smart, you wouldn't be either."

"What? Is he okay? Where is he?"

"I don't know. He went over to Derek's a while ago for band practice. I guess he's still there."

"But—we have the last performance."

"Oh, he'll be there." Michael looked at me, his expression mingled disgust and fear. "Your precious show. You two should get some help, you know that? You should, anyway. *You're* not a total fucking idiot."

He turned and started back to the house.

"Wait—" I began, but Michael looked back and cut me off.

"Get out of here, Maddy," he said. "Now. Just go."

Rogan arrived backstage fifteen minutes before curtain time.

"Hey." He grabbed me and drew me close enough that I could smell marijuana and tobacco and mouthwash, then pulled away. "I got to get ready. See you in a few."

The house was full again. The performances—not just Rogan's, but mine, everyone's—were the best we'd ever done. My relief at not seeing any Tierneys in the audience was offset by the sight of Derek and some of his friends in the front row. I was afraid Rogan would leave with them afterward—our final cast party was supposed to be a wrap party, where we struck the sets.

Instead Derek and the other band members split right after the curtain calls. I couldn't blame them. It was ten minutes before we all stumbled offstage. I was elated despite myself, charged up from being onstage, from being in Rogan's orbit during our scenes together.

And, no matter that my stomach still churned at the thought, the phrase *London…I'm going to London* ran through my head like the opening lines of a speech I'd memorized. As I took my final bows, Orsino's hand in mine, I looked out at the audience on their feet and for a second shut my eyes, imagining another crowd there, another place; an outdoor theater, or an arena stage rather than a proscenium. Real acting teachers rather than Mr. Sullivan; real directors.

A real me, instead of the girl in scuffed tights and thrift shop costume, stepping back so that my cousin could take his customary bow, front and center.

When it was all finished, I changed quickly into the clothes I'd worn over, then looked for Rogan. I found him outside, smoking a cigarette in the brittle black air of early evening.

"Are you going to stay and help take everything down?" I asked.

He drew on his cigarette, then stubbed it out. "In a while. I'm going home first and get a sweater. I'm fucking freezing."

"Okay if I come?"

He grinned. "Sure, Mad-girl. Always."

We walked home. I knew I wouldn't be able to tell him in the secret attic or in his bedroom, or mine, just as I knew I couldn't tell him backstage. So I told him as we walked down the long hill toward Arden Terrace, shuffling through the dirty snow and gritty sand left by the plow trucks. As I spoke Rogan said nothing, only took out another cigarette and lit it, so I could see how his fingers trembled as he cupped the match between his hands.

"Wow," he said at last.

ILLYRIA

We were in the street in front of my house. A car drove past and Rogan stepped up onto the curb, as an arc of slush rose then fell around us. When the car's taillights receded into the night, Rogan turned and started toward Fairview. I ran to keep up with him.

He said, "Don't do it."

"What?"

"Just tell them you won't go." He didn't look at me. "That's all. Just tell them no."

I stared at my feet.

"They can't make you," he said. "Not unless you let them. They can't force you to go."

"I know."

"I wouldn't go. If it was me." A chunk of ice went skidding in front of us as he kicked furiously at the ground. "If they tried to make me go without you. I wouldn't do it."

He turned to me. His eyes looked flat and gray, all the color leached from them. "Maddy."

"I know," I whispered. "I know."

We'd reached the porch. Rogan stood with his hand on the ornate knob of the front door and looked back at me.

"Aunt Kate." He bared his teeth in a grimace. "Aunt Fate. I can't believe you're going to fucking roll over and do what she says."

He went inside, letting the door fall closed on me.

"Rogan. Stop—"

He ignored me and ran upstairs. I followed, not daring to speak again till we reached the third floor. "Rogan, please."

I tried to grab his hand but he pushed me away and headed for his room. "Rogan—"

He stopped in the doorway. "Oh, fuck."

I came up behind him and stopped.

The room had been trashed. Rogan's mattress lay beneath the window, sheets ripped from it and the ticking slashed open. A chair had been smashed against the wall until its legs shattered, a sheet wrapped around it like a torn sail. Books were everywhere, their pages gone, and empty cardboard boxes, ruined Christmas decorations and Halloween masks and ragged pieces of velvet and lace. Fistfuls of coins were strewn across the floor.

Only when I stumbled inside, I saw they weren't coins but foil-wrapped condoms. The air reeked of scorched wool. Ashes covered the floor, and blackened fragments of charred wood; cigarette butts and rolling papers and broken glass ornaments.

"Oh, no," whispered Rogan. "Oh, no, Oh, no."

He knelt beside the entrance to the attic. The door had been torn from its hinges. It dangled from the wall, surrounded by crushed cartons and a splintered wooden panel. On the floor was a heap of shredded paper.

"Maddy." Rogan gathered the wreckage in his hands and looked up at me. "Oh, Maddy."

It was all that remained of the theater: ragged bits of cardboard and tissue, traces of glitter falling from the shattered awning of what had once been the proscenium. I dropped beside Rogan and raked through the drift of torn paper, trying to find something that had not been destroyed.

But there was only shredded cardboard and gilt, matchstick-size splinters that had been topiary trees and damp gauze bearing the faintest shadow of a ship's mast.

"Who—"

Before I could shape the question, someone grabbed Rogan and dragged him to his feet.

"Do you think this is a flophouse?" I stumbled backward as my uncle shouted, his face so red it looked as though it had been boiled. *"Do you think this is your crash pad? Do you?"*

His hand struck Rogan's cheek. My cousin reeled backward and struck the wall. *"You left a cigarette burning in there! You nearly burned the house down—the whole goddamn house—"*

"Stop," I yelled. "Stop, you can't—"

My uncle turned and stared at me, his eyes widening in revulsion.

ILLYRIA

"You get out of here." He began pushing me toward the door. "Get out of here, get out of here—"

I tripped and nearly fell, caught myself, and staggered onto the landing. Rogan got to his feet and looked around wildly until he saw me.

"Maddy," he said. "Go—"

I fled downstairs and back outside. I didn't stop until I reached my own house, empty and dark in the early January night.

It wasn't until much later, when I looked out toward Fairview and the carriage house beyond, that I saw both houses were dark as well. For the first time I could remember, no ghost light burned in Aunt Kate's upper window.

• ◆ •

I DIDN'T SEE Rogan again before I left for London. His parents pulled him from St. Brendan's and sent him to board at Mount St. Michael Academy, an all-boy school in the Bronx run by Marist Brothers. We were forbidden to write or call each other. The truth was that, after three or four days, I was too caught up in a rush of preparation to grieve.

And I was young—I was constantly reminded how young I was, as though somehow my age made an invalid of me.

It didn't, of course. I knew I was being pushed away from Rogan, not just his physical being but his memory, everything connected with him. Which was absurd—he was my cousin; we were tied by blood if nothing else: our shared childhoods, our shared neighborhood, our parents and siblings, the very air we'd breathed for fifteen years—all of these things bound us intrinsically. It was a temporary separation: a few months, a year. Until we were older. Nothing would ever change.

But everything did.

That spring, Uncle Richard and Aunt Pat separated. Within a year, they were divorced—the first divorce in the Tierney clan. My parents didn't separate, but during my second term at the National Youth Theatre they moved. The house at Arden Terrace was sold, a new house bought in a small town fifty miles north of where I'd grown up.

ELIZABETH HAND

I was seventeen before I spent a night in it. My visits to the United States were few and short-lived. I don't know what strings Aunt Kate pulled to get me into the London theater scene, but once she tugged at them, she never let go. Her friend in Hampstead extended his Greek visit by eighteen months, so we remained in his flat, part of a lovely gray stone edifice surrounded by holly trees and rhododendron that bloomed all year long. At drama school I was a quick study; neither brilliant nor beautiful but willing to take on any role, no matter how dour, no matter what short notice.

"A character actor" I was told when, after three years, I finally auditioned for Central. I'd done Viola, and Amanda from *Private Lives*, for my audition at RADA—I now had a perfect English accent—but I wasn't accepted there. Central took me, though. Despite being typed as a character actress, I did my share of ingenues, along with the classics, in school productions of many of the same plays I'd seen years earlier with Aunt Kate and Rogan. Shakespeare, Shaw, Wycherley, Noël Coward's *Hay Fever*, and Alan Ayckbourn's *Norman Conquests*. My parents flew over to see *Hay Fever*, and once VCRs and videotape became popular, I sent them tapes of everything I did.

Aunt Kate was back in the States by then. I moved from Hampstead to share a flat with several other struggling actors in Highgate, all of whom were gratifyingly envious when I got a small role at the Royal Court with Nancy Meckler. A year later, I toured with the Manchester Royal Exchange in *Charlie's Aunt* with Sabrina Franklin, saving enough money to buy a one-bedroom flat near the Angel in Islington. To distinguish myself from my great-grandmother, I performed under the name Madeline Armin.

By the early 1980s I was doing a lot of television work. A girl who got run over by a tram in *Rumpole of the Bailey*, a running part on the soap opera *Emmerdale*, and a nice bit as a female police rookie on *Juliet Bravo*. It wasn't what I'd dreamed of doing, but it was what I'd trained for. I wasn't a star yet. I was something that occasionally seemed even more miraculous, especially among my cohort: a working actor. Still in my twenties, I was young enough to believe that greater success would come; that I wouldn't be frozen forever in those small moments on BBC1; that another, hidden world still awaited me, populated with the parts I was meant to play Desdemona, Lady Macbeth, Noël Coward's Gilda, and yes, Viola.

In the mid-1980s I went to Washington, D.C., for several months, after being cast in a supporting role in *The Good Person of Szechuan* at Arena Stage. I saw Rogan then, for the first time since leaving Yonkers. I'd kept up with his whereabouts through my parents and my sister Brigid. I'd learned not to ask Aunt Kate for news, after she made a brief trip to visit me several years earlier.

"Your cousin Rogan's not doing well, Maddy." She shook her head and stared down at the rhododendrons glistening silvery green in a late November rain. "You know he's a heroin addict, right?"

I turned so she wouldn't see my face.

"No," I said. "I knew he was in a band. I thought they were doing pretty well; Brigid said they had a record deal."

"I saw him at Pat's house and he looked awful. Jaundiced." Aunt Kate's mouth tightened. "Someone should help him. One of his brothers."

I slid a headshot into an envelope and said nothing.

Now, at last, I would see him. I took the train to New York and met him for lunch, all the time I could steal from work. I had suggested Rosoff's.

"Nah. There's a good Szechuan place near Penn Station. In honor of your play." He laughed and gave me the address. Through the telephone I heard the familiar *phhtt* of a match being struck, an indrawn breath. "Go there. I'll meet you at one thirty."

He sat at a table near the front of the restaurant, a narrow steam-filled place where there was more food on the shag carpeting than the tables. "Hey, Maddy."

I could feel him flinch as I put my arms around him.

"Rogan." I pulled back to look at him. "Hi, Rogan, hi..."

Someone had set fire to him and burned away all his youth. The nimbus of golden hair had faded to dull russet, close-cropped and already receding. He was gaunt, his skin so thin I could see the capillaries beneath, a faint blue fretwork starred here and there with red where the vessels had burst. There were already lines across his brow and deep grooves beside his mouth.

And yet he remained beautiful. Not only to me: I saw the waitress stare at him after she'd taken our drink orders and returned to the bar, and the bartender as well, watching us as we ate. His pallor only accentuated his eyes, their aquamarine now darkened to a cold teal blue, and the delicate line of his jaw and cheekbones.

"You look good," I said.

He gave me a twisted smile. "You, too."

I stared at his beat-up leather jacket and T-shirt, scuffed engineer's boots, and filthy jeans. In D.C. the weather had been sultry; I wore a white linen shirtdress and espadrilles, clothes that had seemed elegant, even sexy, when I got on the train at Union Station.

Now I felt dowdy and middle-aged, far older than twenty-six. Beside Rogan I looked ancient.

We made desultory conversation while we ate. I downplayed my modest success, which wasn't hard. I hadn't had a leading role since drama school, and the TV shows I'd appeared in weren't yet broadcast in the United States. Rogan told me about his band's recent gigs in the city and Philadelphia and Boston. I'd imagined this reunion for years, and for the last few weeks had been almost sick with anticipation and yearning—how could a few hours on a Monday afternoon even begin to be enough time to knit our lives back together?

The lunch was excruciating. Rogan wouldn't meet my eyes. I asked after his family and he shrugged.

"I don't see them. You're the first one I've talked to in, I dunno, seven years."

When I mentioned Aunt Kate in passing, he grimaced.

"Aunt Fate." His face contorted into a mask of loathing. "Fucking bitch. I don't want to hear about her."

We finished eating. I picked up the check. Only after we were back outside did he touch me, pulling me to him and resting his head lightly on my shoulder.

ILLYRIA

"Maddy. Thanks for coming up to see me." His tone grew slightly mocking. "It's been a really long time. We're both so busy."

He drew away and reached into the pocket of his leather jacket. "You have a tape player?"

I nodded. "Yeah, a Walkman."

"Here." He handed me an audiocassette. "This is a demo we're putting together. It's really rough, but it'll give you an idea anyway. Sounds a lot better live. You should come hear us sometime."

"I will. You should come see the play."

His eyes grew distant. "Yeah, maybe." He lit a cigarette and looked in the direction of Penn Station. "You better go or you'll miss your train. I'd walk you over but I have to meet someone."

My mouth was dry as I leaned in to kiss him. He gave me a small half smile, turning his head so my lips brushed his cheek.

"See you," he said softly, and walked away.

On the Metroliner back to D.C., I sat beside the window and listened to his tape. A mix of original songs and covers, "Helter Skelter" and "Turn Blue" and "Panic in the World." I had expected his voice to be raw or smoke-coarsened.

But then I punched the Play button and felt my skin grow cold as that same pure, high tenor rang out, so wild and true and utterly unchanged it was like being thrust back onstage with him. I shut my eyes and played the tape over and over, until the train at last pulled into Union Station. I gathered my things, a sheaf of unread scripts and magazines, shoved them into my bag with my Walkman, and made my way to my sublet apartment on Capitol Hill.

◆ ◆ ◆

I HAD ALWAYS imagined my career would be like a series of rehearsals leading up to opening night, followed by a long run and longer semi-retirement, with turns as Lady Bracknell and Juliet's Nurse to buttress solid employment in a critically acclaimed television series or maybe even a movie.

Instead it was an endless audition; a few nice parts in regional theaters before I turned thirty and, almost overnight, the leading roles disappeared. I became trapped in the career immurement that awaits a character actor, shuttling between London and New York, theater and bit parts in TV. Usually I was better than the shows I was in; always I imagined someone else on the stage with me, Rogan's flickering image like the static on a dead television channel, his voice in my head long after the tape he'd given me wore out from being played and replayed for so many years.

When my work was reviewed, critics marveled how I inevitably triumphed over bad material, especially if I shared the stage with weak leading men; how it seemed as if my own presence animated the air between us, as if someone else, something else, moved there unseen.

> Even in this feeble attempt at a post-Stoppard black comedy
> of manners, the redoubtable Madeline Armin walks the stage
> like a woman possessed.

But I would never be a star. Maybe there's only a certain amount of talent that can go around, especially in a family like ours; maybe after hundreds of years, the Tierney gifts had finally died out. Whatever acting talent I possessed, it wasn't enough. I channeled all my energy into my work. I had a few halfhearted relationships, and a drawn-out affair with a married woman, an actress I continued to work with, off and on, until her career outstripped mine. I still read about her occasionally, small items in *Time Out* or *Vanity Fair*. In love, as in theater, I had never had any magic.

True, I never flamed out. And I never shone, not even for a moment, the way my cousin had.

• ◆ •

DECADES PASSED. MY parents retired and moved from New York to Arizona. When Rogan's mother died, I sent him a note of condolence from London, carefully scripted and written on thick Crane stationery. I never received a reply. A few years later, my father told me that Uncle Richard had cancer. Within several months he, too, was dead. This time I didn't write.

The houses on Arden Terrace had long since been sold, all save Fairview and Aunt Kate's carriage house. Two of the bigger heaps were torn down and McMansions built in their stead, but most of the others were restored and carefully maintained by doctors and lawyers and stockbrokers, the same sorts of people who had first colonized Arden Terrace at the beginning of the last century. Aunt Kate remained in her home, attended by a series of loyal and well-paid home health aides who read to her when her vision deteriorated and made certain there was a good supply of audiobooks and cognac when they left at night to their own homes in the Bronx or White Plains.

I visited her whenever I was in New York, but that wasn't often now. I had no work in the city; not much in London, either. I did a series of audiobooks, adaptations of a successful children's series about a brave ant, and that made me enough money to live on.

When I did visit my aunt, the relative prosperity of her home, and the rest of Arden Terrace, made Fairview's gradual decay seem even worse. After Uncle Richard's death, the mansion had been inherited by his sons.

But no one wanted to live in it. Despite a few prosperous neighborhoods, like Arden Terrace, Yonkers had become a ghost city. Gentrification was still a ways off. My cousins were comfortably ensconced in Westchester or Putnam County with their families.

All save Rogan.

Over the years, news of him had filtered to me through family members. Like me, he never married. For twenty years he lived in the city, singing in various incarnations of his original band. He drifted from apartment to apartment downtown and, when he was finally priced out of the East Village, into Brooklyn. In the early 1990s he almost died. I learned about this only a few years afterward, and it was never clear to me what had happened. AIDS, I thought, and felt that same chill as when I'd first heard him sing.

But it wasn't AIDS.

"He's in the hospital," Aunt Kate told me over the phone. Her voice was so frail I didn't ask her to repeat herself. I was afraid she'd lose the strength to talk at all.

As a result, during the next year I received only fractured accounts of my cousin. Rehab. Another hospitalization, a second stint at rehab. Then, surprisingly, a performance at a Tom Waits tribute, or maybe Tom Waits had sung at a benefit for Rogan?

Aunt Kate herself seemed uncertain. She sounded more drifty these days, which was to be expected. I asked her, more than once, how old she was.

She never answered. She had always seemed ageless to me, younger than my own parents. Still, no matter how I did the math, I figured she had to be well into her nineties, if not over a hundred. After 9/11 she grew even more remote: one of my in-laws had been trapped in the towers, and the husband of Aunt Kate's favorite caregiver. I spoke to her less frequently, on her birthday and at Christmas. Finally, six years later, I received a phone call from my father saying she had died.

It was the end of December, the middle of a harsh winter in the Northeast. My parents were too frail to make the trip from Sedona, my sisters too caught up with the aftermath of Christmas and their own children and grandchildren. The rest of the Tierneys were scattered and long out of touch.

So I told my father I'd fly over from London to represent the family at the funeral Mass at St. Brendan's. It was only after I hung up that I realized I'd forgotten to ask what time the funeral was; also, where I could stay?

I rang my father back.

"Your cousin Rogan's made all the arrangements," he said. "He stayed with her, you know. He was there in the hospital when she died. Your mother e-mailed and told him you're coming. Have a safe trip, dear."

ILLYRIA

My plane was late. It was a cloudless blue day. Flying above the Canadian Maritimes and New England, I saw snow thirty thousand feet below, a wrinkled white expanse of woodland dulling into gray urban sprawl, pocked with frozen lakes and reservoirs. In the minutes I stood outside at Kennedy before locating my hired car, my lungs ached from the cold.

"Fucking freezing," the driver told me as we headed toward the city. "Too cold to snow, even. Where's our global warming?"

The car took me directly to St. Brendan's. There had been no wake, and only a few people were inside the church when I arrived. The two middle-aged women I assumed were Aunt Kate's health aides, and the ancient couple I remembered from my own tenure at St. Brendan's.

And Rogan.

"Maddy." He stood in the first pew and waved me toward him. "Jesus, Maddy, I can't believe you came all this way, in this weather."

He was thin, though not gaunt as he'd been twenty years before. He wore a black woolen overcoat over faded corduroys, and a gray henley shirt. His thin russet hair had burned to ash; his eyes were a pale washed turquoise, slightly bloodshot; his face was heavily lined. He looked ravaged; still beautiful, still wrecked.

But his arms around me were strong, and when he drew me to sit in the pew beside him his hand held mine, tightly, until the priest made the final benediction.

Afterward I rode with Rogan to Valhalla for the burial, a ceremony that lasted a fraction as long as the drive there, then back to Yonkers, braving the frigid cold with my window open while Rogan chain-smoked.

"She talked about you all the time," he said on the way home. We hadn't spoken much till then, but it wasn't an uncomfortable silence; more a sort of intermission, while we looked at each other and grew accustomed to once again breathing the same air. "She was really proud of you. The first Tierney in a hundred years to be onstage again."

"Not a hundred years." I gazed out the window. We were on North Broadway, passing houses and storefronts strung with Christmas lights.

A bar was hosting a karaoke Kwanzaa contest. "Madeline wasn't that long ago. And you were onstage. With your bands, I mean. That's performing."

"Not to her it wasn't." He laughed, a faint edge of bitterness to his voice, and tossed his cigarette out the window. "Your TV stuff, that wasn't, either. *Rumpole of the Bailey* or whatever the hell it was. None of that stuff counted. Only the stage. Only the *theater*."

He pronounced it as our great-grandmother might have, *thee-ah-tuh*. "That was the only thing that mattered to Aunt Fate."

We pulled into Arden Terrace. I sat beside him, my heart beating too fast, fear and anticipation and jet lag all crowded into that small car. "How long did you live with her?"

"Two years. Two and a half. I didn't actually live with her, not in her house. She had Luisa and Jadeis for that. They're the health-care professionals." He gave another sharp laugh. "I live at Fairview. I'm, like, the caretaker—Michael and the rest of them, they pay me to stay there and keep it from falling into the ground. Which is a losing fucking proposition, I can tell you. But it's great for me; I can work on my music or whatever, no one hassles me. I never even have to fucking see them. Here we are—"

He slowed in front of the house where I'd grown up. "They shingled it about ten years ago," he said, peering out the side window. "It looked good. Now it looks like it needs some paint. But that's nothing compared to my house. Which looks like the Munsters live there."

The car turned down the long drive to Fairview.

"No kidding," I said.

It didn't look completely derelict, just neglected and sad. Shingles were missing, leaving long gaps like rows of rotted teeth. Plywood covered one of the upper windows, and mats of dead wisteria hung like wet carpet from the porch railings. A few lights glimmered downstairs.

"Aunt Kate's place is in better shape," said Rogan as he parked. "She put a lot of money into it."

I stepped out, shivering, and got my bag from the backseat. "What's going to happen to it now?"

Rogan locked the car and waited for me before heading for the front door. "Actually," he said, sounding embarrassed, "she left it to me."

"Really?" I felt a momentary spike of jealousy, then laughed. "But that's great! Her stuff, too? All those things of Madeline's and, well, everything?"

"Yeah. We went through most of it before she died. She wanted to give it to a museum, or a college—I must've called every school in New York. No one was interested. SUNY Purchase took a few things. I gave some of it to the girls who took care of her—nothing you'd want, just some furniture, blankets, and stuff like that. The rest I packed up. I figured you'd want to look at it and maybe take some of it back to England with you."

"Maybe," I said. "I don't have a lot of room. And, you know, I'm not a citizen. Which these days makes it hard. And it's getting expensive. I don't know how long I can really afford to stay there."

We stepped inside. Rogan switched on a light as I rubbed my arms. "Jesus, it's as cold here as outside."

"Yeah, sorry. Here, I'll put the heat on."

He went into the hall, returning a minute later. "I can't really afford to live here, either." He laughed. "But hey, as long as Michael keeps writing the checks, I'll keep it warm. You hungry?"

I followed him into the kitchen. It was like walking through a haunted house of my own life. Most of the furniture was gone, as well as the worn Turkish carpets and mirrors and ancient theatrical memorabilia.

But enough remained that it was still, recognizably, Rogan's home. Most of the damage seemed to be limited to the house's exterior; the structure was still sound. Rogan showed me where he'd made repairs to the interior walls, replaced some of the old windows with triple-insulated glass, and done a serviceable job of patching a crack in the plaster in the kitchen. There was even a bedraggled Christmas tree in the living room, strung with a few strands of those big, old, multicolored bulbs that are no longer fashionable, and hung with glass ornaments.

"I saved those," he said as we stood and admired the tree. He turned back to the kitchen and began to make coffee and sandwiches from leftover turkey. "After my father went crazy that time and trashed everything. I think that's when my mother finally decided she'd had enough. Not when he was pounding the shit out of me. When he broke all the Christmas decorations."

"Jesus, Rogan."

I sat at the table, still in my coat. He handed me a mug of coffee, turned down the dimmer on the overhead light, and lit a candle in a blue glass holder.

"Hey. I remember that," I said softly. "That was under the porch…"

He seemed not to hear me. "Forget it. It's history. You want a sweater? It'll warm up soon. Last winter I put in a new furnace. Aunt Fate paid for it; Michael was too cheap. I told him when the pipes burst and he had to put in a new foundation he'd wish he'd popped for a furnace, but he said if that happened he'd just tear the whole fucking place down. He would, too. No one cares about this place but me."

He turned and looked at me. He'd removed his coat and, despite the chill, pushed up the sleeves of his shirt, so that I could see how the hairs on his arms glowed in the candlelight. I reached out and touched his wrist, like mine only bigger, took his hand, and laid mine beside it.

"We could have been twins," I said. "I wonder if it would have been different. If there had been a girl in your family."

"They were wrong about that, too." He stared at our hands, then linked his fingers with mine. "All that stuff about us. All that boatload of guilt. People marry their cousins; it's not even illegal. I know a guy in Bay Ridge, he's married to his cousin. Not that he tells anyone," he added and smiled ruefully. "You want a drink?"

He opened a bottle of wine. We ate our turkey sandwiches, and then Rogan handed me a CD.

"Check this out."

The cover was a black-and-white photo of an empty city street, a figure silhouetted beneath a lamppost.

Rogan Tierney: Sad Songs.

ILLYRIA

I looked at him. "This is you?"

He grinned. "Hey, write what you know."

I turned it over and read the back. "Jesus—Nicky Cox produced this? How'd you get him?" I scanned the rest of the names in disbelief. "How'd you get all these guys?"

"You meet a lot of people at NA meetings in New York. I'll play it for you later. I have a whole little studio upstairs. It's pretty cool."

We finished the wine.

"Is it okay that you do this?" I asked as he set the empty bottle in the sink. "If you're doing that whole Narcotics Anonymous thing?"

"I'm straight, not necessarily sober. But I don't do it much." He shrugged, poured us each a tumbler of Irish Mist, then gazed at the bottle. "This was my father's."

He took his drink and walked to a window overlooking the carriage house, the long sweep of darkness to the Hudson. "He used to drink this stuff after dinner every night. After the cocktails, I mean. I found a stockpile of it after I moved in. I'm working my way through it. Not at his rate, though."

I walked over to stand beside him. Outside the night was so clear and black it looked brittle, as though, like ice, it would shatter if you touched it. Stars seemed to stir in the wind. The ridge of trees that bordered the lawn had become so dense and overgrown you could no longer see the lights of the houses below.

Only in the uppermost window of Aunt Kate's carriage house did a single light glow, pale yellow, and cast a bright lozenge onto the ground.

"You kept it on." I began to cry. "After everything, you were the one—"

"Maddy." He turned and put his arms around me and drew me close. "Don't cry, baby, please don't cry..."

He kissed me. He smelled as he always had, of smoke and sweat, his mouth bitter with nicotine. I could feel the wind through the cracks in the walls, and then a slow shifting, as though the entire house moved around us. Behind my closed eyes it all began to take shape again, the carpets in their muted colors unfurling across the wooden floors, white lace curtains at the windows, wisteria blooming on the porch outside, and the echo of footsteps on the stairs above.

"Maddy."

I blinked. There were no curtains at the window, and only worn linoleum underfoot. The kitchen smelled of fuel oil and cigarette smoke.

But Rogan's head rested against mine, and Rogan's voice whispered as he grabbed my hand and stepped away from me.

"Come here," he said. "Upstairs. I want to show you something."

He picked up the candle in its blue glass and walked out of the kitchen, through the hall and into the foyer, and up the curving stairway. I held his hand and hurried after him. On the second-floor landing I peered into a room where a computer blinked on a long trestle table, surrounded by speakers and coils of wire.

"That's the studio," said Rogan. He started up the steps to the third floor. "But that's still not it."

I said nothing, just shivered and followed him. The unsteady candlelight made the dark space seem even colder than the rest of the house. When we reached the third floor, Rogan stopped.

"Close your eyes."

I rubbed my arms. "Do I have to? I can't see anything."

"Yeah. You do. Wait right there."

I flinched as he let go of my hand and stepped away, then shut my eyes. I didn't feel like I had downstairs, when the entire house seemed to knit itself around me. Just cold and a growing unease that was close to dread. I thought of when I had last stood here; of Rogan crouched against the wall and his father shouting at me.

Get out of here, you get out of here...

"Come here." I started as Rogan took me by the shoulders. "Keep your eyes closed. It's okay, I won't let you fall. Come here, but don't look until I tell you."

I took tiny baby steps as he led me across the landing, past the door to Michael's bedroom, and into his own.

"Can I open them?" I knew I sounded anxious and drunk, but I didn't care. "Rogan?"

"Hang on, just a sec—"

He stepped away. For a moment I stood alone, fighting the urge to open my eyes, to bolt. Then Rogan was beside me. His arm settled around my shoulders.

"Okay," he said. "You can look."

I opened my eyes and blinked, staring first at the ceiling, then the floor as I tried to get my bearings.

The room was empty. No books, no bed, no rugs, no drapes; no furniture save a makeshift table made of a sheet of plywood on top of a small desk. At its edge glowed a half circle of candles in colored glasses, cobalt and red and green.

"I know it's late," said Rogan. "But Merry Christmas."

I blinked, unsure what I was looking at.

And then I saw.

It was the toy theater, the fairy stage and proscenium we had shared thirty-odd years before. Only it was no longer a thing of light and shadow but a real theater, torn cardboard and paper carefully reassembled, the broken struts and floor repaired, clumsily in spots, with tape and glue and what looked like dirty plaster. The proscenium arch had been so badly damaged that only a small part of it remained, a fragile gilt arc within a crumpled span of tinfoil etched painstakingly with ballpoint ink in the same design that had been on the original. Crepe paper and a ragged fringe of orange silk replaced the curtains. The topiary trees and snow-capped mountains were a pastiche of torn paper and pictures cut from magazines. The scrim was a piece of mosquito netting, painted with a glowing silver moon and the spidery prongs of a broken mast.

"Rogan." It hurt to speak. I stepped toward the table and knelt. "It's—there are people."

And there were. Dozens of figures, each no bigger than my finger, their heads clipped from old photographs and mounted onto stiff paper and cardboard. There were my parents, heads affixed to the gowns of a king and queen; there was Uncle Richard, incongruously smiling above a hunchback's torso, and Aunt Pat in her wedding gown but with a donkey's long muzzle. There was smiling Mr. Sullivan from the St. Brendan's yearbook, his hands raised like a football referee's. There were my sisters, garbed like princesses or stepsisters or shopgirls; and Rogan's brothers, with monkey's tails or Grecian robes. There were all our friends from *Twelfth Night:* dizzy Sir Toby and dopey Duncan Moss; Maria and Fabian and Malvolio; Orsino and Olivia and Sir Andrew Aguecheek.

And there was Aunt Kate, suspended above the stage by a piece of fishing line, with two sets of wings, a swan's and a bat's.

And there was me.

I stood beneath Aunt Kate in my yearbook snapshot, costumed as Viola. But my head had been replaced, so carefully that only I would know that the little figure brandishing her wooden sword didn't bear my fifteen-year-old face, but the delicately made-up features I bore in my *Playbill* photo for *The Good Person of Szechuan;* the adult Viola I had never played.

"Rogan," I whispered.

I stretched out my hand to touch his image. It stood center stage, slightly in front of mine; a Polaroid retouched with ink. He wore the Pierrot's costume from *Twelfth Night,* his head thrown back and eyes closed with the same rapturous expression he had then.

But this photo was new—it might have been taken that day—and when I touched it, I could feel that it was still slightly damp, as though the glue had not yet dried.

Rogan lowered his head to kiss me.

"'And thus the whirligig of time brings in his revenges,'" he said and began to sing.

> "When that I was and a little tiny boy,
> With hey, ho, the wind and the rain,
> A foolish thing was but a toy,
> For the rain it raineth every day."

ILLYRIA

He sang as he had all those years before; as I'd heard him sing, night after night, alone in bed in my Islington flat; as I'd heard him every time I stood offstage, fighting waves of fear until I could take that first step onto a stage in Manchester or Bristol or D.C. His voice rang so loudly that the candles guttered in their holders; the dark room closed around us until I felt the attic walls and in the corners of my eyes saw sparks of lightning, blue and black and silver.

> *"But when I came unto my beds,*
> *With hey, ho, the wind and the rain,*
> *With tosspots still had drunken heads,*
> *For the rain it raineth every day."*

I blinked. Tears blurred my vision so that it seemed I glimpsed the resurrected theater through a snow-covered window. I rubbed my eyes, then gasped.

It was snowing: tiny whirling flakes like glitter or talc but cold, and wet—snow, real snow, impossible snow, falling in a moonlit column from the ceiling onto the paper stage as Rogan sang.

> *"A great while ago the world begun,*
> *With hey, ho, the wind and the rain,*
> *But that's all one, our play is done,*
> *And we'll strive to please you every day."*

The eddies rose and fell with my cousin's voice, sweeping over all of us in waves, matchstick trees and painted moon and cardboard figures in a toy theater, snow and shipwreck and stage all whorled together into one great bright storm with Rogan and me at its center, motionless in our embrace, long after his voice fell silent, long after first light struck the stony face of the Palisades and the frozen river far below.

Story Notes

LAST SUMMER AT MARS HILL

One of my early stories, and the first one set in Maine. There's a Spiritualist community not far from where I live here, called Temple Heights, set right on Penobscot Bay and dating to the 1880s. Back then, it was a motley assortment of ramshackle Carpenter Gothic cottages, with a Shingle style lodge and narrow unpaved roads. You could go on weekends and have your cards read, or get a reading, or attend one of their services where a medium would give you a message from Beyond. Ellen Datlow and I went once and each got a thirty-minute reading—I think it cost thirty bucks, which was a lot of money but I'd always wanted to do it. Mine was complete bollocks—the guy got everything wrong (he said I played the bagpipes)—but it was still fun. Today, the place is all spruced up, though still a Spiritualist camp. The cottages probably sell for at least half a million dollars, and the sweet, weatherbeaten sign with the sunflowers painted on it has been replaced by something much slicker.

For the story, I changed the name to Mars Hill, not realizing there is in fact a place called Mars Hill in Maine, but the setting is the same. The strange flickering beings known as Them were inspired by a Fred Frith song called "The Welcome," but they're really more like what's described in the Shins song "Those to Come," which came out years later. Martin Dionysos plays a role in my 1997 novel *Glimmering*.

PAVANE FOR A PRINCE OF THE AIR

So many of my stories have turned out to be mementos mori, intentionally or not. This one was intended. My dear friend Ben Smith died after a swift illness in February 2000. I wrote this story in early April. It's an account of my experience of attending his dying, with nothing fictionalized save the appearance of the little bird in the final paragraphs, an homage to "The Juniper Tree," my favorite fairy tale. Ben was a shaman, a friend of Owlsley, co-founder with his wife Cheryl of the Shebang Street Theater, which engaged in neopagan rituals and political activism in our part of coastal Maine. A friend carved a likeness of his face in granite, a memorial which sits on the moss here at Tooley Cottage.

THE BACCHAE

My ecofeminist homage to J.G. Ballard. To this day, I can recall the visceral sense of pain, rage and release I felt when describing that shattered glass fish. All the U.S. genre magazines passed on this, no doubt put off by the subject matter, but David Pringle, editor of *Interzone* in the U.K., snapped it up. The mostly male readership of that magazine hated it and wrote letters to that effect, which is how I knew I'd done a good job and hit a nerve. To me, the story feels more timely now than it did then. Evohe!

CLEOPATRA BRIMSTONE

In 2000, I was driving to the airport to embark upon a long-planned trip to London and Cornwall to see my partner and do research for *Mortal Love*. About half an hour from home, I had a panic attack, the first I'd ever experienced. I drove back home and didn't make the trip. Depressed, I decided to channel my love for London into this story, which is set in Camden Town. I also decided to channel some other things, namely the experience of being abducted and raped in 1979, when I was twenty-one years old. I had only recently learned about Post-Traumatic Stress Disorder, and for the first time realized that my panic attack, along with many years of parasomnia (acting out events in my sleep) were symptoms of PTSD. Janie's experience mirrors my own.

STORY NOTES

Also like her, I was a brainy child who was fascinated with butterflies, and have an early childhood memory of a mobile with monarchs and swallowtails on it. In the mid-1980s I had met a young woman who spoke to me of her own rape, and she told me that afterwards her eyebrows started to grow really, really long, like antennae. "See?" she said, pointing to them. But her eyebrows were perfectly normal.

GHOST LIGHT

The editors of *Lit Hub* asked me to contribute to an anthology of short-short crime stories, which sounded like fun. I always write long, so producing a piece of flash fiction was a real challenge. This is another Maine story, and I asked my friend and neighbor, Tom, for help in figuring out details of the murder. Tom does lighting and sound for local theater companies, and is especially knowledgeable about lights. We had a lot of fun coming up with various scenarios, discounting the more obvious (like falling footlights) before Tom came up with this one.

THE HAVE-NOTS

A story with a divine, or Elvine, genesis. I was alone at the cottage with my one-year-old daughter at ten o'clock on a summer Saturday morning, when out of nowhere I started hearing the voice of a Southern cosmetics saleswoman in my head. Well, maybe not quite out of nowhere—I'd been listening to the great Wall of Voodoo song "Elvis Bought Dora a Cadillac." I immediately put Callie into her playpen, climbed up into the loft, and began writing down what the woman was saying. I stayed up there 'til nine o'clock, when the story was done. (I did take breaks to feed, change, and play with the baby.) Next day I read the story over, printed out a copy, and on Monday mailed it to Gardner Dozois, then editor of *Asimov's*, with a note telling him how the story came to be written. In those pre-internet days, you could wait months or even a year before hearing back from an editor (often with a rejection slip). Gardner wrote back within a week, saying he loved the story and would take it. So that too was a bit of Elvine intervention. In 1999, the story was adapted into a one-act, one-woman play by my old friend Anne Wittman. She performed it as part of London's Fringe Festival, where it was a finalist, and went on to a run at the Battersea Arts Center. Ever since, I've thought of Elvis as my patron saint.

THE MAIDEN FLIGHT OF McCAULEY'S *BELLEROPHON*

For about nine years in the 1970s and 1980s, I worked at the National Air and Space Museum in Washington, D.C., most of the time on NASM's pioneering videodisc project. My colleague on the project, Greg Bryant, became one of my closest and dearest friends. A true visionary artist who worked in an amazing array of forms, Greg produced stunning miniature paintings, woodcut silhouettes, line drawings, and (long after I left NASM), strange, beautiful scale models of fantastical, real-life aircraft that had been designed but never flew (and were never capable of flying). When we worked together, Greg and I would come across archival photos and drawings of these and share them in amazed delight. (One, The Margalis Planets-Plane, became the basis for my story "Snow on Sugar Mountain.") Greg's models were made of plastic soda bottles, tin foil, plastic straws, scraps of paper and the like, then painted with nail polish, in dazzling colors. *Smithsonian Magazine* online did a feature on Greg's work, which you can view here: https://www.airspacemag.com/multimedia/the-weird-world-of-folk-aviators-79582573/

The title for this story, along with a vision of a group of people test-flying a model aircraft on NASM's roof, came to me sometime in the early 1990s, years before the story was written. I saw Greg at NASM when I was in D.C. on a rare visit in 2008. He showed me his models, and the story came together in my head. The island is based on Edisto, one of South Carolina's Sea Islands, where I used to blissfully vacation with a big group of friends when we were in our twenties. And there's an obvious nod to *Mystery Science Theater 3000*.

STORY NOTES

This is one of my favorite stories, for so many reasons, though now it is impossible for me to think of rereading it. Greg died last year, after a long bout with cancer, during which he never stopped talking about his work, which he continued to produce until very shortly before he died—he also wrote pulp fiction, published in *Schlock! Magazine*. To paraphrase Wilbur the Pig's elegy for Charlotte in *Charlotte's Web*, he was in a class by himself. It is not often that someone comes along who is a true friend and a good artist. Greg was both.

EAT THE WYRM

Another bit of flash fiction, this time for Nick Mamatas, who edited an anthology of stories about cocktails. I have longed to visit Greenland for many years, though I never got closer than flying over it en route to Iceland or Sweden or Finland, when I'd press my face to the plane window and look down and see icebergs off the coast. Now of course the entire country is melting, so I tried to cram as much desolation, rage, and also plain old weirdness as I could into a few hundred words.

FIRE.

A few years ago, I was asked to join a government panel of policy wonks, scientists, futurists, and forward thinkers from the U.S. Fire Service and Forest Service, on the topic of the future of fire fighting in the U.S. I was there because I had a history of writing SF that addressed climate change. I knew little of fire fighting and megafires when I started. By the time we were done, I was far more knowledgable, and terrified. The big takeaway was that, when it came to an apocalyptic megafire in the American West, the question was not *if* but *when*.

I wrote this just a few years ago for Terry Bisson, who edits PM Press's Outspoken Authors series, books by writers who confront various political, cultural, and scientific issues. I used my experience with the Fire Futures panel to create a fictional scenario that has now come to life: As I write this, such megafires are consuming California, Oregon, and Washington State. My character Cass Neary is named Cassandra for a reason.

THE LOST DOMAIN—THREE STORY VARIATIONS: ECHO, THE SAFFRON GATHERERS, KRONIA

For the last twenty-plus years, I've engaged in a long epistolary friendship with the writer and journalist David Streitfeld. We first met in the late 1980s when he was at the *Washington Post*, where I was (and am) a book reviewer. We've only seen each other a handful of times since then, and until the pandemic, never spoke on the phone, but we've exchanged thousands of emails, mostly about writing, books, and writers. Our correspondence started on 9/11. We hadn't been in touch for a while (my fault), and when I heard about the fall of the Twin Towers and Flight 98, I emailed to make sure he was okay (he traveled a lot for work). He immediately shot back *Oh sure, it takes a terrorist attack to hear from you!* I wrote this trilogy of apocalyptic stories for him (along with a fourth, not included here).

I think the stories are fairly self-explanatory, so I won't say much more, except that "The Saffron Gatherers," like "Fire," feels all too real. In addition to "The Lost Domain" sequence, David is the dedicatee of my novels *Mortal Love* and *Generation Loss*, and also has a presence in the fourth Cass Neary novel, *The Book of Lamps and Banners*.

NEAR ZENNOR

Another story about and born of loss and grief. I love West Penwith, a remote part of Cornwall, where I have visited many times. Like several other titles, this one came to me years before the story idea did—in Penwith, we would always stay in the tiny hamlet of Treen, which when you look for directions is always described as "near Zennor," a barely larger village where Aleister Crowley, D.H. Lawrence and others lived in the early 20th century.

STORY NOTES

I was in London and had just started writing the story, beginning with the death of the protagonist's wife from an aneurysm, when I got news that Russell, one of my oldest and closest friends back home, had suffered a cerebral aneurysm and was not expected to live. He died a few days later, on the Ides of March. I was in West Penwith by then, and his death haunts this story.

The inexplicable events experienced by the three girls in the story occurred to me and two friends when we were in eighth grade and playing in the woods along the Mianus River Gorge in New York State. I had not read the fairy tale "Cherry of Zennor" until after "Near Zennor" was written, another strange circumstance.

THE OWL COUNT

Same deal with this title as with others. For years, I went on Maine's annual Owl Count with my friend Corelyn, and had long wanted to use it as the basis for a story. I started it eleven years ago, shortly after Russell's death, abandoned it then picked it up again when, early this year, editor Brad Morrow asked me to contribute a story to the Grendel's Kin issue of the literary magazine *Conjunctions*. I've always had good luck with the stories I write for Brad, and this one was no exception. I had just read an account of a family's experience of hearing, and recording, a terrifying and unexplained animal cry in the remote Canadian wilderness. I listened to the recording over and over (and you can do the same here: https://www.youtube.com/watch?v=stISzPngwh4&feature=emb_logo), and it ended up being a central part of the story.

THE LEAST TRUMPS

My first story written for Brad and *Conjunctions*' now-famous New Wave Fabulists issue, this was inspired by another panic attack, and my first tattoo (the two weren't connected). I now have four, all by the same artist, Julie Rose, who has since hung up her tattoo gun but still lives nearby on the Maine coast. I got the tattoo when I heard Joey Ramone had died. I'd wanted once since I was nineteen, and after Joey's death I thought *What the hell am I waiting for?* The books were inspired by John Crowley's brilliant Aegypt sequence, which at the time had not been completed, and I like many readers despaired that they never would be. (The Least Trumps, of course, come from Crowley's equally brilliant novel *Little, Big*.)

I had two endings in mind for this. One would make it a horror story; the other would make it a tale of transcendence. Right up until I wrote the final pages (late as usual on my deadline for Brad), I didn't know which ending I would use. The Lonely House is inspired by Margaret Wise Brown's Only House, owned by my friend Liv on an island near here, which I visited on my first trip as an adult to Maine in the 1980s. The author of the wise Ant books in turn is inspired by Brown, though the books themselves derive from the English writer Angela Banner's Ant and Bee picture books.

ILLYRIA

This is the story closest to my heart of all I've written, and also the story that took my the most time to write. In 1974, my senior year in high school, my boyfriend Steve was cast as Malvolio in his HS production of *Twelfth Night*. Our friend Russell played Feste, the clown, and other friends had supporting roles. John Jay High School (I attended a different school) had a remarkable theater department, with students who went on to have successful stage and film careers—Stan Tucci and Scott Campbell were classmates of my friends, though they weren't in this particular production. I sat in on rehearsals and saw every performance—a transformative experience for me, which started a long love affair for the play, which I've now seen dozens of times. Steve was fantastic as Malvolio, and Russell, in Pierrot garb, remains the most astonishing Feste I've ever seen. He had an incredible vocal range, and was directed to use a falsetto or countertenor for most of his songs. He also sang in rock and roll bands and a barbershop quartet: he just loved

STORY NOTES

to sing. After that initial exposure to the play, I began reading everything I could about it, determined to someday write a story that would capture the magic I'd seen onstage. There are flickers of *Twelfth Night* throughout my work, from *Winterlong* on—the gender fluidity of the twins Viola and Sebastian, the melancholy yet sinister Feste, the overarching theme of the Lord of Misrule and Twelfth Night itself, the Yule celebration that unabashedly displays its pagan origins. But it wasn't until "Illyria" that I was able to do it justice.

In 2006, Pete Crowther, editor and publisher of PS Publishing in the U.K., asked me if I would write the short chapbook that he sent annually to subscribers as a Christmas gift. That October, while visiting Russ and his brother Steve on Norton Island in Maine (inspiration for *Generation Loss*, but that's another story), I decided to write a short story inspired by *The Tempest*—I was on an island, and I was reading Auden's "The Sea and the Mirror," a long essay and poem inspired by *The Tempest*. Out of nowhere, "Illyria" came to me: I suddenly realized that, after thirty-five years, I could write my version of *Twelfth Night*. I wrote the novella at fever pitch over three weeks, and sent it to Pete at PS with apologies—it was obviously not a short story. Pete loved it and decided to publish it the following year as a stand-alone novella, which received the World Fantasy Award, and it was later published in the U.S. Much of my own experience is crowded into its pages—my love of theater, notably, and also my long friendship with Russ. He loved the story, which is dedicated to him, and I was so grateful he was able to read it before he died.

I've never been able to reread "Illyria"—my heart broke writing it, in a good way, and I find it painful to think about, perhaps because it was the single story I always wanted to tell. I usually know when I've hit my mark as a writer—some stories are near-misses—but I knew when I finished "Illyria" that I'd nailed it. The epigraph, which I intended to use from the time I was seventeen, has only grown more poignant since Russell's death of a brain hemorrhage a few years after "Illyria" was published.

"And what should I do in Illyria? My brother he is in Elysium."

Copyright Information

"Last Summer at Mars Hall" Copyright © 1998 by Elizabeth Hand. First appeared in *Last Summer at Mars Hall*.

"Pavane for a Prince of the Air" Copyright © 2002 by Elizabeth Hand. First appeared in *J. K. Potter's Embrace the Mutation*, edited by William Schafer, Bill Sheehan.

"The Bacchae" Copyright © 1991 by Elizabeth Hand. First appeared in *Interzone #49*, July 1991, edited by Lee Montgomerie, David Pringle.

"Cleopatra Brimstone" Copyright © 2001 by Elizabeth Hand. First appeared in *Redshift: Extreme Visions of Speculative Fiction*, edited by Al Sarrantonio.

"Ghost Light" Copyright © 2018 by Elizabeth Hand. First appeared in *Tiny Crimes: Very Short Tales of Mystery and Murder*, edited by Lincoln Michel.

"The Have Nots" Copyright © 1992 by Elizabeth Hand. First appeared in *Isaac Asimov's Science Fiction Magazine*, June 1992, edited by Gardner Dozois.

"The Maiden Flight of McCauley's Bellerophon" Copyright © 2010 by Elizabeth Hand. First appeared in *Stories: All-New Tales*, edited by Neil Gaiman, Al Sarrantonio.

"Eat the Wyrm" Copyright © Copyright 2017 by Elizabeth Hand. First appeared in *Mixed Up: Cocktail Recipes (and Flash Fiction) for the Discerning Drinker (and Reader)*, edited by Nick Mamatas, Molly Tanzer.

ELIZABETH HAND

"Fire." Copyright © 2017 by Elizabeth Hand. First appeared in *Fire*.

"Echo" Copyright © 2005 by Elizabeth Hand. First appeared in *The Magazine of Fantasy & Science Fiction,* October-November 2005, edited by Gordon Van Gelder.

"The Saffron Gatherers" Copyright © 2006 by Elizabeth Hand. First appeared in *Saffron and Brimstone: Strange Stories.*

"Kronia" Copyright © 2006 by Elizabeth Hand. First appeared in *The Year's Best Fantasy & Horror: Nineteenth Annual Collection*, edited by Ellen Datlow, Gavin J. Grant, Kelly Link.

"Near Zennor" Copyright © 2011 by Elizabeth Hand. First appeared in *A Book of Horrors*, edited by Stephen Jones.

"The Owl Count" Copyright © 2020 by Elizabeth Hand. First appeared in *Conjunctions: 74, Grendel's Kin: The Monsters Issue*, edited by Bradford Morrow.

"The Least Trumps" Copyright © 2002 by Elizabeth Hand. First appeared in *Conjunctions: 39, The New Wave Fabulists*, edited by Bradford Morrow, Peter Straub.

"Illyria" Copyright © 2007 by Elizabeth Hand. First appeared in *Illyria*.